THE ROAD
TO HELL

THE ROAD
TO HELL

DAVID WEBER &
JOELLE PRESBY

A Baen Books Original

Baen Publishing Enterprises
P.O. Box 1403
Riverdale, NY 10471
www.baen.com

ISBN: 978-1-4767-8067-2

Cover art by Dave Seeley
Map by Randy Asplund

First printing, March 2016

Distributed by Simon & Schuster
1230 Avenue of the Americas
New York, NY 10020

10 9 8 7 6 5 4 3 2 1

Pages by Joy Freeman (www.pagesbyjoy.com)
Printed in the United States of America

*For Angie and Phil, the friends—and EMTs—
who were there when we needed them most.
Thanks, guys. I owe you.*

CONTENTS

Multiverse:
Hell's Gate Sector

Hell's Gate

New Uromath
256

Nairsom
590

Thermyn
1,210

Resym
2,750

Mahritha
600/2,600

Failcham
1,430

Lashai
800

Erthus
1,400

Karys
1,160

Kelsayr
2,660

Sanchola
910

Garuth
2,000

Traisum

Ilmariya
2,900

Distances shown are the distance
between portals to cross that universe,
given in straight miles.

Where one figure is given, they are
all land miles.

Rycarh
295/4,700

Where two are given, the second is
sea miles.

THE ROAD TO HELL

CHAPTER ONE

Ternathal 10, 5053 AE
(November 29, 1928 CE)

THE VERY TALL, POWERFULLY BUILT MAN STRODE DOWN the early morning hallway like an icebreaker through floe ice. Or perhaps, given his expression, like a battleship breaking an enemy line. The brilliant sunlight of Tajvana shone through the broad windows down the eastern side of the hall, gleaming on floors of polished marble and gathering in rich puddles, dense with color, on the runner of priceless carpet stretched down the passage's center. That same sunlight touched the strands of gold threaded through his dark hair, but it did nothing to lighten the darkness in his gray, shadowed eyes.

He had not slept, though those who didn't know him well might not have guessed it from his appearance. Those who did know him well had no need to guess; they would have known how any trace of sleep must have eluded him in the hours of the night so recently passed. There was bitterness in those gray eyes, and anger. And there was fear—not for himself, but for someone dearer to him than life itself—and there was despair. The harsh, hard, angry despair of someone unaccustomed to powerlessness. The despair of someone who hated himself for his helplessness.

His name was Zindel chan Calirath, Duke of Ternathia, Grand Duke of Farnalia, Warlord of the West, Protector of the Peace, Wing-Crowned, and, by the gods' grace, Zindel XXIV, Emperor of Ternathia and Zindel I, Emperor Designate of Sharona. He was the most powerful man in more than forty universes...and a father who could not save his daughter from the destruction of her life.

*   *   *

1

One of the Calirath Palace maids looked up, saw the emperor bearing down upon her, and flattened herself against the wall with a squeak of dismay. Under other circumstances, Zindel would have paused, smiled at the young woman, asked her name and attempted to set her at ease. This morning, he simply strode past her with a curt nod. He doubted that engaging her in conversation in his present mood could have contributed much to her peace of mind, anyway.

He reached the door of his daughter's apartments, and the pair of grim-faced bodyguards flanking it came to the attention. They saluted sharply, and he nodded in acknowledgment once more, eyes hard with approval this time as he noted the Model 7 shotguns, bayonets fixed, which supplemented their usual Halanch and Welnahr revolvers. The slide-action weapons were ugly and heavy, not at all what a smartly-dressed imperial guardsmen would carry, and they offered less range than a rifle, but inside the confines of the Palace's corridors and passages, they were also far more lethal.

He stepped past them without slowing, but his inexorable progress checked abruptly as he crossed the apartment's threshold and saw the chair outside the closed bedroom door. It was—like all the chairs in Calirath Palace—beautifully made, comfortably padded and richly upholstered. Yet it was intended for people to *sit* in, not as a bed, and the middle-aged woman curled up in it under the light blanket could not have spent a restful night. He gazed at her for a moment, trying to remember if he'd ever before seen Lady Merissa Vankhal without cosmetics, her hair awry. She looked older and somehow worn, even in her sleep, and Zindel's hard, set expression softened as he gazed at her. There were those, he knew—including his daughter, at times—who saw only Lady Merissa's fussiness, her insistence on protocol, her determination that her charge's public appearance should always be immaculate, and overlooked her deep, personal attachment to the imperial grand princess she served so devotedly. Neither he nor his wife Varena had ever made that mistake, and her presence here was not the surprise to him that it would have been to all those other people. She hadn't mentioned her intention, yet he realized now that she shouldn't have needed to. He should have known anyway.

He paused and gently tucked the blanket about her shoulders, then drew a deep breath, squared his broad shoulders, and knocked softly upon his daughter's door.

* * *

Andrin Calirath, Imperial Crown Princess of Ternathia and Sharona, turned in her chair when the tap sounded.

"Come," she called, and the door opened.

Her father stood in the doorway for just a moment before he stepped hesitantly into the room. Sunshine warm as melted honey poured across the small marble balcony where Andrin sat, staring across the quiet morning at the ultramarine waters of the Ylani Straits and the mourning banners fluttering from every rooftop and railing of Tajvana. Her face was worn and tired, her unquiet gray eyes swollen from the tears she'd been too proud to let anyone see in yesterday's tumultuous Conclave meeting. A girl with the vitality of youth, sitting in warm, golden sunlight, shouldn't have looked like ice on a windowpane, so pale light very nearly shone *through* her, and yet there was a hard-won serenity in that tired face. One that seemed to shatter his heart within his chest. The heart which had already lost a son and now had failed his daughter, as well.

"Andrin," he said brokenly, "I'm sorry..."

She shook her head. "It isn't your fault, Papa. There was no other way to secure the accords. I understand that. I don't blame you, Papa. I blame the spineless cowards in the Conclave for not standing up to Chava's demands, but never *you*."

That simple absolution cut Zindel to the bone. She wasn't just his eldest daughter and heir; she was the promise of greatness. And she would never reach it, not under one of Chava Busar's sons. If nothing else, they would kill her in childbed, getting child after child on her. He wanted to wrap his hands around the throat of every rutting royal bastard in Uromathia and squeeze until all that remained was crushed bone and purpled, lifeless flesh. Wanted—more than he'd ever wanted anything in his life—to denounce the accords which made her marriage to a Uromathian prince the price for putting the crown of a united Sharona upon his own head. But duty—that cruel, uncaring goddess of ice and steel which had demanded so much of his ancestors over the millennia—demanded this of him...and of her.

He had an entire world to protect, and protecting *it* meant he couldn't protect *her*.

Gods, he couldn't protect his baby girl....

"Did you bring the list?" she asked softly.

He held it out. It was short. Brutally so. The Emperor of Uromathia had only five unmarried sons. Among them was the crown prince, who was obviously his father's first choice. She scanned it briefly, then handed it back.

"It isn't complete, Papa. Please have it amended."

There was an odd note in her voice, not at all the one he'd expected. It was harder, with an edge of the same steel she'd shown the entire Conclave when she spat her defiance into Chava's teeth, and he frowned down at her.

"What do you mean, 'Drin?" he asked, trying to identify that oddness in her voice.

She lifted her eyes to meet his, and they were no longer dead, filled with burnt-out grief and proud despair. They were violently alive, those mirrors of his own eyes, and there was no defeat in them. Not in *those* eyes. The fierce triumph in his daughter's gaze sent a shockwave through Zindel chan Calirath, and he seized both of her hands, crouched at her feet.

"What is it, Andrin? What have you thought of?"

"It was so obvious we didn't see it," she said. Her smile turned almost cruel, and she gave a strange little laugh that chilled Zindel's blood. "None of us did...except Darcel Kinlafia. Maybe we've just spent too long concentrating on the threat of Chava and his empire for any Ternathian to have thought beyond it, but not Darcel. He and Alazon came to me with the answer in the middle of the night."

"*What* answer?"

"I'm required to marry a royal prince 'of Uromathia.' That's the specific language of the treaty, Papa...but there are more Uromathians in this world than the people who live inside the borders of the Uromathian *Empire*. Chava may've forgotten that when he signed the treaty, or maybe it was just his arrogance. After all, when *he* says Uromathia, it means only *his* Uromathia, because none of those other states matter at all to him. And I realize his negotiators clearly meant 'of Uromathia' to mean the empire. But it doesn't *say* that...and there are quite a number of royal unmarried sons in the kingdoms that govern those Uromathian peoples outside Chava's borders. Unmarried sons like Howan Fai Goutin."

Zindel gaped. She was right. Howan Fai Goutin was the crown prince of Eniath, and Eniath's people *were* Uromathians. Culturally. Religiously. Racially.

"Triad's mercy," he whispered as a crushing mountain lifted from his shoulders, from his chest. He was suddenly able to *breathe* again. The sunlight shone more brightly and the scent of the sea had a saltier tang in his nostrils.

"I ought to have thought of it myself," Andrin said quietly. "I should've remembered that lovely dance I'd enjoyed with Howan Fai at the pre-coronation ball...and the conversation I was having with him and Darcel and Alazon when that awful Glimpse struck. It was so unfair, coming in the middle of a conversation when—" She paused for a moment, then gave her head a little toss. "In the middle of a conversation with someone as sensible as Darcel," she went on in what her father suspected wasn't what she'd been about to say, "and a young man I actually liked, one with enough courage to ask a girl a foot and a half taller than he is to dance with him. I should have *remembered* him, but there was too much crashing down on me. Janaki's death, the accords, Chava...It was all too much for me to think straight, but Darcel remembered for me."

"Shalana be praised," he said, brushing her hair back where the breeze had caught a tendril and wafted it across her face. "You found it. You found the answer none of us could see."

"No, Papa. *Darcel* found it. Although," her lips quirked briefly, "I think he was more than a bit embarrassed to be bringing it up with me."

"Gods, gods," Zindel said softly, tears brimming in his eyes. "This must be what Janaki Glimpsed, 'Drin!"

"Janaki?" Andrin's gray eyes darkened again at her dead brother's name, and Zindel's hand moved from her hair to cup her cheek. "*Janaki* had a Glimpse of Darcel and me?"

"Not a very clear one, love. You know"—Zindel's voice wavered for a moment—"his Talent was never as strong as yours or mine. But he loved you with all his heart, and he knew Darcel Kinlafia would be important to you before he ever sent him to us."

She looked deep into his eyes, as if searching for something which had been left unsaid, and he gazed back steadily. She knew, he thought. She knew Janaki wasn't the only one who'd had a Glimpse of her and Kinlafia, and he wondered suddenly if that was what she'd edited out about her conversation with the Voice. But she only looked at him, then nodded with a maturity that was heartbreaking in someone who was barely seventeen years old. A maturity which realized some questions could not be asked, even of a father.

"I understand, Papa," she said softly, and he felt a fresh pain, because one day, he knew, she truly *would* understand, and Glimpses seldom showed happy or joyful visions of the future.

"I know you do, dear heart," he told her, cradling her face between his hands and smiling sadly. "I know you do. But"—he drew a deep, shuddering breath—"thank all the gods there are that Janaki had that Glimpse. And that Darcel Kinlafia is the man he is."

"In more ways than one," Andrin agreed in heartfelt tones. "I don't think he was deliberately pushing me together with Howan Fai, but he and Alazon were the ones who invited him to join us when I decided I needed a rest. And I think it may have been my telling him how close an ally King Junni's become that made him think of Howan Fai... and remind *me* about him last night, Marnilay bless him! I can't pretend even to myself that I really know Howan Fai, but at least I know I *like* him, and when I think about him compared to Chava's sons..." Her voice wavered with sudden tears. "Oh, gods, Papa, I've been so *scared*."

He caught her close, held her as though she were made of glass. He held her until she stopped trembling. Then held her until *he'd* stopped trembling. When he knew he could actually control his own voice, he kissed her brow and sat back on his heels.

"We'll have an amended list in your hands before sunset, sweetling," he promised, and her eyes softened at his use of her childhood nickname. Shadows of the fear she'd just admitted lingered in them, yet it was a fear she'd conquered. One which could no longer conquer *her*, and his heart swelled with pride in her.

"I don't feel particularly sweet at the moment, Papa," she told him, and she smiled that smile again. The one any hunting lioness might have envied. "At the moment, I feel positively wicked."

He let go a genuine laugh. "You've earned the right, child. More than earned the right." He lifted her hands, kissed each one in turn, then said, "Enjoy the sunlight and the breeze, Andrin. I have a few things to see to, this morning."

He walked briskly back across her bedroom, reaching the doorway in four long strides. He nodded once more as he crossed the sitting room, passed Andrin's saluting bodyguards, and stepped back into the hallway, but this time it was a very different nod and he had to remind himself to maintain the grimly inexorable stride with which he'd arrived. There was no point pretending Chava wouldn't have sources within Calirath Palace's staff, and the last thing he could afford was for one of those sources to see him bounding along with the eager, anticipatory buoyancy which had replaced his morning's earlier despair.

It took him less than five minutes to reach the chamber where his Privy Council had already gathered, despite the earliness of the hour. There were extra armsmen in the green and gold of the House of Calirath outside the council chamber's door, as well, and they snapped to attention as he strode past them.

The assembled councilors rose at his entrance. Their faces were uniformly grim, most of them pale and worried. Partly that was the lingering shock of the news of the crown prince's death and the knowledge that the mysterious Arcanans—the Arcanans who, it seemed, truly did use what could only be described as *magic*—had conquered no less than four entire universes in barely two weeks. But it was also deeply personal, he realized. The grimness of men and women who understood what marriage to one of Chava Busar's sons would do to Andrin yet saw no more way to avoid that fate than he had.

He looked at them, recognizing their grief and treasuring their devotion to his house and family, and then—finally—he let loose his own ferocious smile.

"Shamir!" he crowed, thrusting the list into the first councilor's astonished hands. "Get this thing properly completed immediately. I want the names of every unmarried Uromathian prince from Eniath, from Hinorea, from every damned royal family of Uromathian culture this ball of rock ever produced. Even the ones who've emigrated to the colonies. Andrin's done it, by Vothan! She's found the way out. Well don't just stand there gaping like ninnies! We've only got a few weeks to whittle that list down to a candidate who's actually worthy of her hand!"

Shock at his smile had stunned all of them motionlessness while they listened to him. But now answering smiles—wicked, nasty, *delighted* smiles of sudden understanding—blossomed on every face.

"And need I remind any of you of the need for absolute secrecy on this subject? If Chava gets wind of what we're doing, he wouldn't be above assassinating the best candidates."

Smiles vanished, replaced by angry determination.

"Your Majesty," Shamir Taje's words were chipped ice, "I will personally shoot anyone who so much as breathes a syllable of what you just said."

Zindel saw exactly the same fire in the eyes of every member of the Privy Council and he nodded in profound satisfaction. If he hadn't trusted them completely, they wouldn't have been on his Privy Council. And he knew Security ran periodic probes, from time to time, just to be sure. The families of the personal armsmen who guarded the Ternathian Imperial Family had, for generations, bred some of the oddest, most useful, and occasionally downright terrifying Talents on Sharona. Talents they very carefully never discussed with anyone but themselves and a reigning emperor or empress . . . and which they would be using once again very shortly.

If there were a turncoat on his staff, he'd know it within minutes.

There were times—many of them—when Zindel chan Calirath hated the knowledge that his armsman spied regularly upon honest and honorable men and women who'd sworn solemn oaths of allegiance to him and demonstrated their loyalty so frequently. But when Andrin's life was at stake, he would take no chances. Not even with men and women he'd trusted for thirty years. Not when all it would take was thirty seconds to put his child's life back into the crucible.

Shamir Taje caught his eye. The tiniest of nods told him Taje had guessed far more than he'd been told about Imperial Security. Guessed and approved.

Zindel returned that nod decisively.

"All right, people, let's get to work. We have a royal consort to choose and a war to win. Shamir, I need to speak to you for a moment. As for the rest of you, I suggest we get started immediately. And my friends, I'll make one further suggestion."

The rest of the Privy Council paused, waiting.

"Let's all do our best to continue looking funereal."

Wicked chuckles greeted that piece of advice.

It was a somber, even tearful, troupe that exited the chamber—thespian talent was a requirement for political leaders who operated at their level—and Zindel devoutly hoped Chava Busar would enjoy the reports of his councilors' grief which would shortly be coming his way. He knew he could trust them to maintain the charade, and he'd have to have a word with Varena, as well. Of course, the empress had every plausible excuse to remain in seclusion for the next several days, and no doubt she would. But he'd have to see to it that she was in her box in the Conclave when the time came. He could hardly wait to see the expression on Chava's oily face when Andrin announced her preference next week, and he knew Varena would feel the same. He intended for both of them to enjoy every delicious moment of the bastard's outrage.

He waited until the chamber door had closed behind the others, then turned back to Taje, and his nostrils flared.

"I told the rest of the Council that Andrin found the answer, Shamir, and that's at least partially true," he said. "But it's not the entire truth, and I think it's time I shared something with you about Darcel Kinlafia."

Taje's eyes narrowed with a sudden intensity, but he simply stood there, waiting, and Zindel smiled without any humor at all.

"I know you've realized I've been . . . cultivating and supporting Voice Kinlafia's political future. I notice that you haven't asked me about my motives, however."

Only someone who knew Shamir Taje very well would have recognized the speculation in his gaze, but Zindel *did* know him that well. Kinlafia would very shortly be involved up to his neck in the marathon race of the first world-wide election in Sharona's history. Those elections had been scheduled for two months after Zindel's official coronation, and while the coronation itself had been thrown into a hiatus until the issue of Andrin's marriage was resolved, the Conclave had agreed virtually unanimously that the elections must move forward on the assumption there would be an Empire of Sharona for the winners to govern. Even Chava had agreed to that, given the news from Fort Salby.

"I've assumed that if you thought it was important for me to know why you were doing it, you would've told me, Your Majesty." Taje shrugged ever so slightly. "That's not to say I haven't wondered about it, of course. I've never known you to invest as much effort in support of someone's 'political future'—or to be as discreet about doing it—without having a very good reason for doing so."

"Oh, yes. You could certainly say that," Zindel said softly. "Sit back down, Shamir."

The first councilor obeyed, but Zindel didn't find a chair of his own. Instead, he clasped his hands behind him and began pacing slowly and steadily back and forth across the rectangular chamber's shorter dimension.

"I'm sure someone as astute as you has to recognize how valuable someone like Kinlafia could be to us," he said. "The Voice who relayed Shaylar Nargra-Kolmayr's final transmission. The man who warned all of us that we were at war with another universe . . . and the man whose pain and grief and anger spilled over onto everyone with enough Talent to See that transmission. It's hard to imagine anyone more intensely identified with this entire crisis by the public—unless it was Shaylar herself! That kind of recognition and stature would provide an instant, incredibly strong political base, and there are enough political operatives to grasp that. Janaki"—the emperor's voice wavered, but he went on firmly—"certainly grasped it, just as he understood *someone* would try to make use of Kinlafia, whatever Kinlafia himself wanted. And, as Janaki pointed out, it would be far wiser to attach Kinlafia to *our* interests than to find ourselves in a position in which someone tried to use him *against* us."

He paused, looking down at the first councilor, and Taje nodded.

"I hadn't realized Prince Janaki had directly suggested supporting the Voice, but his potential to assist us—or someone else—was certainly obvious. Yet I have to admit I haven't quite been able to convince myself that's the only reason you've been quietly opening so many doors for the young man." He smiled faintly. "Nor do I think young Kinlafia truly realizes just how many doors you *have* been opening, Your Majesty."

"I think he might surprise you," Zindel said dryly. "He's surprised me more than once, and it would be a mistake to underestimate him. He'd never considered a career in politics before those godsdamned Arcanans blew his life apart with the rest of his survey crew, but there's nothing at all wrong with that man's brain. And whether he realizes it or not, he has excellent political instincts." The emperor resumed his pacing. "In fact, those instincts of his are good enough to have made launching and supporting his political career worthwhile all by themselves."

"Obviously, however, Your Majesty, they aren't 'by themselves,' are they?"

"No. No, they aren't."

Zindel inhaled again, deeply, a man obviously marshaling his thoughts.

"Janaki had a Glimpse, Shamir," he said finally. "One that concerned Kinlafia...and Andrin."

It was Taje's turn to inhale this time, not so much in surprise as at the confirmation of something he'd suspected—even feared—from the beginning. The hallmark Talent, mightiest weapon, and greatest curse of the House of Calirath, were the Glimpses which came to its members. Visions of the future, fragmentary bits and pieces of things to come. Those Glimpses had allowed Calirath emperors and empresses to change the course of history more than once throughout the centuries of the Empire of Ternathia... and more than one of those emperors and empresses had paid the price Janaki chan Calirath had paid when he went knowingly to his death in the defense of Fort Salby.

They were seldom kind and gentle, the Calirath Glimpses.

"Janaki's Talent wasn't strong enough for him to Glimpse exactly why Kinlafia was going to be important to Andrin," Zindel continued. "But mine was." He stopped pacing again, looking directly into Taje's eyes. "He's going to be there for her, Shamir. Whatever happens—to me, to you, to the entire godsdamned multiverse—Darcel Kinlafia *will* be there for my daughter. Just as he was there for her last night when he brought her the answer to the trap that bastard Chava thought he had her in."

The emperor spoke softly, yet his voice was hard with certitude and the Calirath ghosts shadowed his eyes as he gazed down at the first councilor.

"I don't know what's going to happen to me," he continued quietly. "Short of a Death Glimpse—which I haven't had yet, thank the gods!—no one knows that about himself. But I know 'Drin will need him—need him badly—far sooner than I could wish. And I also know his Voice Talent is so strong that he shared at least a part of my Glimpse. *He* knows she'll need him, too, and he also knows I know how much he'll love my daughter. How much he already loves her, for that matter." Zindel's smile was faint and crooked but genuine. "He's the one who came up with the brainstorm about other Uromathian princes, but did he come and tell *me* about it? Hells no, he didn't! And that's because he isn't really a politician—yet, at least. He thought of it because he cares for Andrin, and that's why he went and told *her* about it."

"I see, Your Majesty," Taje said, and his own eyes were dark. Zindel chan Calirath was only in his forties, and his was a long-lived family. Both of his parents had lived past ninety, and Caliraths seldom died—of natural causes, at least—much younger than that. Zindel might not have Glimpsed his own death, but his concern for Andrin sent an icicle down the first councilor's spine. The emperor loved all of his children fiercely, he would die to protect any of them, yet there was something in his eyes, in his voice, that whispered a fear that he wouldn't be there to protect Andrin.

"I imagine you do see," Zindel said, and reached to lay one hand on Taje's shoulder, his expression almost compassionate. He smiled down at the councilor who was also his closest, most intimate friend, then gave his head a toss that pretended to shake off the ghost of futures Glimpsed.

"I imagine you do, and since you do, I'm sure you also understand why it's important to keep the Voice alive. Which is why we're not going to breathe a word to *anyone*—not even the rest of the Privy Council—about who actually found the loophole in the Accords. We're not pasting any targets on his back for Chava. In fact, the longer we can keep anyone from realizing just how good those 'political instincts' of his are—or, especially, how devoted to Andrin he's already become—the better. I want him seated in the House of Talents in the new Parliament before any of our adversaries realize he could pose an actual threat to their plans and strategies."

"And that's why you've been so careful about not supporting him overtly." Taje nodded. His voice was a bit husky with the implications of what Zindel had already told him, and the emperor pretended not to notice as he cleared his throat.

"I believe we have enough Conclave allies to provide the necessary support indirectly and discreetly, Your Majesty," Taje continued after a moment, and managed a faint smile. "Should I assume you'd like me to see to that for you?"

"I see you're as perceptive as ever, Shamir." Zindel gave him a gentle shake and nodded. "That's exactly what I want you to do. And I want you to be your usual, deft, *unobtrusive* self when you do it, too."

"I have just the delegates in mind, Your Majesty," Taje assured him.

"Good!"

Zindel smiled fiercely, but then his expression sobered.

"Good," he repeated more quietly. "But Chava will be apoplectic if he gets even a hint about what we're up to. I want security here in the Palace tripled, and I want someone—one of our own undercover armsmen—keeping an eye on Kinlafia. We can cover some additional security for him because of his relationship with Alazon. Gods know there's plenty of reason to worry about my Privy Voice's security! But I want him covered when he's not with her, too."

"That might be a bit more difficult, Your Majesty. Ah, have you discussed this desire of yours directly with him?"

"No, I haven't. And I'd prefer not to, frankly. One of the more endearing things about him is that he doesn't see himself as the sort of political mover and shaker he has the potential to become. And partly because of that—but mostly because he's so naturally open and honest—he's not very good at dissembling." The emperor's lips quirked. "He'll have to get over that, of course, but I don't think we have time for him to learn the art of misdirection and deception just now. I'm afraid that if he knows we've assigned someone to protect him he won't be able to conceal that knowledge, and I don't want anyone who might wish him ill to realize we've done it."

"Your Majesty, he's a Voice." Taje shook his head. "I know he takes the Voice's Code seriously, but if he's in regular contact with someone assigned to protect him, there's bound to be at least some leakage across his Talent."

"I was thinking about Kelahm chan Helikos," Zindel said, and Taje cocked his head, lips pursed. He stayed that way for a second or two, and then nodded.

"I think that might be an excellent notion, Your Majesty. Of course, Brithum will have a fit when you recall him."

Brithum Dulan, the Ternathian Empire's Councilor for Internal Affairs, was responsible for the empire's counterintelligence services, and he would not be happy to give up Company-Captain Kelahm chan Helikos.

"Brithum will just have to get over it." Zindel chuckled grimly. "Chan Helikos was only on loan to him from the beginning, after all."

"As you say, Your Majesty. But, ah, would it be too much for me to ask *you* to break the news to him?"

CHAPTER TWO

Ternathal 11, 5053 AE
(November 30, 1928 CE)

IT WAS HOT IN FORT SALBY.

Of course, it was always hot in Fort Salby for someone born on Yanohan Bay on the west coast of the green and misty island from which the Ternathian Empire took its name. Back home, they stood on the very lip of winter—not the icy, snowy winters of the 3rd Dragoon Division's winters at Fort Emperor Erthain in Karmalia, perhaps, but winter—and *theoretically* it was almost winter here, as well. To be fair, temperatures at this time of the year were usually quite moderate for the Kingdom of Shurkhal; unfortunately, today wasn't part of that "usually." The temperature hovered in the upper nineties during the day and had been almost eighty even at night for the last freakishly hot two weeks. Fortunately, it was also nearly winter in Arpathia, which meant the stiff, unending breeze blowing through the portal looming above the fort carried a cooler edge between universes, especially at night. Unfortunately, during the day, the local weather seemed rather confused about the season.

Still, Division-Captain Arlos chan Geraith reflected bleakly as he swiped yet again at the film of sweat on his forehead, at least the humidity was blessedly low. And hot as it might be today, it was cooler than it had been last week…in far too many ways.

The division-captain lacked even a trace of Talent, which meant he'd been unable to directly experience any of the Voice reports and images of the Arcanan attack on Fort Salby, but he had a keen imagination and there was more than enough physical evidence of what had happened. The carcasses of flying creatures

14

which could only be described as dragons from the most fearsome fairy tales had littered the landscape. The Trans-Temporal Express's work crews had used steam shovels and bulldozers to bury them, but the damned things were so enormous—estimates ran to over forty tons, and he believed them—that the work crews had been forced to cut (and blast) them into smaller pieces they could handle. Then there'd been the bodies of the "eagle-lions" strewn across the fort's burned and blasted parade ground, the enormous horses—like no horse chan Geraith had ever seen before—which had been killed in the assault on the fort's eastern wall, and the charred ruin of a solid brick and adobe tower which had been pulverized by one of the plummeting dragons.

And there were the row upon row of graves, including, he thought with a pang which had become familiar without becoming one bit less agonizing, the imperial crown prince who'd stayed to fight beside the fort's defenders, knowing he would die, to warn them of what was coming.

It was Arlos chan Geraith's duty to see that none of those men had died in vain. Janaki chan Calirath had entrusted him with that responsibility, and he intended to meet it.

"According to Lisar here," he said, looking up from the map and nodding in the direction of Company-Captain Lisar chan Korthal, his staff Voice, "your heavy artillery should to be arriving by mid-week, Braykhan."

"Yes, Sir," Regiment-Captain Braykhan chan Sayro replied with a small grimace. "I wish we were in a better position to make use of it."

"Patience, Braykhan. Patience!" Chan Geraith smiled grimly at his staff artillerist. "Your 'cannon-cockers' will have their chance. I promise."

Chan Sayro nodded, and chan Geraith turned his attention to Regiment-Captain Therahk chan Kymo, his staff quartermaster. Chan Kymo was considerably taller and fifteen years younger than his division-captain, with a pronounced Delkrathian accent and the dark hair and eyes common to the majority of the Narhathan Peninsula's people. He was also good at his job, which was handy, given that the 3rd Dragoons were at the far end of a thirty thousand-mile supply chain.

"Lisar also tells me Brigade-Captain chan Khartan will be arriving along with Braykhan's guns," the division-captain said.

"Yes, Sir. I already had that information," chan Kymo acknowledged. "Exactly where I'm going to park them all's going to be something of a puzzle, though, I'm afraid."

Chan Geraith snorted. Shodan chan Khartan commanded the 3rd Dragoons' 2nd Brigade, which would add better than three thousand men to his current troop strength when it arrived. An infantry brigade was almost twice that size, but an infantry division had only two brigades, whereas a dragoon division had three, for a nominal total of just over ten thousand men, not counting the inevitable attachments. True, no unit was ever fully up to the numbers in its official table of organization. That was certainly true in the Third Dragoons' case, at least! But moving even a slightly understrength division was a mammoth task, and a staggering total of locomotives and rolling stock would be required to move chan Geraith's entire command down the Trans-Temporal Express's rail line from Sharona.

"I realize space is more than a little tight," he told chan Kymo with massive understatement. "That would be true under any circumstances, and having Engineer Banchu's work trains parked all over the sidings doesn't help."

"We were lucky to have the sidings *to* park them on, Sir," chan Kymo pointed out, and chan Geraith nodded.

The Traisum Cut's narrow slot had been blasted through the heart of a three thousand-foot sheer cliff to connect the universes of Traisum and Karys, which had cost well over four billion Ternathian falcons and taken more thousands of man-hours—and tons of explosives—than the division-captain cared to think about. In the process, Fort Salby and Salbyton, the town spreading out beyond the fort, had been heavily built up as thousands of construction workers and hundreds of thousands of tons of supplies and machinery had been shipped in for the task. TTE had since removed the temporary housing which had been thrown up for those workers, but the miles upon miles of rail sidings remained.

Under other circumstances, those sidings would have provided ample space in which to park the train which had delivered chan Geraith's First Brigade to Fort Salby. Under the circumstances which actually obtained, however, space was once again at a premium. Gahlreen Taymish, TTE's First Director, had sent his senior engineer, Olvyr Banchu, forward to push the railhead across Karys as rapidly as possible as soon as word of the

Chalgyn Consortium's survey team's disastrous first contact with the Arcanans reached Sharona. Banchu had been with his work crews when the Arcanan invasion bypassed them on its way to Fort Salby, but the Arcanan commander had been more than willing to exchange Banchu and his civilian workers—over two thousand of them—and the bulk of their heavy equipment for the prisoners Regiment-Captain chan Skrithik's men had taken during their successful defense of the fort. Chan Geraith very much doubted Two Thousand Harshu had any clear idea of just how valuable all that equipment and all those trained workers were going to prove, and he was delighted to get them back. Yet happy as he was, the massive work trains Banchu had brought back from Karys had already packed much of the sidings' available room solid.

And they'd go right on using up that parking space...unless someone found them something *else* to do.

"I think we'll be able to do a little something about the congestion," the division-captain said now. "First, of course, we don't have much choice but to send our own train back. We're lucky TTE had already allocated so much heavy lift capability to Traisum, but Director Tyamish didn't know we were going to need to supply a major military deployment this far from home. He's building up for it as quickly as he can, but it's not as if he can just turn off the tap on TTE's *other* needs, especially if he's going to build up the nodal infrastructure the Army needs out here. It's going to be two months—at least—before we can get enough rolling stock this side of the Salym water gap to meet our requirement anything near what I'd call adequately. Until we do, we're going to have to make the best use we can of what we have, which means getting the men unloaded and under canvas as quickly as we can."

"That will help, Sir," chan Kymo agreed, "but we're still going to be putting fifty pounds of manure into a twenty-pound bag, if you'll pardon my saying so."

"Nonsense!" chan Geraith said bracingly. "It can't possibly be much worse than trying to put fifty pounds of manure into a *forty*-pound bag! And unless I miss my guess, we should be able to clear out a little more space, as well."

His staff looked at him, and Regiment-Captain Merkan chan Isail, his chief of staff, raised one eyebrow silently. It wasn't much of a change in expression, but chan Isail had been with chan Geraith a long time—certainly long enough for the division-captain to recognize a silently shouted question when he saw one.

"I'm seriously considering pushing an advance down the Kelsayr Chain," he said. Chan Isail's other eyebrow rose, and chan Geraith snorted again.

"I'm fully aware of the potential problems, Merkan." The division-captain's tone was almost as dry as the hot, motionless air outside his headquarters car. "All of them combined, however, can't hold a candle to the problem of getting through the Cut against active resistance, and this entire portal's so damned small—and the approach terrain's so godsdamned bad—that the only option we'd have would be to bash straight down the Cut. Even with Braykhan's heavy guns in support, that'd be a frigging nightmare."

"That's true, Sir," chan Isail agreed after a moment. "But given these people's ability to move troops and supplies by air, they'll have an enormous mobility advantage whichever way we finally go at them. That's going to be especially true in unimproved terrain without any road net or rail lines, and they've obviously been coming up the Kelsayr Chain as well as this one."

Chan Geraith nodded, his eyes dark. Traisum was one of the half-dozen or so "triples" the Portal Authority had explored—universes which possessed three portals rather than the customary two. The Chernoth portal, linking Traisum and Kelsayr, and the Salbyton Portal, linking Traisum and Karys, had been discovered within a year of each other. Unfortunately, Chernoth lay in the heart of New Ternath on the far side of the Vandor Ocean, which had made getting to it just a *tad* difficult. By the same token, however, the *Salbyton* portal (only there hadn't been a Salbyton then, of course) had been one of the most inaccessible ones ever discovered, lying as it did in the heart of the Narhathan Mountains. Given their sheer distance from home and all the manifold difficulties inherent in their development, the PA and TTE had given both of them relatively low priority, at least initially.

When the Powers That Be finally got around to them, the outlay in infrastructure had been enormous. Since the journey between Vankaiyar, the Ricathian city closest to the portal linking Traisum and Salym, and New Ternath included a water gap of over six thousand miles—practically the entire length of the Mbisi and the

chan Skrithik and his men hurt the Arcanans even more badly than we'd assumed."

He flipped the folder open and extracted half a dozen sheaves of thin, tightly typed paper, stapled at the corner, and passed them around the table.

"Obviously," he continued once each of them had a copy, "most of this has to be highly speculative, but at the division-captain's instructions, I've tried to speculate as intelligently as possible. Fortunately, I had Master-Armsman chan Vornos available to help speculate and, ah... restrain any excessive enthusiasm."

Most of the others smiled, and Brigade-Captain Renyl chan Quay, First Brigade's CO, chuckled out loud. Master-Armsman Caryl chan Vornos was close to twice chan Gayrahn's age, and thirty-odd years ago, Junior-Armsman chan Vornos had taken Under-Captain chan Quay under his wing. He'd been polishing officers in the Imperial Ternathian Army ever since, and it was obvious from chan Gayrahn's tone that chan Vornos regarded the battalion-captain as yet another work in progress.

"What became apparent as we looked at the combat reports and our interviews," chan Gayrahn went on more soberly, "is that Regiment-Captain chan Skrithik and his men severely mauled the enemy's 'dragons.' Obviously, the ones killed in the attack, even if we combine the ones picked off in Prince Janaki's ambush with the ones shot out of the sky here at the fort, represent only a relatively small percentage of the total number of dragons the regiment-captain's men observed. But it seems to have been a *significant* percentage, judging by their unwillingness to risk additional losses. I think it's worth noting that in their final attack on the fort, they used their... airborne capabilities only as a feint. They sent in the actual assault on the ground, and once that was broken, they declined to risk their remaining dragons in range of our weapons. I realize Windlord Garsal took several more down with his artillery, but that's almost certainly because they'd underestimated his guns' range. Everything from the way they approached, to the timing, and—of course—to Prince Janaki's Glimpse indicates they never intended to expose the creatures to our fire."

"I agree about their sensitivity to additional losses, Chimo," Regiment-Captain Urko chan Miera, chan Geraith's staff cartographer, said after a moment. "On the other hand, they may just've decided they weren't going to be able to take the fort whatever they did and declined to lose more of the beasties in a losing cause."

"That's certainly possible, Sir," chan Gayrahn agreed. "However, the dragons which actually attacked all seem to have been rather smaller than the ones they appear to use for transport purposes." He grimaced as chan Miera's eyebrows arched. "I know 'smaller' is a purely relative term when we're talking about creatures that weigh forty tons or more, but Chief-Armsman chan Forcal, Fort Salby's senior Distance Viewer, Saw them quite clearly. He confirms the size differential, and there's general agreement that the ones who attacked the fort were all either red or black in coloration. The red ones were the ones who breathed or spat or whatever fire, and the black ones produced the lightning bolts. Chan Forcal and the other Distance Viewers who Saw the remaining dragons during the final attack all agree they Saw less than half a dozen reds and blacks in the diversionary attack. It looks very much like they didn't have many of the... 'battle dragons,' let's call them, to begin with, and they had one hell of a lot *less* after they tangled with Fort Salby's machine guns and pedestal guns."

"There's another point to consider, too," chan Geraith put in. The staffers looked at him, and the division-captain shrugged. "Trying to retake Karys, we could only get at them by fighting our way down the Cut on the ground; their godsdamned dragons can literally fly out of the portal any time they want to. Once Lyskar here"—he nodded at Lyskar chan Serahlyk, his chief combat engineer—"finishes digging in the portal defenses, that'll change. And once Braykhan's guns get here, we'll be able to think about pushing them farther back on the approaches, but for now they've got damned close to completely free passage. That means they have an open road to attack our line of communication, but they aren't doing it. Why not? They have to realize we can't have pedestal guns and heavy Faraikas everywhere, so why *aren't* they trying to circle wide around the fort and the fixed defenses to get at the rail line or our fatigue parties?" He looked around the map table. "Any commander with a scrap of initiative would be probing our rear area defenses, if nothing else, and does anyone in this compartment want argue that someone who managed to advance over four thousand miles in *twelve days* doesn't have at least a trace of initiative? The fact that this 'Two Thousand Harshu' of theirs isn't doing exactly that suggests to me that he has to be extraordinarily sensitive to additional losses for *some* reason. And according to young chan Hopyr he appears to have plenty of men, which seems to add point to the theory that it's his logistics, not manpower, that's the problem."

Platoon-Captain Rynai chan Hopyr was the Distance Viewer who'd gone forward with the escort sent to shepherd Olvyr Banchu and his engineers back to Fort Salby. His was a powerful Talent, and he'd used it to good effect scouting the Arcanans' positions and troop strength. He'd tallied in excess of a hundred and fifty of their dragons and at least six thousand men, twice the 3rd Dragoons' current strength in Traisum. There was no way to tell what might have lain outside his range, but chan Geraith was certain the Arcanan commander had strength chan Hopyr hadn't Seen. Not that what he *had* Seen hadn't been quite bad enough.

"That's essentially my own conclusion, Sir," chan Gayrahn said. "Well, mine and Master-Armsman chan Vornos'. All indications are that Harshu is a determined, ruthless commander—more than ruthless enough to accept casualties and losses as the price of accomplishing his mission. Yet he hasn't even tried to attack the rail line behind us."

"Perhaps he simply doesn't realize how important it is," chan Isail suggested, and chan Geraith nodded. One of the things he most valued about chan Isail was the chief of staff's hardheaded pragmatism. Chan Geraith's own tendency was to think in the most aggressive terms possible. Aggressively enough, in fact, that he sometimes found himself badly in need of chan Isail's willingness to challenge (or at least critically examine) his underlying assumptions.

"I think it's entirely possible—even probable—that he doesn't have a clear grasp of how much we can move, or how quickly we can move it, on rails," the division-captain conceded now. "In fact, I don't see how it could be any other way. They had to be as ignorant of our capabilities as we were of theirs when they set out to attack us, and Harshu wouldn't have been so quick to let Banchu and the work crews go if he'd realized how badly he could hurt us by just hanging on to them."

"You're probably right about that, Sir," chan Kymo said thoughtfully. "I've been trying to get some sort of mental picture of how our transport capabilities stack up against theirs, now that we know about these dragon things of theirs." The quartermaster shrugged.

"I can't be positive they don't have something like our railroads, obviously, but I agree with you that Harshu would never have let Banchu's people go so readily—at the very least, he would've insisted that all their equipment be left behind or destroyed—if he'd had any real grasp of their importance. In fact, I'm beginning to think it's important we not let ourselves be so dazzled by how *quickly* they can move that we overestimate how *much* they can move.

"Assume a sixty-ton dragon can carry its own weight. Frankly, that seems unlikely as hell for any flying beast, but given how 'unlikely' dragons are in the first place, I'm not going to say they can't. But that's still only sixty tons per dragon, whereas we can load a hundred and ten tons into a standard freight car, and the heavy-lift cars can carry almost twice that much. We hauled over *ten thousand* tons all the way from Sharona in a single train. Assuming their dragons really could haul sixty tons apiece, they'd still need over a hundred and seventy of them to match that total...and we currently have two more trains that size following us down the same line, with more loading up right behind them. If Harshu had any concept of what that means, he'd be moving heaven and all the Arpathian hells combined to stop us from doing it."

"Point taken," chan Isail said after a moment.

"I think Therahk may have an even better point than he realizes," chan Geraith said. His subordinates looked at him, and he smiled thinly. "We have to remember both sides are dealing with opponents with completely unknown capabilities. I know I just said that, but it bears repeating because it's something we *have* to keep in mind. At the moment, Harshu undoubtedly calculates—correctly, by the way—that he has every tactical advantage there is in our current standoff. He can't know how good our heavy artillery is, and I think it's obvious that until he hit chan Skrithik here at Fort Salby, none of our people had an opportunity to use their weapons and doctrine effectively against him. He'd've been one hell of a lot more cautious about how he went after Salby if they had. But he's got a better feeling for our capabilities by now, and he's probably licking his chops thinking about what he can do to any assault we might launch down the Cut, right into his teeth. If nothing else, those damned dragons of his mean he could put explosive charges into the sides of the Cut anywhere he wanted to. We've already seen what their equivalent of dynamite can do to a fort's wall, so there's no reason to assume they couldn't do the same things to the *Cut's* walls, now is there?"

He looked around their expressions. Most of them looked as if they'd really like to disagree with him; none of them did.

"One thing we have to remember, though," he continued after a moment, "is that they *have* had the opportunity to observe our capabilities on their advance from Hell's Gate. By now, for example, they must realize our draft animals are nowhere near as big or as powerful as theirs are, judging by those cavalry horses of theirs."

Chan Isail nodded sourly. The "horses" the Arcanans had used in their final assault on Fort Salby were bigger than the largest Chinthai draft horse he'd ever seen, yet according to all of the witnesses, they'd charged the fort's eastern wall cross-country at a speed few Sharonian thoroughbreds could have matched on a racetrack. Obviously, the Arcanans' magic—or whatever the hells they called it—had been at work there, as well.

"I think we also have to assume that they've captured accurate maps of both the Karys and Kelsayr Chains," chan Geraith pointed out. "If they have, they probably realize just how unimproved both chains are beyond Karys and Lashai, not to mention the water gap here in Traisum. Where Kelsayr's concerned, they'll probably assume—logically—that six thousand miles of ocean and another forty-six hundred miles overland must constitute a pretty severe bottleneck here in Traisum, and they'll evaluate our mobility beyond the railheads on the basis of piss-poor roads and trails, wagons, and pack animals. By the same token, even if Therahk's completely correct about Harshu's not realizing how much we can transport by rail, I'll guarantee you he *does* realize we can move one hell of a lot more in a freight car than we could in a six-horse wagon down a dirt trail. So if I were him, and if I could move my entire army four thousand miles in less than two weeks, I wouldn't be especially worried by the possibility of being flanked on a seventeen thousand-mile march by an enemy restricted to horse-drawn transport. Even if he knows about the shipyard at Renaiyrton and the rail line through Kelsayr and Lashai, he'll figure he has plenty of defensive depth on that front."

He paused as if to see if any of his staffers wanted to disagree with him. No one did, and he shrugged.

"So what *I'd* do," he said, "is send word however quickly I could to whoever I'd had advancing up the Kelsayr Chain to turn himself around, backtrack to Thermyn, and then move up to support me in Karys as quickly as he could. I'm sure Harshu committed dragons to support the other advance, as well, so by recalling them, he should be able to regenerate at least a little of the dragon strength chan Skrithik and Prince Janaki cost him here. That would strengthen him against any attack we were foolish enough to launch down the Cut, and it might also give him enough strength to actually try cutting or at least damaging the rail line between here and Salym with deep strike raids into our rear. I think he's expecting to be reinforced—probably pretty damned heavily—as soon as his superiors can get additional men and dragons forward to him. At that point, if I were him, I'd be thinking in terms of using the additional dragons to send a major force through our portal here to drop in somewhere several hundred miles in our rear to cut the rail line and *hold* it. If I could manage that, then eventually I'd be able to starve out Salbyton and any field force protecting the Cut, and if I could interdict movement from Salym *into* Traisum. I'd have both the Kelsayr and Karys Chains without having to deal with the water gap between Chernoth and Renaiyrton. I don't care how 'magical' their damned dragons are, they *can't* be up to a six thousand-mile flight without stopping, or they'd've been one hells of a lot farther up-chain than they are before we even knew they were coming!"

He paused, as if for comments, but once again none of his staffers said anything, and he shrugged.

"Everything makes the advance through Karys the shortest line of advance once he can get past the Cut, and the Cut won't be anywhere near the terrain obstacle for them that it is for us. A *serious* obstacle, but not an insurmountable one like crossing the Vandor without ships. Because of that, and because it's our only present point of contact, he almost *has* to be calling in his secondary advance to strengthen his position in Karys until those reinforcements he's expecting arrive. He'll probably leave pickets along the Kelsayr Chain to cover his back, but I very much doubt he'll seriously expect anyone to attack them."

Chan Isail was looking at him very intently indeed now, and the division-captain smiled again, more thinly even than before.

"My mother always used to tell me a little knowledge is a dangerous thing," he said. "And she used to say it's not what you don't know is so that hurts you; it's what you *think* you know that *isn't* so. At the moment, Harshu knows a lot more about us than we know about him, but no Arcanan's ever so much as heard of a Bison. I realize seventeen thousand miles is a long way, but we've got over thirty-five hundred miles of rail line clear across Kelsayr and Lashai and TTE's already laying track in Resym. For that matter, its advanced work crews are cutting and grading roadbed over a hundred miles down-chain from the current railhead. Since we haven't lost Voice contact with them yet but we *have* lost contact with the portal forts in Nairsom and on Lake Wernisk in Resym, I'm inclined to think that's as far up-chain as they've gotten. What it means from our current perspective is that it's only about seven thousand miles cross-country from the railhead to Hell's Gate as opposed to four thousand miles going via Karys. For that matter, it's barely *three* thousand miles to Thermyn, and at least until Harshu is heavily reinforced, the Cut works both ways as a defensive feature. For that matter," the division-captain's already thin smile became a razor, "he may just find it costing him more than he expects to get his dragons through the portal here even *after* he's reinforced."

"That's true, Sir," chan Isail said. "But the weather's going to be a royal pain in the arse in Kelsayr, and Thermyn and Nairsom aren't exactly going to be picnics this time of year, either."

"At least winter in Serinach will be a change from Salbyton!" chan Geraith retorted, and more than one of his staff officers chuckled again. Serinach, the northernmost state of the Republic of Rendisphar back in Sharona, consisted of most of the vast Serinach Peninsula where New Ternath reached towards the Serinach Strait which separated it from the easternmost tip of Farnalia. For all its stupendous size, Serinach was only lightly inhabited...which had quite a lot to do with Serinach winters.

"The good news," chan Geraith continued, "is that we can move everything by ship and rail all the way from Traisum to Resym, and the construction crews in Resym shifted into high gear the instant TTE heard about Fallen Timbers. Master Banchu's ready to start moving *his* crews and their heavy equipment to Resym, as well, and once they get there, they'll be laying double-tracked line in three shifts. On that basis, they'll be putting in the next best thing to twenty-five miles of track a day, and Therahk estimates that we'll need another couple of months to bring up the rest of the division and prep it for the move. That means they'll have laid another eleven hundred miles across Resym by the time we get there."

He paused, and chan Isail nodded slowly.

"You're right that the weather in Thermyn and Nairsom will be more of a problem," chan Geraith conceded, "but the worst leg from that perspective's going to be in Nairsom, and that's less than six hundred miles. On the basis of our exercises at Fort Emperor Erthain, the Bisons should be able to maintain an average speed of around fifteen miles an hour across the kind of terrain between Kelsayr and Thermyn even in winter. Allowing for the present length of rail, mounted scouts could cover the total distance from Vankaiyar here in Traisum to Fort Ghartoun in about sixteen and a half weeks. Allowing for rail length by the time we could get the Bisons to the railhead, the rest of the division could cover the same distance in about *nine* weeks, and I guarantee you that's one hells of a lot sooner than anyone on the other side's going to be expecting us!"

His staffers were staring at him now. They were silent for a very long moment, then chan Isail cleared his throat.

"Sir, the Bisons have never been tested on that kind of extended advance."

"True enough." Chan Geraith nodded. "But they *have* done the thousand-mile torture test—in winter, through the mountains— and did it damned well, too. And that was *before* we adopted the new rubber-backed track blocks. I know those were only trials, with the best mechanics we had on the spot to put faults right, but that's still impressive as hell."

"I know it is, Sir. But this is a lot longer trip over a lot of different sorts of terrain. However good they may be, there'd be bound to be a lot of breakdowns before we ever got to Thermyn."

"Agreed. On the other hand, we'll have to leave a big enough force here at Salbyton to hold the Cut from our side and to make enough noise to keep Harshu looking this way instead of over his shoulder." Chan Geraith shrugged. "We don't want him to see the Bisons if he decides to risk a few dragons to fly recon-naissance, anyway, so whoever we leave behind couldn't make much use of them here at the Cut. That being the case, we strip the brigade that stands in place and use its Bisons to supplement the flank column's organic transports. And the Army's shipping additional Bisons and Steel Mules forward after us as quickly as it can procure them, along with every steam dray it can get its hands on. Our engineers will improve the roads as we go, so anything coming down the route behind us should be able to move much faster than our main column. Banchu's crews will go right on laying track behind us—and extending the kerosene pipeline, too. They ought to make another six or seven hundred miles good between the time we leave the railhead and the time we reach Thermyn, which will effectively shorten the distance any new Bisons or drays will have to cover. And TTE's already surveyed their entire roadbed. We know where the worst terrain's located, and they can push advance crews ahead of the track layers to begin tackling them. The worst will be getting through the Dalazan Rain Forest in Resym...but that's also where the TTE crews can start improvising bridges and improvising fords out of local materials soonest."

"And those pickets they may've left behind, Sir?" the chief of staff asked.

"I'll grant you they may have all sorts of 'magic powers,' Merkan," chan Geraith said. "And given the way they've managed to shut down the Voice network as they advanced, they must've gotten at least some knowledge of our Talents. But we're the *Third Dragoons*. If there's anyone this side of Arpathia who's as good as we are at scouting an enemy position without being spotted, *I've* never met them. We send a battalion or so down the chain on horseback with enough Voices to maintain constant communication with us. We'll need to get them off as quickly as we can, because it'll take them so much longer to cross the unimproved universes, but there's not a portal in the chain that isn't at least twenty-five miles across. Ask the PAAF how easy it is to 'picket' a portal that size even with a fort right in the middle of it! We send along a full recon section, complete with a Mapper, a half-dozen Plotters to keep an eye on the sky for dragons, and a good Distance Viewer or two to make it harder than hell for the Arcanans to see them coming even if they're mounting standing patrols of dragons around the portals. And we make sure they've got an extra weapons company with mortars and heavy machine guns. They'll have a hell of a lot better chance of spotting a picket on one of those portals than the picket will of spotting them when no one on the other side's going to believe there could possibly be Ternathian dragoons anywhere near them."

"And if they do spot a picket, Sir?" chan Isail asked quietly.

"That's why we'll be sending the mortars and the machine guns, Merkan, because if there *are* any pickets out there, it'll be our turn to shut down their warning network the same way *they* shut down the Voice network." No one could possibly have mistaken Arlos chan Geraith's expression for a smile this time.

"*Exactly* the way they shut down our Voices," he said very, very softly.

CHAPTER THREE

Inkara 9, 205 YU
(November 30, 1928 CE)

COMMANDER OF ONE THOUSAND KLAYRMAN TORALK GLOW-
ered at the report in his personal crystal. It was neatly
organized and illustrated by half a dozen color-coded graphs and
charts—obviously, the intelligence types had figured out how to
get the best out of their word-processing spellware—but it made
grim and ugly reading.

We are so *screwed*, he reflected glumly, and paged ahead to the
latest dispatch from Commander of One Hundred Faryx Helika.

Helika's 5001st Strike had been the weakest of the First Provisional Talon's three strikes when the Arcanan Expeditionary
Force set out on this nightmare journey. That had made it easy
enough to dispense with it and assign it to the purely secondary
advance up what the Sharonians called the Kelsayr Chain, but
that had changed. In theory, an Air Force talon should have
consisted of three full strength strikes of twelve fighting dragons
each. In fact, Toralk's talon consisted of—or would consist of,
after Helika's arrival—the 5001st's three reds and three blacks,
the three blacks which were all that survived of the 3012th Strike,
plus the *single* black survivor of the 2029th. Of course, there
no longer *was* a 2029th; Toralk had officially disbanded it and
assigned its survivors to the 3012th.

Ten, he thought bitterly. *A whole* ten *out of the thirty-six I*
ought to *have, and not a yellow among them. Not that anyone*
this side of a lunatic would send yellows in against Sharonian
defenses that know they're coming!

They'd paid a savage price to discover what alert Sharonian

artillery could do to strafing dragons, and Toralk blamed himself for it. They'd captured Sharonian "field guns" and "machine guns" in their advance from Hell's Gate, and that loathsome bile toad Neshok had actually experimented with them and sent the results of his experiments forward. Toralk could tell himself—honestly—that Neshok's experiments had been far from complete. That Neshok had both underestimated the range their "field guns" could attain, and provided no information at all about "shells" that exploded in mid-air and threw out hundreds of smaller projectiles. He suspected those were probably the "shrapnel shells" which had turned up in the intelligence summaries with a question mark behind them, so perhaps a fair-minded man (not that Toralk had the least desire to be fair-minded where Alivar Neshok was concerned) would have to admit the interrogator had at least given him the best information available. But Neshok hadn't warned him at all about the weapons the Sharonians called "pedestal guns." Not, Toralk admitted bitterly, that it would have made any difference. The thousand wanted to think that if he'd realized there was a weapon which could fire explosive shells at such a high rate he would have re-thought his plan to attack Fort Salby. Unfortunately, he knew better. He'd allowed himself—and the late Five Hundred Myr—to not simply expect the element of surprise but to make their entire attack plan *depend* upon it.

And it didn't help anything when Myr took it upon himself to throw good money after bad. Toralk felt his jaw muscles tensing again and forced himself to relax them. *If the idiot—*

He made himself let go of the thought. He'd been a strike dragon pilot himself in his day. He knew the breed, knew how their minds worked. And because he had been, and because he did know, he understood exactly what Cerlohs Myr had been thinking—or *not* thinking—after the Sharonians somehow managed to ambush his dragons on their way to the target.

Toralk still couldn't see how the Sharonians could have known where to dig in those machine guns on either flank of the approach valley he and Myr had chosen from their maps, yet he'd come to the conclusion they *must* have known. There was no other possible explanation for why those machine guns had been positioned on those hot, dry hillsides so far away from the line of the Sharonian "railroad" and the road running beside it. They'd been in *exactly* the right spot, and nothing Neshok's interrogation teams had wrung out of their prisoners explained how the Sharonians had gotten them there in time. So far, at least, there'd been no mention of any of the bizarre Sharonian Talents which could have predicted Myr's approach route with the necessary precision.

Toralk wasn't ready to conclude that that meant there *wasn't* such a Talent, and Shartahk knew Neshok's interrogation methods were unlikely to encourage anyone to volunteer information that wasn't dragged out of him. If there *was* such a Talent, however, and if it operated with any degree of reliability, the implications were terrifying. How could anyone defeat an enemy who literally *knew* when, where, and how he was coming? But if that sort of Talent existed, how had the Sharonians been so surprised by the AEF's initial attacks? And even assuming it had only come into play after the attack began, he came back again and again to the Sharonian possession of their Voice communications system. If anyone had possessed a Talent capable not simply of realizing an attack was coming but of predicting its exact route accurately enough—and far enough in advance—to dig in heavy machine guns on either side of exactly the one of several valleys the leading dragon strike might have followed, then surely the Voices could have passed that warning farther down-chain, as well. For someone without arcanely aided combat engineers, it must have taken the better part of at least three days' hard labor to prepare the defenses of Fort Salby as thoroughly as they'd been prepared. So if some bizarre Talent farther up-chain from Traisum had managed to predict the attack in time for them to accomplish that much, why hadn't the warning been passed still farther in that ample time window?

Stop beating your head against that particular wall, Klayr-man, he told himself again. *Maybe you were just lucky in Karys. Maybe they* did *send a warning to Fort Mosanik but they had too little advance notice for it to get there before you hit it and took out its Voice. File this one under the "Never, Never, Ever Take Liberties Against Sharonians Again Just Because You Think You Have The Advantage of Surprise" heading and get on with where we go from here.*

He grimaced, wondering if one reason his mind insisted on fretting itself against the question of how the Sharonians had managed it was because of how little he wanted to contemplate the options available to the AEF in the aftermath of Fort Salby. Helika's strike would arrive within the next eighteen to twenty hours, but there wouldn't be any more battle dragons for at least another two or three months. Nor were there any replacements for the eighteen transport dragons who'd been killed or too badly wounded for the dragon healers to return to service. That left his 1st Provisional AATC Aerie with only a hundred and seventy transports, and that was too few for a field force operating the next godsdamned thing to thirty thousand miles beyond the nearest sliderhead.

A single transport could carry loads weighing up to about a quarter of its own mass, which on average came to about fifteen tons of cargo. For short hops that could be boosted to as much as twenty or even twenty-five tons, but the cost in endurance and operational range was high. Levitation spells could double normal capacities, but spells with that sort of power requirement was magister-level work, and the military never had enough magister-level Gifts to meet its needs. The Army Air Transport Command belonged to the Air Force, despite its name and despite strenuous efforts by the Army to hang onto it, and Toralk had put in his own time as a junior officer commanding transport strikes and even talons. As a result, he was well aware of the acute limits on the uniformed personnel who could charge levitation accumulators, especially once they got too far forward to tap the power nets established in more heavily inhabited universes. There were very good reasons the AATC operated from nodal bases where it could assemble its most strongly Gifted techs to charge as many accumulators as possible. It kept such valuable personnel safely out of harm's way, rather than parceling them out in tenth-mark packets, working in isolation too close to the sharp end of the stick, and it was generally simpler and more efficient to ship the charged accumulators—which weighed barely two pounds each, after all—forward to where they were needed.

Except that no one in his worst nightmares had dreamed anyone might ever need to supply such a force this big out at the arse-end of nowhere, and Commander of Two Thousand mul Gurthak had been forced to strip the dozen closest universes of transports to give Toralk what he had. Anything mul Gurthak had left was absolutely essential to maintaining the Expeditionary Force's rear area transport requirements, not to mention the forts and sparse civilian populations scattered through those universes. That cupboard was bare, and there wouldn't be any more dragons popping out of it anytime soon.

That was bad enough, but there'd never been enough accumulators, either. Still worse, the nearest real stockpile had been in Ucala, at the end of the slider net from New Arcana, 24,300 miles behind Arcana's first encounter with the Sharonians, and they'd advanced over four thousand miles since then. That was the next best thing to two hundred and fifty hours' flight time for a transport dragon, and a transport needed periodic breaks in flight and at least several hours rest per day, not to mention downtime for things like eating. All of which meant it was a sixteen-day trip—one way—between Ucala and Toralk's tent here in the universe Sharona had christened Karys. Even more unhappily, the Ucala stockpile had been completely depleted by the heavy transport demands required to build up the AEF's main logistic base in Mahritha and keep moving this far forward. Commander of Five Hundred Mantou Lyshair, the acting CO of Toralk's AATC detachment, was down to an accumulator inventory far below the minimum level specified by The Book, and that was another situation that wasn't going to get better anytime soon.

And because it isn't, the transports Lyshair does have are forced to fly without accumulators, which is exhausting the dragons faster and hauling half the tonnage to boot. And then there's the little problem of fodder and dragon feed, he reminded himself glumly.

The terrain between portals in both Karys and Failcham was hot, dry, and arid. There'd been little Sharonian civilian presence in either of them, which meant there'd also been little farmland to provide fodder for the cavalry's horses or fresh food to vary the men's diet, and there'd been neither domesticated animals nor large herds of wild animals to provide meat for the dragons or the cavalry's unicorns. The wicked losses Gyras Urlan's heavy dragoons had suffered in the final lunge at Fort Salby had reduced the number of horses they had to feed, but there were plenty of the hungry creatures left, and transporting enough food for all of the Expeditionary Force's draft animals—*and humans; let's not forget them, Klayrman,* he reminded himself—only increased the workload on the pilots and beasts of Lyshair's exhausted aerie still further.

We don't have a choice, he decided. *I'm going to have to rotate the transport talons at least as far back as Thermyn to hunt.*

That would be better than two thousand miles, but the portal between Thermyn and Failcham was in central Yanko, and a relatively short hop from there would take them to the vast, rolling plains of western Andara with its endless herds of bison. The hunting would be good, the game would be plentiful, the talon he rotated back would have good eating while it was there, and hunting parties could take enough additional bison to be shipped forward to Karys when it returned.

Of course, it's going to cost me a quarter of my transports, he reflected glumly. *And given the number of carnivorous mouths we have to feed, I'll have to authorize Lyshair to dip into his levitation accumulators to haul the meat back. At least we're in good shape for food preservation spells, so it won't rot before it gets eaten. That's not going to help with the fodder, though.*

He frowned unhappily, then sighed. Two Thousand Harshu wasn't going to like it, but they'd have to send the horses back along with the transports. A winter on the Western Plains of Andara would be no picnic, even for the arcanely enhanced cavalry mounts, but it would be better than trying to graze them here.

Sure, it'll be better, but that's sort of like saying amputation's better than gangrene! Our biggest single advantage over the Sharonians is our mobility, and that's oozing away from us while we sit here. Thank Trembo Fire Heel for the Traisum Cut! At least without dragons of their own those bastards aren't going to be coming down it after us anytime soon. Unfortunately...

He sighed again and paged to the brief report he was going to have to discuss with Harshu. Until that unmitigated bastard Carthos got here from the secondary advance Harshu had recalled, Klayrman Toralk, for his sins, remained the second ranking officer of the AEF. That made him Mayrkos Harshu's senior officer, and that made it his unwelcome job to share his staff's estimates—guesstimates, really—of *Sharonian* transport capabilities with his superior. Frankly, he was half convinced those guesstimates were wildly pessimistic, but only half. And if they weren't, if the Sharonians really could pack two or three dragonweights of freight into a single one of their railroad cars...

If they can, *they may be slower than we are, but they've got the godsdamned railroad built all the way to the portal. Once whatever they have in the pipeline starts arriving in Traisum, they'll be able to build up quickly—probably even more quickly than we*

*could if we had as many levitation accumulators as we wanted!
Each load'll take longer to make the trip, but a single "train" as
long as the work trains that pulled out of Karys after the prisoner
exchange can carry as much as all my transports together. And
that's assuming the transports have the accumulators to double up!*

That, he decided, was a very unpleasant thought indeed.

* * *

Commander of Five Hundred (acting) Alivar Neshok looked
up from the report in his PC as Shield Lisaro Porath knocked
once, opened his office door, and stepped through it. The one
good thing about the abrupt check in the AEF's advance was
that there'd been time for the engineers to throw up quarters
a bit more substantial than tents. The chansyu huts, named for
the legendary immortal Ransaran two-headed, winged lion which
died and was reborn in a flash of lightning, couldn't be erected
quite as quickly as their name suggested, but now that the AEF
looked like spending at least several months in one spot, more
durable quarters were in order.

Neshok didn't like the fact that their advance had come to
such a screeching halt, but he was grateful for the solid roof and
walls—and the warmth—the chansyus provided. The privacy that
came with walls less permeable to sound than canvas was also
welcome, and so was the rather more comfortable set of quarters
attached to the chansyu which housed his office.

Now the shield braced to attention in front of his field desk
and touched his chest in salute.

"Sorry to disturb you, Five Hundred, but Thousand Gahnyr
is here to see you," he said.

Porath—a black-haired, brown-eyed Hilmaran with a thin
mustache—was a solid, chunky, broad-shouldered fellow whose
hard face hinted at the flinty soul of the man who wore it. He'd
been *Javelin* Porath up until about last week, when Neshok had
finally managed to get him the promotion he'd so amply earned.
It was a mark of the way Two Thousand Harshu and Thousand
Toralk were busy pushing Neshok into obscurity now that they
felt they no longer needed him that it had taken so long for
Porath's promotion to come through.

That thought sent a familiar trickle of resentment through the
five hundred, and his lips thinned as he recalled how different
Harshu's attitude had been when the AEF's advance had begun.

No one had expressed any qualms then about how Neshok and his handful of interrogators got the intelligence Harshu needed to plan his movements or Toralk needed to plan specific attacks. Oh, no! All that had mattered *then* was that the information continue to flow!

He treasured the heat of his anger for a moment, warming the hands of his soul's bitterness above the furnace of his fury, then made himself take a mental step back. The truth was that Toralk had always looked down that long, Andaran nose of his at Neshok. In fact, he'd protested to Harshu about the five hundred's methods several times. Hadn't kept him from making use of the information Neshok and Porath and the others like them had obtained for him, though, had it? But now that the brilliant tacticians like Harshu and Toralk were bogged down in front of a bottleneck they couldn't find a way through, now that they might have to start answering awkward questions from their own superiors, *now* they were ready to throw the despised "intelligence puke" who'd brought them this far to the dragon to cover their own arses. They weren't even accepting personal briefings from Neshok any longer. Instead, they sent middlemen like Commander of One Thousand Faildym Gahnyr to see if Neshok had obtained any additional intelligence that might let them somehow crawl out of the pit into which their advance had fallen.

The five hundred squared his shoulders, inhaled deeply, and nodded to Porath.

"Show the Thousand in, Lisaro."

He was rather pleased with how calmly the sentence came out, and he shut down his PC, climbed out of his chair, and straightened his tunic. He caught a glimpse of himself in the mirrored surface of the PC and allowed himself a brief lip twitch of satisfaction. As an intelligence officer, he theoretically ought to have worn the Office of Army Intelligence's gray trousers and maroon tunic with the OAI's unsleeping eye shoulder flash. Instead, he wore the standard camouflage pattern tunic—still the mottled green, black, and brown of summer—of a line Infantry or Cavalry officer. That was more than sufficient to frost the chops of any hard-nosed operational type like Toralk, and Neshok took a certain degree of pleasure in rubbing those aforesaid hard noses in it. He'd been instructed by Two Thousand mul Gurthak himself to avoid OAI uniform, and there wasn't much anyone could do about it as long as he was following the governor's instructions.

He looked up from the reflection and came to attention as Thousand Gahnyr followed Porath back into Neshok's workspace.

"Thousand," he said, saluting briskly, and Gahnyr nodded back with rather less formality.

"Five Hundred," he responded, and accepted Neshok's gestured invitation to seat himself in the chair floating in front of the desk.

Neshok dismissed Porath with a flick of his head, then resumed his own chair and leaned back in it ever so slightly, regarding Gahnyr with an attentive expression.

"How can I help you, Sir?" he inquired as the door closed behind Porath.

"I'm on my way to a meeting with Two Thousand Harshu and Thousand Toralk," Gahnyr said. "It's mostly just a routine base-touching, but I wondered if you'd had time to go over those dispatches from Thousand Carthos? If you've turned up anything new, I thought I'd take it along with me."

"Of course, Sir." Neshok's reply was as crisp as the nod which accompanied it, despite a fresh stab of resentment. Of course Gahnyr would "take it along" with him. It wouldn't do to have Alivar Neshok's pariah presence cast its shadow across Commander of Two Thousand Harshu's latest meeting, would it? Why, if that happened, somebody might actually think Harshu had authorized Neshok's actions!

"There isn't really anything new—certainly not anything earthshaking—in Thousand Carthos' reports, Sir," he continued. "I could wish there were more prisoner interrogations"—his opaque eyes flicked up to meet Gahnyr's briefly—"since that's proven our best source of intelligence, but apparently not many prisoners were actually taken. On the other hand, he'd only gotten about halfway across Resym before he was recalled to join us here, and aside from the fort at the Nairsom-Resym portal, he hadn't encountered anything remotely like resistance, so he probably had less opportunity to secure prisoners than we've had."

"Probably not," Gahnyr agreed in a neutral tone.

The infantry thousand wasn't as imaginative as Klayrman Toralk, his Air Force counterpart, but he couldn't have missed the implication of Neshok's remarks, and the intelligence officer felt a flicker of satisfaction. They'd find it a bit more difficult to dodge the crap Carthos' lack of prisoners was going to splash all over everyone in sight. None of Carthos' reports said so in so many words, but it was obvious he hadn't bothered to *take* any prisoners, and it was difficult to believe every single Sharonian he'd encountered had died fighting.

Not going to be able to sweep that *under the rug, are you?* the five hundred thought coldly. *And Carthos is a regular Infantry officer, not one of those Office of Intelligence types you can shove all your own responsibility off onto, isn't he?*

Indeed Carthos was, and—like Neshok—he enjoyed the protection of no less a patron than Two Thousand mul Gurthak, himself. That was a reflection which brought Neshok quite a lot of comfort upon occasion. Harshu and Toralk might think they'd be able to use him as the sacrificial goat if the time came that some bleeding heart from the Commandery or Inspector General's Office decided to look into any irregularities where the Kerellian Accords were concerned. In fact, he was quite sure now that Harshu had had that in mind from the beginning. He'd throw up his hands in horror when the investigators arrived and tell the multiverse he'd had no idea what his "out of control" subordinates were doing. Of course he hadn't! But, after all, what could anyone have expected? It wasn't as if the Office of Army Intelligence was one of the *combat arms* with a properly developed sense of honor, was it?

But that wasn't going to fly when Neshok and Carthos testified under truth spell that their actions been authorized every step of the way. Especially not when their testimony would implicate not simply Harshu but also mul Gurthak, who was a far larger and more influential fish.

"As for the other material in the Thousand's reports," the five hundred continued after a moment, "his reconnaissance gryphons and dragon overflights have confirmed what we were able to deduce from the captured Sharonian maps, at least as far as everything within a thousand miles or so of the Nairsom-Resym portal is concerned. There's virtually no sign of human inhabitants and the only 'roads' are little more than dirt trails hacked out of the undergrowth. There's no way anyone without dragons could operate in that sort of terrain."

"Good," Gahnyr said. "Can you shoot a summary of his reports to my PC before supper?"

"Of course, Sir."

"Then I think that's about everything." The infantry thousand stood: he did not, Neshok noticed, offer to clasp forearms with him. "I'd best be going if I'm going to make that meeting on time. Thank you, Five Hundred."

"You're welcome, Sir," Neshok replied pleasantly, and came to his feet respectfully as Gahnyr nodded, turned, and left the office.

Oh, you're very *welcome,* the five hundred thought as the door closed. *And I'll be sure to emphasize all those little . . . irregularities Thousand Carthos has been up to. You and Two Thousand Harshu may think you can feed me to the dragon without getting your lily-white hands dirty, but it's not going to be* that *easy. I may be a stinking little intelligence puke, not a proper combat officer, but you're playing on my turf when it comes to information control. By the time I'm done, there's going to be enough evidence tucked away in official records and documentation to lead any IG investigators straight to all of the rest of you, too.*

It might not be enough to save his neck, but at least he'd have the satisfaction of taking all the others down with him.

And the thought of all those smoking dragons hidden away in the files ought to help motivate Two Thousand mul Gurthak to keep his *promises about protection and promotion, as well. Because if he doesn't, I'm godsdamned sure I won't be going down alone.*

*　　*　　*

"You realize Thalmayr would send us both to the dragon if he realized what you and I were talking about," Commander of Fifty Jaralt Sarma observed almost whimsically, arms crossed over his broad chest as he tipped back in his chair and balanced on its rear legs. He was a relatively short, stocky, heavyset young man with unruly brown hair and dark eyes which Therman Ulthar suspected had gotten a lot harder in the last couple of weeks.

"Probably," Ulthar agreed after a moment. "Assuming he didn't just throw us into a cell along with the Sharonians and beat the hells out of *us* every other day along with them."

Sarma's lips tightened, but he didn't disagree. In his own considered opinion, Hadrign Thalmayr was a sociopath. Whether he'd always been one or whether it was a recent development, following his catastrophic showing at the Mahritha portal, was more than the fifty was prepared to say, but it didn't really matter. Regulations, the Articles of War, and the Kerellian Accords were very, very clear and explicit about the proper treatment of POWs. And even if they hadn't been, there were some things Jaralt Sarma wasn't prepared to stomach.

"Actually," Ulthar went on, "if he threw us into a cell with Regiment-Captain Velvelig, he wouldn't get an opportunity to beat the shit out of us. Velvelig would do it for him. In fact, he'd probably reach right down our throats and rip out our hearts with his bare hands." The wiry, red-haired fifty shook his head, his expression even grimmer than Sarma's. "That's a hard man, Jaralt, and I've been watching him. Anyone who can drop a dozen gryphons all by himself—and put a bullet into the last one's eye after he was down with an arbalest bolt in a shattered hip—is *not* someone I want pissed at me. He's already decided what he's going to do. He's just waiting until he has the best chance to take some of us with him before he tries it."

Sarma nodded. He hadn't spent as much time as Ulthar had in Fort Ghartoun's brig—whether as a prisoner himself or since the survivors of the fort's Sharonian garrison had been imprisoned there—for several reasons. The most important of them was his lack of desire to draw Thalmayr's attention to himself, but his own sense of shame was high on the list, as well. On the other hand, *he'd* never been Velvelig's prisoner. He didn't have the personal, searing sense of obligation Ulthar felt. No, *his* shame was for the way in which Thalmayr degraded and dishonored the entire Andaran officer corps by his actions. Not that Thalmayr was alone in that...which presented its own thorny problem.

"The question before the house is what we do about all of this," he said. "We're very junior officers, Therman. Whatever we do is probably going to put us over our heads in dragon shit by the time it all hits the wall."

"*I'd* already be there if you hadn't stopped me," Ulthar replied. "In case I didn't already say it, thanks."

He looked across at the shorter man, his eyes level and his tone somber, and Sarma unfolded his arms to wave one hand in a brushing away gesture.

"Couldn't let you get yourself killed before I had a chance to come along with you," he responded, and the lightness of his own tone fooled neither of them. If he hadn't intercepted Ulthar on his way towards the fort's office block, Commander of One Hundred Hadrign Thalmayr or Therman Ulthar—or both—would be dead by now.

"Maybe you couldn't," Ulthar said, "but this is a lot more on me than it is on you. The bastard's *my* company commander, and

I'm the one Velvelig and his healers did their dead level best to take care of. That makes it personal, Jaralt."

"I know that. But you won't do anyone any good if you try to storm his office. While I'll agree Thalmayr's dumber than a rock, there's a reason he's doubled the sentries on the HQ block. And if I had to guess, I'd guess that reason is named Therman Ulthar."

"Probably," Ulthar agreed.

"No 'probably' about it. You *have* noticed none of those sentries are Scouts, didn't you?"

"Of course I have."

Ulthar sounded irritated, although Sarma knew the irritation wasn't directed at him. Ulthar and Thalmayr were both officers in the 2nd Andaran Scouts, one of the Union of Arcana's elite units. The 2nd Andarans were famous for their high standards, proficiency, discipline... and unit loyalty, and Hadrign Thalmayr had been a member of the 2nd Andarans for less than a month before he got two of its platoons blown into dog meat by the Sharonians. Worse yet, he'd accomplished that by systematically rejecting the advice of Hundred Olderhan, who'd commanded C Company for the better part of two years and whose father happened to be the 2nd Andarans' hereditary commander. There couldn't be much love for Thalmayr among the unit's survivors, and an outfit with the 2nd Andarans' élan and history—with their battle honors and their sense of who and what they were—wasn't going to take well to the dishonor they knew his actions were heaping upon them.

And they're a lot more likely to back someone like Therman Ulthar then they are to obey Thalmayr, if it comes down to it, Sarma thought grimly. *Unfortunately, there're only five of them— six, counting Therman—and Thalmayr's got most of a company of regulars under his command.*

Regulars who didn't have the personal investment of the 2nd Andarans... and who still believed the lies they'd been fed by their own intelligence officers.

"If we were closer to home, we could go to the JAG," he said out loud.

"And if crocodiles had wings they'd be dragons," Ulthar replied sourly. "I'd rather go through channels myself, but from what Iftar said, 'channels' wouldn't give a rat's arse."

"Not anyone *we* could reach, at least." Sarma puffed out his cheeks in exasperation. "Your brother-in-law's right about that, I'm afraid. I told you what happened when I tried to report Neshok's violation of the Accords to Thousand Carthos."

Ulthar grunted unhappily. The Kerellian Accords were the bedrock of the Andaran Army's honor, deep in the bone and sinew of what made Andara Andara. Violating them was a capital offense, but if Sarma and his own brother-in-law, Iftar Halesak, were right, Hadrign Thalmayr wasn't the only one ignoring them. In fact, Ulthar doubted Thalmayr would have had the courage to violate them if they weren't already being violated with the connivance—or at least the knowledge—of officers far senior to himself. No. Thalmayr was a carrion eater, a jackal gorging on the stinking leftovers of someone else's kill. And given the lies the Expeditionary Force had been told—the lies about who'd shot first not just at Toppled Timber but at the Mahritha portal, and, far worse, the lie about Magister Halathyn's death—that someone else was very highly placed.

Under normal circumstances, it was an officer's duty to report any evidence of a violation of the Kerellian Accords to the Judge Advocate General's office. He had no choice about that, and the Articles of War specifically protected him against retaliation even if his suspicions were later deemed unfounded. Of course, what the Articles promised and what practice delivered weren't always the same thing, but at least Sarma and Ulthar could have expected their allegations to be rigorously investigated and that anyone who was the subject of that investigation would be very careful to avoid any open appearance of retaliation afterward.

Under normal circumstances. Under *these* circumstances it was entirely possible that a pair of nosy, holier-than-thou junior officers who dared to rock their superiors' boat might simply disappear. It sickened Ulthar to even think such a thing, but if Thousand Carthos, Two Thousand Harshu's senior infantry officer, and Five Hundred Neshok, who reported directly to the two thousand, were guilty of violating the Accords, why should they hesitate over a few more murders simply because the victims wore the same uniform they'd already befouled? And if those violations were being winked at in the field, and if there was anything to Iftar's belief that the lies the AEF had been told were part of a deliberate disinformation policy designed to whip up the troops' fury, they had to assume *Harshu's* immediate superiors knew about it, too. So any attempt to report their suspicions up-chain to Two Thousand mul Gurthak or *his* superiors was likely to be...poorly received, as well.

"I think," Sarma said slowly, "that whichever way we jump, there's going to be hell to pay. If you or I try to...relieve Thalmayr, you know damned well *he's* going to call it mutiny. Probably mutiny in the face of the enemy, given everything that's going on. And if he does, and if someone farther up the food chain"—even here, and even to Ulthar, he carefully didn't mention any names like "Harshu" or "mul Gurthak" out loud—"really is involved, we could end up looking at a field court-martial."

A field court-martial, he did not point out, whose sentence would almost certainly be death.

"I know." Ulthar's face might have been beaten iron for all the expression it showed, and his voice was colder and even harder. "But if we don't do something, if we don't at least try to stop the rot, then we're complicit in it. I don't know about you, Jaralt, but I can't let that happen. I just can't."

"Well, in that case, I don't suppose we have a lot of choice." To his own surprise, Sarma actually smiled ever so slightly. "On the other hand, I hope you won't object to trying to at least do something *effective* about it. If we're going up against the dragon with a slingshot, I'd at least like to do it in a way bastards like Thalmayr and Neshok can't just sweep under the carpet afterward."

"Oh, I think I can promise you that much, whatever happens," Ulthar said grimly. "I've already sent an outside-channels message home that *nobody's* going to be able to ignore when it arrives."

"You have?" Sarma let the front legs of his chair thump back to the floor and leaned forward, eyes narrow. "How?"

Ulthar smiled crookedly and shook his head.

"It wasn't that hard, really. Thalmayr wasn't with the Company long enough to figure out that Valnar Rohsahk isn't just our platoon RC specialist; he's also our hacker. He didn't even work up a sweat hacking Fifty Wentys' spellware."

"You had him *hack* the censor's spellware?" Sarma asked very carefully.

"Of course I did." Ulthar's smile was considerably broader than it had been. "It's a pity Thalmayr lost the Company files when the Sharonians kicked our arse. If he hadn't, he might know Valnar was honor graduate in the Garth Showma Institute's counter-spellware course. If he'd been willing to transfer to one of the regular regiments, they'd have made him a sword or even a senior sword in their recon section on the spot. Wentys never had a chance after I turned him loose."

Sarma just looked at him for several seconds while his own mind raced. He'd seen Shield Valnar Rohsahk here at Fort Ghartoun, but he hadn't paid him much attention. Rohsahk was probably a year or two younger even than Sarma, with light brown hair and unremarkable features. Like Ulthar, he'd been severely wounded in the Sharonian attack on the Mahritha portal. That was true of all the 2nd Andarans here at Fort Ghartoun; they'd been left by their captors to spare them the additional pain of being transported across such rough terrain by someone who didn't have dragons. He seemed to keep to himself quite a bit, but now that Sarma thought about it, the shield always seemed to have a game or some other app running on his personal crystal. Or at least that was what Sarma had *assumed* Rohsahk was up to....

"And just what, if I might ask, did Shield Rohsahk *do* to Fifty Wentys' spellware?" he asked with a certain trepidation.

"He just hid a file in the letter I sent my wife to tell her I was alive after all," Ulthar said. "It's keyed to the standard extraction code Arylis uses to unpack all my letters, but it won't activate until it hears the code in *her* voice." He shook his head. "If Wentys could find his arse with both hands we'd have had to think up something a lot more sophisticated."

"What if someone farther up-chain is better at his job than Wentys is?"

"They could hardly be *worse* at it," Ulthar pointed out. "I mean, do you really think Five Hundred Isrian left his *best* commo officer here in Thermyn with the gods only know what waiting for the AEF when it finally hits a Sharonian position that's too tough to take?"

That was a valid point, the other fifty reflected. Commander of Fifty Tohlmah Wentys was a Chalaran who'd somehow ended up in the Army instead of the Navy, and he was unlikely to rise much above his present rank. He was a stolid sort—an officer who did what was required of him without imagination, drive, or ambition. He was sufficiently Gifted to perform adequately as a communications specialist in peacetime, but as Ulthar had just suggested, he was hardly the pick of the litter.

And he was also one of the officers who'd swallowed the

official version of Sharonian "war crimes" and what had happened to Magister Halathyn. Sarma doubted Wentys would have had the nerve to beat one of the Sharonian POWs, but he would certainly have held Thalmayr's truncheon for him between blows.

"Well, no. Not if you put it that way," he conceded.

"Wentys officially cleared the file for transmission and sealed it with his personal cipher," Ulthar said. "It's unlikely anyone up-chain's going to go to the trouble of breaking it just to double check. They *can't* do it openly without leaving tracks I doubt anyone involved with some kind of cover-up wants to leave, and if they do it clandestinely, it'll be almost impossible for them to hide the fact. And whether they do it openly or covertly, Valnar set the file to self-destruct if anyone other than Arylis tries to access it. Of course, *Arylis* won't know she's accessing it until it pops out at her. At which point," his smile turned very, very cold, "she goes straight to the duke with it."

"You're sending your wife directly to Duke Garth Showma?" Sarma blinked.

"He's the hereditary commander of the Second Andarans," Ulthar replied simply. "If she takes it to him, he'll read it. And when he does, and when he realizes what one of *his* officers has been doing, hell won't hold what'll come down on Hadrign Thalmayr's head."

"Or anyone else's, I imagine," Sarma said slowly.

"Or anyone else's," Ulthar agreed, but then he shrugged. "Unfortunately, it's going to take over a month for that letter to reach Arylis, and Velvelig's healers'll be dead long before that happens. For that matter, once he actually beats a couple of them to death, I'm pretty sure Thalmayr'll decide *all* the Sharonian POWs were shot trying to escape. Dead witnesses don't tend to dispute live witnesses' version of what happened."

"No, they don't. And you're right about what's going to happen to them if someone doesn't stop it. It's nice to know the duke's going to bring the hammer down eventually, but I'm afraid it's still up to you and me to do something about Thalmayr in the short term."

"Yes, it is. And I'm glad you stopped me from going after him all by myself, Jaralt. I hadn't thought about involving anyone else, especially what's left of my men. In fact, if I'm going to be honest, I'm so frigging furious I wasn't really 'thinking' at all.

Now that you've jogged my brain back into functioning, though, I'd really prefer to work out a solution where anybody who gets killed is one of the *bad* guys. And it occurs to me that you and I probably aren't the only members of this garrison who loathe Thalmayr and his toadies. If we're going to be charged with mutiny, we might as well go the whole dragon, don't you think?"

CHAPTER FOUR

Ternathal 19, 5053 AE
Inkara 17, 205 YU
(December 8, 1928 CE)

THE MAGNIFICENT IMPERIAL TERNATHIAN PEREGRINE GAVE
a shrill cry of disapproval, spread her four-foot wings, and
launched from the saddle-mounted perch. She soared effortlessly
into the clean blue sky, and Regiment-Captain Rof chan Skrithik
looked enviously after her. There was more than a touch of sorrow
in that envy, an aching grief for the death of a prince which had
brought him and Taleena together, yet there was also a fierce
joy as he watched her spiraling higher and higher against the
cloudless blue.

Unfortunately, it was far from cloudless at ground level, and
chan Skrithik tried to be philosophical about that as he climbed
down from his horse, handed the reins to an under-armsman,
and made his way through the incredible racket and blowing wall
of dust towards the officer who stood waiting for him.

Regiment-Captain Lyskar chan Serahlyk was a tallish man,
only an inch or two shorter than chan Skrithik himself, and
although he'd been born in Teramandor and spoke with a distinct Teramandorian accent, he had the tightly curled hair and
dark complexion of his Ricathian father. Of course, the dust
rolling steadily eastward on the permanent, powerful wind from
the Karys Portal to coat everything in sight made it difficult to
judge anyone's skin color just at the moment. It was ironic, really.
Given the mechanics of portal dynamics, the dust cloud—laced
with coal smoke from the heavy equipment helping to spawn
it—blew steadily east *and* west here in Traisum, away from the
portal in both directions like two fog banks fleeing from one

49

another, which meant there was no way to approach the portal without getting grit blasted between one's teeth.

Chan Skrithik tied a bandanna to cover his nose and mouth as he walked, and chan Serahlyk's eyes narrowed in amusement above a matching, dust-caked bandanna. The unseasonably hot weather—for a Shurkhali winter, at least—had finally broken, which was a vast relief. Now if only there'd been anything remotely like rain on the horizon from either side of the portal...

"Good morning, Rof," the Third Dragoons' senior engineer said as soon as chan Skrithik was close enough to hear anything through the background din. He still had to raise his voice, but at least they could talk without shouting.

"Good morning," chan Skrithik acknowledged, reaching out to clasp forearms. "Seen any dragons lately?"

Chan Serahlyk chuckled. It was a serious question, but like most Sharonians, he still found the notion of dragons absurd, despite the fact that his combat engineers had helped to bury the last of the rotting carcasses.

"Not today," he said. "Haven't seen any since that little problem they ran into last week, as a matter of fact."

The engineer's voice was grimly satisfied, and chan Skrithik smiled in satisfaction of his own. The Karys aspect of the Traisum-Karys Portal was four and a half miles across but the entire portal was relatively low-lying, especially from its Traisum aspect. On that side, it was buried—literally—in the heart of the Ithal Mountains, which reached altitudes of over six thousand feet. Getting to it was difficult from ground level, yet it could be done, as the existence of the Traisum Cut indicated. Approaching that aspect from the west, the terrain was even more challenging than from the east.

The Trans-Temporal Express—and the Imperial Ternathian Army and Imperial Corps of Engineers—had dealt with lots of rough terrain over the centuries, however. Division-Captain chan Geraith had made dealing with this particular rough terrain an urgent priority, and Olvyr Banchu had dipped into his copious supply of bulldozers and earthmoving machinery to help chan Serahlyk's 123rd Combat Engineers with their task.

Elevations on opposite sides of portals seldom aligned anything like neatly, and this one was no exception. On the Karys side, the Queriz Depression was over a hundred feet below sea level, which explained the unending wind blowing through from the higher air pressure on that side of it. The portal was also both wider and higher in Karys, where it rose to a height of over four miles above ground level. On the Traisum side, because so much more of its circular diameter was underground, the portal was barely a mile and a half across and its highest point cleared Mount Karek's summit by less than twenty-four hundred feet. Given the mountain's slope and the fact that the portal was somewhat east of its crest, the portal reached to a point about thirty-six hundred feet above local ground level, while its apex was effectively between one and two hundred yards lower than that from the west.

Thirty-six hundred feet—twelve hundred yards—was well within the maximum range of the Model 10 rifle, but the Model 10's *effective* range was only about eight hundred yards, although trained snipers with telescopic sights could score killing hits at twice that range. The twin-barreled, crank-driven Faraika I machine gun fired exactly the same round, and although its ballistics were a little better than the rifle's due to its heavier, longer barrel, its accuracy in aimed fire was poorer, giving it approximately the same effective range. The heavier Faraika II, with its massive .54 caliber bullet, had slightly less maximum range than the Faraika I, but its effective range was actually greater: over fifteen hundred yards. That range would be reduced firing vertically because of gravity, but the Faraika II should still be able to reach thirty-three hundred feet.

Fatigue parties armed with mattocks and shovels had hacked machine gun and rifle pits into Mount Karek's recalcitrant soil on either side of the portal even before chan Serahlyk and Banchu's bulldozers—assisted by liberal applications of dynamite—had gouged out proper approach roads. They couldn't be provided with overhead cover if the weapons in them were going to have sufficient elevation to cover the portal's airspace against the Arcanan dragons, but judging from the attack on Fort Salby, the heavy machine guns outranged the dragons' weapons significantly. Nonetheless, chan Geraith had regarded rifles and machine guns as a purely interim stopgap until better arrangements could be made, which was precisely what chan Serahlyk was doing at the moment. His engineers were emplacing dozens of two-point-five inch Yerthak pedestal guns in permanent concrete-footed and pro-tected positions placed to sweep the portal faces. The four-barreled

Yerthaks had become at best obsolescent in their designed role as light anti-torpedo boat weapons for the Navy's capital ships, but they had a maximum range of over six thousand yards and a vertical range of twenty-four hundred. They also had a peak firing rate of forty-five rounds per minute, and if their explosive six-pound shells were too light to stop warships, the Arcanans had discovered the hard way what they could do to *dragons*.

If there'd been any doubt in their minds on that point, it had probably been resolved last week when a trio of dragons attempted to pass through from Karys. One of them had slammed to earth less than half a mile east of the portal, killing its pilot and nine of the twelve Arcanan infantry aboard when it crashed. A second, obviously badly wounded, had made it back through the portal despite a savagely shredded wing. It had plunged through the opening in obvious distress and clearly out of control, yet somehow avoided plummeting to earth—undoubtedly thanks to yet another of the Arcanans' unnatural magical spells—and staggered in to a clumsy, just-short-of-disaster landing. The third, made wise by its companions' misfortune, had wheeled and fled before it ever crossed the portal threshold into the Yerthaks' range.

Ultimately, the pedestal guns would be augmented or even completely replaced by the heavier "Ternathian 37." Formally the Cannon of 5037, from the year of its introduction, the 3.4 inch weapon was the most deadly field gun in the world, using cased ammunition and firing a nineteen-pound shell at a maximum rate of twenty rounds per minute. It had been in service less than twenty years, but the "37's" reputation for reliability, toughness, and lethality had already attained legendary proportions. The Model 1, the lightweight version designed for high mobility with mounted units like the 3rd Dragoons, had an effective range of nine thousand yards; the Model 2, with a split trail to permit greater elevation and a slightly longer barrel, could reach eleven thousand. First Brigade's artillery had been reinforced when it was dispatched from Sharona, and Division-Captain chan Geraith had peeled off enough of its guns to cover both sides of the portal. Figuring out how to mount even the handy 37 to engage rapidly moving aerial targets offered a nontrivial challenge, but chan Skrithik was confident the Imperial Ternathian Army's artillerists were up to the task, and Windlord Garsal had already demonstrated what shrapnel shells could do to dragons.

On the other hand...

"What about eagle-lions?" he asked, and chan Serahlyk grimaced.

"They got one of those through yesterday," he acknowledged sourly, "but the sniper teams bring down about half of them, and it doesn't look like the bastards have an unlimited supply of the things. They seem to be getting more sensitive to losses, anyway. I just wish we knew *why* they're sending them through."

Chan Skrithik nodded, although he suspected Battalion-Captain chan Gayrahn was probably right about that. Since the eagle-lions weren't attacking anyone and instead seemed content to fly high overhead, chan Gayrahn had suggested they were probably carrying out reconnaissance, and that was a very unhappy thought. The observation balloons in use in Sharona for decades hugely extended visual horizons, and only someone who'd ascended in one could begin to imagine how much detail could be made out from them. No one knew how intelligent the eagle-lions might be, either, or if there was some Arcanan equivalent of the Animal Speaker Talent. There might well be, however, and if an eagle-lion was remotely as intelligent as a dolphin or porpoise, the creatures could be bringing back more detail than anyone could wish.

"Well," he said philosophically, turning beside chan Serahlyk as the two of them considered another dust-spewing worksite about a mile further east, "I doubt getting a handful of eagle-lions past us will tell them all that much about the division-captain's plans."

* * *

It was, perhaps, as well for Commander of Two Thousand Mayrkos Harshu's blood pressure that he was unable to overhear chan Skrithik's observation as he and Klayrman Toralk stood on opposite sides of the floating map table, with Commander of Five Hundred Mahrkrai, Harshu's chief of staff, to one side. At the moment, a selection of imagery from a gryphon reconnaissance crystal was playing out on that table, and Harshu's expression was not a happy one.

The current selection ended, and the two thousand looked up at Mahrkrai.

"That's it?" he asked.

"I believe it covers all the salient points, Sir." The chief of staff's oddly colorless eyes met Harshu's steadily. "There are several hours of total imagery," he continued, "and I've got the analysts going back over it to see if we missed anything on the first run, but I doubt young Brychar did."

Harshu's acknowledging nod was more than a bit brusque, but not because he disagreed with Mahrkrai. Commander of One Hundred Brychar Tamdaran was very young indeed—less than half Harshu's age—and one of the relatively rare Ransarans in the Union of Arcana's armed forces. At the moment, he was none too happy with his two thousand's decision to wink at Alivar Neshok's interrogation methods. Tamdaran didn't know everything Neshok had been up to—Neshok (and Harshu) had kept his operations tightly compartmentalized on a need-to-know basis—but he'd heard more than enough rumors to write up a formal protest, even though he was obviously aware Harshu had tacitly approved the five hundred's actions. That was going to make things even more difficult in the fullness of time, but that was nothing the two thousand hadn't bargained on from the beginning, and he didn't blame the boy. He was rather proud of him, actually.

And however disapproving Tamdaran might be, he was also good at his job. In fact, he'd been responsible for the spellware which allowed his intelligence section to scan captured Sharonian printed maps into properly formatted files and generate accurately scaled and oriented paperless versions. And he also had the patience to wade through hours of recorded images looking for the one key element which might tell Harshu what the Sharonians were up to.

Aside from "no good," that is, Toralk thought sourly. *I think we can count on that much being true, at least.*

"Tamdaran's sure about their 'trains'?" Harshu asked after a moment. "I'd be a lot happier if we had clear imagery of that."

"The Sharonians've gotten damned good at taking out gryphons that come in too low, Sir," Toralk replied before Mahrkrai could respond. Harshu's eyes flicked to him, and the Air Force officer grimaced. "I suspect they're wasting a lot more ammunition than we realize on each gryphon they nail, but they appear to have unlimited quantities of it. And, frankly, the cupboard's pretty close to bare where recon gryphons are concerned. We didn't have anywhere near as many of them as of the strike gryphons when we started out, and we've been losing more than we'd expected to from the outset. I've instructed the handlers to do what they can to hold down additional losses, and they've gotten more cautious about altitudes and evasive routing as a result. I'm afraid it's costing us resolution and detail, but if we send them in for close passes, we'll lose our long-range eyes completely in painfully short order."

"That wasn't a criticism, Klayrman," Harshu said—rather mildly for him. "I do wish we had clearer, more definitive imagery, but I'm not in favor of running any more risks with our reconnaissance assets than we have to."

"Understood, Sir."

"Are we sure we're actually losing them to Sharonian fire?" the two thousand asked, raising one eyebrow, and Toralk sighed.

"No, Sir," he admitted. "But we're not sure we aren't, either. Hundred Kormas and the other handlers are still unhappy about their control spells, and Kormas says he suspects at least some of the attack gryphons broke guidance in the attack on Fort Salby. Unfortunately, we don't have any evidence to prove or disprove the possibility. The strike evaluation crystals on the ones that came back don't show any evidence of it, but they wouldn't, since all of *them* came back, whatever others might have done. We almost lost an enlisted handler day before yesterday, though."

"Spellware failure?" Harshu's eyes had sharpened, and Toralk nodded.

"That's what it looks like, I'm afraid. The safety team put the gryphon down before it could do serious damage—well, damage too serious for the Healers to put right, at least—so we can't be positive. Forensics didn't show any holes in the control spells, though, and the crystal itself tests clean, so we don't have anything concrete we can point to. And the recon gryphons are all females. That means they're less aggressive and at least a little smarter than the strike gryphons"

"Wonderful," Harshu grunted.

He looked back down at the map table, using his stylus to page back through the imagery selections until he found the overhead of the Sharonian rail sidings. It was a low-angle shot from farther away than he could have wished, and no one on the Arcanan side was familiar enough with the Sharonians' "railroad trains" for him to feel truly comfortable with Tamdaran's interpretation, but the hundred was probably right.

He was certainly right that the massive trainloads of construction machinery Harshu had allowed the Sharonians to retrieve from Karys had disappeared, and that was one of many things contributing to the two thousand's unhappiness. He'd come to the conclusion he'd made a mistake there, especially after successive gryphon overflights of the thickening portal defenses showed just how rapidly the Sharonians could push construction projects without the spell-powered tools Arcanans would have used. It seemed those heavy earthmoving machines and gods-only-knew-what other equipment were going to prove far more useful to his adversaries than he'd imagined. If he was right about that, and if he'd been in the shoes of Division-Captain chan Geraith, who'd assumed command in Traisum, he'd have kept it handy...unless he'd had something even more important for it to be doing someplace else.

On the one hand, the work trains had used up a lot of the available sidings, and it wasn't as if they were sliders that could be shunted off the track and parked until they were needed. Given that, it only made sense for the Sharonians to clear as much space as possible for the additional loads of troops and weapons which were undoubtedly headed his way. On the other hand...

I can think of at least one other good reason for them to be elsewhere—like working to increase their supply line capability behind Salbyton, for example, he thought grimly. He'd come to the conclusion that their captured maps were less accurate—or up to date, at least—than he'd initially hoped, for the rail line up-chain from Fort Salby was double-tracked rather than the single-track they showed. His recon flights had gotten that much info for them at least. That meant he had even less of an idea of his opponents' logistics capability than he'd thought he did. *And whatever they're capable of, the bastards can always make them* better. *That has to've been true of every military commander in history! So that's probably what those work trains are doing right this minute, Shartahk take them.*

That was not a happy thought, but at least as long as he kept the cork firmly in the Traisum Cut, all the specialized railroad-building machinery in the multiverse wasn't going to do them a great deal of good right here and now.

And it wasn't as if they hadn't unloaded quite a lot of *non*-specialized machinery before the work trains pulled out, he acknowledged glumly.

He'd vastly underestimated the extent to which Sharonian

weapons could deny portal access on the Traisum side, and from the look of things, that was going to get even worse. The rotating cannons which had wreaked such carnage on Toralk's dragons in the attack on Fort Salby were bad enough, more than sufficient to make the notion of sending SpecOps raiding forces through to Traisum suicidal. It was unfortunate he hadn't realized that sooner, and he couldn't pretend Toralk hadn't warned him before last week's fiasco. Unless he missed his guess, though, the longer, heavier weapons the Sharonians were busy digging in on either side of the portal—the ones their prisoners had called "37s"—were going to be even worse.

Bad as that was, though, there was potentially much worse, and he zoomed in for a close-up of the positions the Sharonians were working on well back from the portal. Those were some really enormous "guns," with differences from the only ones any Arcanan had ever observed that he didn't begin to understand, and they worried him. They worried him a lot, because he rather doubted they were being put into place to shoot the Sharonians' own men. That implied the Sharonians expected to fire them *through* the portal, and they were over three miles *from* the portal. Admittedly, they obviously needed to be emplaced on fairly flat ground, of which here was very little any closer to the portal, but that still suggested an awesome maximum range. It also suggested the Sharonians might well be able to lay down heavier fire than his most pessimistic assumptions had allowed for in support of any attack down the Cut. The only good thing about it was that those massive weapons obviously were nowhere near as mobile as the "field guns" and "mortars" his men had already encountered.

And even if they *could* bring that heavier fire to bear...

"Where the hells did they all *go*?" he murmured.

"I beg your pardon, Sir?" Mahrkrai asked.

"Eh?" Harshu looked up, then realized he'd spoken aloud and shrugged. "Where did that first trainload of Sharonians go?" He tapped the tabletop image in front of him. "This is an entirely different train, Herak. Look—it doesn't even have the same number of 'locomotives' on the front."

"No, Sir," Mahrkrai agreed.

"I know you and Tamdaran are right in at least one respect, Klayrman," the two thousand said, turning his attention to the

Air Force officer. "They can't send individual sliders down those railroads of theirs the way we could, so obviously they have to turn around entire trains. And they can't have an unlimited number of cars and locomotives out here at the arse-end of nowhere any more than we've got a slider line running right up to our backdoor. So it makes sense for them to have sent that lead train back up the line for another load. But where did all the men who were *on* it go?"

"I'm not sure they went anywhere, Sir," Toralk replied. "They've got work parties out all over the place, obviously building a very substantial permanent encampment. And there's an entire tent city over here to the southeast." He used his own stylus to bring up the relevant imagery. "There's more than enough tentage to cover two or three thousand men, and we still don't have any clear idea how many men they have in one of their 'brigades.'"

"That's true, Sir," Mahrkrai acknowledged. "We haven't seen a lot of men coming and going from those tents, though."

"And we haven't been able to keep them under anything like continuous observation, either," Toralk pointed out.

"I'd feel happier if we had been able to," Harshu said sourly. "I don't like not being able to count noses on the primary enemy force in our front."

"There's been one possibility playing around in the back of my mind," Mahrkrai said thoughtfully. "Were you ever stationed in Farsh Danuth, Sir?"

"No." Harshu looked at him. "Never wanted to be, either." He grimaced. "I've been through the region a couple of times, but I was never actually stationed there, thank Graholis!"

Farsh Danuth was an ancient kingdom lying between the Far-shian Sea in the west, the Tankara Gulf in the east, the Shansir Mountains in the northwest, and the Urdanha Mountains in the northeast. It was also the product of ancient Mythalan conquest across Mythal's Stool, the triangular peninsula between the Hyrythian and Farshian Seas. As such, the kingdom had served as the buffer zone—and flashpoint—for hostility between Mythal and Ransar for centuries. Perhaps as a result, it was almost rabidly Mythalan in population, societal institutions, and attitudes, and Andarans were seldom made to feel welcome within its borders.

"Well, this portal's up in the Hanahk Mountains west of Selkhara," Mahrkrai said, "and there's not a lot of grazing in the vicinity. Fort Salby's farther east, on the edge of the Selkhara Oasis, and the grass is probably at least a little better there—it certainly is back home, at any rate, although the portal wind from Karys probably makes the local climate even worse. At any rate, what I've been thinking is that this is a *dragoon* brigade, according to all our information, and that means it has a lot of horses. And horses eat a lot. So if they aren't planning on launching some sort of cavalry charge down the Cut, it would make sense for them to've pulled their horses back along the rail line to somewhere they can supplement fodder with grazing. Gods know we're having enough trouble keeping *our* cavalry fed, and their horses don't have the advantage of augmentation."

"And if they've pulled the horses back," Harshu said thoughtfully, "it would be logical to pull back the *riders*, as well, aside from whatever they thought they'd need to keep us from breaking through and hitting Fort Salby again."

"It would ease the strain on local water supplies, too, Sir," Mahrkrai pointed out.

"That's true," Toralk said, gazing down at the imagery before them, "and it makes a lot of sense. On the other hand, I'm beginning to wonder if they actually had as many men close enough to the front to get them here in the time window as Five Hundred Neshok's interrogations suggested they could."

The other two looked at him, and the Air Force officer shrugged.

"I'm not suggesting his...interrogation subjects were able to fool the verifier spells," he said, unable to quite hide his distasteful tone, "but none of them ever had hard and fast confirmation of exactly what was coming down this railroad line of theirs to reinforce them. All they had was rumors, and gods know we've all heard enough wish-fulfillment rumors in our careers! Maybe the Sharonians were caught even more off-balance than we thought. More off-balance than the *Sharonians* between Hell's Gate and Traisum thought they were. If so, and especially if they're even shorter on railroad trains on this side of the Hayth water gap than we've been estimating, they may have sent a lot fewer men in the first echelon than we'd originally allowed for and they could be spending more time running the trains they do have back and forth."

"I suppose that's always possible, too," Harshu said after a moment, pursing his lips as he considered it. "I don't think it's something we should count on, though. Especially since they obviously did manage to get these"—he tapped the outsized artillery pieces the Sharonians were busily digging in—"all the way up here. Neshok's reports all indicate the Sharonians have cannon even they consider 'heavy artillery,' but that weapons that heavy aren't normally attached to their maneuver formations. Especially not to their dragoons, since they don't have levitation spells or—as Harek's just pointed out about their cavalry—the kind of augmented draft animals we do, either. So if they can dip into their larger formations' artillery and get *it* this far forward, it seems unlikely they couldn't get infantry and cavalry forward at least as rapidly."

"Agreed, Sir." Toralk nodded. "And I'm not suggesting we make any plans based on an assumption that they didn't get just as many men moved up to Fort Salby as we expected them to. On the other hand, we still haven't gotten a recon gryphon close enough for a really good look at those big guns, either. It's always possible they're running a bluff—that these are actually dummy weapons the Sharonians are so busy digging in where we can see them because they *haven't* been able to move up enough men to feel confident of holding a heavy attack. For all we know, they could be the sorts of things we might cobble up with camouflage spells. We haven't seen any sign of that out of them yet, but gods only know what these Talents of theirs are capable of."

"That's true enough," Harshu said even more sourly. "Of course, whether they're really there or not, we're still on the wrong end of an awful solid cork as far as any further advances are concerned."

"The cork's just as bad from their side," Mahrkrai pointed out. "In fact, it's a lot worse. They may be digging in to keep us from getting dragons through the portal, Sir, but *they* don't have any dragons to put through in the first place! Trying to fight their way out of the Cut would be a nightmare, and the demolition spells are already in place to take out the rails—and the Cut—if they try. For that matter, even if those heavy guns of theirs are real, and even if they have the ability to reach four or five miles *this* side of the portal, all we have to do is fall back outside whatever their range is and start picking them apart from the air."

"We'd need more battle dragons for that," Toralk pointed out. "And what the dragons can do isn't going to take them by surprise. Not again."

"No, and they'll undoubtedly factor the possibilities of air mobility into their thinking, at least as well as they can," Harshu observed thoughtfully. "But how well *can* they factor it in without their own dragons to use as a measuring stick? And even if they manage to extrapolate a lot more accurately than I suspect they can, based on what they've seen so far, they can't change the constraints their *lack* of air mobility imposes. Once they're this side of the portal, we can circle as wide as we need to to get around behind them instead of trying to stuff your tactical and transport dragons through the mouth of a jar, Klayrman. We'll be able to get at their lines of communication without running the gauntlet of those rotating cannon. In fact, the farther into Karys they advance, the more vulnerable they'll make themselves."

"Are you thinking about falling back from the Cut, Sir? Giving them a free pass into Karys?" Toralk asked.

"Oh, no! Keeping them out of Karys in the first place, at least until we're properly reinforced, is a lot better idea. And one thing they've already demonstrated is that they aren't idiots, Klayrman! If we were to suddenly and obligingly let them through the Cut without a fight, they'd have to wonder why we were being so helpful. I'm just saying that if they do decide to come after us, and if they do manage somehow to break out of the Cut, we'll be able to hurt them a lot more badly than they may realize."

He smiled almost whimsically.

"I'd like that," he said. "I'd like that a lot."

CHAPTER FIVE

Inkara 18, 205 YU
(December 9, 1928 CE)

"TWENTY FOR YOUR THOUGHTS," JATHMAR NARGRA SAID
quietly, leaning back in the comfortable deck chair.

"I don't know that they're worth that much," his wife, Shaylar
Nargra-Kolmayr, told him with a wan smile.

"Oh, they have to be worth *that* much!" Jathmar disagreed.

Shaylar chuckled, although that chuckle was edged by sorrow
and more than a hint of bitterness. A twentieth-falcon was the
smallest Ternathian coin, so putting that price on her thoughts
didn't set their value very high. But Jathmar shouldn't have
needed to ask her about them in the first place. Oh, the details
of what might be running through her mind at any moment, yes.
But their marriage bond was so strong, ran so deep, he'd always
known what she was thinking, feeling, on a level far below words.

Except that now he didn't. She still wasn't certain exactly
when the bond had started fraying, but it continued to grow
weaker day by day, almost hour by hour, and that terrified her.
It was all they had left to cling to as they traveled steadily across
the faces of far too many universes towards their black, bleak
future of captivity, and it was slipping away, like Shurkhali sand
sifting between her fingers. The tighter she clenched her grasp,
the more clearly she felt it seeping away, blood dripping from a
wound neither of them could staunch.

No, she thought, gazing out through the porthole. *It's not
weakening day by day; it's weakening mile by mile. The farther we
get from home, the weaker it grows, and Sweet Mother Marnilay,
but what in the names of all the gods could cause* that?

She didn't know. All she knew was that it was happening, and she turned away from Jathmar—from the husband who felt as if he were somehow drifting away from her even as he held her hand tightly and warmly in his own—to gaze up at stars which were achingly familiar.

She and Jathmar could at least have an illusion of privacy, and she was grateful to Sir Jasak Olderhan for allowing that. There was no place they could possibly have escaped to from a ship in the middle of the Western Ocean's vast empty reaches, but that wouldn't have stopped all too many Arcanans they'd met on this endless journey from posting guards over them, anyway. After all, they were both Sharonian, with who knew what sort of still undisclosed terrible, "unnatural" Talents? Never mind that the Arcanans could work actual *magic*. Never mind that she and Jasak were unarmed civilians in a universe which was the gods only knew how far from their own. Somehow, *they* were still the threat, and in her more introspective moments she could actually almost sympathize with that attitude. The Talents with which she and Jathmar had grown up, which were as natural to them as breathing, were just as bizarre and inexplicable to the Arcanans as the Arcanans' magic and spells were to her. And whatever someone couldn't explain became, by definition, uncanny and frightening, especially when the whatever in question was possessed by one's enemies.

She understood *that* only too completely, as well, she thought bitterly.

So, yes—whether she wanted to or not, she appreciated at least intellectually why they might be seen as a threat. More than that, she knew Jasak's refusal to post round-the-clock guards was an unequivocal declaration of his bedrock trust in them. Trust that they hadn't lied to him about their Talents... and that even if those Talents might have somehow allowed them to violate the parole they'd given and escape, they wouldn't do it. And Jasak was a man who recognized that that sort of trust was its own kind of fetter, especially for a Shurkhalian who understood the honor concept which lay at its heart.

At the same time, as much as she'd come to value Jasak, to recognize the fundamental goodness and iron fidelity which were so much a part of him, she remembered an ancient Shurkhalian proverb her father had taught her long ago. "Too much gratitude is a garment that chafes," he'd told her. She'd wondered, then, what he'd meant and how he could have said that, for hospitality and openhandedness was at the very heart of the Shurkhali honor code. More than that, Thaminar Kolmayr was the most generous man she knew, someone who was always ready to help, to lend support—the sort of man to whom others automatically turned in need and who was a natural focus for others' gratitude. But now, looking back, she could see that he'd always found ways to allow those whom he'd helped to help him in return, to allow them to repay him with their own gifts or favors.

And she couldn't repay Jasak Olderhan any more than she could forget that without him—without his *protection*—she and Jathmar would be locked up in a cell somewhere, probably separated and subjected to ruthless interrogation ... or dead. He and Gadrial Kelbryan were all that stood between her and Jathmar and death—Gadrial had literally snatched Jathmar back from the very gate of Reysharak's Hall—and it was the totality of their helplessness which made it so difficult to not somehow resent Jasak's generosity. And the fact that he'd been the commander of the Arcanan patrol which had made the initial contact between the Union of Arcana and Sharonians—and killed every single one of her and Jathmar's companions in the horrendous, chaotic madness sparked by Commander of Fifty Shevan Garlath's cowardice and stupidity—only filled her emotions with even greater pain and confusion.

"Really," Jathmar said beside her, lifting the hand he held to press its back against his cheek. "What *are* you thinking, Shay?"

"I'm thinking that looking up at those stars, knowing where we are at this moment, only makes me feel even farther from home," she replied after a moment, and felt his cheek move against her hand as he nodded in understanding.

The ship upon whose deck their chairs stood was slicing through the water at ridiculous speed, and doing it in an unnatural silence. The *night* was full of the voice of the wind, the rush and surging song of the sea as they drove through it, yet here aboard the ship there was none of the vibration and pulse beat of the machinery they would have felt and heard aboard a Sharonian vessel moving at anything like a comparable rate. Jathmar's Mapping Talent had weakened in step with their marriage bond, but it remained more than strong enough to let him estimate speeds with a high degree of accuracy, and at the moment their modestly sized ship was moving at well over twenty knots—probably closer to thirty, as rapidly as one of the great ocean liners of Sharona. The wind whipping over the decks certainly bore out that estimate, yet there were no stokers laboring in *this* ship's bowels to feed its roaring furnaces, no plume of coal smoke belching from its funnels, no thrashing screws churning the water to drive it forward. There was only somewhere down inside it one of those "sarkolis" crystals which Gadrial had tried so hard to explain doing whatever mysterious things it did to drive the vessel forward.

Yet for all the differences between this vessel and any Sharonian ship, these were waters Shaylar had crossed before, often. They'd cleared the Strait of Junkari, between the long, hooded cobra head of the Monkey Tail Peninsula and the thousand-mile long island of Lusaku just before sunset. Now they were well out into the South Uromathian Sea, sailing between the Hinorean Empire on the Uromathian mainland and the vast, scattered islands of western Lissia. Shaylar's mother had been born little more than two thousand miles—and forty-one universes—from this very spot, and Shaylar had sailed these waters many times on visits between Shurkhal and the island continent of Lissia, sixty-five hundred miles from the place of her own birth. But they weren't traveling to visit friends or family this time. They were halfway between their entry portal in Harkala, which the Arcanans called Shehsmair, and the next portal in their endless journey, located in the Narash Islands, which the Arcanans called the Iryshakhias. And there they'd leave the universe of Gryphon behind and enter yet another universe called Althorya.

Even with Jathmar at her side, holding her hand, there were times when Shaylar felt very, very tiny and far, far from home. And the fact that all of those many universes, all those stupefying thousands of miles, lay across an identical planet made it no better. In fact, it made it worse.

"I know what you mean," Jathmar said after a moment, his beloved voice warm and comforting as the ship sliced through phosphorescent seas in its smooth, eerie silence, like some huge, stalking cat. "It seems like we've been traveling forever, doesn't it?"

"That's because we have!" Shaylar's laugh was tart but genuine.

"Yes, but Gadrial says we've only got about another month to go. I can't say I'm looking forward to the end of the trip, though."

"I'm not either, but one way or the other, at least we'll finally know what's going to happen to us," Shaylar said. "I know Jasak and Gadrial genuinely believe Jasak's father will be able to protect us, but I don't know, Jath. Shurkhalis have their own honor code, you know that. And you know how seriously we take it on a *personal* level. But it's probably been broken more times than I could count when it came up against the realities of politics and diplomacy. I find it hard to believe the Arcanans can be *that* different from us, so even if the duke's as determined to protect Jasak's *shardonai* as he and Gadrial both believe he'll be, *can* he?"

"Unfortunately, I only know one way to find out." Jathmar's voice was grimmer than it had been. "That's why am not looking forward to the end of the trip. But you're right—one way or the other, we'll know in about a month."

"What do you think is happening back home?" Despite the weakened state of their marriage bond, Shaylar tasted his half-amused recognition of her bid to change the subject...and his willingness for it to be changed.

"I'd imagine everyone's running around like chickens with their heads cut off," he said tartly. "Probably at least some of them are trying to do something constructive, though. If I had to guess, Orem Limana and Halidar Kinshe are up to their necks in it! And I'd also guess they're in the process of begging, buying, or stealing a real army from someone to back up the PAAF."

"Probably," Shaylar agreed. "Ternathia's, do you think?"

"Well, I hope to all the gods not Chava Busar's!"

"The rest of Sharona couldn't be crazy enough to count on Chava, no matter *how* panicky they're feeling," Shaylar reassured him.

"You're right about that," Jathmar acknowledged. "Besides, when it's time to kick someone's ass, you send the best there is, and that's the Imperial Ternathian Army."

"But can they get themselves organized in time?" Shaylar fretted. "I know it's going to take the Arcanans, even with those dragons of theirs, a long time to move entire armies up to Hell's Gate. I mean, look how long it's taken us to get *this* far." She waved her free hand at the vast, open stretch of saltwater. "But it's going to take Sharona time to move armies, too, and first they're going to have to agree who's in charge! Do we have—do *they* have—enough time to do that?"

would have vastly preferred for that command to have belonged to some stiff-necked, conservative, autocratic, unimaginative, *honor-bound* Andaran—indeed, almost *any* Andaran—instead of mul Gurthak.

"First, there's not a lot of reason to worry about 'security' as far as the Sharonians are concerned," Jasak pointed out. "It's not like they're going to overhear any idle chatter this side of Hell's Gate. Second, nobody's ever managed to put together a security system that actually prevented at least some information leakage along the way. And third, if he didn't make any effort to keep the initial news from leaking, why the sudden silence about what's happened *since*?"

"Since the Sharonian counterattack, you mean." Gadrial's voice was suddenly harsher, its timbre hammered flat by remembered, shattering grief.

"Exactly," Jasak replied grimly. "The whole reason Otwal and Jugthar had to 'reason' with *Zukerayn*'s crew in the first place was how angry they were at the news about the way Thalmayr managed to get his arse reamed and"—he looked at her squarely—"get Magister Halathyn killed. If anyone was interested in keeping a lid on things, trying to throttle back any temptation towards hysteria, they should've kept *that* news under wraps. For that matter, the news that we've got negotiators sitting down face-to-face with the Sharonians would go a long way towards calming things down, I think. But nothing. Not a word. And the lack of any additional information's only causing people to obsess over what they *have* heard about. Worse, it's letting the inevitable initial consternation—and *anger*—set more and more deeply into their minds without anything to counterbalance it."

"So you do think it's deliberate?" she asked so quietly it was difficult to hear her over the wind and the steady sluicing sound of water around the ship's hull.

"Yes." Jasak's voice was flat and he turned to look back along the ship's length toward Shaylar and Jathmar's deck chairs once more, thinking about the hard, hating looks the crew had directed towards the Sharonians. Thinking about the anger and the fear behind those looks. "I know I just said it's hard to prevent rumors and partial information from leaking, but I'll concede that it's *possible* mul Gurthak's sending security-locked hummer messages past us without any leakage. Possible he's keeping the

Commandery and the Union Council fully informed. Graholis, it's even *possible* the negotiations've broken down and the Sharonians have started attacking again! But the fact that he isn't doing a single thing to dispel *any* of the rumors fanning the uncertainty and panic...I just can't convince myself that could be anything *but* deliberate, Gadrial."

"You're scaring me again, Jasak."

"Sorry about that." He smiled crookedly at her. "But what's that old saying about misery seeking companions?" He inhaled deeply and looked out over the phosphorescent sea. "I don't see any reason *I* should be the only one I'm scaring."

*   *   *

At that very moment, almost twenty-four thousand miles away from *Zukerayn*'s decks, an exhausted hummer struck the perch of a palatial hummer cot on a private estate in Mythal. The winged messenger's beak struck the button to sound the chime announcing its arrival, exactly as it had been programmed to do, then settled back to await the result. Its brain was scarcely up to complex reasoning, and even if it had been, it had no way to know what information had been uploaded to the tiny *sarkolis* crystal embedded in its body. And because of those two things, it never occurred to it to wonder why a hummer bearing private dispatches from the Governor of Erthos had been sent to a private citizen who had no official connection whatsoever with the Union of Arcana's military, government, or judiciary.

CHAPTER SIX

Ternathal 23, 5053 AE
(December 12, 1928 CE)

FEAR WAS FAR FROM THE PUBLIC MIND IN WHITTERHOO, a farm town with a train stop in south New Farnal on Sharona. Winter wheat was ready to be harvested, and one of their very own heroes was running for election. Things were a bit different for the "hero" turned neophyte politician in question, of course, and Darcel Kinlafia was only too well aware of how far outside of what his fiancée called his "comfort zone" he was. If he'd had a moment to think about it he would have said he owed it to his old Chalgyn Consortium crew to do exactly what he was doing now, but politics, he was discovering, could be more terrifying than any mere gun battle.

Fortunately, he was too busy to be scared at the moment.

Darcel shook the sweaty hand of the first constituent on the overflowing train platform and was rewarded with a beaming grin. He matched her enthusiasm, delighted to see the crowd had waited through the morning's thunderstorm to see him. His home region in southern New Farnal still felt blessedly solid under his feet even days after the long steamship crossing from Tajvana, but the weather hadn't given him a gentle welcome. The days broke warm and heated his supporters past comfort, and the rains battered his campaign events with squalls.

"Dearest Gods, it's hot again." Voice Istin Leddle wiped sweat from his forehead as he joined Darcel on the train platform.

"Good growing weather!" Darcel answered and put a tanned arm around his campaign coordinator. "He's from Bernith." He explained to the crowd. "They grow ice there this time of year."

71

"That's why we ship them wheat!" a man at the back of the crowd called out.

"You'll get used to it." Darcel patted Istin on the shoulder.

The young man smiled gamely but didn't exactly agree as he used his gangly height to clear a path towards the rented auditorium. A few interns joined his efforts, including one of the newest volunteers, Kelahm something. Darcel couldn't quite remember his name.

Kelahm was brown-haired and brown-eyed just like Darcel himself, and rather below average height for a Ternathian. A late addition to the campaign, he always seemed to be exactly where he needed to be at any given moment, and he was always ready to help with any task, yet somehow he always faded into the background. It wasn't that his personality was *colorless*, exactly. He was simply one of those people who seemed...muted, somehow. Darcel worked hard to avoid the trap of taking volunteers for granted, which seemed to afflict many politicians, and he felt obscurely guilty about the way Kelahm disappeared into the backdrop, even for him. It didn't seem to offend *Kelahm*, but Darcel made a mental memo—again—to get to know the other man better.

A warm, much more memorable presence brushed his mind and Darcel felt his fiancée before he saw her. Alazon Yanamar, former Privy Voice to Emperor Zindel and the exquisite slender, dark-haired woman of his dreams, hopped out of the train car and stepped to his side. He didn't know how she'd justified spending this week on the campaign trail with him. Precious few Voices in Sharona had her Talent; fewer still had developed the political sense she'd earned in her years working at the emperor's side; and *none* of them had been Emperor Zindel's Privy Voice.

Darcel's heart thumped again in astonishment that this amazing woman was here with him. They were soul mates in the magical way two Talents could sometimes find themselves perfectly matched with one another, yet that was only part of what made her so amazing to him. He still found the notion of himself as a politician profoundly absurd in many ways, but that choice wasn't up to him any longer. One way or the other, however preposterous it seemed, he had a political career to launch. Alazon had decided to help him do it, and to his amazement, Emperor Zindel had agreed to let her. As a Voice himself, Darcel knew how incredibly valuable someone with her strength of Talent—and the brainpower to go with it—was to any leader, far less the man who was about to become Emperor of Sharona, yet Zindel hadn't even blinked when she informed him she intended to resign to help Darcel's campaign. Of course, there was the little question of whether or not he intended to allow her to *remain* resigned after the elections, and Darcel strongly suspected that both Alazon and Ulantha Jastyr—her protégée and long-term assistant who'd "replaced" her as Privy Voice—knew her resignation was actually only a leave of absence. In fact, what he *truly* suspected was that Zindel himself had engineered the entire thing, although he knew, as only a Voice bonded to another Voice *could* know—that Alazon hadn't realized it when she initially offered her resignation. She'd expected the emperor to fight her decision, not *support* it, and she still seemed a bit bemused that he hadn't.

Darcel hadn't asked the emperor about any ulterior motives which might explain his willingness to deprive himself of the best Privy Voice in the multiverse, but it would have been entirely in keeping with things Zindel had already said to him. There were more reasons for his entry into politics than an old survey crew Voice's needing a job when a lot of the resources formerly used on exploration were redirected towards war. Prince Janaki had told him he had important work to do for Sharona, but Darcel had found that difficult to believe. He still did, in many ways, but he'd been shaken to his marrow when he'd accidentally shared bits of one of Emperor Zindel's Glimpses and seen himself at the side of a future Empress Andrin. He supposed he'd started down that road when he and Alazon pointed Andrin at the blessed ambiguity of the Unification Treaty's stipulations, but the emperor's Glimpse went far beyond that.

Alazon didn't know everything about that, because he couldn't share the details of that Glimpse with her—much as he loved her, they were both Voices, bound by the confidentiality oaths which went with their Talents—but she clearly understood that the threads of his and Andrin's lives were somehow interwoven, and she was both immensely pragmatic and someone who'd seen imperial politics from their very heart for years. If he was to play a part on that sort of stage, he needed the stature and position from which to play it, which was why she'd insisted Darcel follow through and seek election. At the same time, she'd also insisted he couldn't be directly tied to Emperor Zindel during the campaign, which was the real reason she'd resigned her position at the emperor's right hand. Had she stayed Privy Voice, no one reporting on his candidacy would have let a mention of the campaign be complete without a reference to how close to the Winged Crown's influence he would have to be, and that could definitely have been a two-edged sword in New Farnal.

New Farnal might have been populated and governed initially with significant assistance from the Ternathian Empire, but the public didn't necessarily warm to monarchies now. Even a monarch as generally approved of as Emperor Zindel was still in the words of Darcel's own mother, "An unelected genetic lottery winner. He could easily have been a despot, and Ternathia wouldn't have been able to do a thing about it without one hell of a war, and we've already got enough warfare going on as it is, don't you agree?"

It was in the light of that sort of attitude that Alazon had decided to leave her position as Privy Voice to spend her days and nights with him on the campaign trail. The fact that Zindel undoubtedly expected her back didn't change the fact that she hadn't known that when she handed in her resignation, and Darcel was amazed still she'd been willing to risk her entire career for him.

<*I love you,*> he Sent.

The laugh lines around Alazon's clear gray eyes crinkled in greeting and, possibly in response to his thought, she darted a gentle look towards the waiting voters. Darcel turned back towards the crowd with her hand in his.

The next constituent wore a pin supporting one of the other Voices running for the same seat as Darcel.

She offered her hand anyway, and he took it. He would have done that under any circumstances, but her grip was firm and her gaze met his forthrightly, and he found himself smiling at her. She clearly wasn't going to be supporting him, but Voices were better than most at sizing up others' motives, and whatever her motives for choosing a different candidate, she was open about it. And she was also refreshingly free of the sort of demonization of political opponents he'd already encountered entirely too often.

At least she wasn't one of the conspiracy nut "Truthers" who were trying to deny anything had *really* happened out there on the frontier. Or who believed, if something *had* happened, that the Portal Authority—including one Darcel Kinlafia—had somehow provoked it. For that matter, she wasn't even one of the depressingly large number of people who figured he was only one more political hack who'd vote for *anything* if given a large enough private campaign donation.

Darcel smiled at the open adversary, waved her in the direction of the complimentary buffet, and turned to the next member of this town's League of Women Talents. <*Whitterhoo,*> Alazon supplied with a light mental laugh. <*'This town' is Whitterhoo.*>

Darcel sent a mental grin back. Alazon's mind fitted his own so comfortably he had to keep a tight focus to avoid acting like a lovestruck puppy in front of the crowd of would be voters. There was no hiding that he adored her and that the feeling was mutual, but they were both expert Talents, well able to keep their mental communication private even from the other Voices in the crowd if they stayed focused. And there were always other Voices in the crowd.

His life as a political candidate now included a steady stream of professional news Voicecasters, sometimes following him individually and sometimes simply appearing among the prospective voters. The best of them had a Talent control that exceeded his own and kept complete mental silence until they pounced. The small town reporters like the two from rival news organizations covering this particular stop, on the other hand, leaked like toddlers trying to keep a secret.

Slight shifts in the nearest Voicecaster's level of excitement warned Darcel he expected something interesting to happen.

The next woman in the newly formed line was a gray-haired lady with a self-important if not exactly regal bearing. She held his hand and professed her eagerness to see him take a seat in the new Imperial House of Talents.

"Lady Durthia," Darcel repeated the woman's name back to her and thanked her for the support using one of the standard polite phrases he could now murmur in his sleep. People seemed to appreciate him cycling through six or seven different ways of saying the same thing rather than repeating the same precise lines again and again. Politics. He kept his sigh strictly internal.

The woman leaked irritation at him. In his surprise at having an emotion projected at him, he didn't catch what she actually said.

"I appreciate your support, Lady Durthia." Darcel answered a beat too late, echoing a suggested response from Alazon.

Only the Talented were eligible to vote for members of the new empire's House of Talents, since—like its equivalent in the Ternathian Parliament—it was to be the only part of government authorized to introduce legislation binding exclusively on the Talented population. Since that was the case, Darcel fully expected most of the crowd to be Talented. What he *hadn't* expected was an untrained if very weak projective. She squeezed his hand once, and immediately Darcel had no doubt that, for all her smiles and gentle words, she quite viscerally despised him. And that she also hadn't realized she'd just pushed that angry mental outburst at him.

Not everyone with a Talent trained and used it. This woman should have at least applied a basic effort to learn control but clearly hadn't.

He wanted to take her by the shoulders and shake her. Politeness for the gray in the woman's hair was all that stopped Darcel, a child of New Farnalian university professors, from chastising her on the spot for wasting that shriveled remnant of a very rare Talent.

<*Be nice to the donors, Love,*> Alazon chided him silently. <*Even the idiotic ones.*> She'd felt the projection also, but only because she and Darcel shared the lifemate bond unique to Voices.

"Lady Durthia." Alazon leaned across and said out loud, "Thank you for the kind words. Darcel appreciates your support."

He waved a cordial goodbye at the projective and turned to Alazon during a brief pause in the receiving line.

<*What was that?*> He sent with a pulse of pure bafflement. <*Why is this woman pretending to support me?*>

Lady Durthia fluttered an affected wave at the two of them as she flitted off into the crowd turned campaign stop party. Her beaming face looked as if meeting Darcel had been the best thing in the known multiverses.

<*Oh, I think Durthia will probably vote for you, so she isn't pretending about the support. She's just pretending to like it.*> Alazon answered the wave and subtly nudged his attention back towards the next woman.

Darcel welcomed the next person in line, relieved when she proved to be a soft-spoken Animal Speaker serving as Whitterhoo's veterinarian for all the pets in town. She was also planning to vote for him. A light handshake and a few words exchanged seemed to leave that woman just as happy as Durthia had appeared to be. The line moved on.

Darcel waited for Alazon to continue the mental explanation. Something in the feel of the pause told him she was organizing complex thoughts before sharing them.

<She expected a nephew to have a place in the new parliament. They've been a political family for several generations.>

With so many years as Emperor Zindel's Privy Voice and effective political chief of staff, Alazon held an intuitive grasp of political interactions. Darcel still had to think things through and ask questions to make sure he understood.

<Is her nephew running?> he asked.

<Not at all.>

Startled by her response, Darcel failed to avoid a bear hug from an overly friendly man accompanying the next league member.

The newest intern, the one with the forgettable face, deftly drew the man off before he could follow up with anything more enthusiastic and kept the crowd moving. The political team Alazon had built for him was a masterpiece in action. Darcel credited her practical experience in politics and deep personal network for assembling such a skilled support staff for his campaign.

Kelahm somehow deposited the man farther off in the crowd in front of Lady Durthia, who welcomed the newcomer and his wife with mutual hugs.

<The nephew's family, meaning his Aunt Durthia, just wishes he were running.> Alazon continued after a moment's pause ensured Darcel was able to keep his focus on the crowd and his political duties. *<Unfortunately for what they might've wanted, the nephew found your Voice report compelling. A lot of the younger Talents did. Their generation's been drawn to service more than I've ever seen . . . and many of their parents wish they'd follow in the family businesses instead. Or at least select safer, less dangerous ways to serve.>*

<The nephew enlisted to fight Arcana?>

<Yes,> Alazon confirmed, sending a mixture of deep pride in the many youths rushing to join the Empire of Sharona's armies and equal dismay at the potential loss of so many young lives.

Tears blurred Darcel's vision for a moment before he forced them away. *<Gods bless him.>*

* * *

Alazon Yanamar left Darcel to handle the rest of the long line of well-wishers. The team had finally gotten him off the train platform and into the assembly room proper that had been rented for this campaign stop. They'd also made sure it had a good strong roof to hold off the rain if another squall came through.

He was good at these moment-by-moment meetings with Talents young and old who wanted to lay eyes on their candidate. He'd also work the line faster if she wasn't mentally whispering in his ear, and that meant a shorter wait for those at the end of the line who might simply leave if forced to stand too long.

She scanned the room to reacquaint herself with the mood of the rest of the crowd and caught the nonverbals passing lightning-quick between the Voice she'd drafted for campaign coordination, Istin Leddle, and the double handful of Darcel's political staff scattered across the room.

Two of the staff took station farther up the receiving line to gush about their excitement for the campaign and subtly remind the constituents not to crush Darcel's hands. They might also encourage those at the end of the line to stay for the long wait to see the candidate himself.

The team was good. And Alazon watched her husband-to-be with a deep sense of pride. He was good too. Other campaign managers taught their candidates complex tactics for pretending empathy with potential voters. Darcel didn't need any of that. He liked people, and it showed.

The next pair in line had brought a baby, and Alazon suppressed a laugh as one of her interns produced a baby blanket. Darcel deftly laid it over his arms and bounced the cooing infant without ever touching the child directly. He'd insisted on something being found to keep the babies safe when the first of the mild campaign illnesses caught up with him and even the smallest infants kept being pushed into his arms anyway.

Istin had suggested blazoning the campaign logo across the thing like a banner, but Alazon had nixed that in favor of a discreet appliqué in one corner. The parents loved them. She made a note to order more.

She'd also have to see about getting more regional campaign offices and finding out which of the interns were interested in long-term employment on the Kinlafia staff. It wasn't too soon to plan for Candidate Darcel becoming Minister Kinlafia.

Perhaps a trip outside New Farnal would be good. For this first election, Alazon's goal for Darcel was to secure a position in the new House of Talents by a large enough margin to carry a sense of mandate. The polls showed he was popular everywhere. If a few fellow delegates owed their elections to his support… Alazon began mentally calculating the costs of leaving his base electorate for a day trip or two compared to the impact of merely giving a few supportive Voicecast interviews.

*　*　*

Kelahm chan Helikos, member of the Ternathian Empire's most elite personal protective service, served tea and delicate biscuits to the ladies of the Whitterhoo League of Women Talents waiting in the drizzle outside the packed meeting hall. He'd certainly worked in worse conditions. The crowd was cheerful and no one paid him much attention.

He hadn't even had to provide his cover story yet: Kelahm Helikos, adult middle son of a prosperous Animal Healer, taking a few months off from the family business to volunteer on the Darcel Kinlafia campaign.

Talents that could detect lying, rare though they were in the general population, were too commonly hired to serve as political correspondents for Kelahm to risk any overt falsehoods in his cover story. So everything he said about himself was true. He simply left out many other true things no one would think to ask about.

For example, he wouldn't mention the chan honorific earned from his military service before his recruitment into the Ternathian Imperial Guard. Nor would he mention that his father had also served in the Imperial Guard before retiring to an out of the way game preserve and setting up shop as an Animal Healer just to keep himself busy. And if the *reason* Kelahm had volunteered to join the Kinlafia Campaign had to do with his superiors' orders, as indeed it had, he had no intention of mentioning that fact either.

The other interns clearly didn't care for standing in the warm rain, so he'd arranged his security screen by suggesting they shuttle full carafes of tea and warm covered trays out to him for distribution among the crowd. The bedraggled pair he'd replaced had happily agreed.

Three hours into the shift, Kelahm had to partake of the tea himself when one of the interns started joking that he had some kind of Talent granting imperviousness to weather. He didn't.

But displaying too much self-discipline led to the wrong sorts of questions.

The tea was chilled with ice brought down from the mountains and deliciously sweet on his tongue. The cookies were rich enough to replace his lunch if he could have had a dozen more of the petite dainties. Kelahm brushed the crumbs off the front of his slightly oversized shirt and complimented the Whitterhoo League of Women Talents on their baking skills.

He could easily have refrained from eating the food and drink meant for the voters, but he had to play his part. This first day in a new cover was always the hardest.

He needed to convince the other interns he was entirely as they expected him to be, with his personal depths being limited to quirky tastes in music and perhaps a bit more naiveté about the world than they themselves had. Once they had him mentally slotted he could do whatever he had to do for the real job: Darcel Kinlafia's protection.

Privy Voice Yanamar's blonde assistant brought out the next load of sweets. Kelahm corrected himself, *Voice* Yanamar's assistant. She'd made it quietly clear that none of the campaign workers were to use her previous title while she ran Voice Kinlafia's staff. Especially not here, where feelings about the Calirath dynasty remained a bit ambiguous. That was the sort of detail she never got wrong.

Voice Yanamar was an excellent, if massively overqualified, campaign coordinator, and none of the staff she'd selected were a threat to Darcel, so Kelahm had moved quickly past them after his initial review reconfirmed their loyalty. Unfortunately that meant he'd met everyone but didn't really know any of them yet.

Istin of the pale Bernith Island skin and driven professionalism common to all the Privy Voice's Talented protégés settled beside him as if he'd decided to have some cookies himself while out of sight of the team supporting Kinlafia in the main hall, and Kelahm suppressed a smile. The young man was almost certainly after the same view that had attracted him to the small rise in the first place.

Kelahm hadn't stopped scanning the crowd for threats while taking his break, and he'd picked out a spot where he could see the train station and a good stretch of the track. His Talent worked at close range as well, but he'd already scanned the group inside for the complex instability that might presage an attack on Kinlafia. Outside, he had more range to deal with and redirect those who really shouldn't be allowed within arms reach of the candidate Emperor Zindel had assigned him to protect. Watching the train station let him keep an eye on the cars on which Kinlafia and the Privy Voice would head to the evening's next stop. He couldn't see the backs of the cars from here though, and the crowd looked to be thinning, which marked the nearing end of their stay at Whitterhoo.

Istin was doing a poor job of showing any interest in either his tea or the half eaten cookie in his hand. His head turned back and forth with the careful slow movements used to pass a scene to someone whose inner ear balance couldn't automatically adjust for the regular bobs of someone else's normal head motion—specifically to another Voice. Unless Kelahm missed his guess, Alazon Yanamar had just received an update on how many voters remained outside and how likely they looked to stick around long enough to fit into the packed assembly hall.

Kelahm knew a lot about more Talents than he could count. That knowledge was part of what made him such an effective bodyguard, and so were his own Talents. He was a Chameleon, able to blend so unobtrusively into the background that he could evade even trained security personnel who knew he was there and were trying to keep track of him. He couldn't physically disappear; he was simply . . . not there even for people who looked right at him. It was a vanishingly rare talent, virtually unheard of outside the families who'd served the Calirath Dynasty for generations. And he was also a Heart Hound. He couldn't read minds or emotions, but he could tell, unerringly, when a person was acting under duress or about to do something he deeply regretted. In other generations the Talent might have had the most use in the courtroom; in this one it proved remarkably useful in ferreting out unwilling agents caught in Emperor Chava Busar's cruel control. Heart Hounds were less rare than Chameleons, but the Talent was still highly uncommon, and so long as the Uromathians didn't recognize Kelahm was one, he had a very good chance of keeping Darcel Kinlafia safe. If Chava ever figured out how or who so consistently blocked his infiltrations of the Calirath household, on the other hand, the nature of those attempts would abruptly become much more difficult to detect and Kelahm chan Helikos would become merely an exceptionally dedicated personal guard. And speaking about guarding . . .

He nudged Istin's shoulder when he seemed to have finished Sending.

"Want to go take a walk over to the train station?"

A pale face already beginning to redden in the sun blinked at him, and Kelahm wondered for a moment if Istin didn't know he was trustworthy. Then Istin nodded slowly.

"Yes, let's take a look at the other side of the cars." He paused a moment. "Lufren and Torhm will come out and see to the pastries. We can go ahead. Voice Yanamar expects another hour to go before they break for the overnight trip."

Kelahm tucked the two names away his memory, and noted Istin had just completed another lightning fast communication with their boss inside to ensure the campaign stop continued to run smoothly.

"Okay. Let's go then," he said, and they meandered down across the rails to the other side of the train station. The campaign train with its small private engine and car remained undisturbed.

Istin frowned at it.

"What?"

"We should've had the new engine here by now." Istin's frown deepened. "The new one's bigger and can haul more cars. There's some more campaign supplies coming with it, and it's got a much better paint job, too."

In the waning afternoon light, Kelahm examined the engine in front of them. It looked pristine with clean lines and, to his eyes, a fine coat of road-worthy gray paint, but Istin slapped the side of the machine with irritation.

"This's supposed to say, 'Elect Kinlafia Now' on one side and 'Darcel Kinlafia for Parliament' on the other. We'll update the slogans as soon as he wins, of course."

"Of course," Kelahm agreed though it hadn't occurred to him that anyone would bother to paint political slogans onto a train engine at all. A check of his extended senses gave him no warnings of ill intent, but a thrumming vibration in the railway and the distant shriek of a whistle announced an inbound train.

"Do you suppose that's it?"

Istin cocked his head slightly, and his eyes glazed for a few moments. Not safe, Kelahm's instincts screamed, but the young Voice of course couldn't hear him. He was instead communicating with someone assigned to the railway.

"No." Istin scowled. "Not it. That's the train the railway rerouted our engine for. Diplomatic priority, even though we submitted our timetable first."

A magnificent, if unadorned engine squealed to a halt at the Whitterhoo Station trailing three unusual carriage cars and the normal motley of freight.

Istin Leddle groaned and trailed unwillingly behind him as Kelahm chan Helikos hotfooted up to the train station to see who might disembark.

"Don't talk to them!" Istin called after him. "It only makes them more curious!"

No one had left the newly parked train before Kelahm arrived on an empty platform and discovered he wasn't the only one with a sense of curiosity. He stopped quickly and his eyebrows rose as a dolphin's left eye, set on the side of a long gray face, examined him from one of the windows. What Kelahm had at first taken to be normal carriage cars were actually filled with water and glassed in. The cetacean flipped in place as Istin arrived beside him, and another pair of small dolphins took to examining Whitterhoo from the large window in the next aquarium car.

The young Voice scanned all three and breathed a heavy sigh of relief. "Thank the gods, it's just dolphins and porpoises. At least they can be reasoned with!"

"Really? You're a Cetacean Speaker?" That hadn't been in the file Kelahm had seen on this particular Voice, but the Imperial Guard had no reason to give him full details if Istin was Talented beyond his publicly-acknowledged exceptional Voice Talent.

Not unless they had some reason to classify Istin as a potential threat, at any rate.

"No. I just did an internship at a cetacean embassy." Istin waved off the suggestion. "They'll have brought an interpreter with them. All the cetaceans hear just fine. It's the listening I'm worried about. Just be glad there isn't an orca," he added darkly.

The Voice took his fist to the freight cars and began banging on each in succession until a weary young Cetacean Speaker climbed out of a car stacked high with dried cod. The young woman looked distinctly unwell and stepped gratefully off the train onto the platform.

"I am never, ever volunteering for one of these trips again!" She declared. "Just like being on a boat, my ass!" In spite of the green tinge to her own skin, the young woman turned back to her freight car and began hauling out stacks of dried fish to present to the dolphins and porpoises enjoying the afternoon sun in their cars.

"Trainsick?" Istin inquired.

"Yes!" She groaned. "And we were supposed to be in port and back in the ocean yesterday."

"Oh?"

Kelahm gave the Voice a sidelong glance. Somehow he suspected Istin already knew what the cetacean train's listed schedule had been.

"Yeah." The Speaker sighed heavily. "I'm Forminara Pelgra, by the way." She paused a bare moment for a formal introduction. "These are Nnnnmmmll, Lllllooouooo, and Mmmmunnnll. But they'll try talking to you even if you don't get the pitch right. And don't worry about memorizing the names, if you see them again, they'll probably have picked other human names by then."

"Those aren't human names," Istin pointed out.

Forminara shook her head. "I know, I know. But they like the sound of those letters, and they are human letters. There was this orca, and—"

"Never mind," Istin interrupted. "I understand; I've met orca."

One of the dolphins squealed something that sounded like laughter.

"Oh. And they'd like you to know my nickname is Sings Badly. It's a joke."

The dolphin's musical response raised a blush on Forminara's face.

"Okay, not totally a joke, but," she added defensively, "I'm getting better.

"Say, have you seen any porters around here? We're supposed to have a load of fresh fish at this stop, and there's also supposed to be a politician they wanted to meet. Have you ever heard of a Darcel Kinlafia?"

*   *   *

Her husband knocked lightly on the wood frame doorway of the tidy office Shalassar Kolmayr-Brintal kept for herself at the Cetacean Institute. Once he wouldn't have needed to draw her attention so overtly. But Shalassar was a Cetacean ambassador and founder of the Cetacean Institute in Shurkhal—work that continued even as she grieved for the loss of their daughter—and Thaminar Kolmayr tried to shield her from the overflow of his own mourning while she was working. Even so she felt the pain that mirrored her own and sensed him searching for a light topic for their luncheon conversation.

"Should we support Darcel Kinlafia, do you think?"

Shalassar looked up from the piled correspondence on her desk. She'd forgotten for a moment that the lean, tough man who served as her rock was there in the room instead of pulsing support through their marriage bond from their seaside home.

Grief could black out her world like that. Still.

Thaminar knew her well. He lifted the net bag with their bowls of marinated grilled beef and expertly spiced vegetables and cracked the fitted lid to waft the welcome smells of comfort food. Her stomach growled in response, and Shalassar reluctantly moved back from the desk, her mind shifting away from the pain of their lost Shaylar and back to the present.

Lunch called and the lapping tide outside her window marked the never ending pulse of time passing by, whether she wished it to or not. She followed her husband to the break room for a late lunch, thinking about Darcel Kinlafia as the present political candidate instead of as Shaylar's past colleague.

"Darcel has a chance to win, you think?" she asked him, settling into the comfortable chair at the break room table.

"Yes. The news reports say he's well ahead. Not our district, but some of the letters, from—" He waved at the wall behind her indicating the green star flag hanging over the covered dock on the other side of her office, not visible at all from where they sat in the break room. "—are asking if they should vote for him."

"Oh, them."

The green star flag had been adopted by families who'd lost a child to Arcana, but this one was special. It was the very first green star flag, made to memorialize Shaylar Nargra-Kolmayr. The other survey crew families had needed something too, so the flag had become the banner of a small group of families united by grief. But then, last month, the size of the group had exploded when all Sharona learned the war had been reignited by Arcanans attacking under cover of a truce *they'd* sought.

The war was horrific, in every sense of the word, and to have it resume in the very midst of peace negotiations only made it worse. Even as a diplomat—or perhaps *because* she was a diplomat—Shalassar found she had trouble thinking of the Arcanans as humans, and then the families of fallen soldiers had written her about their lost soldiers and asked to use the flag. She could hardly say no. But still...

"I'd rather hoped they'd stop writing us," she said.

Thaminar paused mid bite to give her a look she didn't need the marriage bond to read.

"Okay. No, not really. I just hoped it would get easier, is all." She sighed. "They're really asking us who to vote for?"

"Not at all," Thaminar said. "They're asking *you*. And reading between the lines, they've already decided. They're asking you to endorse him and want to make political contributions as Green Star Mothers. Most of the letters are only to you and not to me at all."

"Well, I'm not the most famous grieving mother anymore." She pointed out. None of the other extended family members of the lost portal exploration team were as famous in their own right as Ambassador Shalassar Kolmayr-Brintal. And none of Sharona's slaughtered children had been well known as Shaylar Nargra-Kolmayr.

Until now.

<*Janaki.*> Grief over the new losses slipped through Thaminar's best efforts and she pulsed encouragement of her own back at him.

<*At least there's a more famous mother now,*> she pointed out.

Thaminar snorted. "No one's going to be writing Emperor Zindel and Empress Varena expecting a reply or wanting to know if they've gotten their flag dimensions right. As if anyone would be going around policing grief!"

Shalassar's wry return smile matched her husband's. People had tried. None of their true friends were so crass, but the publicity-seeking social commentators who made their livings harassing public figures had reveled in it.

"Speaking of idiots," Thaminar continued, "a rep from VBS stopped by again asking for a meeting off the record."

"Not Krethva?" Shalassar gave him a look. Krethva wasn't the only one to try to market Shalassar's grief or to try to provoke her for shock value with snippy accusations of grieving in the wrong way. But she'd had the sharpest tongue and had inevitably become the one Shalassar publicly humiliated in a live Voicecast. She dreaded the moment when the woman found a way to return the public set down—not because she expected the reporter to be able to find words more painful than the hurt Shalassar already felt, but because she didn't expect to be able to stay civil and coherent if Krethva managed to actually get a display of her grief and rage. Shalassar was half afraid she'd emerge from the interview with blood spattered everywhere and no memory of how it all got there other than a deep sense that Krethva had gotten what she deserved. And that Arcana deserved worse.

"No, not Krethva." Thaminar broke into her red-tinted thoughts. "It was some other VBS Chava-ite. Any interest?"

Shalassar pressed away her emotions. "Sure, why not? Maybe I'll finally be able to get the VBS to take a reasoned stance on respecting cetacean funeral rites." She didn't continue. Thaminar was well aware of her long-standing complaints about the string of Uromathian coastal villages who made toys out of whale bone. She suppressed a shudder. "So creepy."

Thaminar speared another vegetable and ate it. The whales didn't seem to care what happened to their remains after life left their bodies, but any market for cetacean body parts concerned the Cetacean embassy. The Uromathians on Haimath Island also made memorials of their own ancestor's remains, and Thaminar didn't bring that up either. But his silence spoke volumes, and tight marriage bond or not, she already knew by heart the points he'd make.

He and Shalassar had feared they might outlive their daughter when she and Jathmar had become portal explorers, but they'd assumed that even in that horrific eventuality they'd have her remains brought home by the Portal Authority and properly buried. The flags were a thing Shalassar had invented because they had no normal way to mark their loss. And other families had had the same need.

Families of the Fallen Timbers portal exploration crew had started it by making their own flags, with Shalassar sending the first batch of them to her friends among the other families. The beginnings of a sob formed deep in her chest and she forced herself back to the last nonpainful thing she could think of.

"I suppose we should tell people to support Darcel."

Thaminar nodded. "He seemed like a decent enough young man. I hate to see anyone like that go into politics, but maybe he can do some good."

They ate the rest of lunch without much more to say.

Back alone in her office, Shalassar sewed one more flag her-self. She sealed the package and addressed it to Tajvana Palace. Empress Varena could display it in memory of Crown Prince Janaki Calirath or not, but Shalassar would give her the political prop if she needed it.

*   *   *

Campaign travel schedules were always hectic. Making them run smoothly was a formidable task, fit to challenge the best staff, even at the best of times. The New Farnalian winter harvest season, with the railways in high demand to transport food to the more frozen parts of Sharona, was *not* "the best of times" by any stretch of the imagination, and unplanned interruptions didn't help at all. Unfortunately, they happened anyway, and at the moment, the backup engine with its bright "Elect Kinlafia Now" paint job was stalled somewhere behind the aquarium train stuck at the Whitterhoo platform.

The news crews who'd been running commentary stories about Darcel since the campaign began had a field day. One crew reported he was providing a gentlemanly right of way to the cetaceans. A competitor news organization claimed he was being pushed around by a few silly dolphins. They all showed the forlorn little engine alone, without any trailing cars, stuck behind a massive glass-sided aquarium train.

Few reports spared even a few moments for the field abutting the train track, shining with ripe winter wheat. The dolphins watched the harvest with interest while their long-suffering young interpreter attempted to explain why humans went to such lengths to eat plant roe when the oceans were so abundantly supplied with fully matured fish.

CHAPTER SEVEN

Ternathal 24, 5053
(December 13, 1928 CE)

"EXCUSE ME, YOUR HIGHNESS, BUT WHAT ARE YOU DOING at my desk?"

Her Imperial Highness, Crown Princess Andrin Calirath, started guiltily and dropped the page she'd been trying to read in the dim premorning light. Her elbow barked the edge of the desk and nearly toppled one of the stacks of paper filling the half dozen in-boxes of her father's first councilor, Shamir Taje.

The man himself stood in the doorway to his offices in the Tajvana palace, and she felt a flash of guilt go through her. He wasn't merely her father's first councilor; he'd also been her tutor in many things related to the power and might of the imperial government back when she'd merely been studying to support her brother's eventual reign.

"Did you need something?" Taje cradled his first cup of dark morning tea and blinked groggily at Andrin. "Why isn't the lamp lit?"

Because I was trying to sneak a look at these papers without drawing any attention, Andrin thought but did not say. Lazima chan Zindico, her personal guardsman, stood at the side of the room and waited quite politely for the crown princess to explain. She looked up at her old teacher's tired face, feeling her face heat, and drew a deep breath.

"I couldn't sleep," she said. "Too much to worry about—I needed to see for myself."

Taje looked at her, sleepy, and suddenly very old to her eyes. He'd see a young princess with a mess of Calirath black hair shot with gold strands, too tall for proper elegance, and with deep bags under her eyes, she thought, and brushed her hair back with one hand in an automatic attempt to smooth it.

Miss Balithar would have seen to making Andrin's appearance sleek and regal if not actually beautiful and elegant . . . if Andrin had actually woken her staff for proper dressing before slipping off to check on the Privy Council's work. She knew she really should have, but she'd been too impatient, too jumpy within her own skin, to worry about "should haves," and she'd seen no reason anyone else should be dragged out of bed at such an unholy hour. Even Finena, her imperial peregrine falcon, was still back in the rooms resting with her night hood on—the poor bird would squawk enough to deafen a full wing of the Great Palace if she woke with Andrin missing from the room—although at least she hadn't quite been foolish enough to go anywhere without an armed guard.

That much of the duty of a Calirath she'd not failed at this morning.

"Never mind, Shamir. I shouldn't have come out here." She rubbed her own eyes feeling the weight of the lost hours of sleep. "I'd hoped to see the list of marriage candidates, but it was probably foolish for me to come involve myself. I'm sure your council has everything well in hand."

The concern didn't leave the first councilor's face. "Did you have some reason to think it wasn't? Did you have a Glimpse?"

"No." Andrin hastened to reassure him. "Just simple marriage jitters. It's nothing, really. Please, forget I came." At the deepening furrow in Shamir Taje's brow, she added, "I just needed to be sure there'd be at least one good choice on the list."

She lifted her eyes to the first councilor, hoping he would understand all the things she couldn't articulate, sometimes even to herself. Janaki had trained to be her father's heir all his life. Andrin hadn't, and she felt horribly ill-prepared. At this particular moment she felt more like a little girl than a woman about to turn eighteen and make a dynastic marriage to secure the Empire of Sharona.

Taje nodded slowly and took a long sip from his cup, regarding the crown princess with more understanding—and sympathy—than she might have believed he could. But the list she was looking for, the list of all the eligible Uromathian princes from which she must select her future consort, wasn't in the unprotected open on his desk.

The office's security was good enough he could probably have left even so important a document and all its related notes in plain view, but he had far too much concern for Andrin's future—and Sharona's—to do anything so careless. Even in an interior office in the Calirath Palace, with windows that opened only to the secure courtyard and hallways patrolled by the Imperial Guard, some horrible mistake might happen.

So he used the heavy oak cabinets that lined his office study and wore the key to their locks on a chain around his neck.

"One moment, Your Highness. I'll show you the draft. It isn't final, you understand. But I can show you what we have so far."

He made a quick circuit of the room, dropping the window curtains and securing the door while Lazima chan Zindico moved deftly out of his way with the sure experience of a man who knew exactly which security moves to expect. Taje produced his key and opened the largest of the cabinets. For this project, the Privy Council had amassed great piles of notes...and all of them had either been carefully burned and stirred in the study's fireplace or banded and filed here in the wall cabinet. He proffered a few sheaves, and the crown princess snatched them eagerly from his hands.

"This isn't the complete list yet. There are likely a few more names we might add."

Andrin wasn't listening. Her eyes had stopped a third of the way down the second page: Howan Fai Goutin, Crown Prince of Eniath.

"Oh. Oh, good! I suppose there was no reason to worry at all."

She handed the list back to the first councilor, who checked the sheet and smiled at her choice.

"We weren't going to forget the Eniath prince, Your Highness," he said gently.

"Well, no, I suppose not." Andrin acknowledged, ducking her head just slightly. The motion conveyed sheepishness, but, Taje noted, the crown princess' Calirath spine had stayed regally straight. Lady Merissa Vankhal would have approved. "I just wanted to be sure. There might have been concern about his family being too easily pressured by the Busar line, or maybe there were others that would look better on paper, or he could have already been married but not mentioned it when we spoke, I mean, I think he might have mentioned that, but—"

"He is certainly not already married." Taje broke in to soothe the crown princess' concerns. "The Privy Council will be reviewing all the details of these candidates to provide dossiers to you during this week before you meet once more with the Conclave to announce your choice."

"To me?" The surprise in Andrin's tone reminded him just how new his crown princess was to the heirship. She had the backbone to fight Uromathia on the Conclave floor, but demanding her due from the Winged Crown's staff didn't yet come naturally.

"Yes, Your Highness. We'll be making our report to you. Nothing we may find will lessen the importance of your choice, but we hope to provide as much clarity on the candidates as we may." An idea occurred to him. The crown princess' schedule was absurdly busy, but perhaps a few things could be moved. "You'd be welcome to come to our deliberations if you'd like to hear the details."

"Yes." Andrin nodded, slowly. "I'd very much like to hear the details."

Taje responded with a decisive nod of his own. "We've been working through lunch and some of the staff have been all but sleeping in my office. It's a tight fit when we all get in here, but I think it would do the council well to get to know you better anyway. We are your council as well as your father's."

Andrin agreed wholeheartedly, and felt a touch of chagrin as she realized this was exactly the sort of thing Janaki would have done. She should have thought of it for herself, and a part of her scolded herself for failing to do so. But another part of her understood exactly why she hadn't. Intellectually, she knew her brother was dead and gone, leaving her suddenly in the role of heir. She'd managed to accept that much, terrible though the shock had been, but all the other bits and pieces, like sitting in on Privy Council deliberations, still felt foreign and a touch like usurping her older brother's prerogatives.

Andrin quashed the thought. That was a perspective Chava Busar would want her to have—a way of thinking that he could use to keep her ignorant and uninvolved in the workings of the empire—while one of his sons sat in Janaki's place instead of Janaki's blood. As Janaki's sister, she owed it to him to become the kind of empress Sharona needed.

"I'd be very pleased to attend the Privy Council's deliberations. And also—" Andrin caught the first councilor's eyes. "I apologize for sneaking into your office. I should simply have asked."

Taje bowed. "To be sure. But perhaps the Privy Council should have thought to invite you. We still, myself included unfortunately, think of you too much as our emperor's young daughter and not enough as our future empress." He bowed again more deeply. "I, too, apologize."

The first councilor had a few minutes more to consider his crown princess' face as she waited for her guardsman to clear the hallway. The extra security in place in Tajvana felt extreme compared to Ternathia, and yet it was necessary.

The Great Palace had been occupied by the Order of Bergahl for over two hundred years. Outwardly, the turrets, walls, and towers appeared unchanged to the point of disrepair. Inside, the changes were random—likely chosen for modern opulence with little thought for either architectural cohesion or imperial security. Hundreds of years of excess hadn't been and couldn't be put to rights in an instant...and there was always the possibility that the present Seneschal or one of his predecessors might have made changes which had nothing at all to do with modernization and quite a lot to do with less savory considerations. At the moment, however, Taje was more concerned with his princess' emotions than any questions about her physical security.

"Your Majesty," he asked, "are you reassured, truly?"

Andrin looked at him and allowed her expression—for a rare moment—to show her deep concern. "I don't know if I can be reassured, Shamir."

"It's a good solid choice. One that can and will hold the new empire together."

"Yes," his crown princess agreed. "And I should probably be grateful there's just one Howan Fai Goutin. Imagine if there were three good Uromathian princes and I had to roll a die to pick between them. This is how it is though, isn't it? You dance with a decent seeming prince once, politics force the situation, and then you need to marry and hope he's up to the task."

"He should be, but we'll study his background. And there may be others we can find if there's a significant problem with him." The first councilor spoke firmly, his tone confident and reassuring, but Andrin's lifted eyebrow showed he hadn't quite pulled it off. Well, he'd already known she was no one's fool, and the truth was there weren't any others *to* find, really. A few more Uromathian princes existed with less firm ties to Emperor Chava than the man's own sons, but if something were to happen to Howan Fai Goutin, the council would be looking to Howan's brothers, not to some other family.

"I don't need everything coated in honey, Shamir. In fact I think I'll do better if I can hear from the outset if we find any problems," the crown princess said, straightening her shoulders. He bowed in response and secured the precious list before chan Zindico opened the door.

A quartet of night shift guardsmen in thick protective suits wearing braces of throwing knives in addition to their usual gear stepped to the side of the hallway as Andrin came through the door, and the first councilor frowned in surprise.

"Is this a new security measure?"

Chan Zindico shook his head. "No, My Lord, just a practice session. We've been doing these exercises down in the training salles for weeks, but the guard commander decided we should move them to some of the actual hallways we defend."

At the first councilor's startled look, the armsman added, "But only at night. We wouldn't want to skewer one of the staff. And our practice blades aren't poisoned, so it wouldn't be much of a wound anyway. Thrown blades of the type the Order of Bergahl use in their knife dances aren't much of a threat without the poison.

"And the commander's added a few more effective weapons to the training in case local troublemakers decide to be creative." Chan Zindico gestured down to the cross hall away from the direction they needed to go. Something black and feathery shot across the perpendicular hallway; it was followed almost immediately by a yelp.

"They aren't our usual tools," he said, "but we need to be ready to defend against them."

"I see." Shamir Taje rubbed his head, looking distinctly like he could use a second cup of morning tea. "I just wish your definitions of night aligned more closely with mine, Master Armsman chan Zindico." He cast a look at the steadily brightening morning light now spilling in through the window.

"Dawn does some interesting things to shadows in the halls and makes the deflections more challenging, My Lord," the guardsman said, but he also inclined his head in acknowledgement of the first councilor's point.

"So of course you lot had to try it then." Taje shook his head. "You might try just dodging."

"Sometimes, yes, My Lord."

Chan Zindico, the first councilor noticed, didn't point out that none of the guards would be ducking if they thought doing so would let a missile through to any member of the imperial family they'd sworn to protect.

Andrin took in that reminder also. She wasn't the only one in danger if Emperor Chava learned about their subterfuge, and after they announced her marriage, the threat to her father's guards and her own would only increase.

On that sobering thought, Andrin and chan Zindico returned to her suite to face the coming day.

*   *   *

A pair of men had been following Howan Fai Goutin for a day and a half. The Crown Prince of Eniath was certain of that. Well, almost. He was only almost certain because the men kept changing. And there were whole hours at a time when he was very nearly certain that no one but his own personal guardsman, Munn Lii, was consistently with him.

Last night Howan Fai had decided it was all in his imagination, born of spending too much time in close proximity to the Uromathian emperor. Chava VII had no fresh reasons—that Howan Fai knew of—to attack him or any representative of Eniath, but history abounded with enough old reasons to make anyone uneasy, whether Chava had something actively in mind or not.

Chava Busar was certainly not the sort anyone wished to cross lightly, and the avaricious emperor tended to offend with excruciating ease. Eniath had proved too tough to be swallowed easily by the Busars during King Junni's reign, but it was always possible another attempt would be made in this same generation.

Last night's dinner had been at a small Ternathian cuisine restaurant tucked in an out-of-the-way corner of Tajvana. Just a group of his fellow small kingdom princes together in a rented back room for an evening of simple food and very fine beer straight from the tap. The bartender had displayed healthily muscled arms and an even more impressive belly as he regaled the group with stories and elicited the most remarkable outpouring of their own worst childhood antics. The entire room had been laughing at Howan Fai's tale of attempting to induce a stolen goat to eat his tutor's lecture books and instead having the side of his trousers slimed and gnawed as the goat tried to get at the grain and molasses mix which he'd used to attract the beast and then absently stuffed in his own pockets.

If the bartender had somehow lost the gut overnight and grown a nose a size or two larger, he would be the prosperous man of business who'd trailed him through the last three jewelry stores, seemingly just another shopper. A shopper who was always interested in storefronts and stalls that which just happened to keep him on the same meandering path as Howan Fai and Munn Lii. He would have pegged the man as a thief except for the similarly muscled spotter set up at a corner cafe at an uncovered table with a full view of Gem Street. The table should have been empty in the cold winter drizzle, and the spotter should have been a child, or at most a poverty-slimmed man, if he'd truly been dealing with thieves desperate enough to try a snatch in broad daylight in this wealthy part of Tajvana. So *if* Howan Fai wasn't simply imagining things, simple thievery wasn't on the table.

He would have ended the shopping trip early and returned to the somewhat safer apartments being used by all the Conclave members, but family experience taught him not to trust a rented safe house. Besides, Uromathian intimidation tactics were usually much more blatant. These watchers seemed to be merely tracking his routine, so Howan Fai saw no reason to stop what he was doing just to let them get out of the cold.

His mother's birthday was coming up in a few months, and she was far too valuable as a potential hostage to ever leave the security of Eniath. Trapped at home, she always loved it when he picked up something from his travels for her, but everything he'd seen so far could be bought in the flourishing stores of his father's kingdom. He knew how much she'd longed to travel to Tajvana for the Conclave, and he wanted something truly special for her this year.

If Chava VII had him kidnapped, Howan Fai knew with white-knuckle certainty that it would be his duty to do his best to suicide. Unfortunate family experience had shown that tactic worked. One of Howan's own great uncles had proven it.

All the Eniath royals knew how it would go. His father, King

Junni, would pronounce him dead and transfer the inheritance to Howan's younger brother, and Chava would get nothing from Eniath. They'd made certain the Uromathian emperor knew their deadly serious intent, because the knowledge granted the family a small measure of security from abduction.

His mother had every bit of the inner strength necessary to do the same, but she knew what the loss of a beloved wife would do to King Junni, his father. And so she'd put aside her love of foreign places and stayed safe at home for their entire marriage. The least Howan Fai could do was to find her an exotic bit of jewelry for her birthday.

If it weren't so hard to focus, he'd have selected any of a dozen pieces by now, but he couldn't blame his distraction on the shadows. A certain grand princess newly elevated to Imperial Crown Princess had been filling his thoughts. Which, he knew, was unforgivably stupid of the thoughts in question . . . or of the man thinking them, at any rate. He'd probably only ever see her again a handful of times during the rest of his lifetime, so why was his back brain incessantly thinking up ways he might snag an invitation to official events likely to be graced by her presence?

He remembered the reception where they'd first met. Her elegant height, nearly a foot and a half above his own, and her stunning gold-threaded black hair had drawn him across the room, for his mother was not the only one to find the exotic enticing. But then he'd been distracted by Finena her falcon, fallen into real conversation, and been stunned to discover he really, truly liked her.

More than just liked her, he admitted to himself. Oh, Andrin!

Howan Fai glanced down. The matched pair of teardrop rubies he fingered now were an utterly inappropriate present for his mother. She liked darkest green jade that brought out the warmth of her skin and the occasional turquoise or other semiprecious stones for their uniqueness. She didn't like getting precious gemstones. His mother considered those only appropriate for wear at the most official state occasions when, as Queen of Eniath, she'd be expected to don the crown jewels passed down from his father's mother instead of recently purchased gifts from her children.

Still, Howan Fai couldn't help wondering if Imperial Crown Princess Andrin might not like a pair of earrings made up with these. There was no way he could make such a present without also making himself a fool, but he imagined she might very much like them. They weren't the absolute highest quality rubies, so maybe to a Calirath they wouldn't seem so expensive and could be worn almost everyday. And a certain something about the way the fire glinted inside the gems reminded him of her spirit.

With a sigh, he pushed away the beauties and selected a broach formed in the shape of a butterfly with a clever combination of worked silver and dyed pearls.

As he handed the shopkeeper his choice, Howan Fai examined the glass behind the jewelry counter to check his human shadow. The suspicious man was standing in front of a set of ladies' bracelets in a large glass case with a mirrored back side. The man showed remarkably little interest in similar bracelets laid out on velvet without mirroring. And when Howan Fai produced his wallet to pay, the man seemed to decide he couldn't afford the jewelry and wandered out of the store. If the trend continued, the man would find a nice outdoor spot and pass the tail on to a less familiar face.

The shopkeeper wrapped the purchase carefully in a dozen layers of fine cloth, and Howan Fai tucked the package into an interior pocket secure from the quick fingers of the city's clever street criminals. Then he leaned in to exchange a few words with the shopkeeper.

"Master Jeweler. Did you see the large man behind me by the gold bracelets? He was *not* a regular customer, I don't think?"

The owner shook his head with wry disgust. "Haven't seen him before, Your Lordship. Not someone I knew, but begging Your Lordship's pardon, there've been customers come for this Conclave with the look of desert bandits who turned out to be foreign princes. That one had the look of a thief, so I kept an eye out. My goods are all still here."

Howan Fai nodded and didn't correct his title. Tajvana was teeming with foreign nobles these days, and most in the gem-sellers' district had taken to greeting everyone as a lord, just to be safe. Some of his own ancestors had become sea nomads to avoid the land wars which had raged between some of the other Conclave attendees' ancestors—and many of those attendees did look like desert bandits even in Eniathian eyes, far less from the perspective of cosmopolitan Tajvana.

Thievery wasn't an explanation Howan Fai had considered likely, but it made sense from the shopkeeper's perspective, so he adjusted his story slightly.

"That man seems to have been following me, and I'd like to keep the fine jewelry I just bought. There was another one—his partner, perhaps—across the street...."

The shopkeeper lifted the side of his coat to reveal the revolver that looked like the shorter-barreled, lighter civilian version of the Ternathian H&W. It had a well-worn grip, and there were two speedloader pouches on his belt. Howan Fai had expected the owner of a shop with so much valuable merchandise to have guards on staff, and he'd wondered why he hadn't seen any; now he knew why.

"They won't rob Your Lordship in my store. But I could send for an escort if you'd like?"

Howan Fai caught a blatantly skeptical glance from his own guardsman, Munn Lii, which made Lii's opinion about the value of city police for dealing with the brutes the Empire of Uromathia usually hired as intimidators quite clear. A few extra bodies would make it easier for the two of them to escape a bruising if that was all they faced, but unsuspecting men on the police force could easily be maimed or killed in a serious attack by the kind of criminals Uromathia could buy.

Howan Fai shared his guardsman's views in that regard and demurred as politely as he could.

"I'll stay out of dark alleys and my own guard should be sufficient. I just worry that the next customer might not be so wary. Do you think you could provide the city watch with the man's description? If you come to the front I can point out the watcher too."

The shopkeeper readily agreed, and Howan Fai hoped it would at least make this particular criminal's life more difficult if he continued to sell his services to the likes of Chava Busar. Of course when they came to the front of the store both the possible thief and the shivering cafe man were gone.

The shopkeeper claimed the police must have already run them off, but he added after an uncomfortable pause, "At least I hope they did."

He seemed less than certain of that, unfortunately, and Howan Fai found himself regretting that he'd raised the specter of thieves operating with impunity in such a prosperous area of the city. Tajvana might not be the glorious city it had once been under the Old Ternathian Empire, but he began to wonder just how thoroughly the Order of Bergahl had undermined respect for justice in the city if even gemsellers weren't certain criminals would be stopped by the police.

He didn't think his shadows were regular criminals, but now he wondered if the shopkeeper hadn't also noted the excellent musculature and guessed at some more professional organization than the loose bonds avarice would form among common criminals. A check at the doorframe showed the Bergahl emblem was affixed with gold wire next to the certificate of business sealed by the Seneschal.

The establishment certainly seemed paid up with whatever tithes or taxes the Order demanded. Howan Fai's own variant of the Uromathian faith placed the onus for piety on the individual, but some church fathers charged civilian leaders to mandate externally imposed religious observances instead. The quarterly stamps around the Bergahl emblem hinted strongly at a fiscal piety extracted from the well-to-do of Tajvana with the force of law.

"We all pay our dues to the Seneschal, Your Lordship." The shopkeeper acknowledged Howan Fai's careful inspection of the posted certificates. "It'll be better for all of us when this Conclave is over," the man said. "We dearly love the city's visitors, of course, but the Seneschal is Tajvana."

Munn Lii stepped quickly out the front door to check the street more thoroughly. Howan Fai stayed inside, waiting for his guard's all clear and intrigued by the shopkeeper's comments.

"Visitors? I suspect many of us will be staying for quite some time. After the Conclave, we'll have to set up residences for officials coordinating with the unified empire. I'll likely be going home soon, but it'll be good for Tajvana to grow don't you think?"

"As Your Lordship says, that'd be well enough, of course. But the Caliraths, won't they want to get back to Hawkwing in the Ternathian Isles again? They left once, you know."

Through the shop's broad windows Munn Lii gave him the sign to wait and Howan Fai examined the shopkeeper's face. The man didn't seem to believe his own words, quite, but the way he leaned in and pressed his lips together did seem to imply he hoped Howan Fai would confirm them.

"I believe Tajvana should prepare itself to be the imperial seat for the Winged Crown once again," he said finally.

"Oh." The man deflated. "And Your Lordship is quite sure?"

"Yes." He read fear in the shopkeeper's eyes, so he added, "The Caliraths will be good for Tajvana. You've seen the carpenters and masons repairing the Grand Palace." He seized on a point he expected a local merchant to appreciate. "There'll be more fine work ordered after the worst of the damages are seen to. The gilding over the common entry way to the audience hall is missing for instance."

"They'd gild the commoner's entrance?" The man dry swallowed. "Would Your Lordship have heard when the tax for that is scheduled to begin?" When he didn't have an immediate answer, the man continued, "I'll need to sell my gold work before the confiscation. Perhaps Your Lordship has a few friends who'd like to come buy at a discount?"

"The Caliraths aren't thieves," Munn Lii put in as he re-entered the shop. "And our thieves are long gone, Highness."

The shopkeeper flustered through an apology that left Howan Fai wondering what sort of policing Tajvana was accustomed to under the Order of Bergahl. He didn't have to wonder about the tax burden the Order had imposed, though, and he supposed it was inevitable that the shopkeeper would be anticipating the worst. It would be too much to expect him to realize how utterly different from Faroayn Raynarg, the current Seneschal, a man like Zindel chan Calirath truly was. Besides, Zindel wouldn't need to inflate his treasury just to repair the palace. The Imperial Suite had suffered an explosion of gilded surfaces under the Order of Bergahl stewardship. A few chairs from that chamber would provide more than enough gold leaf to set the entire main entranceway to rights; if the bathroom fixtures were replaced with mere solid silver, the Caliraths could build an entire new façade for the north wing! He seriously considered pointing that out, but the proprietor clearly had too many negative experiences to believe him.

Howan Fai gave up calming the man and left the store.

"There's little difference between banditry and taxes in some places, Highness," was all Munn Lii had to say about it.

"This won't be tolerated for long." Howan Fai couldn't help giving a pair of city guardsmen patrolling the street a look of disgust. "I wouldn't tolerate it, and I don't believe Emperor Zindel will accept it either."

Munn Lii was right about their tail and his watcher having disappeared. Howan Fai wasn't sure the two men hadn't simply realized they'd been recognized and left. The crowd filling the street now showed no one who stood out or appeared to be lingering anywhere too long. He sincerely hoped the shopkeeper wasn't too frightened of the criminals' possible Order affiliation to make a report when the city guard eventually stopped by.

CHAPTER EIGHT

Ternathal 24, 5053 AE
(December 13, 1928 CE)

ANDRIN LISTENED WITH RAPT ATTENTION DURING THE afternoon gathering of the Privy Council. Technically it wasn't a formal meeting since neither Emperor Zindel nor a councilors' quorum was present, but the working session was vitally important. And her father would be receiving a detailed report of everything they uncovered.

Privy Voice Ulantha Jastyr, formerly the *Assistant* Privy Voice, sat in the corner making a human record of everything said. She was surrounded by physical reports and notices Andrin vaguely recognized as the routine work of the Privy Voice's aide. Alazon Yanamar's resignation was for public consumption, not reality, and Andrin knew her father intended to have the exceptional Talent back in formal service once Darcel Kinlafia was elected. But Jastyr was an excellent Voice in her own right, and Andrin appreciated having one person on the Privy Council who was closer to her age than her father's.

Andrin added to her very long list of things to accomplish someday, a mental note to find a way to see Jastyr was rewarded for her term as Privy Voice with more than just a thank you and a resumption of her former duties as Alazon Yanamar's aide and protégée. In fact, she supposed it was time she began assembling her own staff—that was another thing Janaki would have been doing if she hadn't been thrust into his rightful place—and one member of that staff ought to be a Voice of her own. . . .

The papers and notes Jastyr was shuffling through at the moment had nothing at all to do with Crown Prince Howan

Fai Goutin or any of the other Uromathian marriage candidates, however. The Privy Voice was managing all the *other* reports and notices that had been forwarded to her father's attention relating to the war, the administration of the empire, and the minutia of coordinating a multi-universe unification.

The other council members focused on the detailed discovery and analysis of marriageable candidates, freeing Jastyr to limit her involvement to making a perfect mental record of the proceedings, and Andrin was deeply thankful for the Privy Voice's ability to multitask. Having heard her recall before, Andrin had no doubt at all Jastyr would be able to provide the emperor with a perfect recitation of everything they discussed when she briefed him at the end of the day. But even more important than updating Zindel, Jastyr kept the secret. No one else could be allowed to know they were working on a way around Emperor Chava's demand until the moment they announced the wedding and Jastyr was playing her part flawlessly. Voices working with the media and serving other royals knew Alazon Yanamar's mind intimately, but Jastyr was new. The change in Privy Voices would certainly help Darcel's chances of securing a seat in the new Imperial House of Talents, but perhaps even more importantly, it also protected the secret. Even Voicecasters who might have realized Alazon was hiding *something* in one of the countless interviews and Voice briefings expected of her position were unlikely to detect those same nuances in Jastyr's Voice. Not until they'd had longer to become accustomed to Hearing her, at any rate.

First Councilor Taje, at the end of the table opposite Andrin, checked off the agenda items and called on Brithum Dulan to handle the presentation on prospective consorts.

"Your Highness." Councilor Dulan nodded to her. "I think we have some useful information to present today. We've had men investigating every candidate Uromathian prince in Tajvana and a few more who didn't come for the Conclave. I'll remind everyone that while every member of the Imperial Guard is loyal, none of the men testifying about their investigations know why they were assigned the task."

The first councilor and the few other council members in the room acknowledged the warning amicably. Andrin—who suspected the real reason he'd mentioned the point had more to do with her presence than with the councilors who'd been working with him since the beginning of the effort—thanked him politely, and they began the day's work.

The subject of the day was the Eniath Crown Prince: Howan Fai Goutin, his family, his background, his connections to Emperor Chava Busar, and perhaps most critically, the detailed minutia of their claim that his qualifications met the terms of the Unification Treaty.

That final piece was easiest to confirm. Everything Darcel Kinlafia and Alazon Yanamar had pointed out about the treaty and Howan Fai was absolutely accurate. The terms of the original treaty called for a Princess of Uromathia to wed the Crown Prince of Ternathia. With Janaki dead, Chava had accepted the modification of Prince of Uromathia and Crown Princess. And as Darcel had pointed out, even though the implication had been Prince of the Uromathian *Empire*—which could be interpreted only as Chava's sons—the treaty itself said only Prince of Uromathia... and Uromathia was a *continent*, not simply a single empire which happened to be located upon it. Howan Fai was a prince, and Howan Fai was Uromathian. All that remained was to ensure he was also a good candidate for consort.

At a nod from the first councilor, Dulan ushered in the first of his men.

Tolleran chan Lofti, a tall, well-muscled man with the extreme physical fitness common in the Imperial Guard, reported with sheepish detail his recent investigation of the eligible Uromathian prince.

"So you said you think the Eniath crown prince recognized you this morning even with the disguise change?" Taje asked.

"I don't think so, My Lord," chan Lofti replied. "I know so. He made me, and it could've gotten quite awkward if I hadn't seen the look he passed to Munn Lii, his guard, and used the back exit instead of the front. In fairness, he didn't guess who was actually having him followed. He seems to have assumed I was a Bergahl hireling, or possibly someone working for Emperor Chava. I'd barely started writing up the report when Munn Lii stopped by headquarters to ask if we'd had warning of any threats against Conclave members from Chava's supporters."

Andrin blanched. "Emperor Chava knows?"

"Knows what?" chan Lofti looked genuinely confused, then quickly amended his question. "My apologies, Your Highness.

But I work outside the Palace most of the time and I certainly don't want to know any more than I need to."

Andrin swallowed her questions and let Taje answer the man.

"We'll take the rest of your report now, I think," the first councilor said smoothly. "If we need to call you back for more questions later, we'll do so."

"Of course, First Councilor." Chan Lofti took a moment to regather his thoughts and then continued. "There was an Order thug at a cafe playing lookout for some kind of strong-arm antics on Gem Street. Either the prince or the merchant, possibly both, associated me with that operation."

"My actual backup, Dorelle chan Whalen, was posing as City Watch for the morning, so he got a full report from the jewelry merchant. It seems the young prince talked the merchant into reporting me in spite of the man's obvious fear of the Order. He gave a pretty good description, too. If I were a criminal, I wouldn't be able to work in Tajvana again."

"Is that some sort of Talent?" Taje asked.

"Hard to say. In the merchant, definitely not. In the prince, maybe. But I think, no. I suspect Prince Howan Fai is simply more observant than usual and something's happened to put him enough on edge that he's paying attention to the crowd even when his mind is wandering."

"Oh?" Andrin leaned in.

"Dorelle said—and he wrote it up in the report if you want his exact words, Your Highness—he said the merchant thought the prince was quite taken with a princess and had trouble making a selection. It could just have been a storekeeper talking up his wares, but there'd be no reason for the man to add that to the telling."

Andrin listened with rapt attention.

"He could have been buying for a girlfriend back on Eniath or even a fiancée," the Privy Voice suggested, glancing up from her stack of paperwork with a concerned glance at Andrin.

The crown princess sat back, disturbed at this new thought. Could her perfect solution be the ruin of Howan Fai's life? His father was a close ally of her father, and with the importance of the Sharona Unification on the line, Howan Fai could be forced to give up a previously formed attachment to become her unwilling groom.

Chan Lofti actually laughed. "I hardly think so. He bought a broach for his mother. The search of his apartments while he was out revealed only letters to his father about the Conclave. And out with his friends last night he was teased mercilessly for not having a prospect for future Queen of Eniath."

"You searched his rooms?" Andrin paled trying to imagine explaining the breach of privacy to the sweet man she'd danced with. "Is that normal?" *Were my mother's rooms searched before she married my father?* She didn't ask it out loud, but the Privy Council members understood the underlying question. Chan Lofti, of course, didn't, but some of the eager delight at the success of his search methods faded in the investigator's eyes as her tone registered.

"Pardon, Your Highness, I wouldn't know about normal. My orders were to conduct a thorough, a very thorough, check of this prince for reliability and security risks."

"Those were, indeed, Armsman chan Lofti's instructions, Your Highness," Councilor Dulan put in. "If the prince was being controlled by Uromathia, we needed to know."

"And by every check we've been able to apply," the first councilor added, "Prince Howan Fai and the rest of the Eniath royal family are exactly as they present themselves: capable rulers of a small historically Uromathian nation fully independent of Emperor Chava's control."

Andrin thought she should have found that reassuring. She did, but she also didn't. The man she'd begun to think of as her prince was eligible, but he might not be truly interested. Perhaps Howan Fai was just like the others at the ball, entranced by her title.

But no, he'd seemed to like her personally too. And Finena had liked him. The falcon didn't warm even to trained falconers very easily, so Andrin counted several points in his favor for charming her feathered companion.

"I see," she said wishing it were safe to talk to Howan Fai directly, "I suppose there's really no way to find out if he has some ugly secrets and really enjoys torturing puppies or, or, really anything."

Chan Lofti bowed deeply to her. "I can assure you, Your Highness, that he doesn't."

Andrin looked at him, her eyes unconvinced, and the guardsman glanced at Dulan. The Internal Affairs councilor looked back for a moment, then at the first councilor. He raised one eyebrow and, after the briefest of hesitations, Taje nodded.

"Your Highness," Dulan said carefully, "you're probably aware the Imperial Guard possesses Talents about which the world in general knows little or nothing. Exactly what all of those Talents are is known only to the emperor or empress. Not even I know all of them. In this instance, however, I assure you that you can take Armsman chan Lofti's word for it."

Andrin looked back at chan Lofti, who smiled slightly.

"When I ask questions, I can get people to reveal quite a bit about themselves, Your Highness," he said.

"I mentioned his conversation with his friends, Your Highness. My cover was as, ah, a server in one of the local restaurants—" for some reason, Andrin had the impression he'd chosen his words with some care "—which gave me an opportunity to speak to all of them. One of them was Prince Yertahla of Rylliath, and I can tell you that, unlike Prince Howan Fai, he's a complete fool. Of course, he's also only eighteen at the moment. In a few years, he might grow out of it, but he might not, either."

"Thank you, chan Lofti." Andrin scanned the table to see if anyone else had more questions for this member of the Imperial Guard. No one did.

"I think that will be all for now." Councilor Dulan dismissed the man, and chan Lofti bowed himself out.

"And," Dulan put in after a slight pause allowed the door to close firmly, "since the Conclave meeting is in only five days, the Council has formally recommended against your choosing Prince Yertahla, Your Highness."

"What about Howan Fai?" Andrin asked.

Councilor Dulan said, "I'd welcome him into the Guard." That was high praise indeed, but it wasn't enough.

"And as Consort?" Andrin asked. "With all honor for the fine work the Imperial Guard does, I don't need a protector. I need a Prince. Is he strong enough for this?"

"I believe he is, Your Highness," Dulan replied. "He's had some hard times in the past. Eniath's struggle to remain independent from Uromathia hasn't been easy on the Fai family, but I judge Howan Fai's emerged from it all stronger rather than broken."

"That's good. That's really good. But, can he handle being consort? I'm—" Andrin blushed. "At least I think I'm trying to be rational about this. He's really amazing, I mean, I like him. But I can't make this choice just based on what I want. I have to choose a man who will be good for Sharona. The gods know Janaki was expected to make a political marriage to help Ternathia, but now the stakes are so much higher. I can't see, and I don't mean Glimpses, though I've gotten niggles of warnings from that too, but I can't see if this choice will ultimately work out.

"I can imagine Howan Fai as an emperor consort, but that shouldn't be for years and years. Father will have plenty of time to train us both, I hope. It's just that I'm coming to this late, too. Do you think he can learn? Sharona is so much bigger and more complicated than the single island of Eniath."

Councilor Yamen coughed to gain her attention. The small birdlike woman specialized in accounts, finances, and banking concerns and provided the Privy Council with her insights on all things financial.

"While it's true Eniath is small and has no physical holdings beyond the home universe, Your Highness, the people were originally nomads, with their range to the east of the Arau Mountains extending to the northern Uromathian coast. At one point Eniathian nomads ranged fairly far south as well. But in old history, several of Howan Fai's many times great grandfathers kept his people free during the Uromath Unification Wars by giving up contested land. One branch of the Eniathians even moved entirely onto their boats when they had to abandon the Uromathian coastline. The Uromathian Empire formed without them, but they kept their independence, and if Eniath's physical holdings now aren't much larger than a postal stamp, their traders, merchants, and bankers are among the canniest anywhere. And, for that matter, as a people of travelers they're quite literally *every*where. There are a few strongholds in the steppes and another couple on some northern islands, but the people of Eniath are still very nomadic at heart."

"Oh yes, I remember learning about that." Andrin replied.

Most of what her tutors had taught her about Uromathia had focused on the Uromathian Empire and its current conflicts with Ternathia, but there'd been a few asides about how the handful of Uromathian kingdoms currently separate from the Empire had come to be. Now she searched her memory for the details of the long eastern Uromathian coast, where the ocean's shallows were filled with floating fisheries and boat cities built by the fishing families who fed the Uromathian Empire.

"I'm sorry, Shamir, but I think I've scrambled some of my history lessons. Does Eniath control the Uromathian fishing industry?"

"Absolutely not," Councilor Yamen replied for the first councilor. "The Uromathian Empire has a strong coastal-based fishing industry independent from Eniath. Some Eniathians do run traditional fish farms and transport their catches widely, but most Eniathian industry is in trade and banking. They've been able to maintain their independence from the Empire for so long largely because of their keen observation and involvement in the Sharona-wide economy. For the last eighty years, that's translated into an equally deep involvement in *inter-multiverse* affairs and commerce, as well. I think we'll find the heir to the Eniathian Crown to be a quick study at inter-universal politics."

"There is one rather significant concern," Councilor Dulan said. "Eniath is prosperous, but not excessively so. For that matter, some of the larger cities of the Uromathian Empire proper could probably match the wealth of the entire kingdom, or come very close to it, at any rate. That means the Eniathian royal house simply can't afford the sort of security Ternathia can. I assess Prince Howan Fai's personal guard to be both loyal and exceptionally competent. If the prince hadn't spotted our investigators himself, I expect the guard would have recognized the tails even with the frequent personnel changes.

"But even the best single guard is weak security. The prince must sleep, and the guard must sleep. That means the prince is vulnerable, if Chava should even begin to suspect what we have in mind. For that matter, his father's security is almost equally weak, and Chava wouldn't hesitate to use threats to the king to sway the prince. At the moment, they're staying in the guest wing with many of the other Conclave attendees, and we can't move their quarters or secure their persons without drawing exactly the sort of attention we're trying to avoid."

"Our best choice is to keep it secret." Yamen agreed.

"But what about Howan Fai?" Andrin asked. "He has to be consulted."

"No, Your Highness," said Dulan. "I'm sorry for the bluntness, but that is exactly wrong. He has to *not* be consulted. For his safety, for his family's safety, and for the good of Sharona, Prince Howan Fai Goutin can't know he's been selected until he's pledging his troth to you in front of the Conclave. He wouldn't thank you for risking his family's health and safety for any advance messages either."

"If he had a Voice with him or even just a Flicker as an attendant," Jastyr mused thoughtfully, before adding, "but he doesn't. So there's no secure way to send Howan Fai anything."

"Princes don't have it any easier than princesses, do they?" Andrin said sadly. Jastyr gave her a slight nod of acknowledgement, but Taje raised an eyebrow and Dulan looked at her inquiringly. "Howan Fai will marry me because he's a prince and that's what princes do," she explained. "Even Chava's sons would do the same if their emperor ordered it."

"Of course they would, Your Highness, but the marriage afterwards is what will make all the difference," Taje said.

"I'd rather not need to have Imperial Guardsmen defend you from your own consort, Your Highness," Dulan added. "So please don't suggest choosing any of Chava's boys."

"So they really are as bad as I've heard?" she asked.

"Probably worse than you've heard, Highness." Yalen said, "There are certain details unlikely to be repeated for a young lady's ears. Certain things I wish hadn't needed to be said to my ears either."

"Likewise." Taje and Dulan agreed.

"Your Highness!" Jastyr pushed her papers aside and glared at Andrin with an expression the crown princess was not used to seeing on councilor's faces. The Privy Voice was angry and very clearly not engaged in any secondary Voicelinks at this particular moment. "Your Highness can*not* be implying you feel sorry for the Crown Prince of Eniath who's looking like he's about to make the match of a lifetime!"

The rest of the council looked thunderstruck. They'd only been listening to what she'd said. Jastyr, mostly silent and listening hard in the moments between her other commitments, had been alert to all the things the crown princess wasn't saying.

"But he doesn't even get asked!" Andrin tried to explain. "My parents had their marriage arranged, but father sent flowers every Vothday for a full year before the wedding and had a full garden planted at Hawkwing as a gift for my mother."

"Wasn't Empress Varena allergic to half the plants in that garden?" Yamen asked, confused.

"Yes, but that's not the point," protested Andrin.

"Your Highness," Jastyr continued severely, "Whichever prince you choose, you're going to have to trust him."

"Trust? This isn't about trust. I'm just trying to find a way to be polite, or chivalrous, or something." Feeling every bit as young as her seventeen years, Andrin tried to find the words to explain her problem to the councilors.

Shamir Taje gently laid the list of names flat on the table in front of them and angled the single paper in front of Andrin.

"Your Highness," he said softly, "Is there any man on this list better qualified to one day serve as Emperor Consort of Sharona than Howan Fai Goutin?"

"No." Andrin bit her lip. "But my Uromathian is still not very good. He speaks some Ternathian, but this could go very, very poorly."

"You'll study. He'll study." Yamen shook her head, baffled. "You don't need to worry about that."

"I don't want him to be forced into this." Andrin tried again to explain.

"Any prince who'd feel forced by this honor, doesn't deserve you." Taje's eye's narrowed with quiet anger at the implication anyone would reject his princess.

"You're my partisans." Andrin couldn't help but smile, but it was a thin faint smile.

"Your Highness," Dulan said, "beside that fact, with which I very much agree, I do believe Prince Howan is already quite taken with you."

"No." Yamen lifted warning finger at the change in Andrin's face. "Your Highness, don't think it. There's nothing wrong with having the special Talents thoroughly check him out. This wasn't any torture chamber session. This prince, and every other we could reasonably consider, has simply had the most thorough background check we could arrange. If they'd known the position they were being considered for—believe us Your Highness!—the ones worth half the gold in their crowns would have volunteered to undergo *far* more than that."

"The reality is, Your Highness," Dulan continued, "that Howan Fai likes you. He might even love you, but this early in a relationship I'd call it deep affection instead. He knows the marital constraints you face and he's a decent man, so he would never over the ordinary course of things even arrange to put himself back in your presence. In his mind, you're meant for a higher marriage. But I have every confidence that he'll be in all ways delighted when he learns he can not only marry you, but in a sense, *save* you from Emperor Chava by doing so.

"You've given him his very own romantic victory, and all he needs to do is say 'yes' at the right moment."

Andrin took a few moments to compose herself. It wasn't every day the succession of an empire was decided, and she wanted to get it right. As crown princess and not yet empress, she wasn't really entitled to the "royal we" just yet, but under the circumstances—

"First Councilor, Privy Voice, Councilors Yamen and Dulan, thank you for your recommendations and advice on Our Imperial Marriage. With due consideration of all candidates, We have made Our decision and are ready to so inform the Conclave."

Taje leaned forward and squeezed her hand. Andrin looked back at her friend and mentor, finally confident.

CHAPTER NINE

Inkara 25, 205 YU
(December 16, 1928 CE)

"I HOPE THIS WORKS," THERMAN ULTHAR MURMURED FROM the corner of his mouth as he and Jaralt Sarma walked placidly across Fort Ghartoun's parade ground towards the administrative block. Their breath plumed in the frigid air, smoke-white in the icy moonlight, and Sarma slapped his gloved hands together as if for warmth, flexing his fingers energetically, and smiled at the other commander of fifty.

"The good news is that if it doesn't work, we probably won't have a lot of time to regret it," he pointed out in turn.

"Oh, *thank* you," Ulthar replied, rolling his eyes.

He heard a snort from behind him and glanced back at the noncom following them across the parade ground. Shield Fraysyr Hathnor was Sarma's platoon clerk, and he was carrying the record crystal which had been carefully loaded with stacks of routine paperwork. None of it meant anything in particular, but if their calculations proved in error and more than the night orderly was on duty, that paperwork would be their excuse to get close enough to take out the extra bodies, hopefully before any alarm was raised.

He looked farther back, over Hathnor's left shoulder towards the stables, and those blue eyes narrowed as he caught a brief flicker of movement. It was as much imagined as seen, something gliding smoothly across a patch of moonlight and back into the darkness beyond it. The moon was almost full, and the splotches of light breaking through the trees the fort's builders had left unfelled to shade its interior were so bright they made the dark beyond them seem even blacker, denser, almost solid. He would have preferred an overcast, or even fog, but the visibility they had was bad enough to suit their purposes.

Probably.

"The truth is," he said, glancing back at Sarma as they started up the steps to the admin block's covered veranda, "I've been looking forward to this ever since that bastard got the Company massacred. I know the dragon shit we're about to step into'll only get deeper if we end up killing him, but I can't help hoping Firsoma lets him be as stupid about this as he is about everything else. I mean, that would only be fair, wouldn't it?"

"You're a very strange man with a nasty sense of humor, Ulthar," Sarma told him. "It's one of the things I particularly like in you."

*　　*　　*

Namir Velvelig's eyes opened.

He woke up the way a septman in the presence of his enemies woke up, which was to say that, aside from his eyelids, not another muscle so much as twitched, and the regiment-captain kept it that way, listening to the deep breathing and snoring around him. The cell in which he and the other officers and senior noncoms of the PAAF garrison had been confined would have provided ample space for a third as many human bodies. There was room—barely—for each of them to have his own patch of floor at night, but anyone who rolled over in his sleep was going to awaken quickly when he was pushed off of whoever he'd rolled onto. On the other hand, there was something to be said for the congested conditions. This far back from the stove, the air temperature was frigid, to say the least, and no one had bothered to issue the prisoners any blankets. The warmth of crowded bodies could be welcome under those conditions.

Velvelig kept his own breathing deep and steady as he tried to decide what had awakened him. He couldn't identify it at first, and his jaw tightened as he heard the catch and painful wheeze of Tobis Makree's breath. The Healer had survived another beating the day before, but he wouldn't survive many more. The Mulgethian was two inches taller than Velvelig, but he'd never been physically robust, and his Healing Talent's sensitivity made him especially vulnerable to the malice and gloating cruelty behind Hadrign Thalmayr's brutality. Velvelig wasn't surprised by his increasing fragility. If anything, he was astounded that the Healer hadn't already willed himself into the merciful escape of death.

He may not be as "robust" as a good Arpathian septman, Velvelig thought, *but he's tougher than an old boot inside.*

It would have been better if he wasn't, the regiment-captain reflected bitterly. It wasn't as if any of the Arcanans' prisoners had any illusions about what was going to happen to them in the end. Especially not Makree or Golvar Silkash. Thalmayr had completely convinced himself that they'd been trying to torture him rather than to Heal his paralysis, and only the intense pleasure he took in beating, kicking, and stomping them had kept them alive—more or less—this long. And of course the Arcanan Healers couldn't be bothered to waste the magical healing abilities which had restored the use of Thalmayr's legs on his victims! There'd be no—

Velvelig's dark thoughts jerked to a halt as the sound which must have awakened him repeated itself. Knuckles rapped on the brig's sturdy outer door, and his stomach muscles tensed. Thalmayr usually waited at least one more day between beatings to allow his victims to recover a bit of endurance for the next one, but he took a special sadistic pleasure in dragging Silkash and especially Makree out of a deep, exhausted sleep to face his truncheon and his fists, his boots and the heated poker he'd taken to using over the last week or so. The regiment-captain turned his head slightly, looking through the bars at the guard room, wondering if this time Thalmayr had screwed up and sent less than four men to collect his prey. If he had, it might finally be time...

The knock came again, and Velvelig's eyes narrowed. It wasn't the usual deliberately thunderous pounding Thalmayr's toadies used to announce their status as Kraisan's own minions. In fact, the three regular night guards went right on snoring.

Despite the tension in his belly and the quickening of his pulse, the regiment-captain felt his lip curl in disdain. He'd learned very little about the Arcanans' military, aside from the fact that Fort Ghartoun's current tenants were quick with a boot or a fist or the butt of an arbalest, but he knew damned well they weren't from the same unit as the prisoners he'd held in custody while the fort had belonged to the Portal Authority Armed Forces. Those had been elite troopers, with a deeply ingrained sense of discipline— both as a unit and personally—who'd maintained their military bearing and dignity even in captivity. None of *them* would have kicked back in chairs around the coal burning stove's welcome warmth and dozed off on duty! And if they had, their officers and noncoms would have sorted them out quickly enough.

But any military unit took its cue from its CO, he reminded himself. He was still convinced that whoever had trained those original prisoners of his, it *hadn't* been Hadrign Thalmayr. No, the slovenly attitude he saw in the guard room's current watch was more Thalmayr's speed.

Whoever was knocking, knocked again—harder—and Velvelig found himself wondering if the real reason the guards dispatched to haul Silkash and Makree back and forth pounded so hard on their nocturnal visits had more to do with the difficulty of awakening their sleeping fellows than a desire to terrify their victims.

Not that they weren't entirely capable of accomplishing both goals at once, of course.

Somebody's snoring hitched, then ended in a raucous, questioning sound, and one of the slumbering Arcanans shoved himself upright in his chair. The knocking sound came yet again, and the roused guard shook himself, then reached out with one foot and thumped one of his companions on the leg. He growled something that sounded unpleasant, and the second Arcanan heaved up out of his chair, stretched his arms high overhead in a spine-popping yawn, and ambled towards the front door.

*　　*　　*

Trooper Zhandru Mysa blinked sleep-scratchy eyes and jerked his camo-pattern tunic straight while Thankhar Zoa and Shield Foswail Tohsar, the guard detail's senior man, climbed out of their own chairs. Shartahk only knew who'd be banging on the door at this time of night, and the odds were that it was going to be bad news for Tohsar's section. Not that it was likely to be too bad, but a man never knew. At least Fifty Varkan wasn't like that prick Sarma or that holier-than-thou pain in the arse Ulthar! Or any of those other Andaran Scout bastards. Of course, even Fifty Varkan would have a little something to say if he had to take official cognizance of someone who'd been catching a few winks on duty. Which was why it was only prudent to let Zoa and Tohsar stretch themselves into a suitable facsimile of awakeness before he opened the door.

He glanced over his shoulder to be certain they had, then shot back the locking bar and pulled the door open with a certain briskness, just in case it really was an officer on the other side.

It wasn't, and his mouth tightened at the unpleasant sight of one of the very Andaran Scouts he'd been thinking about.

"Yes?" he half-growled in a deliberately surly tone. He probably should have shown at least a little respect for a senior sword, but it wasn't like the other man was an officer. And it wasn't like anyone was going to pay a lot of attention to complaints from someone whose unit had fucked up as thoroughly as the 2nd Andaran Scouts had managed to do when the Sharonians took the Mahritha-Hell's Gate portal away from them.

"What d'you want?" he continued, holding the door half open—there was no point letting any more of the guard room's precious warmth leak out of it than he had to—and glowering around it at the newcomer.

"Funny you should ask," Sword Evarl Harnak said pleasantly... and kicked the door as hard as he could.

Harnak's stocky build and powerful shoulders and arms fooled some people into thinking he was shorter than he was. In point of fact, he stood two inches over six feet and weighed a good two hundred and fifty pounds, very little of it fat. When *he* kicked a door, that door opened... rapidly and with a significant degree of force.

Mysa squawked in astonishment—and anguish—as the heavy panel smashed into him like a misplaced wrecking ball. He flew backward, one kneecap shattered, then slammed into the sturdy logs of the guardroom's rear wall. The back of his skull whacked into them with stunning force, and he oozed down into a slovenly, half-conscious puddle.

The door continued its backward arc after hitting him until it slammed into the wall itself, and Sword Tohsar's and Trooper Zoa's mouths dropped open in shock. Astonishment and the rags of sleep held them motionless for perhaps three heartbeats. By the time they started to stir, five men in the uniform of the 2nd Andaran Scouts had stormed into the guardroom, drawn short swords in hand.

"What the fu—?" Tohsar began furiously, only to stop abruptly as the cold, disagreeably sharp point of one of those swords made contact with the base of his throat. The hand holding that sword belonged to Evarl Harnak.

"I never much liked you anyway," Harnak told him pleasantly. "Are you going to be reasonable about this, or do I get to cut your throat after all?"

*   *   *

Namir Velvelig sat up.

There didn't seem to be much point in pretending to be asleep. Not after all that racket, and not when it had awakened eight of the other nine men in his cell almost as abruptly as the door had floored the idiot who'd gotten in its way. The regiment-captain had no idea what was going on, but he felt an undeniable glow as he contemplated the semiconscious idiot in question. It looked as if his nose, at least, was broken, and Velvelig wouldn't be surprised if he'd lost a tooth or two along the way. That was an interesting thought. Could the Arcanan Healers actually regrow missing teeth? If they couldn't, someone was going to need a good set of false ones.

He climbed slowly to his feet, stepping over Makree, who'd been so badly battered he'd actually slept through the hullabaloo. The others got out of his way, pushing back to give him space as he faced the bars and watched what was happening beyond them.

He recognized all the newcomers. They were the ones for whom he'd conceived a special hatred over the last hideous weeks, for every one of them had been left at Fort Ghartoun to be cared for by Velvelig's Healers, and those Healers had given them the very best treatment they possibly could. Unlike Thalmayr, the rest of them had realized what was happening, too. That made their betrayal, the fact that none of them had so much as protested Thalmayr's brutality, even worse than the callous approval the rest of the Arcanan garrison showed for that same brutality. Now he glared at their senior noncom—Evarl Harnak, as nearly as he could pronounce the outlandish name the man had given when he arrived at Fort Ghartoun as a prisoner—while his fellows finished shoving the two regular guards who were still on their feet into a corner of the guard room. They stripped their captives of the swords and daggers Arcanans carried as personal weapons instead of revolvers, and Velvelig's eyebrows rose infinitesimally—the equivalent of a shouted astonishment for an Arpathian—as the guards were turned around and their wrists were fastened together with yet another of the Arcanans' preposterous bits of casual magic.

* * *

Harnak finished securing Tohsar's wrists with the binding spell from his utility crystal, then looked at Trooper Marsal Hyndahr and twitched his head at the moaning heap in the corner.

"Drag his arse over here with the others," he said, and Hyndahr nodded with a certain grim delight.

Hyndahr had a special bone to pick with Hadrign Thalmayr, who'd reduced him to trooper from sword for "insubordination." The insubordination in question had consisted of agreeing with another noncom in a private conversation that Hundred Olderhan's proposal for withdrawing from the swamp portal rather than digging in to defend it had sounded like a good idea. It had been no more than one seasoned veteran talking to another one in the face of potential combat which would involve their squads, quietly, without involving anyone else, but Thalmayr—who'd already been pissed off by the way Hundred Olderhan had made him back down when he tried to put the hundred's *shardonai* in irons—had overheard it. Not simply overheard it, but taken it as a personal criticism directed at him and decided to vent his spleen at Hundred Olderhan by taking out his spite on one of the hundred's men. Given the way Thalmayr had proceeded to get the entire company cut to pieces shortly afterward, it seemed self-evident that Hundred Olderhan—and Hyndahr—had been exactly right. Which, of course, had only prompted Thalmayr to assign him to every shit detail he could find since he'd been given command of the Fort Ghartoun garrison.

Now he crossed to Mysa, grabbed him by one ankle—the one with the kneecap that seemed to have been pushed to one side—and dragged him across the floor to join his mates.

Harnak watched him for a moment, then shrugged and reached into a pocket for his personal crystal. No one except the "designated interrogators"—which consisted mostly of the uniformed thugs Thalmayr had deputized as assistants for his periodic beatings—was supposed to have access to the translating spellware Two Thousand Harshu's troops had brought with them. Shield Rohsahk had hacked Thalmayr's own PC for a bootleg copy, however, and now the sword touched his stylus to the crystal and brought it up.

*   *   *

"Yes, Sir?" the shield behind the desk said, looking at Sarma and ignoring Ulthar, at least for the moment. "How can I help you?"

Ulthar was surprised the noncom's deliberate discourtesy didn't bother him at all, this time. Tahras Bahbar was Thalmayr's senior orderly clerk, and he'd taken his cue from his superior. Under other circumstances, Ulthar would have had him up on charges weeks ago. As it was, there'd been no point, and Bahbar had gotten increasingly insolent—and blatant about it—as a result. Although, to be fair, this time at least the man had a slightly better excuse than usual for ignoring him, since Sarma was officially officer of the watch and Ulthar wasn't. Of course, the main reason it didn't bother him was because their calculations hadn't been in error, after all. Bahbar was all alone, holding down the graveyard shift by himself.

"We need to see the hundred, Shield Bahbar," Sarma replied.

"I'm afraid that's impossible, Sir," the shield told him. "He's been in bed for hours, and—"

"And I'm afraid we're just going to have to insist," Ulthar interrupted him pleasantly, and the shield's eyes flared wide as the commander of fifty's short sword materialized in his hand and its point was suddenly pressed against his chest. "I hope you're not going to be messy about this."

* * *

Javelin Hynkar Vahsk opened the armory door and stepped through it into the welcoming light and warmth. Tarwal Klomis, the javelin responsible for the midnight watch, looked up from the game he'd been playing on his PC with a surprised expression, then stood.

"What can I do for you, Vahsk?" he asked. His tone wasn't exactly warm and welcoming, but the question came out civilly enough.

The men from B Company, 1st Battalion, 176th Regiment who constituted sixty percent of Fort Ghartoun's Arcanan garrison weren't exactly fond of Jaralt Sarma's 3rd Platoon. Partly that was because they were from a different regiment than 3rd Platoon's 343rd Regiment, but even more of that stemmed from the fact that Sarma didn't see eye-to-eye with Commander of Fifty Brys Varkan or Commander of Fifty Dernys Yankaro. None of the fifties made a point out of arguing with one another in public, but the men in their various platoons knew. Just as they knew Hundred Thalmayr wasn't especially fond of Sarma, either. That was why Sarma's platoon had the guard duty at such a godsforsaken hour, since Hundred Thalmayr made a point of assigning them to the most detested duty slots. On the other hand, Javelin Klomis had made the mistake of irritating Falstan Makraik, Fifty Varkan's platoon sword, which was how he came to be sitting here in the middle of the night himself, so he supposed that to some extent, at least, he and Vahsk were riding the same dragon.

"Just passing by and saw the light in the window," Vahsk said now, his tone dry as the twitched his head at the armory's small, barred windows. "How's it going?"

"No worse than usual, I guess." Klomis shrugged. "I know somebody's got to babysit all this shit, but personally, I'd rather be asleep and letting somebody else do it."

"You and me both." Vahsk grinned and pushed the door shut behind him. It didn't quite close completely, although Klomis didn't notice it. "And to be honest, it wasn't so much the light in the window as the smell of burning coal," Vahsk added, moving a bit closer to the stove and holding his hands out to its warmth. "It's cold out there, and the wind's getting up."

"Tell me about it." Klomis grimaced and came out from behind the counter, opened the stove door, and dropped a couple of more lumps of coal into it. Iron clanked as he closed the door again, and he snorted. "Rather be sitting around nice and toasty in a warmth spell, myself."

"Me, too." Vahsk shrugged. "Gods only know how long we're going to be stuck out here, though. Makes sense to go ahead and use up their coal heap first, I guess. At least that way we won't all freeze to death if those idiots in Supply don't get enough heating accumulators shipped forward!"

"Guess so," Klomis agreed, holding his hands out above the stove. "Wish they'd go ahead and haul the rest of the Sharonians' 'guns' the hells out of here, though." He shivered with something besides cold. "Damned things give me the creeps. Not natural, know what I mean?"

"Oh, I agree entirely." Vahsk nodded. "Till we do, though, it makes sense to keep somebody sitting on them, I guess."

"That's what they tell me," Klomis said sourly. "But, getting back to my original question, what can I do for you?"

"Well," Vahsk said as the door he hadn't pushed entirely closed behind him swung wide and half his squad flowed quickly through it, "you can start by staying right where you are and handing me the keys."

*   *   *

Ulthar and Sarma left the shield in the orderly room parked in his chair once again, with the binding spell from Ulthar's utility crystal as a firm suggestion that he should stay there. They crossed the fort commander's office to the door to what had been Namir Velvelig's personal quarters. They belonged to someone else now, however, and the two fifties glanced at one another. Then, in unison, almost as if they'd rehearsed it, each of them drew a deep breath...and Sarma drew his sword, as well.

Ulthar shifted his own sword to his left hand and tried the door's knob gently with his right. It didn't move, and he grimaced. Just like someone like Thalmayr to lock his door at night against imagined boogeymen, he reflected sourly. Then he smothered a sudden, quiet laugh as the absurdity of his disdain for Thalmayr's paranoia struck him, given that two men with drawn swords were standing on the other side of that locked door at the moment.

Sarma looked at him oddly at the sound of his laugh, and he grinned.

"I guess even paranoiacs can have real enemies," he murmured. There was quite a bit of nervousness in the other fifty's answering snort, but there was at least as much genuine humor, as well. Then Ulthar stepped back from the door, drew another deep breath, and slammed the sole of his booted right foot into the door, right on top of the latch.

The door flew open, and Sarma was through it before it had crashed back against the wall. Ulthar followed him, flipping his sword back into his right hand on the move. By the time the Andaran Scout crossed the threshold, Hadrign Thalmayr had already jerked up into a sitting position in bed and Jaralt Sarma had reached his bedside.

The commander of one hundred was obviously confused at being so rudely awakened, but he wasn't confused enough to miss the eighteen inches of steel shining in Sarma's hand.

"What the fuck's the meaning of this?" he snarled.

"The meaning is that I'm relieving you of the duty, *Sir*," Therman Ulthar said coldly, and Thalmayr's eyes snapped from Sarma to him. The hundred's face darkened with fury, and his lips worked as if to spit.

"You motherless bastard," he grated. "You'll go to the dragon for *this* one, Ulthar! And, by the gods, I'll kick your arse into the feeding ground myself!"

"Maybe I will," Ulthar replied in that same, cold voice. "But if I do, you'll go with me."

"Like hell I will! *I'm* not the one committing mutiny!"

"No, you're just the one violating the Kerellian Accords and the Articles of War."

Thalmayr's angry eyes widened in surprise and contempt. There might have been a momentary flicker of concern, as well, but it vanished quickly, replaced by a fresh surge of confidence.

"You're dreaming," he scoffed. "If you think anyone's going to listen to a gutless bastard like you—"

"Oh, I don't know if anyone's going to listen to me out here in the boonies," Ulthar told him with an icy smile. "But that doesn't matter. I've already sent a full report to Duke Garth Showma. I don't know what the hells is going on in the Expeditionary Force, but how d'you think *he's* going to react to the shit you've been pulling here in Fort Ghartoun?"

"You're lying out your arse," Thalmayr shot back, but a shadow of uncertainty and what might have been fear burned under the words.

"It wasn't that hard to sneak past that arse-kisser Wentys." Ulthar's smile turned even thinner. "Believe me, *Sir*, it's in the pipeline where nobody can stop it, and I've named people, places, and times. The duke wouldn't stand for something like this out of *anyone*, and especially not when the sick son-of-a-bitch pulling it belongs to the Second Andarans. He'll insist the Regiment hold the court-martial internally, and guess what kind of sentence the Scouts'll hand down to a worthless piece of dragon shit who got three quarters of his own company killed and then deliberately tortured prisoners of war?"

Thalmayr stared at him for a moment, then wrenched his eyes away and glared at Sarma.

"Are you really stupid enough to go along with this idiot, Sarma?" he demanded.

"Damned straight I am," Sarma replied flatly. "Now, with all due respect, Sir, get your arse out of that bed. We've got a different set of quarters in mind for you—one with bars. I'd suggest you get your uniform on, but we really won't mind dragging you over there bare-arsed if that's what you'd prefer."

"Like hell you will!"

Thalmayr's hand darted under his pillow, then reemerged with one of the Sharonian revolvers. His thumb brought the hammer back, and the muzzle swept towards Sarma.

The Sharonian weapon came as a complete surprise, but Thalmayr was something less than expert in its use and Jaralt Sarma was a stocky, boulder of a man, with very strong arms and shoulders. He also had very good reflexes, and his sword hissed before Thalmayr could get his weapon aimed. There was the sound of a cleaver hitting meat, the beginning of a scream of pain, and then the ear-smashing roar of the revolver.

*   *   *

"What the hells was *that*?"

Commander of Fifty Brys Varkan wheeled away from the hapless trooper whose improperly stowed personal gear had just been dumped across his bunk by Falstan Makraik, 1st Platoon's platoon sword. The platoon had grown a bit lax in Makraik's opinion, and he'd suggested to his fifty that it might be an appropriate time for a surprise inspection. Varkan had agreed the sword had a point, and since 1st Platoon was due to relieve that officious, pain-in-the-arse Sarma's platoon in about two hours, this had seemed like a good time for the aforesaid surprise inspection.

Now he and Makraik stared at one another, his question hanging between them.

"Sounded like one of those Sharonian guns, Sir," the sword said after a heartbeat. There was more than a hint of uncertainty in his reply, but Varkan's face tightened.

"That's *exactly* what it sounded like!" he snapped. "Turn the men to, Sword!"

"Yes, Sir!" Makraik turned on his heel, glaring at the assembled platoon. "You heard the Fifty! *Move!*" he barked.

Varkan left that up to his sword. His own hand darted into his pocket for his PC. He jerked it back out, activated it, and input a command.

An instant later, the alarm began to sound.

CHAPTER TEN

Inkara 25, 205 YU
(December 16, 1928 CE)

VELVELIG STIFFENED AS THE BROAD SHOULDERED ARCANAN stepped closer to the bars. The man was careful to stay out of arm's reach from them, but he was doing something with one of the Arcanans' bits of crystal. Velvelig himself had had very little opportunity to see any of the crystals in use, and his impassive countenance hid a sharp sense of interest and curiosity as he watched the small quartzlike rock glow brightly. The Arcanan looked down into it for just a moment and touched it two or three times with a small stylus or rod—a magic wand, perhaps?—of the same water-clear rock. Then he looked back up as the crystal dimmed once more.

"Regiment-Captain Velvelig," he said, and the words were perfectly clear, with what sounded preposterously like a Shurkhalian accent to Velvelig's ear. They also obviously had nothing at all to do with the movement of his mouth. They were coming out of the crystal, Velvelig realized, and wondered why he wasn't hearing what the other man was actually saying, as well.

"Yes," he said flat-voiced, and the Arcanan seemed to wince slightly before the hard, unyielding anger in his tone. His level green eyes never left Velvelig's, however, and he braced to attention and touched his chest in what the regiment-captain recognized as an Arcanan salute.

"Sir," he—or, rather, the piece of rock in his hand—said, "Commander of Fifty Ulthar extends his compliments and asks you to forgive him for how long it's taken to do anything about the shameful way you and your men have been treated. Hundred

126

Thalmayr's actions have dishonored the entire Union of Arcana Army, and the Fifty's instructed me to tell you that he and Commander of Fifty Sarma are in the process of attempting to do something about that now."

Velvelig's eyes narrowed. The change was so slight that anyone except another Arpathian might have been excused for failing to recognize it, but to one of his countrymen, it would have been as good as shouting his incredulity. He recognized the name "Ulthar," and his brain raced as it ran back over the handful of visits the wiry, red-haired ex-prisoner had paid to the brig since he and his senior surviving subordinates had been confined in it. He'd seen what could only have been anger, even fury, in the other man's eyes. At the time, he'd assumed it was directed at the Sharonians, an echo of Hadrign Thalmayr's; now he suddenly found himself wondering if perhaps he'd misinterpreted the reasons for those emotions.

"And who is Commander of Fifty Sarma?" he asked in that same, flat voice.

"Fifty Sarma has Third Platoon of Able Company," Harnak replied. "Along with the half-squad Fifty Ulthar's got, that's less than a quarter of the total garrison." The Arcanan grimaced in something that looked like shame. "I'm afraid that's why it's taken so long to do anything about your situation, Sir."

This time, even a New Farnalian would have recognized the astonishment and speculation in Velvelig's eyes. Preposterous though it might be, it sounded as if Harnak was suggesting that Ulthar and whoever the hells Sarma was were *mutinying* against Thalmayr. The regiment-captain glanced at the assigned guards, whose invisible bonds had been attached to the brig's sturdy walls in some way, then back at Harnak.

"And what might Commander of Fifty Ulthar and Commander of Fifty Sarma have in mind to do about our 'situation' now?"

"As a matter of—"

The sudden, strident clangor of an enormous bell interrupted whatever Harnak had been about to say.

*　　*　　*

"Shit!" Jaralt Sarma snapped.

His left hand went to the bleeding gash Hadrign Thalmayr's revolver bullet had torn through the outside of his left thigh. Fortunately, it was little more than a shallow furrow. The commander of one hundred had fared less well. The revolver thudded to the floor, still gripped in his right hand, and he screamed again, clutching the bleeding stump of his right wrist with his remaining hand as he fell back flat upon the suddenly blood-soaked bed. Sarma glared at him, then slammed the flat of his sword blade against the side of the hundred's head.

Thalmayr collapsed, and Therman Ulthar jerked his utility crystal back out of his pocket. The UC's spellware menu was on the general side, but it did contain a coagulating spell intended to both stop the bleeding, even from arterial wounds, and prevent infection. It was going to require the healing Gift to do more than that for Thalmayr, but at least he wouldn't bleed to death in the meantime.

He'd barely activated the spell before the strident clangor of an alarm spell pounded over the fort.

"Oh, *wonderful!*" he snarled as he shoved Sarma roughly, turning him to apply the same first aid spell to his leg.

*   *   *

"Oh, dragon shit!" Javelin Traymahr Sahnger growled.

Fifty Sarma had assigned his 3rd Squad to secure the stables while Hynkar Vahsk's squad did the same thing for the armory, Sword Harnak secured the brig, and Sword Nourm and Tolomaeo Briahk's squad secured the barracks occupied by the two platoons commanded by Fifty Brys Varkan and Fifty Dernys Yankaro. Nourm and Briahk had drawn the assignment for both barracks because there'd been only enough "special weapons" to equip a single squad...sparingly. Fifty Sarma and Fifty Ulthar had skimmed enough stun bolts off the top to give each of Sahnger's men one of them, but all the rest had been reserved for 2nd Squad's takedown of the barracks. That plan, however, had been predicated upon achieving surprise. Sahnger had no idea what somebody had been doing up and about to sound an alarm spell at this hour, but the fact that someone had suggested Nourm and Briahk might just have their hands full trying to secure their assigned objectives against someone who outnumbered them six-to-one.

He and 3rd Squad had carried out their own assignment with no fuss or bother, and this was where they were supposed to stay under the plan Fifty Sarma and Fifty Ulthar had worked out. According to Fifty Sarma, Commander of Fifty Sahrimahn

Cothar, whose cavalry troop had been left behind to support Hundred Thalmayr, was no happier about the hundred's brutality than they were, even though Cothar hadn't heard the truth about the portal attack which had killed Magister Halathyn. In theory, that should mean his cavalry troopers were less likely to come boiling in here looking for their mounts than they might have been otherwise. Sahnger couldn't count on that, but it was at least possible, and if Varkan and Yankaro's men figured out what was happening quickly enough, there wasn't any question that Nourm and Briahk were damned sure going to need help....

"Maysak, you and Volmar stay here and keep an eye on those unicorns." He jerked his thumb over his right shoulder at the stalled, restless cavalry mounts. "The rest of you, on me!"

Shield Maysak Uthsamo nodded sharply, and he and Lewak Volmar peeled off as the rest of Sahnger's squad followed their javelin out of the stable and headed for the nearer barracks at a run.

* * *

"I think that's part of your answer, Sir," Evarl Harnak said to Velvelig through the translating spellware while the bell continued to sound.

"What's part of the answer?" the Sharonian demanded, and Harnak scowled.

"I don't have time to explain everything, Sir," he said. "What matters right now is that the way Hundred Thalmayr's been treating you is against the Kerellian Accords. That means it's illegal under our military law. Fifty Ulthar and Fifty Sarma planned to place him under arrest and send word to higher authority, but the people they could count on to back them are outnumbered four- or five-to-one, so they were trying to do it as quietly as they could. From the sound of that"—he jerked his head at the brig door to indicate the bell pealing deafeningly outside it—"something went wrong."

Velvelig looked at him, his face giving no sign of the thoughts racing through his brain. That simple paragraph of explanation stood everything he'd thought he understood on its head. Of course, there was always the possibility the Arcanan was lying to him, although he couldn't think of any sane reason for the man to do that.

"So what happens now?" he asked.

"Sir, my orders are to secure the brig and hold it until Fifty Ulthar or Fifty Sarma tells me otherwise. It's my job to look after you until one of them can get here."

"Does that include letting us out of these cells?" Velvelig demanded.

"Nobody said anything to me about letting you out, Sir." Harnak's tone carried an edge of apology. "And, to be honest, even if Hundred Thalmayr's been breaking the Accords, you're still prisoners of war."

*   *   *

"*Move* your arses!" Fifty Varkan shouted as the men who'd been turned out for inspection started grabbing helmets, sidearms, and arbalests. "Rokar! Take your squad and shag arse over to the admin block! Find out what's going on there and then put yourself at Hundred Thalmayr's orders!"

"Yes, Sir!" Javelin Shelmyn Rokar replied, then jerked his head at the eleven other members of his squad. "All right, you lot! Let's go!"

"Jathyr, you get your arse to the brig and make sure the damned Sharonians are still there!"

"Yes, Sir!" Lerso Jathyr took long enough to salute, then turned for the barracks back door, the shortest route to the brig. The men of his squad followed him in a thunder of boots, most of them still buckling weapons harnesses as they went, while Varkan went on barking orders behind them.

*   *   *

"Oh, crap."

Keraik Nourm, platoon sword for 3rd Platoon, A Company, saw the first man burst out the front door of Fifty Varkan's 1st Platoon's barracks. The man in question was in full combat gear, and he looked disgustingly wide awake. Worse, if *he* was up and about, then—

More troopers erupted from the same door, and Nourm glanced over his shoulder at Tolomaeo Briahk.

"So much for catching them in their racks!" he snarled. "Now we do it hard way."

"Whichever way we have to," the very dark-skinned *garthan* who was 2nd Squad's javelin said grimly.

Like Nourm himself, Briahk had accepted the lies they'd been told about the Sharonians without question. And, even more than Nourm, the javelin had treated the Sharonians he'd encountered with brutality on more than one occasion when he thought Fifty Sarma wasn't looking. Magister Halathyn vos Dulainah had been universally admired and loved by the *garthan* of every explored universe, and the news that he'd been shot out of hand by the Sharonians after he'd surrendered to them had been carefully and coldly calculated to fan the hatred of men like Briahk to a white-hot flame. Now, looking back at his own actions, he was bitterly ashamed of them...and even more infuriated by the way Magister Halathyn's death had been used.

"Drop your weapons!" Nourm shouted at the emerging squad, and heads snapped around in their direction. *"Do it now!"*

*   *   *

Shelmyn Rokar had no idea what was happening. Like his fifty, he'd heard the sound of the Sharonian weapon and, also like Fifty Varkan, he'd automatically assumed the weapon in question had to be in a Sharonian hand. Now he saw a full squad of Arcanans coming at him in an ordered line with arbalests already locked and loaded, and that made no sense at all.

"What the fuck is going on?" he demanded.

"Drop the weapons, I said!" the same voice shouted, and this time he recognized it. It was Keraik Nourm from that pain in the arse Sarma's platoon.

"Like hell we will!" Rokar shot back as his men skidded to a halt and turned instinctively towards Nourm's men. They didn't know any more about what was happening than their javelin did. "We—"

*   *   *

"Take them!" Nourm barked, and 2nd Squad's arbalests spat bolts.

Rokar and two thirds of his men went down like targets on a range, dropping without a sound as the stun bolts slammed into them. The other four gawked in disbelief, then turned and scrambled back towards the barracks door.

"Shit!"

Nourm glared after the escapees. The men who were already down would stay that way for at least twelve hours, but it was unlikely the rest of Fifty Varkan's men were going to be returning fire with stun bolts of their own.

"Brysyl, suppressive fire on the windows!" the platoon sword snapped. "The rest of you, on me!"

Shield Brysyl Vahrtanak and the squad's second section went instantly to one knee and brought their arbalests to their shoulders. The standard infantry arbalest was a heavy weapon, without the box magazine of the shorter, handier dragoon arbalest. It was also more powerful and longer ranged, however, and the spell assist stored in its integral sarkolis crystal allowed a trooper to span the powerful steel bow with a single stroke of the charging lever. The crystal was good for only sixty shots before it required recharging. After that, respanning the bow required six to eight throws and a hell of a lot more muscle, but until the spell was exhausted a trained arbalester could get off at least six aimed shots per minute. There were only two windows in the front wall of the barracks, and Vahrtanak's section broke down into two three-man fire teams. Using sequenced fire, each section sent a stun bolt hissing through its assigned window every three seconds.

Unfortunately, each man had been issued only ten stun bolts. There'd been no way to draw more of them without somebody asking inconvenient questions. Which, given that there were fifty-four men in Varkan's platoon and that not every shot was going to hit its target, meant there were far too few of them to go around.

There was an answer to that, however, and Briahk and the squad's first section followed Nourm as they charged the barracks. Someone inside already had his act together and, despite the stun bolts sizzling through the windows several of Varkan's men were getting shots off in reply. The fire was hasty and not very well aimed, but that didn't mean it wasn't deadly, and one of Briahk's men went down with a cry of pain as a steel-headed bolt drove into him. At least 1st Platoon's dragons were locked up in the armory right beside 3rd Platoon's, so there were no lightning bolts or fireballs coming at them.

Nourm and Briahk reached the boardwalk in front of the barracks side-by-side and flung themselves down, rolling across the rough-surfaced planking until they fetched up against the wall itself, directly beneath the windows. The sword yanked the fist-sized grenade off his belt, twisted the arming knob, and heaved it through the window above him. He heard it thump and rattle on the wooden floor, heard someone shout in alarm, and heard Briahk's grenade land a heartbeat after his own, and then the spells activated.

A shattering blast of light and sound erupted inside the barracks. A stun bolt's spellware had to physically contact its object to take effect. Area spells with the same basic capabilities were possible, but their radius of effect was broader than the range to which the average trooper could throw them, and intervening obstacles offered whoever had thrown them no protection against their paralysis. Flash-bangs, however, were designed to incapacitate without actually rendering their targets unconscious. The sheer intensity of the flash of light they released was sufficient to stun and temporarily blind anyone who encountered it, and the disorienting effect of the accompanying blast of sound was guaranteed to disable anyone who encountered it. While they were classified as nonlethal weapons, they could cause permanent damage to anyone too close to one of them when the spell detonated, and Nourm knew Fifty Sarma and Fifty Ulthar had hoped they wouldn't be required.

Hope didn't win very many battles, however.

He heard voices raised in anguish—probably from men who'd been farther away when the flash-bangs went off, although the barracks bay was too small for anyone to have been *very* far away—and nodded at Briahk.

"All right, you lazy bastards!" the javelin barked to the men of his section. "Let's get in there before they figure out what hit them!"

* * *

Traymahr Sahnger heard the flash-bangs go off inside 1st Platoon's barracks. Varkan's platoon had been Sword Nourm's first target, and Sahnger supposed he was happy for the sword, since detonating flash-bangs had a tendency to settle people down in a hurry. Unfortunately, there'd been only six flash-bangs available, and they'd all been issued to Nourm's squad, since they'd been the ones tasked to deal with the other two platoons.

Which meant Sahnger and his men would have to do it the hard way.

His shoulder slammed into the second barracks building's rear door, bursting it open, and he and the eight men with him went through it in a rush. Unlike Fifty Varkan's platoon, the men of Commander of Fifty Dernys Yankaro's 3rd Platoon, B Company had been sound asleep until the alarm spell sounded. They were still rolling out of their bunks, reaching for their trousers, wondering what the hells was going on, when Sahnger and his men erupted into their midst.

"Just sit where the fuck you are!" Sahnger bellowed.

"Who the hell are y—?"

The shouted question ended in a grunt and the thud of a body hitting the floor as one of Sahnger's troopers hit the loud-mouthed 3rd Platoon javelin center of mass with a stun bolt. At that short range, even a stun bolt could do significant physical damage from an infantry arbalest, but it was unlikely to kill anyone. It did incapacitate its target quite handily, however, and Yankaro's surprised men froze in shock.

"Every one of you back in your racks right the hell now!" Sahnger snapped, taking advantage of the moment of silence. Some of the 3rd Platoon troopers automatically obeyed the bark of command. Others looked at one another with varying degrees of confusion and building anger, and Sahnger nodded to Taswan Slokyr. The burly trooper took one step forward and slammed the butt of his arbalest none too gently into the back of one of the dawdlers.

Slokyr's victim hit the floor flat on his face with a shout of anguish. It was entirely possible, even probable, that he'd acquired a broken shoulder blade in the process, but Slokyr was back in his original position, arbalest in a hip-high firing position, almost before the other man landed.

"I'm not going to tell you again," Sahnger grated.

For just a moment, he felt it hovering in the balance. He and his eight troopers were hopelessly outnumbered by 3rd Platoon's forty-eight men, but none of their opponents were armed and none of them had a clue yet as to what was actually happening. If they'd been willing to rush Sahnger's squad, they probably could have swarmed them under anyway, but they weren't willing to take the casualties. Not yet. Not without at least some idea of what was happening. And so the moment passed and 3rd Platoon's men sank sullenly back onto their bunks, glaring furiously at Sahnger.

*   *   *

Ulthar and Sarma heard the flash-bangs as well as they hurried out of the administration building, leaving Hathnor to keep an eye on the immobilized Thalmayr and Bahbar.

"*That* doesn't sound good," Sarma remarked.

"Could sound a hells of a lot worse, unless you think there's some reason for Vargan or Yankaro to've issued flash-bangs at *their* men," Ulthar pointed out.

"There's that," Sarma acknowledged. "Me to the barracks?"

"And me to the brig," Ulthar agreed.

The fifties separated, running in almost opposite directions.

*   *   *

Javelin Lerso Jathyr heard the flash-bangs go off behind him and swore vilely. He had no clue what the *hell* was going on, but Fifty Varkan's orders had been clear enough.

Two of his men braked to a stop, looking back over their shoulders, and he swore again, this time at them.

"Get your arses back in gear!" he snapped.

"But, Javelin—" one of them began.

"The fifty told us what to do, and we're going to *do* it!"

He glared at the rest of the squad for a moment, then jerked his head and all eleven of them started running again.

Jathyr grunted in approval, even though a part of him wondered if he was doing the right thing. The automatic response would have been to head back into the barracks to find out who was throwing flash-bangs around, but that might well be exactly the wrong thing to do. For all he knew whoever had used the first two flash-bangs had a dozen more of the things, just waiting for him to walk back into range before taking out *his* squad, as well. On the other hand, where the hells would Sharonians have gotten flash-bangs from in the first place? And if it wasn't a bunch of Sharonians attacking the fort, then who the hells *was* it?

Either way, he told himself, his squad would be more useful—and probably safer—doing exactly what Varkan had told him to do.

*   *   *

Keraik Nourm did a quick count of the stunned, groaning men sprawled around the barracks and swore. They were short by at least one full squad, even counting the men they'd stunned on the parade ground. Somebody must have gotten out the back, but where the hells were they?

*   *   *

Senior Sword Barcan Kalcyr rolled out of his bunk even before his sleeping mind had identified the sound of the alarm spell's clangor. The thunderclap eruption of detonating flash-bangs followed, and he scrubbed sleep from his eyes with one hand

and reached for his trousers with the other in pure spinal reflex while his brain fought its way up to speed.

He heard voices now, shouting from the infantry barracks. There were a lot of them, and they didn't sound happy, but *all* of them seemed to be shouting in Andaran. If this was a Sharonian attack, where were the *Sharonian* voices? And if it *wasn't* a Sharonian attack, then who the hells—?

His jaw tightened as a preposterous thought ripped through him. He'd warned Fifty Cothar there was something going on with that lily-livered bastard Sarma! But had his own fifty listened to him? Of course he hadn't!

As Kalcyr buttoned his pants and stamped his feet into his boots he reminded himself he didn't actually know a damned thing about what was going on. He might very well be jumping to conclusions...but he might *not* be, too. And if he wasn't, then what the hells should he do next?

He reached for his tunic and his jaw went tighter than ever as he realized he didn't know the answer to that question. Hundred Worka had quietly warned him that he'd peeled off Fifty Cothar's B Troop to support the Fort Ghartoun garrison because Cothar clearly didn't have the stomach for what needed to be done. Personally, Kalcyr couldn't imagine how any member of the 9th Seignor Light Cavalry could have any doubt about what the Sharonian bastards deserved. Their regiment was the one which had discovered the fire-seared bodies of the troopers who'd been assigned to protect Rithmar Skirvon and Uthik Dastiri while they negotiated with the Sharonian "envoys" at Toppled Timber. They *knew* the Sharonians had shot down at least twenty-one of those troopers in cold blood, then left the bodies behind to burn in the forest fire they'd set. And if there'd been any question about who'd been responsible for that massacre, the bullet which had blown out the back of Dastiri's skull damned well should've put them to bed. The shot had been fired from so close the wound between his eyes was surrounded by a dark powder burn! And gods only knew what the murderous bastards had done with Skirvon and the three troopers they *hadn't* left to burn!

But Cothar didn't seem to see it that way. He'd actually complained to Hundred Worka about the way Kalcyr had made sure the Sharonian Voice he'd been sent to deal with here in Thermyn wouldn't be sending any messages to anyone else. There

was only one way to be sure a Voice didn't get a message off—
Five Hundred Neshok's briefings had made that clear enough!
And what the hells did it matter if the Voice in question was a
frigging civilian? The Sharonians sure hadn't shown any special
consideration for civilians when they murdered Dastiri and vos
Dulinah, had they? From where Barcan Kalcyr sat, that meant
they didn't have any kick coming when the boot was on the other
foot, so why bother to drag the bastard all the way back to the
fort before cutting his frigging throat? But did Cothar see it that
way? Hells, no, he didn't! He'd been on Kalcyr's case for killing
a civilian as if putting down a mad-dog Sharonian "Voice" to
keep the freak bastard from warning anyone else the Army was
coming was some kind of crime!

No wonder the hundred had detached Cothar from the rest
of the company. And he'd left Kalcyr, the company's senior
noncom, here to keep an eye on him and make sure he didn't
give Hundred Thalmayr any of his grief. Kalcyr had done his
best to do just that, but Cothar had been spending entirely too
much time mind hobnobbing with Sarma and Ulthar. Kalcyr had
picked up on plenty of indications that *those* two had their panties
in a wad over Thalmayr's supposed violations of the Kerellian
Accords. As if the Accords applied to Sharonians! He'd thanked
all the gods they weren't *his* fifties, but what if they'd decided to
do something genuinely stupid and sucked Cothar into it right
along with them?

He buttoned his tunic, strapped on his breastplate, checked the
sarkolis crystal in his thigh pocket, and reached for his saber. By
The Book, he should be hunting for his company CO, but under
the circumstances, this time he'd better start somewhere else.

* * *

Movement caught Thermyn Ulthar's attention and he cursed
inventively. Whoever that was, it wasn't any of Sarma's men, and
he knew where all of his were already. There was at least a full
squad of them, though, and they were running hell for leather
towards the brig... just like *he* was.

Fortunately, he was closer than they were, and he dashed
straight towards the door, shouting his name as he came and
hoping to Shartahk that Harnak could get it unlocked in time.

Harnak did. Ulthar actually heard the cross bolt shoot back
through its mounting clips an instant before his shoulder slammed

into the thick, heavy panel. The impact was enough to spin him sideways as he came through the opening, and it slammed shut again almost before he was clear. The bolt racketed back into place, and Shield Sarkhol Gersmyn caught him before he could fall.

"Got a squad right on my arse, Evarl!" he gasped out, and the sword gave him a choppy nod.

"On it, Sir," he said. "Only got one stun bolt apiece, though!"

"Use them first," Ulthar panted.

"Yes, Sir." Harnak looked at the others. "You heard the Fifty."

Acknowledgments were still coming back when the first arbalest bolt drove halfway through the barred door. Lamplight gleamed on the sharp, edged wickedness of its head and Ulthar tried not to think about what one of those would feel like driving through one of his men, instead.

Marsal Hyndahr and Jyrmayn Yanthas had one of the brig's two front windows. Gersmyn and Javelin Rohsahk had the other one, and he heard the thump of a discharging arbalest. He peeked through the small, barred window in the heavy door and saw one of the oncoming infantrymen go down limply. From his companions' angry shouts, it didn't sound as if they realized he'd been hit by a stun bolt instead of something more lethal.

More arbalest quarrels slammed into the brig's walls. One came sizzling in through a window and he heard a Sharonian— it sounded like Velvelig—shouting for the prisoners to go flat. The spellware Harnak had activated was still up, translating the Sharonian words into Andaran, and Ulthar darted a look over his shoulder.

"Stay down!" he barked. "And stay out of the windows' line of fire as much as you can!"

"And what about the cell window if they get around behind you?" Namir Velvelig shot back in a preposterously calm voice, and Ulthar's jaw tightened. He hadn't thought about that!

He looked back through the window in the door and swore again, even more inventively, as he saw three or four men disappearing around the brig's solid northern wall.

"Shit," he said, and grabbed the massive key ring off its hook beside the desk.

"I know all of you are pissed off, and you've got a right," he said quickly, fumbling through the keys to find the one he needed. "If I leave you in that cell, you're going to be sitting ducks for whoever's coming at us. But if I let you out and you screw with us in the next few minutes, *all* of us are likely to get killed."

The Sharonian officer bared his teeth in an expression with only a passing resemblance to a smile.

"Hell of a choice, isn't it?" he asked. Their eyes locked for just a moment, then Velvelig shrugged. "All right. Let us out and you'll have our parole at least until the fighting's settled. Good enough?"

"Good enough," Ulthar replied, hoping to Seiknora he wasn't about to make the worst mistake of his life.

He shoved the key into the lock, turned it, swung the door wide, and stood to one side as Velvelig and his subordinates flowed out of the cell in a tide which somehow kept from jamming solid in the opening. It took them several seconds, and while they were doing that, Ulthar snatched up one of the arbalests the original guard detail no longer needed. As soon as the Sharonians were out of the cell—the last four of them supporting a staggering Golvar Silkash and carrying Tobis Makree bodily—Ulthar charged *into* it.

Before he could reach the window, an arbalest bolt hissed past him. He swerved, dodging the follow-up, then shouldered his newly acquired weapon and squeezed the trigger.

The cell's window was higher above ground level than above the level of the cell floor, and someone cursed loudly as the return fire came close enough to clip a lock of his hair. Whoever it was dropped down below the window sill for cover, and Ulthar plastered his back against the interior wall to one side of the opening and worked the cocking lever.

"*Shit!*" someone grunted, and he looked up to see young Yanthas clutching at the arbalest bolt which had suddenly appeared in his left shoulder.

"Idiot!" Hyndahr barked. "*Told* you to keep your stupid head down!"

The demoted sword had been Charlie Company's senior hand-to-hand and swordsmanship instructor, but he'd been a marksmanship instructor in his time, as well, and Ulthar heard a shrill scream from outside the brig as he sighted quickly and then fired. Hyndahr, at least, was obviously out of stun bolts, the fifty thought grimly.

Someone moved closer at hand, and his eyes narrowed as he saw Velvelig shoving his way back into the cell carrying another of the original guards' arbalests. Ulthar was none too happy to see the weapon in Sharonian hands, but he wasn't exactly in a position to be choosy. He started to offer some quick instruction, then shut his mouth firmly as Velvelig pulled the cocking lever and nocked a quarrel as expertly as if he'd been using an arbalest all his life.

His surprise must have shown, because the Sharonian grinned at him again, much more warmly this time.

"Couldn't afford a decent rifle when I was growing up back home," he said. "Nice piece, though. Cocks really easily, doesn't it? More of that 'magic' of yours, is it?"

Ulthar started to answer, then paused as the Sharonian whipped around and sent the steel-headed bolt back out through the window. An explosive grunt answered his shot, and he jerked back to press his back to the wall on the opposite side of the window.

"Your turn next," he said as he pulled the cocking lever again.

"Fire in the hole!" someone else shouted, and Ulthar looked back just in time to see Sarkhol Gersmyn snatch up the grenade someone had gotten through the window. The wiry *garthan*'s arm whipped forward, throwing it back the way it had come, but its spell activated just as it cleared the window. The outer wall absorbed most of the fireball's fury, but enough of it blew back through the window to sear the Scout's hand to the bone.

He went down, clutching his wrist, jaw muscles standing out like iron as he bit down on a scream of agony, and Company-Captain Silkash shoved himself shakily to his feet. He staggered across to Gersmyn and grabbed the Arcanan's arm, forcing it straight so that he could peer at it through his swollen, blackened eyes. The Sharonian surgeon's own hands were already bloody, Ulthar realized, and another Sharonian, one of Velvelig's senior noncoms, knelt beside Yanthas, putting pressure on the improvised dressing which had somehow appeared.

"We have to keep them out of throwing range of the windows!" he shouted. "If they get another of those things in here we're all cooked!"

* * *

"Mother Jambakol!"

Lerso Jathyr watched the grenade detonate outside the brig and wondered how the hells the bastards in there had managed to get it back through the window in time. They hadn't gotten it clear by much, but close didn't count when there was a solid wall between the grenade and its intended target. Worse, he only had three of them left. Of course, he wouldn't have had any of them, if Bersal Darnaiyr, one of his more idiotic troopers, hadn't tucked them away under his bunk in violation of about five dozen regulations "just in case I needed them."

Well, maybe not that *much of an idiot, at that,* the javelin thought. *Under the circumstances, at least! And at least he hadn't squirreled away any dragon charges to keep 'em company.*

In the meantime, he'd already lost three of 3rd Squad's twelve men, and he had no idea how many opponents they faced inside the brig. Or, for that matter, when somebody else might come running up their backsides.

"All right," he said, raising his voice just enough for the five men on this side of the brig to hear him. "We've got to get close enough to pop another one in on them. Darnaiyr, toss one of them to Tymkara! His arm's at least as good as yours. Lets see if we can't get both of you close enough to give the bastards two of them to deal with."

* * *

Keraik Nourm left Briahk to secure the stunned, disoriented members of Brys Varkan's platoon. The commander of fifty was as singed looking as anyone, but he'd recovered enough to curse Nourm up one side and down the other. He was just getting around to all of the capital offenses the sword had already committed while one of Briahk's troopers used a binding spell to immobilize him, but Nourm had other things to worry about at the moment. He and Brysyl Vahrtanak, Briahk's squad shield, were already headed for the second barracks and Fifty Yankaro's men. If Yankaro's platoon got loose with weapons in hand—

He slid to a halt as Traymahr Sahnger shoved his head out one of the windows.

"We've got this!" Sahnger shouted.

"You sure?" Nourm shouted back, raising his voice to carry above the still clanging bell. Sahnger was supposed to be sitting on the unicorn stables, but under the circumstances, the sword was disinclined to pick any nits about it. "One of Varkan's squads got out the back way."

"Shit! Which way did they go?"

"Damned if I know. How many men do you have?"

"Nine, counting me."

"Okay. You take a section and head for Admin. I'll—"

"Belay that," another voice commanded, and Nourm turned to see Fifty Sarma striding towards him, prodding Fifty Yankaro along at sword point. Yankaro's hands were obviously spell bound behind him, and if looks had been spells, Sarma would have been a corpse.

"I just came from Thalmayr's office by way of the BOQ," the fifty continued. "Nobody passed me on the way here. I'm guessing that means they headed for the brig, instead. Is First Platoon secured, Keraik?"

"Yes, Sir!"

"All right. Traymahr, leave half your men to keep an eye on Third Platoon. Send the other half to take over from Tolomaeo. Keraik, you and I will take all of Second Squad to relieve the brig. Come on, boys—let's move!"

*   *   *

Barcan Kalcyr found himself wishing—briefly, at least—that he was in the infantry. Or that he was wearing infantry boots with their soft, skid-proof soles, at any rate. Riding boots made the gods' own racket trying to creep across a wooden veranda! Fortunately, the godsdamned alarm spell was still making enough noise to hide almost anything.

He'd seen Ulthar and Sarma—he hadn't gotten that good a look at them, but he was damned sure it hadn't been Varkan or Yankaro—rushing out of the admin block. One of them had headed for the brig, while the other dashed across the parade ground towards the officers' quarters beside the barracks. Obviously, his darkest, most paranoid apprehensions had fallen short of the reality, and his face was grim as he contemplated what he was probably about to find. They wouldn't have gone rushing off that way if Hundred Thalmayr had been in any condition to make problems for them.

He'd almost gone after the traitorous fifties himself. Unlike anyone else in Fort Ghartoun, he was armed with a daggerstone. Strictly against regulations, of course, but Hundred Worka had left it with him. It was charged for only four shots, and it was much shorter ranged than any arbalest, but it was also far more deadly and Kalcyr was sufficiently Gifted to use it when the opportunity arose.

His hand twitched around the stone as he watched Sarma disappear between the barracks assigned to Varkan and Yankaro's platoons. Unfortunately, the fifty was already far beyond dagger-stone range. Besides, he had to make sure of what had happened to Hundred Thalmayr before he did anything else.

He peered cautiously around the edge of the open doorframe and his eyes narrowed as he saw the orderly—Bahbar, his name was, if Kalcyr remembered correctly. The shield was seated in his chair, obviously kept there by a binding spell, but his head was free and he'd clearly seen Kalcyr. He kept his mouth shut, but he jerked his head urgently, using it to point in the direction of Hundred Thalmayr's personal quarters.

Kalcyr's heart rose. Bahbar wouldn't be relying on head gestures unless there'd been someone close enough to hear him. And the bastards wouldn't have left anyone behind unless there was someone alive to guard. And *that* meant . . .

He held a finger across his lips, warning Bahbar to go right on keeping his mouth closed, and eased his way into the office space. The door to Hundred Thalmayr's quarters stood ajar and he sidled towards it as silently as he could.

But not silently enough. His boot scuffed the floor and the door jerked open.

Kalcyr didn't know the infantry sword who came leaping through the door, but the short sword in his hand—held low and deadly in a practiced grip—left no doubt about the man's intentions. Kalcyr was a cavalryman, accustomed to fighting from unicornback, not on his own two feet, and the mutinous sword came at him with a balanced lethality which left him in very little doubt about how things would have worked out in a straight up fight. Unfortunately for the mutineer, what Kalcyr held in his hand wasn't a sword.

Kalcyr never knew if the sword had realized what he was carrying. Perhaps he had, given how quickly he tried to close. But he couldn't close quickly enough, and a silent concussion shook the orderly room as the cavalryman triggered the daggerstone.

*   *   *

It was Ulthar's turn to take the shot. The area behind the brig was darker than Shartahk's riding boots, but he caught a flicker of half-imagined movement and sent an arbalest bolt sizzling toward it. Somebody swore in a high, falsetto—the tone of a man who'd been scared spitless by a near miss and not of someone who'd been hit, unfortunately—and he fell back from the window to respan his weapon.

"Watch it!" someone shouted from the office.

Another fireball erupted in the night, but this one hadn't made it through the window, praise Hali! From the sudden smell of smoke, though, it had ignited the brig's cedar shingle roof.

"There, beside the water trough!"

"Got it!"

An arbalest fired and someone shrieked. Which was all very well but wasn't going to help them very much if the brig burned down around them.

*   *   *

Jathyr snarled as another of his men went down, but his eyes glowed with baleful satisfaction as he watched the flames beginning to leap from the brig's roof. Not much longer and the bastards would have to come out where he could get at them or fry—them and the damned Sharonians with them! In another minute or so—

Fortunately for Lerso Jathyr and his remaining men, Tolomaeo Briahk's squad still had almost a dozen stun bolts left.

CHAPTER ELEVEN

Inkara 25, 205 YU
(December 16, 1928 CE)

"AM I GLAD TO SEE YOU!" THERMAN ULTHAR SAID FERVENTLY.

"Likewise."

Sarma's response was a bit more reserved as he watched the released Sharonians intermingled with Arcanans in the bucket brigade working to extinguish the brig's flames before it spread to the rest of the fort. Somehow none of his plans had anticipated letting Regiment-Captain Velvelig and his companions out of their cell—not, at least, until there'd been time to establish certain ground rules. Under the circumstances, however, trying to put them right back into confinement didn't strike him as the best idea he'd ever had. Especially not when he considered how competently Velvelig and one of his noncoms, who looked enough like the regiment-captain to have been at least a distant cousin, were holding the infantry arbalests they'd somehow acquired.

He turned away from the fire for a moment, gazing at the bodies sprawled in the dancing light and shadow from the crackling flames. He couldn't quite decide what he felt. He'd never wanted anyone, Arcanan or Sharonian, to die, yet he couldn't pretend he and Ulthar hadn't always known the odds were very much against pulling off a successful mutiny without casualties. And it could have been far worse, especially if Sahnger hadn't pulled off the stables and moved to neutralize Yankaro's platoon on his own initiative. At least the mutineers—he didn't like the word, but it was the only one which truly applied—had suffered only three fatal casualties. Six others had been wounded, the most seriously of them Sarkhol Gersmyn's savagely burned

145

hand, but none so badly as to surpass the Gift of Commander of Fifty Sorthar Maisyl, the journeyman magistron assigned as Fort Ghartoun's senior healer. So, taking everything together, he supposed they hadn't done too badly. Except, of course, that now they had to figure out what to do with Thalmayr...and how to go about reporting all of this in a way that wouldn't get the lot of them sent straight to the dragon.

"I'm sorry it took us so long to get you out of that hellhole, Regiment-Captain," he said to Velvelig through his own PC's translating spellware. "We couldn't make our move until all the pieces were in place."

"I can see how that might have been a problem." Velvelig's voice was flat, giving away nothing, and his expression gave away even less. "Of course, you two have another little problem now, don't you?"

"We have *several* of them, actually," Ulthar acknowledged with a sour smile. "Which one did you have in mind, Sir?"

"The fact that my people are out of cells and we're not likely to go back into them peacefully. Which, coupled with the fact that by my best estimate you and your men are still outnumbered somewhere around four or five-to-one by the rest of the garrison, suggests you might just find your resources running short if you tried to *make* us go back."

"Frankly, the same thought had already occurred to me," Sarma admitted, and Ulthar nodded in wry agreement. "Believe me, Regiment-Captain Velvelig, Therman and I are both of the opinion that your people have been abused enough. By the same token, I trust you understand why we can't simply stand on the fort's fighting step and wave goodbye as you vanish into the distance. We're going to be in deep enough dragon shit with our superiors for what we've already done, however justified. If we were to, ah...mislay all of you on top of everything else, I'm afraid our word about Thalmayr's behavior wouldn't carry very much weight."

"I could point out that that's *your* fucking problem," Velvelig observed coldly. "We didn't attack you. And we sure as hells didn't launch an offensive while we were pretending to *negotiate* with you! And then there's that little matter of how many of our Voices you bastards murdered along the way here."

"We can't deny any of that," Ulthar said quietly. "I think you know my men and I had nothing to do with any of it, though, since we were your guests right here at the time. And Jaralt's been trying to figure out how to stop as much of it as he could from the very beginning. But we're not very far up the totem pole, Sir. A commander of fifty is only the equivalent of one of your platoon-captains. I know it's a pretty pale excuse after everything you just listed, but we really were following orders...right up to the moment we completely *violated* our orders and put the lives of every one of our men into jeopardy in the process."

Eyes of Andaran blue met dark, hard eyes of Arpathian brown levelly in the firelight. Stillness hovered around the two men, made even stiller by the greedy background crackle of flames, the voices of the men in the bucket brigade, and the hiss when a fresh bucket of water sluiced across blazing timbers. Then, finally, Velvelig nodded slowly.

"Don't expect me to be doing any drum dances or swearing blood brotherhood anytime soon," he said. "But I truly do understand what it took for a pair of platoon commanders to run this sort of risk. For that matter," he added a bit grudgingly, "maybe the fact that the two of you chose to do what you've done proves there really is *someone* in Arcana who understands what honor is."

Ulthar winced, but he didn't look away and he couldn't deny that Velvelig had every right to feel that way.

And he doesn't even know yet about how that motherless bastard Neshok and the rest of the intelligence pukes lied to us every step of the way. I wonder if he'll even believe us if we tell him? Not that he wouldn't find out eventually anyway, even if it's only at Jaralt and my courts-martial!

"I guess I'm glad you feel that way, Sir," he said. "And I'm sorry as hell that it took something like this for us to show you that Arcana—or Andara and the Army, at least—really do have a sense of honor. It's been buried under a pretty damned deep load of dragon shit just at the moment, and cleaning it's going to be a gods-awful challenge, but it's got to start somewhere. It might as well be here."

Velvelig gazed at him a moment longer, then nodded again. He wasn't going to go out of his way to make that chore any easier for the Arcanan Army in general than he had to, but he had to admit these two youngsters seemed to have made a fair start.

"In the meantime," Ulthar continued, "I don't think we have any choice but to keep you and your men in custody—officially, at least. There are only twenty-one of you, so I don't think you could get very far back towards Sharona with Two Thousand Harshu's entire army between you and there. And it's going to be hard enough getting our superior officers to listen to our side of what happened here even with your people available for interviews. If we don't have you around to back up our testimony, they probably won't believe us at all, to be honest."

"We might not be able to get back to Sharona, but we could sure as hells make ourselves scarce enough out there in the wilderness that you people would have one demon of a time finding us again," Velvelig observed rather caustically. "Besides, what makes you think your superiors would be interested in *our* testimony?"

"Sir, I'm an officer in the Second Andaran Scouts," Ulthar said. "That's the hereditary command of the Olderhan family, and Sir Thankhar Olderhan is the Duke of Garth Showma, who also happens to be the planetary governor of New Arcana and one of the three or four most senior officers in the entire Commandery. When he gets involved in something, things happen, and you *don't* want to be part of what he thinks is the problem. I've already sent a full report about what's been happening here to him through a secure channel. He won't have gotten it yet, but when he does, hell won't hold what'll come down on the people responsible. I give you my word of honor on that."

"This duke's going to take a platoon-captain's word for it despite anything his immediate superiors might have to say?" Velvelig sounded skeptical, and Ulthar didn't blame him.

"*This* duke will *definitely* take my word," he replied flatly. "He'd do that anyway, or at least give us a fair hearing, whoever we were. The fact that I'm a Second Andaran will make it easier, I admit. And so will the fact that his son is Shaylar and Jathmar Nargra's *baranal*."

It didn't register for a moment. Partly because the spellware hadn't translated the Andaran term, but then Ulthar's verb tense penetrated and Namir Velvelig's eyes blazed suddenly.

"*What* did you say?" he demanded. "You said '*is*!' Are you saying Jathmar Nargra and Shaylar Nargra-Kolmayr are *alive?*"

Ulthar stepped back half a pace involuntarily, stunned by Velvelig's reaction. The Sharonian reached out with one hand as if to grab the front of his tunic and drag him closer, then closed that hand into a fist so tight the knuckles whitened.

"They were the last I heard, Sir," the Arcanan said cautiously. "Both of them were badly hurt in the original confrontation between our people and yours, and the dragon pulling them back to the rear passed my dragon on the way forward, so I didn't see either of them personally. But Sword Harnak was at Toppled Timber with Hundred Olderhan, and I've had plenty of time to discuss what happened with him. I understand Madam Shaylar had a nasty concussion and Jathmar was so badly burned by an infantry dragon that no one expected him to survive, but Magister Gadrial had enough of the healing Gift to keep him alive until our company healer reached him. Sword Morikan healed him, but Madam Shaylar's injuries weren't immediately life threatening and there was only one of him. They had to triage the wounded, and there were too many critically hurt for him to heal her concussion before she and her husband were pulled back to Fort Rycharn, but I'm sure the magistrons there were able to heal both of them fully."

He glanced at Sarma, who nodded sharply.

"They did," he told the Sharonian. "I came through Fort Rycharn after they were sent further up-chain, and Five Hundred Klian told me they'd been completely healed. They'd have gotten treatment anyway, but after Hundred Olderhan made them his *shardonai* they went straight to the head of the queue."

"'*Shardonai*'?" Velvelig repeated the Andaran word cautiously. "What in all the Arpathian hells is a *shardonai*? And why would this Olderhan have made Jathmar and Shaylar into whatever it is?"

"A *shardon* is...well, a *shardon* is an adopted member of his *baranal*'s family," Ulthar said. He glanced at Sarma again, struck by the fact that he'd never considered that it might be necessary to define something so fundamental to the Andaran honor code. Sarma only looked back at him and shrugged, which was a great deal of help.

"The word '*shardon*' is from very ancient Andaran," he continued after a moment. "I'm a little surprised the spellware didn't translate it, but maybe it couldn't translate it for someone who didn't already have enough of the concept to put it into context. Literally, it means 'shieldling,' I think. Jaralt?"

"That's probably the best way to translate it," Sarma agreed. "There are all kinds of honor obligations tied up in it, though, so it means a lot more than that in practice."

"That's true enough!" Ulthar agreed feelingly. Then he drew a deep breath and looked Velvelig straight in the eye once more. "What matters most in this case, though, is that Hundred Olderhan—every single member of the Olderhan family, in fact, including the duke—is honor bound to die in the defense of his *shardonai*."

Velvelig twitched in surprise, then shook himself and fastened on the most burning of the several questions churning through his brain.

"Why in the names of all the gods and demons of Arpathia did he do that after massacring our people? I don't want to sound like I doubt your word, but that seems like a godsdamned strange thing for a man who'd just butchered an entire party of civilians to do!"

"Trust me, Sir, there are going to be enough Arcanans who wonder exactly the same thing, if not for the same reasons," Ulthar said, still looking him in the eye. "It's not something even an old-school Andaran like one of the Olderhans does very often these days. In this case, though, there's a very specific and special reason Hundred Olderhan declared Shaylar and Jathmar *shardonai*, Sir. A reason Sarma and his people—all of the Arcanans who launched the attack against Sharona—didn't know. Something they were lied to about."

"Lied to?" Namir Velvelig was about as tough-minded as a human being came, but he was beginning to feel decidedly dazed. "Lied to *how?*"

"Regiment-Captain," Sarma said quietly, "I was told—*we* were told—by our superiors that your people initiated the conflict between us, and no one ever told us they were civilians. And on top of that, we were told that Magister Halathyn vos Dulainah, one of our most beloved and respected...scholars was shot and killed by your people after he'd surrendered. That doesn't excuse a single thing that was done to you, but it does explain why so many of our people were so enraged."

"And it was also a complete lie—one that had to be deliberate," Ulthar said flatly. "I know it was a lie, because I was there when your people counterattacked at the swamp portal, and I know Magister Halathyn was killed by friendly fire, by one of our own weapons. And I already told you my senior noncom, Sword Harnak, was there at Toppled Timber when it all fell into the crapper." He met Velvelig's fiery stare unflinchingly. "It wasn't your people who opened fire, it was *ours*. It was a worthless, gutless excuse for a Second Andaran officer named Shevan Garlath, and he opened fire directly *against* Hundred Olderhan's orders. Once he did, and once your people returned fire, there was no way for the hundred to get a handle on the situation and stop it before almost all of your people were dead. That's how this whole bloody, senseless thing started, and that's why Hundred Olderhan took Shaylar and Jathmar under his family's protection. It was his way of admitting responsibility for what happened, even though Garlath acted against his specific order to stand down, and it was also his way of protecting them from any *additional* harm. Sword Harnak was there when Sir Jasak faced Thalmayr down when he tried to put Madam Shaylar and her husband in chains as 'enemy prisoners of war.' It damned near turned into swordplay, because the hundred would've cut Thalmayr down in a heartbeat if he'd pushed it...and it would have been a better damned thing if he had!"

Ulthar drew a deep breath and shook his head as if to clear it.

"But that's what really happened, Sir," he said after a moment, "and I know damned well the hundred would've made a complete and accurate report to Five Hundred Klian at Fort Rycharn. And *that* means there's no way in Shartahk's deepest hell Jaralt and his men could have been told what they were told unless it was deliberate. Somebody—somebody pretty damned high up, I'm afraid; higher than the five hundred, anyway—wanted it to have exactly the effect it did have, and I will be *damned* if I can think of any reason someone would!"

Velvelig's jaw clenched. Everything Ulthar had just said matched with the Voice report Shaylar had gotten out during the savage fight at Fallen Timbers. Oh, there was no way to know whether or not this Hundred Olderhan really had tried to prevent the bloodshed, but there was no question that the first shot had been fired by a single Arcanan to kill Ghartoun chan Hagrahyl, the very man for whom this fort had been renamed. It could have happened exactly the way Ulthar had just described, and the frustrated fury in the Arcanan's expression seemed utterly genuine.

But Shaylar and Jathmar *alive*? That was impossible! *Surely* it was impossible! Why in the names of every god and devil would the Arcanans have lied about *that*?

"Why?" he asked the question out loud, even knowing that Ulthar and Sarma were far too junior to be able to answer it. "Why lie to us about that?"

"About what?" Ulthar asked cautiously.

"About the fact that they're alive!" Velvelig snapped. "Your fucking 'diplomats' told us they were both *dead!*"

"What?" Sarma looked at him blankly. "Told you they were *dead?*" He shook his head. "That doesn't make any sense at all. Not when we were trying to negotiate some kind of settlement!"

"You're damned right it doesn't make any sense," Velvelig said grimly. "In fact, it was godsdamned *stupid* if you people ever wanted to put a lid on this! Bad enough the rest of the Chalgyn Consortium team was massacred, but do you have any concept of just how furious the news *Shaylar* was dead made every living Sharonian? No, of course you don't! This...this 'magister' of yours, this vos Dulainah. You say he was loved by everybody in Arcana?"

"Everybody but the other *shakira,* who thought he was a traitor for treating *garthans* like human beings," Ulthar acknowledged, still cautiously.

"Well, your people had better understand that he couldn't possibly have been more beloved than Shaylar Nargra-Kolmayr. That was probably true even before you attacked her survey team, but *after*? She was beautiful, she was smart, she was one of the strongest Talents we've ever produced, her entire kingdom was proud of her accomplishments, and she was the public face of the entire Portal Authority. Not only that, but she was—she *is*—a *Voice.* She sent back every single detail of that fight. She held onto that Voice link, kept sending back an eyewitness account to us *while it happened,* even while you were blowing every one of her friends into bloody meat around her. Even when her own husband went down, burning alive before her eyes, and she *knew* he was dead. She was still sending that message when whatever caused her concussion knocked her unconscious—we all thought she'd been killed when that happened—and every single Talented person with even a trace of Mind Speech has Seen that message."

Ulthar's expression was sick, but it wasn't sick enough yet, and Velvelig felt something almost like sadistic pleasure, as if he were somehow paying back all of Arcana for every single Sharonian life which had been destroyed, every drop of Sharonian blood which had been shed.

"You don't have Talents, just like we don't have your 'Gifts,' so maybe you don't understand what a Voice truly is. When I say every trace Mind Speaker in Sharona Saw that message, I mean *they experienced it with her.* They felt every single thing she felt. All of it—sights, sounds, smells, even her thoughts and emotions. They were firsthand witnesses to the entire fight, to the entire fucking *massacre,* because they were right there inside her head with her while she experienced it! You think your people are pissed off over being lied to about your magister? You have no idea, no frigging *concept,* of how pissed off and infuriated my entire home universe is, because we absolutely know that every single thing she sent us was completely true! And then, on top of all that, you not only launched this godsdamned attack while we were negotiating for a peaceful settlement but shot every *additional* Voice you could find along the way?" He shook his head. "Trust me, what you've already done is enough to turn every single nation of Sharona against you, and every one of them sees Shaylar as its own martyr. I don't know exactly what's happening back home right this minute, but I don't need to know any specifics to guarantee you that you can't even *begin* to imagine what's headed your way sometime very soon . . . assuming it's not already on its way."

Ulthar and Sarma stared at each other, expressions horrified. They'd thought they understood how bad the situation was. Now they knew their worst nightmares had fallen dismally short of reality.

They were still standing there, still staring at one another, when Valnar Rohsahk, who'd been sent to fetch Fifty Maisyl and his medical detachment, dashed back to them.

"Sir! Fifty Ulthar!" the recon crystal specialist panted. "Hathnor's dead and Hundred Thalmayr and Bahbar are both gone!"

*　　*　　*

"I'd love to have some idea of what we do now," Therman Ulthar admitted wearily and looked around the unlikely group at the huge table in the Fort Ghartoun mess hall.

He sat at one end of the table, despite his lowly rank, as the most senior Arcanan present, with Jaralt Sarma to his right and Commander of Fifty Cothar to his left. The very dark-complected Hilmaran cavalry officer looked less than delighted at the situation, but he'd burned his bridges as thoroughly as any of the others when he didn't join the effort to resist the mutiny. Sorthar Maisyl, Fort Ghartoun's senior healer, sat to Cothar's right, and Evarl

Harnak and Keraik Nourm faced Maisyl across the table. Both noncoms looked acutely uncomfortable at finding themselves in an officer's council, but they'd earned the right to be there and the dragon shit was so deep they deserved the chance to speak up for themselves and the enlisted men who'd followed Ulthar and Sarma into mutiny. Besides, any junior officer who wasn't a complete fool knew enough to listen to his senior noncommissioned officers' advice.

Namir Velvelig sat at the far end of the table, flanked by Company-Captain Silkash, his senior surviving officer, and Master-Armsman Hordal Karuk. Silkash looked enormously better than he had, thanks to Maisyl's healing Gift. The Sharonian surgeon was an Inkaran, from the island off the coast of Shaloma which the Sharonians apparently called Bernith, with sandy hair and blue eyes which were still more than a little bemused from watching Maisyl and his assistants work on the wounded. Tobis Makree was still in the infirmary, although his condition was enormously improved, so Senior-Chief-Armsman Lestym chan Visal sat beside Karuk, and Armsman Thakoh chan Dersain filled out the Sharonian end of the table.

Chan Dersain was both the most junior and the youngest person present, and he looked more than a little nervous. Velvelig had insisted upon his presence, however, and neither Ulthar nor Sarma could fault him for that. The youngster—he had to be at least eight or nine years younger than either of the two fifties—had dark auburn hair and brown eyes. He was from Parnatha, which the Sharonians called Alathia, and his left eye had been blinded in the fight for Fort Ghartoun. It was possible Maisyl would be able to do something about that... but it was also possible the magistron *wouldn't* be able to, given how much time had passed. Yet whatever might have happened to his physical vision, chan Dersain had a very useful Talent for an observer. He was what the Sharonians called a "Sifter," which made him a human lie detector. With him at one end of the table and a sarkolis crystal charged with a verifier spell at the other end, all parties could be satisfied that no one was lying to anyone else.

Gods, I hate to think how the Commandery's going to react to this one, Ulthar thought almost whimsically. *Talk about violating military security—!*

"I think a lot of what we decide to do *now* depends on what you were already planning to do," Velvelig observed in response to his opening remark.

The regiment-captain was the equivalent of a commander of two thousand, which made him astronomically senior to anyone else at the table. He was also at least ten years older than any of the Arcanan officers, and he spoke with a calm sense of assurance and authority which ought to have been out of place in a prisoner of war. Under the circumstances, Ulthar found that more reassuring than anything else.

"What we'd intended to do, Sir," he said now, after glancing at Sarma and receiving the other fifty's nod of agreement, "was to place Hundred Thalmayr under arrest, disarm and secure anyone who opposed our actions, and send a hummer—that's a messenger bird—back to commander of Five Hundred Klian in Mahritha with a report of what we'd done and a request for orders."

"A commander of five hundred is—what? The equivalent of one of our battalion-captains?"

"Approximately, yes, Sir."

"And you thought he'd have the seniority to untangle the mess you were planning to drop into his lap?" Velvelig sounded skeptical, and Ulthar didn't blame him.

"We didn't know whether he'd have the seniority or not, Sir," Sarma put in. "But my uncle served with Five Hundred Klian when they were both squires—that would be under-captains in your Army. He invited me to dinner when I arrived in Fort Rycharn—as the son of an old friend, not one of his junior officers—and my platoon was one of the first ones ordered to move up as reinforcements. I talked to several of the five hundred's men before Two Thousand Harshu or Five Hundred Neshok arrived from Erthos. That's why I knew something wasn't right about the intelligence briefings we were given just before the offensive kicked off. I had a lot better idea of what had actually happened at Toppled Timber and at the swamp portal than anyone else in the Expeditionary Force seemed to have. I couldn't be *sure* what they were telling us was wrong, but it sure sounded that way. And Five Hundred Klian knows *exactly* what really happened when all this started, since he personally debriefed Hundred Olderhan on his way up-chain. If anybody would be likely to believe us and be in a position to give us some kind of advice, maybe even some cover, it'd be him."

"But the fellow in charge of this Expeditionary Force of yours is a commander of two thousand, right?" Velvelig asked. Ulthar nodded, and the Sharonian grunted. "It seems likely to me that, as the CO, he has to have a pretty damned good idea what his intelligence pukes are telling his army. I can't see anybody who could pull off an operation like this as slickly as he has *not* knowing that. In fact, I'd be deeply surprised if he wasn't a part—probably a big part—of the entire story."

"That's why we weren't planning on sending any hummers to *him*, Sir," Ulthar agreed, His expression troubled. "Two Thousand Harshu has a high reputation in the Army, and I really don't want to think he's part of some organized lie. But like you, I can't see how anybody could have pulled it off without his at least giving his unofficial blessing."

"And is this Harshu the sort of fellow who'd come up with something like this all on his own?" Velvelig waved one hand when Ulthar raised his eyebrows at him. "What I mean is, would he try something like this without the approval of whoever's next up in your chain of command?"

"We don't know," Ulthar said frankly. "That's one thing we hoped Five Hundred Klian could advise us on."

"Actually," Commander of Fifty Cothar said, speaking up for the first time, his expression troubled, "I think I might be able to suggest a little something about that, Therman."

Ulthar looked at Cothar with a surprised expression, and the dark-haired, dark-complected cavalry fifty shrugged.

"You're married to Fifty Halesak's sister, aren't you?" he asked, and Ulthar nodded. "Well, my grandmother's a *garthan*, too," Cothar said with a crooked, rather bitter smile none of the Sharonians understood. Ulthar did, though. He nodded again, more firmly, and Cothar looked down the table at Velvelig.

"The senior Union Army officer out here is Two Thousand mul Gurthak, Regiment-Captain," he said. "His headquarters are in Erthos—that's four universes up-chain towards Arcana from here—but he's responsible for a nine-universe command area reaching back from Mahritha, the universe immediately up-chain from Hells Gate, all the way back to Esthiya. He's been pulling in every reinforcement he could dig up from the moment the first hummer from Hundred Olderhan reached him, and he could've taken command of the AEF himself. In fact, that's what he should've done. But instead, he gave it to Two Thousand Harshu."

"And?" Velvelig prodded gently when the cavalry officer paused.

"I don't think he did that because he thought Harshu was better qualified for the command than he was," Cothar said flatly. "He's a *shakira*, and it's not like one of them to let anyone else have any credit he could claim for himself."

"*Shakira*?" Velvelig repeated, and Cothar grimaced.

"They're a bunch of bigoted bastards, Sir. They come from our continent of Mythal—I *think* your people call it Ricathia—and they believe anyone who isn't Gifted is worthless. They'd like to turn all of them into slaves. For that matter, they *did* turn any Mythalan without a Gift into a slave. People like my grandmother's family—*garthans* they call them. They lost the war that broke out back home in Arcana when we first discovered the portals, and the Andarans and Ransarans made them back down on the worst of their bigotry. But they've never forgiven that, and if one of them saw a chance to shove a knife into the Army's back—the Army's Andaran through and through, Sir—the son-of-a-whore would take it in a heartbeat. Or that's my opinion, anyway." He shrugged, his expression bitter. "Only fair to admit I'm prejudiced as all hells where the *shakira* are concerned because of what they've done to my grandmother's family, but I don't think that makes me wrong."

Velvelig glanced back at Ulthar, trying to assimilate the latest overload of information, and the Scout nodded, his own expression just as bleak as Cothar's.

"Sahrimahn has a point, Sir. My brother-in-law thought pretty much the same thing when he found me here in your brig and found out just how thoroughly *he'd* been lied to."

"So are you saying you think this mul Gurthak's really behind all of this?"

"You said you were told Madam Nargra-Kolmayr and her husband were dead, Sir. That means it was the official position of our diplomats when *your* diplomats asked about it. There's only one person out here who'd have the authority to order someone in an official negotiating position to lie about that . . . and only a complete idiot would lie about it without mul Gurthak's signing off on it."

"And it has a sort of *shakira* stink about it, too," Fifty Maisyl said, his expression grim. "I'm not related to any Mythalans by blood or marriage, but I don't have to be to know how frigging arrogant and manipulative they are. Their magisters and magistrons are the most egotistical and condescending bastards in the multiverse, and like Cothar says, anybody who isn't *sha-kira* himself is dirt as far as they're concerned. Hells, their *Book of the Shakira* says that in so many words! And it also teaches them that no *shakira* is under any obligation to deal honestly or honorably with any non-*shakira*. Anyone outside their own caste is their mortal enemy—potentially, at least—so it's actually their *duty* to lie if that helps the *shakira*, individually or as a group, with their 'soul growth.' Most of the *shakira* I've run into really believe that, too."

"They're not all that way," Cothar objected in the voice of a man making himself be fair. "Magister Halathyn wasn't!"

"No," Maisyl agreed. "But that was the reason so many people loved him so much—because he *wasn't* like the rest of the *shakira*. Because he was one of the most powerful magisters Mythal ever produced, one of the highest of all the *shakira*, and he'd turned his back on them and walked away from them!"

"I take it these '*shakira*' aren't universally beloved?" Velvelig asked dryly.

"No one but a fool trusts a *shakira* behind him, Sir," Ulthar said. "By the same token, though, I've tried to bear in mind that just because a group of people has a particular reputation, that doesn't mean everyone who belongs to it deserves the same reputation."

"That's very commendable, Fifty," Velvelig said, "but in this case, it could be a fast way to get you and your friends killed. I don't know anything about your *shakira*, but I grew up next door to the Uromathian Empire. Any septman who takes a Uromath-ian's word for *anything* is too stupid to come in out of the snow. Besides, if this mul Gurthak's the senior officer for this cluster fuck your people've produced out here, then I think you're right that he has to've approved the way it's being conducted. And even if he didn't do that, if he's as unscrupulous as you seem to be suggesting, he's not going to let anything his subordinates might have done splash on *him*. At the very least, he'll do his damnedest to sweep any unpleasant little revelations under the rug, and the easiest way for him to do that would be to sweep you under right with them."

"That may be so, Sir, but we've got to find *someone* we can trust," Ulthar said, his expression grim. "It takes seven weeks to get a message from here to New Andara. That means my message to my wife won't get there for another nineteen days. After that, it'd take another six weeks for any message from Duke Garth Showma to come back as far as Mahritha. And that's for hummers—it'll take twice that long for him or the Commandery to send an actual investigating team clear out here."

"I see."

Velvelig looked at Company-Captain Silkash and Master-Armsman Karuk, and his expression was at least as grim as Ulthar's. They weren't accustomed to thinking in communication delays that long, but the Arcanans didn't have Voices. If Ulthar and the others were right to suspect this mul Gurthak was behind all this, giving him the next best thing to five months to tidy up any inconvenient witnesses before he had to face an inquiry would be a very bad idea.

"All right," he said after a moment. "I realize I'm not in your chain of command and that I'm an enemy officer, but I think you boys are in a hell of the mess, and *my* boys are in it right with you. Mind you, if you hadn't done what you've done, I'm pretty sure all my officers and men would've been 'disappeared' sooner or later by either your Two Thousand Harshu or mul Gurthak, so don't think I'm ungrateful. But the fact remains that we're in the same quicksand and sinking fast, so do you want my advice?"

"Yes, Sir," Ulthar made himself say firmly. Rather more firmly than he actually felt, to be honest.

"All right," Velvelig said again, and there might have been just a hint of a twinkle in those hard, dark eyes of his. "I don't think you're going to like some of it, but as I see it, if you fall back into the hands of Harshu or mul Gurthak before this duke of yours can get some sort of investigation moving out here—an investigation with teeth and muscle—you're dead." He shrugged. "The truth is, you *are* mutineers, and you and your men did kill other members of your own Army. I know why you did it, and from what you've been saying, Duke Garth Showma would not only understand but probably approve. But with five or six months to work on it, the people responsible for this'll have plenty of time to make sure you're all neatly dead and buried by the time his investigators arrive, and there'll be plenty of testimony—most of it *honest* testimony—to justify the court-martial's sentence. You do understand that, don't you?"

"Yes, Sir," Ulthar said quietly. "We'd hoped we could confine Thalmayr to his quarters and keep up the appearance that he was still in command until we'd at least had time to get our message to Five Hundred Klian. Now, though..."

He shrugged, and Velvelig nodded, forbearing to mention just how unlikely they'd been to get away with anything of the sort even if Thalmayr and the missing Senior Sword Kalcyr hadn't stolen unicorns and disappeared into the night.

"We can always hope Thalmayr and the other two will never be heard from again," he said instead. "Frankly, if they're headed for your field army and they didn't have time to grab supplies, that could damned well happen—it's *cold* out there at night, and crossing Failcham without enough water could kill just about anyone—but I'm going to assume your light cavalry's as good as ours. That means Kalcyr can probably keep them alive, and despite your damned dragons, I'm willing to bet there are posts along the way where Thalmayr can resupply and get medical care. And *that* means his version of what happened's going to reach Two Thousand Harshu. I don't think that's going to make Harshu very happy, do you?"

Ulthar shook his head, and Velvelig smiled faintly.

"So you're caught between Vaylar and Sankhar—I mean, you're damned whichever way you jump. Maybe—*maybe*—Duke Garth Showma will eventually figure out what happened and see to it that whoever's responsible pays for it, but you won't be around to see it. I wouldn't like that after the risk you've run for my people. And what I wouldn't like even more, frankly, would be that my people and I would have to be swept under the rug right along with you. As I see it, that means we're in this together. I mean *really* together."

"What are you suggesting, Sir?" Ulthar asked, but his tone said he already suspected where Velvelig was headed.

"I'm suggesting that in the interests of survival, and of possibly getting the truth into the hands of someone who can actually do something to stop this insanity, your men and mine have to work together. We have to combine forces and abilities—Talents and Gifts—and figure out how less than two hundred men can avoid being run down and captured by your entire Army."

"And how do we do that?" Ulthar's voice was edged with bitterness, and Velvelig shrugged.

"I'm an Arpathian, and most of the boys I've got left are veterans. We're used to wilderness and staying alive in it, and I'd bet you 'Andaran Scouts' are pretty damned good at that yourselves. I say we integrate our people—I mean really *integrate*, Fifty Ulthar, into one force—and head for the bush. Go ahead and send your message to Five Hundred Klian. Tell him what you're doing and why and ask him to send *his* report up-chain to your duke, as well. But after you've done that, your duty—your duty to your Army, if what you think is happening really is, and certainly to your own men—is to stay alive until the duke can organize some action in response. The only way you're going to do that is to be someplace Harshu and mul Gurthak can't find you."

"You mean here in Thermyn," Ulthar said.

"There are places in the Sky Bloods where two hundred men could hide from two hundred *thousand* men," Velvelig said.

"But can they hide from aerial reconnaissance?" Sarma asked. The regiment-captain looked at him, and it was the fifty's turn to shrug. "Don't forget we have dragons, Sir. For that matter, we've got recon gryphons. They can search a lot of area in a very short time."

"They wouldn't even have to do that," Maisyl pointed out. "All they'd have to do is trigger the recovery spells."

"'Recovery spells'?" Velvelig repeated, and the magistron nodded unhappily. None of the other Arcanans looked particularly happy either, the Sharonian noticed.

"Every Arcanan soldier is tagged with a recovery spell when he enlists, Sir," Maisyl said. "It's intended to help us locate the wounded after a battle . . . or to recover the dead, anyway. I'm only a journeyman myself, but I could trigger any recovery spell within forty or fifty miles, and my PC would tell me exactly where I had to go to find it after I did. A full magistron like Five Hundred Vaynair, Two Thousand Harshu's senior healer, could probably trigger recovery spells over as much as two or three *hundred* miles."

Velvelig didn't pretend even to himself that he understood how the process Maisyl had described worked, but he didn't need to. It was enough to understand that the Arcanans around him literally *couldn't* hide from their superiors.

"Isn't there anything that could block or cut off those spells?" he asked.

"Nothing we've ever found." Maisyl shrugged. "They're designed to find helpless or unconscious men under the worst possible circumstances, Sir, and they do a damned good job of it."

"Wonderful," Master-Armsman Karuk muttered. Maisyl looked at him, and the graying Arpathian noncom grimaced. "There's been plenty of times I'd've loved to have something like that, Master Maisyl. This isn't one of them."

"No, it isn't," Ulthar agreed. "And I hate to admit it, but it's not something Jaralt and I thought about when we were having the brainstorm that led up to this."

"Wait," Sarma said. The others looked at him, and he held up one hand in a "give-me-time-to-think" gesture, his eyes unfocused in thought. Then he shook himself and looked at Maisyl.

"The recovery spells work through a portal, do they, Sorthar?" he asked intently.

"No. It's about the only place they *don't* work, but then, no spell can be cast across a portal."

Velvelig didn't allow himself to raise any eyebrows, but he filed that bit of information quietly away. Interesting that magic didn't work across a portal threshold any better than a Talent did.

"So to trigger our recovery spells, they'd have to be in the same universe, right?"

"Yes, but what good does that do us? The Expeditionary Force's in control of every universe between here and Mahritha. If they really want to find us, all they'd have to do is cross through into each of them in turn and activate the spells."

"True." Sarma nodded. "But I think there may be one universe this side of Mahritha the Expeditionary Force *doesn't* control."

CHAPTER TWELVE

Ternathal 28, 5053
Inkara 26, YU 205
(December 17, 1928 CE)

IN A QUIET RICATHIAN CORNER OF SHARONA, SOOLAN CHAN
Rahool stretched his toes and sucked coconut milk out
of a freshly broken shell. The rough-barked tree at his back and
the hopeful, grinning Minarti clan youngsters gamboling at the
tree line reminded the simian ambassador just how much he
loved his job. The chimpanzees shrieked in a high glee, making
noises not unlike human toddlers. And he chuckled and laid his
own coconut at his elbow, where it would be handy, to set about
cracking open the pile of coconuts the Minarti clan grandmother
had decided were snack for the day.

The thump of a round rock against a pointy rock made neat
drinking holes in the hairy coconuts. He struck each one twice
for easy sipping, fully aware that one of the older chimps mind-
ing the youngsters was watching him for quality control. Chan
Rahool didn't mind in the least.

He'd served two and a half years in the Ternathian Army
almost a decade ago as a Voice. His superiors there had graciously
marked his early discharge as "due to excess force capacity," but
chan Rahool liked to be honest with himself. He'd been released
from service because he was an awful Voice and a poor fit for
military service in general. His Voice range was barely more
than line of sight at the best of times, his secondary talent as
an Animal Speaker wasn't all that useful to the Army, and the
strictures of military life had simply made no sense to him.

But the simians didn't care that they had to come all the
way up to arm's length to talk to him. And they appreciated

163

that he preferred to wear a webbed belt suitable for hanging many bags of sugared nuts rather than a slimmer one matching uniform trousers and approved of by some uniform board at headquarters.

It amused chan Rahool even now that he owed the military for his dream job. Without the heavy shoulder muscles built from years of punitive exercise, chan Rahool's limited Voice range would have again stunted any hope at a career.

Instead the embassy recruiter had asked that first wonderful interview question: "How do you feel about climbing trees?"

Chan Rahool's answer, "Do I have to wear shoes?" won him the apprenticeship. Being willing to climb triple canopy jungle to visit orangutan nests earned him a career.

Ternathia's Combined Simian Embassies tried hard to be a traditional government organization with hierarchy charts and field position rotations. Chan Rahool found it amusing. His fellow ambassadors were all much like him in their love of outdoor places and a relaxed life with minimal oversight.

Chan Rahool honored his former noncoms' efforts to instill a sense of organizational pride by actually reading all the silly instructions that came from CSE and composing much shorter summaries for his fellow ambassadors. He liked to distill and emphasize the parts that truly mattered. To make sure they got read, he packaged the letters with bottles of his local moonshine.

He'd learned that from the military too. There'd been a supply corps armsman who'd always found a way to incentivize attention when he really needed something.

Chan Rahool's current clan, the Minarti chimpanzees, preferred their alcohol as fermented fruit but they tolerated his preference for the liquid form and would even supply him with armloads of suitable fresh fruit in exchange for a ration of bottles in the dry months between the wet seasons.

That private exchange might have been why chan Rahool was always able to reach his assigned clans. So he wasn't at all surprised when a big chimp, quite a bit more mature than the youngsters he habitually shared coconut with, knuckle-walked up to the official embassy cabin and sat down on the veranda.

Chan Rahool didn't make a habit of feeding the youngsters there, but for the adults he tried to keep drinking in the house or on the porch. The fragility of glass was sometimes a difficult concept, and he didn't want shards scattered in the roots and rocks where they'd be hard for him to clean up properly.

With a grin, chan Rahool began distributing snacks. The young chimps caught the thrown pieces of coconut, and chan Rahool ambled back to do his ambassadorial duty.

* * *

The gray dappling the older simian's back fur distracted chan Rahool momentarily from the sheer mass of muscle underneath it. Then the simian turned and displayed even more muscle and a weapon belt and chan Rahool's eyes widened. He was no chimp. The silverback gorilla's smug expression shocked chan Rahool so much, that he opened the door and invited him in before he quite placed where he'd last seen a look like that.

It certainly wasn't on any simian in the Minarti clan. No, that was the look a veteran infantry armsman had given him once when he'd had a few too many and decided he was tough enough to out wrestle anything. Chan Rahool was significantly stronger now, but he was also far too sober to want to wrestle a silverback... especially a silverback who chose to wear a sharpened eight inch tusk at his belt.

What kind of animal even had an eight inch tusk? Chan Rahool mentally labeled the silverback as Tusk immediately. The simian undoubtedly had a name of his own, but he was unlikely to bother to tell chan Rahool what it was.

Tusk walked straight through chan Rahool's home and opened the back door to admit two more silvers and a smaller decidedly elderly female nearly white with age. White-hair entered with a pronounced, regal assurance and assembled her guard—that was what they had to be—around her as she took possession of the house.

Chan Rahool was quite certain that three such powerful males wouldn't have come to a place pitiful enough to be granted to the CSE for a cabin to fight for territory, and the grandmother of the matrilineal Minarti chimps had assured him that he was considered a youngster for the purposes of male hierarchy and wanted more shoulder mass before he could begin challenging to attract a female. He hoped that would apply to gorillas as well.

"Good morning Ma'am," chan Rahool said. It didn't seem like a bad start. Chimps were usually peaceable, happy creatures with the straightforwardness of a toddler... once he figured out what they wanted. Gorillas, well, chan Rahool had never worked with gorillas. He reached out a hand to touch White-hair's closest knuckle to begin to translate her thoughts.

Tusk made a discouraging noise and batted chan Rahool's hand back.

<A BOWL OF SHRIVELED FRUIT.> Chan Rahool almost fell over. <A bowl of shriveled fruit.> White-hair pushed the picture at him again, a bit more gently but with added details of pink and blue kittens painted on the outer rim of the bowl that chan Rahool recognized as one of the mismatched dishes from his own kitchen.

Somehow he got the sense that she was doing the pictorial equivalent of speaking loudly with exaggerated enunciation. What he strongly suspected might be the most senior simian ever to speak with a CSE representative had come to visit him. And she'd already decided he was an idiot.

The problem was that chan Rahool didn't have any fermented marula fruit. Why hadn't they gone to their own ambassador?

Chan Rahool was rewarded with a series of images in fast succession starting with medicinal plants and ending with giggling chimp babies. *Right.* He'd arranged for the Minarti's exchange of medicinal herbs for periodic medical care. No good deed goes unpunished. *I figured out what grand dame Minarti wanted, so now I get all the hard cases. Of course that one was easy because Dorrick over with the Nishani told everyone about the trade of chimp mineral rights for human medical care. The only tricky part was that the chimps asked me instead of the other way around.*

White-hair grunted to demand back chan Rahool's attention.

<Fruit in a bowl> again. The picture changed flashing through a series of other fruits he might offer instead.

White-hair didn't seem to have any qualms against leafing freely through his mind for useful images. He hadn't known simians even had Voices, if Voice was really the right term for it. For that matter, he hadn't known they had Talents at all! Should he call her a Human Speaker? Or should—

White-hair snapped a command punctuated by clicks and cheek flexing, and Tusk hopped over chan Rahool's kitchen table, landed lightly, and began flinging open cupboards. Chan Rahool followed quickly hoping to catch any falling dishes before they shattered and further ruined the embassy visit.

Tusk snorted.

A much fuzzier picture formed: <*neatly stacked bananas or maybe some type of plantain,*> with an over layer of intense humor from Tusk.

Nothing fell, chan Rahool noted with amazement.

Tusk lifted a bottle from the most recent batch of moonshine and proffered it to chan Rahool: <*an image of an open bottle with shriveled fruit inside.*>

"Oh, right, get the drinks."

White-hair grunted a snorting laughter at the final comprehension.

Chan Rahool put back Tusk's bottle. He grabbed instead the bottle of single malt from the back of a high cupboard. After a moment's reflection, he also pulled out two bags of his favorite nuts. Grand dame Minarti usually wanted just the 'shine, but sometimes she tried some of the snacks he ate along with it, and he considered the dried jerky and the assortment of cheeses and sausages in his cold storage.

<*Cheese.*> White-hair rejected the meats and expressed a decided interest in trying the cheeses. All of them.

*   *   *

Tusk nicked the rest of the single malt when the gorillas left. The other two grabbed the moonshine. Soolan chan Rahool didn't even notice.

The cheese was long gone. Part way through the meeting, he'd been sent back to the kitchen to get all the jerky and sausages, too, but he didn't really care about that, either. No, what he *cared* about was that his job had just gotten a whole lot harder.

These simians weren't actually cheerful happy outdoorsmen. Or they probably were, but they weren't *only* that. They'd obviously been playing their cards close to the chest with the embassies for quite a while. There had to have been humans here and there who'd had higher level contact, but who really listened to that kind of loner?

Today White-hair had decided to go all in. And unless chan Rahool had drastically mistaken something, she was doing it because some really big bluish fish had told them it was a good idea.

Also, she wanted to start colonizing the new universes. Not just move to open jungles in near universes but, if he understood the images right, the White-hair gorilla matriarch wanted tribes of simians moved to the furthest outbound universes bordering Arcanan held worlds. Chan Rahool's mind boggled. None of the simians he'd worked with had ever expressed any interest in leaving Sharona. Sure, some clans were established in nearby universes, but those resettlements had been done on human initiative. He helped the Minarti exchange messages with Minarti sister clans on New Sharona from time to time, but they hadn't seemed to understand when he'd told his chimps about the human war with Arcana. He'd only told them because in his worst night-mares the Arcanans managed a strike deep enough to threaten the simians too.

He hadn't thought they even really understood the concept of other universes. But someone must have figured it out, because White-hair had given him a perfectly clear view of the outbound Sharonian portal.

Chan Rahool vaguely remembered a training lecture mention-ing a few early portal exploration crews who'd taken a pair or two of higher order monkeys with them for deep explorations. It had been one of things he'd disregarded when none of the groups he was assigned to had any interest in multiverse travel.

He rubbed his throbbing head. This was going to be an impossible report to write up for the CSE. So he didn't.

Instead he dashed off a note to Dorrick, who was over with the Nishani chimp clan. Technically, Dorrick was the senior chimp ambassador. There was even a CSE org chart that said chan Rahool reported to him, and chan Rahool grinned evilly to himself at the thought. It was amazing how useful military training could be.

A carefully detailed report, complete with a requisition for more cheese, was folded up and stuffed in the mailbox with Dorrick's name written in bold print on the front. Of course the mail was only taken twice a month when the postal Flicker snatched everything in the box out to the depot, and at the depot they'd sort it and wait another two weeks before sending it on to Dorrick with the routine mail. If Dorrick even read it, chan Rahool would have two more weeks before anything could go back out to the depot and be rushed priority up to CSE.

He felt it was only fair to leave the CSE in the dark for another six weeks. The bureaucrats with no field experience continually tried to claim simians couldn't tell the difference between sweet tree-ripened and cheaper green-picked fruit. They deserved to be left to rot. All they could do was try to stop him, and Soolan chan Rahool did *not* want to be the one to tell that steely-eyed gorilla matriarch he'd elected not to deliver her message because some bureaucrat didn't understand the need.

Chan Rahool didn't understand it either, but White-hair hadn't been much interested in his comprehension. She'd been more concerned about his recall, and after testing that aspect of his Voice Talent with a few memories of what could only have been her great grandbabies bounced back and forth, he'd gotten the distinct sense that he'd passed.

And earned a massive headache. So many pictures, so quickly, and with such intricate detail...they'd hurt. He'd played them back in slow motion and the pain had eased.

White-hair had expressed herself satisfied and had directed him to present these images to his human White-hair. Chan Rahool had thought immediately of Emperor Zindel and the impossibility of a low-level simian ambassador getting a hearing with the Emperor of Sharona.

White-hair had cuffed him lightly and rattled his head. She'd refused to believe humanity could be other than a matriarchy. She'd given him a picture of Empress Varena instead.

How did they know what the empress looked like? The picture was a bit old, but still!

His attempt to explain the difficulty in seeing the empress had been met with Tusk snarling in his face. His old noncoms could have taken lessons from the gorilla.

The report to Dorrick double-checked and tucked carefully into the postal box, chan Rahool set out to arrange a meeting with the Empress Consort of the known Sharonan universes.

He might have had the makings of a soldier after all.

*   *   *

At the heart of the known Arcanan universes, Garth Showma celebrated winter as only Andarans could: with marches, ice dances, and dragon flights over the frozen falls. Snowfall Night, when the faculty and students of Garth Showma Institute filled the fall's basin with floats and hung the sky with faerie lights, drew crowds even from Mythal and Ransara.

Her Grace Sathmin Olderhan capably arranged it all each

year, and this year was no different... in that respect, at least. There were plenty of other differences, unfortunately, all of them revolving around the hideous news which had reached New Arcana less than two weeks ago.

The only good news was that Jasak was alive and unhurt. Which, she had to admit in her fairer moments, was far more important than anything else. But every other word of the terse hummer reports from Governor mul Gurthak in Erthos about events in the universe which had been—all too aptly for her taste—christened "Hell's Gate" had only made the unmitigated extent of the disaster clearer and clearer. That contact with another human civilization, after more than two centuries of inter-universal exploration, should have ended in massacre and carnage was bad enough. The news that Arcana's newly acquired enemies possessed some new, bizarre, and very deadly technology of their own only made it worse. But worst of all, *her* son had been caught in the middle of it—had been the officer whose command first encountered these "Sharonians" and fought the first battle with them.

The public—predictably, in Sathmin's opinion —had reacted to the news with mingled shock, fear, and ferocity. And after digesting Two Thousand mul Gurthak's report, she couldn't really blame the man-in-the-street for reacting exactly that way. Unfortunately, the official dispatch from mul Gurthak differed in several critical particulars from the private message which had already reached Sathmin and her husband from Jasak. There were no aspects of mul Gurthak's report which *contradicted* Jasak's account, but there were certainly some very significant differences of emphasis. Nor had the two thousand's dispatch made any mention of Jasak's decision to declare the two surviving Sharonian prisoners his *shardonai*... or of the reasons which had impelled him to do so. And she knew her husband had cherished some dark suspicions about the reason Jasak's private message had reached New Arcana almost a full week before the governor's *official* dispatch. Given the hummer priority accorded to official messages, if there was a discrepancy in arrival times, mul Gurthak's report should have arrived *before* Jasak's, not after it.

Thankhar had decided to adopt a wait-and-see posture, and Sathmin hoped it had been the right call. It wasn't that she thought they had any other option—the plain truth was that they didn't *know* much more about events than anyone else in the Union's government—but she *hated* the waiting. And she hated the murmurs already floating around where people thought she wouldn't hear about them. While mul Gurthak had expressed his personal approval of Jasak's actions and decisions under the circumstances as Jasak had then understood them, not everyone else agreed. For that matter, even mul Gurthak's approval had been qualified by those deadly words "under the circumstances."

Sathmin Olderhan had not been the Duchess of Garth Showma for over thirty years without learning to read between the lines of official statements and recognize the hidden daggers wrapped in carefully chosen turns of phrase. And mul Gurthak was *sha-kira*. That was more than enough to set her every cat's whisker of suspicion aquiver under the best of circumstances, which these most definitely were not. And much as she loved her husband, he was Andaran to his toenails. He would *not* launch any sort of preemptive defense of his son until he knew to his own satisfaction what had happened, and that was enough to drive even the most loving wife to screaming distraction...at least in the privacy of her own mind. Besides—

Enough, she told herself firmly. *Thankhar's right. You can't do anything about it until you know more, and nothing you can do is going to get Jasak back home one second sooner than he'd get here anyway. And whatever* else *happens, you still have a Snowfall Night to coordinate, so you'd better get back to doing it!*

She smiled slightly at the acerbic edge of her own thoughts, drew a deep breath, and turned resolutely back to her responsibilities.

Magister Loriethe from the college would be arriving for a mid afternoon review with a final update on the Institute's plans for the midnight grand finale, and Sir Kalivar of the Sarkhala Boy's School was begging an invitation to have his students join in the Children's March. Sathmin was inclined to grant the late addition if he'd also be willing to supervise the distribution of candy at the children's pay call.

But first she had to dress. The staff jokingly called her around-the-estate skirts and blouses "women's combat utilities." The clothes didn't have nearly enough pockets, but other than that, Sathmin didn't object to the description. In her younger days, before Thankhar, she would have gone to Snowfall just as she was, watched the endurance competitions and enjoyed camping out on the frozen ground to get the best spot for the dragon flight show. The festival was better organized now, but she also had to put up with being one of the things the people came to see. And that involved hiring a dressing assistant.

Tellemay Lissia arrived precisely on schedule—Sathmin loved that about the woman—and produced a multitude of clothes from her baggage, any of which would certainly do fine. Tellemay always produced outfits that fitted the occasion and Sathmin was blessed with spending no more time deciding what to wear than her husband did. Uniforms were a magnificent invention, in her opinion. It was a pity most women—even in Andara—positively rebelled at the idea of all wearing the same thing. Until Sathmin managed to convince her fellow officer's wives to adopt some manner of civilian uniform, however, she could always depend on her capable dresser.

"Delightful to see you again, Your Grace," Tellemay said. "I've found the perfect things for you today. The absolute perfect! Classic pre-Hathak period reimagined with softened lines and in all the newest colors." The dresser gave Sathmin a measuring look and added, "And yes, I've added pockets. Small ones that don't ruin the lines. Stand just there in the middle and I'll have this fitting done for you in no time at all."

Sathmin complied, and she immediately turned her mind back to more interesting things.

The flights participating in the dragon air show had confirmed. She needed to check with Corilene about the repairs on the estate's second slider car. It would be needed to bring the last demo pilots from the landing grounds back to the falls after they flew their passes. The 2038th training wing had confirmed the extra dragon fodder had arrived. The full storerooms and stockyards should be more than enough to keep all the performing dragons comfortably fed.

"I didn't hear until I went to pick up the new fabric samples, but I suppose you heard with the very first hummer arrival this morning," said Tellemay as she pinned a coat sleeve.

"Pardon, what?"

Sathmin looked at Tellemay in surprise as the dresser's comment pulled her mind back from planning details for Snowfall Night. The woman usually spent these moments talking about fashion and why she'd selected the pieces presented for the day's outfit and hinting about what she was planning for events later in the year, with extra commentary about the occasions when Sathmin would be seen by senior officials or especially large crowds. Those sorts of questions could be answered almost automatically, using only a corner of her surface thoughts to monitor the process, but there was something about Tellemay's tone . . .

"Heard what Telley-dear?" Sathmin asked.

"Oh, you hadn't heard yet!" Tellemay's voice rose in delight to be first with the news. "It's the Sharonians. The truce is over!"

"What?" Sathmin stared at her, stunned by the way the news echoed with her own earlier worried. The truce was over? How? *Why?* And what was it going to mean for Jasak and—

"We're back at war," Tellemay continued blithely. "My cousins are so happy. They were afraid they'd miss it all."

"Miss it?" Sathmin felt vaguely like she'd entered some other dimension—and not one with a portal route back home to New Arcana.

"Yes, Your Grace. Miss the war. We'll trounce them all very soon, so the youngest boys will still miss it. But Ollie's a Trooper out with the Second Andarans now. His brothers are all very jealous that he'll have combat experience and the war won't last long enough for them to get any."

Sathmin placed the names quickly. Ollie Lissia was a reliable young man who'd run his father's textile shop and supplied most of the cold weather gear for the 2nd Andaran Scouts. He'd finally convinced a retired uncle to come manage the place long enough for Ollie to do a two-year enlistment.

Ransarans and Mythalans would never understand, but as an Andaran of course he'd had to do it. Family deferment or not, a well brought up Andaran boy would fight dragons bare-handed if that's what it took to do his basic service tour. And here was Tellemay, his proud cousin, delighting in the chance of her family member returning with a combat service badge on his shoulder. But—

"Are you sure about the truce?" Sathmin clutched at the hope Tellemay had misheard something.

"Absolutely sure. Everyone's been getting hummer messages all at once. They don't say what their orders are or where they're headed, of course. But the war's back on. I'm amazed you didn't hear first. I suppose His Grace was at the Commandery by the time the first hummers arrived." Tellemay paused a moment to adjust and repin a gather on Sathmin's left shoulder. "Everyone's been saying how taken by surprise they were and how the Commandery kept the secret perfectly."

"I don't understand," Sathmin said. "Are you saying *we* broke off the truce talks?"

Tellemay sniffed. "When you say it like that, Your Grace, it just doesn't sound right. I'm sure that couldn't be it. The troop letters just say we won a battle and that they're excited about the next one. The news'll say more in the morning, won't it?"

*   *   *

"They want *what*?" Shalassar Brintal-Kolmayr snapped up from her seat.

Intern Pelgra tried to melt into the Cetacean embassy floor and only managed to look more puppyish instead. *Not the kid's fault,* Shalassar reminded herself, and brushed past the young Cetacean Speaker to confront the orca at the pier herself.

<*What have you taunted this silly intern with, Teeth Cleaver?*>

<*I?*> The black and white cetacean lifted himself for a flip above the water. <*The youngling does anything I ask. I quite like it. I would not taunt it.*>

<*Her,*> Shalassar corrected automatically. The orca had a tendency to not acknowledge genders in preadolescence, but since they didn't attribute gendered pronouns to prey either, she didn't care for the implications.

<*As you like.*> The orca flipped a smiling face above the waves. <*I merely told that girl calf I wanted to take a train migration.*>

Shalassar considered the orca's great bulk. Teeth Cleaver was significantly larger than the dolphins and porpoises who sometimes expressed interest in entering the aquarium cars to take tours of the insides of the shorelines.

<*I suppose you've also got a large-mind or two who'd like to come with you?*>

The orca snorted a cetacean laugh with his blowhole.

<*Little fish bowl trains much too small for large-minds. I will fit, just, if the train's migration isn't too far.*>

<*And why do you want to squeeze and 'fit, just,' for a not too far' trip?*> Shalassar countered.

<*It is practice. If it works, I will tell large-minds and they will sing you reasons.*>

This did not reassure Shalassar. *<Why can't the dolphins do this 'practice'?>* She didn't mention the porpoises. They were included in the mix of sentient cetaceans technically, but the creatures were generally significantly less bright than the dolphins or any of the larger cetaceans. Among all the intelligent sea life, the whales were the deep thinkers, with the thunder-flukes especially reveling in it.

A pod of dolphins played a half mile or so distant, and Teeth Cleaver examined them for a long moment. The orca didn't eat sentients. They were always quite clear on that. But from time to time some of the cetaceans would add in a proviso.

The orca didn't eat sentients, *now.*

The dolphins had been at the pier themselves just an hour or so previously enjoying some of the fish treats provided by the Cetacean Institute. But just this minute, they found reason to play farther away. Teeth Cleaver's presence had nothing to do with it. Of course.

<You see them,> Teeth Cleaver said. *<I see them. They swim, swim, swim always away.>*

<But they can see just fine themselves. What can you do on a train that they can't?>

And why are the thunder-flukes interested? Shalassar added, only to herself.

<I,> Teeth Cleaver said, *<can be orca.>*

Shalassar stopped unable to refute this unassailable argument.

Teeth Cleaver blew a fine mist and settled deeper in the water, all but vanishing. *<I am black.>* He spun beneath the water displaying the clean milky belly that would camouflage him from below. *<I am white.>* He burst out of the water for a high twisting leap. *<I am powerful!>* The splash sent ripples racing in all directions. *<They>*—he snorted a derisive splatter of water in the direction of the pod—*<are merely gray.>*

Shalassar wiped the spray off her face. Cetacean Speaker Talent granted the ability to hear, but not always to understand.

<How far do you think a 'not too far' trip would be?>

<Nine thousand one hundred and eighty miles,> Teeth Cleaver replied promptly. *<Round migration trip.>* He added, *<But for practice, train does not swim away on the rails. I go on stopped train. And train stays stopped as for Sings Badly and the plant roe harvest watching. Sings Badly will do math. Cal-cu-late time*

for nine thousand one hundred and eighty miles. I practice in car for this time. Next to Institute. With fish.>

Shalassar did her own mental calculation of the approximate cost to feed a full-grown orca for days on end.

<Only one orca in the car at a time,> she countered.

Teeth Cleaver agreed with a smile. *<Until large-minds sing otherwise. Only one orca in each car.>*

<Only one car,> Shalassar added.

<Only one car for practice,> the orca agreed.

CHAPTER THIRTEEN

Inkara 27, 205 YU
(December 18, 1928 CE)

IT WAS SNOWING.

The flakes came sweeping in on the teeth of a biting wind that was unusually cold, even for Fort Ghartoun. The weather was going to get worse—a lot worse—before they reached the New Uromath portal, but somehow that failed to make Namir Velvelig feel any warmer just now as the snowflakes touched his wind-chilled face like frozen kisses. Nor did the fact that he'd endured the icy snow and knife-edged winds of northern Arpathia throughout his childhood make him any happier about his current prospects. There was a reason he'd spent so few winters at home since joining the PAAF, after all. This season would not have been his choice for this little jaunt if he'd been given an option. Unfortunately, options were in short supply.

He turned in the saddle, looking behind him and down the length of the small column, and wondered if they were going to get beyond range of the Arcanans' casualty locating spells before someone who could use those spells came looking for them. He was more than a little afraid the answer would be no, but there was only one way to find out.

Of course, he pointed out to himself as he turned back to the blowing snow in front of him and resettled himself in the saddle, *you could always avoid the possibility entirely by simply cutting the bastards loose. Let them evade their own damned army on their own damned terms while you and the rest of your boys skedaddle on your own. Their locator spells wouldn't help them find* you *that way, at least!*

No, they wouldn't. And despite everything, a hard, hating part of him hunkered down, hunched its shoulders, and wanted to do exactly that. But he couldn't, and not simply because Ulthar and Sarma and all of their men had put their necks on the chopping block to rescue what was left of his own command. He might find it difficult to disassociate them in his own mind from the Arcanan sneak attack, yet that attack hadn't been their idea. They'd simply been carrying out the orders they'd given by their lawful superiors, and the Arpathian in him recognized the enormous risk they'd taken by mutinying against those superiors because they believed honor required it of them. And however much he might hate Arcanans like Hadrign Thalmayr and whatever motherless bastards had launched the entire attack, he couldn't deny that the mutineers had acted with decency at enormous risk to themselves.

And that was one reason he needed to get them out of this just as badly as he needed to get his own men out of it. Whether, when, and where he might be able to regain contact with higher authority, it was important for that higher authority to have the window into the Union of Arcana and its military represented by Ulthar Therman and Jaralt Sarma. If the young officers were correct that they'd been deliberately lied to and manipulated by their superiors—and if the "Kerellian Accords" and the standing military law of the Union of Arcana Army truly did prohibit the sort of systematic torture which had been inflicted by the "Arcanan Expeditionary Force"—then it was entirely possible the actual *government* of Arcana genuinely didn't have one godsdamned idea what was happening out here.

That was a staggering concept, one any Sharonian could be excused for finding difficult to grasp. Yet if the hints he'd gotten about just how far it was to Arcana from Hell's Gate turned out to be accurate, and given that this was an entire civilization which had never heard of Voices, it was actually possible. It was almost—*almost*, but not quite—impossible for Velvelig to imagine a civilization which didn't have the ability to pass messages at Voice speeds. It wasn't a lot harder than accepting that magic really existed, however, and if that *was* what had happened, if this entire invasion was essentially a rogue operation launched without the authorization, consent, or even *knowledge* of the Arcanan government, it put a completely different face on what had already happened . . . and suggested a completely different list of options for dealing with it.

Maybe.

On the other hand, it might turn out that the Arcanan government would decide to stand by the actions of its commanders on the spot. And it might also turn out that things had gone so far by now that there was no way back for either side, much less both of them. But if there was the remotest chance this rolling catastrophe could be . . . turned off—*stopped* somehow—then Namir Velvelig was entirely prepared to die trying to bring that about.

Not that he had any intention of dying if an alternative offered, which was the reason they were heading out across the mountains of West New Ternath into the teeth of winter.

There were, however, some unforeseen advantages to having magic on *his* side for a change. Some of the Arcanans' crystals seemed to contain a bewildering array of spells, almost like a magical version of the famous Ternathian Army pocketknife, with its blade or folding tool for every conceivable purpose. Others contained only a single type of much more powerful spell, or perhaps two of them, but with multiple uses of each stored spell. He'd been astonished—and deeply envious—when Fifty Ulthar demonstrated one of the levitation spells. It wasn't that Velvelig had never seen an object invisibly lifted before; one of his own cousins was a Lifter, with a powerful Talent that allowed her to Lift more than twenty times her own body weight unassisted. It required focused concentration, however, and she could only sustain the Lift for about thirty minutes before she was required to rest and recuperate. But the crystal Ulthar had fitted under the center of one of the PAAF wagons left behind at Fort Ghartoun had lifted the entire vehicle effortlessly into the air and held it there until the spell was deactivated.

The standard PAAF wagons were of all-steel construction, which made them much lighter than wooden-framed vehicles would have been, and fitted with heavy-duty axle bearings, leaf springs, and forty-three-inch wheels with tubular steel spokes and wide pneumatic tires, which allowed them to tackle even extremely difficult terrain. They were sized to allow a standard four-mule team to haul fourteen thousand pounds of cargo on a hard-surfaced road and up to half of that across soft terrain, but they were still wagons, and rough going could slow them to a crawl, even with the best draft teams imaginable. The possibility of boosting them almost effortlessly over the worst obstacles was enough to turn any PAAF quartermaster green with envy, and according to Ulthar, a single spell crystal could support up to fifteen tons of deadweight for up to forty-eight hours on a single charge. Not only that, each crystal could contain up to thirty charges. Apparently, when the Arcanans used dragons for transportation, they relied on even more powerful levitation spells, which probably explained a lot about how flying beasts could support the logistic needs of an army capable of advancing across even the roughest terrain with preposterous speed. The levitation spells available to the garrison of Fort Ghartoun offered nowhere near that sort of capacity, but they were going to make an enormous difference to the more pedestrian, ground-based transport of the unlikely allies, especially given the topography they were about to face.

Other specialized crystals offered advantages of their own. One of them, for example, provided the warmth (although not the light) of a roaring bonfire from a piece of rock no larger than a child's fist. The amount of heat it could produce when what Velvelig thought of as "the wick" was turned all the way up was astounding, and at lower temperatures it could produce that warmth for hour after hour. Given the weather and the travel conditions awaiting them, that might well prove the difference between life and death.

Still, marvelous though the Arcanans' magic was, it had its limits. Many of their army's crystals, like the ones he thought of as the Ternathian Army knife, appeared to be designed (if that was the right verb) to be used by anyone who knew the activating sequence. The more powerful, more specialized spells, however, required a Gifted user, which resulted in a basic "technology" with a far narrower...base, for want of a better term, than Sharona enjoyed.

Velvelig suspected that figuring out the parallels and differences between the Arcanan Gifts and Sharonian Talents was going to take a long time, but some of them had already become evident. A particularly strongly Talented Sharonian might have a single primary Talent and as many as two or even three secondary ones which were usually (but not always) in associated areas. Apparently, a Gifted Arcanan might also have more than one

Gift or "arcana," as they were labeled, but such powerfully Gifted Arcanans appeared to be less common than powerfully Talented Sharonians. At the same time, the sophisticated technology of their crystals allowed them to distribute stored spells to a larger percentage of their total population, yet not as broadly or as freely as one might have expected. The bottleneck was apparently the fact that *only* Gifted Arcanans could charge those crystals. Without a Gifted technician to recharge a crystal, it became useless once its stored spells were exhausted.

The fact that Arcanans who were not themselves Gifted could make use of the crystals was obviously a huge advantage, but Velvelig had found himself wondering if the Arcanan reliance on the marvels stored in those glittering pieces of rock wasn't its own potentially crippling weakness. Gods knew most Sharonians would have *loved* to be able to bottle Talents to be decanted at need, and an Arcanan spell might be able to accomplish things even the most strongly Talented Sharonian could only dream of doing. But Sharona's industrial technology had been developed alongside its people's Talents, specifically to be used—and supported—by people who were *not* Talented. He strongly suspected that dynamite was as effective as any Arcanan blasting spell might be, and even though a sufficient quantity of it was undoubtedly bulkier and heavier than a single crystal, workers in the factory which produced it required no special Talent or Gift. *Anyone* could learn to operate almost any Sharonian device, whether on the production floor or in the field, unlike the Arcanan spells whose use was limited to someone with at least a minimal Gift, and no one needed a Gift to charge a cartridge for a Model 10 rifle.

Sure, he thought now, *no doubt there are all sorts of advantages to good, old-fashioned Sharonian technology, but don't pretend you aren't glad to have* Arcanan *"technology" backing you up this time around, Namir!*

Well, of course he was, since he wasn't an idiot. At the same time, he'd been at least equally delighted when he got a look inside Fort Ghartoun's armory and discovered the Arcanans had neither removed nor destroyed the weapons which had been stored there. Some of those weapons *had* disappeared, presumably collected for study and analysis, but most were right where Velvelig had left them. The expeditionary force's commanders had probably planned on disposing of them one way or another whenever they got around to it, but for the moment they'd settled for locking them up securely.

He'd been a bit surprised, despite the fact that Ulthar and Sarma had agreed that the Arcanan mutineers and the erstwhile Sharonian prisoners had no option but to cooperate fully, when neither of them had objected to the PAAF personnel's re-arming themselves. It had been something of an acid test of the Arcanans' sincerity, really, since for all their crystals' capabilities, an individual Arcanan was considerably less lethal than an individual Sharonian equipped with a Model 10 and an H&W revolver. To their credit, the mutineers had passed the test with remarkably calm expressions. In fact, they were clearly as relieved to have that Sharonian lethality on their side for a change as Velvelig was to have their magic on his.

They were short on horses and mules—apparently, most of the Fort Ghartoun stud had been used to feed dragons and unicorns—but one of Fifty Cothar's responsibilities had included looking after a sizeable pool of reserve unicorns for the main expeditionary force. They'd been left at Fort Ghartoun in no small part to take advantage of the opportunity to "graze" on the more mundane draft animals which had been captured with the fort, which left Velvelig and his men with rather mixed feelings where the creatures were concerned. The fact that unicorns appeared to have fractious personalities didn't make them any happier about it, either. But if the mutineers were to be believed (and Armsman chan Dersain's Sifting Talent insisted they were telling the truth) the carnivorous unicorns were capable of incredible feats of speed and endurance. Cothar insisted that they were *routinely* capable of covering a hundred and fifty to two hundred miles *per day* even cross country. They weren't as efficient as the PAAFs powerful, big-boned mules as draft animals—not surprisingly, when those mules went to a thousand pounds each and a unicorn was little more than seven or eight hundred—but they could handle that job when they needed to. And because Fort Ghartoun had been turned into a remount depot, they had enough of them to provide teams for all seventeen of the wagons available to them and still mount all thirty-seven of Cothar's dragoons and half of Velvelig's surviving troopers.

The mutineers' total strength consisted of sixty-three infantry, most from Sarma's platoon, plus Cothar's understrength cavalry troop and the three Healers and eleven of their assistants in addition to Velvelig's surviving forty-one men. A hundred and fifty-five men fell just a bit short of an overwhelming host, but they'd helped themselves to the machine guns and the half-dozen 4.5-inch mortars from the armory, and the Arcanans had over a dozen of the crystal staffs which served them as heavy weapons. They couldn't possibly have enough firepower to stand off the force Two Thousand Harshu could dispatch to run them to earth, but they had enough to ensure that anyone who caught up with them would have one hell of the fight. And between the wagons and the saddle unicorns, they could move much more rapidly than any PAAF mounted force had ever moved before. Each of the wagons had been fitted with its winter canopy, as well—a lightweight, well-insulated shell that bolted into place and turned the vehicle into a reasonably snug hut on wheels. They were fitted with ducted flues to allow the use of coal-fired stoves, but that was unlikely to be needed with the Arcanan crystals to keep them warm.

The majority of what had been Hadrign Thalmayr's garrison had no interest in joining the mutineers' "treason," so they'd been left behind—deprived of weapons, mounts, draft animals, and the "hummers" the Arcanans used as carrier pigeons—while the fugitives decamped. Velvelig wasn't happy about the sorts of troublemaking they were likely to get up to, but he couldn't very well insist that men who'd mutinied to prevent prisoners from being tortured and killed turn around and kill their loyal fellows just to keep their mouths shut and their hands out of mischief. So, since they had to be left behind anyway, Sarma and Ulthar had been careful to "let slip" the deserters' intention to dash across the portal into Failcham.

The arid terrain on the other side of the portal was hardly inviting, but hopefully their supposed route would make sense to any pursuers. The barren desert was no picnic, but it wasn't likely to be lashed with New Ternath's bitter blizzards, either, and they could reach the Sarlayn Valley and follow the mighty river for almost six hundred miles, all the way to the Mbisi Sea. Conversely, they could keep heading east for another hundred and fifty miles until they reached the Finger Sea and cross into Failcham's version of Shurkhal. In either case, the PAAF wagons were designed for ready conversion into pontoons or even sailing craft—not, admittedly, the fleetest and most maneuverable of vessels, but surprisingly stable—which would provide fugitives with a wide option of possible destinations (and hiding places) that wouldn't be frozen solid.

Which, Namir Velvelig conceded as he felt the cold setting its teeth in his bones, actually had quite a lot to recommend it.

"I wish I didn't feel so guilty about leaving the civilians behind, Sir," Golvar Silkash said from beside him, his voice half-lost in the snow-sharpened wind sighing through the pines, and Velvelig turned to look at the surgeon.

Fort Ghartoun's garrison had been badly understrength at the time it was attacked. Unlike the Imperial Ternathian Army, the PAAF's regiments contained only two battalions at the best of times, and out here on the bleeding edge of the frontier, it wasn't unusual for a regiment to have its battalions deployed to widely separated locations. In Fort Ghartoun's case, 2nd Battalion of Velvelig's 127th Regiment had been heavily raided for reinforcements for New Uromath and Hell's Gate following the initial clash at Toppled Timber, while 1st Battalion was still somewhere up-chain from Salym, as far as Velvelig knew. There'd been no great urgency to get them forward to Thermyn prior to the confrontation with the Arcanans, and even after that, Velvelig hadn't expected their arrival for at least another month or two.

The single understrength battalion under his command when the Arcanan attack crashed over the fort had taken heavy casualties, and those casualties had been worst among its officers. Only four of them had survived: Company-Captain Halath-Shodach, Gold Company's CO; Platoon-Captain chan Brano and Platoon-Captain Tobar, who had commanded Gold Company's 2nd and 4th Platoon, respectively; and Platoon-Captain Larkal, who'd commanded 1st Platoon of Silver Company. Although Silkash outranked all four of them in terms of seniority, he was a medical officer, which meant he stood outside the direct line of command. He was ten years older than Halath-Shodach, however, and better than twice young Larkal's age, and he'd become Velvelig's executive officer, for all intents and purposes. It wasn't something Silkash and ever been trained for, but as he'd pointed out just a bit sourly, it wasn't as if the regiment really needed his services as a surgeon at the moment, since Fifty Maisyl and his Gifted healers had the magic touch—literally—when it came to medical needs. And, despite his tendency to deprecate his own competence outside sick bay, Silkash had been a tower of strength during the organization of this hasty withdrawal.

"I don't like leaving them behind, either, Silky," Velvelig said after a moment, "but it's not like we had a lot of choice. Or time, for that matter." He shook his head. "Besides, they're probably safer keeping their heads down where they are than they'd be slogging through the hills with us. Especially if Harshu's bastards turn up and run us to ground."

"I know," Silkash conceded. "It doesn't make me feel any better about it, though. And I don't like thinking about what could happen to any of them who're Talented, especially if somebody like Thalmayr decides to make examples out of them!"

"I don't like that thought any more than you do," Velvelig said. He didn't think it was likely to happen, either, though it was probably too much to ask Silkash or Tobis Makree to expect anything but the worst, given their own treatment at Thalmayr's hands. "On the other hand," he continued more grimly, "I doubt they'd be all that interested in any of the remaining Talents. It's the Voices they've been worrying about, Silky."

Silkash nodded jerkily, remembering Senior-Armsman Folsar chan Tergis. He'd been Fort Ghartoun's senior—and only—Voice, and he'd been murdered in cold blood by Alivar Neshok. That was bad enough, but Sahrimahn Cothar had confirmed that a section of Arcanan cavalry under Senior Sword Barcan Kalcyr had also murdered young Syrail Targal, chan Tergis' student and protégé. They'd been the only two Voices in or around Fort Ghartoun.

"For the most part, the best we can do for all of them is to get as far away *from* them as we can," Velvelig said. "I don't want any of them in our vicinity if it comes to a firefight."

"Understood, Sir. It's just—"

Silkash broke off with a jerky headshake that was as sharp with frustration with himself as with anything else, and Velvelig smiled slightly. It wasn't a happy smile, because he understood exactly what Silkash had just started to say. It was the PAAF's job to protect civilians. For the most part, that might consist of protecting them from fellow civilians with . . . flexible attitudes towards things like law codes and other people's property rights rather than ravening hordes of magic-wielding barbarians, but protection was still the heart of their job description. It felt *wrong* to be leaving any of them behind, and the fact that they'd have been more endangered trying to escape along with the column didn't make it feel any less wrong.

Probably wouldn't exactly be a pleasure trip for them, if we did pull them out with us, though, the regiment-captain reflected. *It's sure as hells not going to be one for* us, *for that matter!*

In theory, it was "only" about fourteen hundred miles from Fort Ghartoun to the portal to New Uromath, located a few miles west of what would have been the site of the small city (or large town, depending on one's perspective) of Wyrmach in the republic of Thanos. Unfortunately, those were fourteen hundred miles as a bird—or one of the Arcanans' dragons —might have made the trip. It would be closer to two thousand for land-bound refugees, and getting through the Wind Peak Mountains east of Bitter Lake City was going to be...unpleasant in the extreme, even with the well marked trails, the wagons' canopies, and the Arcanans' magic to help along the way.

The good news was how much tougher, hardier, and faster the unicorns were than any horse Velvelig had ever encountered. He was sufficiently Arpathian to find that profoundly unnatural and more than a little distasteful, but he was too pragmatic not to be grateful for it. With them for draft animals and mounts and with the Arcanans' levitation spells to boost the wagons across the rougher terrain, they ought to be able to make thirty or forty miles per day even through the mountains and probably up to a hundred miles a day once they were clear of the Wind Peaks. At the best speed they could manage, though, it would take them over two weeks just to reach Bitter Lake City and—hopefully—get beyond the range at which the mutineers' locator spells could be triggered by their pursuers.

The question, of course, was whether or not they'd *have* two weeks.

Only one way to find out, I suppose, he thought now, turning to face back into the snowy wind. *If I were a betting man, I'd probably bet against our pulling it off. Fortunately, Arpathians are so lousy at math that we don't have a clue how to calculate odds.*

CHAPTER FOURTEEN

Darikhal 9, 5053 AE
(December 28, 1928 CE)

HOWAN FAI STRAIGHTENED HIS JACKET FOR THE CONCLAVE, even though it wasn't quite time to head down to the Chancellery. With so few staff traveling with them, he'd prepared first and given his father more time to breakfast. Their few staff had been supplemented, but Howan and his father didn't know these new servants well. And neither did he know their loyalties.

The fact that it had also given him an excuse to avoid breakfast himself was something he'd chosen not to mention to anyone, including his father. Howan Fai had never been the hearty early morning eater his father was, but he had even less appetite than usual this beautiful sunlit morning.

Not when he knew that within the next few hours Andrin Calirath would be betrothed to a man who would do everything in his power to kill her in childbed.

At the moment, King Junni's boots rested on the floor, brushed to a high gloss. The man himself was ruining the press on his court garments by leaning out the windowsill with bits of sweet roll and calling to the birds.

The cheery sounds of vibrant Tajvana covered up any answering hoots or caws the local birds might have made.

"He thought he saw the falcon called White Fire, Highness." Munn Lii explained.

Crown Princess Andrin's imperial peregrine falcon might have flown by the window, but Howan Fai doubted Finena would care to eat breakfast crumbs. He speared a sausage and offered it to his father instead.

They hadn't packed birdfeed. A trip to Tajvana hadn't called for it, but on any normal trading route, King Junni's staff would have provided several trunks of the stuff. The high northern ranges were tough country for any creature, and it was an article of Uromathian faith that a good man returned value to nature for the beauty it gave him. Sharing some seeds with the birds in exchange for the rough fodder the horses consumed along the old caravan ways was as natural to an Eniathian as breathing.

And it was the same on the seas that were home to Eniathians of Howan Fai's mother's branch. The continental shelf was favored by hundreds of bird species, and he often thought his mother knew the names of every single one of them.

Nothing native to Uromathia compared to an imperial Ternathian falcon, of course. Eniath's few inland fortresses and cities did boast many fine falconers and had developed several lines of the fierce birds, but the Ternathian falcons were something more. Still, the study of lesser birds only increased an Eniathian's natural appreciation of the remarkable imperial falcons, and—

King Junni let out a whoop just piercing enough to carry over the city's noise. A blur of silver-white feathers passed by the window before Howan Fai could get a good look, but the satisfaction on his father's face when he pulled back inside confirmed exactly which bird had snatched the last breakfast sausage.

"My son—"

Tears shone in King Junni's eyes, and a flush colored his cheeks that had nothing to do with the exertion of leaning too far out of an upper story palace window. Howan Fai's father wrapped his son in a tight hug.

Pure plainspoken Eniathian-dialect Uromathian rolled off the tongue with the natural open vowels common to the Arpathian wilds. But King Junni spoke barely above a whisper, not in Uromathian, but in thick north country Arpath.

"My son, I think Sharona needs us."

Howan Fai held tight to his father, listening hard. Too many nobles at the Conclave interpreted King Junni's lack of Ternathian language ability as a sign of lacking wits. A prince raised by that king understood it as merely the natural result of a political choice made in his grandfather's day.

"Understand I do not know this," the king murmured. "I do not have any message. I do not have any promises. But I have my guesses, and I need to be sure you are ready, just in case I am right.

"My son, my heir, could you marry the eldest daughter of the Winged Crown's clan chief?"

Shock at the question froze Howan Fai, but he quickly recovered and answered with a nod and a tighter squeeze. If his father was avoiding proper names, *he* wouldn't be the one to say "Ternathia" or "Crown Princess Andrin" out loud.

"You meet the requirements of the agreements between the clan chiefs of clan chiefs." The Articles of Unification, Howan Fai translated. "If we can reach the eldest daughter, we must try."

"Did the white bird carry something?" Howan Fai couldn't hold back the question, but he did his best to pitch his voice low and muffle the words against his father's shoulder.

"No," King Junni whispered. "My audience requests with the Winged Crown were all scheduled for too late. I tried to attract the bird to send a message. Yesterday she would come but not even eat from my hand." Whitefire was well trained. "But the falcon will take food back to the high window. It left with the sausage. And my white jade ring. I trust her falconer will notice the sign."

A remarkable hope began to blossom in Howan Fai's heart. Fear for his family and the Eniathian people bristled in thorns around that hope, but still he hoped. The Ternathian Army greatly outpowered the Uromathian Empire. A direct attack—if Eniath were to be tightly aligned with the imperial house of Ternathia—would be highly unlikely. Emperor Chava was vicious and vindictive, but not a fool. Only if Eniath were to make an offer of alliance and the Winged Crown rejected it would Eniath be at extreme risk from the Uromathian Empire.

King Junni broke the hug, stepped back and clapped his son on the shoulder.

Finena would return to her perch in an alcove in Crown Princess Andrin's rooms and present that beringed sausage to a falconer or quite possibly the princess herself, before the falcon would trust eating something from an unknown hand. The white jade was, Howan Fai hoped, known to the Caliraths as symbol of the Eniath royal family.

King Junni bustled about pretending quite well that no desperate whispering had happened in that long hug. He submitted to having his clothes straightened and to the application of his boots. Rokel Lii, the king's bodyguard, refused to let the staff attempt to iron out the overrobe's creases while the king was still wearing it, so away the garment went.

More staff came and went, clearing the breakfast table. Stains from the windowsill proved too difficult to remove, and the staff changed course to press a new overrobe leaving King Junni in his underclothes in front of the scandalized Othmali kitchen staff. The garments were perfectly modest and provided more coverage than the staff's knee and elbow length uniforms, but that clearly didn't prevent them from striking at the staff's concept of how royalty should be clad.

As usual, the Othmalis pleaded nonunderstanding of Eniath-accented Uromathian, so Junni turned to gestures and communicated mock horror at his state of undress, then exaggerated pride in his physique when the youngest maid blushed. No matter how scandalized they might be—or pretend to be—there was no resisting Junni when he chose to be charming and his performance earned delighted laughter and smiles from them all.

Howan Fai was happy to see it, yet even as he smiled back at them, he couldn't put aside the internal wariness he never quite dared to relax anywhere outside Eniath. The Grand Palace at Tajvana had some servants who'd arrived with the Caliraths from Hawkwing or followed later. Some others had continued on after service under the Seneschal. Still more had been hired to support the Conclave visitors, but the ones who cared for the apartment assigned to Eniath were all of the last two categories. And however innocent they might be, some of these same Tajvanese staff also visited the apartments assigned to the Uromathian Empire each day, where they might be receiving small gifts to repeat back anything they'd seen and heard. King Junni tipped them each generously, after Eniathian custom ... and a reasonable sense of caution. A well-inclined staff would intuitively protect patrons in ways more neutral servants would not.

Howan Fai wondered if some of these would ask to follow them home after the conclusion of the Conclave. A part of the palace staffing increase would be temporary work, due to end after most of the foreign kings and princes returned home, and King Junni was an exceptionally easy royal to serve, especially when compared to some of the others in residence. Of course, any who might wish to return with them still had much to learn about Eniath and its customs. What the staff missed in their surprise about the king in his underclothes, for example, was the nature of the garments themselves.

His father had gone traditional today, with a djadja berry treated underjacket and loose trousers. The tough deep brown fabric protected a fisherman from rough barnacles and fishhooks, but it could help turn a knife too. Howan Fai wore much the same thing under his dress jacket, but with a long shirt rather than the full underjacket. Kings wore full overrobes, but princes only had to wear elaborate jackets.

King Junni joked that the first Eniathians to take to the seas hadn't stolen enough fabric to drape everyone with it, so they'd settled on only making the king wear three bolts worth of silk and treated every other bit of line or yarn they had with djadja berries to make sure the stuff would endure as many centuries as they had to wait for peace to break out again on the Uromathian subcontinent. It was only partly a joke.

Munn Lii and Rokel Lii wore uniforms of the same tough fabric a few shades darker. Howan Fai could tell the guards especially approved of their royal charges' choice of clothing today. He hoped it wouldn't be tested.

King Junni had the fresh, pressed overrobe draped over his head by a Tajvanese footman. As usual the presence of a local man reminded Howan Fai of just how short Eniathians were compared to the parts of Sharona beyond Uromathia. The footman was probably only average height for Tajvana, but he was a full head taller than the king and even Howan Fai looked eye-level at the man's chin. It did make the dressing process easier though.

Perhaps the footman would be among those seeking to follow them back to sea and to Eniath. The man could include in his list of skills a notation that he was professionally tall. And he might even not be a spy.

The clock still read too early an hour to head directly to the Conclave, and in truth Howan Fai couldn't think of a plan for how to get to Crown Princess Andrin or Emperor Zindel to point out his father's insight. If the Goddess Mother Marthea had kept direct control over humanity instead of gifting Her children with free will, a marriage between the Ternathian Empire and Uromathian Empire would peaceably unify Sharona. But the Uromathian Empire itself was only about a generation shy of dissolution. Maybe, just maybe, two generations. King Junni and Howan Fai had discussed it at length—with equally great discretion—and neither of them saw any way it could last much longer than that.

Emperor Chava, called the greatest Busar to hold the name by his scions in the Court of the Uromathian Empire, possessed the combination of attributes necessary to hold together a disparate empire through personal charisma and fear. Unfortunately, he clearly saw no reason to acquire any other attributes...or create a regime which could be held together by someone who lacked his own "gifts." Indeed, he'd dismantled—or allowed to atrophy—any tools or institutions which stood in the way of his preferred governing technique...and none of his sons and nephews possessed those skills. Nor were any of them a Calirath to hold the loyalty of an empire through the sort of personal courage and devotion to country that inspired so much patriotism in Ternathia's subjects. In part that was Chava's own fault for executing a few consorts who'd shown signs of excess independence, but the end result was ominous to consider. The possible heirs to the Uromathian Empire were all cruel enough to match their father, but none inspired the loyal following the current emperor did, and King Junni's assessment was that none of them would be able to do so, even if Emperor Chava eventually selected just one as heir and set to training him properly.

Not that Chava gave any signs of doing any such thing. The brood currently ran wild between periods of banishment or genteel confinement, seemingly arbitrarily applied. The view from Eniath provided Howan Fai with plenty of details about their various excesses, and he knew only too well how they'd modeled their behavior on their father's example. That would have been bad enough under any circumstances, but it was even worse because none of them seemed to recognize their father's internal discipline. Chava Busar was a ruthless, unscrupulous, vile, utterly amoral human being, without a trace of pity or compassion and much given to personal excess—the sort of man who never forgot an injury and would wait decades, until the time was ripe, to avenge himself. But, give Kraisan his due, he *would* wait. He understood the need to work, plan, and discipline even his own inner furies. His sons did not.

And that was the true reason Chava's example of adopting

any strategy or using any tool—no matter how hideous—had made this current Unification Treaty all but impossible. Even Chava hadn't planned it that way, and some of the daughters were reasonably rational. He'd seen a use for them and ensured they were raised to be both deeply loyal and reasonably attractive to allied powers (which meant being at least a few strides short of outright insanity), and Howan Fai suspected Prince Janaki would have been more than up to the task of managing his own household. The sons were a very different matter, unfortunately. It was they who were contenders for the throne of Uromathia, so it was they who were encouraged in excess and feral appetites by their father's example and the nature of the court he'd built.

Somehow the new Empire of Sharona would need to find a way to stabilize and restore the Uromathian Empire even as Chava continued to rule it. It would be too late to restore it after his death, but finding some way to accomplish that impossible task with Andrin married to one of Chava's sociopathic sons...

Howan Fai shuddered at the thought. She'd need guards to protect her from her husband as well as from her enemies.

Or from her *other* enemies, at any rate. And once an heir was born...

One small signet ring seemed such a paltry tool to begin a campaign to save an empire. He hoped it would be enough.

Crack!

Finena, talons grasping the edge of the still open window, flapped strong, broad wings to stay a moment on the sill. Then the imperial falcon gave a great push with those same wings and lifted away.

The ring lay on the tile floor just inside the window, jade fractured clean through. What did it mean? Was the cracked stone a sign from the crown princess? Or had it broken only when the ring dropped from the window to the floor?

King Junni twitched his overrobe quickly to settle in a flare over the ring, but it was too late.

Both the footman and the youngest maid stared at that corner of the king's robe and silence hovered for a long, still moment. But then banged fists on the doors startled everyone, turning them quickly towards the palace hall. Munn Lii flung open the door with Rokel Lii ready to shoot or skewer anyone who threatened to enter unwelcome.

A pair of Imperial Ternathian Guardsmen stood there, and other similar knocks echoed down the hallway.

"Your pardon Your Majesty. And yours, Your Highness." The guard bowed to both of them. "Some miscreant has attempted to injure an imperial falcon. If you'll allow a speedy check of the premises, we'd like to ensure the troublemaker didn't use this apartment."

Rokel Lii stepped back and translated quickly for King Junni's benefit.

The footman and maid exchanged quick glances.

"There weren't no birds here, guardi." The maid offered a quick curtsy with her lie.

The second guard flinched. Probably a Sifter, Howan Fai guessed.

"Quite. Exactly as she says, guardis. We didn't see any falcons here." The footman volunteered, making a small bow of his own.

Howan Fai thought the second guard's left eye was beginning to water. It was either that or the man had developed a sudden and unexplained eye twitch.

King Junni gestured for the guards to enter and spoke Uromathian flatly to Rokel Lii.

"Tell them I offer any bird that comes to me the remains of a fine meal, as is custom in Eniath for good luck. No harm has ever been intended."

Rokel Lii didn't have a chance to speak before one of the guards replied in the same language.

"Of course, Your Majesty," he said, then cast a glance back down the hallway as the sounds of angry shouting drew closer.

Both Guardsmen stepped quickly inside and two others appeared, bracketing a florid-faced Uromathian in heavily jeweled cloth-of-gold festival dress. The man looked more ready for a coronation than a Conclave.

"Prince Weeva of the Busars."

He introduced himself, and rudely poked a fat finger at the ribs of the closest Imperial Guard.

One of Chava's special police did trail the little party, as well, dressed in the brilliant crimson imperial uniform with father-of-pearl hilted pistols on each hip. But the specialist showed no interest in restraining his emperor's son.

Prince Weeva was the fourth acknowledged son of the Uromathian emperor, child of a now deceased courtesan, and Howan

Fai examined him critically. Weeva—they all adopted a "va" suffix to honor their father—was considered the most attractive of the emperor's boys. Which, in Howan Fai's opinion, wasn't saying much. True, the black hair almost matched Andrin's but it lacked the fine gold strands. And the sneer was most definitely unattractive.

"Dogs." Weeva spat the pejorative Uromathian term for police and snapped his fingers. "I told you I saw the cutcha's bird being lured down here." He pointed a finger at Howan Fai. "That one. The Eniath princeling did it. The coat sleeve was colored just like that."

The staff held complete silence about the recent change in King Junni's overrobe, and Howan Fai saw the maid slip farther back into the apartment out of line of sight from Prince Weeva. Reputations had been earned in the Grand Palace already, he noted.

"That hasn't been established, Your Highness." The guardsman behind Weeva tried to soothe him, while the ones who'd arrived first all but locked shoulders to prevent the Uromathian prince's entry.

"Understandable. You're just a dog who doesn't speak the Tongue of Emperors." Weeva lifted an eyebrow at King Junni. "Even if your version is horridly bastardized. I can almost smell the rotting fish guts every time I hear an Eniathian speak."

"What do you want, Prince Weeva?" Howan Fai asked.

"You." He wiggled a finger like a hooked worm. "Since you can call that bird, I want you to attend on me after the Conclave. If the cutcha picks me, I'm going to have her kill that bird. If she doesn't, I'm going to have you kill it."

The special policeman just closed his eyes and shook his head with the air of a long-suffering attendant.

Prince Weeva snorted laughter, turned to his own guard, and threw an arm around the Uromathian man.

"Did you see their faces? I want game bird recipes! Have the staff begin looking for them immediately. I want a good selection to review as soon as this dull ceremony's over. Maybe something can be done with stewed redberry, or currants, but whatever it is has to be delicious so the cutcha'll eat it before she recognizes what it was."

The four Imperial Guardsmen still stood at the Eniath apartment. Indeed, they'd *solidified* somehow, drawing together in some invisible fashion, as Weeva laughed. Their stony faces were too well trained to reveal what they might be thinking, however, and one with senior armsman stripes bowed deeply to King Junni and issued an invitation.

"Your Royal Majesty, I'd prefer to escort your party to the Conclave, if you're prepared to go." Rokel Lii translated at the king's ear.

Prince Weeva grimaced pettishly, but he nodded with brusque contempt and allowed himself to be escorted away.

"No one'll be touching any imperial falcons," one of the remaining Ternathians muttered, not far enough under his breath for politeness. He was the one with the Sifter Talent, and his expression staring after Prince Weeva indicated entirely too much confidence that the Uromathian prince intended every word of his threats.

King Junni responded to the Imperial Guardsman's tone without bothering to wait for a second translation.

"Rokel Lii, we will go. Assure them no harm will befall White Fire at our hands. And have someone tell the maid the threat has passed at least as far as down the hall."

                    *   *   *

The enormous Emperor Garim Chancellery was packed with bodies—some even as resplendently dressed as Prince Weeva. King Junni pressed right past their usual seats near the middle, halfway back from the places of high honor, and strode straight for the front.

Weeva caught their eyes and laughed, then huddled in close to Emperor Chava and began a wildly gesticulated story with arms mimicking an imperial falcon's flapping, and Howan Fai watched the emperor's face. Chava looked at them and frowned, not seeming to enjoy his son's latest antics. Whatever his other faults, Chava had finesse, and the hijinks Prince Weeva planned both lacked that and needlessly complicated Uromathia's push for greater power in the new Sharonan Empire.

Only when Chava's eyes suddenly narrowed did Howan Fai realize he and his father had reached the very front of the room... and that the Imperial Guard had let them without the smallest word of restraint.

He turned away from Chava and bowed to the Ternathian emperor. Zindel looked at him with an odd light in his eyes, and none of the astonishment Howan Fai had expected to see as the result of their effrontery. He almost faltered in surprise, but a quick touch of King Junni's elbow encouraged to him to speak.

"Your Imperial Majesty, may I have the honor of a word with the Imperial Crown Princess?"

"Yes!" Delight filled Emperor Zindel's face. "Why, yes, you may."

Then the princess was there. Andrin, face tilted down towards him with a hopeful lift on her mouth, reached out and took his hands. He started to speak, still not sure exactly what he meant to say, but she overrode him before he could open his mouth.

"I need to marry you," she whispered urgently. "Will you do it?"

Howan Fai was a prince. Of a small kingdom, perhaps, but still a prince, born and bred to the job and well trained in its responsibilities. That was the only reason his eyes didn't flare wide and his mouth didn't drop open in astonishment and disbelief. Instead, he dipped his head in a courteous nod, as if that was exactly what he'd expected to hear, although he suspected the light blazing in his own eyes gave that notion the lie for anyone who could see it.

"Of course!" he replied in the same whisper and kissed her hand. "I can imagine no greater honor. When?"

"Now." She squeezed his hands tightly. "Father will see to it. But we marry now, in front of the Conclave, where no one can challenge the validity. Are you ready?"

"Absolutely."

He released her hands to press a fist to his heart, bowing as if they'd exchanged the merest pleasantry, then stepped back beside his father as Andrin and Zindel continued to their places on the dais at the heart of the Conclave chamber. Shamir Taje accompanied them and waited while they took their seats before continuing himself to the podium at the lip of the dais and reaching for his gavel.

That gavel rapped once, twice, three times, the sharp sound cutting through the muted burr of conversation. Stillness fell—a taut, singing stillness—and he cleared his throat.

"The Conclave will come to order," he said calmly into the silent tension.

The first councilor's smooth, unruffled control of the packed Conclave's members and their invited guests soothed Howan Fai's jangled nerves. But he also knew that in the next few moments he'd pass beyond the level where enmity from fools like Prince Weeva mattered and attain in its place a personal enemy in the ruling emperor of the Uromathian Empire.

The rest of the opening ceremonies, unavoidable even here, on this day, flowed past him in a blur. He tried to concentrate enough to pay attention—he truly did—but Andrin's whispered words replayed themselves in his head again and again, drowning out everything else while he grappled with his astonishment and tried to sort out the wild mix of surprise, joy, determination, and fear. He hadn't made a great deal of progress by the time the inevitable ceremonial was completed. And then—

"Lords, Ladies, please stand for the commencement of the Conclave. I present the Imperial Crown Princess Andrin Calirath, Heir to the Winged Crown and the Empire of Sharona."

Taje's words snapped Howan Fai's whirling brain into sudden, razor-sharp focus, as if he'd just hurled a bucket of icy water into the prince's face. The young Eniathian stiffened and the huge chamber went deathly silent. A quarter of the room turned towards the knot of Uromathian imperials, but Emperor Chava said not a word.

Andrin stepped up beside the first councilor and called out in a loud, clear voice:

"I am here to complete the unification of the Empire of Sharona, to meet the requirement of the Articles of the Unification, and to marry a Prince of Uromathia. I present to you my choice of consort: Prince Howan Fai Goutin of Eniath."

She held out her hand, and Howan Fai rose, the sound of his feet loud in the deafening stillness as he crossed to the dais. He made himself walk slowly, calmly, and mounted the steps, bowing to Emperor Zindel as he reached the top, still wrapped in the electric cocoon of the Conclave's astonished stillness. Then he bowed again, even more deeply, to Andrin, stepped up beside her, and took her hand in his.

They turned to face the Conclave together, and its silence shattered. The sudden, surging thunder of cheers as the Conclave's members came to their feet was deafening, rolling up like the sea, pressing against Howan Fai's face, and Andrin's, like a powerful wind. It was a storm, a tempest whose like he'd never imagined in his wildest dreams, and Finena on Andrin's shoulder added her own piercing war cries to the tumultuous cheering.

The response from Emperor Chava was absolute silence.

*   *   *

Andrin looked across at Howan Fai, her prince—about to become her husband—and breathed a deep sigh of relief. The secret had held!

Chava Busar, three rows back, and cosseted all around by his Uromathian courtiers, had earlier taken a seat with his sons rather than at the higher place his imperial precedence ranked. Now those other, unchosen princes stood frozen in the tumult of the cheering nobles. Rage and envy marked some of their faces, but the dominant emotion was fear, perhaps even terror, and every one of their sidelong glances tracked towards their father.

The Emperor of Uromathia, however, wore a calm, pleasant expression. He simply waited while the wild cheering spent its strength, the Conclave members seated themselves once more, and something like silence returned, then rose from his own chair, standing to seek recognition from the Conclave's Speaker.

Shamir Taje stepped back to the podium and tapped his gavel once, sharply.

"The Chair recognizes the Emperor of Uromathia," he said calmly, and a fresh, even tauter tension gripped the great hall.

Andrin more than half expected a screaming rant to disrupt the Conclave—expected him to denounce her choice, demand she wed one of his sons, whatever the exact language of the treaty—but he simply nodded courteously at Taje's response, and his voice was as calm as his expression when he spoke.

"I crave the Conclave's indulgence," he said then, "but I would seek a point of clarification." His smile was just a bit tighter, showed just a bit more tooth, than the rest of his expression, but he had himself well in hand and his control was formidable. "No one disputes Her Imperial Highness' right to choose any husband she wishes from the list of appropriate candidates, yet it was my understanding that the treaty provided that this wedding was to be between the royal houses of Ternathia and Uromathia."

He raised his eyebrows calmly and politely, and Taje nodded gravely.

"The House of Fai *is* a royal house of Uromathia, Your Majesty," he replied. "If you will review the actual language of the treaty, you will find it specifies a marriage between the heir to the Winged Crown and a princess—or, in this case, a prince—of Uromathia. Her Imperial Highness was presented with a list of *all* royal princes of Uromathia and, after much thought and serious reflection, made her choice."

"I see."

Andrin braced herself afresh for the inevitable denunciation, but Chava only stood for a moment, head slightly cocked, like a man considering a new, unexpected, and mildly interesting insight. Then he nodded to Taje.

"I see, indeed," he repeated. "Clearly"—despite his calm voice, his brief smile was colder than a dagger's blade—"I was operating under a misapprehension, and I thank the Speaker for the clarification."

The silence was deafening as he resumed his seat, and Andrin heaved a huge mental sigh of relief. She could hardly believe it, even now, but Taje and her father had been right. Chava Busar was as calculating as he was ambitious. The Conclave's thunderous response showed only too clearly how the rest of its members would respond to any tirade on his part, and the letter of the treaty was against him. It said exactly what Taje had just said it did. If he protested now, tried to set aside her choice, it would only make him look ridiculous and petulant. Worse, it would make him look incompetent by simply emphasizing his failure to recognize the ambiguity of the language he himself had insisted be inserted into the treaty. And, worse yet, it was entirely probable that that treaty's other signatories would not hesitate to enforce it anyway—by force of arms, if necessary—and his empire could never stand against an entire world united against it.

No, he'd been outmaneuvered—for now, at any rate—and the Emperor of Uromathia would not allow the fury consuming him behind that calm façade to betray him into a disastrous false step. He'd make no political moves until he'd had time to think, time to find a response which benefited him. But he'd remember this moment—not simply as a political defeat but as a personal, unforgivable insult to his dignity—forever. She shivered at the thought and looked away from him, searching for King Junni, her soon to be father-in-law.

The short, stocky king of Eniath rewarded her with a brilliant smile. Good! He did understand what was going on, and even better, he approved! The white jade ring was missing from his finger, but Finena chose that moment to leap from Andrin's shoulder and fly to King Junni.

The Eniathian king lifted his forearm to grant the imperial falcon a perch, which, wonder of wonders, the bird accepted. Finena might shred that fine overrobe with a brush of her beak or an injudicious talon scratch, but the sheen of King Junni's sleeve looked like he'd come prepared.

Howan Fai's warm hand squeezed hers.

"Sister of White Fire, your falcon has a new admirer."

"Yes. Your father's been sending her jewelry." She returned the squeeze. "It was a lovely gesture. I'm glad the guards were fast enough getting to you. Emperor Chava's retinue made a fuss, and I thought we'd been found out too early."

Howan Fai lifted her hand to his lips. "Not found out. Only Prince Weeva saw, and he didn't know what he'd seen. So he came to make threats rather than telling his father."

"Threats that should concern us?" Andrin tensed.

"No. Not any more. The emperor, his father, won't let him act. We'll face more intelligent enemies now."

"What was it he threatened?"

"Finena." Howan Fai gave a minute headshake. "Prince Weeva's a fool. White Fire would eat out his eyes before he could even unsheathe a meat cleaver for the game roast he threatened."

Andrin's falcon stretched wide her wings at the sound of her name, but stayed settled on King Junni's arm.

There'd been no arrangement made for a translator, and she'd just stolen Howan Fai who usually performed those duties at the Conclave, but King Junni made small hand motions encouraging her to move along to stand in front of the priests and begin the wedding ceremony.

Andrin locked fingers with Howan Fai, and they took their places at the center of the dais. Acolytes summoned from the Temple of Saint Taiyr marched braziers of incense up and down the aisles of dignitaries. Devotees of Vothan, Shalana, and Marnilay, originally present to bless the assembly, came forward, and followers of Tryganath, Marthea, and Sekharan were sent for to serve as the gods' witnesses for each of the six members of the Twofold Triad.

"We need a Uromathian priest, as well." Howan Fai spoke in her ear, and while his lips never even twitched, his dark eyes smiled as he nodded to an elaborate tapestry of Bergahl the Just in his incarnation as Vindicator.

"Of course," Andrin said, then caught her father's eye and inclined her head towards a familiar round figure. Who better to serve as senior officiant than the highest priest in Tajvana—the Seneschal for the Order of Bergahl?

"My friends," Emperor Zindel's powerful voice rolled out across the chamber, "I realize this may seem a bit sudden, but—"

*   *   *

This was... it was...

Whatever it was, Raka couldn't call it Just. The sudden changes in what everyone had expected to happen had surprised everyone in the Emperor Garim Chancellery, including Raka, and it had only gotten worse from there. The crown princess had selected her Uromathian prince, but it was just the Prince of Eniath, not a relative of Emperor Chava at all. That was a sufficient affront to Raka's sense of what was right and proper, but it hadn't ended there. Oh, no! Not content to simply announce the betrothal, Emperor Zindel had announced a *wedding*, as well. Now. *Immediately*, before this cloud of court-dressed nobles. And he'd called on His Eminence, Raka's master, to serve as one of the officiants.

Clergy for all six gods of the Double Triad—Vothan, Shalana, Marnilay, Tryganath, Marthea, and Sekharan—were represented as well, of course, which was another affront to Raka's sense of propriety here in Bergahl's own city! Not that anyone cared what *he* thought. Now each deity had at least one priest, monk, or priestess scampering down the aisles with unholy glee to join the wedding party, and it was all Raka could do not to glower openly at the uncouth horde.

He recognized the Sekharan monk Nekhaan, who wore braided rawhide for a belt even for an event with emperors in attendance. Nekhaan spent too much time among the poor and forgot the dignity of a god's servant. And if the Vothanite priest Lavo was turned out immaculately, as all of the six should have been, he still sported a muscled physique more fitting to a day laborer. The truth was that all six of the Double Triad clergy who served as chaplains to the Winged Crown were affronts to the dignity of their priestly calling in one way or another.

The Marthean priestess Thea-Nami had the gall to be leaking tears of joy. She at least sported a rotund figure befitting the wealth that came with a god's blessings, but the child-sized jam handprints at knee level were probably real. A Marthean attendant behind Thea-Nami swung ginger incense back and forth behind her mistress's steps, and Raka wrinkled his nose. Of course she was pregnant again. No doubt Marthean devotees would consider it an extra blessing on the marriage.

They were all contemptible, in oh so many ways, but what could one expect? The Double Triad clergy were simple tools, compliant in a way His Eminence the Seneschal had never allowed himself to be. They were nonentities, supremely unimportant. When one came down to it, there were three men in this Conclave who mattered, and Raka studied them, hoping to guess their thoughts.

A vein pulsed in the Holy Seneschal's forehead, Emperor Zindel smiled ever so blandly, and Emperor Chava watched, showing nothing at all. The Seneschal seemed to see something in that utterly flat expression and his steps moved faster. As a loyal servant of Bergahl's highest priest, Raka hurried after him. Raka couldn't guess what the emperors intended, but his master's response was clear.

The center dais should have collapsed into a hundred thousand splinters if the weight of the Seneschal's angry outrage had been made manifest by Bergahl in that moment.

"This is hardly appropriate." The Seneschal's protest came in the calm and measured tones of a revered church leader, and pride rose in Raka's chest. He straightened the trailing end of the Seneschal's court robe so the thread of gold showed properly.

Nekhaan, the only clergy member to make it to the dais ahead of them, looked from Raka's master to the Crown Princess of the Sharonan Empire and obviously decided otherwise. Ignoring the Seneschal, the young monk filled his lungs and shouted out the beginning of the Double Triad marriage ceremony.

"Glory to Sekharan that I am allowed this day! Praises to Him and honor to his Brother and Sister Gods!"

Nekhaan had a voice trained to carry in alleys and market-places. The amplification of a room designed for the less rough voices of kings and emperors made him sound like the voice of Sekharan himself. The lines were familiar to the many followers of the Double Triad present among the assembled members of the Conclave, and the crowd knew their response.

"May His blessings endure forever!" they rumbled back like human thunder.

Nekhaan raised his hand in benediction, beaming out across

the crowded floor. Then he glanced at the Seneschal and lowered his voice considerably.

"There's a shrine to the demon of lost causes across in the poor quarter if you want to cause trouble, Your Eminence," he said under his breath. "But this is a state wedding, and it will be held in all honor if I have to skewer you with one of your own knives."

From still halfway up the north aisle came the next line in the liturgy:

"Thanks to Tryganath that this joy should fall to me! Praises to Him and honor to His Brother and Sister Gods!" Tryganath's priest had a powerful voice too.

"May His blessings endure forever!" the crowd gave back, and Finena added her own loud cries in emphasis. His Eminence the Seneschal cringed at the falcon's cries. Raka wished Emperor Zindel had at least had the damned bird caged for the ceremony.

"Reverence to Marthea that I live in this moment!" Thea-Nami reached the dais and achieved a creditable soprano roar. "Praises to Marthea and honor to Her Brother and Sister Gods!"

"May Her blessings endure forever!"

Thea-Nami took her place, completing the opening liturgy which honored the Veiled Triad, and the Seneschal shifted in frustration, curling the edge of his train. Raka straightened the fine cloth again and retreated to the back of the dais.

All eyes were on the Seneschal, and Raka almost laughed aloud when he realized the reason for the growing silence.

This point between the Veiled Triad's invocation and the Elder Triad's invocation was when other gods and goddesses included in a Double Triad ceremony were invoked—or not—by their respective priests and priestesses. And the Seneschal obviously intended not to. His master would refuse to officiate at the ceremony by not invoking Bergahl. It was a dignified way to object, and Raka imagined explaining it to some of the less devoted Order worshipers who'd begun to be overawed by the Caliraths. His Eminence the Seneschal could not bless a union so newly announced. It was concern for the young crown princess that stayed his hand, his priestly concern that she be properly counseled and instructed before taking this monumental step. Yes, that would strike the right note to remind the people of Princess Andrin's youth and her obviously few years of experience with the elements of high statecraft. The Seneschal only needed to remain disapprovingly silent to stop this entire outrage in its tracks and remind all the world of who truly held power in Tajvana, the Queen of Cities.

Raka watched his master take in the whole crowd who moved restlessly, waiting on words he was sure the Seneschal would not speak. The paper notes for the carefully drafted blessing of the crown princess' betrothal to a son or nephew of Emperor Chava were still in the Seneschal's right hand. His master crumpled them, deliberately. Only the first few rows could hear the sound, but Emperor Zindel and Empress Varena sat in those rows.

Someone whistled softly and Raka began to enjoy the growing sense of embarrassment he thought he could detect in Empress Varena's increasingly colorless face.

Nekhaan said something to Lavo, but it was too low voiced for Raka to make out. The silence stretched, ringing in the stillness—

And then Finena, the crown princess' bird, chose that moment to fly from King Junni's shoulder. The bride and groom kneeling on the dais facing all seven representatives of the gods leaned together, and Howan Fai kissed his bride. Just quickly and lightly, but the Conclave took the opportunity to cheer. And in that distraction, the crown princess whistled sharp and clear to her falcon.

The bird spread its wide wings, circled the dais, and in a lightning fast dive ripped the prayer notes from the Seneschal's hand before settling—not back on the crown princess' arm or even at King Junni's side—but on the Seneschal's own shoulder.

Raka stared in horror as his master stood frozen. Lavo and Nekhaan, with a few low voiced exchanges that sounded far too much like laughter, clamped themselves on either side of the Seneschal and retrieved the notes, while Raka's master stood unmoving in terror and the falcon watched. Raka couldn't read an expression in the feathered head, but that wicked sharp beak gleamed inches from the Seneschal's eyes.

"Bergahl honors this union." Lavo read out in a loud carrying voice. "As Bergahl is Just, so is this completion to the Articles of Confederation. Blessings of glory, honor, and wisdom on the Prince of Uromathia chosen this day to wed our own Crown Princess—"

The words continued and Raka stood as frozen as his master. They were exactly the words on the papers, but they'd never been intended for this!

Sparing the Seneschal nothing, Lavo read every word with
Nekhaan holding and turning the pages. Then the three Elder
Triad gods had their traditional invocations. And all the while
Finena turned her feathered head this way and that, studying
the Seneschal's eyes.

All seven of the holy men and women clasped hands together,
with the Vothan and Sekharan priests giving the Seneschal no
other option, and the priestess of Marnilay pronounced the final
words.

"In the names of All Gods, Ternathian and Uromathian, we
and Sharona Entire bless our daughter Andrin and our son Howan
and join them before all people as one house. And in this holy
joining we renew our blessings on the People of Sharona and
the united Empire of Sharona. Rise daughter and son, wife and
husband, Crown Princess and Prince Consort."

The Seneschal opened his mouth, but no sound came out.

"In the names of All the Gods," the Double Triad six called
out together, "Blessings, blessings, seven times blessings!"

*   *   *

"That conniving little whore!" Raynarg snarled. "I had to bless
them. *Bless* them! While those six tridiots fawned over the sanc-
tity of marriage and acted oh so delighted to preside over that
six times damned farce! She should be whipped in the streets!"

Chava Busar watched the spittle-flecked would-be holy man
with partially concealed disdain. "I'd settle for dead. In childbirth
would be appropriate, but we probably shouldn't wait that long."

Faroayn Raynarg offended Emperor Chava's sensibilities. But
the price of empire demanded using tools like the soft man in
front of him. Ternathians dismissed "His Crowned Eminence" as
a buffoon, because he was one. But Chava could use buffoons as
handily as he could men of capability. In fact, handled properly,
buffoons could be far more valuable than more capable—and
wary—tools.

"Zindel Calirath, the father, is our true enemy here, remember," the Uromathian counseled. "The girl is just his blood, and
not yet out of her teens, to boot. Trouble enough in time, but
for now she's still untrained."

"She offends me." Raynarg ignored this comment, not pausing
in his furious pacing to actually acknowledge the wisdom being
offered him. "I'll cut her. Cut her where it hurts."

Chava sighed inwardly and continued, pointing out more Calirath weaknesses that would never apply to a Uromathian imperial heir.

"Zindel's children do not compete amongst themselves for heirship, so when he lost the boy he lost his only truly trained heir. Princesses are only good for alliances. Admittedly, our bride chose poorly, but such errors can be...corrected. So, certainly, if your knives get an opportunity, kill her."

"Yes!" Raynarg clenched a fist in a manner probably meant to be threatening and collapsed into a heavily padded chair exhausted by the few minutes of pacing.

The emperor hid his personal contempt for the qualities which made the Seneschal so attractive as a tool. The man was a fat toad. He was a pure terror to small men, the flies—like those acolytes in the Order of Bergahl who wanted to serve the gods rather than enrich their order's leader—but he appeared utterly impotent against a force like the Caliraths. Yet that very incompetence was what made him valuable in Chava's present need. The Seneschal of Othmaliz would never be taken seriously by even the extremely thorough Ternathian Imperial Guard, and so a strike using his Order had a far better chance of succeeding than one might have expected from so feckless a leader. The unholy cleric just needed to be properly led.

"But Zindel is the one who stole your palace and presumes to rule us, not—at least not yet—this girl." The emperor pointed out. "*He* represents the true threat. Still, it *would* be as well to eliminate this new heir of his before he has a chance to train her as he did his son. If a chance arises, I trust your Daggers have enough sense to make a cut?" He lifted his glass in inquiry.

"Absolutely!" Raynarg slammed his fist on the table, rattling the glasses. It was no way to treat the gently aged vintage in the crystal decanter between them, but Chava had long since determined that the self-absorbed man before him only desired the finer things in life, without the true refinement to actually identify quality in his possessions.

"My informants, trusted loyalists you understand, tell me the new consort's mother has asked for a visit," he said now. "The newlyweds will hide with the Caliraths for a time. But eventually, and count on it to be sooner than later, they'll want some manner of honeymoon. The royal yacht has been sent for an overhaul. The next voyage may have the crown princess and her prince consort aboard. If they take that honeymoon by sea, they could visit Eniath."

His spies had had reported nothing of the sort, but if an imperial yacht left the harbor chances were high *someone* Zindel cared about would be onboard, and he continued the lie fluently with a fine salting of truth.

"They would be at their weakest when out of sight of land, with no reinforcements near to call. But they'll also be readiest then. I suggest your men examine the palace's harbor and its approaches. You may find some most unique Talents available to you among your newest supplicants."

Raynarg's eyes lit as Emperor Chava had expected they would. Lending the Seneschal a few exceptionally capable men was, he deemed, absolutely necessary to provide a decent chance of breaking through the Ternathian Imperial Guard. Fortunately, Zindel wasn't the only emperor capable of searching his lands for useful people and enticing them into his service. Certainly the Ternathians had an unusual number of such capabilities born to families of those already in service, but Chava suspected that came of having started the process centuries earlier and somehow managing to keep whole families in service instead of simply the young men.

Not for the first time Chava longed for a way to make slavery desirable. If he'd just been born a few thousand years earlier, he could have established a stronger Uromathian tradition for the Talented to be wards of the state. Property of the state would have been better, but his otherwise competent ancestors had denied him that possibility. When the Talents which had first arisen in Ternathia finally found their way into Uromathian bloodlines, the rulers of the kingdoms which had predated his own empire adopted many of the Ternathians' practices in order to encourage their growth. He liked to think they would have showed more wisdom if they'd realized where it would lead, and at least they'd stopped short of the more ridiculous of the Ternathian excesses, but they'd established early on that the Talented were exempt from enslavement except after conviction for certain very specific crimes. By the time of Chava's birth, those traditions were too ingrained to be overcome in a single generation. He was working on it, of course, and the empire did have the tradition of service, but something stronger than that—something which allowed the assigning of spouses and obligated apprenticeships—would be so much more useful.

Perhaps a breeding program . . . The idea intrigued him. Not all the Talents would be willing, but surely some could be enticed. And other Talents were valuable enough they didn't *need* to be willing.

But that was later. For now Chava needed to tone down the Seneschal's aspirations. A public flogging of an imperial princess would never happen. The man was a fool to even speak of it. Positions and titles must be respected or the public might come to think they could live without emperors and kings. Or even seneschals.

This had to be an assassination, and a speedy one, because the attacking team itself would never survive the Calirath response. Of this Chava approved. An emperor should be properly ruthless.

For that matter, the entire Order of Bergahl was unlikely to survive a less than fully successful attack on the Caliraths, not that Chava intended to mention that to Raynarg. And such a neat clean up would be distinctly convenient for Emperor Chava—a reality the Seneschal failed to note and which the Uromathian emperor carefully declined to reveal to him.

A certain breed of man-eating fish could be adapted to survive in saltwater and be trained to enjoy the taste of warm-blooded cetacean, but as soon as the orca became aware of their presence, that nest was as good as eaten. The Bergahldian could make for a useful toothy little fish. If Faroayn Raynarg thought of himself instead as a shark, Chava would let him continue in the delusion.

*   *   *

Drindel Usar received his recall orders two hours later— the time required for a trusted Uromathian courtier to decode Emperor Chava's orders and issue all the necessary secondary commands required to see His Excellency's will accomplished, plus a terrifying hour and a half for the Haimath Island Director of Talents to actually find the grubby Talent.

Drindel had neither updated his residency card nor filed his papers with Haimath Prefecture and thus was guilty of several small felonies. These would have to be immediately lost in governmental paperwork, because the seal on the Flicker-sent summons meant the missing Drindel Usar was required for Service to Uromathia.

No mere prison term could be allowed to stand in the way.

The director wished fervently for an option to have Drindel locked in a dank cell overnight first, but dared not report to the Imperial Court that he'd taken any action other than performing his own Service to Uromathia as expeditiously as possible. So he settled for slapping the papers in Drindel's face and storming out of the rundown dockside establishment in which he'd finally found the man.

The director left too quickly to notice Drindel's pleased mis-interpretation of the slight. In the young Talent's mind a local bureaucrat had hand-delivered his orders and left with all speed, honoring the importance of Drindel's work, while the director's silence proved the petty rules of Talent registration were beneath one such as Drindel Usar!

Drindel took great pleasure in tearing open the missive immediately. He scattered wax bits all over tavern the floor and ground some into the space between the boards for the wait staff to crawl after.

Rena would probably be the one bent down on her hands and knees. He hoped she saw the slight gleam in the wax and spent the evening on the floor picking up each little bit to gather the minuscule amount of gold fleck added to the wax of an Imperial Order.

Her father Toruph certainly wasn't going to do it. Drindel shot a dark look at the old man, but he was careful to keep his own head down and his eyes lidded. Old Toruph's arms were as wide around as some of the shark jaws adorning his tavern walls, and he'd never needed a bouncer to keep order in *his* tavern. That didn't mean he had any right to keep Rena working in the back just because Drindel was in town, though!

But he'd deal with that later.

"I am recalled to active service!" Drindel announced to no one. He lifted the papers with a flourish anyway.

He waved a hand at the stacked glasses and plates: one of everything and no matter that he couldn't eat that much and didn't care for the taste of any of the liquors available in his hometown. He dumped the drinks he hadn't touched on the floor to ensure Toruph didn't pour them back into the bottles to serve him again next leave.

"Charge these to Uromathia."

Drindel had no right to authorize anything, but his hometown had chaffed him irritatingly. And he wanted to hear all about Toruph trying to get a reimbursement from the Empire. Maybe the Prefecture could take care of Toruph for him. The man's skill with a sea spear made the usual methods too challenging.

Drindel stomped out of the tavern into the brisk evening air holding tight to his papers, but under his swagger there was an edge of disquiet. They were marked urgent, and a cold knot of fear squeezed his belly.

What if the fearful Director of Talents had found the right ear to whisper into? The island administrator might lay the blame for a slow start on Drindel Usar—instead of on the sloppy care the Prefecture provided for their elite Talents.

He forced himself to calm. No. The orders had come only on paper without a member of the emperor's special police to oversee their execution. This wouldn't be noticed.

And besides, who was the Director of Talents to be listened to? The administrator probably had just one name like most of the rest of the Haimath. Drindel was no longer just little boy Drindel, or worse, Drindel son-of-Drand. No, he was Drindel Usar—a man of rank who'd taken a second name to honor his emperor.

And he wanted to visit his mother. There should be time to see his Maman Usar, before he headed as directly and quickly as possible across the inlet to catch a night train across Uromathia.

Maman jumped to her feet and ran to see him when he knocked at the door.

She respected him, oh yes.

A dinner, a lunch, and copious extra tidbits—she pressed on him for the journey. Maman Usar had proper respect for his work and the honor bestowed on him by selection for Service to Uromathia.

As for Drand, well, his father was a long time ago.

And it hadn't been his fault, really. The way Drindel saw it, and the way he'd convinced Maman to see it, was that all of the mess truly had been Drand's own fault. The old man had been a Talent himself and never even registered: a crime. And worse, his father's Talent had been to call fish easily into the nets, despite which they'd been only a moderately prosperous fishing family. Drand should have brought them the best and largest fish every day, with never a boat trip returning with empty nets. But no, the old man had been too squeamish about the registration and always hid the Talent away.

Drindel had the better Talent. The regular fish ignored him entirely, which had seemed a deep misfortune at first, until he found that the sharks would follow him for miles and not just the little ones that got caught up in the nets.

His father, Drand, had been a criminal. That was the important part. Drindel using his Talent to teach a criminal a lesson was almost a Service to Uromathia, really.

All that had been before Drindel was old enough to formally register and have his own Talent tested. And some of the comments the Prefecture Mind Healer had made to Maman had been sadly lacking in perspective. But that man had transferred inland before Drindel's first home leave, so Drindel had never had a chance to even things up properly. Some of the locals still thought he'd been sent into Service as some kind of punishment. Drindel kept track of who said such things and who wasn't appropriately kind to his mother.

Maman had lists for him every home leave of who to teach lessons to. Everyone was very nice to her. Now.

Toruph was about the only one left who didn't make a point of greeting Maman cordially on the street and sending her things now and again to ease her troubles. His Maman deserved the best of life while her one son was off working so hard for the good of Uromathia.

A boat ride across to the mainland was easy to cadge at the docks, with half the local fishermen falling over themselves to offer him a trip across. Drindel accepted the one with the largest boat and seated himself carefully in the center of the vessel. He hated being on the water. He always tried to blank his mind as much as possible to reduce the chance of even the smallest tendril of his Talent squeezing out. It was just that he wasn't always successful.

This trip across was uneventful, for which Drindel thanked Heaven most fervently, but only in the confines of his own heart.

Outwardly, he took care to pose as if he'd known exactly what went on beneath the surface of the waves and had all the ocean's mysteries under his complete dominion.

The truth, Drindel had to acknowledge, if only to himself,

was something significantly less comforting. He could call sharks, all kinds of sharks and especially the biggest of the white ones. And the sharks would come great distances for him, even without enough food and without the energy to do more than wash up dead on the beaches once they arrived.

But they would come. He just couldn't direct them to do a single thing once they arrived. And deep down Drindel wondered if they didn't all come in hopes of finally getting a bite of him, snapping him in half with those great teeth, and tearing out mouthfuls of his liver and lungs. Those open jaws seemed like they would do anything to stop the compulsion to come, to follow, to swim to wherever he was.

The compulsions he couldn't find a way to stop sending. Drand had said the Talent could be controlled with mental exercise and should be expanded only most carefully after control was proven. The work of control had hurt and left him exhausted, though, and Drindel was now sure it had been no more than a trick his father had played on him. There was certainly no pain and exhaustion in *expanding* the summons! When Drindel unfurled his Talent, it felt like Arcunas Himself had descended from the Heavens to kiss his brow.

The euphoria was better than anything. In fact, Drindel couldn't stop calling, at least softly, even if he wanted to. And he wasn't sure he could imagine ever wanting to stop. It wasn't like the sharks should really mind. They were cold, wet, and heartless creatures.

The biggest ones would just eat the smaller ones he'd also called, so Drindel didn't feel like he really starved them all that often. It wasn't fair of them to blame him for anything, if indeed they did want to eat him.

The qualms he sometimes felt were just echoes of the foolish things Drand had said about the sea needing its balance.

But Drindel did have the nightmares. At the frazzled edges of the euphoria, where he couldn't tell real from phantasm, he sometimes saw his father. The Drand in those fever dreams wore the body of a great shark with a pale gray, almost white, skin, and it swam from sea to sea, looking for him.

That one couldn't possibly be real. But Drindel was careful never to embark on too small a boat or come too close to the side of a larger vessel. Starving sharks could do quite a lot to get at meat. Especially if his Talent let the flare of the Call get too loud.

Fortunately, this time he was summoned to Othmaliz, to the City of Tajvana, and that meant no more boats. Safe inland travel would bless him all the way to Tajvana's magnificent confluence of seas.

*   *   *

Drindel Usar picked up a tourist packet at a train station hub during the transfer to the morning train that would take him most of the rest of the way to Tajvana. From the pictures, Tajvana was a massive place.

He couldn't actually read much of the descriptions that went with the pictures, but the pictures were really all he needed to know. His orders always came in a code he'd been suffered to learn along with the basics of his letters.

Uromathia did not abide ineptitude in its servants.

But when Drindel hadn't wanted to learn more, he'd been allowed to stop his studies there. The Service instructor might have called him a fool to his face and spat at him for quitting, but what did he know?

The instructor's slight Talent in Mind Healing had been applied, quite properly in Drindel's opinion, to easing the challenge of code-based studies. That hardly made the man qualified to judge the value of the supposed literacy he also wanted to teach!

The instructor had never even seen an ocean, nor, after a disdainful look at Drindel, expressed any interest in visiting one.

Maman always said that if a thing actually mattered, everyone would be talking about it anyway, so there was no need to hurt your head learning to puzzle out words on a paper.

Drindel bent his thoughts to his work in Tajvana. It was a city built for seaborne commerce: oceans to the north, oceans to the south, a twisting strait connecting them, and inlets scattered nearly everywhere. Water meant sharks. Perhaps not the biggest, and perhaps not all the species of sharks, but there would be at least a few waiting for him and he'd Call more.

The fear in his stomach eased a bit. This might be a simple assignment after all.

He boarded his train and eased into a comfortable seat. A quick riffle through his luggage produced a pleasant breakfast from Maman's parcel, and he leaned back and let his Talent go.

Perhaps some sharks would try to fight up riverways until the lack of food and heavy currents forced them back. He didn't care. It felt too good.

Around lunchtime, Drindel finally tapered back on his Talent and dug into Maman's sack for more food. There was salted fish and the good thick bread she did best. He chewed with pleasure.

Perhaps the Tajvana job would rank among his favorites too.

It couldn't be the best though. Surely nothing could ever top that ocean prison with the very efficient warden. Drindel had only had to really work to Call the sharks for a few days. After that the warden used the condemned prisoners to keep Drindel's listeners used to legged prey. Well-fed sharks stayed and fed even better any time an escape was attempted.

If Drindel could stand just on this side of Tajvana's strait and not need to cross over while Calling, it would be an entirely safe job. It'd be just like the way he'd stood on the nice rocky beach mainland while Calling every great monster he could to that island prison. The shoals and reefs were surely bare of other fish by now, but if the warden had kept his word those sharks still weren't hungry.

Yes, that'd be good. Drindel promised himself he'd find a way not to get on a boat at all this time. *Maybe there'd even be a big crowd. Some mass of people to get bitten, tasted, and spat back out—where it didn't matter who died and who didn't. I could just Call, fill the beach waters with fins, and walk away.*

Or the people could be on boats even. Big sharks could overturn boats, and skiffs for sure. Maybe even some smallish ships if the sharks're really hungry and the big big ones.

Swimmers're always easy, but how do I get 'em in the water after a Call? Unless it was night...

Drindel pondered some more, trying to guess who his targets might be.

The instructions in the orders this time were odd. He was to present himself as a new acolyte for a religious sect and follow whatever directions they gave him. *The Order of Bergahl.* The tourist packet had a picture of a robed man wearing cloth-of-gold with the letters matching the sect's name included in its caption. He might be the boss. Drindel shrugged to himself. If he was, someone would say so.

Drindel opened up the last packet from Maman and had a nice sandwich.

CHAPTER FIFTEEN

Darikhal 10, 5053 AE
(December 29, 1928 CE)

THE SENESCHAL OF OTHMALIZ STOOD BREATHING IN THE incense, listening to the majestic music of organ and woodwinds, and the bathed in the glorious polychromatic chiaroscuro light pouring in through the Temple of Taiyr's stained glass dome and managed—somehow—not to curse.

It wasn't easy.

He held the golden staff of his high office in his right hand, but he would vastly have preferred a dagger. The memory of the previous day's insult burned deep within him, like poison, and there was only one way that poison might be purged. Yet today he had no choice but to absorb yet another insult, yet another affront to the dignity of his office, and yet another nail in the coffin of the Order of Bergahl authority here in its own city.

He'd considered—considered long and hard—pleading illness and remaining closeted in his apartments with his personal Healer. No one would have believed it for a moment, and that would have been fine with him. It would have been one way to repay at least a little of the calculated insult he'd been offered in the Emperor Garim Chancellery during that travesty of a wedding. Unfortunately, he'd discovered—or perhaps *re*discovered—just how much he truly feared those Ternathian barbarians. The unspeakable Zindel had the bit well and truly between his teeth at the moment. The Seneschal wouldn't put it past the emperor to send his personal armsmen to drag a recalcitrant cleric to the temple. After all, he'd stood there and *smiled* while his bitch of a daughter used her godsdamned bird to terrify and humiliate him in front of the entire Conclave!

Still, he would probably have dared Zindel's wrath—no, he told himself, he would *certainly* have shown his steel by defying the Calirath tyrant—if not for the message from Chava Busar.

The Seneschal knew that at least half of Tajvana was waiting, agog to see how Chava would react to the Coronation now that he'd had thirty-six hours to recover from the shock of that over-sized cutcha's scandalous, bizarre betrothal and wedding. However pleasant he might have forced himself to appear in the Chancellery, no one could doubt the bitter bile he'd swallowed as Zindel and his daughter brazenly circumvented the clear intent of the Articles of Unification. He was a proud man, Chava Busar, and one who had agreed to subordinate his own empire to this worlds-wide mon-strosity the Conclave had forged only after the interests of his own dynasty had been safeguarded. Whatever he might have chosen to show on the surface, the abrupt destruction of those safeguards in a flagrant reading of the treaty's literal language rather than its obvious intent, must have struck him like the cut of a whip.

The Order's ears were everywhere, and the Seneschal knew the betting was over three-to-one that Chava would change his tune here at the Coronation. That he would denounce the entire proceedings, denounce the treaty itself, and storm back to Uromathia. After all, he had scores—*hundreds*—of Uromathian jurists who could provide him with any number of precedents to base that defiance upon. And if they couldn't *find* the precedents they needed, they could certainly have manufactured *them* in the ensuing day and a half.

But the betting was wrong. The Seneschal's new friend hadn't shared all of his reasoning with him, but the Uromathian emperor had suggested—rather more forcefully than the Seneschal was accustomed to—that it was essential the Coronation proceed. Personally, Faroayn Raynarg considered it anything *but* essential, and he'd been very strongly tempted to tell Chava that. But only *tempted*. Given the last day or so's events, the necessity of an alliance with someone like Chava, someone with the wherewithal and...intestinal fortitude to defy even the fabled Calirath Dynasty, had reasserted itself in the clearest possible way.

And it was obvious from Chava's message that whatever posi-tion he might adopt for public consumption this day he had no intention of acquiescing in the Calirath tyranny. In the fullness of time, he would take back what was rightfully his, and in the process the Seneschal and Order of Bergahl would take back what was rightfully theirs, as well. But for now, for today, they must bend their necks and bear the unbearable—with a *smile*, gods damn it!—if they would preserve the freedom of maneuver to strike back when the time was ripe.

At least his part in the proceedings would be relatively brief. Of course, he'd have to stand here, lending his official countenance and blessing to the travesty, for *hours* before he would be able to escape. But despite his prestige as the senior prelate of Bergahl, and despite the fact that Tajvana was Bergahl's own city, he would have no active part in the coronation itself. He would simply join all of the other senior priests and priestesses in bestowing a final, parting blessing upon the newly crowned and consecrated Emperor of Sharona.

He was grateful for that, and yet the reason for it was simply one more insult delivered to both himself and Chava, for the Articles of Unification specified that the ancient Ternathian coronation rites would be extended to the Empire of Sharona. It was preposterous! *Outrageous!* Yet Zindel had been inflexible upon that point. He'd flatly refused to accept the planetary crown the fawning fools of the Conclave were so eager to place upon his head unless everyone else on the entire planet accepted the *Ternathian* ceremony. And under the terms of that ceremony, only the clergy of the Double Triad would be permitted to officiate in the coronation itself.

Ecumenicalism stretched only so far as suited the Caliraths, it would seem.

He felt his teeth grinding together and made himself stop, then stiffened as the temple's massive, magnificently sculpted portals swung open at last to admit His Imperial Majesty Zindel XXIV, Duke of Ternathia, Grand Duke of Farnalia, Warlord of the West, Protector of the Peace, Wing-Crowned, and by the gods' grace, Emperor of Ternathia.

Zindel chan Calirath was a tall, powerfully built man, with the sheer force of Calirath personality even the Seneschal had to admit was formidable. Yet in that moment, as he walked slowly down the temple's long nave, between the packed pews, his appearance was shockingly at odds with the magnificently garbed onlookers crowded shoulder to shoulder to witness this pivotal moment in history.

He wore a plain shirt of white linen, its full sleeves gathered at the wrists by cuff bands of Calirath green. His breeches were of the same green, yet they were also starkly, almost brutally plain, and instead of the elegant court shoes every other occupant of that temple wore, his feet were encased not in shoes, not even in boots, but in plain, calf-high rawhide sandals, and more rawhide served as a belt. He was bareheaded, with no attendants, no servants. The golden-stranded black hair of his dynasty gleamed in the sunlight pouring through the temple dome, his only diadem, and he carried no dress sword, no dagger, no jewelry beyond the golden marriage bracelet around his left wrist and the emerald signet of the House of Calirath on the second finger of his right hand.

The music had stilled as the temple doors opened. There was no magnificent fanfare to play Zindel down the nave. There was only silence, and the quiet, clear slap of the soles of his sandals on the polished marble floor of the temple.

The Seneschal curled a mental lip of scorn. Why, Zindel might have been any menial, a mere *servant*. For that matter, the staff of Tajvana Palace was *better* garbed than he! But did he show any awareness of that? Of course not! And yet, Raynarg reflected, was that not the ultimate statement of arrogance? It said, as clearly as if he had shouted it into the witnesses' faces, that he—a *Calirath!*—had no need for mere finery, no need for the trappings of power. He could come before them dressed like *this*, and still they would bow their heads before him and submit to his mastery.

Zindel walked alone through the ringing silence to the rail about the temple sanctuary, passing his watching wife and daughters, seated in the temple's front puke, without even acknowledging their presence. He bent his head reverently, raising his hands, the first three fingers of each spread to signify the presence of the Double Triad, then folded those hands—fingers still spread—across his breast, fingertips touching each shoulder, and sank to his knees before Chezdahn Myrkosah, High Priest of Vothan and the senior cleric of the Ternathian Empire.

Myrkosah was an old, old man, yet his spine was straight, his silver hair still thick, his beard immaculately clipped. His robes were far less ornate than the Seneschal's splendor, cut in a style which was—literally—thousands of years old, yet he wore them with an assurance that, like the plainness of Zindel's clothing, was its own form of arrogance, Raynarg thought bitterly.

"Who comes before the gods to seek their blessing?" Myrkosah intoned. Like every Ternathian cleric, he possessed a rolling, powerful voice that filled the temple like a living thing.

"My name," the kneeling emperor replied, "is Zindel."

"And why are you here, Zindel?" Myrkosah asked.

"To take up my burden."

"What burden?"

"The burden of service," Zindel said, his deep voice even more powerful than the high priest's, and yet somehow hushed, almost humble.

"And who calls you to assume that burden?"

"The people of Sharona."

"And by what right do you answer that call?"

"I am the son of the House of Calirath, descendent of Halian and Erthain the Great."

"And what service do you offer to the people of Sharona?"

"The service of heart, of mind, of body, of spirit, and of Talent," Zindel replied unflinchingly, lifting his head to meet the priest's searching gaze.

"And what is your duty to the people of Sharona?"

"To stand between." The words came out levelly, almost softly, yet they reached every ear in that temple. "To stand between evil and its victims, between darkness and light. Between right and wrong. Between my people and their enemies... and between the people I am sworn to protect and death."

"And will you meet that duty?" Myrkosah's level voice was the very balance scale of the gods, and Zindel chan Calirath's nostrils flared.

"With my life. *Chunika s'hari, Halian. Sho warak.*"

"Will you pledge that upon the Winged Crown? Upon the Sword of Erthain? Upon the altar of the Double Triad and under the eye of the gods themselves?"

"I will so pledge."

"Then we will hear your oath, Zindel," Myrkosah said, and the High Priestess of Shalana and the High Priestess of Marnilay joined him.

They formed a triangle about the kneeling emperor, reaching out their arms, fingers spread in the presence of the Double Triad as they held the Winged Crown of Celaryon above his head. It was over forty-eight hundred years old, that crown—a heavy, angular thing of thick gold plaques and the outstretched wings of a falcon, forged by the goldsmiths of Farnalia to commemorate the treaty binding their land to Ternathia. It had been used in every coronation of every Ternathian emperor or empress in all those long, dusty millennia, and now—as they held it above his head—their fingers hummed with a silent vibration only they could perceive.

They stood a moment, and then Myrkosah said, "The gods are listening."

Zindel drew a deep breath. This was an oath he'd sworn before, and unlike the watching Seneschal, or Chava Busar, or anyone beyond the House of Calirath and the high priest and high priestesses standing about him at this moment, he knew what that oath truly meant. It was not a simple formality, not a mere promise.

Much of Sharona—perhaps most of it—believed that Erthain the Great was mere legend, a figure of myth created by the Calirath Dynasty to justify its claim upon the imperial power. But the emperors and empresses of Ternathia knew better than that. *Zindel* knew better than that, and he remembered every time he'd cursed that "legendary" ancestor, for Erthain had been the very first Calirath to possess the Calirath Talent, and his Talent had been a tsunami. The secret records of the House of Calirath had not recorded what Erthain had Glimpsed in the moment his Talent awoke, but they did record what he'd done about it, and five thousand years of Caliraths had bound themselves to that same unforgiving, merciless oath.

Not all of them had lived up to the totality of its harsh, unyielding demands. Some had broken under its weight... and under the weight of their Talent. But the compulsion Erthain had set, the compulsion with which Celaryon had imbued his crown, held them all. They must take that oath willingly, but once taken, it could never be *un*taken. Perhaps some of them hadn't realized that before they swore it, but afterward... afterward they knew.

And now, the oath, the compulsion—the Talent—which had bound all those countless generations of Caliraths to the service and protection of Ternathia would henceforth bind them to the service and protection of all Sharona. They might make mistakes, they might be guilty of misjudgment, they might misunderstand a crisis, they might be unequal to the task, but they would *meet* that crisis... or die in the trying.

And so Zindel chan Calirath looked into the eyes of the High Priest of Vothan and opened his mouth.

"I, Zindel, son of Kairnos, descendent of Halian, descendent of Celaryon, descendent of Erthain, do pledge myself and my House unto the end of time to the service, the guidance, and the protection of the people of Sharona. I will bear true service to them all the days of my life. I will stand between them and the darkness, between them and danger, between them and death. I will offer to them the very best that I have of heart and soul and Talent, and may the gods themselves deal with me as I deal with them."

CHAPTER SIXTEEN

Darikhal 14, 5053 AE
(January 2, 1929 CE)

THE ELEGANT CROWD ASSEMBLED AT THE SENESCHAL OF Othmaliz's new private residence swirled around Darcel Kinlafia in a deceptively accepting and supportive murmur. Alazon Yanamar watched them and they watched her with the wariness the polls deserved. The latest numbers from New Farnal were excellent, and the powerbrokers had all accepted that her fiancé would be elected to the House of Talents in two weeks time. So had she, and while she wasn't going to allow herself—or Darcel—any premature victory laps, the pressure of the election itself had definitely eased. That meant it was time to begin looking *beyond* the election to the pragmatics of wielding power, and that meant finding potential parliamentary allies. With that in mind, the amount of publicity this event was drawing—especially combined with those New Farnalian numbers—had been enough to warrant a return trip to Tajvana.

Just yesterday Darcel's last remaining serious competitor had formally withdrawn his candidacy and appeared in a Uromathian-station Voicecast personally endorsing Darcel. The SUNN correspondents following the campaign had been unable to reach the man for follow-up interviews.

Alazon didn't trust it. Her work as Zindel's Privy Voice had always involved more political interactions than she cared for, yet that did have its benefits. The job alone didn't make her good at politics, but it gave her the instincts to know no one was ever elected to these levels of political power without some kind of fight.

Certainly the emperor's support had been a significant aid, especially with setting up a campaign staff and getting the relatively quiet and unassuming man she loved ready for the invasive personal questions SUNN reporters asked in hopes of getting interesting answers to amuse and engage their viewers.

But even the least astute observer could tell the Seneschal considered himself no friend of the emperor. This gala, for instance, was nominally in memory of the late Crown Prince Janaki, but the guest list quite noticeably omitted the emperor, the empress, Crown Princess Andrin, the prince consort, either of the younger grand princesses, or any other blood relative of Janaki's. Pretending to honor Janaki the platoon-captain who'd died in combat—probably through his own ineptitude... or that of his superiors—instead of Janaki the Crown Prince of Ternathia who'd used his Talent to intentionally place himself in mortal peril to stop the Arcanan invasion was... foul.

Of course, Alazon hadn't been given an opportunity to peruse the guest list when they accepted Darcel's own invitation. She supposed that should have raised warning flags, but it hadn't.

She'd wanted to wring the Seneschal's neck when she figured it out. Instead, she walked politely around the room on Darcel's arm greeting recognized supporters and being friendly with the rest of the crowd of faces. Being the candidate's wife was harder than she'd expected.

Relatives of the soldiers from Fort Salby and other forts farther down the chain dotted the crowd, recognizable by their red eyes and obvious discomfort. They'd been trickling in throughout the evening, with honor bells rung for each new group while the Order of Bergahl's musicians played variations of the Mother's lament for her children.

Needing a few minutes away from the pressing throng, she let go of Darcel. The crowd drew him away.

Alazon wondered if the invitations for the guests of honor had been timed for quarter hour arrivals or if the Seneschal had all the bereaved sequestered in a side room to arrive a few at a time as pleased his sense of political blood theater.

The next one to enter was dressed as elegantly as any of the local powerbrokers, but Alazon nearly lost the light supper she'd worked so hard to glean from passing hors d'oeuvres trays when she heard the majordomo's announcement.

Dr. Shalassar Kolmayr-Brintal kissed the Seneschal of Othmal-iz's cheeks as warmly as if she were merely a dowager socialite.

Shaylar Nargra-Kolmayr's mother, the whispers swept the crowd immediately, but the longtime ambassador slipped into the crowd with much the same ease as the cetaceans she normally Spoke with slid below the waves.

...and with much the same smiling menace as the black and white whales, Shalassar emerged from the crowd not by Darcel Kinlafia but just in front of Alazon. The Voice barely avoided snapping the stem of her wine glass.

*   *   *

The finger marks on Alazon Yanamar's forearm were likely to bruise by morning and despite her frantic looks at the assigned imperial security not one of them had come to rescue her. Looking for physical threats, they dismissed Dr. Kolmayr-Brintal entirely, but at this range Alazon wondered why the Calirath line hadn't been exterminated already if the guards couldn't recognize the raw menace in Shalassar's expression. Only Kelahm, the intern newly assigned as Darcel's personal aide, had even looked her way.

"Sit." Shalassar pointed at the chairs in the little alcove she'd led them into. "I'm not going to bite, Ms. Yanamar."

Alazon sat.

"My daughter is dead," the woman said, watching her intently. "Your husband received her last transmission. I Saw it myself half a dozen times, until it burned into my nightmares and I couldn't watch anymore. But would you believe the tales I've been receiving about what those Arcanan negotiators said and didn't say?"

As former Privy Voice, Alazon Yanamar did, actually, and she froze. There were bits and pieces which had led to guesses about Arcanan military capability, but most of that had been rendered thoroughly obsolete by the much less theoretical experience of fighting Arcana to a stop at Fort Salby. The rest were guesses about how Arcana was politically organized, the rare details with which Emperor Zindel might arm future negotiators at another peace table, but only if Sharona could be convinced to attempt another peace.

Ambassador Kolmayr-Brintal didn't look like a woman willing to countenance any peace with her daughter's killers, and if this woman wanted to unite Sharona's will, Alazon was afraid she might very well be able to do it—even if Emperor Zindel threw all his own power into stopping her. But surely she had to understand negotiation had to happen again *sometime*, or did—?

The intensity of Shalassar's eyes, boring into her own, worried Alazon. How much of the ambassador's telepathic Talent for cetacean speech transferred to humans?

"That seven-times damned reporter was right then." Shalassar's fierceness faded and those fiercely erect shoulders sagged ever so slightly. "They're going to say she could have still been alive, and you won't have a thing to say back. Not one. Still no body at all, and where she died is five universes beyond the front now."

Alazon cursed herself silently as she abruptly recognized the core of Shalassar's anger. This woman needed her *help*, not her suspicion.

"Ma'am, I'm so sorry for your loss. Darcel and I would be delighted to host you and your husband—"

"No." Shalassar forced her face back to blankness and straightened her spine before continuing softly. "I'm sorry, dear. I don't believe that would be a good idea. This is just scum-eater politics. A VBS reporter came to me for confirmation, probably knowing the whole thing was a farce. He's lucky I didn't toss him in the ocean and make him swim back to port."

Alazon nodded uncertainly, not sure how to calm the alternately infuriated and grief-stricken woman before her.

"Then after I heard the idea," Shalassar confessed, "I just had to ask. It's an entirely foolish hope, I know. Thaminar tried to talk me out of even coming, but I had to ask."

"Of course." Alazon Yanamar looked Shalassar Brintal-Kolmayr dead in the eyes and said, "We are absolutely certain Arcanan military forces killed Shaylar and every one of her companions."

"And there's no doubt at all?"

"None. I'm sorry. The Arcanans burn their dead." And in a momentary lie designed to ease Shalassar's pain, she added a small embroidery on what Sharona knew absolutely, "They burned each one of ours too. It's how they do respectful funeral rites. A kind of purification from their perspective, I understand."

"Please, no one tell the cetaceans that." Shalassar shuddered. "Only demons would use fire to consign their dead. It'd be like praying for the departed to be accepted into hell."

"But the smoke rises to the heavens?" Alazon suggested.

"Heaven is in the deep. It's a warm place with a gentle current full of kelp and fish, where lungs never empty, and dorsal muscles stay strong forever. I've explained to them that humans hope for a different kind of place, so they've allowed that heaven might have an island or two. If, that is, the better humans aren't reborn with fins."

A few guests drifted near their corner alcove, heard the mention of death and just as quickly found reasons to melt back into the crowd. Shalassar laughed a bit bitterly.

"I'm not the light-hearted dolphin lady they used to love to have at parties anymore," she said. "I suppose I have too many other things I care about now."

They sat gazing at the crowd for a few more moments. Then Shalassar stirred and turned to look at Alazon once more.

"Oh one more thing," she said. "Watch the Order. The Seneschal in particular. He seems to think I'm here to humiliate your fiancé and destroy his political chances."

"And why would he think that, Madam Ambassador?"

Shalassar's smile once again reminded Alazon of oceanic predators. It was comforting to see the flashes of old confidence showing through her grief.

"I might have mentioned that I wanted the invitation in order to tell candidate Kinlafia I expected him to do his very best to turn the bastards that attacked my daughter into shark chum. I trust you'll convey the message for me." She clutched Alazon one more time. "I can't have my Shaylar back, Madame Voice. But I will have the Arcanans who murdered her and desecrated her corpse pay for their crimes. Tell your fiancé that and tell that to the emperor."

"I'm not Privy Voice anymore, Madam Ambassador."

Shalassar dropped her voice. "If Our Emperor doesn't have you back in service of one kind of another the very instant it's politically feasible, he's a fool. And I hope to Vothan he's the furthest thing from a fool."

She stood, nodded once, and flowed away into the crowd once again, more like a dolphin than ever. Alazon Yanamar watched her go, then rose from her own chair and worked her way through the gala towards Darcel, glad Shalassar Brintal-Kolmayr was on their side.

*   *   *

The unexpected guests of the evening didn't end with the Cetacean ambassador. A Simian ambassador arrived as well, but unlike Dr. Shalassar Brintal-Kolmayr, he wasn't on the guest list. Darcel suspected the man had snuck in through the staff entrance while the overworked caterers were distracted.

He introduced himself to both of them as Soolan chan Rahool, followed by a series of clicks and a puffing out of his cheeks. Then he reddened and switched to a more normal conversation mode.

"I'm sorry about that, but my clan is very particular about certain things. They'll ask if I introduced myself properly, and by that they'll mean by the name they've given me and all that." He shrugged. "I've gotten used to it, but talking to weak-arms, I mean humans, well it does sometimes put people off."

Chan Rahool seemed to feel badly out of place in his present surroundings, so Alazon offered him one of the appetizer trays as a distraction while he composed himself. His eyes lit immediately.

"Oh! You understand." He selected a bacon wrapped plum confit and crunched it with relish. "I do so love working with people who understand simian relations." He licked his lips. "Quite delicious, too. I will have to have the name of your caterer later. If I bring them back a sample of the food you greeted me with, they'll be oh so pleased with you and encouraged by the warm reception." The man fairly beamed at them both.

Darcel immediately denied any knowledge at all of simians other than what any school boy gathered from elementary school about the great apes—the mountain gorillas, chimpanzees, orangutans, baboons, some of the higher monkey species, and so on—though Darcel did admit to dedicating one summer to an attempt to reproduce a triple canopy jungle tree house.

"Good thing you didn't manage it." Chan Rahool shook his head mournfully though it was clear from his eyes he regretted it not at all. "A little two-story treehouse combined with a minor Voice Talent, and my whole life went straight to the monkeys." He winked. "Now, would you like your hair checked for lice?"

Alazon began to suspect the man had an incurable sense of humor.

"Why help yourself," Darcel replied, "Just promise us we can wrap anything you catch in bacon before you eat it. I wouldn't want to damage relations with the New Farnal simians by offering substandard bugs."

Chan Rahool chuckled. The chuckle was genuine, but Alazon suspected he had something rather more serious than badinage on his mind, and so did Darcel. Her fiancé might be new to politics, but no one could accuse him of lacking wits.

"I thought the great apes didn't much care what we did," he

said. "And you came from Ricathia, not New Farnal. Why would they have any interest in me?"

"I was actually hoping to speak with your wife." Chan Rahool lifted his arms in an overlarge shrug that made him look something like a chimp himself. "And who can say why the other sentients do anything? Sometimes their motives are as clear as a human toddler's interest in a new toy. But when the grandnanas get involved I often end up wondering if we aren't the less intelligent species."

Alazon blinked.

"Oh, on average we're definitely smarter, but not everyone is average... on either side." The ambassador flapped a wrist at her. "Not an official reporting for the emperor or anything. Just that the Minarti are matriarchal. There's a grandmother that runs everything season by season, but there's also a group of older women who don't seem to be necessarily related to the grandmother at all.

"When the first reports of the Arcanans came in—by which I mean your report, of course—" He nodded to Darcel. "I was very concerned and tried to tell the grandmother about it. Some of the Minarti have split and established new clans in the nearer universes, and I thought if a war went poorly there might be great apes cut off out there thinking an Arcanan was one of us." The man grew serious as the lines on his face showed just how deeply he feared for the simians he worked with. "The lady chimp just patted me on the head, like she usually does, and told me to go have more babies.

"I thought that was the end of it, but last week a delegation of silverback gorillas and their matriarch came to me with a message. They tried to explain things to me, and I'm... Well, this sounds insane, but as near as I can figure, the simians do have some kinds of Talents themselves just as we humans do. And the lady gorilla gave me a near Voice-style sending for our human clan leaders.

"Oh and they want you to tell Empress Varena—they've never quite accepted that Emperor Zindel's in charge; they seem to think it's a polite fiction—that they're concerned about the war. In fact, they're much more concerned than I'd realized, and some of them want to go colonize the border universes. I think they meant to fight.

"Also..." He winced. "The gorillas have offered nursemaid services and open foraging to human females with young to help support wartime population expansion. That's an extremely generous offer, you understand."

Chan Rahool finished his recitation with palms held up.

"I know none of it makes any sense from a human perspective, but I'm their ambassador too. They wanted the message delivered, so I needed to take it to Empress Varena."

He looked pleadingly at Alazon. "I heard you'd stepped down as Privy Voice, but perhaps you still have contacts? If you could just take the transmission, I could say I'd given it to a woman in the empress's service. I think the gorillas would accept that."

Darcel handed the now obviously distraught ambassador the rest of the appetizer tray and sent his wife a speaking glance. This was clearly a question for the former Privy Voice, and Alazon sighed.

"I can relay your gorilla's message and this conversation exactly as we've had it to the emperor...and," she added at his cough, "to Empress Varena as well. But you'll have to explain to them that humans don't order other humans to procreate the way it sounds like the simians can."

"Yes. Yes. Already done three times over," the ambassador said. "But at least I can tell them I passed on the message. They don't normally cling to things this long. I thought sure migrating for the dry season would put it out of their minds, but almost a full month since the last rain and they're sending me off with messages like I'm one of their teen boy chimps. That's what the clicking and cheek blowing means, you know: human grandmother's little boy chimp." He winced. "If you must tell the emperor about that bit, please do include that I had no idea at all what it meant when I first agreed to the name."

Alazon nodded gravely, trying very hard to keep her lips from twitching in amusement.

"They're willing to change the name for me," chan Rahool continued, "but they insist that I should kill a tiger with a spear I carved myself first. And then I'll be an adult and the male chimps have said they'll need to fight me from time to time just to help me keep in shape.

"I'd really rather not complicate the ambassadorship with all that, if you didn't mind terribly."

Chan Rahool's head turned, following a tray of food in a passing waiter's hand. "Say, do you have any more of the crunchies?"

CHAPTER SEVENTEEN

Hayrn 17, 205 YU
(January 9, 1929 CE)

GARTH SHOWMA.

Jasak had forgotten how much he loved it...until an unwary glance out the slider window snatched him up out of the briefing he'd been conducting for his *shardonai*. The sight of the first cluster of snow-draped forest pulled the heart-hunger up into his throat, with a fierce power made even stronger by how many terrible things had happened since his last visit home, and he stared out that window, unaware of emotion which had transfigured his expression in that moment. The winter-struck trees of the ducal estate, which ran in forests thirty miles on a side, had been lovingly maintained in their pristine, virgin condition over most of its vast extent, and he drank in their icy beauty like strong wine. Despite two full centuries of settlement, Garth Showma was a jewel of natural beauty, punctuated by the massive Showma Falls.

He'd been showing Jathmar and Shaylar the maps as they traveled by slider for the last portion of their three-month long inter-universal journey, comfortably ensconced in their own private car.

And comfortable in more than one way. That thought sent a wave of mingled darkness and satisfaction through him, pulling him back almost brutally from his thoughts of home, and his glance moved from the trees to the end windows where another slider car was now coupled to the rear of their own. It bore the colors of the Dukes of Garth Showma, that other car, nor was it alone; there was an identical car coupled to the *front* of theirs, as well.

231

Jasak's messages to his father had reached home just over a month ago, and his father's reply had been waiting at the incoming slider station in the city of Theskair in New Ransar—three universes, eight thousand miles, and fourteen days' travel from Garth Showma. He'd expected a hummer message; what he'd gotten was a security team—a very professional, highly trained, very dedicated, and heavily armed security team from the Garth Showma Guard commanded by Commander of One Hundred Hathysk Forhaylin.

Forhaylin's presence had been all the message Jasak really needed about how seriously his father took events down-universe. Hundred Forhaylin had served in the 2nd Andaran Scouts with Thankhar Olderhan and Otwal Threbuch. When the duke retired, Threbuch had stayed in the Scouts, but Forhaylin had followed his duke out of the Union Army and become second in command of the Garth Showma Guard, the personal guard whose men—whose *Andaran* men—were all sworn to the service of the Duke of Garth Showma as their liege lord, not as the Governor of New Arcana. They answered to Thankhar Olderhan directly... and Hathysk Forhaylin was the man he sent out when he *expected* blood in the streets.

Jasak was just as happy Shaylar and Jathmar had been unaware of that minor point. And he was also happy Forhaylin had briefed him very privately on the occasional anti-Sharona riots which had already occurred.

"His Grace," the dark-haired, bearded hundred had said, sunlight bright on the silver beginning to color his temples, "is... perturbed by the dearth of additional formal reports from Hells Gate." He'd met Jasak's eyes levelly. "The absence of official dispatches has left people—and the news services, of course—free to make up whatever rumors they want, and some of them are pretty damned ugly. It didn't help when word that hostilities have been resumed arrived without any real explanation of *why*, either. The natural assumption in New Arcana is that the Sharonians must have broken them off, but we don't actually *know* anything about the circumstances. I believe His Grace shares your own suspicion that the absence of any official explanation—or several other critical aspects of events out there—may not be accidental."

That was certainly one way to describe his "suspicions," Jasak had thought grimly, and he'd hated having to share the news that the fighting had flared up again with his *shardonai*. They'd taken it just as badly as he'd expected them to, and it had taken almost a week for them to regain their comfortable relationship—or as comfortable as it had ever been—with one another.

That reflection finished the process of drawing him back to his present duty. They didn't have that much longer until they arrived now, and he smiled a brief apology at the others for his distraction and bent back over the map on the table.

"The Duchy of Garth Showma stretches from the Ocean of Storms in the east to the western-most of the Great Andaran Lakes," he said, and pointed to an immense span of territory that corresponded, roughly, to the Republic of Faltharia where Jathmar had been born.

"Technically, we own all of it," he continued, smiling at the Sharonian's expression, "but the vast bulk of it's been permanently deeded to freeholders of one sort and another." He shrugged. "Unless someone dies intestate or the land is seized for nonpayment of taxes or something like that, we don't really have much to say about its disposition. The family's personal demesne, Garth Showma, itself, is much smaller, of course. It lies here, where the Showma River drops over a horseshoe-shaped cliff that forms the Showma Falls. They're one of the two largest waterfalls on New Arcana—and every other universe, of course."

Jathmar nodded. "In Sharona, we call it the Grand Emlin Falls. I was born here," he pointed to a spot on Jas Olderhan's map, "in the city of Serakai in the Republic of Faltharia."

"How did you like growing up with all those winter blizzards?" Jasak asked. "I got so tired of them as a kid."

Jathmar chuckled. "Serakai means 'city of snow.' I can remember winters when blizzards piled up drifts thirty feet high."

"So can I," Jasak told him with a grin, and the two of them turned in perfect unison, as though they'd rehearsed it, to check the cold clear skies out the window.

Shaylar, who'd grown up in the hot deserts of Shurkhal, looked from one to the other, then grimaced at Gadrial.

"I'd never even *seen* snow, until I married Jathmar. We held the wedding at his parents' home, as Faltharian custom calls for, during the mid-winter solstice festival," she said. "Winter solstice is considered a fortunate time for weddings in Faltharia. Personally, I think that's just because there's nothing else to *do* in Faltharia during the winter." She shivered. "It took weeks to get warm again."

"We just missed Snowfall Night," Jasak said wistfully. "It lasts a fortnight, but all the best parades are on the shortest day of the year."

"So you two think you've seen *snow*, do you?" Gadrial asked, looking back and forth between the two men, and laughed softly. "Babes in arms, the pair of you! If you want to see *real* weather, you should try spending a winter in *Ransar*. It's not uncommon for the temperature to drop thirty or forty degrees below zero, for weeks at a time. My first winter away from home was a delightful shock. I didn't have to bundle up in furs or tie a safety line to my waist even once, just to keep from losing my way between my parents' house and the barn to feed the livestock."

Shaylar shuddered. "Thank you, but I'll pass on that offer."

"That sounds remarkably like how people in Sharona deal with blizzards. There's not some magic to find your way through the snow?" Jathmar said.

"There's a whole field of applied magic for that," Gadrial explained, "but when it gets cold enough, sarkolis gets brittle. When that happens, the crystals tend to crack—which does horrible damage to the stored spells. It's best to have a safety line."

Jasak tapped the map to bring their attention back to his lecture. "Ahem. Now, then. The demesne lies along the river. You can see the falls from the ducal palace, which is my parents' main house. They maintain another in Portalis, the city that sprawls along both sides of Arcana's first portal." He tapped the map, where a symbol in red ink marked the location of the portal.

"My father lives on the estate and governs all of Garth Showma directly in his own right—it's complicated," he added as Shaylar and Jathmar frowned at him. "Like I said, in theory the Olderhan family owns the entire duchy; actually, it's more a matter of everyone who lives in it owing fealty to the Duke of Garth Showma as their liege lord. But that's a *personal* relationship between him and them. He governs the *rest* of New Arcana in the name of the Union of Arcana, and none of the other citizens of New Arcana owe him any sort of personal fealty."

"But the governorship is also hereditary, right?" Jathmar asked in the tone of someone wanting to be very sure he has something straight.

"Yes," Jasak agreed, nodding encouragingly.

"Then how can the people he governs not owe him personal fealty?"

"Like Jasak said, it's complicated," Gadrial put in with a wry grin. "In fact, it's complicated even for an Andaran. Just take his word for it that Duke Thankhar has two different personas: one is Duke of Garth Showma and the other one is Governor of New Arcana. They just happen to both live in the same body."

"Right. 'Complicated,'" Jathmar muttered, and Jasak chuckled.

"Don't worry too much about the details, Jath. The important point for us is that my parents can get away with living on the estate because of how close it is to the capital, Portalis. Or, rather, to the side of the city on New Arcana, not the side on Arcana Prime. Of course, when his duties call him to the capital, he and mother stay in their town house in Portalis, which is considerably smaller than the ducal palace."

"Hah!" Gadrial interjected once more. "Small is relative. I've never been to the ducal palace, mind, but I've passed that so-called town house hundreds of times. It fills an entire city block. Not one side of the block; the *whole block*."

Jasak looked exasperated. "Well, it has to be large, since it houses the government administration staff for the whole of New Arcana, Gadrial! The family lives in a very small portion of the house."

"How many rooms?" she asked in a sweet tone, and he scowled.

"I don't remember, exactly," he muttered.

"Oh, just a close estimate will do." She actually batted her eyelashes. Jasak turned red, and Shaylar suppressed a splutter of laughter as she recognized the ploy.

"Uh . . . maybe thirty?" he said finally, and Gadrial sat back in queenlike satisfaction.

"I rest my case."

Shaylar couldn't help it. The laugh she'd struggled right womanfully to restrain broke loose in a bubble of delight, and Gadrial nodded to her in the shared satisfaction of their gender while Jasak rubbed the back of his neck, which was as hot as his face. Then he stopped rubbing and grinned sheepishly, and that let Jathmar's chuckle surface, as well. He glanced at Jasak with a look that said, very clearly, *Women. Can't live with 'em, can't drown 'em, might as well love 'em.*

Jasak's return glance agreed with that assessment.

Shaylar, dying of curiosity by inches, asked in the same sweet tones Gadrial had used, "Are those your parents' only houses?"

"Well," he said cautiously, "ah, no. Actually, there are two more. There's a manor house at the demesne in the Earldom of Yar Khom and another smaller demesne property in the Barony of Sarkhala. Neither of those is in New Arcana, though. Those are the oldest family titles, the oldest family estates. The duke-dom wasn't created until the portal formed, two centuries ago. They're located here," he pointed to his map, "but in Arcana Prime, of course."

He swept his hand down the map, indicating two tracts of land some eleven hundred miles south of Garth Showma, but on the same continent.

Yar Khom encompassed a long, narrow peninsula of sub-tropical land at the southern extremity of that continent, which jutted into the warm waters that formed—on Sharona—the meeting point of the North Vandor Ocean and the South Vandor Ocean.

"Andara," Jasak explained, "is first and foremost a military power. Before the creation of the Union, we had the largest army on Arcana. We also had the second largest navy, for that matter. We're an aristocracy, with a military tradition that stretches back centuries. My father's other Arcana Prime estate, the Barony of Sarkhala, lies here." He pointed to the large island off the south-ern tip of that long peninsula.

Gadrial chuckled. "The democratic republics of Ransar like to say that Andara is an army that somehow acquired a state. We're not entirely sure *how* they managed that, since it makes no sense to us, either, but that's essentially what they did."

Jathmar blinked in surprise. "Your country's a democracy, Gadrial? Governed by the people?"

"Oh, yes. Ransar"—she pointed to the vast sweep of land that to Sharonan eyes corresponded to the various kingdoms and empires of the Uromathian peoples, plus the entirety of the Arpathian Septentrion—"is comprised of several independent republics, with elected presidents and legislatures. We're all part of the Union of Arcana, of course, just as Andara is, but demo-cratic principles are very important to Ransarans."

"Mmm," Jasak commented.

Gadrial's eyes sparkled. "Go ahead, Jasak. Don't let your

chivalry or stiff-necked Andaran pride stop you from commenting." She grinned to take any implied criticism out of her comment and rolled her eyes at Jathmar and Shaylar. "'Those unstable, chaotic Ransarans,'" she murmured in pedantic tones, "'with their lunatic notions of personal freedom and the worth of individual initiative. They'll be the ruin of the Union.' You know it's been said," she added when Jasak gave her The Look.

"More often in Mythal than Andara," he replied, and the sparkle of humor in her eyes flashed into a sudden anger that surprised Shaylar.

"Yes, it has," the magister half-snapped. "Which undoubtedly explains why Ransar has the highest standard of living on Arcana, why Ransaran manufacturing capacity is twice the size of every other nation's—or culture's—in the world, including those self-worshipping *shakira* narcissists in Mythal!"

Her anger was growing almost exponentially as she very nearly spat out her words.

"And that 'unstable chaos' is obviously why Ransarans consistently produce more applied magic innovations than the rest of Arcana combined!" she continued, still building steam. "Not to mention the most advanced high-tech magical industry in the history of Arcana, despite the over-hyped, over-confident, self-satisfied, power-worshipping, gods*damned* Mythalan control of theoretical magic research."

The anger in her eyes had gone volcanic and she turned her furious gaze away from Jasak to meet Shaylar's gaze.

"The *shakira* spend their time sitting on their backsides for long, arduous hours, toying with the interlocking magical building blocks of the multiple universes and wondering which is more profound, the religious underpinnings of the multiple universes or their own elevated place in the multiple cosmos. And while *they're* staring at their navels and pondering the imponderable, *Ransarans* develop the tools and the technology that make their lives comfortable and easy enough to spend those lives sitting there, doing damned near nothing else. Of course, their slave labor policies are a big help. It gives the *shakira* lords a lot more spare time to devote to doing nothing! If I could, I'd rip their whole ugly society to shreds and send *them* into the fields and factories to get a dose of reality!"

"Peace, Gadrial." Jasak leaned across and touched her wrist

very gently. "I hate the *shakira* caste system almost as much as you do, and not because of what they've done to *me*. My family's always sided with the *garthans*, and you know it, so don't think I don't have your back on this one. After the way they mauled you at Mythal Falls Academy, you've got every right to feel that way, and I'm ready to stand in line to help you! But don't let your hate for what *they* are turn *you* into something you don't want to be."

Rage transmuted into sudden tears and she bit her lip. "I'm sorry," she whispered, squeezing shut her eyes. "It's just... I have to see Halathyn's widow... tell her what happened, out there... and that's raked up all the old agony, again."

Jasak abandoned his seat and joined Gadrial in hers, and she turned toward him, resting her head against his shoulder. Shaylar recognized the tenderness in his expression and wondered if he, himself, had realized, yet, how deeply he loved Gadrial Kelbryan. While he held Gadrial close, Jasak spoke very softly, telling them what had happened to her as a student, the prejudice, the accusation of cheating, Halathyn's defense of her, the whole sordid story.

"Did I come reasonably close?" he asked finally, looking down at her as he finished at last, and she nodded.

"Very," she whispered. Her eyelashes were wet. "Oh, Jasak, it still hurts so desperately...."

He actually kissed her hair. She sniffled and sighed, then scrubbed her face with the back of one hand and sat up, again. She met Shaylar's distressed gaze.

"I don't blame you for his loss, Shaylar. Truly, I don't. It wasn't your fault that Halathyn..."

Her lips trembled as memory burned in her eyes, and she bit the lower one again, making herself pause and draw a deep breath.

"It wasn't your fault," she continued once more after a moment, her voice more ragged than she would have liked. "But Halathyn was the finest man I've ever known, the most gifted theoretical magister I've ever met, and the only Mythalan *shakira* who deserved courtesy and respect. As for the rest of them..."

Her eyes went hard as granite. "I detest Mythal and all the magic-using Mythalans in it! And thanks to what Halathyn built in New Arcana, we don't need the Mythalan *shakira* to understand the multiple universes *or* theoretical magic."

"What Halathyn started and what *you* built," Jasak said

mildly. When she looked uncomfortable, he chucked her chin, very gently. "Those are Halathyn's words as much as mine. He was deeply proud of you, Gadrial. With good reason."

Her eyes went wet again.

Jasak fished out a handkerchief and handed it over, then looked back at the two Sharonans.

"Now, then, getting back to our original conversation," he said more briskly, "Gadrial's made several very valid points. Not the least of which is that compared with Ransar, we Andarans are little more than barbarians with clubs in our hands."

Gadrial chuckled, wetly—but it was a chuckle, nonetheless. "Well, yes, but you're such *adorable* barbarians, it's easy to overlook your shortcomings." She leaned up to give him a swift kiss, an endearment that reflected the increasingly intimate relationship Jathmar and Shaylar had watched blossom over the course of their long journey.

Jasak's face scalded. Even his ears turned red.

Shaylar had to admit that he did look awfully adorable, sitting there in his uniform, flushed with embarrassment and looking like a man who couldn't make up his mind whether to bolt for the nearest exit or grab Gadrial by the shoulders and show her just how well barbarians *could* kiss their women.

He settled for clearing his throat and bending over his map again.

"Where were we?" he muttered. "Oh, yes. Explaining Garth Showma to you. Arcana's first portal opened here, in the Grand Duchy of Tharkan, an imperial territory of the Kingdom of Elath."

Shaylar peered at the map and frowned. The Grand Duchy was located smack in the center of what would have been the Ternathian Empire, on Sharona, and that puzzled her, since the kingdom that controlled the Grand Duchy was located on Arcana's analog to New Farnal. Elath was all the way across the North Vandor Ocean, sandwiched between the southern region where Jasak's father owned an earldom and a barony and the northern sweep of land that corresponded to Jathmar's birthplace. It seemed an...odd arrangement. On Sharona, Ternathia and Farnalia had colonized and controlled, at least at first, the two connected continents of New Ternathia and New Farnal. On Arcana, the political control had run in the other direction, eastward across the North Vandor instead of westward.

"Elath was desperate to hold onto the portal, so they asked their Andaran neighbors for help. Which was immediately forthcoming, of course, since even an army that's managed to acquire a state," Jasak continued, eyes glinting as they met Gadrial's, "could see the value of controlling that portal."

Gadrial refused the bait. She merely gave him a charming smile and waited for him to go one and he grinned.

"At any rate, everybody could see the value of that portal, which meant no one wanted anyone else to control it. Particularly not Ransar and Mythal, not to mention Lokan and Yanko," he added, touching in succession landmasses that corresponded to Arpathia/Uromathia, Ricathia, New Ternathia, and New Farnal.

"The upshot was a very nasty, intense war that lasted about five years. It fueled a truly appalling arms race as both sides developed more and more powerful battle spells. Some were literally powerful enough to wipe out whole cities. Those spells were banned, after the war came to a negotiated end.

"That war brought us right to the brink of Sharskha," he said very quietly. Jathmar and Shaylar looked perplexed, and he grimaced. "Sorry. It's from one of Andara's oldest myths—a final battle between the forces of light and the forces of darkness which ends only in the entire world's death."

Perplexity was replaced by something else, something with an edge of disbelief, perhaps. Or the look of someone who recognized hyperbole when he heard it. Jasak saw it and laughed harshly.

"I'm not exaggerating," he told them. "Some of the spells they came up with *were* so destructive they could have wiped out entire cities. One of them was used by the losing side in a major battle and effectively annihilated every man in *both* armies—over a hundred and ten thousand men gone, like *that!*" he snapped his fingers, eyes bleak. "And the researchers weren't stopping there. They were still coming up with worse ones when the war finally ended! Thank all the gods they were banned under the terms of the final peace treaty."

Shaylar and Jathmar exchanged horrified glances, appalled by that simple, dreadful recitation. *Spells that could destroy entire* cities? *Would the army that had acquired a state pull those banned spells out of mothballs and use them against Sharonian cities?*

"At any rate," Jasak continued, unaware of their sudden fear, "the same treaty created a new world government—the Union of

Arcana—which took control of Tharkan, where the portal was located. And that's how the city of Portalis was born. The Arcanan side of the city is the capital of the Union of Arcana. The New Arcanan side of the city is the capital of both New Arcana and houses the Union's Commandery, where the Union's Army, Navy and Air Force are headquartered. It's also where the Union's officers are trained and where enlisted men are given basic training.

"The land for a radius of seventy miles from the New Arcanan side of the portal was originally given to old Sherstan Olderhan, the first Duke of Garth Showma, as his personal desmesne during the war, as one inducement to back up Elath's bid to keep control of the portal. The rest of the Duchy was added later, under the peace treaties, once the Union took over the portal. The new government had to reach a negotiated settlement with Sherstan, as well as Elath, and the truth is, they came out much better with Elath."

Gadrial made a rude sound and Jasak's lips twitched.

"Sherstan was tenacious and he wielded enough military power to come out of that negotiation very well placed." He conceded. "He kept most of the original land grant ceded him by Elath, the Duchy of Garth Showma was created and placed under his direct, hereditary rule, and he ended up named Governor of New Arcana, as well. At the time the entire planet amounted to a howling wilderness, so it probably seemed like a reasonable bargain to the Union's negotiators. Of course, things have changed a bit over the last couple of centuries.

"Anyway, in return for its concessions to Sherstan, the Union received everything within a twenty-mile radius of the portal, on the New Arcanan side. The seated duke owns the next fifty miles in every direction, which forms the demesne of Garth Showma. A fairly large chunk of that land's rented—technically sub-enfeoffed—to the city and the Union's Commandery, though. The city of Portalis expanded across the entire twenty-mile swath of land controlled by the Union pretty quickly, and the Dukes of Garth Showma wanted to see the Union prosper, so they were inclined to be reasonable. For certain values of 'reasonable,' at least.

"Early on there was a lot of bluster about convincing the King of Elath to change the terms of enfeoffment to give the entire original demesne to the Union, instead of just the inner twenty-miles. But old Sherstan was a stubborn fellow, and since the territory of the duchy and its demesne were a part of the Union's founding treaty, the King of Elath—who happened to be his first cousin, did I mention that?—had no interest in bowing to outside pressures. Besides, Sherstan had no desire to be *too* greedy. Not only did he want to see the Union prosper, he also recognized that being too unreasonable might just convince his cousin the king to go along with the folks doing all of the blustering. So he made a counter offer.

"That's how the Union ended up renting part of the ducal estate, instead. My ancestors have kept the rents very low, but the Union needed a *large* parcel and the rents were assessed per acre, on a sliding scale to reflect changing land values over time. Over the two centuries since that agreement was signed, those rents have provided my family with a very comfortable income."

"*Comfortable?*" Gadrial echoed. "Sweet Rahil, Jasak, your father's the richest man on New Arcana! Maybe the richest back on Arcana Prime too."

"No, not on Arcana," Jasak corrected her promptly. "There are at least half a dozen Mythalan *shakira* caste lords that outstrip his total portfolio, some by a considerable margin. But on the whole," he agreed, "we've done well for ourselves. And I'll admit we periodically bless Great-Great-Great-Something-or-Other-Grandfather Sherstan's stiff-necked Andaran stubbornness. Otherwise, we'd have blue blood, a lot of beach sand in Andara, and not much else."

Gadrial leaned back in her seat, chuckling. "It's impossible to remain exasperated with you, Jasak. If I were in your shoes, I'd bless him, too."

"I'm glad you approve," he replied mildly. "Now, then, back to our discussion..." He met Jathmar's gaze. "You and Shaylar will be staying with my family, permanently. You'll move with us whenever we shift residences, whether it's moving into the townhouse in Portalis for the social season or traveling through the portal and crossing the original Ocean of Storms on Arcana Prime, to spend part of the winter at the Earldom of Yar Khom or the Barony of Sarkhala."

"I thought we were required to live with *you*, Jasak. You don't have your own house?" Jathmar asked, surprised, and Jasak shrugged.

"I keep an apartment in Portalis, but I don't use it all that often. Both the ducal palace and the town house are large enough, my parents and I can live in the same house and still maintain our privacy. The palace has four wings, all connected to the central tower, and each wing has about eighty rooms."

Shaylar's mouth fell open. "Mother Marthea!" One *wing* of that house was larger than the King of Shurkhal's entire palace!

"That's where we'll stay, at any rate, and I think you'll like it better than the town house. The portion of the estate not rented to the Commandery's been left largely pristine, still covered in heavy mature growth forest. That's where I learned my basic woodcraft as a boy."

"That's something else we share, then," Jathmar murmured. "I learned mine in the Kylie Forest, which corresponds almost exactly to your demesne. It's a major national park, set aside for public use. I very nearly lived in that forest, as a boy."

The two men looked at one another with a shared smile, and Shaylar's heart warmed as she saw it. She and Gadrial had become close friends, during their journey, but Jasak and Jathmar had remained at a distance from one another, for reasons she understood only too well. Her husband had lost his closest friends in the savagery of Toppled Timber—friends he would never be able to replace, given their status as permanent prisoners in their captors' society—and he bitterly missed the easy camaraderie of the explorer's lifestyle.

As a Voice, Shaylar had always been connected back to life in Sharona through the Voice network. Some of the team had craved that connection and routinely wanted updates on the settled universes they'd left behind, but Jathmar had never been like that. As intimately connected as their marriage bond made them, Jathmar could have relived news updates as vividly as if he were a Voice himself. Instead he'd reveled in the experience of the new universes and the time tracking through pristine worlds with their team. The Union of Arcana and Jasak Olderhan had taken that away from him. Their lives and the lifestyle they'd loved were gone for good.

But here in New Arcana, Jasak's family had preserved a piece of Jathmar's home forest, kept it nearly as pristine as in a brand new universe, and Shaylar watched the two men lean in to discuss childhood woodsmanship and identical landmarks in very different universes with a glint of hope.

If Jasak and Jathmar could somehow learn to trust one another enough to become friends—genuine friends—Shaylar would be grateful for the rest of her life.

She sighed and sat back in her seat. After the intense stress of capture and the unending strain of imprisonment, it would be wonderful to stop traveling, to settle down in one place, a private home, no matter how large that home might be. She ached to crawl into a bed, knowing she'd actually sleep in it more than once or twice. And it would be a major blessing to never again sprawl wearily in a succession of military forts, slider cars, ships, or dragon saddles.

It had been so long since she'd lived in a real house, rather than a tent or the temporary accommodations they'd used on this long journey, that she'd nearly forgotten what it was like. And if that house was to be their prison, there would at least be a beautiful forest to walk through. If, she bit her lip, they were *allowed* to walk through it.

Or, for that matter, if it was *safe* for them to walk through it. She'd noticed how carefully Jasak didn't speak about the reasons Hundred Forhaylin and his men had joined them in New Ransar. She didn't think he'd have been so reticent if he hadn't wanted to shield her and Jathmar from still more bad news, and they'd seen more than enough hostility out of all too many of the Arcanans with whom they'd come in contact on their journey from Hell's Gate.

Jathmar caught a glimmer of her feeling and slid an arm around her. She leaned against him, much as Gadrial had leaned against Jasak, and drew great comfort from the warmth and the aura of protectiveness that wrapped around her. But even that was a source of sorrow. It continued to be more and more difficult for them to "read" one another, despite the marriage bond. They still hadn't spoken to Gadrial or Jasak about it, and nothing had changed their reasons for that. If something was weakening their Talents—and it was getting even worse; even the range of Jathmar's Mapping Talent had been drastically reduced and continued to dwindle almost daily—that was potentially deadly military intelligence. They couldn't let *anyone* know, not even Jasak and Gadrial, but the steady erosion distressed them both, and the fact that they couldn't explain it—to themselves, much less to anyone else—only added uncertainty to the distress. And there was already more than enough of both those things in their lives, without adding more to the load.

At least Jasak had done what he could to reduce their worry about the end of this journey. And much as she suspected she wouldn't have liked *all* the reasons Duke Garth Showma had sent Hundred Forhaylin to escort them, she was also profoundly grateful for his presence for at least one reason. Like Jasak, the duke appeared determined to minimize the temptation of the Arcanan high command—the "Commandery," Jasak called it—to break its own custody rules and seize Jathmar and Shaylar. That could have happened at any of the weary progression of military dragonfields and forts through which they'd passed, out of sight of any civilian agency or witnesses, and the temptation to do just that must have grown steadily greater as the ominous official silence from the war front stretched longer. That was the real reason, she knew, Jasak had used commercial sliders rather than using military transport ever since they passed through the universe of Pegasus, two universes before even New Ransar.

Shaylar had begun to truly believe how wealthy and powerful the Olderhan family was as she watched Jasak chartering private slider cars—not just tickets, entire sliders—in his father's name...and had seen the alacrity with which everyone from station masters to concierges to maître d's scurried to do his bidding. That belief had been an indescribable relief as it seeped into her bones, and Hundred Forhaylin was further proof of the power of the family whose sense of honor had become her and her husband's only protection.

There'd been another sign of that family's—or at least their *baranal*'s—sense of honor, too. Jasak had picked up a new dress uniform from the post store at Shaisal Air Base, just outside Chemparas, the largish city at the portal between Basilisk and Manticore. But the base didn't have anything suitable for Jathmar and Shaylar or Gadrial. He'd apologized to them all for that, but it wasn't until Forhaylin and his men turned up in New Ransar that she'd realized why apologizing was all he'd done. Once the security team was on-site with them, he'd taken all three of them on a shopping spree in Theskair...with a wary-eyed squad of the Garth Showma Guard prominently displayed everywhere they went.

The shopping trip had surprised them, since Shaylar and Jathmar had picked up practical Arcanan-style clothing along the way; but Jasak hadn't wanted them to arrive in Portalis wearing workmen's sturdy clothes. They might be prisoners, but they were political prisoners more than anything else, and their status was high enough to warrant the finest clothing available. Particularly since Arcana had done them sufficient injury to make any reparations he could offer them a high personal priority.

First impressions were also important, he'd explained with a very sober expression. His parents would do their best to see Jathmar and Shaylar as foreigners, not bound by the same social conventions as Arcanans—any Arcanans, let alone Andarans— but having them show up in the kind of clothing the family's gardener wore would make it difficult for *other* people to treat them with respect.

Gadrial had been impressed that he'd recognized the problem, when he broached the subject with her earlier. And when he'd asked for her advice, she'd plunged into the spirit of things with childlike glee.

The results were well worth it. Shaylar had been transformed from a sturdy, tough-as-hickory pioneer into a stunningly graceful young woman. She wore the silks Gadrial had chosen like a queen, and the current Arcanan ladies' fashions, with their nipped-in waists and clean, elegant lines suited her petite stature. She would've been swallowed whole by the ruffles and flutters that had been popular when Jasak had left New Arcana for the frontier, but now—! If she'd been single, instead of married, Jasak would've been hard-pressed to turn away smitten suitors, her status as political prisoner notwithstanding, Gadrial thought, watching Shaylar run her fingers down a long, silken sleeve with absent sensuality.

Not that Shaylar had been the only one to profit from the expedition.

Now Jasak had to swallow a laugh as he, too, watched from the corner of one eye as Shaylar stroked her shirtwaist's sleeve and remembered the other side of the excursion...and his own reaction to it. Gadrial was close enough to Shaylar's shape and size for the styles and silks to be stunning on her, as well, and he'd gotten his first taste of jealousy when they left the first boutique, with Gadrial and Shaylar each wearing one of the ensembles they'd just purchased. The long, appreciative male glances at Gadrial, in particular, had left Jasak with rising blood pressure and a need to stomp hard on an equal rise in irritability. He'd gotten used to being the only unattached male in Gadrial's company.

He hadn't liked the change.

The intoxicating scent she'd picked up hadn't helped. The perfume was some earthy and exotic Ransaran concoction that punched him in the gut with the first whiff. Whatever it was, it smelled totally different on the two women despite the fact that he'd seen them both dabbing various pulse points from the same little bottle. On Shaylar, it was evocative of the wilderness and endless forests drenched with patches of sunlight and droplets of water from the last rain.

On Gadrial...

It should've been illegal on Gadrial.

To distract himself, he'd studied Jathmar critically, comparing him with the well-dressed men on the streets and in the lines at the slider station, and he'd come to the conclusion that Gadrial and the salesman had done equally well by Jathmar.

Jathmar was a rather nondescript fellow in a lot of ways, the kind of man most people wouldn't glance at twice, neither handsome nor homely. But he was in very good physical condition, if not the hardened, top-notch condition of military veterans on active duty. He not only wore the current styles well and contrived to look surprisingly distinguished, he moved well in them, with the kind of catlike grace trained athletes possessed. Once the uneasiness at finding himself in unfamiliar, expensive clothes wore off, he'd been transformed from a man who faded into the background into one who commanded intent glances from unattached women. He would certainly pass muster with Jasak's family and servants.

On the whole, the shopping trip had been well worth the time and money spent on it. As their slider whipped silently across the miles, following the shining dotted path of crystal control nodes, Jasak felt better about their reception in his parents' household. As to their reception into Arcanan society... That, he knew, would depend largely on how the press chose to portray the events at the frontier, and that wasn't looking good. By now, everyone knew the fighting had resumed, but *still* there was no official explanation of how and why, and in its absence, the rumors only grew more extreme every day.

Now, watching Jathmar and Shaylar, particularly the lovely

woman his men had come so close to killing, Jasak felt an ominous foreboding about the future—his own and theirs and both of their people's. Jasak's culture and theirs should have been able to meet one another peacefully, for they shared enough common ground to form genuine friendships. Watching Shaylar and Gadrial together was proof of that. If only that incompetent bastard Garlath—

He cut short that thought. Yes, Garlath had effectively started the war, but Jasak had been Garlath's commanding officer. The *blame* might be Garlath's, but the *responsibility* had been his, and he fully expected a court-martial. But the question of how the Commandery's officers would *vote* on that court was as up in the air as everything else, and until that court-martial was out of the way and resolved, one way or the other, he could make no plans for his own future.

His stomach seemed to congeal inside him as that familiar thought went thought him once more, and his glance lingered on Gadrial, who was busy poring over her PC, studying the Sharonian primer she and Shaylar had put together. She was now very nearly as proficient in their language as the Sharonians were in Andaran, and her expression was rapt with a scholar's joy as she worked on becoming even *more* proficient. Jasak's heart twisted as he watched that expression, watched the light play across Gadrial's face while the slider whipped across the last hundred miles toward home.

He wanted Gadrial to share that home with him.

Desperately.

He hadn't spoken to her about that. Not yet. And as the final miles flashed past, all the reasons he hadn't—the reasons he *couldn't*—crashed in upon him. It was like a vast weight, slamming down on him, blotting away the amusement he'd felt only a moment before. The moment was coming when he'd *have* to say something to her . . . one way or the other. And he couldn't. He simply couldn't.

He wasn't free, couldn't be free, to say a single thing to her about his hopes and dreams. He didn't want to think about what it would mean to him, personally, if a court-martial found him guilty, and not because of whatever sentence it might hand down. A woman like Gadrial deserved the very best in life, not a future tied to a man drummed out of the military in disgrace. He wouldn't—could never—even ask her to endure that.

Yet even if he was acquitted, would a Ransaran whose deeply held convictions about personal worth had been tested and turned to granite in the volcanic fires of Mythalan prejudice, even be willing to accept a proposal that would tie her to an Andaran officer and aristocrat? Submerge her in the suffocating web of obligations and honor-debts that comprised the only world Jasak truly understood? She'd had years of experience with Andaran customs during her time at the Garth Showma Institute, but that was a very different thing from *joining* that culture. She and Magister Halathyn had been enormously respected scholars and teachers, and that's what she still was. In their cases, Andaran custom had accommodated itself to *them*, not the other way around, and rightly so. But if he asked her to share his life, he wasn't simply asking her to live in Garth Showma with him, or even to accept the outer forms of culture and custom. He was asking her to marry the *heir* to Garth Showma, to accept the knowledge that one day he would become duke... and *she* would become duchess. One of the things he'd learned about her—one of the things he most *loved* about her—was that she would never, ever shirk an obligation she'd assumed, and she wouldn't shirk that one... *if* she accepted him.

He didn't see how she could.

True, one day he would be Duke of Garth Showma, a man of immense political power and wealth, whatever happened to his military career. Assuming, of course, that none of the charges which might be levied against him carried the death sentence. But the mere inheritance of a title would carry less weight with Ransarans than with almost anyone else in the Union of Arcana. Many of them actively *despised* hereditary titles and the—in their opinion—unearned power that went with a mere accident of birth. Gadrial wasn't one to be prejudiced against someone by the mere fact that he possessed a title, but she was no friend of aristocratic privilege, either. If she ever had been, her time in Mythal would undoubtedly have cured her of the infatuation!

Why should one of the most gifted theoretical magisters—*Ransaran* theoretical magisters—in the entire Union chain herself to a man who might soon find himself stripped of his commission and utterly disgraced? A lesser woman might accept him based on the Olderhan wealth and title, but no amount of money could make a man worthy of Gadrial Kelbryan. She was too exceptional, too accomplished, too brilliant in her own right—too *strong*—to ever live as a man's shadow. She deserved everything. He could only complicate her life and add extra responsibilities to interfere with her passion for magical research.

And even if she might be willing to entertain the thought of accepting his proposal, what about her family? How *did* they feel about aristocrats? What if, unlike her, they *did* despise the very concept of aristocracy? And how would *they* feel about his dishonor if the court-martial did strip him of his rank and expel him from the military in disgrace? About the part he'd played, whatever a court decided, in launching the first inter-universal war in human history?

He was afraid to even suggest his parents travel to Ransar and speak with hers, for what could Sathmin Olderhan say in his defense? "He didn't mean to" was such a paltry apology for the man who'd begun a war that had already claimed the life of Gadrial's mentor. Not the kind of troth gift that convinced a family to permit an engagement. But the thought of her going out of his life—the thought of one of those men on the streets of New Ransar standing beside her, instead—left him feeling like the ashes of last week's campfire: cold and gray and utterly desolate.

Perhaps it was the intensity of his inner turmoil or perhaps it was just the helpless stare that he couldn't help, unable to pull his eyes away from her face, but she lifted her head, abandoning the display on her personal crystal to meet his eyes. The instant their gazes touched, a jolt like lightning blasted through him. Blessed Torkash, how he wanted this woman to stay in his life!

Gadrial, too, jolted when their gazes met and she saw the look—the longing, the hunger...and the fear—in his eyes. She knew in that moment, as clearly as if she'd had Shaylar's Talent as a Voice—*exactly* what he was thinking, exactly what he feared... and why. She *knew* it, yet for a long, wrenching moment, she didn't know what to *do* about it. Anything she said or did—or didn't say or do—was likely to push him in a direction she didn't want him to go. Then she thought about what a future without Jasak Olderhan in it would do to her.

She put away her personal crystal with brusque movements, quite suddenly angry clear through. Angry over the massive injustice of the whole situation, angry that he would back away without ever giving her the chance to say yes or no to whatever it was he wanted to say or ask her. So she stuffed her PC into its carrying case, jerked to her feet, and strode over to his seat. She felt Shaylar's startled gaze follow her, with Jathmar's joining it an instant later.

"Jasak," she said in a low voice, "would you walk with me for a moment?"

Surprise flared in his eyes and a frown of uncertainty drove between his brows, but he stood up without a word. Once she was sure he'd follow, Gadrial turned and marched toward the door that led into the enclosed space between their private car and the one behind it. The instant Jasak had joined her there, closing the door behind him, she turned to glare up at him.

"Gadrial?" he asked warily, reacting to the anger surging through her.

Anger at the enormous, insufferable, idiotic weight of Andaran pride and Andaran stupidity stacked against her, against Jasak. Against *them*.

"You look like a man about to make a decision, Jasak Older-han," she said in a low, hard voice. "An irrevocable decision."

His eyes widened. She read alarm and the beginning of genuine panic in his expression. She didn't give those reactions time to solidify.

"I just want to make one thing perfectly clear, before you start making decisions your insufferable pride won't let you back away from or reconsider."

She grabbed his uniform lapels and jerked hard. He might be well over a foot taller than she was, but Gadrial was in superb physical condition and he wasn't expecting her to jerk him forward, off balance. The instant his head was in range, she let go of his uniform, plunged her fingers through his hair, and kissed him with every ounce of creativity and passion she could summon from her admittedly limited repertoire.

Apparently his repertoire was even more limited than hers, because he simply stood there in utter shock for long seconds while she did everything she could think of, short of ripping his clothes off and seducing him right where he stood. She did things with her lips and tongue she hadn't realized the human mouth was physically capable of doing.

A long, deep shudder ran through his whole body...

Then a groan tore loose, like a tree in the dead of winter, splitting down the center with a thunderous snap. Quite suddenly her feet were no longer touching the floor and Gadrial discovered that his repertoire was considerably more inventive than hers, after all. Her senses swam as he crushed her close, nearly breaking bones as he pulled her against a chest that was hard as granite.

She didn't care.

Every inventive touch of his lips, his tongue, and his hands on her body wreathed Gadrial in wildfire and smoke. When they finally came up for air, she was shaking violently. And so, she realized with a sense of marvelous satisfaction, was he. They stared into one another's eyes. His were wide and shocked.

"Does that clarify things a little, Jas Olderhan?" Her voice was soft and husky, and he swallowed once. Then—

"Yes," he whispered. "Yes, I do believe that does, Magister Gadrial."

"Good. Now if you'd be so kind as to put me down, we can both get on with what we were doing when you started to make a decision without all the facts."

"What?" He blinked, then realized he still held her nestled tight against him with both feet off the floor. A sheepish look stole across his face. "Ah . . ." Then he muttered, "Oh, what the hell . . ."

By the time he broke the second devastating kiss, Gadrial's knees were such jelly that if he *had* put her down, she would very probably have collapsed. One corner of his mouth crooked into a satisfied little smile as he set her down at last. To her amazement, she *didn't* collapse . . . probably because he still had one arm firm around her.

"Does *that* clarify things a little more?" he asked, and brushed one fingertip across her cheek as the sense of his words finally sank in. Her breath stuttered under that exquisitely gentle touch. Then she breathed out.

"Oh, yes . . . that clarifies things very nicely," she allowed.

"Good."

He held her a long, long moment longer, then took his arm back with manifest reluctance, led her back into their slider car, and guided her back to her seat. She couldn't have made it there unaided. And when he settled her solicitously into her seat and handed her the carrying case with her PC, she simply held it in limp hands, still reeling from the aftershock of that second fusion of lips and thundering heartbeats.

Jasak opened the case for her and put her PC back into her hands, then resumed his own seat.

Jathmar was staring in bafflement, but when Shaylar caught Gadrial's stunned gaze, she grinned and winked. Gadrial found herself answering that grin with a sheepish smile.

She also spent the next quarter of an hour staring at the same line of Ternathian script, without once taking in the shape of the letters, let alone what the words meant.

She was too busy being deliriously delighted with the outcome of that little experiment in cross-cultural communications. Whatever happened when they reached Portalis and Garth Showma, Gadrial had made sure Sir Jasak Olderhan understood exactly how she felt. She wasn't going to let anybody—neither the Commandery of Arcana nor Jasak Olderhan, himself—wreck what they could build, together.

Not without a down-and-dirty fight!

CHAPTER EIGHTEEN

Hayrn 18, 206 YU
(January 9, 1929 CE)

SHAYLAR SAT BESIDE THE SLIDER WINDOW AND PEERED OUT
with rising excitement. They were very near the end of their
journey, at last, and she was eager to see the Union of Arcana's
capital city. The universe explorer in her had longed to stop and
do surveys all along the way here, but as prisoners of war, even
honored *shardonai*, they didn't control the itinerary. And despite
the length of their journey, they'd seen very little of Arcana's cities.

They'd spent most of the journey through the outer universes
flying on military dragons, which landed on military bases, not
in civilian cities. Once they'd reached the inner universes, they'd
boarded sliders, which passed through every crystal-controlled
traffic junction at high speed. Some truly enormous towns for
frontier universes had hung tantalizingly on the other side of
the slider windows, but they'd been so busy *passing through* that
there'd been no time to really study anything.

The only real Arcanan city they'd even spent an hour in
was Theskair. While Shaylar had been amazed by that city—it
had a population of almost two million—it was little more than
a sleepy, backwater town compared with Portalis, according to
Gadrial. Now that they were close enough to actually see Portalis
in the distance, she knew the other woman had been right. The
capital of New Arcana stunned the senses.

Tajvana was a large city, the largest Shaylar had ever visited.
During the years she'd spent at the Portal Authority's academy,
she'd marveled at the city built on both sides of the Ylani Straits.
But Portalis made Tajvana seem small.

Their final approach wasn't made at ground level. The slider's crystal control network lifted into the sky, running alongside a wide pedestrian bridge which floated nearly eighty feet above the earth, skimming well clear of the magnificent winter forest below. The vast expanse of trees was the estate where Jasak had grown up, and he hadn't exaggerated his description of the lands. She could tell at a glance that she was looking at pristine, old-growth forest, truly untouched despite two centuries of settlement. Even with only winter-bare branches, it was breathtakingly lovely.

That soaring bridge should have been impossible. On Sharona, it would have been. The crystals that guided the sliders were embedded only now and again in the bridge rail, and the towers connected to the bridgeway from below were very nearly gossamer structures, like spiders' trailing lines that must surely sway to the touch of any breeze. Those slender towers couldn't possibly be structural supports for the bridge, let alone the sliders floating past on either side.

"Why is the sliderway so high, here?" Jathmar asked as they hurtled silently over the treetops, and Jasak's mouth crooked in a half smile that was part embarrassment.

"When the Union wanted to put in a slider path, several decades ago, my grandfather—who, just coincidentally, also happened to be named Sherstan—refused to allow the construction battalion to cut down any trees. He said that forest had been held in a pristine state for a century and a half and no transport clerk was going to cut the heart out of it with a slider right-of-way."

He rolled his eyes. "Grandfather was fond of colorful exaggeration. All they wanted to do was cut down enough trees to entrench a control lattice, something on the order of fifty feet wide. But Sherstan was a stubborn old . . . gentleman," he said carefully, causing Shaylar and Gadrial to glance at one another in amusement. "He told them," Jasak continued, determinedly ignoring their suppressed laughter, "that if they were so set on building sliderways to hook Portalis to the rest of the multiverse, they could by Torkash run the sliders *over* the forest. Which is exactly what they did.

"So many people stopped their sliders along the route to take in the scenery that they ended up building the pedestrian bridge too and modding the guidance crystal spellware to ensure all the sliders keep moving. My family added the lifts later—"

he pointed to the towers "—to allow people to walk around in the forest itself."

"But weren't there already roads cut through it?" Jathmar asked. "If this is the main portal out of Arcana, there must be roads leading out of the city, through your family's land?"

"There are," Jasak nodded. "Those roads were built at the same time the Union formalized the treaty conferring property rights on my family. The city and the Union can maintain and widen *those* roads as necessary, which they've done many times. For all practical purposes, there's only one portion of the original land grant still in forest cover." He pulled over the map again and zoomed in to show them. "This section, surrounding the falls, across to here, is still in forest. The rest of it's been leased out to the city and to the Union—for the military bases, primarily, but also for access corridors to the suburbs that extend for many miles beyond the leased land.

"That's why Portalis is lopsided, like this." He zoomed back out and pointed to the irregular blob of the city, which bulged and fanned out across the map on the sides away from the forested estate. "What the Transportation Corps wanted to do was run a line through the inviolate section left in old-growth forest. Grandfather refused to cut down even one more tree of what was left."

"That doesn't seem unreasonable to me," Shaylar said, studying the map and glancing out the window. "When one has a legacy to protect, one has to be adamant about such things. Otherwise, there'd eventually be nothing left to conserve."

Jasak smiled. "That's precisely how he felt and frankly, I agree with him. For one thing, it would've robbed the citizens of Portalis, since the section they wanted to cut the line through runs through a section of the forest that's open to the city as a public park."

Shaylar broke into a delighted smile. "That's a wonderful thing to do for your neighbors!"

Then the slider rounded a curve on its approach to Portalis and Shaylar got her first close look through the wide train windows.

"Oh..."

The single word was a soft exhalation of wonder.

Portalis was a magical city...literally. The dominant feature was, naturally, the portal. It wasn't the largest she'd ever seen, but it was a whopping big one, nonetheless, and every single mile of that immense hole in reality was jammed with roads, control towers for sliders, floating highways, and what looked like flocks of migrating birds, except these "birds" were dragons of so many bewildering sizes and hues the air seemed to shimmer from all their wings. They flew in what seemed at first to be total chaos, but as she stared, entranced, she began to discern patterns.

Beasts of a certain size flew in one line, on what was clearly a well-established flight path. There were dozens of such lines, each with dragons of a different size, going at different speeds. Some of the small beasts were falcon-fast, making impossible maneuvers as they shot over and around other flight paths.

There were smaller winged creatures, as well. The gryphons they'd seen again and again at military bases whipped through Portalis' skies at phenomenal speeds, intent on errands Shaylar couldn't even guess at. Other flying things registered as she gazed in wonder at the astonishing panorama ahead, and what looked like small lozenges floated well above the ground, although still far below the sliderway, moving at a surprisingly rapid pace.

"What are those?" she pointed.

Gadrial answered. "The very latest in transportation. They're automated carriages, powered by the latest motive spells. The official name is 'automoticars,' but that's too big a mouthful. The advertisers are calling them 'motics,' although I'm not sure the name's going to catch on. At this point, they're still new enough, the public really hasn't decided, yet, *what* to call them."

"Why so new?" Jathmar frowned. "Those motic things are much smaller than a slider. Why weren't they developed first?"

"Ah," she smiled. "The problem was one of steerage. Sliders are guided by the control net and even dragons are guided by pilots. Gryphons are small enough and smart enough to avoid mid-air collisions, but the idea of hundreds of ungoverned vehicles—even thousands of them—flying anywhere people chose, straight through established flight paths, flown by anybody with enough cash, not by responsible, licensed pilots, buzzing across roads, whipping around people's houses and through city streets..." She shuddered. "The very idea horrified city councils. Most cities passed laws prohibiting ungoverned flying vehicles piloted by nonlicensed pilots.

"Things stayed that way for a long time, until a very bright spellcaster—a Ransaran, of course," she added, eyes sparkling with mischief and challenge, "figured out how to cast a motive spell that follows predetermined flight paths, responding to a series of permanent traffic pods put up in a grid all over the city. Once he did that, the door opened and the djinn was out of the bottle, so to speak.

"Although I've never understood why any rational person would actually want to let a djinn out of its bottle," she added in a surprisingly grim tone. "They're bad-tempered, incurable liars who invariably cheat any fool stupid enough to fall for their promises. Of course, they do provide a decent living for spell-casters who specialize in personal disaster and curse reversal, not to mention attorneys representing people damaged when some idiot wished for the most beautiful women in the world, which caused a djinn to yank a thousand or so perfectly innocent girls out of their houses, offices, or schools with no warning at all and no way to get home again, without suing the irresponsible worm responsible for djinn-napping them."

Shaylar and her husband gaped at Gadrial.

"You...are joking, aren't you?" Shaylar gulped.

"I never joke about women wronged through no fault of their own," Gadrial said, grim as any soldier on the way to combat.

"It's a recurrent problem," Jas said quietly. "The military's returned victims home many times, as a public service. There are djinn-victim aid societies, too, and it's illegal—profoundly so—to traffic with a djinn. But idiots and reckless, irresponsible jackasses keep risking it, convinced *they'll* come out ahead. They never do, but the challenge and the lure is just too irresistible for some.

"It doesn't help that djinn are almost impossible to control, once released. There's a whole branch of the UBI—the Union Bureau of Investigation—devoted to tracking the magic trails left by renegade djinn some fool's let loose, but it takes a powerful spell-caster to re-bottle a djinn. It usually requires a team of them, acting in concert. More than one team's subsequently encased a djinn bottle in concrete, to keep anyone from releasing it again, but the black market thrives on stealing bottled djinn out of holding facilities and selling them at huge prices to gullible fools. We can't just dump them into deep ocean water, because some black marketer would use lifting spells to bring the bottle back up to the surface. And you can't drop a djinn's bottle into a volcano, either. That just melts the bottle and lets it out, again.

That was tried, once, with genuinely horrifying results. You can't kill a djinn by roasting it in lava, but you can make it furious enough to level a city."

Shaylar stared in horror and Jasak shook his head, partly in sorrow, partly in obvious disgust.

"Some people are just too stupid or too desperate to pay attention to public warnings or the mandatory prison sentences for anyone trafficking in djinn, whether it's selling a corked bottle or uncorking one for gain or revenge. Those are the worst cases, by far—the revenge cases. Trying to undo a revenge-motivated djinn attack can be a nightmare. People have died, from it. *Lots* of people, over the years. There's a reason for those mandatory sentences, and anyone responsible for a djinn episode that kills someone is tried for voluntary manslaughter even if that was never his intent. If it *was* his intent, it's an automatic charge of premeditated murder, whatever he may claim about extenuating circumstances."

Jathmar's jaw muscles quivered as fury swept through him. "Just how the hell did these things come to exist?"

"They were created, we think," Gadrial replied when Jasak hesitated. "During the Arcanan portal war, two centuries ago. By Mythalan *shakira* caste lords and their greatest magisters. The Ransarans lodged massive protests when the Mythalans turned the djinn loose against Andaran armies and ships—in fact, that's what brought most of Ransar actively into the war on the other side—but the protests didn't do any good. We've been trying to bottle them back up—permanently—for two hundred years. So far, no one's succeeded."

"There's no way to destroy the things?" Jathmar demanded, and Gadrial bit her lip.

"The last team that tried it..." She shuddered. "No one's tried actually killing one since, although we've been working on an approach we *think* would work at Garth Showma. The problem is that we aren't *sure* it'll work, and it's the sort of field test that only gets to go wrong once. Sooner or later, we may have no choice but to give it another try, and we intend to go right on refining our R and D until we *have* to trot it out. In the meantime, fortunately, they can be forced back into bottles, eventually, with enough sufficiently Gifted magisters. But trying to kill one just makes it desperate enough and mean enough to get truly ugly."

Her voice turned bitter.

"They know being bottled won't be a permanent state. Most of them think it's an amusing game, being released and having their fun, trying to elude capture in the chase, then being cornered and put back into a bottle, then waiting for some black marketeer to steal the bottle again so some other idiot will open it. They actually make a contest of it, amongst themselves. They're hoping that eventually, we'll get tired of chasing them down and leave them unbottled."

"Which is something we don't dare do," Jasak added grimly.

"Why don't they just kill anyone who tries to bottle them?" Jathmar asked, still seething with anger.

"Because it isn't sporting," Jasak growled. "Their creators gave them a sense of humor and a twisted sense of respect for anyone clever enough to re-bottle them, as well as an appetite for creative ways to dupe their victims. So far, that seems to be holding true, but as Gadrial just implied, we can't be certain it'll stay that way forever. And, of course, the day it stops being true is the day some poor team of magisters is going to find out about it the hard way. The magisters know it, too," he said grimly, his eyes flicking sideways to Gadrial for just a moment, "but they have to go right on bottling them and pray each time that *this* isn't the moment the djinn stop playing games and start slaughtering magisters. That," he added with a vicious snarl in his voice, "is another reason I hate most Mythalan *shakira*."

Shaylar stared from Gadrial to Jasak and back again, then shuddered.

"Every time I think I've gotten used to your culture, something like this knocks the props out from under me, again, and I end up feeling like a lost and scared little girl. Again."

Jathmar slipped an arm around her, and she needed it. If they were willing to do that to one another, she thought, what would they do to Sharona? Would their Commandery decide to uncork those bottles and turn the djinn loose against Sharona's forts? Sharona's *cities*? She leaned against her husband's shoulder, trying to blot that ghastly image from her mind and not succeeding very well.

Jathmar's worry for her prompted him to change the subject, bringing the conversation back to the one they'd been discussing before their unexpected digression.

"So these 'motics' respond to programmed pods that steer them?"

Gadrial nodded, and her expression was relieved.

"Yes. The pods keep them in clearly marked lanes high enough above the streets and houses not to endanger anyone on the ground but low enough to avoid collisions with other air traffic. A car's owner must tell the vehicle's guidance crystal where he or she wants to go, and the GC is programmed to contact the nearest traffic control pod by means of a short-range communication spell. The pod sends back a response call that gives the car's GC the flight path to reach the next pod in the system, leading the car from pod to pod until it reaches the its destination."

"It sounds complicated," Shaylar put in, grateful that her voice didn't shake as much as her insides, which were still quivering.

"It *is* complicated. The initial spellware was very complex to build, and it took the designers and city traffic engineers a couple of years to set up the grid, put the pods in place, test the system, and work out the kinks even after the initial spells were created. Then they had to convince the air traffic controllers and the city councilors it would work and that it would be safe. But they finally did it and the system went live a few months before I left to join Halathyn. Motic sales soared so quickly the makers couldn't produce them fast enough to fill the orders."

"If there was so much resistance from the government, what gave the companies enough incentive to go ahead with them?" Shaylar wondered.

"The military wanted them," Jasak explained. "For the officers' corps, mainly. It's cumbersome to schedule a pilot and dragon to fly across town, but that's usually the fastest way to get around, especially in a city as large as Portalis. We have the best mass transit system in New Arcana, but the public sliders make so many stops it can take double the dragon flight time to reach anywhere in Portalis even with the faster slider speeds. And the portion of the city in Arcana, beyond the portal, wasn't built for the public city slider system, but the pod control system's flexible enough to be made to work even in Old City Portalis. Of course, motics can't cross a portal threshold any better than a slider can, and that's going to be an ongoing problem for their owners. You've seen the elaborate arrangements the slider stations have for transferring passengers between coaches at a portal, but how does the owner of a private motic manage that?" He shook his head.

"I think they'll manage it in the end," Gadrial said confidently. "There's been some fundamental research into purely mechanical ways of getting entire sliders across thresholds, Jas. If we can make that work, we can scale it down for motics. And there'll be a lot of motivation to do just that." She shrugged. "As you say, it's flexible enough to make it work *anywhere*. Eventually, *every*one's going to want one of them, so the pressure to make it work will certainly be there!"

Shaylar glanced out the window, where the vast spread of the city stretched for miles. "I can well imagine. It's certainly faster than any carriage I've ever seen! And some of our largest cities are a nightmare to navigate during peak traffic times."

Curiosity touched Jasak's eyes, but he was careful about pushing Shaylar and Jathmar for details they were unwilling to share. She and her husband both knew how fortunate they were that to have avoided falling into the hands of someone like Hundred Thalmayr. He would have treated them like criminals. Or worse. Each time Jasak Olderhan showed restraint, Shaylar and her husband gave thanks for their good fortune.

So she said, "What did you want to ask about our cities, Jasak?"

Surprise lit his eyes. Then he leaned forward. "You've never told us what the capital city of Sharona is called. Will you at least tell me that?"

The unspoken, "So I'll have something concrete to tell my superiors" was clear, and Shaylar glanced at Jathmar, who met her gaze with as much dismay as she felt. Neither of them knew what to say. Sharona had no capital city because it wasn't a unified world, the way Arcana was. Yet admitting that would only make Sharona seem weak and disorganized. Even Shaylar, about as unmilitary as a person could be, realized the danger inherent in that.

She felt her husband's desire to handle this one, so she let him speak. His answer surprised her, but it made sense, as well.

"The city's called Tajvana. For several thousand years, it was the capital of Sharona's largest and most ancient empire, called Ternathia."

"The name of the language you taught us," Gadrial said in surprise.

Jathmar nodded. "Ternathia either controlled or colonized at least two thirds of the world. Today, Tajvana is the seat of world governance. Even our Portal Authority is headquartered there, despite the fact that no portal lies in or near Tajvana."

Shaylar could very nearly see the thought that formed behind Jasak Olderhan's eyes: *Their capital city is protected from direct invasion through a portal.* She managed to hold in the shiver that touched her spine, feeling glad—very glad—Jathmar had answered. She would've bungled it, she knew, but Jathmar hadn't actually lied, not once.

Which hadn't prevented him from leaving the distinct impression of a long-unified multiverse government. The failed truce in Hell's Gate had been called under the auspices of something called the Sharonan Empire, but neither of them knew if that really existed as more than a polite fiction useful for negotiating with the Union of Arcana. Yet if Sharona as a unified political entity *had* come into existence after Toppled Timber, Tajvana was the city most likely to be named as the seat of that new multiversal government.

Who would head it and what form it might take were unknowable. Shaylar couldn't even hazard a guess. So she sent a flood of gratitude to Jathmar over the weakened bridge of their marriage bond and turned her attention back to the city they were approaching. The closer they got to Portalis' heart, the more amazing it grew.

Buildings soared to impossible heights, rising at least forty or fifty floors above the streets, and the shapes were even more astounding than their height. One immense building resembled a butterfly, with wings outstretched beyond a central tower shaped like the long, slender body of that delicate insect. The windows in those "wings" dazzled the eye, catching the sunlight with myriad colors, mimicking real butterfly wings with uncanny success.

Others had fantastic, soaring arches that spanned entire city streets, connecting buildings, allowing people to cross busy thoroughfares without leaving a covered building. Yet those arches seemed gossamer thin, like bridges made of spidersilk and thistledown and soap bubbles. She couldn't imagine how they didn't fall apart or plunge into the busy streets below, let alone support so many people's weight as they crossed along the soaring spans.

Other buildings had strange projections, like shelf mushrooms made of glass and what caught the sunlight like metal. Only these "shelves" were the size of large houses, projecting sixty and seventy feet from the sides of buildings, with no visible support. Their walls and roofs were almost entirely glass and they were undeniably beautiful, but Shaylar would have been petrified just nerving herself to step out onto one of them. When the slider slowed and the sliderway angled down to a height merely twenty feet above street level, she stared in wonder at yet more sights nothing could have prepared her for.

Everywhere she looked, there was something new and marvelous, so much, her senses began to overload. She couldn't take it all in. Little flashes now and again came clear in the blur of unfamiliar sights. People rising up the sides of buildings in lines like marching ants, to reach doorways cut into the sheer, vertical sides of those buildings. Many of those doorways were cut into the sides of the strange, cantilevered "shelf mushroom" extensions, which she could see more clearly, now that they were actually inside the city.

She saw street entertainers performing complex acrobatics and dances, while hovering mid-air. They whirled like spinning tops, made prodigious leaps, turned graceful somersaults like a high-trapeze artist, except there were no apparatuses to assist them. They simply danced and whirled and leapt like birds who'd decided to take up acrobatics.

Sidewalk artists painted the air. Glorious swaths of color burst into being as they swept their hands in complicated patterns, creating breathtaking works of art that shone with unearthly beauty. Some glowed with soft tones, others glittered like gold dust, and still others scintillated like sunstruck opals. As Shaylar watched, entranced, a girl pointed to one of the patterns hovering mid-air and the whole glowing "painting" floated gently over to an easel, where it landed on what looked like a sheet of that strange, glassy substance that stored spells.

The artist picked up the sheet and handed it to the girl, who passed money to him, then walked away with her artwork, smiling happily. The other patterns floated over to other sheets of that strange glassy material, creating yet other paintings the artist then stacked up beneath the easel, and Shaylar sighed as she sat back in her seat.

"What's wrong, Shaylar?" Gadrial asked in sudden worry.

She turned her gaze away from the astonishing city. She was still so amazed by what she'd just seen, she blurted out precisely what was on her mind.

"I wanted one of those glorious paintings. The ones that artist painted in the air." Then she reddened and covered her face with both hands. "I can't believe I just said that," she said, aghast.

Jasak laughed softly. "If you want a spell painting, Shaylar, I believe I can afford to buy one for you."

She lowered her hands to meet his gaze. "I didn't mean—"

"I know you didn't," he said gently. "But it's my fault you're here, unable to leave. If you want something beautiful, that's only natural. And Shaylar, if you ever need *anything*, tell me. Please. My responsibility for you is as deep as though you were members of my own family. I'm bound by honor to provide you with everything you need, and the friendship I've come to feel for you makes me want to provide you with gifts, as well—things you might have purchased for yourself, before all of this happened.

"At some point, it's my hope we'll be able to help you work in some fashion, to earn your own money. I know it must gall to be totally dependent on what you surely view as charity or the grudging support of a jailor," he added, looking into Jathmar's hooded eyes, as he spoke. "You probably think I don't understand how you feel, and I will admit I probably don't.

"But I do understand wanting to feel like I've accomplished something on my own merit. Neither I nor my sisters have the slightest need to work, but we all do, nonetheless. Except for the youngest, who's still in school. Working, contributing to society, earning your own money—that's something important to self-esteem. But until we can find some way for you to do that, until we can help teach you to live safely in Arcanan society, you must rely on my help, financially.

"You've been watching the city with wonder and fright in your eyes. Now that you've seen some of the things that happen on an ordinary city street, I think you have a better understanding of the fact that we have to teach you how to live, here. How to avoid unseen dangers, such as accidentally stepping into a spell-field that sends you thirty stories up the side of a building when you're not expecting it. That will take time, as well.

"I *hate* seeing you virtually helpless as young children, when both of you are extremely intelligent, well-educated, talented—and Talented—" he added with a very serious expression of respect, "people, highly skilled at what you do."

Shaylar, seated on a train in the middle of the most amazing city she'd ever seen, met Jasak's worried eyes and bit her lower lip. "I'd like to work, somehow. But there's very little I can do, here."

"You and Jathmar could find some way, surely, to put your Talents to use," Gadrial said.

Shaylar glanced at her husband, trying to send a silent question to him. It was like trying to walk through thick syrup, now, to reach his mind, and what little she could still sense took as much mental effort as it had once taken to connect another telepath at the very edge of her eight-hundred-plus-mile range.

His glance into her eyes was hooded and wary; then a sigh escaped him and he shrugged.

"We might as well tell them," he said softly. "Maybe Gadrial can tell us why."

"Tell you what?" she asked as Jasak leaned abruptly forward, gaze sharp with sudden interest.

Jathmar lifted one hand to touch Shaylar's face, then turned to Gadrial. "We can barely Hear one another, now."

Gadrial blinked. "I don't understand."

"Neither do we," he said.

"What, exactly, do you mean?" Jasak asked.

Shaylar tried to explain. "At one time, I could touch Jathmar's emotions, his feelings, so easily, I could often guess what he was thinking. You saw, yourself, what happened on board that first ship, when I was so distressed. Jathmar felt my chaotic emotions so clearly, he came charging into Gadrial's cabin from ours. That's gone," she whispered, very nearly in tears. "I have to very nearly Shout to make Jathmar sense my emotions through the marriage bond, now. And it's terribly difficult for me to sense his. Even sitting close, like this, it's hard to do. When we're in different rooms, now, we can't Hear each other at all."

Jasak stared from one to the other and back. "That makes no sense."

"You think we don't know that?" Jathmar demanded in a harsh voice. "We've lost everything else. And now we're losing the most precious thing our marriage gave us: the telepathic bond between us." Pain and anger throbbed through his voice.

"Why didn't you say anything sooner?" Gadrial asked, baffled. Jathmar only looked at her, but, after a moment, Jasak answered for them.

"Because it's important data, Gadrial," he said. "Militarily important." He sounded weary, frustrated. It came as a shock when Shaylar realized he felt that way because of the added pain it was causing them. When Gadrial still looked baffled, Jasak explained.

"If their Talents don't work as well here, their military's greatest advantages—including their Voice network—disappear. That places their soldiers at a serious disadvantage."

"But *why*?" Gadrial wondered. "If their Talents don't work as well here, would our Gifts not work as well on their homeworld?"

"You tell me," Jasak said quietly. "With Halathyn gone, you're the best theoretical magister we have. The team you've built at the Garth Showma Institute is as good as anything in Mythal. Surely there's something you can do to figure out why something like this might be happening?"

Gadrial's eyes reflected one moment of stark terror as the sudden responsibility for answering a question of that magnitude landed on her slim shoulders. Then the muscles in her jaw tightened and the look in her eyes shifted from fear to determination.

"All right," she said, her voice hard with purpose. "We'll do everything we can to figure it out."

She frowned in thought for several seconds, then raked one hand through her hair with a grimace of what looked very much like irritation.

"It occurs to me," she said slowly, "that we—theoretical magisters—have overlooked something very important. Something that was dismissed out of hand... and that I suddenly suspect shouldn't have been. The last year I was at the Mythal Falls Academy, I ran across an entire file of reports while researching a major project for Halathyn. They'd been files by early portal explorers, Gifted ones, who reported magic didn't work quite as well in pristine universes as it did here in Arcana. No one paid much attention to it, certainly not in academe. The analyses I read treated it almost as a joke. At best, a curiosity, but more likely just a mistake by people with poorly trained Gifts. And don't look at me like that," she added tartly when Jasak glared at her with a flash of irritation. "I don't mean to belittle the soldiers who reported those observations, let alone suggest they were incompetent. We hadn't seen anything significant, though, and what little was reported was a small enough difference to fall inside measurement error. Besides, *I* wasn't the one who dismissed their reports!

"Remember, Jasak, for most of the last two centuries, the only people doing research in the field of multi-universe theoretical magic fields were *shakira*. To them, any non-Mythalan is an unreliable observer, particularly when it comes to something as genuinely complex as theoretical magic and the way portals interact with the magic field. The Garth Showma Institute's the first non-Mythalan academy we've ever had that could match the Mythal Falls Academy."

Jasak managed a sheepish smile, mollified by her explanation.

"Sorry about that, Gadrial. I've just heard snide remarks from *shakira* a shade too often, myself, belittling anyone in the Army. Any non-Mythalan in the Army, at any rate. My father's position's meant I've seen and heard more *shakira* than most other Andarans."

Gadrial's expression softened. "Of course, Jas. And I realize the stress you're under, as well. I'm sorry I snapped at you." Then she frowned in an abstracted way. "If there *is* something about the way universes interact that make certain things possible in some universes but not in others, we need to know what it is and why it operates."

"Yes, we certainly do," Jasak agreed. "Urgently."

Gadrial's eyes glinted, and she nodded.

"Yes, I can see that, too," she said. "All right. I'll pull together the best theoreticians we have and sic them onto this question as our top priority."

"Thank you, Gadrial," Jasak said quietly. Then he turned to Jathmar and Shaylar. "And thank you, both of you, for telling us this. I understand the risk you've both run, revealing that. I can't even guarantee Arcana won't use that information against Sharona, should we somehow fail to stop the shooting war we've started, out there."

"You've been as honest with us as you can," Jathmar said slowly. "I appreciate that. Our situation..." His mouth tightened. "I could try for the rest of my life to explain it and you still wouldn't understand the depth of what we feel, cut off from everything and everyone, unable to reach our own families to tell them we're safe. Unable to trust your superiors, your government, unable to trust even *you* as fully as we might if we'd met under other circumstances. And now this. If Shaylar and I have to lose a vital piece of who we are, if our souls have to be ripped apart, as well as our lives... we'd at least like to know *why*."

Gadrial bit her lip. "I'll do everything I can to find that answer for you," she said in an unsteady voice.

"Thank you," Jathmar said softly. "That's all we can ask."

Before anyone could say anything further, the slider glided down a low slope to street level and slowed even more. A moment later, they were pulling into a long, low building. It was far more graceful than most of the slider stations they'd passed through on their endless journey, and it was adorned with magnificent frescoes and glowing sculptures of light, but none of that hid the utilitarian aspects of its design. Shaylar saw the multiple rails of guidance crystals that made it easy to shunt slider cars from one track to another, and one entire wall of the building opened on what she thought of as the equivalent of the Trans Temporal Express's switching yards. The broad pads used to recharge levitation accumulators stretched away from the covered passenger platforms in neat rows. There must have been at least a hundred—possibly twice that many, really—some of them empty, but most with sliders parked on them.

They'd reached Portalis Station.

Journey's end. She fumbled for Jathmar's hand and clutched it tightly. Physical contact improved her ability to read his emotions, and she could tell he wanted to put himself between her and any danger. Her hand trembled in his, and he turned and rested his brow against hers, trying desperately to restore the easy exchange they'd enjoyed since the day of their marriage, if only for just a moment or two. She could feel the love flowing from him, the fear for their future, the determination to protect her at all cost.

She lifted her face to look into his eyes and pressed a single, soft kiss to his lips, sending back all the love and reassurance she could. He even managed to smile. Then the slider sighed to a halt and a light blinked at the door leading to the station plat-form, letting passengers know the vehicle had settled to the same level as the platform. Jasak rose and extended a hand to Gadrial. She took it as she came gracefully to her feet and collected her equipment bag—*that* never went anywhere without her, although the arrival of Hundred Forhaylin and his men had at least given them plenty of other hands to carry their suitcases!

Jathmar pulled down a deep, deep breath, then he, too, rose and assisted Shaylar from her seat. Beyond the windows, the platform was a sea of people, all streaming from the dozens of other sliders, all greeting other people who waited on the platform. Shaylar could see happy reunions, almost hear the glad voices and laughter as families and friends were reunited, despite the sealed window.

Her chin quivered just once.

Then she followed silently as Jasak led the way out of the slider.

*   *   *

Sir Thankhar Olderhan met the travelers not as the Duke of Garth Showma, Governor of New Arcana, or any of the rest of his titles but as a father. He waved a barely recognizable crab-handed reply to the salutes hurriedly offered by Trooper Sendahli and Chief Sword Threbuch and wrapped his boy Jasak in a big bear hug. Jasak had outgrown his father by a good three inches sometime in his early teens, but the older man still managed to project power and strength.

Thankhar hadn't thought about those intangibles in years, but if asked, he wouldn't have been surprised to learn that the reporter across the street using image capture spellware managed to capture clear beautifully framed shots of familial bliss. It also would not have surprised him to learn that later the editor would throw the recording crystal at the reporter's head and send the young woman back out to get an image that could actually be used with the story headline: OLDERHAN HEIR RETURNS IN DISGRACE!

Instead he released his son from the hug and warmly greeted Gadrial, Shaylar, and Jathmar. The last two were family now, even if the Sharonans hadn't quite internalized just how much Jasak had meant that when he explained the *shardonai* term to them. As for Gadrial . . . well, he'd read his son's messages, and he had every hope she might be family one day too. He ushered them all into a palatial motic not so very much smaller than the slider they'd just left.

His staff coordinated with Forhaylin, Threbuch, and Sendahli to fill other vehicles, manage the luggage, and convey the rest of their gear the remainder of the way home.

*   *   *

Lady Sathmin Olderhan would have loved to have been waiting at the slider station for her oldest child's return. But before the scheduled arrival, there'd been a spate of tiny disasters uniquely suited to the duchess' touch. So she'd stayed behind expecting to follow after her husband in a second motic and still reach the station well before their son's slider arrived.

She was still home when the master of the sword in crimson full dress uniform knocked at the private entry to the ducal apartments, however, and she *stayed* home to keep the Master there to deliver his summons privately. She only stepped out into public view when the staff told her the motic was nearly home.

The reporter stationed outside the gate snapped *that* shot just fine: Sathmin Olderhan, Duchess Garth Showma, outside the ducal apartments looking deeply worried as the motic bearing Jasak and his party crested the rise on its way home. A little fiddling with the lighting to make the expression deeply foreboding and the image was fit to run on page one.

*   *   *

"Welcome home Jasak!" Sathmin embraced her son in a hug just as fierce as the one he'd received from his father at the station. "It's been far too long."

"Thank you, Mother." He hugged her back, holding her for several breaths, then inhaled deeply and stood back to do the introductions. "Mother, I believe you've met Magister Gadrial before. Maybe through your support of the Garth Showma Institute's veteran scholarship fund? These are Jathmar Nargra and Shaylar Nargra-Kolmayr, my *shardonai*. They've had a very long trip and would rather be home, but—"

"Of course I understand." Sathmin welcomed the group and ushered them all inside where a small army—*another* small army—of staff was on hand to make off with the luggage and carry it to the private suites assigned to each guest.

A quick word in her husband's ear was enough to have him vanish into the comfortable office where she'd convinced the master of the sword to wait, then she turned back with a smile to try to calm her guests.

"Jasak's written me, though not as much as I'd like." She arched a brow at him, and her son chuckled in response.

It was an old joke between them that she always wanted more letters home though in reality she was usually quite satisfied with the ones he did send. Normally she had more than enough information to put her heart at ease while he and his troops worked on the edges of the explored universes.

"Anyway," she waved a hand. "I do what every Andaran mother must, and spend hours and hours just pining away imagining horrible things—" She was already halfway into the familiar joke before she suddenly realized it had lost a lot of its usual humor. She paused, then shook herself.

"I imagine that for about a half second," she said composedly. "And then I remember Chief Sword Threbuch is there and I'm put entirely at ease. How is your family, Otwal? I saw your niece and her new baby just a few weeks ago. I hope everyone's doing well?"

Otwal ducked his head in acknowledgement. "This was our first stop, Your Grace. I actually haven't been to see the family yet."

"Of course." Sathmin pulled herself up straight. "Don't let me keep you. I did prepare some places for you here if you'd like to stay with us, but I certainly don't want to hold you to ceremony when there are people in Portalis you haven't seen in ages."

Otwal shook his head. "I wouldn't mind another night of easy sleep before meeting the newest rug rat. And I'm a bachelor myself, so there's no particular urgency to see the extended family."

He didn't add that reporting to the inquiry board would be easier to do from here than from his brother's place on the outskirts of Portalis on the Arcana Prime side of the city. The chief sword had seen the duke leave, and she suspected he'd correctly interpreted what it meant when a staff member discreetly called Jasak Olderhan away.

Sathmin didn't ask after Otwal's parents since she'd attended both their funerals several years past and, like many of the families with a long history of service in the Andaran Temporal Scouts, their ashes were scattered at the military memorial parade grounds maintained by the duke's private purse.

The ashes of the troops fallen in this current conflict were due to begin arriving back home soon, and Sathmin expected to be attending all the services. The memorial grounds were a quiet, serene place that until relatively recently had seen only weekly or monthly use as the elder and infirm passed on at great age. She didn't look forward to their new more frequent use or the changed tone that would come when services for old veterans were replaced by services for young men killed in combat.

They names of the dead and news of their loss had, of course, out paced the arrival of their ashes. And while Sathmin's routine visits to the bereaved were no less necessary, in some cases they were significantly less welcome when the shock of loss turned to anger. Worse, sometimes the family chose to blame the Andaran Army—especially in the absence of the official dispatches which might have explained *why* the young men they'd loved had died—since there were no Sharonians at hand. And through that tenuous contact, the fury made its mad connections to direct itself at Andara's highest commanders including the Duke of Garth Showma and thus also his wife, Sathmin.

"I understand, Otwal," she said. "Then you're welcome to stay with us, and I shall ask Cook to do her very best to tempt you to stay for just as many meals as you can possibly manage." She turned to Trooper Jugthar Sendahli. "And a very fine welcome to you also Trooper. I'm sorry I'm not acquainted with your family, but the same offer applies to you. We can speed you or your way or host you with us in whatever way makes you feel most comfortable."

Trooper Sendahli executed a deep bow that caused Gadrial's brow to furrow. Sathmin recognized it, too, as the greeting of a lowest *garthan* to a high caste *multhari shakira*.

"Oh please my friend, none of that! I'm an Andaran woman. If you start treating me like a Mythalan I'm sure I'll mess up all the ritual responses." That wasn't even remotely true, but it was the response she needed to make. Both the trooper and the magister relaxed immensely to hear it, and Jugthar Sendahli even gave her a tentative smile. Sathmin reached out and clasped his forearm, entirely giving herself away by using the *garthan* to *garthan* welcome between friends with a purely Andaran nod to complete the motion.

Gadrial's laugh was music to Sathmin's ears. She hadn't totally failed the first introductions at least, and she ushered the party in for lunch after ascertaining that Trooper Sendahli didn't mind staying to eat and that his family was, as she'd guessed, not housed anywhere near Portalis anyway. It would be here or the temporary barracks for him, and she had every intention that it would be here.

After the court took Sendahli's testimony, he'd be assigned to a local garrison, and she also intended to ensure that any duties that might naturally be assigned to a visiting trooper were kept flexible enough to allow him a week or two off to visit his family on the far side of the continent.

If army commitments wouldn't allow that, she'd try to arrange for some of Jugthar Sendahli's family to visit Garth Showma as her guests. Those invitations were easy enough to arrange between Andarans, but her interactions with *garthan* ancestry Mythalans were hit and miss. A wrongly phrased invitation could be too easily confused with a Mythalan *shakira's* order for a *garthan* peasant to become a house servant, and Sathmin had no desire to inspire fear. A family recently escaped from Mythal might have any number of psychological wounds she didn't want to open.

Sathmin danced through the polite social forms carefully. It wasn't easy—not when Jasak held his shoulders lower than she'd ever seen and had aged more in the last year than he should have from a strict counting of calendar days. And the unease in Shaylar and Jathmar's faces cried out to her heart, however bravely they tried to hide it . . . and not just because they were her son's *shardonai*. But that, at least, she could do something about, she hoped.

She personally showed the Sharonians to the green suite and offered other rooms to Threbuch and Sendahli. For Gadrial Kelbryan there was a lady's retiring room and a suite as well, but she expressed a desire to stay at her own home on the Institute grounds. Sathmin had half-expected that and tried not to push as she insisted the offer would remain open.

"If you'd ever like to stop by or perhaps visit for a bit, a tea, a meal, you're always welcome."

"Thank you." Gadrial said. "That was a formal summons from the Commandery wasn't it?"

Sathmin nodded, grim.

"I'd hoped we could all have one night's rest first," Gadrial's tone was harsh, "but I suppose the military's waited long enough for us to get here." She paused. "I saw the red uniform through the doorway when Jasak went in after the duke. Is it an inquiry or a court-martial?"

"Formal summons to a court of inquiry. But—" Sathmin couldn't leave the magister with false hope "—there will be a court-martial too. Thankhar will have to call for it if no one else does."

"Of course. An officer does the best he can in a horrible situation, and his supervisors have to dissect his every decision the instant he returns home." Gadrial laughed with an edge of bitterness. "Welcome to Portalis."

Sathmin grabbed the magister's hand. "He has us. We'll get him through. And his father will ensure he's treated fairly. Portalis is an odd mix of Mythal, Ransar, and Andara, but there's honor here. And the Union has to learn *why* it was horrible out there. You were there and I wasn't, but it doesn't sound like everyone else was trying to do their best."

"No." Gadrial agreed. "They certainly were *not*. And I'll be testifying to that if I have to enchant the doors of court myself to gain an entry."

"I'm sure that won't be necessary." Sathmin assured her as she walked the magister out.

CHAPTER NINETEEN

Hayrn 18, 206 YU
Darikhal 21, 5053 AE
(January 9, 1929 CE)

EMM VOS SIDUS HATED PORTALIS. HE HATED THE CROWDS of people, the racket, the disgusting mélange of Gifted and non-Gifted, and the need to pretend he *didn't* hate all that. Even the pristine magic source of the falls emitted a frost-coating mist instead of proper humidity.

The high-climbing city structures were filled with offices and manufactories, with not a palace in the lot. Portalis, on either side of the portal, hardly deserved the name of city. Even the Duke of Garth Showma's own family had little apartments in the city. A *shakira* with that demesne would level the mess of trees, build a proper villa with orderly plantings and garden the grounds. Emm would add a few dragon breeding fields and set *garthan* to working fields and livestock across the larger duchy to support the elite in the city, but Thankhar Olderhan did nothing so useful.

Instead the duke had his sizable living quarters in a corner of the Garth Showma demesne quite a ways distant from Portalis, leased property to merchants and army clerks, and allowed the masses to harvest deadfall timber from his private woods. The Olderhans didn't even stock the forests with predator game animals.

The Duchy of Garth Showma could be bearable in the summer months, when the wet of the falls cooled the skin instead of freezing to it. Not so in midwinter. Pretending to like Garth Showma's Snowfall Night festivities was yet another thing Emm hated about Portalis.

As a member of the *shakira* sent to treat with the upper crust of Andara, he had to lodge in what passed for elegance in a hotel near Garth Showma Institute. The lobby's wide windows proudly showed the falls choked by ice and snow with only a few of the base station chargers online to repower accumulators. Winter always affected the falls...yet another reason the flawed diamond of Andara could never compare to the brilliance of Mythal.

The Andarans grouped their hotel rooms in squads, small cramped rooms all of a size circled a common room. The clerks assumed a senior officer would share the same quarters and provisions as his men, and that any business traveler with his staff would likewise imitate Andaran military customs.

Andarans were idiots.

Emm vos Sidus took a full grouping. His staff were *garthantri*, drawn from the subclass who'd demonstrated personal loyalty to their betters for at least three generations. They were as magicless as all *garthans* but the very the best of their kind and they would adjust the place to better suit his needs while he took a leisurely lunch with an old friend. The common area would be his main chamber with most of the quartering spaces to become holding areas for his clothing, personal necessities, and bathing room. The lot of them would take turns sleeping in the remaining pair of rooms and use the bath down the hall.

They wouldn't bother him with the details, so vos Sidus put it from his mind. He was *shakira*. His task was the work of magic and those small duties assigned to him by his seniors, and his job today was a lunch, so a lunch he would have.

The "old friend" in question was a contact and not actually a companion in any true sense, but Emm vos Sidus did what his superiors asked, even if that meant taking up a friendship with an only barely gifted Andaran. And Nosak Urrihan *had* risen to the highest ranks of the Andarans now. It was only appropriate, vos Sidus agreed, for a person with some magic ability to be placed over so many with absolutely none, but if the man had been Mythalan he would have been carefully ringed all round by a cohort of many-generations-loyal *garthantri*. And probably with an equally carefully selected tutor. *Someone* needed to turn Nosak Urrihan's dabblings into something approximating competence, anyway.

The thought wasn't entirely fair. Back in his youth, when his duties had been limited to riding dragons, Urrihan might even have been a capable officer, but now the man was retired from military service and held a political appointment in the Andaran Air Force: Undersecretary, Office of Dragon Warfare. Urrihan could be relied on to fly his favorite old dragon breeds every chance he had. For everything else—policy making, the organization of branches and forces—he wasn't just uninformed, he was actively disinterested in ever becoming more knowledgeable or remotely capable. That made him an exceptionally useful idiot.

Emm vos Sidus made it a point to visit Urrihan at least once a quarter to maintain the fiction of their long-time friendship. Mostly they spoke of dragons. Emm's family bred the seadrakes, which Urrihan disdained as not true dragons, but since Urrihan didn't really consider transport dragons worthy of being called true dragons either, it was a friendly old argument.

And the shared luncheons and dinners weren't *that* terrible, either, since Andarans made a point of serving their troops good hearty meals whenever possible. Urrihan always made that observation, and Emm vos Sidus always agreed. And he actually meant it. Some truly excellent cuisine was available at this heart of Andaran power. They didn't serve the exquisite delicacies of Mythal, but there was something to be said for being able to dispense with a taster and enjoy the pantomime play that came with a trip outside his family estates.

In Garth Showma, vos Sidus pretended all people were equal and that he didn't even notice the poor quality of the spellware hanging about or that those who would have been trained up as *garthan* in a proper household were to be found here and there begging on street corners. In Portalis, some of the magicless pretended to be artists and played off-key music for coins in a hat and Urrihan seemed to enjoy hearing military marches butchered by street players, so vos Sidus even tossed the savages coins himself now and then.

Mostly he made charitable little gestures in Urrihan's company, but just in case someone in the Andaran's extended family ever smartened up enough to run some kind of inquiry, he did it while on his own as well. His duties outside the home estate were clear: make contacts, keep them at a distance, and plant servants in their households.

The girl he'd placed overtly with Urrihan was doing well. No complaints at all. In fact Urrihan was effusive in his praise and a little concerned that her period of study might end too soon, calling her back to Mythalan Falls Academy and leaving a hole in his staffing.

There was no notice at all of the others placed in the man's employ or the handful vos Sidus recruited among the *garthan* Mythalan immigrants living in the town. Those were utterly unreliable, since they'd abandoned their original lords and selfishly destroyed the trust their families had spent generations building, but a few words here and there via his own staff would always get them to feed him what he wanted to know.

Combine enough independent semi-reliable sources and a reasonably accurate piece of general intelligence could emerge. Currently he was interested in the mood of the city, and it was leaning strongly against the war.

The common people were horrified by the reports they were hearing. But they were still Andarans at heart, so they supported the soldiers: their brothers, sons, and grandsons in the forward universes. That meant the discontent had to go somewhere else, and it was beginning to focus on the Andaran Army's senior officers. That was too soon for the plan, but there'd always been a certain flexibility to the schedule, and no one could have anticipated the boon of the encounter with the Sharonian barbarians. Indeed, it seemed likely a good dose of fury towards the Sharonans would help spice everything up...and the Duke of Garth Showma's own son had brought back two Sharonan prisoners under the odd Andaran honor code.

Emm vos Sidus considered. *Yes. Yes. That should do nicely... and I won't even actually have to do a single thing!*

That was good. It would require no extension of his assets or risk exposing anything. The natural fury of an untrained mob of *garthan* was about to hit the lords of Garth Showma.

The High Lords would be very pleased. Vos Sidus would make the suggestion in his report and then ensure he was nowhere near Portalis in the next few months, when all this came to a head. He'd seen a rough report of the events at the front—as an Andaran handler he was entitled to that information—and the news that currently riled the Andaran people wasn't going to get any better. Oh no, not by a long shot.

Emm vos Sidus boarded the transport dragon for home content with the multiverse... and pleased with the hell about to rain down on his Line Lord's enemies.

*   *   *

The salt and foam of the Strait of Tears lifted her easily while the porpoises played about her. Whale song ran out at a distance, and Cetacean Ambassador Shalassar Brintal-Kolmayr floated with an ease that belied her inner turmoil.

Her ocean guardians didn't notice the distress. A pod of porpoises crested and dove with the waves around her. The peaceable, friendly creatures were clearly taking turns swimming beside her in case she grew tired and needed a tow back to shore. They were mostly younger ones who hadn't yet decided who they were with enough conviction to select adult names, and Shalassar floated with the waves, reaching out and listening to the many others speaking and singing in the oceans today.

The cetaceans were discussing things she thought had been decided absolutely a long time ago. The topic at hand was whether or not to consider Arcanans sentient. It was clear that all of the speakers knew beyond any doubt that Arcanans could think, but a more fundamental question was at stake.

The orca wanted it formally agreed that the Arcanans could be eaten freely. Most of the dolphins agreed quite readily with the idea of the Arcanans being eaten, but given their digestive preferences did not intend to actually bite the bad human flesh themselves. Most of the various whale types were somewhat less accepting of the idea.

The discussion hinged on the interpretation of how a finned creature would know if a particular stranded human flailing about at sea was of the Sharonan pod or of the Arcanan pod.

Shalassar listened with growing horror as some of the orca, who had multiple representatives instead of just a single primary, provided detailed descriptions of the taste, crunchiness, and texture of human meat that could be compared with any samples of Arcanan meat if it were ever tasted. Teeth Cleaver, newly elevated to hunter-scout within the pod for his week in the aquarium car, swam a careful distance from these toughest of orca.

One of the porpoises nudged Shalassar gently and informed her that humans hadn't been intentionally killed or eaten even by the orca in a very long time. Shalassar reminded herself of the

cetaceans' long memories and oral tradition of passing down all
knowledge without screening out distasteful bits of history in the
way human cultures tended to do. The cetaceans had no paper
records to hold the details of things that had happened but which
the current generation preferred not to think on too much. For a
cetacean everything was either remembered in living minds and
passed on via song to the young ones or else it was entirely forgotten.

The cetacean Remember Talent made it possible for those
mammalian histories to keep their vivid accuracy over centuries.
They had none of the telepathic component of a human Voice
Talent, but the ocean's transmission of sound carried their songs
through the deeps just as well as Voice transmission might and
no psionic Talent was needed to hear the Rememberer's song.

And so Shalassar heard in detail about the taste of humans
and how the orca used to hunt fishing vessels and overturn them
to get at the meat of the large floating clams. The details about
breaking the boats and only taking the ones that had drifted
out of sight of the others suggested a full understanding that
the creatures they'd been eating were thinking beings who could
retaliate if allowed to know just what had been hunting them.
The orcas weren't the ocean's finest hunters by accident. The ease
with which they'd once hunted man without humanity managing
to notice gave her a chill.

It was also highly informative, however, and Shalassar couldn't
help filing the information away as an explanation for why the
orca in particular had never taken offense at the human history—
ancient records from before the emergence of Talents—when
humans had blithely slaughtered intelligent cetaceans. And the
larger whales whose ancestors had been the primary targets of
those genocides had also not complained so very much either. The
singing thunder-fluke reached an interlude about using a strong
tail to destroy boats too tough in construction for an orca pod
to take apart, and it occurred to her—not for the first time—how
lucky humans were to have developed Talents and to have chosen
to stop preying on the cetaceans. There'd been a war, and the
humans hadn't even known they were losing it.

The old history made the water feel colder than the sun's
warmth should have made it. Enough so that for a long moment
she even felt uncomfortable floating in the deep waters with these
cetaceans she'd been talking with and listening to for years.

The deeper side of this discussion was the absolute certainty the cetaceans had that they would be involved in the portal wars. These weren't idle plans. The cetaceans fully expected to meet Arcanans one day, to fight alongside Sharonan warships and feast on the flesh of their enemies. The dolphins and porpoises planned to pull away the Sharonans and leave the Arcanans for the orca. The great whales wanted the details of Arcanan ship design so they could break open the hulls more efficiently. They even suggested the Sharonans might build mock-ups for them to practice with. The cetaceans were preparing for war.

Shalassar hoped by the Double Triad that war would never come so far as the Sharonan home universe. The cetaceans hummed their throaty agreement...and sang of portals, great tanks, and traveling out universe.

*   *   *

Emm vos Sidus had always loved the sea. High waves crashed against the good Mythalan rock as the two natural powers of stone and sea warred against each other, and the native magic soothed his very blood. At home everything felt right. The sea salt flavored each breath, and in the distance his youngest sister could be heard squealing with glee over the frolicking of the newborn hydra seadrakes. It was good to be back on the family estate.

The *garthan* manufactories and boarding houses hugged the earth out of sight of their betters. A *garthantri* carrying a filleted pigfish destined for dinner paused for an obeisance before continuing on his run from the butchery to the roasting house. Vos Sidus favored the servant with a nod and the man immediately deepened his bow at the honor of being so noticed. Had he not been carrying food meant for a *shakira*'s table, the *garthantri* would have fully abased himself from the first, but one made allowances to ensure an unpoisoned meal.

The *Book of Secrets* taught that remnants of old curses seethed invisible in the very soil, so the pure ate only of clean food prepared by the hands of the washed. The *Book* told of many other things besides, but that one was permitted to be known by *garthan* and was spoken of so widely that even children in Andara and Ransar practiced the ablutions of health before preparing and consuming their meals.

The *garthantri* held the pigfish high so not even the tail touched the ground as he stopped again for another obeisance at the drake nursery pool. This time the man bowed only once, vos Sidus noted with pleasure. His youngest sister had outgrown her habit of speaking with every *garthantri* she saw, an unfortunate legacy of a brief fosterage with an Andaran family now corrected.

The raising of a *shakira* was a complex art with far more challenges than arose in educating *garthan* children. Vos Sidus was proud to have had a youth of his immediate family selected by the Line Lord as precocious enough to build lines of false obligation with outsiders before even her Mythal Falls novitiate induction. Already little Bre received letters from Andaran girls signed "sister."

Vos Sidus himself had passed through novice, journeyman and magister training at Mythal Falls Academy with fine marks several years past and then been assigned his lifework by the Line Lord. But as a trained Mythalan magister of good family, it was only natural he would also take up a hobby.

He had. His passion was for the biggest and strongest drakes, known for their stunning ocean gladiatorial contests. It was quite incidental that Andarans mistook that hobby for his true work.

Seasprite, his current favorite, lifted a long gray-green head and nuzzled at his cheekbones with the exquisite delicacy required of a creature nearly ten times human size. Her other two heads remained submerged in the pool snapping and gulping the farmed fishes his family's *garthan* servants raised for her feed. These animals had less financial use than their more lucrative flying cousins, but the Sidus family had always enjoyed expanding the scope of the possible with their breeding programs. The hobbies had been mistaken for a family business for quite some time now.

They'd proved with one of Seasprite's great grand dames that all three heads could be made fully functional. Certain Ransaran magisters had argued it could never be done. And they were undoubtedly right about their own abilities, but no Mythalan *shakira* had so little faith in the power of magic.

The practical issues of a three-headed beast *had* presented some formidable challenges, however.

For example, when the originally vestigial secondary heads became equally capable of controlling the body after the prime head was loped off it did create certain control issues. Then there was also the difficulty of controlling the bleeding. But any drake put into the arena these days wore specialized spellware tourniquet collars, so very few of the powerful beasts were lost to head amputation injuries, and crystals embedded in the center of each of the three foreheads controlled which mind dominated. Training varied by beast of course, but Sidus drakes usually had two fighting styles and a third mind trained for docile transport and feeding.

Passivity wasn't usually a desired setting among any of the families that chose to buy seadrake young, but vos Sidus enjoyed having the beasts entirely calm and nearly puppy like for transport. The best money to be had was for the pit fighters, to be sure, and for those, all three heads needed to be as vicious as possible. Other drakes, with shepherd training and control spellware, were used to corral the pure fighters and move them from training pits into arena-bound slidercages.

A clear sky with brilliant sunlight pouring over the ocean surf marked this morning as a very good one for the day's fight, and float-bespelled spectator palanquins were just beginning to jostle for position around the distant island.

The Sidus VI breed was being tested against a new Vacus line. They'd captured and bred a kind of shark creature that breathed through gills instead of lungs. Vos Sidus thought it might have some small use as a guard fish around prisons and the like, but the gladiatorial sales would be miserable. The beasties were smaller and tended to clutter the view of carnage with blood and entrails. If it were only the entrails, many *shakira* would enjoy watching, but put too much blood in the water and even the clearest pools suddenly showed nothing but boring red.

Breeding a special kind of prey fish that didn't cloud up the waters had been tried, but the interesting fights were always the ones that involved humans in some way. Vos Sidus's aunt had tried bringing in the great whales for fights, but those fights were too dull. Some pleasure boats still went whale hunting—which was to say they followed behind a pair or a small nest of seadrakes and watched as they found and devoured the larger cetaceans— and vos Sidus had been on a few of those pleasure cruises as a child. Aunt Kellbok had pointed out the *garthan* ship captains' maneuvers to set the drakes against only the very largest and toughest of the whales, but he'd agreed with his aunt: cetacean prey wasn't tough enough for a drake. Whales lacked sufficient intelligence and cunning for a decent fight.

Sometimes, when Aunt Kellbok had used just one drake and set up an ocean arena around a full pod of masked whales—the ones with the black and white coloring that hid so well in the water—she'd entice cetacean combatants to perform a show worthy of a *shakira* audience. But even then, she'd had to send in a drake youngling bloodied from an earlier fight. When it got dull—because it *would* get dull—she'd signal the show master to release the mother drake to empty the seas as a grand finale.

The best argument vos Sidus had seen for cetaceans having some modicum of intelligence—more than, say, that of a barnyard cat—was that the larger whales all avoided the Mythalan coasts. That the masked whales still came said something else, but Aunt Kellbok insisted insanity had entertainment value.

Universes beyond Arcana Prime allowed for more varied open ocean shows. In New Mythal, there were still oceans where native creatures didn't know to swim for their lives the moment they tasted drake blood in the water or heard the bellows of a hunting drake reverberate across the ocean bottom.

Of course Union law forbade the release of drakes into the wild, but a breeder couldn't truly know his training held until it was tested. The Seadrake Owners' Association understood that, so from time to time vos Sidus could fill his slidercages and transport a nest of seadrakes to a preserve on New Mythal owned by a cousin of Aunt Kellbok's.

Sometimes training failed. In those cases, he'd make a discreet report to the Seadrake Owners' Association and send in a troop of *garthan* for cleanup. If the team was too slow, a few ships would be crushed or a crew might be eaten, but the accidental fodder were generally *garthan* of low value, with few years of service left, and the SDO paid well for the use of the land. Every *shakira* with property near by knew when tests were scheduled to be run and would remove their persons and *garthantri* well in advance. But there was no point trying tell that to an Andaran or a Ransaran! They didn't understand that acquiring true wisdom required a certain amount of... breakage along the way.

Every monument worth building killed a few *garthan* in its construction. That might be unfortunate for the *garthan* involved, but better a dozen *garthan* lost than a single *shakira* maimed, and even the Ransarans understood the value of experience. "A burned hand is the best teacher." That was one of their own proverbs, although they turned their noses up at the Mythalan equivalent, of course. "Blood buys true value," as the great vos Hardyna had observed thousands of years ago, and it was true. It was *always* true, and if the barbarians thought it applied solely to *garthan*, that only showed how stupid they truly were. Vos Sidus had memorized every proverb in the *Book of the Shakira* at Aunt Kellbok's knee before his tenth birthday—most non-Mythalans were still playing at learning their sums at that age—and he knew that proverb applied to *all* Mythalans. Even the blood of a thousand *shakira* was nothing to the honor due a Line Lord.

Non-Mythalans didn't understand context. The SOA used only drake males for arena events outside Arcana Prime for that precise reason. An escaped drake gone feral in Delkor had devastated a fishing community for several decades before a passing magister put the beast down as a favor to a *shakira* cousin. But when a breeding pair had escaped on New Mythal, it had taken a full company of magisters over a month to hunt down the creatures and all their offspring. If it happened again, the Union of Arcana would expect exactly that second level of effort, even if it were just to clean out the oceans of a wilderness world hardly worth preserving. These annoyances were the cost of working with the uninitiated, but one day every Arcanan would bow to a Line Lord and hold the teachings of the *Book of Secrets* more valuable than their own hearts.

That would be a lifework worthy of Line Lords. Emm vos Sidus had his own small part to play in the great glory of Mythal, and in the between times he had the drakes. All too often, he found himself wishing he could uncage a nest of seadrakes in the Garth Showma Falls Basin and remake the Union in a bloody baptism, but that, sadly, was not his assignment.

The sand-in-silk frustration that annoyed him the most was that the Andarans had never recognized the military power inherent in the proper use of seadrakes. He blamed their focus on land. Sure people lived on land, but any fool could see over a third of the Arcanan-discovered frontier universe transits required ocean passage to reach the next portal—not to mention that two of the five newly taken portals were on those universe's equivalents to the North Mythal River and the Evanos Ocean. Now that war with these Sharonian barbarians was afoot, perhaps it was time to finally put together a multiverse nautical power with more teeth than the Union of Arcana Navy. Let the Andaran Army struggle with the arcane logistics of a cross portal war with "gun"-carrying Sharonians. The Mythalan Navy could save them all with a simple seadrake barricade.

And slipping drake mating pairs into hostile universes' oceans could do wonderful things for the destruction of their economies, vos Sidus reflected dreamily while he petted Seasprite's long neck.

The great benefit of the seadrake's amphibious nature was that these beautiful creatures didn't just hunt the oceans. They claimed the beaches and seaside cities as well...and if Sharonians were anything like Arcanans, more than eighty percent of their population lived on ocean coasts and riverways.

Any trained Arcanan with the right spells could control a drake, but Sharonians didn't use magic. Every single one was *garthan,* and their ignorance made them nothing more than walking meat for the seadrakes' triple rows of teeth.

Vos Sidus scratched the underside of Seasprite's vestigial wing and she lifted all three heads to hiss in pleasure. Then the dexter side head suddenly snapped to the right, the whole drake launched across the pool, and the delicate plantings screening the handler station broke instantly.

Vos Sidus shook his head in resignation and waited for the gurgling scream to stop before he keyed the spell to force the docile head to resume control. The new servant hadn't worked out. Seasprite went through handlers faster than his other drakes, but then she also cost less to feed. Unless one started counting the cost of a *garthan* against her food bill, which he was beginning to seriously consider. These weren't his valued servants, of course. He used only pit drake handlers on Seasprite. That kind of *garthan* one bought by the dozen from the prison system, with special care taken to ensure no past members of one's own estate were included in the lot.

He held Seasprite bespelled with no backup handler for three full minutes, patting her noses, and using her scrub brush to get the worst of the carnage off her faces. Then he stepped back through the bars of her enclosure and retreated across the white sand circle that marked the far edge of her bite reach. Just beyond the line, he released her. The timbre of her hiss changed, but not one of the three heads made a lunge for him. Seasprite knew her range.

A pair of *garthantri* with long tongs worked from the opposite side to withdraw the remains of the body. Seasprite watched their progress coldly with her sinister head while the other two quite reasonably remained fixed on the magister who'd most recently held control of her minds.

When the *garthantri* finished retrieving the corpse, one made the sign of Mithanan and spat on the body. Emm couldn't hear what the other said, but neither showed any care when they dumped the parts into a wheelbarrow and trundled it off to a convict's pit. Funeral pyres were reserved for honorable servants.

He shrugged mentally, dismissed the *garthantri* from his attention, and turned back to his original train of thought.

Anyone could operate the precharged spells to control a seadrake, he reflected, although few demonstrated the persistent, careful attention required to become a veteran handler. Yet if the Sharonians lacked not only magisters but also even the most rudimentary understanding of the principles of magic, nests of drakes could be sent in entirely handlerless. The Mythalan Navy could never do that in a war against a civilized nation, because the opponent's magisters or even ground troops armed with spellware would simply take control of the drakes. But Sharonians might not even realize it was *possible*. This kind of opportunity had never existed before.

There were potential difficulties as well, of course. For example, uncaged drakes in Mythal found without a handler would be re-enchanted by a neighboring house and claimed as feral foundlings under the old estray laws. That sort of carelessness could lead to a century or more of careful breeding going to enrich a rival drake line without even a sum of coin or lot of chattel in exchange. The Siduses had taken a few such opportunities in the past, as had every other member of the Seadrake Owners' Association when granted the chance, but he certainly didn't care to give away his stock easily, and he considered the legal difficulties of free roaming drakes in the frontier universes. Some type of branding could work, he decided. And he would have to insist marked drakes be reclaimed only by the respective breeder houses after the end of the war, with offspring to be divided on a pro rata basis determined by share contributions of the possible parent drakes released in each universe.

And the Union of Arcana would need to pay rental fees to the breeders for the use of the animals for the duration of the conflict. It wouldn't do to have the Union's other members just assuming that Mythal would pay the heavy blood price of war simply because they were best suited to it and were the only ones who had prepared to fight properly at sea.

*   *   *

Ullery the Fool patted each long neck of his drake and paced around the beast examining every inch of her armor. The sand of the small, created island off the coast of the Sidus estate burned Ullery's bare feet, but he did his best not to limp. The *shakira* would be watching, and Ullery kept all his attention on Silverstreak's hide as he scratched the base of her dexter neck carefully. The scales were thinner here at the very back of the animal in the indentation where a drake's *garthan* driver latched in. The spiny ridges on either side had small, carefully drilled holes which gave the purchase needed to attach his ropes and body netting.

The crystal implants in Silverstreak's center head were giving her trouble again. Ullery could tell from the way her neck ticked that head in an uncontrolled spasm every few minutes. If they were still back serving the House Belftus, he would have known which of the *shakira* lords to go to and could have gotten it fixed. But since their sale to House Vacus a fortnight ago, he hadn't been able to figure out which, if any, of the *shakira* masters actually cared about maintaining their drake property.

He'd been born a *garthan* servant, and from certain of his features, he was fairly sure his father had been a member of the Belftus family. But since no Gift had manifested, his bastardry was an embarrassment to be hidden from other *shakira*. A lord was supposed to only breed true.

Ullery himself had continued to expect to be taken into the family proper long after he should have realized it was never going to happen. Still, his unusually advanced early education had granted him a few advantages. Those had kept him alive when no Gift manifested and his early mistakes earned him a place as a drake rider on the animals used to host spectator fights for *shakira* amusements. Ullery did at least understand magic theory, even if he utterly lacked the spark necessary to cast spells. He knew how the drake's spellware worked, and he had the sense to be very, very careful with the control crystal belted across his waist.

The other *garthans* of the Belftus House had been careful not to offend Ullery lest his possible *shakira* father choose to take offense. And since Ullery didn't complain and managed his drakes so cleverly that they never *quite* caught anyone who tried to swim the straits to leave *shakira* service, he'd been treated well by his fellows.

But that had been in the last household. In House Vacus, Ullery knew far too few people to really know what his place was. He was beginning to suspect that the reason for the chill distance was that none of the other servants really wanted to get to know him. They'd prefer not to know the man-like-object who'd end up mangled by their House-bred drakes during the next exhibition event.

It was a fair assumption. Except that the last two weekends had passed without a drake-on-drake fight. And just recently orders had come down to begin seeing if any of the drakes could be trained to work together. He'd overheard one of the Vacus handlers muttering worriedly about it. They didn't seem to think it could be done. And maybe with Vacus drakes it couldn't. But House Belftus had done it any number of times. The trick was to keep the calm driving head dominant during all the close maneuvers.

Ullery could show them all how to do it...if he survived the next few hours.

The fins in the water around the island were moving in ways he didn't think were natural. A shark's head came up with far too wide a mouth for the body and snapped at empty air.

The glare on the surface of the ocean blinded him for a moment, and then Ullery saw the creature clearly in the passing foam. Not natural at all. There were *sarkolis* crystals on the monsters' flanks imbedded just before the dorsal fins. Idiotic placement for water flow, but no one asked a *garthan*'s opinion.

Just *behind* the fin was the vortex null where natural water magics amplified *sarkolis* enchantment, but some imbecile had implanted the shark's control crystals higher up the spine at almost at the spellbreak point. Which meant the ocean would polish imperative-strength spell commands down to mere nudges with every passing wave.

Squeals above from young *shakira* voices revealed that the controllers had discovered that exact error.

Ullery marked the width of the island. It was all soft sand that felt steady underfoot but the edge dropped off sharply just beyond the waterline. Only about twice the diameter of Silverstreak's length from bite to tail, it was a created island, probably on a float spell that could drop to the bottom of the sea on a word.

He ran soothing hands down each of Silverstreak's necks rubbing out tension and encouraging her to stretch and flex. She was going to need to shark hunt for him today. Bludgeoning tail strikes and rapid *sarkolis* cracking bites should work if he could keep Silverstreak's delicate inter-talon webbing protected from the razor teeth.

Dark trails followed the sharkbeasts already. The kids had enchanted the teeth to enlarge and sharpen them without considering the damage to gums and jaws.

The mouths were too large for the gullets too. These sharkbeasts wouldn't be able to feed themselves. Some out of favor *garthan* would have to do it.

He shivered and Silverstreak vibrated in response. He forced himself to still and calm her anxiety. No good panicking about what might happen at the feed pits this evening when he hadn't yet survived the afternoon.

A child, announcing himself as master of ceremonies, blew a great horn. The poorly tuned blat earned an eruption of laughter from his fellows.

A teacher of some sort confiscated the horn and restored order.

"*Shakira, Multhari,* and guests—welcome! The fosterlings and young ones of the House of Sidus present for you this afternoon's entertainment. Monsters of the deep patrol a classic drake deathmatch!

"Step right up to the red palanquin if you'd like to take your turn handling a sharkbeast. We've colorized the *sarkolis* and the controllers for you so it's easy to see which beast is yours, but if you have any doubt at all, we have a spotter next to each control."

Rousing cheers and a flurry of nursemaided small ones hopped onto small platforms and converged on the red palanquin.

"Ask any of our *garthantri* servants if you need anything at all. Remember your sharkbeasts can't breath air, so just snap at the drakes when one throws the other into the water."

A slidercage was beginning the slow float from Sidus Proper to Arena Island. Ullery had heard of Sidus. Every handler had heard of the nightmare Sidus V line. But this cage was big even for a Sidus V, and Ullery had the sinking feeling that the long awaited Sidus VI line might be coming out for first blood.

Silverstreak's center head let out a low moan and jerked again. She'd seen the cage coming too.

Ullery tested the tension on his straps and practiced deep breaths. If he had to go into the water, he needed to be able to match Silverstreak's lung capacity. He'd give near anything for an air spell right now, but he'd've needed four of them, one for each of Silverstreak's three heads and one of his own, for it to make any difference.

Belftus had had short-duration breather spells, but Vacus hadn't bothered to refresh anything to do with his belt crystal. Ullery figured he might have a few gasps left on an old air spell, but if he tried to use that enchantment it might empty the accumulator too much to maintain the control spells. Silverstreak had never yet tried to take a bite out of him, but if the fight ran on long enough she'd get extremely hungry.

Ullery did his very best not to test his drake like that. He'd rather be eaten alive by something else.

The massive slidercage dragged to a stop on empty sand in the middle of the island. And Ullery the Fool finished belting himself in. However bad this got, he'd have the best survival chance on his drake's back.

The horn sounded again, and the cage bellowed in response. Then all four sides clanged flat into the sand and the roof flew up and away to spiral high over the tops of the audience palanquins.

Ullery didn't wait to hear the splash. He hunkered Silverstreak down and clamped his precious belt tight against her back. The cloud of dust risen from the cage opening would give him the first and only cover he'd get during this fight. He urged Silverstreak to sidle around the island, feet and tail kept carefully out of the water.

"The House of vos Sidus presents Blackfang Heartripper of their Sidus VI line! And awaiting on Arena Island, from the breeders at Belftus, we have Silverstreak Fleshrender!"

Children cheered. Some threw down pieces of cookie, inadvertently giving away Ullery's attempt at subterfuge.

He let Silverstreak snap the sweets out of the air before they reached the sand and was rewarded with more substantial cuts of roast and sausages. Iridescent horned crests streaked down all three of his seadrake's heads, straight to her great club of a tail. She was a lovely creature, and it wouldn't hurt to have some of the audience on her side.

Silverstreak preened at the sky, and from out of the cloud of sand in the center of Arena Island, a massive black seadrake raised two heads and howled fury. The third head twisted back and struck cobra fast to rip its handler out of the harness straps.

Blackfang's third head swallowed his handler's skull. Then all three heads ripped at the corpse's soft entrails, and gasps from the audience mixed with laughter and applause to acknowledge the fight's first blood as Blackfang flung limbs and bits of flesh in all directions.

Ullery patted Silverstreak's neck. A leg still encased in loose trouser cloth landed nearby. It had a shoe.

Blackfang's sinister head paused long enough to hiss in Silverstreak's direction. She hissed back and lifted her body high, trying to look bigger and intimidate the much larger beast.

Ullery looked into the sinister head's eyes and was all but certain it would be impossible to intimidate the uncontrolled monster. Blackfang was operating on pure instinct now, and the sinister head returned to gnawing the body, but the dexter head curled back to watch them. With the control spell broken so abruptly, the large Sidus drake might not even have a dominant head.

Ullery took a wild chance and directed Silverstreak to do something he'd never thought he'd tell a drake to do.

Silverstreak complied instantly. She snapped her center neck forward and closed her jaws around the still dripping human leg. Ullery prayed she would obey the rest of the order too, and somehow—miraculously—she did. She arched her neck and hurled the leg in a high arc. Up, and up...Then it hit the floor of the red palanquin and splashed into the ocean. Blackfang's dexter head had tracked the full motion. The other two heads snapped back and forth, tracking the sharkbeasts circling the spot where the stolen piece of their kill had hit the water.

The red palanquin veered back, and children clamored at the controls while sharkbeasts swarmed after the leg, some controlled and some not, fighting each other for the taste of blood in the water. That was a mistake, and all three Blackfang heads roared in chorus.

The whole drake dove into the ocean. Nothing got between a

seadrake and his kill, and Ullery imagined the points about his tactics that the vos Vacus tutors in the palanquins above would be making to their charges right now.

Silverstreak shivered and trembled with her need to follow, but Ullery held her back with every bit of will he could muster. He let her pick at a bit of cake, dropped from above and missed in the handler's slaughter, but he had no desire to enter the fray he and Silverstreak had arranged for Blackfang.

But then his drake shied right as a bottle was hurled down at them. It shattered on the beach nearby, and Ullery realized some of the yells above were directed towards him. He glanced up to see Kon vos Vacus gesturing urgently at him to enter the fight.

Ullery didn't go so far as to shake his head at the Master, but he had no intention of obeying. Still, the spectators needed a show, and as the only remaining handler, it was up to Ullery to give them one. If he didn't, they'd change something about the arena fight, and it probably wouldn't be survivable, so he urged the quivering Silverstreak to slink around the edge of the low dune island to give him a view of the ocean melee.

Blackfang's dexter head cracked the spine of a sharkbeast and tossed it high overhead. It missed the red palanquin but not by very much. Small arms reached out trying to touch this second bleeding projectile before it fell back into the sea.

The crowd roared approval. And cookies rained down from the heavens.

Mostly they fell on Silverstreak who caught them with elegantly arched necks and flicking tongues.

Blackfang's center head took a frosted coconut puff to the nose and went cross-eyed staring at the thing lodged between the horns of his muzzle.

And that was the point at which Ullery's drake, dancing in the fall of sweets, slid off the island into the waves herself.

A sharkbeast bit her. Probably entirely by accident in the chum-thickened waters, but Silverstreak's center head responded with a lightning-quick jawlock on the beast's dorsal fin and a flip that snatched the creature into the air. And then, just before the jaw should have released for a clean upward toss, the center head spasmed.

The stunned sharkbeast tumbled tail over rictus mouth directly at Blackfang.

The drake's dexter head caught it just by the tail fluke. The sinister head crunched through the shark's skull, and the center curved back and forth watching Silverstreak.

Ullery pressed his drake towards the island and she took an unwilling half step in the direction of partial safety.

Then Blackfang's center head tore out the sharkbeast's liver and tossed it in a clean throw straight at Silverstreak who swallowed it whole.

There weren't enough sharkbeasts in the water to satiate both seadrakes, so in the end Silverstreak licked the frosted coconut puff off Blackfang's nose while Ullery tried to keep his pulse steady and his breath even. Someone else, someone with magic, would have to be the one to tell Silverstreak Fleshrender and Blackfang Heartripper they wouldn't be permitted to mate.

High above, adults hurried to end the children's party before the events on Arena Island became too explicit to explain to inquisitive young Mythalan nobles.

CHAPTER TWENTY
Darikhal 16, 5053 AE
(January 4, 1929 CE)

"THANK YOU FOR COMING ABOARD, MASTER YANUSA-
Mahrdissa," Battalion-Captain Hymair chan Yahndar said,
standing behind the desk in his cramped—*extremely* cramped—
shipboard office. There was too little room, as his Karmalian grandmother would have said, to swing a sheep. Of course, chan Yahndar
had never understood who'd *want* to swing a sheep, but the phrase
certainly offered all of the earthy color anyone could have desired.
And however tiny his office was, he was lucky to have it. TTE's
mass-produced steamships were scarcely noted for their palatial
accommodations, and *Voyager Osprey* was no exception to that rule,
although—thank all the gods!—she'd at least been intended as a
transport from the beginning. That meant he and his men hadn't
ended up stacked in six-high pipe-frame bunks in a converted
cargo hold whose last contents had reeked to the gods themselves.

"Well," the dark-skinned Shurkhali said with an expression
halfway between a grimace and a smile, "given all we've got
to do, it seemed like a good idea to get started early. I've been
practically camped on that damned dock for two days, now."

"Sorry about the delay." Chan Yahndar's expression was all
the way over on the grimace side of the scale. "We lost thirty-six
hours getting the horses loaded. They didn't much care for the
princely quality of their accommodations."

Which, he thought dryly, *once again demonstrates how superior
"horse sense" is to* human *sense.*

"And I don't envy the crewmen who have to muck out the
holds, either," Yanusa-Mahrdissa observed.

"Don't feel too sorry for them," chan Yahndar said dryly. "The ship masters are pretty damned insistent about who's doing what before our baggage gets released."

"Trans-Temporal's ship masters are about as ornery as they come," Yanusa-Mahrdissa agreed with something suspiciously like a chuckle.

"True, but they got us to Shosara in handsome style once everyone was onboard," chan Yahndar conceded. "And now that we *are* here," he continued, waving his visitor into the sole vacant chair, "I suppose we'd best get down to it."

He waited while the civilian seated himself, then swept his hand in a gesture which indicated the other two officers squeezed into the compartment.

"Master Yanusa-Mahrdissa, allow me to present Company-Captain Grithair chan Mahsdyr and Battalion-Captain Francho chan Hurmahl. Company-Captain chan Mahsdyr has Gold Company of Second Battalion, and Battalion-Captain chan Hurmahl has the Fourteen-Oh-Seventh Mounted Engineers."

Yanusa-Mahrdissa nodded to the other two Ternathians, and chan Yahndar leaned back in his chair while he contemplated the task which confronted them. He'd always known Division-Captain chan Geraith wasn't afraid to think outside the box, but this was considerably farther outside than even the division-captain was accustomed to straying, and if even one thing went wrong...

He shifted his contemplation to the maps on the office's bulkheads and tried not to shudder as he thought about the sheer scale of the task before them. Even assuming the Arcanans truly didn't know they were coming, and that they weren't spotted en route by one of their godsdamned flying beasties, simple logistics were enough to make the mission a nightmare. But in the words of one of the Imperial Ternathian Army's legendary commanders, if a job was easy, they wouldn't need Ternathians to get it done.

And just your luck you've got no less than two deployments to the PAAF on your résumé, isn't it? he thought dryly. *When the division captain needed someone who'd spent time crawling around the backside of nowhere, he didn't have far to look. And it's a* damned *good thing young Grithair can say the same.*

The truth, unfortunately, was that for all its immense experience and proud traditions, the Imperial Ternathian Army had never operated as a unit outside its home universe. There'd never been any need for it to...which meant it had no experience as an institution of the rigors of moving from one universe to another. That wasn't as simple as a walk in the park—not when the two sides of any given portal might literally be halfway around the world from one another. The transition from scorching summer to the middle of a howling blizzard was nothing to take lightly. In fact, far too many men had died because of just that sort of shift, and the need to supply both tropical and arctic equipment—and to haul it along as they went—was a quartermaster's nightmare.

And it's exactly what we'll have to do moving from Resym into Nairsom, too, he thought grimly.

The good news was that the Army, like the Imperial Marines, had been loaning personnel to the PAAF for over seventy years now. Many of its senior noncoms and officers—like Hymair chan Yahndar himself—had amassed plenty of universe-hopping experience along the way. Which was how the 12th Dragoon Regiment in general and Gold Company in particular had been picked for their present duties.

"How thoroughly has Master Banchu briefed you, Master Yanusa-Mahrdissa?" he asked after a moment.

"Please, call me Ganstamar," Yanusa-Mahrdissa said. "Most non-Shurkhalis seem to find my last name a bit of a mouthful." He smiled crookedly. "And, in answer to your question, I think he brought me as close to up-to-date as anyone could." His smile faded and he shook his head. "Frankly, I don't envy you, Battalion-Captain."

"There are times I don't envy myself," chan Yahndar admitted. "On the other hand, most of your sympathy should probably go to Grithair. And any you have left over should go to Francho. The rest of us will be pretty much following in their wake, after all."

Yanusa-Mahrdissa nodded, but if he was taken in by chan Yahndar's dismissal of the scope of his own task, he showed no sign of it.

"Well," he said, "we've been extending the line like mad ever since Fallen Timbers." His affable expression hardened. After all, Shaylar Nargra-Kolmayr had been a countrywoman of his. "Fortunately, there are no water gaps along the route—well, no *ocean* gaps, anyway; there're more than enough rivers to be a pain in the arse—but our priority was reduced compared to the Failcham railhead even before we encountered the damned Arcanans, so we haven't made as much ground as I might like. We can get you all the way across Lashai by rail and a thousand miles or so into Resym, and we're laying more track like mad. But you'll still have somewhere around two thousand miles, a lot of it rain forest and jungle, before you get out onto the plains in Nairsom, and you'll be doing all of *those* miles the hard way."

"Which, in winter, is going to be even harder than the hard way usually is once we get *out* of Resym," chan Yahndar agreed.

"The good news is that the entire route's been surveyed all the way to Fort Ghartoun and we've gotten a head start on improving some of the worst portions of roadbed," Yanusa-Mahrdissa pointed out. "We started sending advanced parties down-chain the instant Division-Captain chan Geraith alerted us to his plans. They've already made a start on putting in the bridges—or improved fords, at least—through the Dalazan. Mind you, I don't think some of our supervisors really believed the loadbearing requirements we gave them, but they're used to working with locally available materials. Most of those bridges are going to be temporary—*very* temporary—structures, but they'll get the job done. And given that we've surveyed the route clear through to New Uromath, we know exactly what you're going to need in the way of bridging supplies once you get beyond our own advanced crews, too, and I've been working on running them up out of available materials. There's not much I can do about the girders you'll need in Thermyn, but I understand the shipyard's working on that?"

He raised an eyebrow at chan Yahndar, but chan Yahndar tossed the question to Battalion-Captain chan Hurmahl with a sweep of his hand.

"Master Banchu assured us he has the situation in hand, Master Yanusa-Mahrdissa," chan Hurmahl said. "I don't think anyone's exactly pleased over how difficult we expect it to be to make all of this come together, but Master Banchu went over the inventory you sent him with the Renaiyrton yardmaster, as well as kicking his requirements up the Voice chain. By the time Division-Captain chan Geraith's ready to follow us across, he should be able to bring almost everything he'll need with him."

"The shipyard's able to supply what we'll need for Coyote Canyon?"

"Assuming the work crews' diagrams and measurements are accurate, yes." Chan Hurmahl grimaced. "I understand the main girders were already en route when all this blew up. In fact, they got shunted onto a siding in Camryn to clear the mainline for troop movements, so it's only a matter of getting them inserted back into the pipeline behind us. The shipyard says it can run up everything *else* we'll need—again, assuming the diagrams and measurements are good—and combine it with the girders into a single package. Getting all of that delivered to the Near Ternath side of the pond's going to be a bit of a hassle, but the yard master says TTE's used to that sort of challenge."

"In a normal sort of situation, that's certainly true," Yanusa-Mahrdissa said. "But this situation's just a bit *ab*normal, and that brings us to what's really my major concern. Once you're beyond the railhead, transporting that kind of tonnages is going to be a nightmare, especially when you think about the Coyote Canyon loads and all the coal I understand you're likely to need."

"No one in this office is stupid enough to think it'll be easy," chan Yahndar replied. "On the other hand, if the Bisons perform as advertised, it should at least be *possible*. Under the circumstances, that's about the best anyone could ask for."

"I'm not familiar with them myself," Yanusa-Mahrdissa said. "How likely are they, really, to be up to the task?"

It was a very good question, and every man in that small cabin knew it. The Bison—technically, the Transport Tractor of 5051, from its year of adoption—was a completely new departure in military transport. In fact, it was so new there was still a fair degree of confusion in nomenclature, with most people referring to it by its assigned name of "Bison" while others referred to it as the Tractor 51.

"We'll be swaying the first of them ashore in about two hours," chan Yahndar told him. "Hopefully, you'll be able to form your own opinion. All I can say is that they've performed remarkably well in our exercises at Fort Erthain. We had some initial problems with breakdowns, but, frankly, I think that's mainly because dragoons are more accustomed to horses than machines. Grooming, horseshoes, and riding tack we understand, but we tend to be a little short on steamer mechanics. If we can't feed it or muck out its stall, we're not real sure what to do with it."

The Shurkhali snorted, although he'd had enough experience introducing neophytes to steam-powered machinery and the mysteries of hydraulics and pneumatic drills and machine tools to understand exactly what the battalion-captain meant. By the same token, chan Yahndar was certainly exaggerating. There were more than enough steam drays and personal steamers on the Ternathian Empire's roads for at least some of the Third Dragoons' personnel to be comfortable with wrenches and screwdrivers.

"I understand they're based on our Ricathian Buffalo?"

"They are," chan Hurmahl replied, "and I've had plenty of time during the crossing to watch Battalion-Captain chan Yahndar's men performing routine maintenance." He smiled slightly as his eyes met Yanusa-Mahrdissa's, and the TTE engineer nodded. Even vehicles parked in a freighter's hold or—especially—secured as deck cargo needed constant monitoring and maintenance if they were going to be ready for use at the end of the voyage. A lot of people didn't understand that, and he was glad the 3rd Dragoons did. "Trust me," chan Hurmahl went on, "the battalion-captain's men are better mechanics than he chooses to admit. In fact, I was almost as impressed with their crews' proficiency as I was with the Bisons themselves."

"I don't doubt that," Yanusa-Mahrdissa said, "but I can't say I'm not worried about reliability, especially given the tightness of the schedule. The 'Devil Buffs'"—the TTE's personnel had bestowed the nickname of the enormous, ferociously-horned, unpredictable, and usually vicious Ricathian Buffalo on its huge, steam-powered bulldozers—"can move the gods' own pile of dirt, but nobody ever called them *fast*."

"Maybe not, but they've always had plenty of horsepower and plenty of torque," chan Hurmahl pointed out. "And the Bison's suspension and tracks were completely redesigned. All the engineers really used out of the Buffalo was the power plant and the basic chassis; everything else is new, and I've seen one of them moving along a prepared surface with a thirty-ton trailer at better than thirty miles an hour."

Yanusa-Mahrdissa blinked, impressed despite himself. Of course, the army officer was right about the Devil Buff's sheer power. It wasn't at the very top of Ram's Horn Heavy Equipment's line of bulldozers. That distinction belonged to the Black Rhino, the largest and most powerful bulldozer ever built (yet), but the Devil Buff was no slouch. Like everything else in RHHE's catalog, it was built "Ram Tough" and its uniflow six-cylinder engine—two banks of three cylinders each mounted back-to-back—produced pressures of up to five hundred pounds per square inch and gave the bulldozer almost sixteen horsepower per ton. The obstacle it couldn't move was rare, but its maximum speed was no more than ten miles per hour under ideal circumstances, and even then the operator was taking far too many hours off its tracks' design life.

"When the Army approached RHHE about the Bison, their track designers thought the quartermaster general was out of his mind," chan Mahsdyr put in with something suspiciously like a grin. "The Artillery was already experimenting with steam tractors as prime movers, especially for the heavy guns, but Division-Captain chan Stahlyr's ideas were a lot more...ambitious than that. In fact, I think at least half the Army thinks he's out of his mind." The dragoon company-captain shook his head. "He has this idea the entire Army—infantry, dragoons, artillery, and all—should be what he calls 'mechanized.' He wants to move *everything* cross-country as fast or faster than cavalry could cover the same terrain."

Yanusa-Mahrdissa started to chuckle. Then he realized the company-captain was completely serious and glanced at chan Yahndar, who shrugged.

"It's not as crazy as it sounds, really, Master Yanusa-Mahrdissa. The emperor's been quietly pushing the Army's modernization for more than fifteen years now. The Empire hadn't fought a major war in over a century before he took the throne. We've been involved in the occasional peacekeeping action, but not against a first-rate opponent, and His Majesty felt we'd allowed our doctrine and thinking to stagnate, especially given the advances in steam engineering TTE's expansion has been driving. Division-Captain chan Stahlyr's only about fifty-two years old, but the heads of the Artillery, Cavalry, Infantry, and Engineer Boards are almost as young as he is and they're all what His Majesty calls 'forward thinkers.' He told them to think about Army doctrine and equipment as aggressively as the Navy thinks about designing the next class of battleships, and Division-Captain chan Stahlyr obviously took him seriously."

"That's certainly true," chan Hurmahl agreed. "He had a pretty damned clear idea what he wanted, and he wasn't about to take no for an answer. At first, Ram's Horn told him that if he wanted those sorts of speeds, he should just buy commercial steam drays, but they didn't have the capacity or the cross-country capability he wanted. So they came up with a design based on a modification of their standard eight-ton dray which is pretty impressive. They call it a 'half-track,' since it has a tracked suspension in the rear and steering wheels in front, and it can handle terrain that would kill any wheeled vehicle. They were damned proud of it, because it really is a huge improvement over existing drays, and the QMG was happy to get it. In fact, the Army standardized it as the Halftrack of 5051—the troops named it the 'Steel Mule'— and ordered over two thousand of them, but it still couldn't meet his specifications, especially for payload and towing power, since its maximum capacity's only about a ton and a half, so he sent them back to the drawing board for something better.

"When he insisted he was serious—and they realized he wasn't going to go away just because it was impossible—they actually *looked* at the problem. And since they'd been right that no existing suspension could give him that kind of performance, they had to come up with a new one. Once they recognized that, they got into the spirit of the thing, accepted the challenge, and came up with a pretty damned radical solution. Instead of conventional leaf springs like the Buffalo's, the Bison uses *vertical* springs. The height of the spring well was still too limiting, so they added a bell crank to swing vertical motion to the rear, in addition, which reduced the vertical stroke by about twenty-five percent. The combination means the Bison's road wheels can displace over twenty inches vertically, and the new springs are actually tougher than the old-style leaf designs. I'll let you imagine what kind of obstacle that means it can handle."

Yanusa-Mahrdissa pursed his lips in a silent whistle, and chan Yahndar snorted.

"Don't let him pull your leg too hard," he suggested, and the Shurkhali looked back across the desk at him. "Oh, the Bison's suspension can do everything he's claiming for it, but the *tracks* are still more fragile than we'd like. RHHE's retrofitting the newest design, with rubber-backed track blocks, to everything coming down the line behind us, and we're supposed to be getting an ample supply of spares by the time the main body's ready to follow us. Unfortunately, we don't know for certain they'll get here, just like we don't know how well the new design'll hold up. And even if all the new hardware works perfectly, trying to take one of them cross-country at anything like its top speed will jar your teeth right out of your head. The nosebleeds can be pretty bad, too, and if there's any unsecured gear flying around the black eyes get positively spectacular. And it took some bright lad at Ram's Horn over a year to come up with the notion in the first place. Then they spent most of *another* year working out the bugs in the original concept. And they only reached the deployable stage a little over two years ago, so no one has enough experience with them to know whether or not Division-Captain chan Geraith's idea is really going to be workable."

"I imagine not," Yanusa-Mahrdissa said after a moment. "It does make me feel a bit better about the whole notion, though."

"Like I say, they're shipping additional units and replacement tracks forward as quickly as Ram's Horn can get them off the assembly lines," chan Yahndar said. "And the Mark Two uses kerosene instead of pelletized coal. It's got a more powerful engine and a longer range, too."

"How *much* range are we talking about?" Yanusa-Mahrdissa asked.

"Under decent conditions in open terrain, the Mark One's good for over two hundred miles on a single bunker of coal, and it carries enough boiler feed water for at least four hundred. I understand the Mark Two will be good for two or three times the Mark One's range, given the advantages of kerosene. The Mule can make three hundred miles on roads and about two thirds of that cross-country, as long as it's not too heavily loaded and the going's not too soft."

The Shurkhali was impressed afresh. The Devil Buff devoted so little of its volume to fuel, since refueling was seldom an issue, that he would have been astonished if one of the bulldozers could have traveled as much as *one* hundred miles before refueling. He was less surprised by the feed water endurance, however. The Devil Buff's coiled monotube boiler used very little water—less than two gallons for the entire system—under very high pressures, and the uniflow engine was downright miserly in steam loss compared to older style expansion engines. And chan Yahndar was right about kerosene's advantages over coal. Not only did it have a higher caloric efficiency, but a given volume of kerosene contained none of the air spaces between individual lumps or pellets of coal. The powdered coal used in most maritime and industrial power plants had many of the same advantages, but installing the crushing machinery to powder coal on-site in a land vehicle was hardly practical, and Yanusa-Mahrdissa would rather try to transport old-fashioned black powder than pulverized coal. It would certainly be a less explosive challenge! That was the reason the pelletized fire boxes had been developed for vehicular use. The coal was powdered, then mixed with water and a bonding agent and forced through dies which produced uniform pellets about half an inch in diameter. It wasn't as efficient as injecting the powder directly into the flues, but the pellets packed "tighter," with smaller air spaces, than lump coal, and they were both easier to shovel and could be fed into the fire boxes mechanically in most cases.

Despite which, kerosene was a *far* better fuel choice in the end. That was why TTE was converting a lot of its heavy equipment to liquid fuel.

"That's going to make things at least a little easier," he said out loud, "and I realize we're talking about a single division, not an entire corps. How many Bisons are we actually going to need?"

"The Model A's the personnel-carrying version," chan Yahndar replied, "and each of them can transport two cavalry squads—minus their horses, of course. Assuming we had enough of them for the entire division, we'd need almost five hundred." He smiled faintly at the civilian's horrified expression. "Fortunately for your logistics concerns, we don't have anywhere near that many, though. For that matter, the Army's been buying about three times as many Model B's—the pure tractor variant—as Model A's. We'll be lucky if Division-Captain chan Geraith is able to scrape up *two* hundred of the A's. We'll probably have several hundred Mules to support them, though, and the Mules run on kerosene, like the Mark Twos."

"That's still going to burn Saramash's own pile of coal," Yanusa-Mahrdissa pointed out. "Then again, we've already *got* Saramash's coal pile right here at Shosara." He smiled another crooked smile. "Our own heavy equipment's got quite an appetite for it, you know. Moving it's still going to be a pain, though."

"That's why the Army's also scraping up every dray it can find up-chain from here and shipping them forward. I understand TTE's combing out its own steamer fleet, too, even if no one had come up with any hard numbers for the division-captain before he sent us on our merry way. I think we can confidently assume there'll be quite a lot of them, and we'll probably end up using some of them to move troops, as well, especially after the first infantry comes forward to join us. And at least we won't have to move as much fodder! That's one thing a dragoon's used to calculating. It doesn't feel right leaving the horses behind, but the Bisons will actually move a lot more cargo per ton of 'fuel' than animal traction can. And each ton of it will be a lot less bulky than fodder, too."

Yanusa-Mahrdissa nodded silently, his brain grappling with the quantities of coal, kerosene, and other supplies which would have to be transported through what amounted to a howling wilderness.

Resym was going to be bad enough. The railhead had already extended the next best thing to a thousand miles beyond the entry portal, located near the site of the small town of Shdandifar in the New Farnalian republic of Darylis, but it was almost *three* thousand miles—over a thousand of them through the heart of the Dalazan Basin's rain forest—to the exit portal, near where the Limathian river city of Paditharyn ought to be. They were fortunate the existing rail line covered over half of the rain forest crossing, and even more fortunate that TTE survey parties had already laid out the railbed for the entire trip. The fact that the Portal Authority had surveyed dozens of identical planets meant picking a route was seldom that great a challenge, although there were exceptions, of course. But someone still had to go and hike or ride the entire route to be sure there weren't any surprises; local and ground erosion, watersheds, landslides, tree growth patterns, and even earthquakes could provide plenty of those.

In this case, though, they knew now where to expect the greatest difficulties, and the Portal Authority's standard practice of using the rail line's planned route for the initial animal-drawn traffic of exploration meant there was at least a rough roadbed hacked through the jungle. It was little more than a muddy trail in far too many spots and the speed with which the jungle encroached on and reclaimed roadbeds had to be seen to be believed. Nor had that trail ever been intended for vehicles as heavy as the 3rd Dragoons Bisons and Steel Mules or for the sheer quantity of traffic which would shortly go streaming down it. But his own advanced construction parties were improving it steadily. It would offer a starting point, at least, and if the Bisons' towing capacity was really that great...

"How many Bisons do you have available right now, Battalion-Captain?" he asked.

"We've got about a dozen aboard the other ships," chan Yahndar replied a bit cautiously. "We didn't see any point in bringing along more than that, especially with how tight shipping is and how much heavy construction equipment Master Banchu needs to move this way. Besides, the entire idea is for our initial scouting efforts to be carried out on horseback. The kind of smoke trail a column of Model A's throws up would be a bit hard to conceal."

"I understand that," Yanusa-Mahrdissa said. "But one of the key things we need to worry about is getting enough heavy equipment far enough forward for our bridge builders. For that matter, moving the bridging *materials* is going to be a problem, and there are areas—especially in Resym—where we're simply going to have to do major road improvement—a *lot* of major road improvement—if it's going to support the amount of traffic Division-Captain chan Geraith's talking about putting down it. The tractor-trailer steamers we'd normally use to transport our bulldozers, graders, and steam shovels are bigger than hell and not very well suited for breaking trail through the middle of a rain forest. But if we can tow the flatbeds behind your Bisons instead of the regular wheeled tractors we can probably move the heavy stuff a lot farther forward a lot faster. And if you're going to be moving on horseback initially, anyway..."

"I see your point." Chan Yahndar nodded. "We may be able to trade off to some extent. I know you've got a lot of standard steam drays working around the railhead. Maybe we could give up a few Bisons for heavy towing and replace them with wheeled drays which are individually lightly loaded enough to get through and give us the capacity we'll need. For that matter, we could trade them out for Mules as they come forward. In fact," he frowned in sudden thought, "I think we need to suggest just that to Division-Captain chan Geraith. We didn't have any of the Mules here in Traisum when we started out, but if he can get enough of them forward to support us while we scout the route, it would help a lot from a tactical perspective, as well."

"How?" Yanusa-Mahrdissa asked curiously. "I thought they didn't have much payload capacity," he added, and chan Yahndar snorted.

"They don't, compared to a Bison, but they're faster than a Bison, so they wouldn't have much trouble catching up to us well before we hit Thermyn, and we won't have anywhere near the logistical requirements the main column will. More to the point, though, they burn *kerosene*, not coal, and they burn hot enough there's no visible smoke. We'd be a lot harder for some dragon or eagle-lion to spot, and we'd be able to leave all of our Bisons with you for the heavy hauling."

"I think that's certainly an idea worth looking into," the Shurkhali agreed. "And I know Master Banchu plans to transfer all his heavy equipment and heavy lift transportation to this side of the Vandor as quickly as he can find shipping for it. Eventually, we'll have plenty of steamers available to move stuff forward from Shosara; the problem's going to be how quickly we can improve the roadbed enough for them to do the moving."

"The division-captain's given me pretty much carte blanche on how I use the transport assigned to me," chan Yahndar said. "Why don't you and Battalion-Captain chan Hurmahl put your heads together and come up with the best estimate you can for how we divvy up our resources while we wait to find out about the Mules' availability?"

"We can do that. Of course, anything we come up with at this point's going to be pretty much a WAG."

"Understood. On the other hand, you're going to have at least a month before the division-captain gets the main column as far forward as Kelsayr, and any of the infantry's going to be more than a month behind *that*."

"Granted, but sixty days isn't anywhere near as long as it sounds, especially when we'll need to be setting up forward fuel and supply dumps. Which brings me to another point. What kind of depths can one of these Bisons ford?"

"They're designed to ford up to five feet of water," chan Mahsdyr replied for his CO. "The Mules can ford up to about the same depth, and I've seen Bisons manage just over six. Of course that was crossing a streambed where we knew exactly what the bottom conditions were. I think the Mark Twos, at least, can be fitted with a deep fording kit that would get them across up to ten feet if they seal all the hatches and openings. At that point all that would be above water would be the exhaust and the snorkel, so steering would get problematical as all hells and the risk of stranding one of them permanently in the middle of a river goes way up. Crew risk goes up, too. And the Mules can't go anywhere near that deep. On the other hand, *they* can use a standard scissors bridge or pontoon bridge, and the Bisons are too heavy for that. But you can probably count pretty solidly on five or six feet for either of them, especially if your fabricating crews are up to bashing a deep fording kit of our own."

"Really?" Yanusa-Mahrdissa brightened. "That's better than I expected. In fact, it's probably good enough to get us across eighty or ninety percent of the water obstacles in Resym. That would ease the strain on our bridging crews a lot!"

"I know we have to worry about getting across Resym," chan Yahndar said, "but all we really have to worry about there is the terrain. Once we hit Nairsom, we're going to be crossing 'only' five or six hundred miles of Roantha and northern Thanos in the middle of winter. It'll be a lot flatter, and we won't have triple-canopy jungle to worry about, but the temperature's going to be a bitch. And *then*, assuming a blizzard doesn't come along and kill all the damned horses, we'll hit the Chindar Portal in Thermyn."

The others looked at him without saying a word, and he snorted mirthlessly at their expressions. From their entry portal just south of the small, dusty town of Chindar in the Kingdom of West New Ternath to Fort Ghartoun was only a little over a thousand miles, and the weather would be far milder than anything they were likely to experience on the winter-struck high plains of New Ternath. But the terrain was also far more rugged, water supplies would be few and far between, there would be far less to conceal them from enemies who could fly, and the minor obstacle of Coyote Canyon would have to be dealt with somehow.

At least there was some good news to go with the bad. Coyote Canyon was well over five hundred yards across and over eight hundred feet deep at the point the TTE survey crews had selected for Thermyn's version of the Coyote Canyon Bridge. That was enough to give anyone pause, but in the carefree days before the Arcanans had darkened the horizon, work crews had been sent forward from Karys to begin work on the bridging project. They'd lacked the heavy construction equipment necessary to do a complete job of it, but they'd packed in enough picks, shovels, steam drills, and wagon loads of dynamite to make a serious start on the preliminaries. The access cut to the river had been blasted out of both sides of the canyon to permit heavy construction equipment to reach it once the railhead arrived. There was still a lot of spill from the blasting strewn about, which might well prove a major pain, but the maps and blueprints chan Yahndar had seen suggested that infantry and cavalry—and Bisons—would be able to negotiate the steep slopes, assuming they could get across the river itself.

And assuming the godsdamned Arcanans and their frigging "dragons" aren't sitting right on top of us when we try, he reminded himself grimly. *Of course, the whole idea's that we're coming at them from a direction they won't expect, but still...*

He decided to keep that particular concern to himself. If it should happen that the Arcanans were worrying about rats in the Thermyn woodwork, the preparation work already done at Coyote Canyon would certainly have a tendency to draw the eye. On the other hand, that work was four hundred and eighty miles from Fort Ghartoun as a bird—or a dragon—might fly. Even if the Arcanans had noticed it, that was a long way from anything worth defending.

And if they have noticed it and they're thinking about possible threats that might be coming at them from the back, Hymair?

That, he told himself firmly once again, looking back at the bulkhead maps, was something to stew over after it actually happened. Gods knew he had enough to worry about just getting there, first!

CHAPTER TWENTY-ONE

Hayrn 18, 206 YU
(January 9, 1929 CE)

THE FIRST INDICATION OF TROUBLE CAME WITHIN HOURS of their arrival.

Shaylar and her husband, exhausted by the long journey, had gone to bed early after being shown to the enormous bedroom set aside for them in the duke's Portalis townhouse. She jolted awake an unknown stretch of time later, groggy with lingering bone-deep fatigue, but gripped by a rising tide of fear, a brooding sense of danger she couldn't shake. When she peered at the chronometer glowing beside their bed, she realized she'd been asleep less than thirty minutes, yet it was impossible to get back to sleep. Weariness dragged at her, left her feeling bruised, but her sense of impending danger kept getting stronger—so much stronger, she finally couldn't bear to lie in bed any longer.

Not wanting to disturb Jathmar, she wrapped herself in a luxurious house robe made of velvet and tiptoed from the bedroom, out into the sitting room. The duchess had given them a beautiful suite, by far the most elegant and luxurious place Shaylar had ever stayed. Now silver light flooded through tall windows, nearly as bright as daylight thanks to the full moon visible high above the rooftop. She curled up on a cushioned window seat, resting her brow against the chill glass, trying to understand the disturbing mood that had gripped her so unexpectedly. She knew there was danger for them here, but she wasn't accustomed to having waves and waves of threat crashing across her senses.

She bit her lip and wondered what was happening, out there in the capital city, tonight. The hummers with news of the initial

311

conflict had beat them to Portalis by over a month followed by word of the failed negotiations and the resumption of hostilities, but it was clear Jasak and Gadrial were right about the effect the lack of official news *since* then was likely to produce. In some ways, she was grateful for the news blackout, if that was what it truly was. At least no one had associated her or Jathmar with the conflict brewing down-chain from Hell's Gate when they went clothes shopping! But she dreaded what was likely to happen when the long-delayed news did reach Portalis.

She bit her lip harder, dreading *everything* that lay ahead of them. Because there was nothing whatsoever she could do about any of it, she sat in her window seat, peering out through the window, and tried to calm her unsteady nerves.

A large garden, right in the middle of the vast structure, split the duke's townhouse in half. Open to the sky, it was filled with trees, carefully tended shrubbery, flowerbeds, beautifully fitted flagstone pathways, statuary, and a truly spectacular fountain, and it divided the public half of the house from the private portion. The offices from which Jasak's father governed New Arcana lay on its far side, and she was unsurprised to see lights in many of the rooms in that half of the house as she gazed across the garden. Clearly, their arrival had inconvenienced a fair number of public officials and their support people.

She leaned listlessly against the glass, and her head throbbed as the sense of danger tightened like a steel band around her head. It wasn't getting better; it was getting *worse*, and she was finally driven to seek assistance. The duchess had told her to press a small plate set into the wall of each room in the house if she needed to summon a servant. Now she slid out of the window seat and padded barefoot across the room, locating the faintly glowing bell-plate in the moonlight, rather than switching on the main lights. She didn't think she could bear bright lights with her head throbbing like this. She wasn't sure what Arcanans did about headaches, but she was in pain and needed assistance. At home or even in the field, she would simply have reached for a packet of herbs to calm the throbbing, but here she had nothing.

She touched the wall plate, which began to glow softly. Aside from that, however, nothing happened. She stood there for several moments, wondering if she'd misunderstood the instructions. After waiting for a minute or two—and feeling both awkward and a little silly standing there in the dark—she retreated to the window seat.

She was still sitting there, massaging her pounding temples, five minutes later, when a brisk knock rattled the door. It was sudden enough, and loud enough, to startle her, and she twitched in surprise before she stood, shook herself, and headed across the room to the door. She opened it—then hissed aloud and stumbled backward two full steps. The *hatred* seething in the housemaid's eyes sent a jolt of pure terror through her and her breath froze in her lungs under the brutal force of the woman's murderous glare.

"You wanted something?" the servant snarled.

Shaylar stood frozen in place, so stunned by the other's fury that she literally couldn't speak. She could only stand there, staring up at the tall servant and wondering what to do if the woman actually attacked her, and the hatred in the housemaid's eyes was overlaid with something else: contempt. The Arcanan woman waited a moment longer and then, when Shaylar still couldn't speak, growled something under her breath which sounded like a curse, whirled around, and stormed off, yanking the door closed behind her. It slammed shut with a bang, rattling framed pictures on the wall, and Shaylar sagged to her knees, trembling. The servant's lethal hatred had been so strong, even her dimmed Talent had felt it without physical contact.

She crouched there in the moonlight, gasping for breath, bludgeoned by a blow far more vicious than any physical attack. That sort of concentrated hate would have constituted a savage assault on a Voice under any circumstances; coming totally unexpectedly, with no warning, no opportunity to shield or brace herself in any way, its effect had been devastating. Her mind literally refused to work, yet she felt the tears beginning, felt her heart pound with the need to flee, to find some sanctuary, some hiding place. But there *was* no sanctuary, not here in his hideous alien world with its monstrous creatures, its hate-filled people and grotesque magic! There would *never* by any sanctuary! Never any—

And then Jathmar was at her side, jolted awake by the slamming door and her terror, and his arms closed around her like a fortress against her horror.

"What just happened?" he demanded urgently, and she trembled against him, clutching him with desperate strength.

"I don't know!" she cried. "I had a terrible headache. I woke to a feeling of danger. I couldn't sleep, it kept getting stronger, and my head was aching, throbbing. So I did what the duchess told us, pushed the wall plate, there." She pointed to the still-glowing rectangle in the wall. "The maid who answered the call wanted to *kill* me. I could feel it, like a sledgehammer. She wanted to murder me, Jathmar, and I have no idea why!"

He held her tightly while reaction tremors shook through her. None of the servants had done anything like that earlier in the day. What in Marthea's name had brought it on *now?* When a second, much quieter knock, sounded at their door, she flinched and clutched Jathmar even harder.

"Who's there?" he snarled.

"It's Gadrial. Please unlock your door. I have to talk to you! I need to show you something important."

Jathmar stood, glaring at the closed door for at least ten seconds, his arms still around his trembling wife. Then he growled something under his breath, released Shaylar with obvious reluctance, and opened the door.

Gadrial stood in the hall, in a house robe as elegant as the one Shaylar had donned, and her expression tightened as she saw Shaylar's ashen, tear streaked face.

"You already know," she whispered.

Shaylar shook her head. "I don't *know* anything! I just woke up. Something felt dangerous. My head ached. So I rang for servant. The maid wanted to kill me."

Jathmar closed and locked the door behind Gadrial, then drew Shaylar across the room and eased her down in one of the comfortable chairs. The magister crossed to a handsome sideboard, found a decanter of some kind of spirits, and splashed some of it into a glass.

"Sip this," she said.

Shaylar took a deep sip, shuddered, and gulped down the rest. Then she looked up to find Gadrial with a crystal in one hand, biting her lip in obvious distress.

"What's happened, Gadrial?" she demanded. "Why did that woman want to kill me?"

"Jasak is furious. Cursing and snarling." Gadrial's voice was tight with obvious anger of her own, and also with something that sounded almost like . . . shame. "Even the duke is in a towering rage, and *I'm* so upset, I can't stop shaking. It's this," she held up the crystal. "It's dreadful, what they've said in the headlines, the articles, the picture captions, everything."

"Show us," Jathmar growled.

Gadrial touched a lamp, which lit with a mercifully soft light. Then she handed the crystal to Shaylar and tapped it with a stylus. It immediately began to glow and a sheet of light appeared above it, looking for all the world like a Sharonian newspaper page, although no newspaper Shaylar had ever seen printed its banner headlines in blood-red ink that *flashed* as a reader looked at it. That was her first thought... but then the one-word headline actually registered:

MURDERED!

Just below was a picture of the man Shaylar and Jathmar had met so briefly at the swamp portal, the man who'd made the fire rose, who'd been a second father to Gadrial. The fact that Halathyn vos Dulainah's picture was printed in color, not the black and white of a Sharonian photograph, registered only as a mild surprise. What caught her attention was the caption:

"The death of Magister Halathyn vos Dulainah, above, beloved of millions, at Sharonian hands has been confirmed."

Other article headlines jumped out from the page as she swept disbelieving eyes across it.

Arcanan Diplomats Murdered in Midst of Peace Talks.

Casualties Much Heavier Than Initially Reported: Mass Funerals Planned.

Garth Showma Heir Arrives in Disgrace!

Shardonai War Criminals? No Explanation from Duke

The articles were even worse than the headlines. The words were a blur, hard to read because Shaylar's eyes kept filming over with tears of shock and horror. She had to scrub her eyes again and again just to see them.

The Portalis *Herald Times* has received information which makes it disturbingly clear that the initial confrontation with the so-called "Sharonians" was far more catastrophic than the citizens of the Union had been led to believe.

As previously reported in these pages, the first contact between Arcana and the violently aggressive "Sharonians" ended in a total slaughter. Magister Gadrial Kelbryan escaped death by a hair's breadth and Commander of One Hundred Sir Jasak Olderhan, only son and heir to the Duke of Garth Showma, was nearly killed when an entire platoon of his company of the 2nd Andaran Temporal Scouts was butchered. He barely escaped the ambush with his life, a tiny remnant of his shattered platoon, and Magister Gadrial.

As our readers know, the entire remaining strength of his company was killed or captured in a nighttime sneak attack through the portal between Mahritha and the universe which has since been dubbed "Hell's Gate." What our readers *did* not know, however, was that Hundred Olderhan had succeeded in capturing two of the murderous Sharonians alive following the original, savage attack on his platoon and had been ordered to return them with them to New Arcana for interrogation. Despite some concern over freedom of information, this journal must concede that it was proper for that information to be withheld from the public in the interest of security. What this journal has only now learned, however, is what *else* was withheld.

Magister Halathyn vos Dulainah, a national hero in Ransar, founder of the New Arcanan Academy of Theoretical Magic, and the most Gifted magister Arcana has ever known, has been foully murdered. The unarmed magister, present with Hundred Olderhan's company purely as a civilian consultant—without uniform or weapon—was shot down without pity or mercy when the brutal Sharonian attack overran the 2nd Andarans. Armed with weapons even more terrifying and destructive than initial reports had suggested—weapons capable of hurling explosive spells *through* a portal—the attack overwhelmed our troops almost immediately. And as Magister Halathyn attempted to aid a wounded soldier, one of the attackers cold-bloodedly shot the elderly, unarmed magister with one of their hellish weapons.

Despite the brutality of the attack, whose full details have not been officially acknowledged even now, Governor Nith mul Gurthak attempted to establish diplomatic contact with the Sharonians in hopes of avoiding additional bloodshed. As our readers will recall from earlier articles, he directed Rithmar Skirvon and Uthik Dastiri or the Union Arbitration Commission to seek a truce with the Sharonians for the purpose of negotiating some peaceful alternative to the carnage which appeared to be their preferred mode of contact. Our readers will also recall that those negotiations failed and active operations were subsequently renewed.

What we did not know, and have only now learned, is precisely *how* those negotiations failed. The exact details remain unclear, but the *Times Herald* has learned that the murdered bodies of every member of our diplomats' security detail were discovered—left lying where they fell and badly burned by a fire clearly set by the Sharonian murderers to cover their own flight from retribution. The body of Envoy Dastiri was also recovered, and Army forensic Healers have determined that he was shot directly between the eyes at very short range by one of the devilish Sharonian weapons. Perhaps even worse—and far more ominous—the body of Envoy Skirvon has *not* been recovered, leaving one to wonder what still worse fate may have befallen him.

In the meantime, personal messages beginning to arrive from the handful of prisoners from the 2nd Andarans who have been rescued tell grim tales of torture and brutal mistreatment in which even rudimentary Healing was denied our heroic wounded. In other news just received from the front—

It went on and on, article after article, lie after lie, distortion after distortion. Shaylar finally lifted wet and streaming eyes to meet Gadrial's stricken gaze.

"But it's not true!"

"I know," Gadrial bit out. "That's why Jasak and his father are so furious. They don't even know where the *Times Herald* got its information. There are more facts in those articles—distorted, twisted, and perverted, but still with a kernel of fact—than anyone in the Union *government*'s officially heard even now! The *Times Herald*'s always been one of the journals which feels out-universe exploration should be managed by civilian agencies rather than the military. If the duke—or anyone else in the current Government—tries to lean on them for their sources, they'll clam up and refuse to say a word. And if the duke insists they reveal those sources, they'll positively *welcome* the chance to be sent to jail until they give up the names. Which they won't do, of course. The Union's freedom of the press laws would protect them in the end, and they'd gain a huge amount of prestige for their 'principled stand.'

"The fact that someone obviously fed the *Times Herald* all this distortion is bad enough, but even if Jasak and the duke manage to get the *truth* out, it may not help. Worse, without some official news from mul Gurthak or *someone* out-universe from Mahritha, they can't even tell anyone what the truth *is* because they don't know what's happening themselves. Not really. And other journals and news outlets have already pounced on the *Time Herald*'s reportage. It's spreading like wildfire, all over New Arcana—and probably Arcana Prime and all the rest of the multiverse by now, as well! So in a lot of ways, it doesn't even *matter* what the truth is. The damage is done, and the duke doesn't think it can be undone."

She paused, her expression miserable, while the stunned Sharonians stared at her. Then she squared her shoulder and bit her lip.

"And I'm afraid there's more, as well," she told them in an utterly miserable tone. "Please get dressed, both of you. There's something else you have to see."

"*What?*" Jathmar bit out.

"It's—" Gadrial sighed and shook her head. "The duchess saw this coming, I'm afraid. Saw the potential for it. That's why she put you here, in rooms whose windows overlook the garden, rather than the street."

Those words sent a shudder of fright through Shaylar. What was out there, in the street they couldn't see? She looked at Jathmar for a moment, and then the two of them returned to their bedroom and dressed in silence.

Gadrial led them through the house, until Jasak and his father met them in a corridor near the front of the vast townhouse. The duke spoke briskly.

"I don't want you to be too alarmed, when you look out there.

The security system is on and armed. Nobody can actually reach the house, not physically and not with a malicious spell. You're under my protection," he added, "and I'm serious about that duty."

He looked back and forth between them for several seconds, his expression hard and determined. Then he motioned courteously for them to follow him, and Shaylar groped for Jathmar's hand as he led them into a large and beautifully appointed drawing room or parlor. The duchess was already there, standing beside a tall, curved window that overlooked the street at the front of the house. They were a full story above that street, looking down into it, and a mutter of sound reached them, rising and falling like a distant sea. It was too indistinct for Shaylar to determine what it was, but it set her teeth on edge. The sense of danger—and her throbbing headache—worsened drastically, and the duchess turned toward them, her expression grave. She held out one hand.

"Come, stand beside me," she said gently.

Shaylar and her husband crossed the room. The closer they came to the windows, the louder that sound grew, until they reached it and Shaylar blanched. The street was jammed with people. Thousands of people. *Angry* people. Waving signs and shouting. The low roar was the sound of fury and hatred. She could read some of the signs, while others had been written in languages other than Andaran. The ones she could read chilled her to the bone.

These people wanted to kill her.

"They can't see us," the duchess murmured when Shaylar flinched back from the tall window. "We've set the defensive spells to block the view of the windows. *All* the windows. The people out there see the windows as they ordinarily look. They can't see us standing here."

"Why did that newspaper tell such horrible lies?" Shaylar demanded. "Why does someone want *them*," she pointed at the screaming mob, "to kill us? We're *helpless!*"

"They're being manipulated." Jasak Olderhan's jaw muscles were bunched and fury crackled in his eyes. "The *Herald Times* is bad enough on its own—I don't doubt for one minute they'd love to embarrass the Government and Father any way they could—but they wouldn't go *this* far from the truth unless someone had fed them carefully doctored information. Unfortunately, we don't know who's doing it . . . but we intend to find out."

"But *why*? From everything you've said we would have frightened them, anyway! Why paint us as such monsters?"

"I don't know," the duke answered in a voice ribbed with iron, "but as Jasak says, I damned well mean to find out! I started digging into this the moment I saw that journal. It arrived shortly after dinner, which means that collection of crap hit the streets three hours ago. And *that*," he nodded toward the mob outside in the street, bathed in the double glow of arcane streetlamps and moonlight, "is too big and too organized to be entirely spontaneous. Someone organized the kernel of it; then started spreading the word. Three hours later, we end up with a riot on my doorstep.

"My people have dug out a few facts, already. This so-called story was leaked by someone in the civil government, not the Commandery. Someone very highly placed wants the story told this way, and I suspect whoever that someone is, he's been sitting on dispatches from the front that have *not* been shared—officially, at least—with anyone in the Army or with the Cabinet. I intend to find out who that person is, but I already know—or suspect—his reasons."

"For lying?" Jathmar demanded. "For deliberately misleading the public? Inciting them to murderous demonstrations? When my wife rang for a servant to ask for something for her headache, the damned maid who answered was on a hair-trigger edge of killing her!"

The duchess blanched, and the duke scowled even more furiously than before.

"That will be dealt with at once," he said in a growl that Shaylar trusted implicitly. Then he sighed. "As for the rest... As Jasak says, the *Herald Times* is anti-Government and anti-Army at the best of times. This was exactly the sort of raw meat anyone could predict its editorial staff would pounce on. And once their version of the 'truth' hit the street, every other news outlet picked up on it. Some started reporting it and—of course—speculating wildly in the process, but even the more restrained papers had to at least acknowledge it. Partly, it's just the news industry's tendency to exaggerate things, to whip up interest amongst their readers and capture new readers. The more details they can offer—even when they don't *have* details—the more likely people are to buy *their* newspaper, not their competitor's."

"You said the story came from someone in government," Jathmar bit out.

"Yes. It did. Or perhaps it would be more accurate to say it came from someone engaged in *politics* at the highest level. Someone with contacts and allies—tools—in the government, whether or not he's actually in government service himself. And that, I'm afraid, leads to several possible scenarios. What better way to unite public opinion than to paint the other side as entirely evil? And the fact that Halathyn vos Dulainah was killed offered a perfect mechanism for implementing that strategy. He *is* dead, after all; none of us can dispute that. If whoever this is can convince the public he was murdered out of hand, it'll be like applying a flame spell to a haystack! *My* question is one of motive. Was this done purely to unite factions that will be jockeying for control? Or for some more sinister reason?"

"What sort of reason could justify *this*?" Jathmar demanded. The duke's jaw tightened, but when he responded, his reply seemed curiously oblique...at first.

"Andara's controlled the Union of Arcana's military for two centuries," he said. "That's not because we've snatched the reins of power, either. Primarily it's because nobody else wanted the job." He shrugged. "We Andarans enjoy the military lifestyle. Neither the Mythalans nor the Ransarans do. In fact, most of them despise and disdain it. Some *individuals* from Mythal and Ransar enlist, whether from patriotic commitment or—more commonly—as a way to better their stations in life. But nobody else has wanted control of the military.

"The fact that you exist, however, and that we've met violently, has changed everything, rather abruptly. Quite suddenly, Mythal and Ransar must face the reality that their survival lies in someone else's hands. Andaran hands. I know Mythalans and Ransarans," he glanced apologetically at Gadrial, "well enough to know certain factions of those societies will suddenly discover, despite lifetimes of disdain for the military, that *they* want control over the means of defense. Some of that's inevitable—when someone feels threatened, of course he wants to be sure he and the ones he cares for are protected the way *he* wants them protected, and Shartahk take anyone who gets in his way.

"But I suspect what's really driving this—what the manipulators want—goes far beyond that natural reaction. Some people have never been comfortable with the extent of Andaran influence on the military, not because *they* wanted to control it, but because the military's been a huge factor in stabilizing the Union from the very beginning. Some of them want to rock that stability because the collapse of existing power relationships may let them build new ones more...beneficial to their own interests. Others see the military as the primary support for Andara's influence within the Union—its power base—and want to break that power base in order to improve their own. And now those manipulators finally see a chance to accomplish their goals.

"There's just one problem. How does someone take charge of a military whose control is so entrenched in Andaran hands? The easiest—and the one I fear most—is by discrediting Andara. By making Andaran officers appear incompetent. By vilifying the enemy in the worst possible terms, exaggerating the threat, and then howling that the Andarans can't protect Arcana from that kind of threat. Not when they bungled the first contact so badly that they allowed themselves to be wiped out virtually to the last soldier and couldn't even protect an inter-universal hero like Magister Halathyn!"

"But that isn't what happened," Jathmar protested. "Your son lost only a *third* of his men and that included the wounded, not just the dead. The rest of his men weren't taken prisoner until the second confrontation. And they certainly didn't mention that we were civilians—that *we* were the ones brutally slaughtered! They didn't mention the little detail that your own soldiers killed Magister Halathyn or that Jasak's replacement tried to kill an unarmed man asking for civilian survivors, either. What kind of government do you have, that would lie so hideously to its own people?"

"This *isn't* the Government," the duke said firmly. "As Governor of New Arcana, I'm a member of Speaker Skyntaru's Cabinet, and I will guarantee you that neither he nor any other member of the Cabinet's received any of that news about what happened to Skirvon and Dastiri—not through any *official* channel, anyway. *Some* information, like how Magister Halathyn actually died, we've known about ever since Jasak's initial report arrived, and I've argued in favor of releasing it in full from the beginning. I can't argue too strenuously, though, because someone will claim I'm only trying to hand out sketchy, incomplete information in the best possible light to protect Jasak from the consequences of this disaster. So the decision was made to withhold some of the more potentially inflammatory information until we knew more.

"And now we have this." He jerked his head at the mob beyond the windows, his expression one of disgust. "I'm not saying that someone in the Government—inside the Cabinet—isn't involved in what's happening, Jathmar. I'm only saying that it sure as Shartahk isn't anyone who's a *loyal* member of that Cabinet. This is directly opposed to the Speaker's policy! I've known Misarthi Skyntaru for thirty years, and believe me, the *last* thing he wants is for this situation to get any worse. He and I have argued for years over how big a chunk of the Union budget the military 'sucks up,' as he likes to put it, but he knows how thin we're really stretched. Even if he didn't hate the very thought of how many people are likely to get killed, he knows how costly it's likely to be and how ill-prepared we are for it. He's been trying to keep a handle on emotions—that's the real reason he decided to sit one the news of Magister Halathyn's death—until he could find out what in Mithanan's name is going *on* out there!"

The fire in Thankhar Olderhan's eyes could have reduced the entire city of Portalis to ash...without magic.

"Who's behind this—and why—*will* come out," he said coldly. "We'll make damned certain of that. Whether or not the truth will do any good at that point remains to be seen." He gestured at the crowd and said, "I felt it was important to show you this, so you'd understand what you—and therefore we—are up against, here."

"Political in-fighting and power grabs are never pretty," Jathmar muttered. "Innocent people tend to get hurt during them. Or killed."

"Then Sharona has the same difficulties in that area that we do," the duke rumbled.

Jathmar's laugh was humorless. "We may be from a different civilization, sir, but we are human. Wherever humans live, that problem will always rear its ugly head. We're far more alike than they," he nodded toward the window, "would care to admit."

The duke's glance was piercing. "Well phrased and well thought-out. And that's also the reason why war between us is now an absolute certainty. We," he nodded toward his son, his wife, and Gadrial, "will do our best to shout the truth of what happened from the rooftops. But..." He didn't have to elaborate. "The Mythalans were dead-certain to fear and hate you sufficiently to demand war no matter what, and whoever was behind that garbage in the newspapers this evening knew full well how to manipulate the masses. Ransar will never forgive Sharona for Halathyn vos Dulainah's death."

"But we didn't kill him!" Shaylar protested.

"That won't matter," Jasak growled with an angry glance at the crowd.

"But won't they be angry and upset when they discover they were lied to, about the way he died?" she demanded, and Jasak rubbed the back of his neck.

"Some will. Most won't. Even if we get the truth out, the anger will've set too deep for most of them to be willing to give it up. Thinking about something this emotional is harder work than they'll be willing to undertake! So instead of thinking about that, they'll just point out that if it hadn't been for you," he nodded toward her and Jathmar, "your soldiers would never have attacked his camp and he'd still be alive. So, of course, even if he was accidentally killed by an Arcanan *weapon*, it's Sharona's fault there was any fighting for him to be killed *in*. We'll do our best, but you have no idea how popular Magister Halathyn was in Ransar."

Shaylar and Jathmar stared at one another, shocked by the notion of a society that not only could lie to its people on this kind of scale, but whose people wouldn't *care* they'd been lied to, or why. It was more alien than anything else they'd yet encountered, including the existence of dragons and gryphons.

The anger that blazed in Jathmar's eyes licked like flame through Shaylar, as well. She would not spend the rest of her life cowering in terror of these people. If they killed her, so be it. But she would not live in fear. As she stared, narrow-eyed with fury, at the mob screaming for Sharonian blood, she realized her headache had vanished, and she bared her teeth in something which definitely *wasn't* a smile.

She'd always heard that a headache was one of the hallmarks of the Calirath Talent. That many of the Caliraths who'd manifested their family's Talent experienced pre-Glimpse headaches... and that the stronger the glimpse, the worse the headache. She'd never demonstrated even a normal Clairvoyant Talent, much less the Calirath Talent, but in that moment she wished, bitterly, she *could* Glimpse their future. It would be useful to know how to sabotage Arcana's preparations for war.

If a way existed, she'd find it.

And use it.

CHAPTER TWENTY-TWO

Hayrn 18, 206 YU
(January 10, 1929 CE)

HORVON FOSDARK, EARL OF BRITH DARMA, SAT BACK IN HIS chair as Chief Sword Otwal Threbuch saluted, executed a perfect about face, and strode briskly from the room. The other Arcanan officers empanelled to conduct this board of inquiry sat back, as well. The man with iron gray hair and the rigidly starched crimson uniform to his left was Fleet Third Kordos, who held the third-highest rank a naval officer could attain. On his right sat the white-haired Commander of Legions Shorbok Githrak of the Arcanan Army. He wasn't the highest-ranked officer in that army, but he had headed the Intelligence Corps for a staggering twenty-three years.

"What a damnable mess," Kordos muttered.

Brith Darma agreed. Profoundly. He'd sat on dozens of boards of inquiry during his career. None of them came even remotely close to matching this.

"Our job," he said, "is to sort out this damnable mess, and the two toughest witnesses are still waiting for us. Does anyone want a brief recess before we tackle the Sharonians?"

They'd already taken the statements of Hundred Olderhan and Magister Gadrial, in addition to Chief Sword Threbuch's. His brother officers shook their heads.

"No," Githrak replied, "let's get this over with. I want to hear their testimony before we break for lunch. We can call them back this afternoon for closer questioning if we need to, but I'd just as soon have a complete preliminary picture to mull over while we eat."

"Agreed." Brith Darma nodded. "Very well, gentlemen, which shall we question first? The Voice or the Mapper?"

He used the titles deliberately, just as he'd been thinking of them that way since reading the first report arrived. He didn't want to humanize them prior to seeing or hearing them. Thinking about the Voice, in particular, as a frightened girl far from home would have led him to sympathize with her, rather than focus on the critical military aspects of what she was: a mind-reading communications specialist. One whose existence was a profound threat to Arcana's ability to conduct military operations against the people who'd produced her.

"The Voice," his fellow officers agreed unanimously.

"Let's face it," Githrak added, "she's the one we've all been worried about since the reports arrived. Or at least if either of you *hasn't* been worried about her, you've got no business on this board."

Kordos just snorted rudely and Brith Darma's lips twitched sardonic.

"I won't say I've lost sleep over her," he said, "but I've had some damned unpleasant nightmares."

Githrak nodded. "Well put. I've got a much clearer idea, now, about what happened out there on our side—initially, at least. I still don't have a godsdamned clue what mul Gurthak and Harshu have been up to since!" The Intelligence officer clearly didn't like that admission, but he made it unflinchingly. "Having said that, though, I damned well want to know a hells of a lot more about these people and their mental weapons. And more about their physical weapons, as well. And frankly, I want to see these terror weapons in operation. Hundred Olderhan's descriptions were brutal. Chief Sword Threbuch's were ghastly. And I'm in awe of Magister Gadrial. A civilian, a *woman*, caught in the middle of that, with men whose wounds leave me queasy, just trying to picture them. But she was in there treating those wounds, damn near killing herself with exhaustion keeping those men alive. The woman deserves a medal."

"Damned good idea," Kordos agreed. "I'll bring it up with the commander general. I'm scheduled to have dinner with him and his wife, tonight."

Brith Darma nodded. "Yes, please discuss it with him. I'd like to see her get something more out of this than a disrupted life, days of questioning, and a brusque thank you while we rush out the door to prepare for battle."

A brief silence fell as the officers contemplated the enormous task facing them. Gods, a war fought through multiple universes...

Brith Darma brought his attention back to the matter at hand.

"I've already made arrangements to have Hundred Olderhan demonstrate the enemy's weapons this afternoon, at the officers' firing range. He's brought samples of their long weapons, their hand-held ones, and several other intriguing pieces of their gear, shipped with him the whole damned, long way."

"That ought to be interesting," Kordos muttered. "Try as I might, it's hard to imagine building a civilization without magic."

"Why," Brith Darma gave the Fleet Third a sardonic smile, "do you think I've been having those damned nightmares?"

Githrak sat forward in his chair, pouring more water into his glass from the self-chilling carafe on the long table at which they sat. He sipped thoughtfully for a moment, then leaned back with a shrug.

"Right. Let's see what this Voice has to say," he said crisply. "I want to take her measure as a person, as well as a weapon. She claims she's the first woman allowed to work with their point survey crews. I want to see what sort of woman our enemy considers qualified enough to do that tough a job."

"Agreed. Particularly since *we* do that job with soldiers." Fleet Third Kordos toyed with his stylus, his expression frankly worried. "That girl's going to tell us a hell of a lot about these people, no matter what she says or does."

Brith Darma glanced at their Master of the Sword, whose job it was to secure the door and usher those being questioned into and out of the room.

"Call the Voice, please, Master Sword."

The noncom saluted and opened the door to the adjoining, sound-proofed chamber, a small room where witnesses awaited their turns for interrogation.

"The Board of Inquiry commands the presence of the Sharonian Voice. Enter the Inquiry Chamber, Shaylar Nargra-Kolmayr."

Brith Darma expected several things. He expected a frightened civilian. Even Gadrial Kelbryan, who was merely a witness, with no personal consequences hanging over her testimony, had shown signs of stress and worry, so he fully expected to see signs of prolonged strain in this Voice. He also expected uncertainty and quite possibly a few legitimate tremors and tears.

The witness was in a terrifying situation, totally helpless, and fully aware of the hatred rampaging through Arcana's populace as conflicting versions of events at the frontier were splashed across the journals and public message crystals. He even expected questions about what would become of her.

He did not expect what walked through the door.

The Voice was tiny. She was a slip of a girl, smaller even than Gadrial Kelbryan, who was a slender, petite Ransaran. Brith Darma didn't like the instantaneous reaction he felt at first sight of her: a rush of chivalric protectiveness. She was so small... and so self-controlled and poised, it shocked him. She marched across the room in her rustling skirts as regally as any duchess and halted when the master of the sword told her to stop.

Then she stood there, hands folded neatly in front of her, her silence and her stance as solid as any soldier braced to attention. She met Brith Darma's gaze with stunning power, neither flinching from his cold, deliberately hostile stare nor losing her composure when he ran his gaze rudely up and down her body. When he identified the emotion that simmered deep in her alien eyes, a shockwave ripped through him.

She was *angry*.

"State your name and occupation," the master of the sword intoned.

"I am Shaylar Nargra-Kolmayr, employed as a civilian exploratory survey crew Voice by the Chalgyn Consortium, a privately owned company engaged in the exploration and development of newly discovered universes. I hold a survey license from the Sharonian Portal Authority. My mother is an ambassador to the Kingdom of Shurkhal, where I was born, a nation that is more than three thousand years old. Who are *you*?"

That took Brith Darma aback. All of it did. Her command of the Andaran language was *terrifying*. Her grammar was perfect, her word choice flawless, and her accent less pronounced than most Mythalans and Ransarans he'd encountered. And she continued to hold his gaze, ignoring the other officers. Someone had told her he was the Board's presiding officer. Either that, or she'd plucked the fact from his mind. His intellect was inclined to believe the former, with Magister Gadrial as the likeliest source.

But the deeper part of his mind shouted a warning of intense and incredible danger. *She's a living weapon!* He drew down a deep, silent breath, taking care to breathe from the diaphragm so that his chest didn't rise and fall, and narrowed his eyes, watching her closely even while he wrestled with his own mind. He'd vowed to conduct this proceeding with honor, and if he allowed irrational fear to rule him, he would learn nothing from her.

He decided to begin with something she might not be expecting him to ask.

"Why are you angry?"

He didn't throw her off stride. Instead, her eyes sizzled even more ferociously. She looked like a dragon in the instant before it spat searing flame.

"Why am I angry?" she repeated softly, the question on a rising note of utter contempt. Then her voice went hard as flint, and she spat out her answer like hailstones. "I was hunted down like a dog and nearly murdered. I watched my friends, my professional colleagues, slaughtered without pity. My crew leader was shot through the throat with a crossbow bolt. Why? For the crime of standing up without a weapon and saying in a calm and reasonable tone 'That's close enough.' Have you ever watched a man choke to death on steel and blood? A man you'd spent months with, working together under exhausting, dangerous conditions? A man who'd saved your life at least three times? A scholar who taught young people how to build cities, who came to the frontier to find new places to build them? Your soldier *murdered* him! And you ask why I'm angry?"

He started to speak, but she wasn't finished.

"My *husband* was burned *alive*. The only reason he didn't die of those horrifying burns was the mercy and Gift of Magister Gadrial Kelbryan. Have you ever seen human skin touched by the fireballs your weapons produce? It cracks and turns black. You can see the flesh beneath it through those cracks. It blisters like paint on a skillet that's been shoved into a campfire. Have you ever *smelled* what that unnatural fire does to human flesh? Some of your own soldiers *vomited* from it. From smelling the remains of young boys who'd just left school and wanted to build something wonderful for themselves and the families they hoped to start. And you can sit there and ask why I'm *angry*?"

She didn't move a single step closer, didn't even unclasp the hands folded before her, but he suddenly felt an irrational desire to back away from her as if she'd crossed the room, slammed her fists on the bench in front of him, and shouted in his face.

"My freedom is gone. A career I fought an entire *world's* rules to establish has been ripped out of my hands and smashed to pieces. My family—my mother and my father—no doubt believe I'm dead; that I was savagely murdered by barbarians! I have nothing left. No money, no home, no possessions. I don't even own the comb I used on my hair, this morning, or this dress." She lifted her arms at last to display the well-made but admittedly plain gown. "And you have the *gall* to ask why I am angry?"

He swallowed down a throat gone terribly dry.

"You pompous, arrogant jackass! My husband and I lie awake each night wondering if you or someone in your government will override Jasak Olderhan's authority over us. That you'll seize us and use some ghastly form of questioning to learn what you want to know. We've read your journals. We've seen the lies in them. And we've seen the demands Mythal is making. I believe the term is 'mind ripping'? Stripping every fact out of a victim's mind, leaving behind nothing but a piece of meat that still breathes?

"What you would do to *us* is terrifying; what you would do to an unborn child I might carry if my husband lies with me—*that* goes beyond terror to *nightmare*. Yet you can sit there in your brave uniform, wearing your brave medals—decorations you earned for facing situations far less deadly than what your army did to *me*—and dare to ask me why I'm *angry*?"

He blanched whiter with every word.

"As if that weren't enough," she hurled those furious words at him, "*someone* in your government and your military is deliberately lying to the public. They're lying about me, my husband, my people. They're lying about the actions of your soldiers. Even the Governor of New Andara's furious about it. Yet you sit there and ask me why I'm angry? Holy Triads preserve us, do you expect me to be *happy*?"

A dreadful silence crashed down across the interrogation chamber. Brith Darma was breathing hard, and he didn't have to glance at the officers on either side of him to know they'd been hammered just as hard by her stinging accusations as he had. He could hear it in the way they were breathing. What was even worse was the lethal accuracy of those accusations. Someone—and he'd give his right arm to know who—*was* leaking systematic lies and distortions to the news services. And some of the more rabid, ultra-conservative *shakira* lords *wouldn't* be above harming a child, unborn or otherwise.

But he dared not show her how badly she'd rattled him.

"Happy?" he echoed softly, forcing his voice to remain steady. "No. I don't expect that." Then he put a whiplash in his voice. "But I do expect prisoners of war to show respect to their captors!"

"*Respect?*" Her eyes went incandescent and her small hands clenched into fists that nearly shredded the skirt under them. "I gladly give my respect to those who earn it. Gadrial Kelbryan's earned my respect for life. Jasak Olderhan did his damnedest to *kill* me, just as I did my damnedest to kill him; but he's earned my respect again and again, for the way he handled the men of his command in combat, for the way he cared for his wounded, for the respect and the mercy he accorded me when my shock was so deep I could barely keep my sanity from disintegrating in my hands.

"I respect Otwal Threbuch for the incredibly difficult tasks he performed. He survived that first firefight, when we were shooting down every man we could center in our gun sights. He managed to reconnoiter our portal fort, survived the *second* battle, and slipped across to the Arcanan side of a guarded portal without being caught. *Any* man who can do that has my respect. But he deserves my respect far more for the way he broke the news of Halathyn vos Dulainah's death to Gadrial."

That surprised Brith Darma.

"Why?" he frowned.

"He had to tell her that a man she loved as a second father had been killed—*by his own soldiers.* I've seen a lot of soldiers. Every portal my crew passed through has a fort sitting in it. We stopped at every one of those forts, picking up supplies, replacing gear. I've seen a lot of men like Chief Sword Threbuch, the kind of men who find it difficult to talk to civilian women, to talk about *anything* emotional, whether happy or painful. Yet he broke that ghastly news to her gently, on his knees and with tears in his eyes. I *profoundly* respect a man like that."

Then her voice went scathing, again.

"But *you*," she raked him with her gaze just as rudely as he'd raked her, "haven't even bothered to give me your bare name. I don't know how things are done in your society, but in *mine*, gentlemen and soldiers—particularly *officers*—are neither deliberately arrogant, nor rude, nor cruel to women."

The second silence was even worse than the first.

This woman was *dangerous.*

Brith Darma sat rigidly still, staring down at her through eyes trying to widen in shock and dismay. She might be a prisoner, but she was neither cowed nor frightened, and she was far, far from alone and broken. Despite every ordeal this woman had endured, despite facing a lifetime of house arrest, she retained enough spirit to spit in his eye and make him cringe in shame.

If a Sharonian civilian, a *woman*, displayed this magnitude of sheer guts, it was little wonder the men who wore the Sharonian uniform had smacked Hadrign Thalmayr into the mud like a swatted mosquito. These people were *trouble*. Brith Darma studied her in silence for a moment, mulling over possible responses. He decided to address her barbed and accurate accusation of rudeness with an attempt to judge her reaction to authority.

"You want to know who we are? Very well. Fleet Third Kordos is on this board as a representative of the Arcanan Navy. His rank is the third highest possible for a naval officer. Commander of Legions Githrak is the head of Army Intelligence. And I am Horvon Fosdark, Earl of Brith Darma and Commander of Wings for the Arcanan Air Force. My rank is the second highest in the Air Force."

Her smile and formal curtsey shocked him. "Thank you, My Lord. I won't say it's any kind of pleasure to meet you, but it's much nicer to at least know *who* is shouting at me." She then folded her hands neatly in front of her once more and waited.

He sat blinking in consternation. She was too damned *small* to be this much trouble. He frowned down at her where she stood simply waiting for him to bring forth his next shout, and her attitude and accusations stung even deeper than she probably realized, since one of the tenets of the Andaran code of conduct was the importance it placed on how an officer and gentleman, particularly one born into the peerage, treated ladies. Worse yet, the fact that she surprised him on a constant basis worried the hell out of him. If he couldn't accurately predict the responses of a civilian prisoner of war, how poorly would he and his brother officers fare against *her* world's officers?

"You said our soldiers hunted you down like a dog," he said finally. "Explain."

Her recitation was cool, detailed, and astonishingly clear, both in the sequence of events and thoughts and emotions she'd experienced at the time. She even repeated the shouts she and others nearby had traded, fighting off the attack from flanks and rear. He finally interrupted with a question.

"How is it you can give us such a detailed description *weeks* after an event that was emotionally and physically traumatic? None of the other witnesses recalled the kind of detail you've been so glibly repeating."

She didn't react angrily to what amounted to an accusation of lying—or more accurately, stretching the truth. Nothing she'd said had triggered the lie-detection spells, which would have caused an indicator light on the wall behind her to glow instantly. Given her earlier reactions, he expected her to spit in his face, again, for such a criticism, but she didn't. She merely blinked in surprise.

"Of course they couldn't. They don't have my Talent. Jasak and Gadrial are Gifted, but they can't do what I do. I'm a Voice."

Brith Darma frowned in confusion. "I don't understand. What do you mean by that? What does being a Voice have to do with describing something that happened to you?"

"Voices have perfect recall."

Brith Darma blinked in surprise, this time.

"Perfect recall?" His voice was flat with disbelief.

"Of course. All Voices do. It's part of the Talent. We have to transmit long, complex messages, whether we're in government service or work in a corporate office, sending complex legal documents to another company's Voice or working in the news business, transmitting news stories. Perfect recall's been bred into us, so to speak."

Githrak leaned forward abruptly. "Prove it!"

She repeated every word she and Brith Darma had spoken since her arrival in this room. She got it right. Terrifyingly so. She repeated things Brith Darma had already forgotten. She captured the intonations of his voice with a stunning mimicry, duplicating the emotional effect he'd striven to portray with eerie, chilling accuracy. She even described things she'd merely observed: facial expressions, movements, Kordos' habit of toying with his stylus while listening.

A swift glance as Kordos and Githrak revealed horrified expressions. Brith Darma understood that reaction in his bones. Not only could the enemy transmit across vast distances, the enemy could do so with terrifying accuracy, not only what they'd heard, but what they'd seen, every tiny detail of it. Even a prisoner of war could transmit critical intelligence data. It was one thing to read Hundred Olderhan's report that this woman had transmitted every instant of the Toppled Timber battle; it was quite another matter to have that report graphically demonstrated.

Brith Darma deliberately drew another slow, careful breath, then asked, "How many Talents are there?"

"What?" Surprise touched her eyes. "Clarify your question, I mean, so I'll know how to answer."

Why did such a simple question surprise her?

"How many Talents are there? We have two prisoners. You and your husband. Both have Talents. *Different* Talents. Here, a Gift means you can manipulate magic. Some people have stronger or weaker Gifts: magistrons are Gifted in portions of the magic field touching upon living things; magisters work primarily with *non-living* things, but within that broad categorization, a Gift merely means an ability to work with spellware and the magic field. There's no . . . specialization within Gifts. But you and your husband are fundamentally *different* from one another. How many different Talents are there? And how many of your people have them?"

She held his gaze steadily when she answered. "I don't know how many different Talents there are. New ones appear unexpectedly from time to time, which makes it difficult to count them. I know or have heard of dozens."

"And how many of your people have them?"

"About eighty percent."

The truth spell light never even flickered, and horror cascaded through the Earl of Brith Darma. *Eighty percent* of their population were Talented? Barely *twenty* percent of Arcanans were Gifted! If they had that huge an edge in these "Talents" of theirs . . .

He fought to control his expression, but some tiny glitter of satisfaction in her eye told him he'd failed. He sat there for a moment, trying to think of where to go next, feeling irrationally as if *he* was the prisoner and she the captor. But then Commander of Legions Githrak cleared his throat.

"If I may, Sir?" he said calmly. Brith Darma nodded brusquely, and the intelligence specialist looked at Shaylar. "And are all of them as strongly Talented as you and your husband, Madam Nargra?" he asked.

Something other than satisfaction flickered in her eye, but she smiled very slightly, like a fencer acknowledging a hit.

"No," she said courteously. "One of the qualifications for a Voice with one of the survey teams is a particularly strong Talent. Obviously, the same is true of every other Talented member of a team like ours, given how far from our home base and any support we operate."

Once again the indicator light remained dark, and Brith Darma felt a cautious sense of relief.

"I see," Githrak said. "And what percentage of those with 'Talents' are sufficiently powerful to be trained to use those abilities? In a professional sense, I mean. As a way for them to earn their livings?"

"Perhaps twenty out of a hundred," Shaylar replied, manifestly wishing she didn't have to.

Again, the indicator light remained dark, and the relief surging through Brith Darma became a torrent, although he did his best to conceal it. Their *effective* percentage of Talented people was no higher than the Union of Arcana's percentage of Gifted people. Of course, depending on how large their population was, the total number of Talented people could still far surpass the Union's Gifted population. And if it did, their non-Talented population would be far larger, as well, an eventuality he did not enjoy contemplating.

"How large is Sharona's population?" he asked, taking back control of the interrogation . . . and reminding himself *very* firmly not to give the intelligence officer a grateful look.

"I have no idea."

He stared hard at her. He wanted to accuse her of lying, but the lie-detection spells still refused to trip the warning light.

"Why not?" he asked.

"We've spread across so many universes, I'm not even sure how many we've colonized. We've never done a formal census to count how many of us there are. We're more interested in exploring, colonizing, building factories and forts, mines and farms than we are in counting people. Why waste time when there's so much work to be done, building a multi-universe civilization? One that's strong and healthy and productive. Our priorities are focused on building and living, not pigeonholing and counting and controlling everyone."

The lie-detection light remained stubbornly dark, and Brith Darma sat back, contemplating her, what she'd said. She simply stood there, calmly waiting for the next question. A group of people who didn't know how many members it had sounded like a slipshod bunch of backwoods barbarians, but for one thing. Their technology—the weaponry and other equipment—as well as their extremely effective use of it in combat suggested otherwise. Strongly so. Underestimating them could well prove fatal. Of course, so could *over*estimating them.

Before he could frame the next question, Kordos glanced at him and arched one eyebrow.

"May I?" the Navy officer asked, and Brith Darma nodded. Then Kordos leaned sharply forward, scowling thunderously at Shaylar. "However many of you there are, do you seriously expect us to believe that these mental Talents of yours aren't weapons?"

"I don't expect you to believe anything I say." Her glance at Kordos was cool and appraising. "I've never met such suspicious people in my life."

"*We're* suspicious?" Kordos snapped. "Your people launched a full bore attack through a portal—an attack that, unlike the affair you describe—most definitely *wasn't* the result of confusion and a sudden encounter! It was clearly carefully planned before it was executed, and you massacred a complete company of our troops! And then, according to what little information we do have, your 'negotiators' *murdered* our envoys and their entire security escort. And you call *us* suspicious?"

For just an instant, Brith Darma thought they'd found the way to frighten her. The Voice's face went parchment white and a tremor shook through her. Then she exploded.

"Don't you *dare* sit there on your sanctimonious Andaran arse and regurgitate the same swill your 'journals' printed! Otwal Threbuch admitted your officer in charge of that 'complete company' of yours tried to kill an unarmed Sharonian officer asking for *me*—by *name*, damn you—under a flag of truce! That officer tried to commit *murder.*

"By all the gods and goddesses of Sharona, the bastards in that camp deserved what they got! Most of them had tried to kill me. Tried hard. If you expect me to feel sorry that some of those men were already wounded because I shot them, you'll be waiting a long time for it. The only man in that whole camp I shed tears for was Halathyn..."

To Brith Darma's horror, *that* was what broke her.

She stood there, shaking and magnificent, her eyes rimmed red, and wept while talking about roses made of light and child-like wonder and kindness to terrified, traumatized captives, and all the other reasons a whole civilization had loved Magister Halathyn vos Dulainah.

And the lie-detector light remained dark.

If this wisp of a girl was Sharona's norm, Arcana was in desperate trouble, and he had a sinking, hollow-gut feeling that there were altogether too many people just like her on the other side of the portal she'd walked through before running into Jasak Olderhan's platoon. She'd been wronged. Hugely—*devastatingly*—so. Worse, her people knew she had. And they knew Hadrign Thalmayr had exhibited the moral judgment of a jackal.

Worse, if her "Voice" ability functioned the way she said it did—if the rest of Sharona had received the terrifyingly accurate report of what she and her comrades had endured that he was sink-ingly certain they had—there was only one way they could possibly respond. They'd be out in force, demanding blood vengeance, and he couldn't find it in himself to blame them. Yet it was his job to defend the Union of Arcana and its vital interests. As disastrous a course as it was bound to be, the Union would have no choice *but* to fight these people, and it was up to him and his fellows to do that fighting ... however much they privately sympathized with Shaylar, her husband, and their dead companions. They had no choice, and he wanted to scream at the utter damned fools who'd botched this so badly and landed Arcana in such a foul snare.

The trouble was, the fools he needed to scream at were either dead, prisoners of war, or over 85,000 miles from where he sat, on the far side of Hell's Gate and being *damned* chary about sending timely reports back to their superiors. The only other candidate handy was Jasak Olderhan. Brith Darma was sinkingly aware of where that was likely to end, and he hated the thought of trashing the career of an officer who showed as much prom-ise as Sir Jasak. But that was for later. For now, they still had a difficult and exhausting inquiry to get through and the witness of the moment was trembling, wiping her face with her hands, and trying desperately to regain her composure.

"Master of the Sword," Brith Darma said, tone gruff to hide the emotion in his voice, "please be kind enough to fetch a chair for this lady."

When she stared at him, he said, "Like you, I give respect when and where it's earned. You and I are enemies. I can't tell you how profoundly I regret that, but neither of us can change it. Not at this point. But you're a worthy opponent—and, so far as I can tell, an honorable one—and I won't add to the burden on your shoulders by treating you harshly when you're intensely distressed. Particularly since your distress is for one of *us.*"

"Thank you," she whispered, almost voiceless.

When the master of the sword brought a chair, she sank down onto it, trembling. When the stoic, stone-faced master produced a handkerchief from his blouse pocket and handed it to her, fresh tears welled up and her second "thank you" was entirely voiceless. She dried her eyes, got her snuffles under control, and took several deep, calming breaths.

Then she surprised him again.

"May I reassure my husband that you're not torturing me, in here? He can feel my distress and it's driving him nearly frantic."

Both officers flanking Brith Darma hissed softly under their breath. So did Brith Darma. Jasak Olderhan's report had mentioned a strange mental connection between this woman and her mate, but he hadn't thought to see it demonstrated so quickly.

"Master of the Sword, allow Jathmar Nargra to enter."

The instant the door swung open, Brith Darma braced for assault. Jasak Olderhan and Gadrial Kelbryan were grappling with Jathmar Nargra, who was trying to reach the door, apparently intent on *kicking* it down while a ghastly combination of terror and rage blazed in his face.

The massive master of the sword whipped his sword out of its scabbard and braced himself for assault.

"Let him enter!" Brith Darma called out sharply.

The master of the sword snarled a curse under his breath and retreated, backing up with sword held at the ready. He kept himself and his blade between the crazed prisoner and the officers of the board.

"Hundred Olderhan! Let him go!"

In the instant, Jathmar exploded through the open doorway. He swept his wife into his arms, jerking her off her feet and dragging her out of the interrogation room. She was speaking urgently in a language that was not what Gadrial Kelbryan had recorded. She was clearly trying to reassure him, because the wild rage gradually seeped out of him. He shuddered. Set her on her feet. Buried his face in her hair.

When he lifted his face again, it was a mask of helpless agony. He brushed wet strands of hair out of her eyes where her upswept hair had come loose and been plastered to her face by her own tears and his. He was whispering her name. Over and over. Just her name. Brith Darma was so shaken, he couldn't even look away. When Fleet Third Kordos started to speak in an undertone, the earl lifted a hand, warning him to silence. He didn't want *anything* setting off that man's hair trigger.

He wished to hell he'd worn his own sword.

When Jathmar had calmed sufficiently to release his hold on his wife, and the look he turned on Brith Darma and the other officers might have frozen a sun. Silence hovered, and the earl neither moved nor spoke. The absolute last thing he wanted to do was provoke the master of the sword into disemboweling the Sharonian.

Shaylar spoke again and touched his face, turned it back to look down into hers. At length, he nodded and caught her face in both his hands, pressing a gentle and desperate kiss to her lips.

Brith Darma said in a low whisper, "If either of you even *suggests* we try to continue questioning her alone, I will personally loosen your teeth."

"No argument from me," Kordos muttered, and Githrak merely lifted one eyebrow.

"I wouldn't dream of it," the Intelligence officer murmured. "The amount of information I just took in was extraordinary. Although I must admit, I'd prefer the next burst of data to come with a little less personal peril. I don't suppose anyone thought to set the automatic defense wards around our bench?"

Brith Darma slid one hand carefully to press the stud under the lip of the table, just above his lap. "Oversight remedied."

When Jathmar released his wife from the kiss, Brith Darma judged it safe enough to address the man directly.

"Mr. Nargra?"

The knives leapt back into the Sharonian's eyes as he jerked his gaze up to meet the earl's. He didn't say a word. Just stood there in the open doorway, glaring at Brith Darma and gripping his wife tightly again.

"Mr. Nargra, I will say only this. I have the deepest respect for your wife, her courage, and her strength. I won't even ask you to leave her side for the rest of this session. In fact, we would vastly prefer for you to stay with her."

His eyes narrowed. "Why?"

That single word was harsh with hatred and suspicion.

"Because I have no desire to see the results if we goad you into attacking us to defend her. I do not want to watch you die, sir."

That caught him by surprise.

"Master of the Sword, please bring in a second chair."

"No, Sir."

He stayed right where he was, sword drawn and held in defensive posture between the threat and three of the highest-ranked—and currently unarmed—officers in the Arcanan military. Brith Darma didn't swear aloud; nor did he say, "It's all right, Sword Master, I've set the wards." Instead, he said, "Quite right. My apologies. Hundred Olderhan?"

"Yes, Sir," the younger officer said crisply, swinging up an empty chair from the waiting room and depositing it beside the one Shaylar had abandoned. When he stepped back into the waiting room, past Jathmar and his wife, he spoke quietly. "I gave you my word, Jathmar, that they weren't hurting her in here."

The prisoner's gaze locked with Hundred Olderhan's. "Physically, no. You're in no position to judge *anything* else."

"No. But I am in a position to guarantee your safety."

Shaylar said something soft, too soft to hear, even if she'd been speaking in her astoundingly good Andaran. Whatever she'd said, Jathmar gave a stiff, reluctant nod.

"Very well," the prisoner said in a low growl. "I'll hold you to that guarantee."

The young officer smiled. "I know you will."

That smile and those words were exactly the right touch, at exactly the right moment. That, alone, told Brith Darma what he needed to know about Jasak Olderhan's judgment under pressure. It was a damned shame, he thought bitterly, because there wasn't a prayer that they could do anything but recommend a full and formal court-martial. Some days, Horvon Fosdark, Earl of Brith Darma, Commander of Wings, genuinely hated his job.

CHAPTER TWENTY-THREE

Hayrn 20, 206 YU
(January 11, 1929 CE)

GADRIAL PEERED AT HER REFLECTION WITH CRITICAL EYES.
The burgundy silk gown the duchess had ordered her private dressmaker to run up for her was a glorious confection, but she was in no fit state to truly appreciate it.

Yesterday, after the long day waiting on the Board of Inquiry, she'd finally accepted the duchess' offer and taken a suite in the Portalis ducal apartments, which stood so much closer to the Commandery offices used by the Inquiry. This morning her hostess had provided everything she needed. Nor was Sathmin Olderhan alone in "looking after" her.

Many of the Olderhan staff might believe Shaylar and Jathmar were the villains the news painted, but not one believed the slanders whispered against Jasak Olderhan. They'd helped raise that boy into a man. And now they clearly very desperately wanted Gadrial to like them. It was almost overwhelming how well they were treating her. This dress wasn't just from the duchess, and she knew it. Yet as much as she appreciated their remarkable welcome, it was impossible for her to respond the way she knew she ought to. However hard she tried, she simply couldn't see past the horror of what the Union of Arcana's Commandery might do to Jasak.

She gave her reflection a brave attempt at a smile. It failed miserably, so she gave up, closed her eyes, and covered her face with both hands. *Help me get through this day, Rahil,* she prayed. *And please, I beg of you, help Jasak. He's not Ransaran, but he needs your help.*

341

Needed it desperately...

Gadrial slipped off the burgundy silk. She'd hoped it might cheer her up a little, but her eyes were so damp she was afraid of dripping on the dress and ruining it with water spots. Given what the duchess had paid for it, she didn't want to ruin it the first time she took it out of the closet, and she'd forgotten to ask the designer if the silk had been treated to repel water. She wasn't sure of the wording for a spell that would accomplish it, either, which made her wary to experiment on so expensive an item.

So she dutifully stripped it off, hanging it carefully in the closet where a magic field kept garments floating at the perfect height for the wearer, kept any of them from touching and wrinkling any others, and served, as well, to repel dust, moths, and anything else that might nibble on them. She'd never seen a closet like it, *ever.*

Before the news had come, night before last, she'd vowed to build the spells necessary to replicate it in her own closet, at home. She still intended to do that. She really did. Just as soon as her life settled down enough to make going home again possible. That threatened to start the faucet flowing again, and she drew a deep breath to calm herself, pulled out a suit to replace the burgundy silk, and dressed quickly.

She'd already planned a whirlwind of a week, meeting with her Academy staff, with the duke and several of his political supporters, and with Halathyn's widow. When the summons for the Board of Inquiry came immediately, she'd canceled or delayed everything she possibly could—except for Mahritha vos Dulainah. Halathyn's widow would actually have understood if she hadn't come. The woman's generosity of spirit overflowed even now, and she'd done her very best to comfort *Gadrial.* If Halathyn had been her second father, Mahritha had been her second mother, and she'd watched that second mother's eyes fill with tears at last when Gadrial told her Halathyn had named the very last universe he would ever explore in her name. *That* was what had finally broken her composure, and Gadrial wished desperately that she'd had some miraculous piece of magic to wash away the pain of Halathyn's death.

But today promised to be worse. So she dressed quickly, then spent a great deal of care over her face and hair, using cosmetic spells to tint eyelids and cheeks, to smooth over the dark smudges under her eyes, put there by sleeplessness and strain, and to repair her dry, bitten lips so they were moist and expertly shaded in her best, most flattering colors. For her hair, she wanted a simple, businesslike look and she murmured spells from the latest fashion crystals, grateful she could do the job, herself, rather than having to pay a Gifted hair and makeup artist to do it for her.

Of course, she could always borrow the duchess' in-house artist...

Gadrial sighed while her hair lifted itself into the upswept style from the crystal, tucking itself into the proper configuration. Once she had it smoothed to her satisfaction, she set the spell with a simple holding incantation and clipped her favorite bracelet around her wrist. She checked the results carefully in the mirror, then nodded, satisfied.

Sleek, simple, professional.

All signs of stress carefully obscured.

Except her hands, which shook. She dragged down another deep, desperate breath and told her eyes to stay dry. *I will not cry, I will not cry, I will not...* Word had come at dinner, last night. Without waiting for the Board of Inquiry's report, Parliament had announced War Hearings and the Commandery had declared sufficient grounds to begin court-martial proceedings.

Jasak was being court-martialed.

She snarled a curse under her breath, snatched up her crystal case, and strode out of her beautifully appointed suite. The actual court-martial—the trial, itself—would run concurrently with a hellish schedule of Parliamentary hearings, both set to begin today.

Every single one of the "witnesses" who'd returned from the frontier had already given their preliminary testimony to the Board of Inquiry, which had been used as the basis for the decision to proceed with a formal court-martial. Now all the witnesses, including that snake of a Mythalan, Bok vos Hoven, would be questioned again—and again—minutely, as the officers of the court attempted to determine Jasak's guilt or innocence on a number of charges.

That nightmare was scheduled to begin this morning, at North Hathak Army Base. This afternoon, it would be Parliament's turn to poke and prod and drain them dry. They would undergo interrogation on that schedule for as long as it took to find Jasak guilty or innocent of the military charges and for the members of the War Operations and Intelligence Committee to obtain what they termed "sufficient information to pursue national defense," keeping their personal lives on hold while they wobbled back and forth like marionettes on strings.

Rahil's mercy, but she dreaded the next several days. Or weeks. Surely it wouldn't last for *months*?

She drew another breath and focused on what was on her plate for today. She'd never testified at a court-martial. She'd never been called before a parliamentary committee for official hearings, before, either. Halathyn had, in his capacity as a theoretical magister, several times, and she was trying to recall everything he'd said about the process, but her nerves were so jangled, it was difficult.

Her role today would be similar to his, with the emphasis being on what she'd seen and heard from the moment that first rifle shot had split the air on the morning Yurak Osmuna and Falsan chan Salgmun had shot one another. She had her notes, in the slim case she used to carry her PC, and held more of her research data on additional data crystals. She wasn't sure she'd need it, but she wanted to be prepared if Parliament's newest standing committee asked for particulars on what she and Halathyn had been working on.

What maddened her more than anything was that neither Jasak nor his father would comment on anything that was happening. They were perfectly prepared to discuss the general news, to share her fury at the obvious distortions in the journals and public crystals. And they made no bones about their wrath at the way Jasak's *shardonai* were caricatured and demonized in those accounts. But she couldn't get a word—no one single, solitary *word*—out of either of them where the implications for *Jasak* were concerned!

She'd thought she'd come to some acceptance of the way she felt about Jasak Olderhan. The way she felt about living in his world. But during the past five days, the Jasak she'd known during their long journey had utterly vanished. She didn't even know the cool, remote stranger who pretended to be the same man she'd ended up kissing so passionately during their final run into Portalis. The tears prickled again, and she swore savagely under her breath and told them to go right back where they'd come from.

It didn't work.

She was busily engaged in the mortifying business of scrubbing her cheeks fiercely dry with the backs of both hands as she stepped into the magical drop-field that wafted her from the fourth-floor bedroom suites to the ground-floor area where meals were taken, visitors were met, and life was generally lived. Even with a direction finding spell, she could barely find her way around beyond the immediate environs between her assigned suite and the dining room.

They'd been gathered in that dining room for a late supper when word had arrived. Jasak's only comment had been that the court's investigators had promised to be impartial, thorough, and scrupulously honest. He'd actually told her to *trust* the court's officers! *Oh, yes, certainly*, she'd fumed through a haze of anger and horror. *Trust them. They're impartial. Honest. They'll reach the right verdict. Right. And if Jasak or his father or those officers expect me to believe* that, *they're either arrogant or fools! Or both…*

She didn't trust any of them. Not as far as she could throw them, which was about as far as she could pick up and throw this sprawling townhouse. *Trust* them? Hah! She didn't even *understand* them. They were *Andaran*. She'd spent the entire night alternating between sobbing into her pillow and throwing the pillow—and everything else within reach—at the walls.

Court-martial!

He hadn't done anything wrong!

Didn't anyone besides her *see* that?

It had taken Gadrial a shame-faced hour, this morning, to repair the damage she'd wrought with spells that put the broken pieces of the duchess' lovely knickknacks back together.

Now the drop-field set her gently on the ground floor and she set her teeth and stepped out into the corridor, heading grimly toward the dining room for yet another meal she didn't feel like eating. When she'd tried to talk to Jasak after dinner last night, he'd taken both her hands in his, said, "I really can't talk to you right now, Gadrial. Not until the court's finished questioning you as a witness." And then he'd kissed her—on the cheek!—and vanished through a side door.

She'd wanted to scream at him.

She still did.

When she reached the dining room, a waiting maid redirected her to "the breakfast room." Gadrial hadn't even heard of that room, since breakfast had invariably been served in the same chamber in which they'd eaten dinner and luncheon, but she followed the maid through a maze of corridors, expecting to find the entire family, comprising the duke and duchess, Jasak, his youngest sister, and Jathmar and Shaylar. Instead, she found the duchess, by herself.

Jasak's mother glanced up when she halted in the doorway.

"Come in, Gadrial, dear," she murmured, beckoning her over.

Uncertain what to expect, Gadrial crossed the sunny, cheerful little room—little by the townhouse's standards, anyway—and set her PC case down on an upholstered chair no one would be using.

"Sit down, Gadrial," the duchess said, patting the chair beside her own.

She took her seat with great hesitation and the duchess gazed at her, then nodded.

"Mmm-hmm, as I suspected. You've spent a night as miserable as mine. More miserable, I should expect, since you're so unused to Andaran ways."

"How could you tell?" Gadrial asked in a hoarse voice. "I was so careful, this morning, to erase the signs."

"Yes, my dear. I know." The duchess' smile was surprisingly sweet. "But you've been a leading light at the Institute for years. All those breakthroughs in magic theory have had you in the crystals countless times. And this is the first time I've ever seen you—in person or in the news—when your makeup and coiffure have been perfect."

"Oh." Gadrial bit her spell-tinted lip. "In my defense, things in the lab can be messy, and I never quite knew when reporters might be stopping by."

"But we know there are plenty of reporters watching now." The duchess nodded again, gently. "And you care a great deal about what happens to my son."

She nodded. And then, to her horror, the faucet started running again. She waved her hands in helpless apology, then gave up and simply accepted the linen napkin the duchess had rescued from the table's place setting and handed to her. A moment later, Gadrial found herself in Sathmin's arms, sobbing miserably. The Duchess of Garth Showma didn't complain about the tears soaking her five-figure silk suit. Instead, she kissed Gadrial's hair, rocked her, even crooned a soft little tune that reminded Gadrial—achingly—of home.

"Wh-where did you learn that song?" she quavered.

"Mmm? Oh, in Ransar, my dear."

Gadrial sat up, astonished. "Ransar? You've been to Ransar?"

"Oh, yes." She gave Gadrial a conspiratorial wink. "It was a perfect scandal in the family. I insisted—forcefully—on applying to the Ransaran Academy of Fine Arts and Magic. When I was accepted, I turned our household into a living hell until Papa finally agreed to allow me to attend. Poor Papa. He never did understand why it was so important to me."

She tilted her head and peered down at Gadrial.

"I'm profoundly glad I spent those four wonderful, illuminating years in Ransar. Particularly now."

"I don't understand. Why particularly now?"

"Because, my dear, when my son finally recovers from his bull-headed, stubborn insistence on doing this his own way, without the slightest assistance or advice from anyone, he's going to find himself in need of a new career and someone to help him put the pieces back together in a totally new configuration."

"You think he'll be found guilty?" Gadrial asked softly, and pain ran through the duchess' eyes.

"I don't know," she said. "But in a very real sense, it makes very little difference, since Jasak's military career is likely over, whatever the final verdict." She bit her own carefully spell-tinted lip, allowing Gadrial to see *her* distress. "Even as an Andaran, myself, I'm sometimes appalled by the way our menfolk embrace the absurd code that regulates the way officers are allowed to function."

"*You're* appalled?" Gadrial gasped, and the duchess' eyes flashed.

"You think it's easy to watch a husband or a son pay fealty to a set of rules that chew them up and spit them out through no fault of their own? I understand why they do it—why it's important to them—better than you probably ever will. But Gadrial, child, it hurts to watch them *do* it, knowing they're innocent of any wrong-doing and knowing it's tearing them apart, inside, too."

Gadrial felt quite abruptly small and selfish and mean.

"No, dear, don't feel that way," the duchess said, deciphering her stricken expression. "You've no idea how comforting it is, knowing Jasak has someone as wonderful as you waiting to help him when he finally lets you back in."

"Why has he locked me *out*?" she wailed. "I don't understand it. Not at all! It can't be this folderol about being a witness. We spent months together getting back home. If 'witness contamination' was going to happen, it already would have!" Then she lifted her hands to her cheeks, which scalded hot. "Oh, Rahil..." she whispered. She met the duchess' gaze, eyes wide with horror. "It *did*. I fell in love with him."

She covered her eyes, moaning, and Jasak's mother gathered her in again and kissed her hair once more.

"I know. Which is precisely why you and I are having our breakfast alone this morning. I told Thankhar to take himself off with his son and fend for themselves, and Jathmar and Shaylar are enjoying breakfast in bed. And I've already promised both of them that I will personally be present during *their* questioning, whether by military or civil authorities."

"I don't understand," Gadrial murmured into the duchess' silk-clad shoulder, which was obviously spell-protected, since the material was not only unspotted, it wasn't even wet. "How can you do that?" She sat up again, peering curiously into the duchess' face. "You're not a soldier or a witness, so how can you attend the court-martial? And the duke said the parliamentary hearings will be closed sessions, too."

The duchess chuckled. "My dear, you're not Andaran. Trust me. I'll be granted admission, whether *they* like it or not."

Gadrial frowned in confusion.

"I think I'd better find out what you mean. I'm in love with the heir to a dukedom," she said, feeling more than a little dazed at the notion, "and I have no idea what that entails, politically. Or even *socially*." She bit her lip. "How can you possibly keep all those crazy rules straight? And why would you want to be present when Jathmar and Shaylar are questioned? I mean, they're the reason your son's being court-martialed. Why would you want to protect them? You haven't known them long enough to consider them friends, the way I do."

The duchess sighed and gave Gadrial an odd little smile.

"You do have a way of getting to the heart of things, don't you?" she said. "Very well, let me start with your last point. Why do I want to protect them? Because they're helpless. And because it's my *duty* to protect the helpless. That would be the case even if they hadn't become part of my family, my household."

When Gadrial just stared at her, totally mystified, the duchess settled back with the unmistakable air of someone about to launch into a lengthy lesson.

"An Andaran noblewoman has a lifelong duty to help anyone who's helpless, whether they ask for assistance or not. I know very well what you Ransarans think of the notions we Andarans hold dear, the concept of service before self. But it's very real for us, very serious. We aristocrats enjoy great privileges, but they come with great price tags. Sometimes those price tags can bring terrible pain, even rip your world apart."

Gadrial's eyes widened.

"Oh, yes," the duchess nodded. "You may laugh at our militant notions all you like," she said, arching one brow in a delicate challenge Gadrial had no intention of taking up, "but many a case of serious injustice has been set right by an Andaran noble-woman who's taken up the cause of the person being wronged.

"We may not serve in combat, but we do fight." The duch-ess leaned in as if bestowing a secret. "At school in Ransar, I learned that Ransarans and Mythalans think Andaran women are oppressed. Yet they somehow never noticed that Andaran men are every bit as controlled as the women are. They fight the wars, and we ensure the home front is worth their sacrifice. Sometimes that involves a bit more force than some of the administrators who *think* they run things quite expect.

"Andaran women aren't in uniform, but we might as well be. If the Union of Arcana expects otherwise, they're in for quite a surprise. The Andarans at the Commandery are fully cognizant of our power...and more than a little wary of our wrath. And before I'm done with this business, the *rest* of the gentlemen who think they run our worlds will be more than a little wary, too. I promise you that!"

Her eyes flashed in a way that delighted Gadrial.

The duchess was a fighter!

"Having said that," the duchess continued smoothly, "let's turn to Jathmar and Shaylar. They're utterly helpless and at grave risk of enduring serious further injustice on several levels. That makes them my business. My official, Andaran-duty business. But it doesn't end there, my dear. Since they're Jasak's *shardonai*—a decision on his part which I wholeheartedly support—they're not simply in the *custody* of my family; they *are* my family, and that makes those duties even heavier and more vital for me to uphold."

Gadrial's brow furrowed.

"You're serious about that. It isn't just some abstract concept for you, is it?"

"No, indeed, it is not. Jathmar and Shaylar are legally a part of my family, part of *my* household."

"*Your* household?" Gadrial echoed. "I thought Andaran men were in charge of Andaran households."

She could hear the outrage in her own voice. So did the duchess, whose lips quirked again.

"That's the general perception. But as with many other things about Andarans, it's, ah, somewhat less than accurate. Thankhar is the lawful head of the family, but by long tradition, an Andaran wife is expected to run everything—and I do mean everything—about the home front when the men leave for war. It's been so long since the Portal War that some people have forgotten about times when nearly every Andaran governorship was being managed by the governess, but that is and remains the Andaran tradition.

"The fact that far too many men and women—and too many of them Andarans, like that toad Thalmayr, I'm sorry to say—have forgotten how Andaran women fight is secondary to this discussion, however. The point that *is* pertinent to this discussion is this: the duties and obligations of the Andaran code are as binding on its women as on its men. And that, my dear, is where I shall nail their balls to the floor."

"Oh!" Gadrial couldn't help it. She gaped openmouthed in astonishment; then clapped both hands over her lips. "Sorry," she gasped. "I just had no idea it really could work that way."

"It does and it will," the duchess assured her. "Under Andaran honor codes, *I* am the one responsible for the safety and well-being of every member of my household. That's true whether they're blood-kin, servants in my employ, or invited guests. I'm required, under a fairly stringent set of rules, embodied in Andaran *law*, to ensure their comfort and their safety.

"An Andaran woman who deliberately allows a member of her household to be injured can be punished quite severely under those laws. I don't mean common accidents, which can't be foreseen. I mean if she allows *anyone* to deliberately injure them. It's a serious charge and therefore a serious obligation.

"Its origins lie in the endless wars between various noble houses during the pre-Union centuries. A woman who aided her husband by luring his enemies into the home under a guise

of hospitality, then betrayed them, was rightly viewed as a dis-
honorable murderess. That's why the law is so stringent on that
point. And that law has all kinds of ramifications in the modern
world, which we Andarans understand quite well. Unfortunately,
those ramifications are poorly understood outside the Andaran
nations, and it's been entirely too long since they were publicly
reasserted—and demonstrated.

"What that translates to in our current situation is simply this:
I'm legally obligated to protect Jathmar and Shaylar, which means
I must ensure their safety, which means I cannot allow anyone
to bully, browbeat, threaten, or batter them, even emotionally.
Not while they remain part of my household. And since they're
a *permanent* part of my household, that duty's legally binding
upon me in perpetuity, either for the duration of their lives or
mine. Oh, and should they have children, that duty will extend
to *them* as well.

"I cannot *perform* that legally-binding duty if I'm not present
during their interrogations. Therefore, I must be granted access
to the hearings, whether military or civil. They *must* allow me to
attend. Even if they desperately want to keep me out, they can't."

"*Can't?*" Gadrial's eyes widened, and the duchess smiled serenely.

"Can't." She picked up her cup and sipped hot bitterblack.
After so many years married to an Andaran, she'd actually
developed a taste for the Union Army's beverage of choice. "It's
always possible they might be foolish enough to try. In fact, I
rather wish one of them—a Mythalan, by preference—*would* be
that foolish, although I doubt they'll oblige me. I would *so* enjoy
'bringing the hammer down,' as Thankhar so charmingly put it.

"But, as I say, I very much doubt any of them will be that
stupid. And since they can't keep me out, they must adjust their
behavior accordingly. Politicians—and officers—who might not balk
at savage attacks in my husband or son's presence will think twice
before indulging that sort of nastiness with *me* in the chamber."

Her Grace's eyes twinkled.

"Thankhar is a politician and bound by the rules of his office,
whereas I'm *not* a public-office holder. That gives me far more
latitude in which to kick up a fuss. I assure you, Gadrial, I can
be every bit as difficult, stubborn, and cantankerous as they are,
when I put my mind to it. And unlike *them*, I'm perfectly prepared to take every single archaic, persnickety, underhanded, and

devious advantage that antiquated social code you dread bestows upon us 'poor, downtrodden women.'"

Gadrial stared at the Duchess of Garth Showma in genuine awe.

"Perhaps it's impertinent of me, Your Grace, but I'll say it, anyway. Jasak has a *seriously* wonderful mother."

"Thank you, my dear." The duchess' smile went tender and abruptly watery, and she lifted one hand to touch Gadrial's cheek. "I've hoped for a long time that Jasak would find someone very special. He's going to need you."

"He won't even talk to me," Gadrial whispered.

"No. Not yet. He's like his father, that way. I can't tell you the number of times I've wanted to put Thankhar's head through the nearest wall. Try to understand, Gadrial. Jasak's entire focus over the past several months has been getting you and the Sharonians safely home, with as little further hurt as possible. He's also had the responsibility to bring back a prisoner who quite seriously wants him dead. I refer to the *shakira* he caught abusing a *garthan* under his command. And he's also had the worry of making sure Otwal Threbuch and Jugthar Sendahli reached home safely, as well."

Gadrial blinked. "Why would he worry about a pair of veterans who can take care of themselves very capably?"

"Two reasons. One, Otwal must testify before the Commandery and the court-martial board, which means his life's as greatly at risk as yours until this whole mess has come to an end. The Olderhans have enemies, Gadrial, a fair number of them. That's something you must understand from the outset.

"If you link your life to my son's, you'll also become a target of those enemies. In the main, that means political swipes, violated privacy, and the occasional attempt to destroy one's reputation—or career. That's a very serious matter for you to consider, Gadrial, which is another reason I wanted to speak to you privately.

"More importantly, as far as Otwal's concerned, the man Jasak is responsible for handing over to the Judiciary General on capital charges is a Mythalan with high family connections. Very, *very* high. If the witnesses whose testimony can exonerate my son—if that's possible—were to suffer accidents prior to testifying, the court would almost certainly hold against him."

Gadrial nodded.

"Yes, I understand that. In fact, the duke mentioned it the

day we arrived. I just hadn't realized Jasak was thinking about possible attempts to kill us *during* our journey. But that's the real reason the duke sent Hundred Forhaylin out to New Ransar, isn't it? Not just to insure our privacy once we got closer to home."

"Did Jasak tell you that was why Hathysk was sent to meet you?" the duchess asked, arching both eyebrows, and Gadrial shook her head.

"No, but he did let me leap to that conclusion without disabusing me of it," she replied a bit tartly, and the duchess chuckled.

"I do love my son, but he *is* very like his father, isn't he?"

Their eyes met with a shared warmth, amusement, and exasperation, but then the duchess sighed.

"Unfortunately, you're quite right about the reason—*reasons*, plural, I should say—Thankhar sent him to meet you. A piece of advice, my dear, from a veteran of the nasty little game of politics: never, *ever* underestimate what a *shakira* will do to protect himself, his family line, and his culture. Before you point out that you're only too familiar with *shakira* machinations, let me say this. There have been times when Thankhar's put our entire residence and every member of our family under the heaviest wards money can buy from the top security magisters in the business. Ugly accidents tend to befall people who go head-to-head with line lords or who merely incur their wrath.

"Jasak believed that the initial hummer dispatches had delivered the news of both the battle between his platoon and the Sharonians and the news about the arrest of Bok vos Hoven. Given who vos Hoven is related to—*closely* related to—it was quite reasonable for him to assume a hummer message could have been sent back down the transit chain with instructions to *shakira* operatives to arrange a nasty little surprise for your traveling party. Without Otwal's and Trooper Sendahli's testimony—or yours—the chance of his conviction would have gone up astronomically. And, of course, if they'd managed to kill *all* of you, there'd be no need of a court-martial at all, from their perspective."

Gadrial swallowed hard. "That's ghastly."

"Yes," the duchess said simply. "It is."

Anger licked Gadrial's nerves like tongues of flame, and the eyes which met hers this time held no warmth at all.

"Forewarned is forearmed, Your Grace. Thank you for that warning."

"You're welcome. Now, then, if Jasak is found guilty in his court-martial, the odds go up that this slimy little *shakira* won't be found guilty of his crimes, even with Trooper Sendahli's testimony."

"I don't understand," Gadrial moaned, holding her throbbing temples. "He was caught in the act. How much more evidence would the army require?"

"An officer cashiered for poor judgment is an officer whose judgment—and motives—are suspect in *all* things. Including the arrest of a *shakira* allegedly caught beating and extorting money from a lower-ranked soldier. The Olderhans are widely known for opposing the Mythalan caste system, and Sendahli, as a *garthan* would have an obvious motive for wanting to see a *shakira* convicted, rightly or wrongly. And I truly hate to say this, my dear, but virtually everyone in the multiverse knows how *you* feel about *shakira* . . . and you happen to be one of the finest theoreticians in all the known universes. If anyone could hack the court's truth detection spellware to let him lie successfully, it would be you."

"I see." And she did, clearly and hideously. "They'll say Jasak trumped up the charges against an innocent man, out of prejudice, and that Jugthar went along with it. And you're right; the *shakira* would *love* to drag me into it, as well, wouldn't they." She grimaced. "And the court will call that worm vos Hoven as a witness in Jasak's court-martial, too, won't they?"

"Yes." The duchess nodded. "He was present at the battle that's the basis for the charges pending against my son."

Gadrial's heart went a little colder and she swallowed hard.

"Surely the court's officers will realize that nasty little slimeball will do and say *anything* to ensure Jasak is destroyed."

"Of course they will . . . but that may not be enough to save the man we both love." She bit her lip again. "I must ask, Gadrial. Did you actually *see* the battle?"

"No," she whispered. "When we reached the clearing, Jasak realized immediately that the Sharonians might've taken refuge in all that storm debris. It was a perfect spot for an ambush, if that was what they intended. He wouldn't put me at risk. So he assigned two soldiers as bodyguards and kept me back, out of sight. But I *heard* it all very clearly."

Her Grace, Sathmin Olderhan, Duchess of Garth Showma, closed her eyes for a moment. Then she got them open again.

"Well, that's better than it might have been," she said. "You may not be an *eye*-witness, but you're aware of what happened, when it happened, and in what order. That's something the court will have to pay attention to, at least."

"I'm sorry I didn't *see* it, Your Grace," Gadrial whispered.

"Don't fret too greatly, my dear," Jasak's mother said firmly. "And given what we've just been discussing, it's time to drop this silly formality. My name is Sathmin. And don't even try to protest," she added. "One of the greatest joys of the four years I spent studying in Ransar was the delight of having people use my *name,* rather than my title or its related formal address."

Her smile was soft with memory.

"Those four years were so...liberating. It took some getting used to, at first, but I missed it desperately when I came home and discovered that my father had set up a marriage arrangement for me."

"He *arranged* your marriage?" Gadrial gasped, horrified.

"Oh, yes. Most Andaran marriages are carefully arranged by the parents on both sides of a prospective union."

Gadrial's heart sank.

"Oh, no, dear child," the duchess said firmly, "none of that! If I thought you weren't suitable, we wouldn't be here, this morning, having this conversation."

When she finally managed to speak, Gadrial's voice was filled with wonder. "That's the second-highest compliment I've ever been paid."

Sathmin Olderhan blinked, startled and obviously puzzled for a moment; then her eyes softened.

"The highest was when Halathyn vos Dulainah agreed to train you?" she asked gently.

"You're close. That was a profound compliment to a country girl barely turned eighteen. But the highest compliment was the day he resigned from the Mythal Falls Academy. He was furious over the accusations against me, but I couldn't believe it, when he resigned his faculty post. He was Chairman of the Department of Theoretical Magic Research, the most coveted and honored position in the entire academy. And he threw it away. Threw it into their *teeth*, like a hurled stone. Over *me*. I wasn't worth it," she whispered.

"My dear," Sathmin murmured, taking Gadrial's hand in hers, "I beg to differ. You most certainly *were* worth it, or he wouldn't have done it. You forget how many conversations I've had with him, in my role as an Institute advisor and sponsor. Moreover, I've watched the Garth Showma Institute prosper and grow and outshine the Mythal Falls Academy again and again, under your leadership. To succeed wildly in an endeavor in which your enemy has attempted to make you fail, Gadrial, is always the very best revenge. Trust me; you've accomplished *that* many times over."

The duchess smiled again, sweetly.

"And by placing *me* in the same company as Halathyn vos Dulainah, you've paid me one of the highest compliments *I've* ever received. So, having settled how admirably suitable you are for my son, let's get some breakfast into you."

Sathmin touched a spell accumulator beside her chair. Nothing happened here, but Gadrial knew the spell would inform the staff that the duchess was ready for the rest of her breakfast. Less than one minute later, that breakfast arrived, set out efficiently by the maids who looked after the family meals. The spell-enhanced serving dishes were the best on the market, programmable for various temperatures, with a simple dial on each serving dish allowed the staff—or diners—to dial the holding temperature up or down, as desired.

She settled in and tucked into her meal as Sathmin worked exceedingly hard at putting her at her ease. Within minutes, she'd relaxed enough to actually enjoy the stories of Jasak's childhood mishaps, hijinks, and triumphs. She needed that, and she blessed Jasak's mother for helping her prepare for the coming ordeal. And she prayed to Rahil, as well. Prayed hard, hoping that what she'd heard that terror-filled, agonizing day in a forest far from this lovely breakfast room, would save the man they both loved.

The alternative was unbearable.

CHAPTER TWENTY-FOUR

Hayrn 22, 206 YU
(January 13. 1929 CE)

THE DOOR CHIME RANG AS THE HUMMER BATTERED ITS BEAK against the bell mounted beside Arylis Ulthar's porch door.

She turned from the cake she'd been frosting, and her eyes widened as she realized how exhausted that hummer was. The wings were missing a few iridescent green feathers, and whatever Novice or Journeyman had been supposed to recharge the levitation spell at the last way station to help the small beast's natural magic maintain its breakneck speed had obviously bungled the job. The creature had settled, exhausted, into the open wire cage by the doorpost instead of taking any number of more natural perches in the small yard or nearby trees.

Strong compulsion spells gave the hummer no choice in its destination, and the crystal chip in the base of the cage glowed as it transferred the message from the travel-worn creature. Arylis wanted that message—wanted it badly—but she knew hummers well enough to realize how thoroughly distressed this one was. The message would be there whenever she got to it; the hummer might not be, if something wasn't done about its exhaustion.

She'd worked summers as a hummer trainer and run a hummer nursery business with her sisters before marrying Therman Ulthar. It was the sort of support work—on the edge of the Army but not quite in it—many Andaran women did between school and marriage and sometimes after, and her family was *garthan*. They'd found refuge from the nightmare of Mythalan society under the protection of Andara, and like most refugees, their patriotism and devotion to their new home burned hot and fierce, which had

357

made that support work even more satisfying. The young hummers needed about a year's growth after leaving the nest before they gained enough strength to receive their enchantments, and her family had bought hummer chicks from Gifted breeders and fed them up before reselling the strong, older birds to the Union Army and private communications services. She'd come to love the swift, jewellike little creatures, and she didn't bother to close the cage door or slip on the bespelled handling gloves hanging under the cage before she reached for this one with her bare strong, dark-skinned hands. She knew hummers too well to bother with them, and she didn't care to mess the inside of the gloves with cake frosting from her interrupted baking.

She hand-fed the creature a couple of ounces of honeywater with her icing bag. The small magic in the icing tip wasn't designed to feed birds, but it worked—beading in a fat wet globe at the end of the bag between the hummer's red-throated gulps. It was very hungry, and she wanted the worn creature fed before she confirmed the download from its message chip and let it follow its next spell-compulsion to streak back to the North Portalis Hummer Aerie. She hoped it would receive a gentle grooming and a few days rest before its next long message route.

Her half-iced cake had been more in the way of practice than actually needed for a gathering, so she didn't mind interrupting her decorating efforts to ensure the little creature at least got some sugar in its system before powering back home again. Not only had she spent years raising them for the mail service, but more recently, sleek-winged hummers who'd probably never flown farther than the outskirts of Old Portalis on Arcana Prime arrived weekly with short messages from the Commandery's Bureau of Family Relations and Military Support Services. That always happened when a unit was deployed, and Arylis had grown accustomed to their general nothing messages about Therman's unit when it was on deployment.

Of course, those messages had been anything *but* "general" or "nothing" since the first news of the clash with the mysterious Sharonians had blasted over the entire Union of Arcana. The nightmare of not knowing for almost two weeks what had happened to him—if he was even alive or dead—had been horrible, despite the way in which all the 2nd Andarans' wives and family members had rallied about one another. But then had come the wonderful news that he *was* alive and recovered from his wounds, although he was now stationed in a universe called "Thermyn," which she'd never even heard of. Once she'd gotten over the shock—and finished weeping in joy—at the news that he was alive, she'd been a bit amused that his current post's universe bore a name so similar to his own.

But she hadn't heard a great deal directly from *him* yet. There'd been a brief note from her brother Iftar, telling her Therman had been found alive and rescued. And there'd been an even briefer standard Military Support Services survivor's message, from Therman himself. Aside from that, there'd been nothing, which suggested the censors were clamping down pretty hard. Arylis had enough of a *garthan*'s suspicion of those in authority to make her uneasy over that silence, but she trusted the Army to tell her if anything bad—anything *else* bad—happened to her husband.

This message might well be from BFR or even from Therman himself, which was why her fingers itched to check its contents, but she made herself take the time to finish caring for the hummer. Hummer stations could transfer the messages from creature to creature as they came down the line, but the hummers didn't get immediately sent back after long trips, either. So if the message was from *Thermyn* and not the BFR office right here in Porta-lis, this hummer might have been the one to bring her message much of the way across New Arcana from the outbound portal to New Andara. Or it might have brought some other message and simply been reused for a purely local message by a sloppy handler who hadn't noticed the creature's need for rest.

If it had been Threeday, she'd have been certain it was just another Bureau of Family Relations nothing message. But today was Fiveday and she'd already gotten one of those this week.

The hummer finished the last bead of sugar water, pressed its needle-sharp beak against the back of her hand with feathery gentleness, then squirmed until she released it. It hopped back into the cage, crossed to the cage's message chip, and tapped the chip once with that same beak. Its complex enchantments had completely transferred the message to the sarkolis chip in the base of the cage, and it was clearly impatient—thanks to those same complex enchantments—for her to confirm receipt and send it upon its way once more.

She had no intention of doing anything of the sort, however. It needed a longer feeding, and so she refilled the icing bag with more honeywater and hung it from the top of the cage before she extracted the crystal from its receptacle. then she latched the hummer into the cage to ensure it would get to finish feeding before the homing compulsion forced it on.

Arylis tried not to hope for too much when her shaking hands slotted the message chip into the carved lines of the family's old message reader. A family with a magister, or even a novice in its household, would use a PC for this and a multitude of other tasks. Since neither Arylis nor Fifty Ulthar had a scrap of Gift between them, she used reliable single purpose spellware for the few things in their homelife that required enchantment or disenchantment.

"My name is Arylis Ulthar." She spoke carefully into the device, enunciating, and projecting her voice a bit more than normal to make sure its aetheric energy made a strong enough field for the old spellware to work.

The carved lines marking out runes and amplification circles around the message chip glowed a familiar solid blue, and Arylis relaxed. The old device hadn't chosen this moment to stop working.

The chip slowly warmed until it too glowed. Then it did exactly what she expected.

"Personal message from—" the spellware paused to access the sender's name and then continued, and Arylis' heart leapt as Therman's familiar reference number rolled out of the reader "—soldier 2AS-50C-03-73524. Speak access code to retrieve message."

"I love you Therman. It's Arylis." She wiped a little wetness from her face. It was hard to deliver her personal access code in the deadpan tone necessary for the spellware, but she managed. Sheer stubbornness kept her from changing it, even as difficult as it sometimes was to speak the phrase clearly on the first try.

The hummer chirped happily. She glanced up and saw it return to feeding.

"Message decryption in progress. Please wait."

She waited.

And waited. And *waited*. It was one of the hardest things she'd ever done. This message was *far* longer than the MSS survivor's message had been, and she *wanted* it—wanted it more badly than she'd ever wanted anything in her life! But it would take however long it took, she told herself firmly... and was just about to poke at the crystal chip to see if it was seated properly when it finished.

"Arylis, my love," Therman's voice said from the reader, clearly him, but with the extra rasp camp-recorded messages always had. "I'm fine. Things have been rough out here. I'll tell you about it when we all get home. The war, well, its war, but I'm okay and I've seen Iftar. He's fine, even if he isn't any happier about this whole damned mess than I am. Pass that on to your sisters and give them my best, as well. And I'm sorry about putting you in this position, but I knew you'd find a way. I love you."

The message continued with just soft rasping over silence while Arylis stared at the crystal chip. *He was sorry? About what position?* Then the reader's spellware clicked on a second time.

"Personal message for soldier 2AS-Actual. Message decryption in progress. Please wait."

Arylis' mind froze. *2AS-Actual?* That was...that was *ridiculous!*

Her husband, Fifty Therman Ulthar was 2AS-50C-03-73524, the fifty commanding Third Platoon, Company C, Second Andaran Scouts and assigned the lineal number of 73524. But 2AS-*Actual* was the commander of the entire Second Andaran.

That was the Duke of Garth Showma himself.

She was still staring at the reader in shock when the hummer tilted its long beak away from the tip of the icing bag and gave a bright *chee-dit*. It was done feeding, and her hands moved as if they belonged to someone else as they loosed the fine bird. It tapped the cage's floor once, its complex enchantments received the signal that the message had been completely transferred, and with a blur of wings, it was gone. Arylis' eyes tracked it automatically as it disappeared.

"Decryption complete," said the message crystal reader. "Message ready for replay."

*   *   *

The well-fed hummer landed at North Portalis Hummer Aerie. The delay while it was fed had also delayed its confirmation that its message had been downloaded to Arylis Ulthar's reader. That meant its implanted crystal had been active when Arylis spoke her access code and Therman's brief message played itself. That wasn't supposed to happen, but it did occasionally, and the privacy laws were clear. When it did, any scrap of personal information which had made its way onto a hummer's crystal was immediately deleted. But in this instance, when it returned to its aerie and the scrap of conversation uploaded to the central traffic crystal, someone who shouldn't have even known about it *read* it before it was deleted.

*   *   *

"Straight to the duke," Arylis told herself. "Just take the message straight to the duke." She almost laughed. Of course Therman had thought that would be easy; he hadn't been living in northern Garth Showma these past six weeks. He didn't know what they'd been hearing about the war. Instead he'd been experiencing the truth of it.

She shivered at that thought, because it shouldn't have been that different. What she'd been certain of and believed with absolute conviction and what she thought was probably true now, after hearing Therman's version—they shouldn't be so opposite.

Not knowing what else to do, she packed up the half frosted cake in its beautiful red striped carrier and matching satchel. One of her sisters had given her the thing. A cake carrier bespelled for freshness and balance to keep the frosting from messing even if the whole thing was tumbled end over end...and just a little greater in diameter than the flat, round spellreader. She put the reader into the fitted satchel first, then slid the cake carrier on top. The rosy bubble over the cake stuck out a half palm's width more than it should have, but with a little effort Arylis still got the satchel to close. Tinkling bells played a soothing arpeggio and the Ransaran company logo on the satchel changed from pale rose to burgundy. Good, it had sealed.

She hung her apron on its hook, wrapped the satchel strap twice around her wrist for a good hold, and set off for Portalis. The duke was in residence, and he wasn't likely to be anywhere else when she arrived. Not with the news services' daily, breathless reports about the closed sessions of the courts-martial.

Arylis Therman didn't follow those reports...mostly because she already knew *exactly* what their outcomes should be. Her family's memories of Mythal were long, deep, and bitter. None of them had ever been bound in service to the vos Hoven line, but one *shakira* clan was very like another, and what she'd heard of the charges against him told her precisely what sort *he* was. Magister Halathyn would have spat on his shadow, she was sure.

The memory of the dead magister sent a fresh stab of grief through her...and an even hotter stab of fury. She hadn't actually read Therman's message to the duke; that was between him and his CO. But he'd wanted her to know at least some of why it was so important for that message to be delivered, so he'd included a brief synopsis just for her. Which meant she now knew that the official stories coming from official government spokesmen—the stories she'd put down to an effort to control the rage of every *garthan* in a hundred universes—were actually the truth. That they *hadn't* been fabricated to still the outrage, as journals like the *Herald Times* trumpeted in every issue. That the "scoops" from "official sources speaking on condition of anonymity" were the lies. The Sharonians hadn't killed the magister; their own troops had! And like her brother and her husband, Arylis could think of only one reason—and one group—with the motive to lie so consistently, so passionately, and so *convincingly* about it.

And vos Hoven's part of that same stinking, lying, twisted *sewer of* shakira, *isn't he?* she thought bitterly. *Well, at least maybe* he'll *get what he has coming! And if Ulthar and Therman are right, the duke may just see to it that* another *batch of the scum get what* they've *got coming, as well!*

She hugged that thought to her, but at the same time, a fresh shiver of concern melded with the hot fury, like an icy wind through the throat of an angry volcano. If Therman was right about what was happening, then the odds against Sir Jasak Older-han were even worse than she'd feared they were. Like virtually every *garthan*, Arylis knew about the bitter hatred between the Olderhans' faction of the Andaran nobility and the *shakira*. That was one reason she'd been so proud when Therman was assigned to Hundred Olderhan's company. But if Therman was right about how high the lies and the manipulation had to go, then Sir Jasak had to be in the sights of whoever was truly behind it. And no one had to tell a *garthan* how deadly any *shakira* line lord's malice could be. And if there truly was some sort of general *conspiracy* behind all of this...

Arylis hugged the float-assisted cake carrier to her chest as she walked into the public slider station and checked the sched-ule. She found the connection she wanted, bought her ticket, and settled into an available seat with the cake carrier cradled in her lap, and her mind went back to the questions and speculation buzzing through it like Mythalan mosquitos.

There was no news about *either* of the courts-martial, and there wouldn't be, until they were concluded one way or another. The

Union Army's tradition—adopted from the Andarans—was that the public was entitled to full disclosure of charges, testimony, evidence, and verdicts in any court-martial...but only after the trial was completed. The accused was guaranteed the protection of confidentiality until his guilt or innocence was determined, and that confidentiality could be extended still further if he was convicted and chose to appeal...assuming the Judiciary General's Office granted an appeal hearing. That was another reason she'd avoided coverage of the trials; all the reporters and talking heads could do was rehash rumors, speculation, and more of those "confidential sources," and she didn't trust *any* of them as far as she could spit.

Well, they'll have something else *to chatter about after the duke reads Therman's message,* she thought grimly, and tried to suppress a fresh pang of fear—this time for her husband—as she considered how a *shakira* was likely to respond to being dragged out of his foul, comfortable concealment by a mere commander of fifty.

I'm not going to think about that, she told herself firmly. *Not right now, anyway.*

She pushed the thought from her mind—or as close to from her mind as she could get—and tried to distract herself by watching the scenery flow past the slider window.

The slider system trundled through Portalis, making its many stops to deliver her with thorough, if not speedy, efficiency to the Central Portalis Station. The ducal town house was only a few stops farther, but this was where the sliders really began to pack in with fellow travelers. There were a lot of them—more than there should've been—and heavy bags with broom handles and folded bits of sheeting poking out of them filled the overhead luggage compartments. The conversation around her was filled with none-too-suppressed anger—and fear—and Arylis didn't care for it a bit. There was also a lot of talk about forming up at the last stop and marching to the Garth Showma House together.

What especially disturbed her was the percentage of the protesters who were clearly *garthan*. Their anger was even more searing than that of the Andarans flocking to demand a more rigorous prosecution of the war. The fury over Magister Halathyn's "murder" was to blame for that, of course, and she wanted to shout out the truth. But she dared not. Even if they believed her, it would be a betrayal of Therman's charge to get word secretly to the duke . . . and odds were they *wouldn't* believe her. The rage was so profound, the notion that the *Sharonians* had killed the magister had burned itself so deeply into their minds, that they'd almost certainly turn on anyone who tried to deny the "truth" they knew like rabid animals. Indeed, some of them reminded her of rabid animals—of the very stereotype the *shakira* had tried for so many decades to sell to the rest of the Union—and their assumption that she was one of them made her toes curl. Of course she looked the part: younger, female, obviously Mythalan and working class (and thus automatically a *garthan* herself), and out during the middle of the day without an obvious work errand at hand. One or two of them tried to talk to her, but she only nodded politely and returned as noncommittal a reply as possible.

The crush getting out of the slider was dreadful, and try though she might, she couldn't break free from the tide of bodies flowing through the streets. By the time she reached Garth Showma House, the group from her slider—and far more people beside—packed the wide avenue from one side to the other. She couldn't see very clearly; she was too short to see over the sea of heads between her and the townhouse, but the chanting was in full swing and if they'd ever formed up in any sort of order they'd long since fallen out into a rough mob, swirling like a storm-lashed ocean. Fortunately, the high walls around the front of the public-facing building, which *looked* ornamental, were proving to be a solid defense. But broomsticks intended to hold painted sheets tied between them were now being banged against the wall in tempo to the chanting.

Arylis pushed her way through, using the cake satchel as a prod to force a place for herself. It didn't have the sharp corners of a sturdy traveler's trunk, but the rounded shape worked better in this already hostile mob. The spirit of the crowd was too uneasy, filled with too much sullen anger—and fear, probably—and she really didn't want to crack the dragon's egg without family around to back her up in a fight. Even with the chanting and banging, people were too upset and too quiet, and she had a skin-prickling sense of latent violence swirling all too near the surface of their uneasiness.

A knot of women blocked her way with tightly locked arms. They swayed together with the motion of the crowd's cheers and sobbed in time.

Arylis called out her apologies and tried to push between two of them.

Tear-streaked faces about her own age in shades of brown looked down on her. There were older faces—most more starkly Andaran-pale but some almost as dark as Arylis own skin—among them. An Andaran family with *garthan* immigrant parents or grandparents, she realized, and from their expressions they were almost certainly here to mourn Magister Halathyn and not to lash out like so much of the rest of the crowd.

"The guards won't let us in," one of them told her sadly.

"I just need to try," she replied, although she really wasn't sure what she'd say to get admittance even if she managed to reach the front of the crowd.

The words didn't mean anything particular, but the women loosened their grips on each other just enough to let her through and she plugged gamely on until she was close enough to duck under the stick wielders themselves. One of them nearly hit her—by accident, she thought—but she managed to block the stick with her cake carrier.

"I'm trying to get in!" she told the man with the stick as he glared at her as if it was *her* fault he'd almost hit her. She had to shout to make herself heard, and his expression made her go on quickly. "I just want to ask—"

It was the wrong thing to say.

A woman with a voice amp heard it and the chant changed.

"We want in! *We want in!*" it roared, and the crowd surged in response.

Arylis was suddenly mashed against the wall around the townhouse. A quick turn saved the reader inside the cake carrier, but put the force of the impact on her left hip and shoulder for two surges of the crowd. It knocked the breath out of her, as well, and she staggered for balance, suddenly terrified she might fall and be trampled underfoot. But she managed to keep her footing, somehow, and sucked in a deep breath of relief.

On the next pulse in the chant, she regained her momentum and spun the cake carrier on its side, with the reader pressed into her belly, while she used the cake as a pillow against the wall, pushing inch by inch closer to the entry.

A stone handrail to the entry stairs blocked her path almost at the goal, and she gave up on gentleness, using elbows and kicks to push the precious feet straight back into the crowd to get around the side rail and up on the stairs themselves.

Two javelins and a sword of the Garth Showma Guard stood at the head of those stairs. They were armed with peacekeeper staffs and, judging from their expressions, furious as they glared at the crowd.

One of the javelins was saying something to the sword, utterly inaudible over the chanting of several hundred angry voices. He got a headshake in response, but the first one gripped his staff as if he was going hit the crowd with it, and Arylis flinched back. She had absolutely no desire to be struck by accident. For that matter, she wasn't sure that if the javelin hit her it *would* be by accident. There was no way the guardsmen could differentiate between her as separate from the rest of the crowd, after all.

The peacekeeper staffs had a rough look to them. They were solid eldritch oak, with rounded sarkolis caps that glowed faintly and ominously, and Arylis wished she could pull back well out of the crowd control weapon's fifty-foot range. Getting struck with one wouldn't kill her, but being unconscious and alone in a crowd this angry could be deadly all on its own.

"Please," she tried to yell over the roar of the crowd, "I just need to come in!"

A crash sounded somewhere behind her, and she dared a fearful look over her shoulder into the mass of people. Had more people joined in since she worked her way to the front of the townhouse?

And then a dragon bellowed suddenly and she found herself in what had abruptly become a great deal of open space. She looked up . . . and swallowed a squeak of terror as a yellow—young to be ridden—soared over in a slow pass. The crowd roared back at the sky, even the chanting lost in momentary surprise. Some of the protestors recognized the threat inherent in that pass, but at least half the crowd had misinterpreted it as no more than a surprise bit of airshow. After all, for all their fury, they knew it was the Air Force's job to *protect* the Union's citizens, not threaten them with lethal force!

The pilot turned the dragon and began a second pass, coming in so low this time that Arylis could feel the air pressure change as the spells pulled in aetheric power to hold the beast aloft.

She clambered a few steps up and crouched against the rail wall to the side of the stairs her arms still wrapped around the cake carrier. Groups at the edges of the crowd had begun to move away and the center moved back with it. The chanting was gone, replaced by individual yells and shrieks, and she drew in a deep breath of relief. They'd all go home now, she thought, and in a few moments she might even be able to speak loudly enough to be heard over the din and possibly gain admittance at least into the public reception hall.

She looked back to the guardsmen and saw not calm, but horror sketched across both their faces. They were screaming at the pilot, who certainly couldn't hear them. She snapped her head back the other way and saw the dragon open its mouth.

Two shots burned over her head passing a warmth and numbness across the back of her neck. Through a darkening sight Arylis saw the pilot collapse limp in his straps and the dragon's mouth go slack and snap shut.

*   *   *

"What the hell was that?"

A noncommittal grunt answered.

Icy fingers running down the back of Arylis' neck cut through the thumping in her head. She awoke, still on the steps to Garth Showma House, but with a nearly empty street in front of her. The yellow perched on a nearby building roof and lowed mournfully, its pilot limp in his cockpit.

More people in GSG uniforms scurried from huddle to huddle in the street giving aid or assistance as needed to those left behind by the crowd.

She moaned and found one of the guardsmen immediately at her side.

"Awake now, Missus?"

She nodded slowly, surprised to find her neck functioned just fine and that the pain in her left arm was only the too tight tangle of the cake carrier's strap.

"Why don't you head on home then? We're going to help a group down to the slider station nice and slow here in a minute if you feel you can stand?"

"No." *I need to go see the duke.*

"That's alright, you can rest a few more minutes, and we'll get someone to carry you. Maybe there's someone you could send for?"

"I need to get in," Arylis said and was rewarded with a long sigh for her accidental repeat of the chant. "No, not that—" she tried to explain "—I'm trying to see the duke." She pointed her cake in an effort to explain.

The man cursed softly. "A cake delivery? In the midst of all that? I'd hate to have your boss, Missus."

He didn't get it right, but the door was opening and another retainer was summoned to help her up and walk her inside. Arylis saved her explanations for further inside the townhouse.

She found a comfortable chair in the receptions office and settled into it. Office doors were flying open, and staff were rushing about entirely too quickly to catch their attention immediately. She rested, for just a moment.

"I don't believe for one moment the Undersecretary for Dragon Affairs personally authorized that disaster!" The voice echoed down the hall.

"I'm just telling you where the staffer I spoke with said the order came from, Fifty."

"That pilot up there isn't even a commissioned Twenty-Five."

"Hope to Graholis he never gets a commission either, Fifty."

"Hm. Kid might not even be alive."

An inarticulate grumble answered that one.

"Trooper's right, Fifty. I don't want to serve with anyone who'd even think about firing on civilians."

"He's going to say he didn't mean it. You *know* he's going to say he was just faking to scare the crowd, and he'd *never* have dropped gas on anyone!"

"Don't they gas people sometimes in Mythal?"

"I don't care what the spell-blasted Mythalans do. We *don't*, and that boy up there needs a healer. The dragon probably caught some of the blast, too. See about finding a dragon healer while you're at it."

Arylis let herself slip back into a dozy gray while she waited for the public offices to calm.

*   *   *

Later, hours later, Thankhar Olderhan, the Duke of Garth Showma personally opened the door and bowed to the fifty's wife as she dropped him a curtsy and prepared to withdraw from his private office. She still seemed more than a little awed that the duke himself had wanted to hear her story, and she'd been more than a little nervous when she entered the warm, wood paneled room with its comfortable chairs, large desk, and the PC which now held a certified copy of her husband's shocking message. He'd spent over an hour taking her back through every aspect of the extraordinary circumstances which had brought her to Garth Showma House—and damned nearly gotten her killed—and everything she'd said had only made him even more grimly confident that she was absolutely trustworthy.

"Thank you, Madam Ulthar," he said as she rose from her curtsy. "It's my honor to have men like your husband in the Second Andarans, and I genuinely can't tell you how deeply grateful I am for your own integrity—and courage—in bringing his message to me so quickly. Magister Halathyn would be as proud of you as I am, I'm sure."

"Thank you, Your Grace." The words came out husky and the young woman's beautiful brown eyes filled with tears. "I only... I mean, it was Therman who did it, really. And—"

"Your husband, Madam Ulthar, would be the first to tell me what a critical and personal service you've done me and my entire house, as well as the entire Union," he said firmly. "And I'm very much afraid he may have put you at risk by asking you to undertake it. Because of that, you'll be moving into Garth Showma House—unless you'd be more comfortable at Garth Showma itself?—until we know precisely what's going on out there."

"Oh, Your Grace, I couldn't! I mean—"

"My dear, *Her* Grace has already spoken in this matter," he told her with a faint smile. "I assure you that *I'm* not foolish enough to argue with her about it, and I'd recommend *you* not argue, either. It will be safer for both of us."

The young woman was obviously flustered, but as she looked up into his face, she realized he meant it and her protests faded. He took her hand in both of his and gave her another bow—which only flustered her even more deeply, of course—and turned her over to one of the assistant housekeepers. Then he returned to his office, dropped into the comfortable chair behind his desk, and glared up at the ceiling while his mind raced.

He'd ruthlessly shoved the job of unraveling the chain of incompetence behind that fool trainee pilot onto the desk of Five Thousand Rukkar. The entire thing was a mess. The yellow wasn't even a proper battle dragon—just a youngling on loan from Mythal Air Expeditionaries for a breeding experiment that probably should never have been approved. MAE was as undisciplined a group as ever claimed commissions, but Mythalan private families paid for the feeding and care for MAE's fleet of dragons—a relief on the Union of Arcana's military budget too large for Parliament to decline. The old practice of an airknight paying for his own equipage and fodder was darn useful in that respect, but other Mythalan habits didn't mesh well with Andaran sensitivities. Among other things, they conducted side line breeding efforts and produced special dragon lines for crowd control, which had to be one of the stupidest godsdamned ideas Thankhar had ever heard of. And what kind of frigging idiot authorized a *yellow* for "crowd control"?

He shuddered as he thought about it. *He*'d never heard of a yellow which produced nonlethal gas, and he doubted like hell that anyone in Mythal was interested in producing one, whatever they might claim. And he had his doubts—*serious* doubts—about the rider's claim that he'd never intended to *actually* fire on the crowd. Hells, he doubted he'd believe it even if the kid repeated it under a dozen truth spells! No, that little prick had been ready to gas the street in front of Garth Showma House, and what kind of miserable bastard used *poison gas* on a crowd of bereaved women and children?

As soon as the healers had that trainee back on his feet, Sathmin would have him at a meeting with the spouse's club to make a very heartfelt and public apology. Sathmin would make it work, but the real apology should be coming from someone far more senior who'd allowed the almost disaster to launch. Rukkar had better figure out who'd started it, or Thankhar would have to.

He didn't care how mild the MAE's hundred who'd claimed credit for the idea thought the yellow's gas was. That idiot had also been shocked—or *claimed* he had, anyway—that the crowd hadn't instantly dispersed the moment yellow wings flared overhead. He'd clearly never met an Andaran woman. And he equally clearly hadn't figured out how much of that crowd had been *garthans* who didn't give a single solitary *damn* about any *shakira* ever born. Once they got out from under the bastards' thumbs, there was no stopping any *garthan*. It was one of the things he most liked about them...and what was making it so godsdamned hard to get them to stand back and believe the truth about how Magister Halathyn had actually died.

And now this. What in all Shartahk's Hells was going on at the front? He'd had his doubts, had his concerns, but *this*—!

His staff commo officers, with some assistance from Magister Gadrial—he wasn't going to let a possible forgery slip by when he had a theoretical magister of her caliber on hand—had confirmed the message was legitimate. Arylis Ulthar hadn't faked it, and the original message had definitely been recorded on a hummer at the front. He had to bear in mind the theoretical possibility that Fifty Ulthar hadn't sent the original message, but the chance of anyone's getting a successful forgery past Gadrial Kelbryan was virtually nil. Which only made it even worse, in a way. Ulthar had a solid performance record before his posting to the frontier, and Jasak had flatly stated that he'd been the best fifty in C Company. There was no reason—no *sane* reason Thankhar could think of, at any rate—for a man like that to invent an elaborate story, especially one like *this* . . . which meant what he'd reported was almost certainly true.

And that meant Thankhar had to assume the events at the front really were as bad as the message claimed. He needed to find out what was going on out there—*everything* that was going on out there—and he needed to find out yesterday. Most people would have felt the meat of Ulthar's message was all about the violation of the Kerellian Accords and the truly horrible treatment of Sharonans held under Arcanan military authority, and Thankhar Olderhan's fury had burned fiery hot as he read that part of it. Yet under the fury had been something far, far colder.

The Commandery knew the truce had broken down, that Two Thousand Harshu had led a counterattack deep into the Sharonian-claimed universes, and that the initial offensive seemed to have done well. But aside from that bare notification and the report that at least some Second Andaran survivors had been recovered alive, there were *still* no additional official messages. It was preposterous—or worse—but the most recent *reliable* information they really had was Jasak's report, and *that* was both suspect in certain quarters and locked down, denied public release, until after his court-martial had delivered its verdict.

It wasn't unheard of for there to be delays—sometimes very *lengthy* delays—in reports from the frontier when officers were overwhelmed dealing with some crisis. The Union of Arcana had learned long ago that it couldn't micromanage affairs over a communications chain that could take weeks or even months to pass a message one way. The military *had* to trust the judgment of the officers on the spot, and those officers were often more focused on the problem at hand rather than on writing reports for superiors who couldn't do one damned thing to help them, anyway. So, yes, there'd been *lots* of examples of that sort of delay over the years.

But it *also* happened when officers were doing something profoundly stupid and thought they could fix it before the Commandery found out, and Thankhar Olderhan had decided weeks ago that that was almost certainly the case this time...unless it was something still worse. In fact, he'd been inclining further and further towards that "still worse" hypothesis even before Jasak, Gadrial, and Jasak's *shardonai* reached Portalis. Now, with what Therman Ulthar had said about intelligence reports which contradicted what he knew first hand to be true added to what Jasak and Gadrial had already told him...

For anyone who'd spent as many years as he had fighting corruption and facing down one scheming political maneuver after another, the possibility that Army and Air Force personnel were being deliberately lied to by their own superiors raised questions which were far more chilling even than the violation of the Accords. Ugly questions about who was doing what, who was covering it up, and—above all—*why* he was covering it up. And when that was added to what was clearly an orchestrated campaign to leak the false narrative from the front to the news services which were most hostile to the current government...

He needed an investigation, and he needed it now. And whatever team he sent down-chain needed the military teeth to be listened to and the strength to withstand whatever threat the Sharonan military—and, much as he hated the possibility, its *own* military—represented. Collecting evidence in an active war zone was not for the faint of heart.

Lucky for him, Thankhar Olderhan was an Andaran, and Andaran inquiry officers didn't come in faint of heart.

CHAPTER TWENTY-FIVE

Hayrn 24, 206 YU
(January 15, 1929 CE)

THE WINTER AIR WAS CRISP AND THE SUNLIGHT CRYSTAL-
line as it drenched the target range on the outskirts of
Portalis. The temperatures had been freezing since Jathmar and
Shaylar arrived, but Arcana's use of magic to heat their homes
and offices had produced one consequence no Sharonian would
have anticipated: no coal smoke. As a result, the distant tree
line was a sharp, dark thicket of bare branches, undimmed by
the gray smudge of urban smoke. They were as clear here with
Jathmar's eyes wide open as they would have been in this same
meadow in Sharona if he'd closed his eyes and stretched out his
Mapping Talent.

He drew a deeper, fuller breath than any he'd taken since their
arrival at Portalis. He didn't try his Talent—he had no desire to
face either a headache or the heartache of its extremely reduced
range. It was enough to enjoy the familiar bite of cold air and
the joy of being outdoors. They'd been confined in one room or
another since their arrival, allowed outdoors only long enough to
dash into or out of the duke's motic or ornate, improbably speedy
coach for trips between Garth Showma House and wherever the
current day's inquisition happened to be located.

For this trip the shiny new motic and its driverless GC had
been deemed unacceptable. The angry crowds outside the huge
townhouse undoubtedly had something to do with that—the
motics' restriction to pre-set, predictable routes would have
been a nightmare for the duke's security personnel—but Jathmar
wasn't sure he wouldn't have preferred a vehicle controlled by

the central traffic system. It might have been more susceptible to ambushes, but at least he'd have been confident the journey *itself* wouldn't kill him!

The duke's black coach horses, on the other hand, had whipped through the city streets so fast his hands had gone white-knuckled gripping the seat arm while Shaylar leaned against him, eyes shut tight, the whole way. He'd braced for collision so many times he'd spent the whole city portion of the ride stiff as a brick. Yet not even that speed had prepared him for what those horses could do on open roads, like the one leading to this army post.

He'd been convinced they'd sprout wings and *fly*. Instead, they'd merely whipped along the open highway so fast their coach might well have outraced a bullet. Not one from a modern gun, of course, but they'd have given one of those early, slow-moving balls from a Ternathian matchlock a real run for its money.

The journey to this firing range had scared him nearly piss-less. But now that they were here . . . He could actually *breathe*, out here. The knowledge that they must go back to those hateful walls, which pressed more closely and more unbearably with every day, was a physical agony he could scarcely bear. Confinement was killing them. Slowly, cruelly killing them, and they had no hope of clemency from their captors.

Jathmar intended to enjoy every moment out here to the fullest, despite the unexpectedly large, avidly curious, openly hostile audience. He turned his gaze to the viewing stands where the entire Commandery sat in a glittering array of gold and silver and bronze devices on their fancy dress uniforms: forest green and gray for the army, a crimson as vivid as any tropical fish for the navy, and the velvet-ink black of night skies for the air force. He hadn't seen anything resembling Marines and had opted not to ask, since giving his captors new military ideas was not on his agenda.

Also seated in the viewing stands were the members of the newly appointed Parliamentary War Operations and Intelligence Committee, led by the Speaker of the Union, himself. The committee's interest in their planned demonstration was both obvious and intense and, unlike the military's board of inquiry or court, the committee included two Mythalans: one *garthan* and one of the *shakira* he'd heard so much about, during their travels and since their arrival.

The *shakira*—Gerail vos Durgazon, the Union minister of industry—wore a supercilious sneer that appeared to be permanently etched into his face. Jathmar had detested him on sight, and not just because prior experience had amply confirmed Gadrial and Jasak's attitude towards *shakira* in general. No, he had a very specific and personal reason to detest this *individual* representative of Mythal's hereditary overlords: the truly filthy way the man had looked at Shaylar. Part cold-blooded hatred, part carnal lust, and part thwarted rage, that smugly superior, violently hostile look told Jathmar Minister vos Durgazon had no intention of abiding by military regulations or Arcanan law, should Shaylar ever fall into *his* custody.

The *garthan*, on the other hand, had the gentlest, kindest eyes Jathmar had ever seen. He hadn't expected that, particularly from a Mythalan, but Gadrial had told him Jukaru Tumnau, the minister of health, although unGifted, with no trace of the Healing capability, was one of Arcana's best psychiatrists. He'd also been a close personal friend of Halathyn vos Dulainah—which helped explain the notorious bad blood between him and vos Durgazon. Tumnau wasn't about to accept anything the Sharonians told him without considering it very, very carefully, but he wasn't automatically hostile, despite vos Dulainah's death. In fact, what Jathmar read most strongly in Tumnau's eyes was an almost childlike curiosity, which rippled through a deep and glimmering compassion.

A long table stood just in front of the viewing stands. That table provided seats for the officers of Jasak's court-martial. There were five: three Andarans, one Ransaran, and one Tukorian, and Jathmar already had cause to view all of them with a cold hostility. They'd spent the entire day, yesterday, questioning each of the witnesses in what they referred to as a mere "preliminary inquiry." Those questions had been fairly sharp when directed at Jasak Olderhan, patient and attentive when directed at Otwal Threbuch, grim and scornful when leveled at Bok vos Hoven, and gently respectful when addressed to Gadrial Kelbryan.

As for Jathmar and his wife...

The officers had badgered them with a remorseless barrage of questions that were hostile, scathing to the point of deliberate cruelty, and contemptuous of every syllable they uttered in response. The board of inquiry before which they'd first appeared had been difficult enough initially, but its members had quickly taken their tone from Commander of Wings Brith Darma and become almost courteous. Not so the court-martial board. If he'd been inclined to be charitable—which he wasn't—Jathmar might have put that down to the fact that they were scared to death by what had already been reported to them and were taking that fear out on the closest example of what they were frightened of. The reasons for their attitude didn't much concern him, however; its *consequences*, on the other hand, most assuredly did.

Of course, he thought with a certain bitter amusement, *I have to say* they *learned better, too, didn't they? And a godsdamned sight quicker this time around.*

His lips quirked in a smile of memory, and he shook his head. There were huge differences between Sathmin Olderhan and his own mother, but under the skin, the New Ternathian farmer's wife and the Arcanan duchess were more alike than either of them might have believed. Duchess Garth Showma had already tolerated quite as much abuse of her son's *shardonai* as she intended to, and she'd sailed into the hearing room at Shaylar's side like a Ternathian battleship breaking an enemy line.

Commander of Twenty Thousand Helfron Dithrake, Count Sogbourne, the senior and presiding member of the empaneled court-martial, had been less than pleased to see her, though he hadn't been stupid enough to say so in so many words. His courteous suggestion that Her Grace might, perhaps, want to await the witness in the lounge had been answered only with the sort of cold stare with which governesses reduced unruly children to terrified obedience, and the count had shown he was even smarter than Jathmar had thought by dropping *that* line of suggestions immediately.

Some of his colleagues had been rather less discerning, however. They'd intended to treat Shaylar as a hostile witness, and treat her as a hostile witness they had. Squadron Master Olvarn Gerandyr, the court-martial's Navy representative and second ranking member, had led the way. Gerandyr was a Chalaran, from the Arcanan equivalent of Esferia, the enormous island off the peninsula of Yar Khom, and Thankhar Olderhan (who'd known him for over twenty-five years) had warned Jathmar he was about as tactful as a brick at the best of times. He was also, the duke had said, a man of honor who would do his best to consider the evidence, but it had been obvious the squadron master was one of those who regarded all things Sharonian—and especially Sharonians with those unnatural "Talents"—with profound suspicion.

"So, Madam Nargra-Kolmayr," he'd begun in a sharp, aggressive tone, "you continue to assert that your 'party of civilians' had nothing but peaceful motives, do you? Perhaps, then, you'd care to explain why all of you were armed to the teeth? And why, when you realized there was another survey force in the area your immediate response was to run—run in a body—for the nearest portal rather than sending a single member of your group, or even a small delegation of it, to attempt to establish nonviolent contact with it? Surely people with these 'Talents' of yours should've been able to locate and contact Hundred Olderhan's platoon without precipitating a bloodbath if you'd chosen to make that effort instead of settling into what can only be described as an ambush position!"

Shaylar had stepped back half a pace, wincing under the power of the emotions rolling off of him. Then she'd rallied.

"I'm not 'asserting' anything," she'd replied in an equally sharp tone. "I'm telling you what actually happened—*exactly* what happened—and your own lie-detection spells should tell you I'm doing it as honestly as I possibly can."

"Oh, really?" Gerandyr had scowled. "And how do we know our spellware even *works* against someone with your 'Talent'? All we have is your word for that. And, frankly, I'm not at all convinced we should accept it. Besides that—"

"Magister Gadrial's also explained that—" Shaylar had begun, but Gerandyr's palm had slapped the top of the bench before him like a gunshot.

"I was *speaking*, Madam!" He'd glared at her, flushed with anger. "You'd do well to remember your situation here! In the eyes of this court, you and your husband—"

"Are my son's *shardonai*." Sathmin Olderhan's cold, clear voice had cut through Gerandyr's bluster like a scalpel. It had also snapped the ship master's eyes to her, and her smile had been even colder than her words.

"Shaylar and Jathmar come under the house honor of House Olderhan and the civil protection of the Duchy of Garth Showma under the provisions of the Code of Housip," she'd continued with merciless precision, "and that code—like the Kerellian

Accords—was given formal force of law *and* incorporated into the Articles of War—by the Union's Constitution at the time it was drafted. They are members of *my* family, Squadron Master, and I'll thank you to remember that!"

"Your Grace," Gerandyr had started, "I was merely—"

"I know *precisely* what you were doing, Olvarn Gerandyr," the duchess had said crisply. "However, you will *not* verbally abuse, or threaten, or attempt to frighten a member of my family! Shaylar is not *your* prisoner, nor is she accused of any crime. The worst that can possibly be alleged against her is that she and her companions defended themselves against attack by a far larger force of trained soldiers. That they did it superlatively well is to their *credit* and no grounds for abusing her when she and her husband are captives so far from home! If you wish to lodge formal charges against her, then I invite you to do so." She'd bared her teeth. "I don't think you'd like how that would turn out, Ship Master, but by all means try, if that's what you want. In the meantime, however, you'll keep a civil tongue in your head when you interrogate a member of *my* family." She'd paused, sweeping the assembled, momentarily petrified court with cold eyes.

"I trust," she'd added then in velvet tones wrapped around a dagger of ice, "that I've made myself clear?"

She had.

Under the circumstances, the court had decided to excuse Shaylar from any further examination that day and allowed her to return to Garth Showma House. Clearly, they'd hoped the duchess would go with her.

She hadn't.

With Shaylar absent, Jathmar had, perforce, borne the brunt of the officers' questions about Sharona, but with the duchess sitting silent and watchful at his side, they'd been remarkably calm, even courteous about it. They hadn't been any less suspicious or thorough, but they'd *definitely* watched how they asked those questions, and he was just as happy they'd been asking them of *him*. He might not be good at lying and prevaricating, but he was better at it than Shaylar. He'd succeeded in tiptoeing through the brutal day without once tripping the lie-detection spell's alarm, which he considered quite an achievement.

But today, thank all the gods of Faltharia, he wouldn't be

formally testifying in a witness chair. He had little doubt he'd be questioned; but he felt more capable out here, more in control and far more comfortable with the subject matter at hand. Even breathing fresh, clean open air helped.

Jasak was explaining his plan to the officers of the court. Jathmar watched their faces, predicting an outburst at any moment. That outburst came twenty seconds later.

"Are you *mad*, sir?" Count Sogbourne demanded incredulously. "Allow a prisoner to touch—to operate—a terror weapon? In the presence of the Commandery of Arcana and the entire War Ops and Intel Committee? Including your own father and Speaker Skyntaru? Not to mention *us*? Are you mad?"

The "us" in question was the glittering row of officers selected to try Jasak, who remained perfectly calm and formally at ease.

"Jathmar Nargra is the most appropriate person to demonstrate these weapons, Sir," he replied in a patient, firm tone. "My father, by the way, concurs with that opinion, because Jathmar understands their function and operation far better than I do. And he's not going to commit suicide and leave his wife alone to face a lifetime of imprisonment, either, I assure you!"

His argument made perfect sense to Jathmar, but no member of the court was likely to care very much what *he* thought. For that matter, they didn't seem overly impressed by what Duke Garth Showma thought, either.

Under the circumstances, he wasn't surprised when Sogbourne insisted Jasak conduct the demonstration. In fact, they'd all expected that reaction, and Jathmar had spent two and a half hours the previous evening coaching Jasak on how to load and operate the rifle and handgun they planned to use today. Jasak had already fired each type of weapon, but that had been weeks and eighty-five thousand miles—and a multitude of universes— ago. Firing a weapon someone else had loaded, just enough times to realize its true power, was hardly sufficient preparation for a demonstration of this kind.

So Jathmar had coached him, resisting the fleeting notion of teaching him an incorrect technique that would cause the Commandery to dismiss the guns as unreliable and far less effective than they really were. It was so tempting he could taste it, but he couldn't do that without putting Jasak at risk of serious injury, and he wouldn't—dared not—risk the death of Jasak Olderhan.

He needed Jasak to stand between them and the rest of Arcana, beginning with the men in those bleachers. And truth be told, he liked Jasak. They were enemies, yet in an odd way he also regarded Jasak as a friend. Not a confidante. That was impossible. Nor did Jathmar feel the same easy camaraderie that he'd shared with his fellow survey crewmen. That, too, was impossible.

But Jathmar knew he could rely on Jasak Olderhan. He'd seen enough of Jasak's interactions with superior officers, during "conversations" where he and Shaylar had been the sole subject of discussion, to know nothing would cause Jasak to deviate from the protection he offered. Watching Jasak's father and even—or perhaps *especially*—his mother had merely reinforced Jathmar's inclination to trust Jasak Olderhan's word.

Those parents had raised the man who'd courteously but firmly refused every threat, bribe, and offer made in demand of turning them over to the speaker of the moment, in a dizzying and depressingly long line of speakers and tense moments. And that mother had descended upon the court-martial board which had traumatized Shaylar like the gods' own wrath because Jasak had given his prisoners his word that he and his would protect them from *anything*. Whatever else might happen, Jathmar trusted Jasak Olderhan's word, in a world where he could trust no one and nothing else.

So he'd gone to Jasak's apartments and carefully and correctly taught him how to safely load, fire, and chamber a new round to fire again until convinced that Jasak could perform the drill on his own—*safely*—with a live-fire demonstration.

And so it was Jasak who strode out to the shooting bench on Fort North Hathak's target range. Fortunately for him, there was very little breeze today, so he wouldn't have to contend with bullet drift caused by high gusting winds. It had snowed a little overnight, but the sky was perfectly clear now.

Jathmar watched Sogbourne with a sense of intense satisfaction. The true danger this morning hadn't been the threat of arming a prisoner in the presence of senior officers. It had been the inadequacy of High Hathak's shooting range.

Its earthen berms were built to stop arbalest bolts, which had a maximum range of no more than eight hundred yards even from the Arcanan Army's spell-assisted weapons. They were, to put it mildly, insufficient to stop heavy rifle bullets from a weapon with a maximum range which was four or five times that.

The look of horror on the faces of the Arcanan officers when Jathmar explained the problem during the questioning yesterday had been grimly satisfying.

"A mile?" Sogbourne had gasped. "Your hand-held weapons can kill a man a *mile away*?"

"There are some rifles that can take down a target even father away than that. Actually, the maximum range of the most recent rifles is as much as *three* miles, but I've never met anyone who could actually hit a target at that range. On the other hand, there are specially tuned weapons—we call them 'sniper rifles'—which can hit a man-sized target at two thousand yards," he'd added.

"'Sniper'?" the count had repeated the Sharonian word carefully.

Jathmar had enjoyed that reaction, as well.

"Yes. The men who use them are called snipers. Their job is to find a vantage point like a branch in a tree or a spot partway up a rocky hillside or on top of a cliff. Once hidden, they locate and shoot specific targets—high ranking officers, artillery crews, soldiers who are particularly effective on a battlefield, or even visiting civilian dignitaries."

He'd met horrified stares with a cool, level gaze and let the protests roll off his back.

"That's murder!"

"It's barbaric!"

"As barbaric as burning a man to death?" He'd raised an eyebrow. "I assure you, from personal experience, I'd far rather be shot from a mile away by a trained sniper than roasted alive."

The silence in the courtroom had been profound, to say the least. If they'd expected him to be cowed they'd been grievously disappointed. He hadn't been rude. He hadn't been aggressive. He hadn't even been belligerent. But he wasn't going to roll belly up and let them eviscerate him, either—not yesterday and not ever. Pride was damned near all he had left.

Wringing sweat from the officers of Jasak Olderhan's court-martial board was a fair accomplishment for a man figuratively in chains. As for the weapons demonstration, Jathmar had suggested stacking up piles of sandbags to strengthen the range's berms, and now he felt a stir of satisfaction as he noted how high and deep the soldiers of Fort North Hathak had piled them. The targets they'd be using were, according to Jasak, standard military arbalest targets, and the range officer had set up a series of them at varying distances to demonstrate the effective ranges of both the handguns and the rifles.

Now Jasak picked up a scissor-action rifle and carefully loaded it with one round. He used great care in following the drill Jathmar had taught him, loading the tube-fed magazine through the loading gate, working the action to chamber the round, releasing the safety, lifting and anchoring the buttplate in the pocket of his shoulder, aligning the sights and carefully, gently squeezing the trigger.

Jathmar heard a faint mechanical click.

That was all.

Jasak stood uncertainly where he was, not sure what to do next. He glanced over one shoulder, carefully keeping the muzzle pointed down range.

"Jathmar? What happened? What did I do wrong?"

"I don't know," he replied, genuinely baffled. "From what I could see, you didn't do anything wrong. Work the action to eject the cartridge, then lay the rifle on the firing bench and bring me the cartridge case."

Jasak nodded and followed his instructions meticulously. When Jasak handed him the unfired cartridge, Jathmar frowned. So did Shaylar, peering past his shoulder.

"That's odd," she said, gazing down at the cartridge on his palm.

"Yes. It is." Jathmar scratched the back of his neck. "I'm damned if I can figure it out."

The firing pin had punched a neat divot in the primer cup, a small metal cup inserted into the base of the cartridge case. Just as it should have done. But the primer had failed to ignite the powder.

"Maybe there was no priming compound in the cup?" Shaylar suggested.

"Maybe." Jathmar was dubious, despite its being the likeliest explanation. Their ammunition was one thing on which Ghartoun chan Hagrahyl had refused to cut corners when it came down to supplying his crew. Ternathian Imperial Armory case-stamp was the only ammunition he'd allowed them to carry. And Jathmar frowned as he met Shaylar's perplexed gaze.

"If this was one of those fly-by-night Uromathian brands, slopped together by a manufacturer more interested in profits than turning out a reliable product, I'd suspect something like that. But this is Ternathian Imperial Armory."

"It's the civilian case-stamp, not the military, but I've never—not once—seen a TIA cartridge misfire. Neither had Ghartoun. That's why he insisted we carry it. Even Barris Kassell agreed, and he'd been in the military before he joined our crew. That's why most survey crews carry TIA cartridges and reloading supplies: primer cups, powders, and bullets."

"Well, *something* went wrong, love," she pointed out practically, and he nodded.

"Yes, it did," he agreed, and turned back to Jasak. "Pull five rounds of the correct caliber from five separate boxes of ammunition, Jasak, just to be sure we haven't got a bad batch. If the rifle doesn't fire, work the action to eject the cartridge and pull the trigger again."

Commander of Twenty Thousand Sogbourne stared intently at Jathmar.

"You think like a soldier," he said.

"A soldier?" Jathmar echoed. "Hardly, Sir. I don't know the first thing about the military. Faltharia doesn't even have an army. We've never needed one," he added, as shock detonated in Sogbourne's eyes—and Jasak Olderhan's, as well. Jathmar shrugged. "I'm a good outdoorsman, is all. I've spent most of my life in wild country, whether it was a major wildlife park on Sharona or the wilderness of a barely settled or newly discovered universe at the frontier. When your life depends on attention to your equipment, you're careful with everything related to the weapons you count on. You develop the same careful habits I've seen in Hundred Olderhan when it comes to caring for and using a tool as important as a sword and arbalest... or a rifle."

Sogbourne's eyes narrowed slightly. "There's a great deal of interesting information in what you've said. Very well, Hundred Olderhan, pull the ammunition from different boxes and let's see the results."

"Yes, Sir."

Jasak returned to the shooting bench. He pulled out the ammunition. Loaded the rifle with great care. Lifted it to his shoulder. Took careful aim. Pulled the trigger. Worked the action. Pulled the trigger again. The result was five mechanical clicks, five perfectly punched primer cups, and zero fired rounds. When Jasak recovered the rounds from the ground and brought them over to him, Jathmar stared at the unfired cartridges in baffled consternation.

"It can't be the ammunition," he frowned. "Did you bring any of the reloading tools out here with you, Jasak?"

"We brought one of everything we found in your camp. Including the loaded gear bags."

"Good. I need to see them."

Jasak escorted Shaylar and Jathmar out to the shooting benches, since she insisted on coming along. Commander of One Thousand Solvar Rinthrak, another of the officers from Jasak's court-martial, also insisted on following them, and while the others watched closely, Jathmar used the tools in the reloading kit Jasak had brought to pry the bullets out of the cartridge cases. He tipped out the powder, piling it up on the table, then used a punch to remove the priming cups. He felt squeamish about doing that to "live" primers. There wasn't enough explosive compound in a primer cup to do real damage, but the very idea of hammering on a primer that hadn't been fired went against the grain.

Once he'd removed all five primer cups, he tipped them over in his palm and examined them closely. There was nothing wrong with them. The dried film of liquid explosive used as priming compound coated their interior exactly as it was supposed to. That film was shock sensitive, igniting under the sharp jolt of a firing pin, and he could *see* the primer painted into the cups. There were no voids, no spots where the coating was thinned out to let bare metal show through.

They should have fired.

Shaylar echoed that thought aloud. "They should have fired, Jathmar."

"It's the damnedest thing I've ever seen. And that's saying a hell of a lot, considering where we're standing, right now."

Shaylar had the temerity to chuckle, which startled Sogbourne into staring at her.

"Well, it *is* funny," she told him, meeting his rather hostile scowl with a smile. "We see things that are flat-out impossible every day. Every *hour*. Even the way the *bathroom* works is weird enough to raise gooseflesh. But even with all of that, I have to agree with my husband. Those cartridges *should* have fired. But they didn't. And that's just as impossible as anything we've seen in your civilization."

Sogbourne's scowl shifted into a thoughtful frown.

"Maybe I did something wrong?" Jasak suggested.

"I was watching you very closely and I didn't see you do anything wrong. Certainly not wrong enough to cause this." He held up the five unfired cartridges, then added the first one Jasak had tried to fire to the pile. "One might be a fluke. But six..." He shook his head. "I don't know why, but they simply failed to fire, and they *should* have."

Gadrial, who'd been sitting quietly in the row of chairs reserved for witnesses, called out a request to join them.

"Yes, please, Magister Gadrial." Sogbourne nodded. "Perhaps you can explain what's going on."

She crossed quickly to the shooting bench and stood beside Jasak while Jathmar explained the problem.

"How are they supposed to work?" she asked.

Jathmar glanced at Shaylar, who shrugged. He started to refuse, but then he returned her shrug, instead.

Why not? he thought. *They can't duplicate a formula that tricky to make from a generalized description.*

So he explained the process of manufacturing the liquid explosive, explained how and why the spark from a tiny, controlled explosion caused the powder charge to burn, generating gas that was confined in such a small space that it pushed with terrific force against the place of least resistance: the bullet, which was merely held in place by a small crimp in the metal rim of the cartridge case. The one thing he didn't explain was the ingredient list for the priming compound and powder. He preferred to keep that secret for as long as he could.

"It's a very simple, very basic process of chemistry and physics," he finished the explanation, "but the manufacturing process is something I don't understand very well. I'm told it's difficult to make some of the ingredients and the steps in combining them are very complex. Even small variations can ruin a batch. But I've given you the basics as I understand them."

When Sogbourne glanced at Shaylar, she said, "Don't look at me. Jathmar knows more about it than I do. I can shoot a rifle or a handgun and I've learned how to reload cartridges, but I don't have the slightest idea how they make the components." When Sogbourne looked at her with a clearly skeptical frown, she said, "Does a non-Gifted person have to understand how the spells that operate a cook stove are put together? How and why they work? Does a non-Gifted person need to know every single line of the incantations that run a slider chain or operate the controls that heat or cool your house?"

"Point well taken." Gadrial nodded. Then she grinned. "Very well taken, in fact."

Sogbourne glared at Gadrial and Shaylar with a belligerent air, then he muttered, "Oh, all right. Point taken." But his eyes remained suspicious.

"So the primer explodes, which causes the powder to burn, which creates pressure?" Gadrial asked.

"That's right."

"How much pressure?"

"It varies from one type of gun to another and it varies from one type of ammunition to another."

"Why?" Sogbourne asked, frowning again.

"When the length of the cartridge case changes, you can either pack in more powder or be forced to put in less, depending on whether it's larger or smaller. The size of the grains of powder and the number of those grains determines how much pressure will develop inside the case. Beyond that, some gun types are more robust than others, which means you can safely add more powder to a cartridge, generate higher pressures, and end up with higher speeds for the bullet when it leaves the gun barrel.

"When you start reusing them in the field, you also have to take into account how old your cases are. If a case is new or nearly new, you can put more powder into it than into an older case. Older ones are more brittle from the heat generated by repeated firing, which can cause them to split or tear apart inside the chamber if you load them as heavily as you would a *new* case.

"You also have to consider how high the metal quality is to start with. The metal in the gun, itself, is a factor. An old gun that's been fired thousands of times is more likely to crack or split during use than a new gun. If the metal quality's lousy to start with, you can create problems from the very outset. I've seen guns with parts that sheared off, from cheap metallurgy and shoddy manufacturing and poor maintenance, and a couple of those broken guns caused serious injury to the men shooting them. So you see, there isn't an easy or definitive answer to your question."

"Well," she responded reasonably enough, "what about this gun?" She pointed at the rifle Jasak had tried to fire. "With this ammunition?"

"That combination would yield about forty thousand pounds per square inch of pressure inside the cartridge case and the rifle's chamber. That kind of pressure would propel a bullet of this size, shape, and weight at a bit over two thousand feet per second at the muzzle. The speed drops, of course, once it leaves the gun, but it's still moving fast enough to kill a man a mile or more away."

Sogbourne stared at him, his horror at the weapon's power once again clearly evident. "No wonder those accursed things blow flesh apart!"

"Yes," Gadrial said, but she was frowning thoughtfully. "But if this is merely a physical process, a simple burning of natural compounds that works in your universe, but not in ours, we need to find out *why* it doesn't work here. It may be that some step in the manufacturing process used to make these cartridges renders them inoperable here, although I can't imagine what that might be."

"Neither can I," Jathmar agreed.

"I find it interesting that your Talents don't work as well here and your weapons apparently don't work at all. It's odd... very odd...."

Her voice trailed off, and then a sudden flare of inspiration lit her eyes. She met Sogbourne's gaze. "I want Jathmar to try shooting the rifle."

"What use would that be?" Sogbourne asked sharply. "And I still don't want a prisoner to handle a weapon."

"If it doesn't function in our universe," Gadrial said in a patient, reasonable tone, "there's no risk in letting him hold it. It wouldn't be anything more dangerous than a simple wooden stick. Speaking as a scientist, Twenty Thousand Sogbourne, I want as complete a dataset as possible. Right now we have only one set of data to work with: the priming compound doesn't ignite the powder, *or* it doesn't ignite the powder because Jasak Olderhan is operating the rifle."

Sogbourne stared at her as though she'd taken leave of her senses. So did Jathmar. Even Shaylar was astonished. He could feel it even through their malfunctioning marriage bond.

"Frankly, Sir," Gadrial went on, raking one hand through her hair, which promptly rearranged itself into the sleek coif she'd laid a spell to create this morning, "that's seriously insufficient data. Scientific research demands that we find a way to prove that something will work. We already know this weapon works under some conditions. What we need to know is how to make it work under *our* conditions. That's the basis of good magisterial science."

Jathmar blinked in surprise. "Your science is based proving something *can* work, instead of looking for conditions that prove it *doesn't*?"

Gadrial blinked in turn. "Your scientists look for ways to prove a theory *doesn't* work? How in the world do you ever manage to invent *anything*?"

"I don't mean inventing technology," Jathmar tried to explain. "I mean coming up with ways to explain how the universes work. You start with a hypothesis, an idea. You test it every conceivable way to see if any of those conditions cause the idea to fail. If it fails, your hypothesis was wrong. Only after multiple people have tested it in many different ways, over a long period of time, does everyone assume it's true, that it's an accurate description of how the universes work.

"But it's still considered only a theory. If any new data come to light that causes the idea or even part of the idea to fail, then the theory has to be revised or eliminated and replaced with a new theory that includes the new discovery. Then that new idea is tested again and again before it's assumed to be valid."

Gadrial looked stunned. "That's... my God, Jathmar, that's *backwards*, totally opposite of the way magisters approach scientific research—"

"I fail to see the need to discuss this nonsense," Sogbourne growled. "We're here to demonstrate Sharonian battlefield equipment, not develop new explanations of science! We don't have time to waste on folderol and curiosities of the magisterial mind!"

Gadrial's eyes glinted. "Oh, really? Then you'd better resign yourself to losing this war."

"Why?" Sogbourne demanded.

"Because this," she pointed at the malfunctioning rifle, "is the greatest scientific mystery to come along in two centuries. Their Talents don't work properly in our core universes. Their military technology doesn't work properly here, either. If their technology doesn't work in our universes, it's logical to assume *our* technology won't work in theirs."

Sogbourne swallowed hard. "Oh, dear gods..."

"Yes. This isn't some mere 'curiosity of the magisterial mind.' It's a matter of Arcana's survival if we can't find some way out of this shooting war with Sharona. This," she touched the rifle, "is simply an object. It either works or it doesn't work. It worked in the battle of Toppled Timber, in a pristine universe. It worked on the way back to Arcana, when Jasak and Otwal Threbuch and I fired them at targets made of paper. But it doesn't work *now*. To find out why it doesn't, we have to start testing it under as wide a variety of variables as possible, to see if we can find a condition under which it *does* work. The most obvious variable is also the easiest and fastest to test. Jathmar's people built this object. Jathmar's used it many times, and so has Shaylar. Let one of them operate it and see what does—or doesn't—happen."

Sogbourne frowned. "I don't like it," he muttered. "You don't hand a prisoner a weapon."

"There are enough armed soldiers here to turn Jathmar into a crisped pincushion if he tries to attack one of us. Are you planning to stand there quoting regulations or do you intend to try *winning* this war?"

"Magister Gadrial—" Sogbourne glowered at her. "You're obviously going to be as great a pain in the arse as Magister Halathyn ever was. Maybe greater. Oh, all right, I withdraw my veto. Conduct your research. I just hope to hell you know what you're doing."

"I haven't a clue," she said brightly, "But I mean well. And I guarantee I'll know more in just a few moments." She rested a hand on Sogbourne's arm and said more seriously, "You have your duty to Arcana, Sir, and I have mine. You may trust that I'll take that duty very seriously, indeed."

He sighed and nodded. "Very well, let him proceed."

"Thank you, Commander." She turned to Jathmar. "All right, Jathmar. Let's find out what happens."

Jathmar turned to Jasak. "Will you go with me to the firing line, please? I'd like someone from Arcana to observe closely what I do. I don't want anyone to doubt my actions—or my intentions."

The request caught even Jasak by surprise, but the hundred's eyes glinted with amusement. "Of course, Jathmar. That's a very accommodating request. In fact, I'd like to ask an officer of the court to accompany us to the firing line, if you don't mind?"

"That's a good suggestion," Jathmar nodded.

Sogbourne stepped forward briskly. "Let's go," he said, eyeing Jathmar with curious speculation.

Jathmar pulled ammunition from several boxes, as he'd asked Jasak to do, then loaded carefully. "Very well, gentlemen, shall we see what happens when I try to fire it?"

Sogbourne nodded.

Jathmar lifted the rifle with care, moving slowly enough to keep the suspicious guards satisfied that he wasn't going to shoot any of the officers or ministers of Parliament. He sighted carefully, acquired the x-ring on the paper target, and squeezed gently on the trigger. He wasn't entirely certain what to expect, having witnessed that inexplicable series of misfires.

So he squeezed gently down on the trigger, taking up the slight amount of slack, waiting for the crisp snap as carefully machined inner parts sent the firing pin forward through the breechface, into the primer.

A sharp *c-r-a-c-k!* tore the crisp morning air. The rifle had fired. But the buttplate had barely nudged Jathmar's shoulder. He stared down the barrel past the front sight at the target, which was pristine. It was only fifty yards away. There was no wind. His sight alignment had been perfect, he *knew* it had been, but the bullet hadn't struck the target. He hadn't missed a shot *that* simple since childhood.

He peered at the rifle in consternation. It had fired, which was comforting to his violated sense of normalcy, but the recoil had been so puny as to be almost nonexistent and the bullet had failed to punch a target only fifty yards away. Even the sound of the rifle had been off. That sharp crack wasn't anything like the deep-throated bellow the Ternathian Model 9511 was famous for producing when fired. That characteristic roar had earned the rifle its most common nickname: Thundergun. Only *this* Thundergun had barely wheezed.

Jasak's voice punched through his shock.

"It fired!" Jasak was saying again and again. "It *fired*. But why? I don't understand. It *fired*."

"Ye-e-s-s," Jathmar said slowly, "but it didn't fire properly."

Sogbourne frowned. "What do you mean by that? Explain."

Jathmar scratched the side of his head, trying to figure out where to begin. He was still scratching when Gadrial called out a request to join them at the firing line. A moment later, she and

Shaylar were standing beside the shooting bench, staring down at the rifle in Jathmar's puzzled hands.

"Well," Jathmar said, "for one thing, the sound was wrong. Much too quiet."

"Quiet?" Sogbourne gaped. "That hellish crack was *quiet*?"

"You know," Jasak frowned, "now you mention it, the noise was louder the last time we shot this gun."

"Yes," Jathmar said, although his voice was distracted by the thoughts colliding uselessly in his head. "For another thing, the recoil was all wrong. It was much too soft."

"Recoil?" Sogbourne asked.

"Yes, the recoil that occurs when the gun is fired. The release of all that gas pressure moving forward shoves the butt of the rifle, this part," he carefully moved the rifle into a new position, muzzle-up, to show them which part of the rifle was the butt-plate, "back against my shoulder."

"Why?" Jasak asked, looking mystified.

"Because of physics. For every action, there's an equal and opposite reaction. When the gas propels the bullet forward at such a high speed, with all that tremendous gas pressure, the energy released propels the rifle backwards, in an equal and opposite direction. The bullet goes one way and the rifle goes the other way, so it punches your shoulder. The faster the bullet moves out of the gun barrel, the more energy there is to slam backwards. If you have a big, heavy gun, some of the weight will tend to compensate, but there's still an opposite reaction. The gun will travel backwards while the bullet travels forwards, and there's nothing you can do about it."

The Arcanans, he discovered, were staring at him as though he'd lost his mind.

"Ah, Jathmar," Gadrial said carefully, "that's a very interesting theory. But it doesn't work that way here."

Others were shaking their heads.

"But that's impossible," Shaylar said. "There's *always* a reaction."

"Oh, well we're familiar with the idea of recoil," Gadrial reassured her. "We just don't let it get in the way."

"*'Get in the way'*?" Jathmar repeated. "That's one of the basic laws of physics. It underlies *everything*. It *has* to 'get in the way,' Gadrial!"

Gadrial's brow furrowed. "Not here. Half of what we do on a daily basis wouldn't work if that was a physical law underlying *everything.* Heavens above, dragons couldn't fly if we had to worry about silly things like *recoil* all the time!"

Jasak Olderhan exchanged a long and worried look with Commander of Twenty Thousand Sogbourne.

"I want to shoot this," Gadrial said abruptly. "I shot it before. I want to shoot it again. Jathmar, I've forgotten how to operate it. Could you show me again, please?"

"Well, certainly, if you really want to." He loaded it for her, slipping half-a-dozen rounds into the tube-fed magazine, worked the action to chamber a round, then showed her again how to hold it, how to aim it, and how to fire it. She had trouble holding it steady and on target, because the weapon was much too heavy for her, but she did a creditable job of aligning everything, and then she squeezed the trigger...

It clicked.

Just clicked. Not even a crack, let alone a roar.

Jathmar stared in utter consternation.

"*That's impossible!*" he blurted. "Why didn't it fire? It should have. It just did!" He did something he shouldn't have done. It wasn't safe. It certainly wasn't smart. He took the gun from Gadrial, thumbed back the exposed hammer to cock it without working the action, tucked it against his shoulder, and squeezed.

C-r-a-c-k!

The buttplate jostled his shoulder. The target remained pristine, but the cartridge that had failed to fire for Gadrial had fired on the first try for him. He nearly dropped the rifle. In fact, he had to fumble for it as the gun started to slide out of his numb hands and a film of sweat broke out across his whole body. His hands actually shook as he lowered the rifle gingerly to the shooting bench.

Jathmar stared at Gadrial.

She stared back.

"That's impossible," he said, voice flat with shock.

"Why?" Jasak asked, brow furrowed.

"It just is," Jathmar insisted. "The primer should have worked for Gadrial, too."

"Does this kind of thing ever happen in Sharona?" Gadrial asked.

Jathmar started to answer, then halted. "Sometimes," he said slowly, "there are misfires or hang fires. A misfire is a cartridge that doesn't function at all. A hang-fire is one that for some reason doesn't ignite properly. It goes off more slowly, usually due to the powder not burning at the proper rate, which is one reason we always point a gun's muzzle downrange, away from anything we don't want to shoot. A hang-fire can go off a second or two later."

"Maybe," Jasak suggested, "we should experiment with more shooters?"

Jathmar nodded, feeling dazed.

Ten minutes later, he was so confused, he could barely think straight. It was flatly impossible, but they'd given it a thorough, rigorous testing. When Jasak Olderhan, Gadrial Kelbryan, or Twenty Thousand Sogbourne tried to fire a Sharonian gun, nothing happened. When Jathmar or Shaylar pulled the trigger, the gun fired—but with only a fraction of its original power. A bullet that should have nailed a target a thousand yards away wouldn't travel fifty. They had to move the target back to the twenty-five yard line before Jathmar's bullet would even reach it.

Even Twenty Thousand Sogbourne was puzzled by the admittedly weird performance of Jathmar's hunting rifle. "What's going on, Magister Gadrial?" he demanded in exasperation.

"I don't know. Jathmar, tell me again how the guns work. What makes the bullet leave the gun?"

Jathmar drew a deep breath and launched into another explanation of powders and primers and gas expansion. He told her what gunpowder was, how and why it burned, what priming compounds were and why and how they exploded when struck with a sharp blow. He didn't do a very good job of it, in part because he was thoroughly rattled and in part because he wasn't an expert in arms manufacture or the chemistry of weapons development. But he told her what he could.

Gadrial listened intently.

"In essence," she said with a frown that only seemed abstracted, since Jathmar was perfectly well aware of how agile her mind was, "what you're describing is the incarnation of motive energies, which are harnessed through a distillation process that transfers their latent arcane energy from the etheric plane to the physical, and the action of this device, this 'fire-making pin,' is a physically expressed incantation that causes the latent motive energies distilled in these various compounds to combine in a sudden, complex spell of release. Ye gods, Jathmar, it's mind boggling!"

Jathmar's mind was certainly boggled, since he hadn't understood a single word of that crazy mishmash. Judging by their expressions, neither had Shaylar or even Jasak Olderhan and Twenty Thousand Sogbourne. Gadrial, however, was gazing at the rifle with a smile of childlike delight. She moved with sudden authority, taking Jathmar by surprise.

There were five more rounds loaded in the magazine. Gadrial racked the action like a seasoned pro, creating a crisp, metallic *shlack-shlack*, the characteristic sound of a cycling scissor-action. Before Jathmar could even open his mouth to protest, Gadrial had lifted the gun to her shoulder, more-or-less sighted on the target, and yanked the trigger.

C-R-A-A-A-C-K!

Gadrial dropped the rifle.

Then stood there, gulping hard and staring down at the gun as though it had transformed itself into a venomous snake. She finally looked up. Looked around, searching almost frantically for Jathmar.

"It worked," she whispered. Her lips had gone unaccountably dry.

"I noticed," he croaked. His voice emerged as a hoarse, froglike sound—a hoarse, froglike sound even feebler and far fainter to ears stunned by the thunderous blast of a Thundergun which had just functioned perfectly.

"No," she shook her head, eyes wide in growing fright, "you don't understand. It *worked*. Not the rifle. I mean, that worked, too. It wasn't the rifle I meant. Wasn't the rifle I was talking about. Or testing."

"Gadrial," Jasak said in a down-to-earth voice, "you're not making sense."

She didn't even seem to hear him, because she was too busy turning parchment white and battling the tremors that had begun to shake through her slender body.

"It shouldn't have worked!" she said on a note of rising alarm that was heading rapidly toward panic and the onset of hysteria. "I didn't expect it to work!" she gasped. "It was just a crazy idea, a half-baked notion that flashed into my head, an idea so nutty, I didn't even stop to think it through. If I had, I would never have tried to shoot that...that *thing*." She shuddered, staring down at the rifle on the ground with genuine horror in her eyes. "It was just a crazy idea, but my God, it worked. Rahil's mercy..." She wrapped both arms around herself. "It's impossible," she whispered, lifting her gaze to stare into Jathmar's totally bewildered eyes. She was shivering so hard, Jasak peeled off his uniform's coat and wrapped her up in it.

"Jasak," she gripped one of his hands in both of hers, "Jasak, what I just did—" she gulped. "I just took everything we thought we knew about reality and turned it inside out and upside down and raveled out half the garment we call physics." She stared down at the rifle again and bit her lip. "Jasak, I'm *scared*."

Jathmar glanced from Gadrial to Shaylar, who was as baffled as he was.

"But why?" Jasak asked. He, too, was bewildered. So was Sogbourne, by the look on his face, and more than a little worried, as well, since whatever Gadrial had just done had terrified a woman who was high on a very short list of candidates for the best theoretical magician in the whole of Arcana's civilization. When Jathmar realized that, he felt an abrupt stab of sudden, unadulterated terror. What the *hell* had Gadrial just discovered?

"Gadrial," Jasak said in a tone that was abruptly stern, "what have you done, just now? What have you discovered? And why has it scared you out of your seriously intelligent wits?"

"What?" she asked as though dazed.

He took her by the shoulders in a grip so firm, it was just shy of shaking her. That grip forced her to meet his gaze. "What have you just discovered?" he asked again. "And why has it scared a year off our lives?"

She gulped. Shivered. Pulled Jasak's coat more tightly about her shoulders. "The connection I made," she whispered, "about Jathmar's ability to shoot the rifle you couldn't. It isn't what their *weapons* can do, Jasak, that's a danger to Arcana. That's so minor, it's hardly worth mentioning—"

"Now see here," Sogbourne snapped. "What the devil does that mean? Their terror weapons are minor? Weapons that blow apart human flesh? That can destroy an entire platoon in a matter of minutes? Have you lost your Ransaran mind?"

"No. I haven't." Gadrial's hoarse whisper sent chills down Jathmar's spine. "But what their weapons do is the least of our worries. It's what they *believe* that will destroy us. Unless we're very, very careful."

*　　*　　*

Thankhar Olderhan sat gazing into the heart of the message crystal badged with the logo of Halka & Associates while cold, dark despair flowed through him.

He stared at it, longing for some spell to obliterate it, to change history so it had never been sent—*would* never be sent. But no magister had ever devised that spell, and no power in all the universes could protect him from what he had to do now.

He set the crystal on his blotter and leaned back in his chair, massaging his temples with both hands, trying to grapple with all the implications. Trying to imagine all the things he still didn't know about this entire Jambakol-spawned monstrosity... and about who was deliberately shaping it into an even greater monstrosity.

He knew Commander of Two Thousand Mayrkos Harshu. Not well, but he'd met the man, spoken with him—even been briefed by him once. What he didn't know was how the man he'd thought he knew could have lent himself to something like this, whatever the "military necessity" which might have justified it. Gods! How could someone as intelligent as Harshu fail to understand what this would do to the Army—to the entire *Union*—when it inevitably got out?

And deservedly so.

Yet even that paled beside what he knew he had to do now. Not in its inter-universal implications, perhaps. But on the *personal* scale, the scale where the things which made a man of honor who and what he *was* mattered, it was infinitely worse than any macro political considerations could ever be, and he wished with all his heart that he *wasn't* a man of honor, because then he could have avoided it.

He lowered his hands to the blotter, laying them on either side of the crystal, and sat for another thirty silent seconds. Then he drew a deep breath and rose with the expression of a man about to face a firing squad.

*   *   *

Shaylar looked up from the Andaran history book displayed on the crystal in her lap as the soft, musical chime sounded. She glanced across at Jathmar, who was immersed in quite a different book. His Andaran was still weaker than her own, but he'd been wading through the crystal—*A Basic Introduction to Theoretical Magic*, by Halathyn vos Dulainah—ever since the firearms demonstration. Gadrial had provided it at his request, and he was determined to somehow reconcile the differences between the Arcanan and the Sharonian concepts of science.

Somehow, she doubted he'd have much luck in that endeavor. Not that there was the remotest possibility of dissuading him from the attempt.

The chime sounded again, and she smiled faintly as Jathmar read on, oblivious to everything outside his crystal. Obviously, it was up to her.

She set her own book aside, climbed out of the comfortable, floating chair, and crossed the sitting room. She opened the door, and her eyebrows rose as the servant in the hallway bobbed a curtsy.

"Yes?" Shaylar asked as pleasantly as she could.

The acute hatred which had poured off of some of the Olderhan servants had eased considerably over the last week, for which she was grateful. The most hate-filled had simply disappeared, although she didn't know if Sathmin Olderhan had found them other positions on another of the Olderhans' many properties or simply fired them. Most of the remaining staff continued to regard her and Jathmar as profoundly unnatural beings from an alien and threatening universe populated by the gods only knew what monstrous threats, however. As Jasak Olderhan's *shardonai* they were entitled to service and respect—even to protection, since those servants were also part of the extended Garth Showma household—but nothing seemed capable of banishing that penumbra of fear.

"His Grace's complements, Madam Nargra-Kolmayr, and he requests that you and your husband join him in the Blue Salon."

"Did His Grace say why he'd like us to join him?" Shaylar asked in some surprise, and the maid shook her head.

"He just told me to ask you to join him, Milady."

"I see." Shaylar gazed at the other woman for a moment, then shrugged.

"Please tell His Grace we'll be there as soon as possible."

*   *   *

The Sharonians stepped through the door to the enormous room called the Blue Salon holding one another's hands and paused, just inside the threshold, in astonishment. They'd expected a private meeting with Thankhar Olderhan, but the Duke of Garth Showma wasn't alone.

Jasak stood by the windows, gazing out into an evening which had turned gray and cold, burnished with a swirl of snowflakes and polished with wind moan. Gadrial stood beside him, her expression worried, and Sathmin Olderhan sat in one of the elegant, impossibly comfortable armchairs. Shaylar and Jathmar hadn't expected the others, but at least they knew who all of them were. They had no idea who the man standing beside the duke might be, however.

He was a nondescript, brown-haired fellow in civilian clothes, yet Shaylar had the strangest impression that he ought to be in a uniform of some sort. Of course, that seemed to be true of an awful lot of the Andarans she'd met since that hideous day at Toppled Timber.

"Thank you for coming," the duke said, crossing the room to personally usher her and Jathmar to a small floating couch which faced his wife's armchair.

He waited until they were seated, then stepped back and clasped his hands behind him. There was something...frightening about the way he stood facing them, like a soldier bracing against an enemy charge. That was Shaylar's first impression. Then she was sure she'd imagined it...until she glanced at Jasak and saw him watching his father with exactly the same sort of wariness *she* felt.

"I asked you here," the duke's voice was strangely formal, "in the presence of your *baranal*, because it's my duty, as his father, as an officer of the Union Army, and as Duke of Garth Showma, to tell you—all of you—what I've learned this very evening."

He paused and inhaled, nostrils flaring, then took one hand from behind him to indicate the stranger, still standing beside his desk.

"This is Sertal Halka. Once upon a time, he was Commander of Five Hundred Halka and served with me in the Second Andarans before he was invalided out of the service after the same fracas in which Otwal Threbuch saved my life. Since then, he's had an...interesting career in Intelligence, and he and I have stayed in touch over the years."

He beckoned, and Halka crossed to stand beside him. The retired five hundred walked with a slight but noticeable limp, favoring his left leg, which struck Shaylar and Jathmar as odd in a culture which had Gifted healers. Having seen people snatched back from the very brink of death—having been snatched back himself, in Jathmar's case—by Arcanan healers, they had to wonder what sort of injury those healers hadn't been able to completely cure for Halka.

"I asked Sertal to join us this evening because, at my request, he's been investigating certain outside-channel reports which have reached me. In particular, I asked him to investigate a report from Fifty Therman Ulthar."

Jasak's eyes narrowed suddenly, and his father glanced at him and nodded ever so slightly.

"I apologize for not sharing the contents of that report with you sooner, Jas," he said. "And I appreciate your patience, since I know how impatient you must've been to hear whatever he had to say."

"Should I assume you're about to share them with me now, Father?"

"Yes," the duke said heavily. "And I wish to all the gods I didn't have to. Unfortunately, you and I both have obligations which leave me no choice."

"Thankhar," his wife said quietly, "you're frightening me."

"I'm sorry, my dear. I didn't mean to. But there was a very good reason young Ulthar sent me that message. He's concerned about violations of the Kerellian Accords." The duke's voice was flat, hard as hammered iron. "*Deliberate* violations of the Kerellian Accords."

Jasak snapped fully erect, so suddenly Gadrial reached out and laid a concerned hand on his arm, and Sathmin Olderhan stiffened in her armchair, her expression shocked. Shaylar had no idea what the "Kerellian Accords" might be, but her hand tightened on Jathmar's as she sensed the sudden storm of tension rising all about her.

"Violation of the Accords?" Jasak's voice was even flatter than his father's had been, with an over controlled calm that sent icy fingernails up and down Shaylar's spine.

"That was one of the things he reported," his father confirmed in a voice hewn from granite. "His report was...comprehensive and very informative, and I took it seriously. In fact, I've already dispatched an inquiry team in response to it, although it will be some time before it can reach Thermyn to verify everything in it. Under the circumstances"—he met his son's eyes levelly—"I sent it on my own authority, as hereditary commander of the Second

Andarans, without involving the Commandery. The allegations contained in his message were that serious. But it was clearly incumbent upon me to verify anything I could from this end, as well. Which is how Sertal got involved."

All eyes returned to the brown-haired man who squared his shoulders under their weight.

"Sertal left official government employment some years ago," the duke said. "He established his own security firm, and he's assembled a highly competent staff which has handled my personal security needs from the time he opened his doors. I want all of you to understand that there isn't a man in the entire Union I trust more implicitly and completely then Sertal."

He paused a moment, as if to allow that to sink in, before he continued.

"It turns out we've had at least some piecemeal communications from Commander of Two Thousand mul Gurthak which haven't been made public. For reasons which I strongly suspect we won't like very much once we find out what they are, the two thousand still hasn't filed any official dispatches dealing with this material with the Commandery, even though the communications which have reached Portalis contain significant military information. Instead, they were sent to the Ministry of Exploration and the Directorate of Intelligence."

He must have seen from the Sharonians' expression that his last sentence meant little to them, because he grimaced and explained.

"The Ministry of Exploration is the civilian ministry charged with overseeing our exploration policies, and the Directorate of Intelligence is a civilian intelligence service. The Ministry's in charge of developing the infrastructure in the explored out-universes and of coordinating our *general* exploratory policy, but the actual exploration mission belongs to the Army, and the Ministry has no direct authority over that aspect of its operations. And the Directorate of Intelligence is a department of the Ministry of Justice, not of Exploration or the Army. In fact, there's been an ongoing turf war between the Directorate and Military Intelligence for at least fifty years, just as there are those in Exploration who've argued for years that *they* should control the actual exploration rather than leaving it in 'the Army's clumsy hands.'"

"Which would imply," Jathmar said slowly, "that mul Gurthak

wanted to avoid sharing his information with anyone in your military? Or even that he wanted to share it with someone who didn't *like* your military very much?"

"It *could* imply that," the duke corrected him. "It could also simply be a case of sloppy clerical work in the midst of an ongoing crisis. Sertal managed to . . . acquire copies of the material for me, and it's not in the form of a formal report. Instead, it looks like some sort of internal memo that hasn't yet been put into its final form."

"So you're saying it wasn't supposed to be sent at all?"

"No, Jathmar, I'm saying it may have been sent by clerical error . . . or that it was deliberately sent in a format which would allow it to *appear* to have been sent by clerical error."

"But why would anyone do that?" Shaylar asked, sounding totally confused because that was exactly what she was. Voice transmissions didn't get sent by "clerical error," and she couldn't quite wrap her mind around how that could happen to *Arcanan* reports.

"We don't know that yet," the duke told her. "I have some unpleasant thoughts in that regard, and Sertal's helping to determine whether or not my paranoia is justified. If it is, then I'm afraid the entire Union of Arcana may be about to discover that we face more than simply external threats. That, however, is something for us to worry about, not you and your husband. The only reason I've described this aspect to you is so that you can understand why and how I've discovered what *does* concern you."

"In what way?" Jathmar's tone was courteous but sharp, honed with formless dread born from too much bitter experience.

"As you know, all the public's been officially told—all anyone outside a handful of highly placed officials at the Ministry of Exploration and the Directorate of Intelligence knows—is that negotiations broke down, virtually all of our own negotiating team was killed in some sort of confrontation, hostilities have been resumed, and Two Thousand Harshu has advanced beyond Thermyn," the duke replied flatly. "And all of that's true. But if the information Sertal's people have turned up is correct, the real reason those negotiations 'broke down' was because—according to Rithmar Skirvon and Uthik Dastiri—the Sharonians 'made their warlike intentions clear' from the outset by failing to stipulate that there would be no attack during negotiations. Because that clause is an essential hallmark of all serious diplomatic efforts to negotiate a cease-fire agreement, it was clear to Skirvon that Sharona had no intention of signing any peace treaty and intended to keep its hands free to attack at a time of its own choosing."

"*What?*" Jathmar stared at him. "That's crazy!"

"In fairness to Skirvon's interpretation, the agreement by both parties not to attack during negotiations is, indeed, a fundamental part of traditional Arcanan diplomacy," the duke said heavily. "*Traditionally,*" he emphasized the adverb heavily, "there was no *obligation* to agree to any such thing, and it was understood by all parties that unless it was specifically agreed to, either side was free to—and probably would—resume active operations at the moment it felt would be most advantageous. Mind you, no one's negotiated any peace treaties since the establishment of the Union, so I think it's safe to say our procedures are a little rusty, and we haven't had any true 'diplomats' in the better part of two hundred years. I'd think that gave us plenty of opportunities to get it wrong from our side, as well. More to the point, it doesn't seem to have occurred to anyone that we're dealing with someone from a completely different—a totally *alien*—society which might not understand all of our own diplomatic niceties."

"Diplomatic *niceties?*" Jathmar visibly gripped his temper in both hands. "No Sharonian would even *think* about that! It's obvious that anyone seriously interested in negotiating a cease-fire wouldn't be planning to *attack* in the middle of the talks! One of the first things each side's Voices—"

He broke off, and the duke nodded unhappily.

"Exactly," he said softly.

Silence hovered for the better part of a minute before he cleared his throat.

"One of the minor points which hasn't yet been officially reported to Parliament or the Commandery is that the 'diplomatic incident' which resulted in the deaths of at least one of our negotiators and most of their military escort occurred because Two Thousand Harshu's offensive began with a *preemptive* attack predicated on the supposition that Sharona was preparing to attack *us*. In other words, contrary to what most of the citizens of the Union believe, there was indeed treachery and a 'sneak attack,' but it wasn't launched by the Sharonians.

"Skirvon and Dastiri were involved in face-to-face negotiations with the representatives of the Sharonian Empire when the attack kicked off. They were supposed to keep the Sharonians talking right up to the moment our troops arrived. In fact, although there's no way to confirm it at this point, I suspect our 'diplomats'' ceremonial guard detail was supposed to kick off the entire operation by capturing—or killing—the entire Sharonian negotiating team."

The duke's expression showed what he thought of that tactic.

"Unfortunately for the attack plan, that particular bit of treachery apparently came a cropper. By the time our cavalry reached the negotiation site, the Sharonians were long gone, leaving behind the bodies of Uthik Dastiri and most of the 'ceremonial guards.' As far as I'm aware, the Sharonians are still at large somewhere behind our lines."

Shaylar felt her hand tighten like a claw on Jathmar's, yet it was obvious the duke wasn't done. There was worse to come, and she tried to brace herself to meet it.

"There are suggestions in the material," he continued, turning to glance at his son instead of the Sharonians, "which appear to confirm Fifty Therman's report of Kerellian Accord violations. At the moment, I can't even begin to decide which of the ones he's reported is the most egregious. There's going to be hells to pay over any of them, but the worst are that the head of Two Thousand Harshu's intelligence staff—a five hundred named Neshok—is using torture to—"

"*Neshok?*" Gadrial blurted, then blushed as she realized she'd interrupted the duke. The senior Olderhan paused, cocking an eyebrow at her, and she had the oddest sensation he was actually grateful for the discourtesy surprise had startled out of her.

Or for the *interruption*, anyway.

"That was the name, Magister Gadrial," he said. "An Alivar Neshok, I believe. According to the memo that went to the Directorate of Intelligence, he was specifically requested by Two Thousand Harshu and given the acting rank of five hundred so he'd have the necessary seniority. Should I take it you met him?"

"We *all* have, Father," Jathmar said grimly. "At least I'm pretty sure we have. Hundred Alivar Neshok was the officer who wanted to separate Shaylar and Jathmar from us in Erthos. The one Gadrial backed down when she told him to put her in the same cell to make sure nothing...untoward happened to them. Are you saying *he's* who's been in charge of Two Thousand Harshu's intelligence this entire time?"

"Yes, I'd say I am, although I confess I hadn't connected him with your description of your time in Erthos." The duke's tone was even grimmer than his son's had been. "I don't think the name's a coincidence, at any rate. And apparently he's been just as . . . untrammeled by any scruples as Gadrial was afraid he might be. Therman informs me that there have been numerous reports of torture and of prisoners dying under questioning. In fact, he says that according to healers to whom he's spoken, they've flatly refused to heal prisoners undergoing interrogation because healing them only allowed them to be tortured even further."

Jasak's face could have been hewn out of granite. Gadrial held his hand tightly, her own expression anxious as she looked up at his profile. Despite the weakening of her Talent, Shaylar physically felt the fury raging through him behind that stony mask, and she found herself clutching Jathmar's hand even more tightly.

"I wish I could say that was the worst thing Fifty Ulthar had to report," the duke said even more heavily. "Unfortunately, it isn't. According to Therman's brother-in-law, the lie that Magister Halathyn was shot down in cold blood by the Sharonians *after* surrendering, not in a ghastly friendly fire accident, isn't just a wild story concocted by rumor mongers and so called reporters desperate for a story. According to Ulthar, the troops have been told—told *officially*—the same lie by their own intelligence officers."

"*That's insane!*" Gadrial snapped, and this time there was no hint of apology in her expression when the duke looked at her. "One of the few things we knew for *certain* before we ever started for home was that Magister Halathyn was killed by one of our own infantry dragons! That was absolutely established in the earliest reports, whatever lies may've hit the crystals since!"

"Precisely." The duke shook his head, looking older in that moment than Shaylar had ever seen him look. "Precisely. Apparently whoever's feeding the troops the false reports is at least attempting to cover himself by saying his information is 'unconfirmed,' but as far as I'm concerned, that's simply a glaring tipoff that it's deliberate and authorized at the highest levels. Harshu *has* to know the truth. For that matter, he has to know that eventually the truth is going to *come out*. But it's evident from Ulthar's report—assuming he's got it right, and I'm very much afraid he does—that at the very least none of the Expeditionary Force's senior officers are attempting to correct the 'rumors' sweeping through the ranks. And you know as well as I do, Gadrial, exactly how that's going to inflame our people. Especially the *garthans* like Ulthar's brother-in-law. I can't think of anything better calculated to generate atrocities than to allow our own troops to believe the *Sharonians* routinely commit them."

A crackling silence invaded the room, lingering like a static electricity on the skin, until Shaylar broke it.

"You Grace," she said very, very carefully, "why do I think those 'atrocities' are the reason Jathmar and I are here this evening?"

"Because they are." The duke faced her squarely, and his shoulders braced. "I'm afraid Two Thousand Harshu, faced with your own people's huge advantage in communications—apparently on the advice of Five Hundred Neshok—settled on a technique to prevent your Voices from warning anyone up-chain about our advance."

Shaylar blinked. Sharona had been forced to develop techniques for neutralizing the Voice Talent long ago, but it hadn't been easy and it had taken centuries. How could the Arcanans, who'd never even *heard* of Talents before Toppled Timber have devised one so quickly?

Then she felt the spike of pure, unadulterated fury coming off of Jasak and the sudden horror radiating from Gadrial. The emotions were so powerful—and so focused on *her*, for some reason—that they almost knocked her breathless despite the weakening of her Talent.

"I don't care *who* he is, Father," Jasak snapped. "I'll cut his black heart out on the dueling ground!"

"I understand your sentiments, Jasak," the duke said. "And I share them. But that's getting ahead of where we are now. What we have to do now is find out if what Ulthar's reporting is true. We have to *confirm* that, with evidence that will stand up before any tribunal, before we can do anything else. And we have to find out whose idea it *really* was. Harshu's for the dragon as far as I'm concerned, no matter who came up with it, but given how this information's reached Portalis—and who in Portalis has it—I have to wonder who else could be manipulating the situation . . . and why?"

"*Mul Gurthak*," Gadrial hissed. "We keep hearing about Harshu, but mul Gurthak's his *superior*, and this has the stink of *shakira* all over it, Your Grace!"

"That's exactly what I think, my dear. Unfortunately, we can't *prove* it. In fact, at the moment, we can't prove *any* of this."

"Any of *what*?" Shaylar demanded. "What do you all talking about, and why is Jasak so...so *furious* about whatever it is?"

Jasak crossed to the couch upon which she and Jathmar sat. He dropped to one knee in front of her, reaching out and taking her free hand in both of his while he looked straight into her eyes with that unyielding personal integrity she'd come to know so well.

"I'm furious because I'm your *baranal*," he said. "Because you and Jathmar—*all* your people, even those I've never met—have already suffered and lost so much because of this entire stupid, unforgivable nightmare. And because whoever came up with Harshu's 'technique' for neutralizing your Voices only knew they had to be neutralized in the first place because *I* reported the capability."

"That's not fair, Jas!" Gadrial said sharply. "You *had* to report that, and you had no idea—no idea at all—anyone would use that information for *this!*"

"For *what*?" Shaylar demanded again, and Jasak drew a deep breath.

"There's only one way we could 'neutralize' a Voice, Shaylar." His voice was gentle, yet it was cored with steel, hammered on the anvil of his fury. "We don't have a spell to do that. The only way *we* know to...'turn off' a Talent is to kill whoever has it."

Shaylar stared at him for a second or two longer, unable to process what he'd just said. And then understanding filled her like a sea of poison. It rushed into her, filling every nook and cranny of her soul with a black, crushing tide of horror. And of guilt. And of hatred.

She snatched her hand out of Jasak's and slammed back against the couch's luxurious cushions. Of course that was what they'd done. It was what they did. They *butchered* anything they didn't understand! But they couldn't have done it—couldn't have *known* to do it—if not for her. If she hadn't survived, if she hadn't told them about her Talent, if *Jasak* hadn't passed that information along, then Sharona couldn't have been surprised the way it clearly had been! And all of those Voices, all those people whose only crime had been to be Talented...

"*Monsters*," she whispered, staring back and forth between Jasak and his father. "You're all *monsters!* Mother Marthea, how do you *live* with yourselves? I *knew* some of those Voices! I've touched their minds, shared their thoughts. They were *part* of me, and some of them were only *children!*"

Jasak reached out to her again, but she shrank away, shaking her head convulsively.

"Don't *touch* me, Jasak Olderhan!" she snapped. "*Don't!* Not now!"

"Shaylar—"

"No, Gadrial." Shaylar shook her head again, even harder. "I don't want to hear it! Not now." She released Jathmar's hand to wrap her arms about herself, huddling in on her bones as if she were freezing. She rocked on the couch, like a mother mourning the deaths of her own children, and tears ran down her face.

"I don't want to touch an Andaran—*any* Andaran. I want to wake up and find out this was all some hideous nightmare, but that's not going to happen. I'm going to have to live with this. I'm going to have to live with knowing what monsters you can be and knowing *I* helped you. I *helped* you, Gadrial—whether I wanted to or not—and the gods only know how many others— how many other *Voices*—are dead because I did that!"

"No, you didn't," Jasak said stonily. "You were a prisoner. *You* did absolutely *nothing* wrong, Shaylar. And you're right, the people who did this, who ordered it—who *permitted* it—*are* monsters. I promise you we *will* find out who those people are and why they've done what they've done. And I promise you—*I* promise you, not the Union of Arcana—that when I do find out, they'll face justice for their actions. I don't care who they are, I don't care who tries to protect them, and I don't care whether or not I can do it through the courts. I *will* find them, and they *will* pay."

She stared at him, hating him in that moment with every fiber of her being, but she couldn't shut down the incandescent edge of sincerity and determination blazing from him like the sun. And when she jerked her eyes from his face, looking over his head at the Duke of Garth Showma, she saw only matching fury and the same flinty determination. The pain and the guilt and the anguish within her fought to reject that recognition, but she couldn't. As hard as she wanted to, she couldn't.

"I can't give your people back their lives, Shaylar," Jasak Olderhan told her very, very quietly, "but I *will* see to it that whoever took them pays for it."

CHAPTER TWENTY-SIX

Hayrn 25, 206 YU
(January 16, 1929 CE)

THE AIR IN PORTALIS WAS OPPRESSIVE. THE WALLS OF THE duke's townhouse, where he stood, alone, staring out at the city from his bedroom window, were worse than oppressive. They seemed to close in around him like the jaws of a vise until he felt himself gasping like a winded runner.

There were doubtless some Sharonians whose hearts were large enough and gentle enough to forgive Arcana—or at least those Arcanans not directly responsible—for what Harshu the Butcher had done. Jathmar wasn't one of them. He wasn't sure he could ever forgive these people for that series of atrocities. It was all he could do to forgive Jasak and Gadrial and Jasak's parents, all of whom had gone to great extremes trying to make what amends they could.

It wasn't enough. The score Jathmar needed to settle just kept getting larger by the day, and he cherished his anger, rubbing the hands of his soul above its heat. Yet even as he did, he knew a very real component of that anger was directed—irrationally, to be sure, but still directed—against *himself*. Against his inability to *do* anything to protect himself, his world . . . or Shaylar.

Standing now in front of the carefully spelled window that would neither allow him to leave nor allow anything from the outside to enter, staring in silence at the capital city of his captors, Jathmar was forced to admit that not all Arcanans were outright monsters. Indeed, the fact that Shaylar wasn't with him today only confirmed that. The duke had flatly—and curtly—denied every request that she return to the court-martial for further

409

testimony. For that matter, the duchess had actually picked up a daggerstone and promised to kill any soldier who tried to drag Shaylar back into a courtroom—*any* courtroom.

The Commandery, thrown into total disarray, had backed down, which was why Shaylar remained safely at the Ducal Palace outside Portalis, where the duchess had vowed to remain at her side during every moment of Jathmar's absence. She'd canceled every other appointment and made it perfectly clear that during her husband's absence, *she* commanded Garth Showma's personal armsmen and that the Garth Showma Guard would meet *any* attempt to intrude upon Shaylar with unyielding force. The depth of the duchess' devotion to Shaylar had caught him by surprise.

Even more telling, in some ways, was the duke's reaction. Jasak's father had presented Jathmar with documents bestowing a lifetime income—a very comfortable income, so far as Jathmar could tell—upon him and his wife. Half of it came from a trust funded entirely by the duke and his wife, which hadn't really surprised him, given how seriously they took Jasak's position as their *baranal*. What *had* surprised, him, however, was the fact that the other half had come from the Union of Arcana's Parliament as the result of a piece of legislation Thankhar Olderhan had rammed through Parliament in less than twenty-four hours.

Jathmar doubted any of the legislators who'd voted for it had the least idea what had driven the duke's unyielding determination. They didn't know—yet—what their army had been doing in Sharona's universes. He found it very hard to remind himself of that, and part of him burned with the need to hurl his own knowledge into their teeth. But he couldn't. There were so *many* reasons he couldn't . . . including the fact that they had no official proof of what was happening.

Jathmar hated admitting that. And that burning part of him didn't really *care* about all the reasons to keep his mouth shut. The shame and the rage the duke and Jasak felt was genuine. He knew that. But Arcana wasn't *his* country, and the fact that someone might be trying to manipulate the situation to undercut Andara and the Union Army meant exactly nothing to him. *Let* them come down in ruin! *They* were the ones who'd killed his friends, almost killed him and Shaylar, invaded the universes claimed by Sharona treacherously, under cover of negotiations, and slaughtered every Voice in their path!

That part of him wanted only to hurl the money back into Thankhar Olderhan's face, but he couldn't. First, because he was a penniless beggar with a wife and one day, if the gods were kind, a family to support, and beggars couldn't afford pride. The money would at least give Shaylar and him a measure of independence. They could pay for their own clothing, their own personal items, without the indignity and shame of having to ask for such basic necessities. And, second, because another part of him did know Olderhan was just as determined as his son to find the men behind the Union of Anccara's murderous crimes and bring them to justice.

So he'd accepted the money, if not the conciliatory gesture Parliament's contribution to it represented. That, he would never accept, and he'd told the duke so while signing the requisite records with a stylus that recorded his signature in the personal crystal designated to hold Jathmar's financial affairs. Still, it was a beginning, at least. A first painful step on the road toward true autonomy. At times like this, alone in a spell-locked room, waiting for Jasak's trial to resume tomorrow, the dream of freedom to come and go as they chose seemed so remote, so unattainable, he might as well have reached for the moon by climbing a ladder too short to touch the sky.

Shaylar, love, I need you beside me tonight. Separated like this, Jathmar felt only half alive, as though his soul had been ripped down the center. Shaylar was too far away for him to sense her through their damaged marriage bond, and he regretted, again, his decision to support her crusade to join a survey crew.

It was undoubtedly as irrational as blaming himself because he couldn't protect her now, but that made the regret no less bitter, no less intense. Reasonable or not, he simply could not shake off the belief that *he* was the one who'd brought her to this, to such terrible suffering. Had he known...had he even *suspected*...But this was one risk they'd never considered.

Tomorrow he must face his captors' relentless questions alone. He knew, already, that he'd spit in their faces before he would reveal anything of military value. He didn't care, any longer, if their lie-detection spells caught him in an outright fabrication. The rules had changed, permanently, when the duke shared his suspicions with them.

In his memory, he saw again the crossbow quarrel slam into Ghartoun's throat, choking him to death on blood and steel. Saw again the lightning bolt slam into Barris Kassell. Felt, again, the searing agony of the fireball igniting his hair, his clothing, his very skin. Saw the dragons attacking Shaylar outside a fort. Saw the whole sorry parade of soldiers, politicians, and even servants who looked at them with hatred, with the desire to injure, to strip their very minds bare.

The hatred in his heart ran to the bottom of his soul.

But how could one prisoner exact retribution?

He stood in front of his darkened window, gazing out at the blazing sea of lights that sparkled and glittered and danced across Portalis' rooftops, domes, spires, and crystalline towers. Another fireworks display detonated in the darkness above the city, spreading a sparkling pattern of light across the stars.

They weren't true fireworks, of course, since there was no gunpowder involved. They were silent light displays, sent racing skyward by Gifted wizards who performed "sky light" shows for momentous occasions such as state anniversaries, religious holidays, or the celebration of invading and slaughtering people who'd never done Arcanan citizens harm.

From his room high above the rooftops, Jathmar could see the crowds in the streets, tonight. There was a festival underway in Portalis—a rally in support of the Union of Arcana's "heroic defenders." He'd seen news crystal reports of other rallies just like it, watched the recorded images as people danced and laughed, consumed sweetmeats and sparkling wine and made toasts to the downfall of Sharona's portal forts and towns.

Now, as he watched those distant fireworks, the pain in his heart was too deep to express in mere words. Somehow, he vowed, someday, Sharona would avenge those murdered Voices. Someday, somewhere in the widely scattered universes, a Sharonian soldier would avenge the slaughtered civilians in those towns, in Jathmar's crew. Somehow, Sharona would force Arcana to pay for its sins. All Jathmar could do was pray for that moment to arrive before too many more innocents lost their lives.

He turned away from the "sky light," soul-sick. He dimmed the window, using a spell-powered controller to turn the "glass" opaque, so the celebration wouldn't shine into his eyes all night. That done, he climbed into bed and turned out the lights. Tomorrow would be here all too soon.

He needed to be ready for it.

CHAPTER TWENTY-SEVEN

Darikhal 31, 5053 AE
(January 19, 1929 CE)

"WELL, IT'S NICE TO KNOW THE CORPS-CAPTAIN DOESN'T think I've gone completely mad," Arlos chan Geraith said dryly, gazing down at the typed transcript of the Voice message which had arrived the night before from Corps-Captain Fairlain chan Rowlan. Then he glanced up at Brigade-Captain chan Hartan. "I half expected him to relieve me and put you in command, Shodan. Very restful it would've been, too."

The other men seated around the large meeting table chuckled or smiled, depending upon their seniority and nationality, and he leaned back in his chair to contemplate them for a moment.

They sat in the conference room attached to the office which had been made available for him in the town of Salbyton. It felt a bit odd to be quartered outside the precincts of Fort Salby, but the evacuation of the town's civilian population had been completed, and the substantial brick house into which he'd been moved had once belonged to Salbyton's mayor. It also stood directly adjacent to the town hall, which was far bigger and offered much better—and more efficient—accommodations than anything inside the crowded fort. And it was also considerably more comfortable than the fort's barracks, which was a nontrivial point in its favor. The fact that he would have displaced Regiment-Captain chan Skrithik if he'd located his HQ in the fort CO's offices had been another part of his thinking, although he hadn't cared to discuss it with the regiment-captain himself. Rof chan Skrithik had amply proved his right to that command and to those offices, and chan Geraith wasn't going to step on that right.

In addition to any considerations of common courtesy, there was a potentially delicate point of authority involved. Although chan Skrithik was a serving officer in the Imperial Ternathian Army, from which he'd been seconded to his present duty, he held his command as an officer of the Portal Authority Armed Forces, not the ITA. It had been made clear to all concerned that the local PAAF units came under chan Geraith's command—and would come under Corps-Captain chan Rowlan's command when 5th Corps' commanding officer arrived—but the PAAF was still a separate military entity. Its standing units would almost certainly be folded into the unified Imperial Sharonian Army which must inevitably emerge from the new political structure. Until that happened, however, it was incumbent upon an Imperial *Ternathian* Army officer to tread carefully, and not simply—or even primarily—because of the Portal Authority's sensitivities. Despite the surface calm being reported from Tajvana, Emperor Zindel's relationship with Chava Busar remained as... fraught as ever—probably even more so, given the violence Busar's matrimonial plans had suffered—and the Uromathian was no doubt searching every nook and cranny for some fresh reason to take umbrage. As such, it behooved chan Geraith to be more cautious than ever about appearing to overreach.

At the moment, he had a remarkably good relationship with Sunlord Markan and Windlord Garsal, which he intended to keep that way, but neither they nor the units of the Imperial Uromathian Army they commanded had been placed under his orders. They'd been ordered to cooperate with *chan Skrithik*, and they'd been specifically placed under the PAAF officer's command—as a PAAF officer—for the defense of *Fort Salby*, but their exact relationship with chan Geraith, chan Rowlan, or the ITA had been left completely undefined. Which was why they, as well as chan Skrithik, had been invited to the present meeting in the most scrupulously courteous fashion and as allies, not subordinates.

Now Markan smiled ever so slightly—an enormous concession from a senior Uromathian officer in the presence of Ternathians—and shook his head.

"You may be surprised he has not decided to relieve you, Division-Captain, but I am not. And while what I understand about your intentions could certainly be described as...audacious, I believe they fall somewhat short of insanely reckless, despite any apprehensions you may cherish about your potential madness."

"I appreciate your courtesy, Sunlord," chan Geraith replied, careful, as always, to use his aristocratic title rather than his military rank, "but I'm not sure how *far* short of 'insanely reckless' my current brainstorm actually is."

"I have observed from my study of military history that the difference between insane recklessness and inspired genius is often difficult to parse. Unfortunately, only time will tell us which way future historians will describe your current intentions," Markan observed, and chan Geraith chuckled.

The Uromathian was almost certainly correct about that, he reflected. Fortunately, the Ternathian tradition was to encourage officers to utilize their own best judgment and to think for themselves, and audacity—or at least a willingness to run calculated risks—in the accomplishment of their missions was expected of them. In this case, however, the risk he was running was impossible to quantify, far less calculate, ahead of time, and the gaping holes in his information about the other side and its capabilities only underscored that difficulty.

He glanced down the table at Battalion-Captain chan Gayrahn. The youthful Bernithian was working hard to improve their knowledge and understanding of the Arcanans. Many of the POWs who'd been moved farther up-chain after Prince Janaki's arrival at Fort Salby had since been returned to Traisum, now that it was securely held. The others had continued their journey towards Sharona, but it had been evident to chan Geraith—and approved by higher authority—that it was essential at least some of them be kept where chan Gayrahn and the Voices and Mind Speakers available to the 3rd Dragoons could work with them. The men at the sharp end of the sword needed the best available information as quickly as they could get it, and quite a few useful nuggets had already emerged from the Talent-assisted interrogations.

A lot of what chan Gayrahn was learning about the Arcanan military, or about the Andaran culture which seemed to permeate that military, at least, seemed hopelessly at odds with the Arcanans' observed actions, however. Indeed, quite a few of their prisoners flatly refused to believe Sharonian claims about how the rest of their military had conducted itself. They were less inclined to reject the notion that the Union of Arcana had reacted to the initial clash between itself and Sharona by launching an attack, but they indignantly denied that the Arcanan Army would have been guilty of simply shooting civilians out of hand. Chan Geraith ought to have found that at least somewhat reassuring, and yet...

I wish I had a copy of these "Kerellian Accords" they keep talking about, he thought now, moodily. *However much I hate to admit it to any one else, I can actually understand how a military force with no equivalent of Voices might be do whatever it took to shut down our Voices. For that matter, it's hard to see how they had any other choice, and it fits exactly with* Sharonian *military policy before the protocols for shutting down the Voice Talent were devised. It's a bit difficult to demonize them for doing exactly what our ancestors did, especially when they don't have any Voices of their own or any way* short *of shooting them to neutralize them.*

Of course, the fact that those protocols had been available for well over fifteen hundred years meant it had been a while since any Sharonian military organization had found itself in the quandary the Arcanans currently faced. It was unreasonable to expect even the minority of Sharonians who studied such ancient history in the first place to let present day Arcanan "atrocities" pass simply because their own great-great-whatever-grandparents had done the same thing seventy or eighty generations ago, and he expected public opinion back home to demand accountability and punishment. For that matter, chan Geraith wasn't exactly prepared to give the Arcanans a pass himself. Yet what worried him much more was the Arcanan commander's refusal to return any Sharonian POWs taken before his repulse here in Traisum.

From Regiment-Captain chan Skrithik's reports about the magical translating ability of their crystals, it seemed likely that Arcanan interrogators must have already gotten any vitally important military information their prisoners might have had. That was what bothered chan Geraith. If Commander of Two Thousand Harshu wasn't hanging on to them for the intelligence they could still provide him, logic suggested he was hanging on to them because of the intelligence they might have provided to *chan Geraith.* There were all sorts of things Harshu's enemies might have found it useful to know about the Arcanans, and it was reasonable to assume he'd prefer they didn't find out what those things were. Yet it was also possible there were things Harshu didn't want his enemies to know about how the forces under his command had dealt with the survivors of the Sharonian units they'd overrun on their way to Fort Salby.

And it's also *possible you're indulging your own paranoia*, he reminded himself. *The fact that the bastards killed Crown Prince Janaki's likely to predispose you to think the worst of them in every conceivable way, now isn't it? And if it makes* you *feel that way, what do you think it's going to do to all the men under your command when they find Arcanans in their sights?*

"At least we have all of the division as far forward as Salym, Sir," Regiment-Captain chan Kymo pointed out.

"Yes, we have," Brigade-Captain chan Kartan said rather sourly, and chan Geraith grinned at him.

"Someone has to mind the store here in Traisum, Shodan, and you're already on the spot. Don't worry too much about it, though. When the Twenty-First gets here, Division-Captain chan Jassian will be taking over Traisum. He's got more manpower than a dragoon brigade to begin with, and given all of the Bisons we poached off of him to get the Third on its way, he wouldn't have the mobility for his entire division to keep up with us, anyway."

Chan Khartan's nod might have been just a tad short on enthusiasm, but he knew he didn't really have a lot of room to complain. He'd still be on the road to the Renaiyrton wharves in plenty of time to catch up with the division's spearhead. Assuming chan Geraith's entire strategy didn't come crashing down in ruins, of course.

"I know you'd like to come along with us as well, Regiment-Captain," the division-captain said now, glancing down the table to where Rof chan Skrithik sat. Taleena waited on the sturdy perch erected for her, motionless with the patient stillness people unfamiliar with imperial Ternathian peregrines always found profoundly unnatural. "Unfortunately, Fort Salby's your command responsibility."

"I understand, Sir," chan Skrithik replied, and chan Geraith was fairly confident the regiment-captain really did.

It had to be galling for chan Skrithik—and, for that matter, Markan and Garsal—to be left behind after they'd fought so magnificently to hold Salby in the first place. But neither chan Khartan's dragoons nor the infantry brigade which would relieve them here sometime in the next three or four weeks was going to be staying in Traisum. Assuming chan Geraith's plans worked, chan Khartan would be following the 12th Dragoons and the rest of Renyl chan Quay's 1st Brigade down the Kelsayr Chain quite soon now. Chan Jassian's 21st Infantry Division would also be moving out—probably very rapidly indeed—down a rather different axis of advance sometime in the next two or three months, and there were still all those nasty political considerations to bear in mind. Chan Geraith couldn't very well order chan Skrithik to join the advance from Traisum without taking Markan and Garsal along as well, unless he wanted to offer the Uromathian emperor a mortal insult by depriving his personnel of the honor of the advance after they'd fought so gallantly at chan Skrithik's side. But neither could he let them come along without offering Chava an equally useful pretext for taking offense by taking Uromathian units under Ternathian command without prior approval.

Why can't at least part of this frigging operation be at least remotely simple? he wondered. *For that matter, why can't the Arcanans be the only opposition I need to worry about?*

"In the meantime," he continued more briskly, "I'm rather relieved by the reports from Battalion-Captain chan Yahndar, Master Yanusa-Mahrdissa and Master Banchu. I especially like Yanusa-Mahrdissa's plans for getting heavy equipment forward, and we damned well should have thought about sending chan Yahndar the Mules from the get-go."

A grimace of disgust accompanied the second half of his last sentence as he castigated himself once more for not having had the same thought in time. Mostly, he supposed, because he'd been so focused on the Bisons and their massive towing capacity, but he still ought to—

"We should have thought of that, Sir," Regiment-Captain chan Isail agreed in the overly respectful tone he saved for times when his superior was being unreasonable with someone else... or himself. "Except, of course, for the minor fact that while we were planning this entire movement at Fort Emperor Erthain no one expected them to get forward as quickly as they have. *I* certainly didn't, and neither did Therahk." Chan Geraith's chief of staff nodded in Regiment-Captain chan Kymo's direction. "Neither did Corps-Captain chan Rowlan or anyone on *his* staff, now that I think about it." He shrugged slightly. "We put this entire deployment together so quickly it's a wonder our *organic* transport units got forward with us more or less in order, much less any of the QMG's attachments. For that matter, all the movement arrangements up-chain from here are *still* a little... chaotic," he added dryly, and despite himself, chan Geraith snorted at the massive understatement.

"I like Yanusa-Mahrdissa's suggestions, too, Sir," Regiment-Captain chan Serahlyk put in. "At the same time, I'd really like to pull out the Hundred and Twenty-Third and take them across to New Ternath. Chan Hurmahl's going to need all the help he can get."

"Agreed. But he's got Yanusa-Mahrdissa's work crews, not to mention the crews Master Banchu will be moving across. That's a lot of skilled manpower and equipment, Lyskar, and it's equally important that we keep the Arcanans' attention fixed here on Fort Salby. The more dust you and your people kick up preparing for us to either advance from here or go over onto the defensive and dig in as deeply as possible, the better."

The dark-complexioned engineer didn't look particularly convinced by the division-captain's logic, but he didn't raise any further objection...for the moment, at least. Chan Geraith was prepared to settle for that. Chan Serahlyk's engineers were occupied very obviously further improving the approach roads to the Traisum Cut. They were also building a truly impressive encampment for the thousands upon thousands of infantry who were clearly en route to Traisum. Only a handful of the Arcanans' eagle-lions were getting through the portal these days, but a trickle still seeped past the defenders on a semiregular basis. Chan Geraith hoped their masters were enjoying whatever reconnaissance they were bringing back, and he was perfectly happy to use their recon capabilities against them by giving them all sorts of preparatory activity to see right here in Traisum.

And, of course, if his hopefully brilliant flanking maneuver blew up as spectacularly as it had the potential to blow up, they might just end up actually needing all of chan Serahlyk's preparation work here in Traisum after all.

So far, however, none of the wheels had come off. Or not any that he knew about, at any rate. The delays in Voice transmissions to and from Sharona imposed by the water barriers in Haysam and Reyshar were sufficiently irritating, was one reason he was so profoundly grateful chan Rowlan's HQ had moved as far forward as Camryn. Bottlenecks in transportation were likely to keep the corps commander in that universe for at least another month or two, unsnarling the endless snafus which were inevitable when such a massive troop movement was undertaken on so little notice. It was unlikely he'd be moving any farther down-chain until at least one of his two infantry divisions could come up, but the Voice chain meant he and chan Geraith were in effective communication. It took only a few hours for messages to be transmitted as far as Camryn, which made it even more frustrating that it had taken the better part of nine *days* for chan Yahndar's report from the other side of Traisum's Vandor Ocean to reach him.

Don't complain, he told himself sternly. *If the Authority hadn't already brought up and assembled the relay boats it would take a hell of a lot longer than that!*

That observation didn't make the delay a lot more palatable, although he knew he would have been much unhappier if it hadn't been true. The Portal Authority had shipped forward a half-dozen of its prefabricated small, extremely fast steamships to shuttle Voices back and forth to get them into range of one another. The relay "boats" displaced almost two thousand tons, so they weren't exactly tiny, but they consisted of remarkably little besides fuel bunkers, boilers, and engines, and those engines were twin-shaft turbines, not the more fuel efficient reciprocating engines TTE's *Voyagers* used. That gave them a top speed of almost thirty-five knots in calm sea conditions, but not even that fleetness made the vast, wave-tumbled wilderness of the North Vandor in winter any narrower.

Still, the messages did get through, and chan Yahndar and Yanusa-Mahrdissa seemed to have matters under control. Chan Geraith felt his own nerves itching to move forward to the New Ternath side of the Vandor, but—like chan Rowlan in Camryn—he was far better employed where he was, at least for the moment. It was his responsibility to coordinate the movement of the rest of the 3rd Dragoons to Kelsayr; this was the best place for him to do that coordinating, and there'd be plenty of time to relocate his HQ before young chan Mahsdyr reached Thermyn.

Assuming he does reach Thermyn, of course. And that he doesn't get spotted after he gets there. And that we're able to get the rest *of the division up to him without being spotted. And that we're able to pounce on Fort Ghartoun and take it before Harshu reacts. And—*

He made himself stop worrying at all the things that could still go wrong like a terrier worrying a dead rat. There wasn't a thing in the world he could do to prevent any of them from happening, if that was what the gods had decided to allow. So it made a lot more sense to concentrate on getting the parts he *could* control right and hope that someday history would confirm Sunlord Markan's diagnosis of "inspired genius."

CHAPTER TWENTY-EIGHT

Darikhal 31, 5053 AE
(January 19, 1929 CE)

LARAKESH CITY, ON THE SHARONAN SIDE OF THE PORTAL to New Sharona, wasn't a place to be. "Being" was too stagnant a verb to describe anything in Larakesh. The portal city in the birth universe of Sharonan civilization was all movement.

Trans-Temporal Express Director Tyamish had offices somewhere in the space between all the rail lines, but Larakesh's schedule—her beating heart—was in the keeping of her hand-picked stationmasters.

The mass of train tracks running in and out both sides of the portal bristled off into dozens of yards with cars waiting for engines and full loads waiting for their timeslots to run hurtling down-portal to New Sharona, Haysam, and beyond. Larakesh the city had given way entirely to the needs of Sharona's TTE railways, and Port-of-Larakesh extended the massive rail yard of a city out to the Ylani Sea, an ocean port almost as busy as Portal City Center itself. The deadhead trains once sent empty or nearly so down-chain were deadheading no more. Instead, troops assembled and marched aboard transports bound for the outer universes. Supply cars with weaponry, munitions, and food fitted into every available siding, with shunters busy shuffling the cars as needed to keep the portal tracks hot with constant traffic.

Stationmaster Rinlin Torrash all but tore his hair out at the latest request from TTE, and he didn't have very much hair left to spare.

"Whales now? *Whales!*" He stabbed a finger at the train priority list. "I have troop transports to work in and supplies!

Entire doubleheaded heavy loads to send down-chain, and who is this lady?"

"Cetacean ambassador," Fadar Shelthara supplied. Shelthara was the current shift freight manager for Larakesh Central, which made him effectively Torrash's second in command. "Very important woman. Kingdom of Shurkhal's Cetacean Institute. Skip the request from the simians if you have to, but you probably want to fit in at least a few cars for the whale lady."

"You sure about that, Fadar?" Torrash pointed at the now empty tin of honeynuts in the outer bay. "That Mr. Monkey Man bribed the stevedores, and you know we can't get a darn thing done without the stevedores. They'll be putting aquarium cars on the lines with potted banana trees and gorillas in them if I insist on granting all the cetacean requests and none of the simians'."

"They were good snacks." Shelthara acknowledged. "You don't suppose he'll drop by with some more if we expedite, do you?"

That earned him the snarl he'd expected.

"No one bribes the TTE in this office!"

"Of course not." Shelthara didn't point out the sugar crystals on Torrash's shirtfront. "Just wondering is all, Boss. Very tasty they were, very tasty."

Torrash snapped his fingers, coming to a decision. "I'll give 'em the Uromathian slots. That's enough space for both of 'em for the moment."

"And when the Uromathian troops show up?" Shelthara asked.

"Thirty-two percent!" Torrash slapped the table. "I had plans and loading documents all worked out, and their last troop train mustered with only thirty-two percent of the scheduled load out."

"They'll have to be coming later though, right?" Shelthara did insist on bringing up the human issues behind the headaches in Torrash's life. The trains planned for Uromathian units and their supplies hadn't been light because someone packed exceptionally well. They'd been light because the units had been so badly understrength, and the ones who *had* reported had been equipped but not particularly well supplied. It'd surely play hell with the Sharonan Empire's military logistics down-chain, but for the moment, Torrash had made the best of it and slotted in available cars of Ternathian Army supplies to make up weight for what the assigned engines could pull.

The Windlord arriving with yesterday's Uromathian troop

transport concerned Torrash. The man had clearly expected to meet up with more men and supplies here at Larakesh. It'd been all Torrash could do to convince him to keep to his transport time and go with the assigned engine at least as far as Haysam. At least a Windlord was senior enough to understand the value of keeping the logistics lines as smooth as they could be when subjected to volumes of transport so much greater than the portal could easily manage. Of course, there was the little matter that the Uromathian *commander* in question had expected more troops. If their logistical planning was so bad their own officers didn't know what was really on its way…

Portals were a chokepoint—as simple as that—and Larakesh's portal was the Sharona side of the most developed and populous Sharonan universe at the top of the long chain. Everyone knew that—or damned well ought to—and it bothered Torrash that the man's reaction to missing troops had been a desire to turn straight around and head back to his corner of the Uromathian Empire with all the troops he *did* have instead of proceeding to the reporting location.

The Larakesh track was red-hot for the duration of the war, as far as Torrash was concerned, and he wasn't about to let track be wasted on deadheading.

One of TTE's stevedores—Ratatello Dolphar—beat a fist against the door to get their attention and then stuck his head in.

"Thought you'd want to know, the Voicenet just announced the election results. We've got us a parliament to go with our empire now. Gorda's got a list of all the reps if you want to see. He's going to paste it up on the staff board. But let's see. Fadar, you're from New Farnal right? You've got Kinlafia for the House of Talents, just like they said. And, Boss man, you've got Ruftuu. There's a whole group of them, the newly elected I mean, talking about forming a caucus and passing a bunch of statutes to get the supply situation for the war going more smooth-like."

"About time," Torrash grunted.

"Damn sure, Stationmaster." Dolphar agreed. "Know what I'd like to see is more of that chan Rahool character. You see the size of the arms on that guy?" He patted his own, far from insignificant biceps. "I felt like I was a new kid having my first day on the job again when he shook hands all gingerly-like."

Shelthara laughed. "Now you know what we little office workers suffer through all the time. Women at the bars offering to hold our mugs for us 'cause our toothpick arms look too scrawny to lift 'em."

"Right." The stationmaster shook his head. Shelthara had a natural charm and never seemed to lack for female companionship. It was a source of continual amazement to the stevedore crews that the freight manager managed to do so well for himself with such a thin physique. "And excellent taste in trail food had nothing to do with the simian ambassador's charm did it?"

"Hey now." Dolphar objected. "He didn't try to give us liquor like the more mercantilist types do. That chan Rahool's a working man. He understood all about regs, and staying clearheaded while working the track. In fact he's a veteran too! Might even be returning to active service with the war, for all you know."

"Doubt it," said Shelthara. "Looked too old to me."

The three men exchanged a moment of understanding that cut across their work divisions. All of them were too old for enlistment, though Shelthara might be able to get in with the help of a recruitment officer's blind eye, so Shelthara was the one who volunteered the next tidbit.

"The guy said he wasn't much of a Voice, if you can believe it. Darn fortunate to be able to communicate across species lines and happy to have the simian ambassadorship, he said." Shelthara nodded to Dolphar. "Did he warn you he thought chimps would want to help with loading?"

"He might of said something like that. I sent him off with one of my loading crews. Said he spent the day with 'em lifting as much as anybody and asking questions the whole while. He's a quick study. He'll do plenty fine."

"You can't draft an ambassador." Torrash glared warningly at his senior day shift stevedore. "Don't even try."

Dolphar laughed. "Don't worry, Bossman. I won't try to impress anyone who can hold his own with gorillas. I know my limits."

The glint in the man's eyes hinted to Torrash and Shelthara both that Dolphar knew no such thing, but that at least his efforts to recruit the simian ambassador when next he came through wouldn't be physical. Rumor had it that the stevedores had already taken the ambassador out drinking after shift in an effort to get him to join the crews and found his tolerance far exceeded their own.

"Did your boys talk to the cetacean ambassador too?"

"Yup," said Dolphar. "That job's going to be tough. The port haulers are doing most of the work setting up the aquarium cars for us. Talked to my cousin at Port-of-Larakesh about that, but the lady'd already worked it out with him. Very efficient. Not so friendly as the simian, but I figure she's got her reasons to be glum."

They nodded. Everyone knew the story of Shaylar Nargra-Kolmayr, and while they didn't all know Cetacean Ambassador Shalassar Brintal-Kolmayr, no one had failed to make the connection once they'd heard her full name and seen the family resemblance.

A triumphant train whistle cut through their conversation, and they all paused a moment to savor it. It was 3:05 pm, and that was the steam blast of a Paladin—the mammoth workhorse engine of the TTE—set to begin her straight transit from Larakesh through the New Sharona portals direct to the Haysam coast city of Cejyo. She'd reach the enormous seaport in eighteen hours and twenty minutes, arriving at 9:25 am on the dot. Trains were a beautiful thing.

When the whistle from the departing ten thousand-ton haul cut off at the portal boundary, Torrash turned back to the two men.

"Think this Parliament will be a help for the war? That they'll actually do anything that makes sense or that it'll just be people making decisions about stuff they don't really understand?"

"Can't say. But I hope they know what they're doing," Dolphar said, grimly.

Shelthara puffed up his chest. "We've got Darcel Kinlafia in office. He's not a railroad man, but he's been out as far as the lines go. He'll make sure they don't go making decisions in Parliament that are better made at the railhead—or the *trail*head for that matter. I bet you he backs TTE on everything we need and pushes the rest of the reps to get the Army what *it* needs. We'll be winning those lost universes back in no time once we get enough troops and guns down-chain."

"Everything's pretty hard to muster. We need some more signalmen further down track. And lay crews—lots of lay crews from what I hear." Torrash mused.

"Figure TTE's asking them for everything we need?" Dolphar asked.

"I imagine so, but who's to say." Shelthara looked questioningly at Torrash.

"The director's on it. Don't worry that the emperor isn't being asked. Might not prioritize us as high as we'd like, but you can be sure Director Tyamish's talking to the Privy Council regular and probably even plans on meeting with the Parliament as soon as they sort themselves out in committees and all."

"News says some of the representatives are forming advisory staffs. You interested, Boss?" Shelthara asked, "Wanna go meet your Parliamentary Representative?"

"Not one bit, Fadar. We've got too much work to do here. Tell you what though, you slot in the cetaceans and the simians like I said, and send off to the ambassadors so they know when to have their cars ready. The bit the Cetacean ambassador included about feed cars is a real good idea. You might drop a note about that to the big guy with the gorillas. I imagine a gorilla's going to want to eat more than the dining cars usually stock. And warn the stations down-chain about all the unusuals coming. Especially the portal junctions near the ocean need to be warned about the cetaceans. They don't all have rails that go all the way to the ports. I'm not sure what the whales are planning on and I don't want any cetaceans dying on our watch."

"Sure it won't come to that, Boss," Shelthara said.

"You're damn right it won't, and that's 'cause we aren't going to let it."

"Do you think we need to report to somebody about the military trains that've been coming in light?"

"Already wrote it up for Director Tyamish, but you go ahead and write to Parliament about it, if you like. This isn't proprietary or anything you need to keep quiet on noticing."

"Good," said Dolphar, who'd been listening quietly for the last few minutes. "I'd wondered about that Windlord. My sister's boys signed up. I don't want their commanders finding out the reinforcements're light only when the trains arrive."

"Right." The stationmaster acknowledged the stevedore and with a furrowed brow added, "And Fadar?"

"Yes, Boss?"

"Better tell the Voice to make sure he passes it along in the next transmission window, too. Hadn't thought to tell the down-chain military channels about it. Gotta remember to do that now, too, along with updating the stationmasters. Remind me."

"Will do, Boss. Will do."

*   *   *

The Seneschal of Othmaliz took the election, the war effort, and the entire mess of recent events less well than the men at the Larakesh TTE office. His Eminence considered the entirety of it a bitter draught to be endured while he worked to put in motion all the events his pride demanded for a proper resolution to the situation in Tajvana.

A middle-aged Bergahldian lay brother had managed to win election to a seat in the region of Othmaliz immediately outside Tajvana, but that was the extent of their electoral success. Too many of the locals were besotted with the Ternathian prince's sacrifice and the old pageantry of the Calirath family's return to their ancestral seat.

The print news was even calling the Crown Princess Andrin a beautiful bride—a depiction Faroayn Raynarg found personally offensive. He preferred his women small and delicate. The princess' sheer height appalled and repelled him, although it would never do to admit that was because she also intimidated him. Andrin was irritatingly mannish in appearance, he'd decided. The new Crown Prince Consort Howan Fai, all dressed up and looking absolutely delighted with her, in spite of standing significantly shorter than Raynarg, made it even worse. The Seneschal despised them all.

That creepy bird she insisted on bringing everywhere, and the wedding! The disgraceful demand for his services with no notice and no consideration for his status! The Caliraths were beyond vulgar. It was settled.

But his spies were doing good work. A lot of the information was actually coming from his new dear friend, Chava Busar, but Raynarg didn't let that concern him. Uromathia was far away; the Caliraths—curse them—were right here. Ternathia had owned Tajvana before and unless he struck soon, the Caliraths might very well rule *his* capital again.

Chava's tendency to tell him what to do and how to use the Order of Bergahl annoyed him, but Raynarg only needed his help to get rid of the Ternathian emperor. After that, he could have his palace back and return everything to the status quo he'd enjoyed before the Caliraths' arrival.

He did acknowledge that Chava was right on one point. It was important to choose his target carefully and then focus his resources to accomplish a proper terror-inducing, successful strike. Then the crowds would be remember who the true power in Tajvana was. And that, Raynarg knew from old experience, would make the second, third, and fifteenth strike so much more successful. But Chava didn't appreciate the true nature of the threat . . . or the proper way to deal with it. No, he was positively *obsessed* with Zindel, Zindel, Zindel—as if there weren't another Calirath in the entire multiverse!

The hints, oh so many hints! Chava made Raynarg's head throb with his endlessly repeated hints, his focus on one hard and fast attack on Zindel. He never actually said it in so many words, of course . . . just as he never admitted his insistence stemmed from fear. He wanted to destroy their opposition in a single strike, before Zindel could see it coming, because he was afraid of what Zindel might do if he somehow survived that strike. A part of the Seneschal could recognize the Uromathian's logic, but however reasonable Chava's caution might sound in the palace, in his own temples, it tasted excessive.

Well, the emperor could drop all the hints he liked; the Seneschal had his own choices to make. He agreed that his true enemy was Emperor Zindel. But he wanted the man to suffer.

Zindel couldn't die until he was broken. The Seneschal wouldn't allow it. He'd seen the arrogance of Ternathia drain right out of the Winged Crown with the news of Prince Janaki's death was confirmed and he was determined to see it again. And again and again and *again.* That, and only that, was the price he would exact for Zindel's sins against Tajvana.

He would have preferred to start with little Anbessa and slit the throats of each Calirath, from youngest to oldest. Unfortunately, the two younger grand princesses rarely left the palace. That made reaching them . . . difficult, and Janaki was already dead. Raynarg regretted that. Satisfying as Zindel's reaction to his son's death had been, that reaction hadn't come from the Seneschal's own hand. That would have been *so* much better! And since he couldn't have that, he longed to embrace the pattern, instead, and kill each heir, one by one. He allowed himself a delightful moment imagining the horror in Emperor Zindel's eyes when his youngest daughter was finally made crown princess after losing all three of her older siblings.

But there were limits in all things, he reminded himself, and the Caliraths' security was too tight for the sweet, extended revenge he craved. And he didn't truly need it, when all was said.

It was all too probable that he'd have to restrict himself to a single attack, yet one would be enough if it was executed properly. Even if it fell somewhat short of his heart's true desire, it would be enough to send them packing. After all, the Caliraths had left Tajvana once before. If they left again, Chava Busar could see to the rest of the Calirath brats elsewhere. The Seneschal would wish him success, and perhaps he'd loan the Uromathian some muscle, just as Chava had done for him.

When it came down to it, the Seneschal considered himself a reasonable man. He only wanted back his palace, his city, and the adulation he deserved from the people of Tajvana.

*   *   *

"Show me."

Acolyte Raka pointed at the muddy, pier-spined inlet. The Ylani Strait running through the center of Tajvana had many of these side waterways, and Drindel Usar knew what the Bergahldian wanted.

He'd been Calling for hours to get his creatures in range, yet these weren't their normal waters. The temperature wasn't completely horrible, but it should have been much warmed and there were nowhere near enough fish.

Another Uromathian padded along beside Raka's group of Bergahldian toughs. Drindel didn't recognize his countryman, but he knew from the man's stance that this was another Talent trained up for Service, and he refocused on Calling, lest he make a bad impression on a likely senior.

He got a very small toothy shark pup to come to the surface. It wanted to be a man-eater one day, but it was only about three feet long so far. And from its starved length, it would never grow to four feet. The creature would die within the week unless someone fed it, and Drindel didn't have access to enough raw meat or fish to make a difference. At least the cold would dull its senses somewhat.

Raka grunted and led the group mercifully back away from the water.

That night Drindel took a risk and contacted his assigned handler with a simple coded message. He wanted to say, "This place is colder than a cutcha's privates, with less fish than a desert stream. I'm a Talent, not *Arcunas*. Send me home and let's do this in the summer, when there's enough warmth for algae to bloom, fish to school, and sharks to fill the whole Ylani with shore-to-shore fins!" But he only had code, so all he could send was: "Now. Water cold. Few shark. Small shark. Hungry. Give three month. Many shark. Big shark."

The answer came back. "Understood. Stop contact. Will inform if directions change."

Drindel was relieved. Sometimes his handlers were less than understanding about the physical limits of nature. It was good to have a reasonable one; his fellow Talent must have made a good report on him. They were finally taking the details of the Calling Talent seriously!

In a ledger in a small room deep inside Uromathia, Drindel Usar's name had a small mark added next to it. At the bottom of the page, that mark had a notation: "Weak Talent. Expendable."

CHAPTER TWENTY-NINE

Molidyr 2, 206 YU
Cormas 5, 5053 AE
(January 24, 1929 CE)

COMMANDER OF ONE THOUSAND TAYRGAL CARTHOS SNARLED behind his goggles as his command dragon spiraled earthward. The pilot was too busy looking down to notice Carthos' expression and there were no other passengers to see it, since he'd deliberately flown ahead of the main body of his once independent command. His subordinates could oversee the rest of the movement, and he'd decided it would be better for him to meet Mayrkos Harshu with as few witnesses as possible. He doubted the upcoming interview would do anything to improve his relations with the AEF's commander, whatever happened, and it might be wise to not have any of his subordinates or aides where they might inadvertently offer... unfortunate responses to questions. Better to get the lay of the land so he could brief them on how best to characterize their independent operations in the Nairsom-Kelsayr chain.

Their *abortive* independent operations, he thought bitterly. He remained far from certain why Harshu had diverted him to that long, roundabout advance, but however hard he'd tried, he'd been unable to think of a single *good* reason for it. There'd never been any real point from a strategic perspective, even if he'd managed to secure every universe from Nairsom to Kelsayr, given the water gap in Traisum itself. Without ships, getting across the Treybus Ocean—especially in winter!—would have been flatly impossible, even assuming they *had* managed to take the entire chain and been able to maintain a supply line through it. That had been obvious to Carthos from the moment he'd received his orders.

But it had to have been equally evident to *Harshu* before the two thousand sent him off anyway, and he'd never provided the support a serious advance through four universes would have required. In fact, he'd proceeded to starve Carthos of even minimal supplies on the pretext that his own advance required everything the AATC could haul. If not that excuse, he would've found another, Carthos thought with a fresh surge of anger. He was sure of it, the only question in his mind was why Harshu had shoved him down a useless rathole and then jammed a cork into it behind him.

They'd never liked each other, but this went further than that. He'd pushed Carthos aside, cut him out of any hope for glory, and picked that Air Force prick Toralk to share the spotlight with him. And there'd been something else, something in Harshu's manner that went beyond anything so simple as dislike. It got a lot closer to scorn, possibly even contempt, and Carthos had found himself wondering if Harshu had somehow discovered the financial transactions between himself and the Mythalan banking interests. The ones Nith mul Gurthak had helped arrange.

It wasn't as if Tayrgal Carthos were the only Army officer to have skated around the edges of legally allowable loan agreements, but he'd dipped far deeper into those prohibited waters than the majority of his fellows. Worse, the fact that he had gave mul Gurthak a degree of leverage that was...unfortunate. Carthos would have shed no tears over any unpleasantness which befell these Sharonian bastards under any circumstances, but mul Gurthak had made it clear he wanted the gloves to come completely off from the very beginning. Carthos knew the same suggestions had been made to Harshu himself, but mul Gurthak had been more subtle—or perhaps cautious—in the way he'd approached his fellow two thousand. In many ways, Carthos had enjoyed watching the Mythalan manipulate Harshu, maneuver him into deciding on his own to give Alivar Neshok his head. However little Carthos might like dancing to mul Gurthak's tune himself, seeing a man he detested—and who he knew detested him in return—abandon his high and mighty principles and unknowingly put his entire career into the hands of someone like mul Gurthak had been gratifying.

The fact that his own career was already in mul Gurthak's hands had been a less pleasing thought, and the Mythalan had been less delicate in his approach to Carthos. His "suggestions" had amounted to scarcely veiled orders delivered outside official channels, and while Carthos would have been inclined in the same direction himself, there'd been no question about how far mul Gurthak wanted him to go. Nor had there been any question about what mul Gurthak intended to happen to Harshu in the end. Carthos didn't know *why* the Mythalan had decided to destroy Mayrkos Harshu, but he'd recognized the noose tightening around the other officer.

Harshu had appeared oblivious to the threat, but over the last month or so, Carthos had begun to wonder if he truly had been. If he hadn't, if he'd seen this coming all along, and if he'd realized Carthos was effectively mul Gurthak's creature...

The dragon spiraled lower, the flat, brown terrain below taking on texture, and the sheer, knife-sharp cliffs of the portal located near where the Shendisfalian city of Tayrmek ought to be rose before them. Carthos tightened his seat belt for the landing and worked on getting his expression under control. Whatever Harshu's reason for diverting him from the main advance, the arrogant bastard had changed his mind after his own operations turned into an unmitigated cluster fuck. His losses in the thoroughly bitched up assault on Fort Salby had compelled him to recall Carthos, but the tone of his orders had scarcely been anything one might call cordial. No, whatever else happened, Tayrgal Carthos hadn't been summoned to Karys to give him an opportunity to shine. Somehow—he wasn't sure how, but he was certain Harshu would find a way—he'd be shoved aside again, denied the chance to acquire any credit.

Yet there might be a bright spot after all, he told himself, leaning back as the dragon's powerful legs reached for the ground. Given how completely Harshu had fucked up, his own relief was inevitable, probably sooner rather than later. And that arse-kisser Toralk would be tarred with the same brush. He'd have to go, too, and he was junior to Carthos, anyway. Which meant all Carthos had to do was bide his time, watch his back, keep his own skirts clean, and the command would almost certainly devolve upon him in the end. For that matter, as much as he resented—and feared—mul Gurthak's power over him, that very relationship might act in his favor. Carthos still hadn't figured out what mul Gurthak's real motives might be, but he rather suspected the

Mythalan would prefer to have someone he could...strongly and directly influence in Harshu's place.

I can wait, arsehole, he thought, glaring in the direction of the encampment where Harshu awaited him. *I've waited this long, and I can wait a little longer. Because in the end, mul Gurthak's going to put the blocks to you and I'll be standing on the edge of the pit while you slide straight down to the dragon.*

*   *   *

Commander of Five Thousand Pardinar Rukkar wasn't exactly looking forward to this meeting.

His old friend Thankhar Olderhan had been stalking Portalis, white-lipped and vibrating with fury for days, but Rukkar had to acknowledge his longtime comrade had kept up with every one of his duties despite his inchoate rage. The work of governing an entire planet didn't stop just because the Union was at war. Or because his heir was on trial. None of which had made Olderhan's task one bit easier, of course.

As he followed the liveried footman in Garth Showma's colors down the hallway, the five thousand made a mental note to treat the duke gently.

The footman reached the door to the duke's private study and rapped once, sharply, on the frame. Then he opened the door.

"Your Grace, Five Thousand Rukkar," he announced.

"Show him in, by all means, Larsu!" Olderhan's deep voice replied.

The duke rose to greet his guest, reaching out to clasp forearms as Rukkar entered the study, and despite his own mood, the five thousand smiled in familiar amusement at the contrast between them. Thankhar Olderhan looked every inch the Andaran duke he was, and Rukkar...didn't. A small ruddy-featured man, the five thousand looked as if his first ancestor had been decanted by Mythalan magisters expressly as the first rider of the first dragon—which was fitting. Rukkars had been flying Andaran dragons almost as long as Olderhans had been commanding Andaran armies.

And that was why Sir Pardinar Rukkar had been chosen to run the investigation into the shit storm with the yellow. He'd sent updates over the last several days, but he'd come to deliver a summary of the final report in person.

Now he lowered himself heavily into a well-worn leather chair at the duke's gesture and drew a deep breath as he prepared to do that delivering.

"Thankhar, it's a mess," he said frankly, skipping any honey coating preamble. "I know it's to be expected, given what it takes for this kind of cluster-fuck to happen, but—" He grimaced. "There're going to be people who'll never believe my report, and I don't know as I'll blame them. For about the first twenty-four hours, I thought it was a clear-cut case. Stupidity all 'round—but simple. And I still think it is, really. But then things got a lot less clear-cut."

Olderhan leaned back in his own chair, listening but certain he wasn't going to like what came next.

"A hundred with Mythal Air Expeditionaries took full credit for sending one of my boys still in flight training out to scare off the crowd in front of your offices. Someone'd told them you'd asked for assistance with a riot. The boy needed saddle time, so this Hundred mul Belftus gave him the mission.

"So far so good, I thought at that point. But when my investigator asked mul Belftus where the hummer was who'd brought that request message from you, the hundred died."

"He *what*?" Olderhan jerked upright in his own chair, and Rukkar winced. There was no easy way to explain the oddities of the report.

"His heart, the healers said." He threw up his hands. "And it gets worse. My boy flying that yellow—I know he was a fool to take the mission, but before that he was shaping into an excellent flier. He was a third-generation Andaran pilot, and he'd been flying retired transports at home since his arms were long enough to reach the controls. I had to write his parents a letter. He never woke up."

"From a *crowd control* spell?" Olderhan wasn't taking this nearly as calmly as Rukkar could have wished.

"Two blasts from peacekeeper staffs at focused max power." He corrected. "Unusual, but not unheard of for that to be fatal."

"Even at that range with him at least partially shielded by a dragon's body?" Thankhar shook his head disbelievingly.

"I know," Rukkar said. "If I hadn't been running this investigation, I'd be a skeptic myself. But for any other explanation, I'd have to believe someone walked into the hospital and shot the boy with a daggerstone at exactly the same angle as he'd been hit by your retainers. Angles," he corrected himself. "It'd need to be two shots to the same spots. It's ridiculous."

Thankhar Olderhan looked at him, his expression absolutely blank, and Rukkar raised an admonishing index finger.

"Don't be thinking that, Thankhar. People're stupid far more often than they're wicked. Mythalans do things like gassing their field hands if they try to riot. We'd never do it, but to someone like mul Belftus, it wouldn't have seemed so outrageous under the circumstances."

"Slaves, Rukkar." Olderhan spoke through gritted teeth. "They gas their *garthan* slaves and do it for revolts, not riots."

"You know what I mean." Rukkar regretted mentioning the Mythalan practices.

"And I never sent a hummer," Thankhar said. "None of my Portalis staff sent a hummer. None of the Garth Showma Househummers left their coops within four hours of that dragon's arrival."

"Maybe someone on your staff forgot to log it, or—"

"No, I'm telling you a message was never sent!"

"Old friend, I understand," Rukkar said, "but there's no proof of that. You weren't at home yourself until afterwards, so you can't swear to it of your own knowledge. And no one's staff would have the clearest recollection of what happened after that kind of surprise."

"You don't believe me." The look in Olderhan's eyes was not friendly.

"That's not what I said." Rukkar tried to calm him. "I only said there's no proof, and I have a sworn statement from Hundred mul Belftus that *someone* sent him a hummer. And there's a note in his office log that he *did* receive one. You say you didn't send it, and I know you too well to think you'd say that if it wasn't true. But think about it. Mul Belftus' senior commo clerk—an Andaran, not a Mythalan—noted a message from someone at exactly the time mul Belftus said he'd received one, and why would anyone *fake* a message like that?"

Sir Thankhar Olderhan looked very old. "If that horror had happened, I'd look like someone who'd kill my officers' wives and sisters on a whim. I'd be a pariah, a man no one could trust, much less believe."

Rukkar shook his head. "It didn't happen."

"Only because the chief sword who manages my duty roster

decided he needed to stand a ceremonial door watch himself that morning. I usually have two *lances* in that position, Rukkar! Lances!"

Rukkar raised his hands again. "Your staff did very well. It was brilliant. Almost anyone else would've stepped inside and sealed the doors instead of shooting at the yellow's pilot."

"The same staff you believe uniformly lied to your investigators about not sending the message supposedly asking for that mission." The iciness in Olderhan's tone began to frustrate Rukkar.

"I'm not the enemy here, Thankhar!" He shook his head. "I admit the coincidence of mul Belthus and the pilot both dying like that looks odd. Maybe even suspicious. But I did my investigation, and I had the medical examiner run detailed forensic exams on both bodies. There's absolutely no evidence the hundred died of anything but natural causes, and the pilot's death was clearly the result of the crowd control spells your people hit him with—entirely justifiably, under the circumstances! It was a mess, and I'll say so. But there's no evidence of any conspiracy. Some of the MAE pilots thought a new breed of yellow had been flown in—one with a very mild breath weapon the *shakira* claim to have used on, yes, *garthan* slaves with no long-term injuries—and that that wingling was one of those. The pilot trainees who weren't picked for the flight thought it was, too."

"And was it?" Olderhan's voice was flat.

"No. But that doesn't change the fact that everyone who was on-site *thought* it was. And before you say another word, everyone in the Air Force understands how near this horror came to happening. I have a debrief with the Undersecretary for Dragon Affairs himself. We'll ensure controls are put in place so that nothing like this can ever happen again."

"You didn't have controls already?" The tone was deceptively mild.

"We damned well had controls! But the wing deputy, Hundred mul Belftus made an exception and no one questioned it because they thought the Governor of New Arcana was being assaulted *in his home* by a mob!" He winced. "And I know you weren't *actually there*, but they scrambled that mission thinking they were helping you and your family. I understand how pissed off you are, and under the circumstances, I don't blame you for questioning the likelihood of that many fuck-ups piling on top of each other. But you spent enough time in the field yourself to know crap like this *does* happen. And"—the five thousand looked his old friend straight in the eye—"there's absolutely no evidence—*none*, Thankhar—that this was anything but just that: an effort to get help to your townhouse as rapidly as possible that almost blew up in everyone's faces!"

The duke looked back for a long, silent second, then nodded minutely.

"Shartahk spare us all such 'help,'" he said, and Rukkar made an averting sign against the devil. Olderhan matched the sign, and rose to walk him out.

"Thank you for taking the time to give me the report in person," he said. "I know it wasn't a pleasant chore."

It was obvious to Rukkar that the duke wasn't about to accept his conclusions, but Olderhan's tone acknowledged that there was no evidence to support any other determination. And, if he was honest with himself, Rukkar didn't blame his old friend one bit. In fact, he was prepared to admit there was a distinct whiff of something rotten about the entire affair, but he'd taken too much testimony under lie-detection spellware. Every witness— every *surviving* witness, at any rate—said the same thing, and that was that.

"Of course I brought it in person," the five thousand said, and grinned crookedly. "Knew I *had* to bring it in person, because you'd damned well've taken the head right off anyone else I'd sent, now wouldn't you?"

The duke's lips twitched in a small, unwilling smile, and Rukkar snorted. Then, on a wall in the outer office, he spotted an old picture of himself and Olderhan as squires. Rukkar's first black lifted a wing in the background to frame the two men for the image spell capture, and the five thousand smiled more naturally and tapped the picture to draw the other man's attention to it.

"Remember my first dragon? She was a beauty, wasn't she?"

"I've never been very fond of dragons."

Rukkar shook his head. Olderhan's perspective had never been comprehensible for him.

"I love 'em," the five thousand said simply, then racked his brain for something neutral to part with. Nothing came for a moment, but then he nodded.

"Say, I received an interesting bit of correspondence from a colleague on New Mythal the other day," he said. "A man from the vos Sidus family. He served a few years as an Air Force officer a decade ago, but his family's been breeding dragons for ages. They're old money, though. No transport dragons or regular combat types for them; they do sea dragons. They call 'em drakes or hydras. Strong swimmers. A few of them fly, but mostly they're sea creatures—great for securing coasts and rivers, he says. Monsters, really, since the Mythalans breed 'em for those nasty spectator fights, but he wanted to press a proposal for the creatures to be used for military purposes. He's going to pitch 'em to the Navy. Doesn't that sound interesting?"

"I think it sounds horrible," Olderhan said. But after a pause he admitted, "Still, they might be useful, I suppose. Are they docile enough for transport?"

"I'm not so sure about that. These are fighter lines. They're worse than combat dragons. They're bred to fight each other, not just selected enemies."

"How barbarically Mythalan." Olderhan grimaced. "Do they have any officers for them?"

Rukkar shrugged. "After a fashion, but I can't say I trust any of 'em. And none of them are actual operators. The Mythalans use *garthans* with the drakes, not *shakira*—the operators often die in the gladiator shows, and no *shakira*'s signing up for *that!*—and no *shakira* would ever consider making a *garthan* an officer, either. So if we want officers with hands-on experience, we'll have to commission *garthans*, and you know how *well* that's likely to go over with Mythal. And, truth to tell, they aren't the most genteel folk to invite into an Air Force officer club."

Olderhan's lips tightened, and Rukkar shook his head.

"Don't get me wrong, Thankhar. I'm just saying that these aren't emancipated *garthans*; they're still literal slaves and the Mythalans seem to treat them like just another animal to go with the drakes. And less valuable *than* the drakes, come to that, because the drakes are at least carefully bred and trained. Not surprising the poor bastards won't come equipped with the attitudes and...call 'em social skills we expect in our officers. But Torkash knows we can't allow the *shakiras'* attitudes to spread to the Air Force, so I'm recommending to the undersecretary that if we make these into some kind of Air Force Naval Auxiliary, we have to insist on commissions for the drake riders, anyway."

Olderhan actually laughed at that. "You hate the very idea, but you're going to push them forward anyway just in case they're useful in the war effort. You're Andaran to the core, Rukkar! Sometimes I wonder about the sorts of people who want to spend so much time with dragons, but then I think of you, my friend, and I know we'll be okay. Andara's in good hands as long as five thousands like you run the Air Force."

Rukkar brushed the compliment off, but he was deeply relieved to feel back on easy footing with Olderhan again.

"That's just ground pounder jealousy because some of us get to freeze solid during the long travels and then spend our days digging latrines and building up the frontier fort while you marching lot take your sweet weeks-long promenade across perfectly flat looking ground to get to the place we have all set up for you by the time you get there," he said.

Olderhan smiled at the old joke, not as widely as Rukkar would have liked, but there was a faint smile there. Rukkar knew full well that marching over a bit of ground and flying over it were two drastically different propositions.

CHAPTER THIRTY

Molidyr 9, 206 YU
(January 31, 1929 CE)

COMMANDER OF TWO THOUSAND MAYRKOS HARSHU'S
expression was bleak as his orderly escorted the exhausted-
looking, travel-stained commander of one hundred into his
chansyu hut office. The sarkolis-crystal heater filled the office
with a comfortable warmth, but none of that warmth had leaked
into the two thousand's cold eyes.

"Hundred Thalmayr, Sir," the orderly—who could read his
two thousand's moods unerringly after so many years in his
service—announced in a somewhat flattened voice, then withdrew
as Hadrign Thalmayr braced to attention and saluted with the
stump of his right wrist. Not even the best of Gifted Healers
could regenerate a totally lost or destroyed limb.

Harshu returned the salute with a curt nod, not even glancing
at the other two officers he'd asked to join him here. He already
knew what he would see in Herak Mahrkrai's and Klayrman
Toralk's expressions. They'd read the brief hummer message
Thalmayr had sent ahead of him, and neither of them was stupid enough to miss the weasel-wording of that dispatch...or the
holes in it. Nor had they missed the fact that it had arrived less
than twenty-four hours before Thalmayr himself. Worse, they
probably understood the reasons for the tardiness of its arrival
as well as Harshu did.

The hundred's journey—flight, more accurately—from Thermyn
to Karys had begun over a month earlier. True, he'd spent much
of that time on unicornback, covering the vast distance between
Fort Ghartoun and the first of the AEF's airheads in Failcham,

but he'd still had ample opportunity to send word ahead if he'd wanted to. For that matter, he could have gotten higher priority for air transport if he'd been willing to tell Toralk's AATC station commander what had happened in Thermyn. The dispatch he'd finally written could say whatever it liked about maintaining security to prevent rumor mongering, but the truth was obvious.

He hadn't wanted anyone else to know about it before Harshu because he hoped the two thousand would protect *his* worthless arse the way he had Neshok's. That he'd wink at Thalmayr's barbarities because he'd allowed so many others. And the hundred was so concerned with covering up his own actions—and their consequences—that he didn't give a single solitary damn how much additional damage the time he'd wasted might have caused.

Well, Mayrkos, you always knew the gryphon would get loose in the henhouse sooner or later, didn't you? Not that you ever expected it to happen this *way.* His iron expression never wavered, but internally he winced. *On the other hand, you knew no plan survives contact with the enemy, too, and you ought to've borne* that *in mind while you were deciding what kind of shit you were willing to let people like Neshok get away,* he reminded himself. *Thought you could keep it from getting out of hand, did you? Sure, you knew that stinking* shakira *bastard would've just shuffled you out of the way and given the job to that arsehole Carthos, and only the gods know how much worse it would've been with* him *in command. No way you could've gotten anyone back home to override the son-of-a-bitch in the available time, either. So you went all Andaran-noble and decided to jump down the dragon's throat to keep as much control as you could. And the fact that you* really *needed* that *info—that keeping your own men* alive *required it—made it easier, didn't it? Besides, you were so damned sure you could keep it from splashing on anyone else when the time came, weren't you? Well, guess what? If what you think happened really did...*

He let the silence linger, watching the tall, broad shouldered commander of one hundred's face as that silence worked on his nerves. For all his powerful build, the dark-haired, dark-eyed Thalmayr's body language was stiff, defensive, as if he were bracing for a blow. His eyes were nervous and a muscle in his cheek quivered as his stiffly squared shoulders seemed to hunch under the weight of the two thousand's silent gaze. The hundred was obviously exhausted, as well he should be, given the journey he'd undertaken to reach this office, but the sweat smell which hung about him carried a stronger stink of fear than of exertion.

"Very well, Hundred," Harshu said at last. "I suppose we'd better hear your report, hadn't we?"

"Yes, Sir." Thalmayr swallowed visibly and his nostrils flared. "Last month," he began, his voice harsh with fatigue and something else, "two of the officers under my command at Fort Ghartoun—"

*   *   *

"—until I arrived here this morning, Sir," the hundred finished. He'd spoken for little better than a half hour, interrupted by only a handful of questions, but perspiration gleamed on his face.

Silence fell, coiling in the corners like a serpent, and he swallowed again, harder than before, as Harshu gazed at him with the hooded eyes of a hunting dragon.

"And you had no intimation that such an obviously well-organized mutiny was being prepared in your command?" the two thousand asked finally.

"No, Sir." Thalmayr's remaining hand clenched tighter on his right wrist behind him as he stood in a position of parade arrest.

"And how do you think that happened, Hundred?" Harshu's voice was icy.

"I don't know, Sir. In retrospect, I *should* have known, of course. Fifty Ulthar always resented my authority, and I believe he blamed me, rather than Hundred Olderhan, for what happened to Charlie Company. And Five Hundred Isrian did remark when he left me in command of the fort that Fifty Sarma had a reputation as a complainer. But I never anticipated something like this, and if there were any warning signs, I missed them. I shouldn't have."

"You should have known," Harshu repeated softly, and Thalmayr seemed to wilt a little further. The hundred's cheeks, chapped and reddened from his winter dragonback journey from Failcham, turned paler, and Harshu smiled thinly. "Yes, I think we can all agree about that."

Thalmayr said nothing. There was very little he *could* have said.

Harshu let him stand there for several more heartbeats, then exhaled harshly.

"Is there anything you'd care to add to your report?" he asked. "Any additions or ... clarifications?"

"No, Sir." The muscle in Thalmayr's cheek twitched harder, but there was an almost defiant glitter in his eyes, something composed of far too many emotions for easy analysis. "Not at this time."

"I'll expect a formal report in my PC by tomorrow morning," Harshu told him.

"Yes, Sir."

The hundred didn't look happy to hear that, Harshu reflected with a certain satisfaction. And he was going to look one hell of a lot *less* happy before the two thousand was done with him.

"Very well, Hundred Thalmayr. That will be all for now. My clerk will see to your billeting."

"Yes, Sir!"

Thalmayr saluted again, turned on his heel, and marched out of the office, and Harshu sat back wearily in his comfortable chair as the door closed.

It was very quiet—quiet enough the voice of a distant sword could be heard through the closed office window, counting cadence on one of the drill fields—and the two thousand pinched the bridge of his nose.

"Perfect," he said into the silence. "Just perfect."

"Not the word I'd choose, Sir," Toralk said, and Harshu snorted. Trust the Air Force officer to get right to it, he thought.

"I suppose that's fair enough," he replied. "And," he confessed, lowering his hand and turning his head to look Toralk straight in the eye, "it's nothing you haven't been trying to warn me was coming, either, Klayrman."

Toralk nodded, and to his credit there was barely a trace of I-told-you-so about that nod, despite his own obvious dismay.

Harshu pinched his nose again. The only good news, such as it was and what there was of it, was that Thalmayr had not only kept his mouth shut on his way from Fort Ghartoun to Karys but also failed to send word back to Two Thousand mul Gurthak's headquarters in Erthos. He'd done it for all the wrong reasons—in fact, from Thalmayr's viewpoint, it almost certainly would have worked out better if he *had* reported it to mul Gurthak—but that didn't mean Harshu wasn't grateful.

"How do we want to handle this, Sir?" Mahrkrai asked.

The chief of staff's tone made little effort to hide his own unhappiness. He'd never criticized Harshu's decisions in the run-up to the AEF's advance—not openly, at least; he was far too loyal for that—but private conversations with his superior had been another matter. Under those circumstances, he'd never tried to hide his reservations about where those decisions might ultimately lead. The consequences and wreckage they might leave in their wake. Even his worst fears, however, had fallen short of the situation Thalmayr's report suggested.

If one read between the lines of what the hundred had actually said, of course.

"The first thing is to find out how much that piece of dragon shit's lying to cover his arse," Harshu said grimly. He gripped the arms of his chair and shoved himself to his feet so he could pace properly about the office's tight confines. "I know godsdamned well he *is* lying; resentment and malingering are piss-poor reasons for a pair of fifties to mutiny against their CO in time of war, and I don't believe for a minute that's why they did it. And it was obvious from every word he said how he feels about Sharonians. He wouldn't have spent so much time on how they'd used 'their sinister mind powers' to influence Ulthar and Sarma's men into following their 'treasonous' lead if he wasn't trying to set up some sort of defense for any reports that might come out about how he treated the POWs he was responsible for. So the only questions in my mind are how big his lies are and how much worse than we already know this clusterfuck really is. And before you say it, Klayrman, I know whose fault it ultimately is."

Toralk's jaw tightened slightly, and Harshu shook his head.

"Sorry. I don't imagine you really were going to say it, but I know damned well you were thinking it, because I'm thinking exactly the same thing. And I can't—and won't—pretend you didn't warn me about it every step of the way. I can honestly say I never wanted anything like I'm pretty godsdamned certain happened in Thermyn, but I damned well set up the conditions to *let* it happen. There's an old Chalaran proverb that says a fish rots from the head, and there's no point trying to deny that's what's happened here."

He stood still for a moment, meeting the Air Force officer's eyes unflinchingly, then gripped his hands together behind him and resumed his pacing in silent, frowning thought.

"How bad do you think it really is, Sir?" Toralk asked after a handful of minutes, and Harshu grunted.

"Bad," he said flatly. "The way Thalmayr was dancing around the edges of 'prisoner discipline' and the way he kept watching my expression when he did it is enough to tell me that much. The arse-kissing bastard's hoping I'll clean up his mess to keep it from splashing on me when the IG starts investigating. He's wrong about that, as it happens, but I'm not going to start issuing any orders about how to deal with this until I've had the chance to have him questioned under a verifier spell—and not *Neshok's* verifier, either." The two thousand showed his teeth in a tight, feral grim. "We can't afford to allow any gryphons of a feather to flock together on this one, and Neshok's been busy trying to bury his own bodies for weeks now. We need someone who's not likely to help him shovel more dirt back into the holes."

"I think young Tamdaran might be the man for that job, Sir," Mahrkrai said, and Harshu grimaced. Not because he disagreed but because he knew exactly how the youthful Ransaran was likely to react to what he, Mahrkrai, and Toralk all knew a close interrogation of Thalmayr would reveal. Nonetheless...

"You're right, Herak," the two thousand sighed. "And it makes sense to get him involved early on. He's almost as pissed with me over this as Toralk here, so he'll go after Thalmayr like a dragon after a bison. And given his position on the intelligence staff, he's likely to be a critical witness at the court-martial, after all."

"At whose court-martial, Sir?" Toralk asked. Harshu glanced at him again, and the Air Force thousand shrugged. "You and I both know *Thalmayr* deserves a court," he pointed out grimly. "I could fly an entire strike of dragons through the holes in that cover-your-arse story, and any serious interrogation's going to nail him right to the wall. When it does, you've got more than enough officers of sufficient rank to impanel a summary court under the Articles, and frankly, I think you ought to seat one as quickly as possible." Harshu raised one eyebrow, and Toralk shrugged again, a bit more sharply. "Morale's already sagging, Sir, and word of this is bound to leak. When it does, we're going to have to deal with it, and this is probably a time to cauterize the wound as quickly as possible."

Harshu grunted. He couldn't argue with anything Toralk had just said, although he might have chosen a stronger verb than "sagging" to describe the AEF's current confidence. That was probably inevitable, given how decisively the Sharonians had rebuffed their attack on Fort Salby, and the bloody repulse had hurt even more after how rapidly—and with such light casualties—they'd advanced up to that point. The further proof of the efficacy of Sharonian weapons and the extent to which their air power had been whittled away with a machete weren't calculated to make the men feel any better, but underlying all of that was the sense that they were out at the shaky end of a very long limb. They were well aware of how tight the logistics situation was—the number of cavalry mounts, gryphons, and dragons who'd been pulled back from Karys to graze or hunt was proof enough of that—and there was no sign that situation was going to improve anytime soon.

Personally, Harshu didn't blame his men for wondering what had become of the reinforcements Two Thousand mul Gurthak had promised to send after them, and his own worry about that question had hardened steadily into conviction rather than simple suspicion. It wasn't surprising, perhaps, that no additional manpower or dragons had actually reached them yet, given how far from home they were and how scattered the Union's armed forces were along this distant frontier. But by now, mul Gurthak had had plenty of time to at least determine what reinforcements were available and how soon they might arrive, and Harshu hadn't heard a peep out of him. That would have been worrisome under any circumstances, but coupled with the tone of the official dispatches from mul Gurthak which had made their way to Harshu's HQ it became downright ominous.

If there'd ever been any doubt in Mayrkos Harshu's mind that mul Gurthak had deliberately maneuvered him into the position of the officially out-of-control field commander in order to make him the scapegoat when the official lightning bolt came down from on high, it had long since disappeared. And as Toralk and his single exhausted, overworked Army Air Transport Command aerie struggled to keep the existing Expeditionary Force fed and supplied with essential matériel, the men under his command had clearly started to sense that all was not well. When word got out that the Union Army had just experienced its very first mutiny on top of everything else...

"I understand your point, Klayrman," he said, after a moment. "But if what you and I both think happened actually did, I can't do that. I can't do it for a lot of reasons, but especially not given the fact that it's Thalmayr's senior surviving subordinate when he was in command in Mahritha and the Sharonians overran the portal in Mahritha who's apparently mutinied against him. You think anyone's going to believe Fifty Ulthar would've done that if he thought Thalmayr had done a *good* job defending the portal? Or that he and his men—men who were *there*—agree with the intelligence analysis Neshok produced...and I used?" He shook his head. "That's going to point a big, ugly finger at what happened at the Swamp Portal in the first place...and shine a big, bright spotlight not just on Neshok and me but on Thalmayr's treatment of the prisoners under *his* charge. The Andaran Scouts aren't exactly a low-profile outfit, and given the present situation, any questions about Thalmayr's conduct would turn into a political nightmare, with senators and delegates crawling all over them, even without my own ineffable contribution." He shook his head again, harder, his expression grim. "At the very least, that's going to get Duke Garth Showma and the Commandery involved, and the Army can't afford any hint that anything's being swept under the rug at this point."

He held Toralk's gaze again, and the silence in the office seemed to buzz about his ears with the weight of the dozens of things which weren't being said. Enough ugly things had been strewn about in the AEF's wake to destroy a score of senior officers' careers, after all, and Mahrkrai and Toralk knew it as well as Harshu did. How much additional damage could one more...irregularity do?

But that wasn't really the point, and Harshu knew Toralk understood that, as well.

"All right," the two thousand said, turning his attention back to Mahrkrai. "Before we do anything else, we definitely need to wring Thalmayr dry and find out what the hells really happened in Thermyn. Let's get Brychar in here so I can give him the bad news and discuss Thalmayr's interrogation with him personally. Once we've done that, I'll have a better idea of what to do next."

*   *   *

"Good morning, Hundred Thalmayr," the smartly uniformed Ransaran said, laying his briefcase on the table and opening it to withdraw a PC. "My name is Tamdaran, Brychar Tamdaran. I'm on Two Thousand Harshu's intelligence staff, and I have a few questions to ask you."

"Questions?" Hadrign Thalmayr shifted uneasily from the other side of the table. "What sort of questions?"

"There are a few points which Two Thousand Harshu would like clarified," Tamdaran replied, and brushed his fingers across the PC's surface. "And, for your information, and pursuant to the requirements of the Articles of War, I'm notifying you that I've just activated verifier and recording spellware."

Thalmayr stopped shifting and froze. His remaining hand locked on his wrist stump in his lap under the concealing table-top, and his eyes narrowed.

"Verifier spells? Why?"

"Hundred Thalmayr," Tamdaran said patiently, "you've just reported that troops under your command have mutinied when we're in a de facto state of war. That's a capital offense, as I'm sure you're aware. Obviously, the two thousand doesn't want there to be any ambiguity when he convenes the court-martial himself or sends his recommendation for one further up the chain of command."

The Ransaran watched Thalmayr relax ever so slightly and kept his own expression bland and thoughtful. Tamdaran intended to be as objective as possible in his questioning, but he'd read Thalmayr's written report carefully. Carefully enough that he was already confident of where his questions were going to lead. That confidence sharpened the edge of his own bitter disappointment in Mayrkos Harshu, yet the two thousand had ordered him to get to the truth, whatever that truth might be. If Tamdaran was right—if *Two Thousand Harshu* was right—about what had really happened at Fort Ghartoun, the consequences for Harshu would be devastating, but he'd instructed Tamdaran to write up his own independent report of this interrogation for the Inspector General and the Judge Advocate's Corps. And that, in a strange way, proved that despite the way the two thousand had sacrificed the Kerellian Accords and Articles of War in the name of expediency, he was ultimately true to them in the end.

And if Brychar Tamdaran could help drop kick a prick like Thalmayr into the dragon pit along the way, so much the better.

"Now, Hundred," he said briskly, bringing up his own copy of Thalmayr's report, "let's go through this from the beginning. You say the first intimation you had that Fifty Ulthar and Fifty Sarma were conspiring against you came when—"

*   *   *

"So there it is," Mayrkos Harshu said grimly, looking across the steaming cup of bitterblack at Klayrman Toralk. He held the cup in his right hand and tapped his left index finger on the sarkolis crystal on the breakfast table between them. Sunlight streamed in through the chansyu hut's window, pooling in the crystal's heart with eye-hurting intensity. "The bastard tried to weasel out of it, but his lies started coming unglued from almost the very first question. Brychar got it all out of him in the end. And it's all verified, all true."

Toralk's own cup sat on the table beside his plate, and he felt no temptation to touch either of them. The acid-churning lump in his stomach saw to that.

"The only thing I can say on his behalf—not in his *defense*, because I don't think anything could constitute a defense—is that he seems to genuinely believe the Sharonians were deliberately torturing him and trying to 'steal' his mind. Apparently, the fact that the Sharonian healers at Fort Ghartoun testified under verifier that they'd only been doing their best to *help* him wasn't sufficient to convince him. So he decided to return the favor and spent the next several weeks systematically beating them to death one inch at a time. From the sound of things, he'd've been doing even worse than that if his senior healer hadn't refused to patch them up between sessions. He tried to emphasize the fact that he wasn't really trying to kill them—after all, they'd've been dead long ago if that was what he'd wanted!—but the real reason for his 'restraint' was that he didn't want them to die and deprive him of his entertainment any sooner than he could help."

Harshu's eyes were as bleak and grim as Toralk felt, but he sipped from his bitterblack cup and unlike the Air Force officer, he'd cleaned his plate. Of course, he'd had a bit longer to think about it, Toralk supposed.

"It's impossible to be certain of everything that happened at this stage," the two thousand continued, lowering his cup again. "I think Brychar's pieced it together accurately, but all the verifier spell can really tell us is whether or not Thalmayr *believes* he's telling the truth, not necessarily what the truth actually is. I'll see to it that you get a complete transcript of the interview, but I'll warn you now that he's about as self-serving—and as able to convince himself that what he *wants* to be true *has* to be true—as a man could possibly be."

"Are you saying he's one of those...what-do-you-call-them... 'sociopathic liars,' Sir? Or that he's so delusional he genuinely doesn't think he's done anything wrong?"

"I think he'll lie his arse off to stay out of the pit come dragon-feeding time." Harshu's tone was as hard as his expression. "Whether that makes him a 'sociopath' or not is another question. But while I'm godsdamned sure he feels *justified* in his own mind, there's no question that he understands damned well that nobody else is likely to agree with him. And unfortunately"—for the first time, the two thousand looked away from his breakfast guest—"the fact that he headed for Karys rather than Mahritha and didn't say a word to anyone about it on the way through or send any reports back up-chain suggests two things to me.

"First, he may claim he kept his mouth shut because he didn't want to spread any confusion or panic, but that's as full of dragon shit as everything else he's said. The truth is, he hoped like hell he'd be able to cover up what he'd been doing. He wanted me to hear *his* version, and he wanted me to hear it before anything could force my hand when it came time to deal with it. If Ulthar and Sarma's actions had become general knowledge before he got here, I'd've had to set the official wheels in motion before he had an opportunity to spin the story in his favor. As far as I'm concerned, that's proof he damned well knows he's violated the Articles of War left, right, and center, however 'justified' he might have felt. An effort to conceal is pretty strong evidence of guilt."

Harshu paused for a moment, gazing down into the PC on the table, and his dark eyes were as stony as the crystal itself. Then he looked back up at Toralk.

"That's the first thing it suggests to me," he said flatly. "But the second thing—the *worse* thing—is that the reason he wanted to get his version to me is that he hopes I'll clean up the mess to protect my own arse. He hasn't said so in so many words, but it's pretty damned obvious what he really wants is for me to send out an air-mobile detachment with orders to run down the 'mutineers' and shoot to kill when they do. Dead men make piss-poor prosecution witnesses."

"I imagine they do, Sir," the Air Force officer agreed after a moment, meeting those stony eyes levelly.

"Well," Harshu took another sip of bitterblack and cradled the cup in both hands, "I'm afraid he's going to be disappointed. I'll be sending an air-mobile battalion back, all right, but its orders will be a bit different from the ones he wants. I want Ulthar, Sarma, all their men, and any surviving Sharonians apprehended, but I want them taken alive, and I'm sending Thousand Stanohs to personally see to it they are if it's humanly possible."

He paused, and Toralk nodded. Valchair Stanohs commanded 2nd Battalion of the 703rd Infantry Regiment, and although he was junior to Tayrgal Carthos or Faildym Gahnyr, he was smarter than Gahnyr and far less loathsome than Carthos. More to the point, as the senior officer present, he was the acting commander of the entire 703rd, which made him Five Hundred Chalbos Isrian's CO, and it was Isrian who'd selected Thalmayr to command Fort Ghartoun when his own battalion was called forward. Stanohs and Isrian didn't much care for each other, and the fact that Stanohs' one thousand's rank was only an acting one—that he was Isrian's commander on the basis of less than three months' seniority—hadn't made the five hundred any fonder of him. Nor did the fact that they didn't exactly see eye-to-eye on the treatment of Sharonian POWs.

"I can trust Stanohs to do his damnedest to pull it off," Harshu continued, "and once he finds them, a full battalion ought to be enough to convince them resistance would be hopeless. I hope so, anyway, because I really, really want those men—*all* of those men—back alive, and then I want them immediately deposed under verifier and their depositions handed directly to the IG and Judiciary General. I don't want them coming across my desk at all, I don't want to know what's in them, I don't want anyone to even think I had the opportunity to tweak them, and above all"—his expression turned as hard as his eyes—"I don't want Two Thousand mul Gurthak even finding out they exist until backup copies are safely out of his reach on their way back to the Commandery."

Toralk looked deep into his eyes, then nodded slowly. If those reports went to the IG and the Commandery, they'd inevitably spark a massive investigation of Harshu's conduct and the Kerellian violations at which he'd winked. The consequences would be profound, yet he felt gratified—almost but not quite *pleased*—by the proof Mayrkos Harshu truly did intend to face his responsibility for those violations. It wouldn't undo a single thing he'd done or allowed someone else to do, but it might go a *little* way towards restoring the Army's honor.

But underneath any satisfaction he might feel in that regard there was a cold ripple of fresh concern as he considered Harshu's final sentence. There was no legitimate reason for Harshu to keep mul Gurthak in the dark. The Mythalan was not simply his direct military superior but the designated governor in whose area of responsibility the conflict with Sharona had begun. Legally, Harshu was *required* to report something as serious as a mutiny to the local military and political authorities. That meant mul Gurthak, and as Klayrman Toralk thought about the carefully worded directives Nith mul Gurthak had sent forward after the offensive he'd ordered had kicked off, he found himself wondering just how thin the ice under the Expeditionary Force's feet truly was.

*   *   *

"You're sure about this, Lisaro?" Commander of Five Hundred Neshok tried and failed to disguise the intensity of his gaze as he looked at the noncommissioned officer of the other side of his desk.

"No question about it, Sir." Lisaro Porath shrugged and stroked his thin mustache with an index finger. "I got it from Falmyn."

Neshok pursed his lips thoughtfully. Shield Tyzar Falmyn was a clerk in Brychar Tamdaran's cartography section. He stood well over six feet, with a powerful physique, but he was no more than nineteen years old, and while he was obviously devoted to Hundred Tamdaran, he was also a long way from home and more than a little homesick. "Home" in his case was the continent of Shalomar, but his Shalomar lay in New Tukoria, thirteen universes down-chain from Arcana. That universe had been settled just over a hundred years ago, primarily by colonists from the Hilmaran Kingdom of Tukoria, and his coppery skin and dark eyes reflected those ancestors. That heritage might also be one reason he'd become such a close friend of Lisaro Porath, given Porath's Hilmaran birth back on Arcana itself. Aside from their ancestry, Porath and the youngster actually had very little in common, although Falmyn might be excused for not realizing that. Porath was almost twenty years older than he was, and it had no doubt been flattering—as well as comforting—to be taken under the more senior noncom's wing, and Porath could be surprisingly charming when he put his mind to it.

Which was exactly what he'd done when Neshok pointed out to him how useful a window into Tamdaran's shop might prove.

"And Two Thousand Harshu's orders were definite?" the five hundred pressed.

"He was pretty damned clear, Sir...according to Falmyn, anyway. He wants Ulthar, Sarma, and the others taken alive—especially any Sharonians with them—and he's sending Thousand Stanohs back to handle it very quietly."

"I see."

Neshok nodded slowly, drumming his fingers on his desk while he considered the news. His sources had reported Hadrign Thalmayr's arrival almost before the dragon landed, and he'd had a quiet word with Senior Sword Kalcyr that same afternoon. Kalcyr had worked well with Neshok in the advance from Hell's Gate, but he'd been less forthcoming than Neshok had anticipated. It had taken the five hundred the better part of an hour to worm the story out of him, because Thalmayr had ordered him to keep his mouth shut. And now Harshu was sending out his own troops to look for the mutineers under remarkably constraining orders.

And he's not telling mul Gurthak about it. Neshok's fingers drummed harder. *That's not a frigging oversight on his part, either. It's deliberate. And if he wants those Sharonian bastards back alive, it's not for any reason the two thousand's going to like.*

He caught his lower lip between his incisors as he tried to evaluate how this latest disaster was likely to affect his own precarious position. It was obvious there was no love lost between mul Gurthak and Harshu, and Neshok had quite a lot riding on the relationship between the pair of two thousands. There were times when he wished he'd gotten mul Gurthak's instructions in writing before he'd been transferred to Harshu's command, especially now that he found himself drifting in an ambiguous no man's land between the Mythalan and his field commander.

The one thing I can be damned sure of is that someone's *going to be scapegoated now that the Sharonians have stopped that arrogant smartass Harshu in his tracks. I wonder...I know the bastard's getting ready to dump everything on me if the IG starts nosing around about the Kerellian Accords, but did he realize from the beginning that the two thousand assigned me to him specifically to keep an eye on him? Did he plan to drop me to the dragons all along, no matter what happened, just to get rid of me?*

The thought made a certain disturbing sense, but if that was what had happened, what did he do about it? It was possible, given the obviously...cool relationship between Harshu and Thousand Carthos that he might find an ally there, but how useful could Carthos be? He was too junior to be used as an active weapon against Harshu, and Neshok's contacts reported that Carthos had operated far from gently against the Sharonians during his advance up the Kelsayr Chain. Unless the five hundred missed his guess, that meant Tayrgal Carthos was in very much the same fix as he was. So would any...arrangement with Carthos be a case of two men guarding one another's backs, or would it be a case of two men fighting over the same life preserver?

No. Unless he discovered some presently unknown factor that changed things, he was on his own, and it would be wiser for him to make his plans on the assumption that he'd stay that way. But that, unfortunately, left the question of what sort of plans a man in his position *could* make. He'd kept his records, written his reports, done everything he could internally to protect himself, yet there was no point pretending. Without a patron of his own—a patron like Nith mul Gurthak—he was dragon-bait whenever Harshu decided to toss him into the feeding pit. And without something to make him valuable to mul Gurthak, there was no guarantee the two thousand would remember his promises. In fact, without something to make him valuable, it would probably suit mul Gurthak's purposes far better to quietly forget about those promises and hang Neshok around Harshu's neck like another anchor.

But there's valuable, and then there's...valuable, isn't there?

He thought about it a moment longer, recognizing the risk, yet the water was neck deep and showed every sign of rising higher. Perhaps it was time to take what an arrogant bastard like Harshu was fond of calling a "calculated risk."

"All right, Lisaro," he said. "Thank you for bringing this to my attention. I don't want you squeezing Falmyn too hard, but if he drops any more tidbits on you, I want to hear about them. Clear?"

"Clear, Sir."

Porath nodded, saluted, and disappeared, and Neshok leaned back in his chair, toying with his PC while he considered how best to play what could only be described as a risky card. He was pretty sure no one on Harshu's staff had tumbled to his discreet, private communications channel to mul Gurthak, just as he was pretty sure mul Gurthak didn't realize just how much his good friend Alivar Neshok had recorded during his private briefings and instructions. He might not have gotten mul Gurthak's orders in writing, but he'd managed to record enough of his conversations with the two thousand to make very interesting hearing for any representative of the Inspector General or Judiciary General. Clearly it was time to make Two Thousand mul Gurthak aware of the situation in Thermyn which Two Thousand Harshu was deliberately concealing from him. And when he did, perhaps he should use the same opportunity to make mul Gurthak aware—discreetly, of course—of the ... potentially awkward information in his possession.

The trick, of course, was how to phrase his message most felicitously.

CHAPTER THIRTY-ONE

Darikhal 12, 505s AE
(January 31, 1929 CE)

"COME ON, CHAN RESNAIR! IT'S A FRIGGING GANGPLANK, not the grand staircase at Hawkwing Palace, for gods' sake!"

Arlos chan Geraith smiled as the leather-lunged chief-armsman remonstrated gently with the petty-armsman staggering down the gangplank to the Shosara docks under his heavy pack and shoulder-slung rifle. The unfortunate chan Resnair didn't look as if he felt particularly well, which really shouldn't surprise anyone. The North Vandor in winter could be as unpleasant as any body of water in the world, and the division-captain didn't doubt two thirds of his men had found themselves wondering whether or not seasickness was fatal.

From chan Resnair's looks, the petty-armsman might well be among the sizable minority who'd wished it had been.

"At least none of the ships actually sank, Sir," Regiment-Captain chan Kymo observed dryly, as if he'd read chan Geraith's mind. "A time or two, there, I was pretty sure one of them was *going* to," 3rd Dragoon Division's quartermaster added.

"Nonsense. Nonsense!" Chan Geraith slapped the taller and much younger chan Kymo on the shoulder. "Why, I never doubted the splendid seaworthiness of those transports for a moment! After all, the sea runs in Ternathians' blood!"

"But not even Ternathians can *breathe* it, Sir," Regiment-Captain chan Isail pointed out.

"A mere bagatelle which shouldn't have occupied your minds for a single instant," chan Geraith said sternly.

"I'll try to bear that in mind next time I'm aboard a transport

458

that seems intent on standing on its head, Sir," chan Isail assured him, and chan Geraith chuckled. Not that chan Kymo and the chief of staff didn't have a point.

"The important thing," he said rather more seriously, "is that we've got everybody across now except for the Ninth and the Thirty-First. And we've got enough shipping to bring both of *them* over in a single lift. That means we can have them here and ready to move out in less than three weeks."

Chan Isail nodded. They hadn't managed the movement in as orderly a fashion as they'd hoped, which shouldn't have surprised anyone, given the speed with which the entire operation had been thrown together. Brigade-Captain chan Khartan was still in place at Salbyton and wouldn't be able to pull his remaining regiment—the 9th Dragoons—out of the defenses there until the first brigade of Division-Captain chan Jassian's 21st Infantry Division arrived to replace him. Brigade-Captain chan Ursan's lead regiments should reach Salbyton within the next three days, however. At that point, chan Quay would entrain back to Renaiyrton, link up with Brigade-Captain chan Jesyl's 31st Dragoons—the last unit of Brigade-Captain chan Sharys' 3rd Brigade, which was currently still en route from Jyrsalm, where it had been awaiting additional Bisons and Steel Mules—and follow the rest of the 3rd Dragoon Division to Renaiyrton and across the ocean as soon as the TTE transports could return from Shosara. The rest of 5th Corps's infantry and supports would be arriving in Traisum over the next couple of months, aside from Brigade-Captain Desval chan Bykahlar's 3rd Brigade of the 21st Infantry, which would be following chan Geraith's division down the Kelsayr Chain.

The movement, which undoubtedly had every TTE traffic manager between Traisum and Sharona tearing his hair, wasn't pretty, and it bore precious little relation to the tidy paper studies the Imperial Ternathian Army's staff college was accustomed to putting together. It was, however, *working*, which was not a minor consideration for the largest trans-universal troop movement in history. Although, judging by the Voice messages coming down-chain, it was only the beginning of what the emperor had in mind.

Of course, the other side's probably thinking a lot of the same things we are, chan Geraith reflected. *That could make things… interesting. If our flanking move happens to run into a division or so of Arcanans headed to reinforce Harshu…*

No doubt that was true, but given the concentrated firepower the 3rd Dragoons represented, he'd take his chances against an Arcanan division in the open field.

"All right." He turned away from the tall-sided ships lying against the docks and headed purposefully for the steamer sedan on the quayside with the faint heat shimmer of a kerosene-fired boiler dancing above its exhaust. It flew a fender-mounted flag with the two gold star bursts of his rank, and the driver popped out, opened the rear door, and saluted sharply as he and his staff officers approached.

"The first thing is to get ourselves to chan Quay's HQ and check in," the division-captain continued as he settled into the forward-facing rear seat and chan Isail and chan Kymo took the rearward-facing seat across from him. "The next order of business is to get a Voice message off to Battalion-Captain chan Yahndar and make sure everything's still proceeding more or less to plan at his end."

CHAPTER THIRTY-TWO

Cormas 19, 5053 AE
(February 7, 1929 CE)

NORIELLENA DRUBEKA, ONE OF DOZENS OF SUNN CORRE-spondents assigned to cover the newly elected members of Sharona's Imperial Parliament, flipped through notes and prepared to throw her life away over a handful of interview questions. Voice Kylmos Trebar watched her do it with a carefully suppressed sigh.

Their assigned region of Uromathia included Emperor Chava's capital city, but they didn't have to be in his waiting room or attempting to get in to interview the emperor to do their jobs. They could have stayed in Tajvana, interviewing MPs representing that part of his empire instead of following a very dangerous man back to his home country after the conclusion of the Conclave.

Correspondents all over Sharona's populated worlds were interviewing the members of parliament and trying to get reactions from public officials about likely power blocs in the new Parliament. But Drubeka wasn't satisfied with that approach. Years ago, as a beginning SUNN hometown news correspondent, she'd asked Ambassador Shalassar Kolmayr-Brintal to comment on a Uromathian ambassador who'd proposed euthanizing elderly cetaceans for their whale oil.

Shalassar's response still replayed in the Voicecasts, and he could tell Drubeka was hoping for another career-making interview.

She'd initially planned for a single question, if they could only manage to intercept Emperor Chava in transit: "SUNN is honored that you'd take this interview, Your Majesty. Please, tell us just what would it take for you to support the Imperial Parliament's war caucus?" But it looked like they'd be getting a full formal interview with the emperor, instead.

The war caucus had other, longer names. "The Sharonan Imperial Defense Group," for one. Then there was "MPs for the Restoration of the Frontier Universes and Defeat of the Arcanan Scourge," which was just the beginning of an unwieldy mouthful of a name advocated by MP Ruftuu. Whatever they called it, the MPs who'd joined it were in agreement about supporting the war. The conflict was on *how* to support it, and the group most reporters were calling the "war hawks" were pushing to extend the policies begun as Emperor Zindel's executive orders.

No surprise to political observers, the New Farnalian MP Kinlafia was one of the many representatives expected to vote with that power bloc. The Uromathian MPs—both from the Uromathian Empire and other historically Uromathian nations—were also supporting the war, however, which was enough to make anyone suspicious, given Chava's influence. Virtually every one of SUNN's political analysts expected them to become the opposition party, but as yet they hadn't formed any distinct caucus of their own or even explained exactly *how* they intended to support the war, and Drubeka wanted answers about what they were *really* up to from the power everyone knew was writing their marching orders.

The waiting room lacked mirrors, so Drubeka used Trebar's eye for her final pre-Voicecast touch ups. The Shurkhali Voice took no special care for his own appearance, beyond buckling on platform shoes to raise his height of eye from five foot three to five foot eight. Viewers liked correspondents at eye level and Drubeka stood five seven in flats and five eight in the pastel court attire selected to complement her olive skin and contrast nicely with the audience chamber's carpet, where she expected to make her obeisance before and after the interview. SUNN might cut it to show only a cordial bow for the 'cast shown in regions outside Uromathia, but that would be for other staffers to decide. Trebar would capture the best lighting and angles and try to keep Drubeka in sight as much as possible.

Voices were never harmed in Uromathia except by chance street violence. Critics without the Voice ability to send an exact record of their final moments did not fare so well. But there were more kinds of power than back alley brutality. Drubeka knew that as well as he did, but she was betting the Emperor of Uromathia would see the value of occasionally giving his version of events directly to the people of Sharona.

If the worst happened and she vanished, SUNN would give her memory as many headline stories as it could, but Drubeka wasn't planning to die. There was still too much news to find and tell.

The correspondent's carefully practiced sexy but still serious personality had a lot of fans, including the court page managing the order of the supplicants to see the Emperor of Uromathia. The young man controlled the political factions in the room without a blink, but his interactions with the famous must have been few. He fairly melted when Drubeka spoke to him and eagerly complied with any requests Trebar conveyed.

Now Drubeka set aside her notes and nodded to Trebar.

A word to the page about the need for processing time before the evening Voicecast saw their audience shuffled forward to next in line. A quickened pulsing at Drubeka's temples caused Trebar to reach for a hairbrush. He could adjust her hair to mask more of her temples, but she lifted a hand and he held back. That wouldn't be the right look for Drubeka's public personality, and Emperor Chava was unlikely to be fooled into believing he didn't scare them.

Trebar applied a light coat of powder to hide the shine on her forehead.

"We can walk out of here and catch a train back to Tajvana. Get some interviews with the MPs themselves. Noriellena, we don't have to do this," Trebar said. He didn't like to see her sweat.

"I've got this," Drubeka said. She was deepening her voice and lengthening the vowels to stretch her normal speech patterns— getting mentally ready to be on. "SUNN needs this interview. We're going to bring in ratings gold on this one."

"You can't move up to Special Correspondent if a third of the features are in areas SUNN can't send you because Chava has you declared persona non grata." Trebar reminded her. "Go easy, Noriellena. Just remember he's an emperor and this is his seat of power. Don't push too hard. Promise me, okay?"

"No promises; no lies, Kylmos." Drubeka rolled back her shoulders and smoothed her dark hair, tucking a lock behind her ear in her signature interview pose: Noriellena Drubeka, SUNN, listening for you. "How do I look?"

"Ready as always," Trebar replied, just as the page gave them the nod and opened the double doors of the entry hall. They were on!

"Good. Let's do this." She flashed her classic grin.

*   *   *

Chava Busar, Emperor of Uromathia and power behind a dozen or more theoretically independent polities, understood perception—and how to create it—well. He met the SUNN team on his own terms a few steps inside the audience chamber.

The emperor wore normal street wear and held his formal court robes tucked over one arm, as if he was a mere justiciar who'd just finished ruling on a long case, without a legion of servants to take that heavy brocade and see it cleaned and pressed for his next audience.

Drubeka in her SUNN personality began a very creditable obeisance for a woman who'd spent the last several years interviewing small town fishermen and plebeian business magnates. She got no further than the initial bow, because the emperor stepped in close and clasped both her arms in the warm greeting of colleagues. That caused the robe to slide, and Drubeka caught it.

Emperor Chava laughed out loud, the handful of courtiers attending to business around the room chuckled in pure delight... and a chill ran down Trebar's spine.

Chava's eyes twinkled inviting all of Sharona to share in the joke. The Uromathian-based Voice Broadcast Service had accused SUNN of carrying the robe for Emperor Zindel. The phrase implied an ugly willingness to do distasteful things to further the desires of the robe's owner—an insinuation SUNN Voicecasters had simply ignored. Now VBS would play the nasty comment to the hilt with their audience if SUNN used the interview.

"Mistress Drubeka." The emperor chuckled. "You SUNN correspondents simply cannot help yourselves. I shall have to ask the VBS to take your natural inclinations into account when they make their news bulletins." He tipped his head at a courtier standing a half dozen paces back up the entry wearing, Trebar noticed belatedly, the sash of office adopted by Voices in the employ of VBS.

So they could be sure this interlude would run tonight whether SUNN showed it or not, he thought. SUNN in the person of Noriellena Drubeka would be accused of being Emperor Zindel's robeholder, and the VBS report would surely expand that to imply Drubeka was so used to being Zindel's servant that she'd reached out and grabbed Emperor Chava's robe too out of helpless habit. Regrettably the other man had had a better view of the whole exchange, and Trebar moved quickly around to position himself for the rest of the interview.

Drubeka rallied by offering the robe to the VBS Voice...who avoided ruining his version of events by making a leave-taking bow to Emperor Chava and exiting the chamber. At a crook of the emperor's finger, a servant relieved Drubeka of the heavy garment.

"Please, please." Chava motioned to an alcove, clearly set up specifically for this meeting. "Let us sit. My page, he tells me he is a big fan of your work, but you have questions about the new Parliament, of course. And you would like to ask me about the war caucus. Is that not so?"

Trebar was already very still taking the record. Drubeka only froze for a fraction of a second. Then she smiled right back at the emperor.

Chava Busar was good. He'd had to be to build and hold the political position Uromathia had maintained for the last decade, but in Ternathian-influenced areas of Sharona it was too easy to discount the man as a power-mad aristocrat more likely to be killed by his own kin than to survive to old age.

The emperor sat and the interview began.

Drubeka skipped the formal, flowery intro she'd practiced. This had become Chava's Voicecast, not hers. He was setting the tone and she'd have to scramble to slip in her best questions wherever she could make them fit. The plan had been to distract him with a few cetacean rights questions, the topic she was known for pursuing in many of her interviews, and then shock him into an unplanned response with questions about the MPs who might emerge as parliamentary leaders.

Clearly surprise was now out of the question. She could ask about the cetaceans after all, but that was old news, with well-worn talking points he'd already spoken to with a dozen VBS reporters. Drubeka had pursued this audience to get something fresh, and the war caucus was the topic of the day.

The group supported Emperor Zindel, celebrated the unification of the Sharonan universes, and sought to transfer as much power as possible to the Winged Crown. One MP had even suggested folding existing national police agencies into a single imperial police force—far beyond anything Emperor Zindel had requested. The obvious question was what the Uromathian emperor would have to say about this support for his rival's objectives.

Drubeka didn't do obvious, but she didn't normally interview emperors, either.

"Mistress Drubeka." She'd waited too long and Chava was taking the interview's reins again, and the correspondent clenched her teeth at the thought. "Why is it, exactly, that your news organization, this SUNN, is so negative towards all things Uromathian?"

"Your Excellency, I'm no emperor to speak for all of SUNN." Trebar breathed relief as Drubeka rallied enough to speak calmly. "Personally, I find Uromathia a lovely place and, as you yourself mentioned, we have many fans here, including Master Rihva your Excellency's Court Page."

She didn't take the bait and attempt to defend the reporting, for a lot of reasons. One was that it was *true* reporting, highly critical not of Uromathia itself but of Uromathia's current emperor, as she and her Voice were in a far better position than most non-Uromathians to know. Kylmos Trebar and Noriellena Drubeka were among the many who'd been greatly relieved when Zindel had emerged as Emperor of Sharona instead of Chava. Another reason, of course, was that attempting to defend it would give Chava exactly what he wanted: legitimization for the VSB's claims of bias. The SUNN correspondent had obviously been scrambling for an explanation of Chava's legitimate question, their mouthpieces would opine. It wouldn't matter what she'd actually said, either; they were past masters at twisting clear, simple declarative sentences into pretzels to make those sentences say exactly what they *wanted* them to say.

"Your Excellency," Drubeka said instead, "while I have this wonderful chance to ask, and I must say it's beyond gracious of you to have allowed this interview, I must ask some questions myself. So I suppose I should start with a question your page told me he hoped I would ask: Who's your favorite MP?"

It was a simple question, she'd never thought to ask, but after the page had mentioned it, Drubeka hadn't been able to let it go. If Chava answered, he'd probably name the man he'd chosen as leader of the opposition and she'd be able to stop leaning on the SUNN analysts' guesses about which Uromathian MPs had influence and which didn't.

Emperor Chava smiled indulgently, as Drubeka held her breath waiting to see what he'd say.

"Here in Uromathia," he said. "All our MPs are the exquisite flowers of their districts, as difficult to chose between as an orchid over a rose. So I would not normally answer this question." Emperor Chava leaned in with a knowing look directly at Trebar. "But for my friend Mistress Drubeka who sees the loveliness of Uromathia, I tell this secret. My favorite is the fine Mister Darcel Kinlafia."

Trebar blinked quickly. He needed to focus and catch all this.

Kinlafia had no connection to Uromathia. The MP's district was in New Farnal, which had been populated by settlers from Ternathia not Uromathia, and the MP's wife was even Emperor Zindel's former Privy Voice.

Someone was being played right now. Quite possibly it was all of Sharona, but it might be just SUNN and Drubeka. Trebar couldn't tell where this was going and he needed to see and hear what Chava decided to announce next.

Drubeka glanced downward with an eyelash flutter that was something of a signature expression for her. It gave the viewers a distraction while she thought.

And she might not realize it, but Trebar knew she used it far more often when she thought the interviews were going exceptionally well than when she thought they were out of control. Not for the first time he wished she'd been at least a trace Mind Speaker so he could whisper a warning as she played with a black tendril of hair by her ear.

"Oh my, that is a secret." Drubeka tilted her head with another eyelash flutter at Trebar inviting all of Sharona to join her and the emperor in this interview-turned-intimate-conversation. "I know all the women out there agree Darcel has that wild universe-explorer handsomeness, but tell me really, what attracted Your Excellency?"

Kinlafia was on the wrong side of average in Trebar's opinion, but the right angles and lighting could make anyone look good, as every SUNN correspondent certainly knew.

"My girl Krethva," the emperor named a Uromathian society journalist for VBS who certainly wouldn't disagree with any words he put in her mouth, "tells me the strong shoulders are more than sufficient reason to favor a man.

"But," he continued with a side look at Trebar, proving himself an adept at Voicecast interviews, "We all know the famous Mistress Drubeka does not fall for just a pretty face."

He made a mournful expression inviting the audience to sympathize with him for not personally attracting the correspondent in that way. Then he winked as if to tell the viewer he knew full well that he, one of the most powerful men in all of Sharona, had not a chance with their darling beautiful newsgirl.

It wasn't the truth, but perception, even on live Voicecasts, showed only the surface. No emotions were permitted in commercial Voicecasts without the express permission of the interviewee. And without that, no amount of additional commentary would convince the audience which Saw this that Emperor Chava was really a dangerous man who'd have a pretty reporter slaughtered like a farm animal if he found her responses disrespectful.

Drubeka blushed, and Trebar thanked the Double Triad that she was a capable actress.

"Many of my viewers have quite the crush on you, Your Excellency." She covered the emperor's implied self-disparagement, carefully.

Chava shrugged off the flattery, this time not quite managing to appear unconceited. He acknowledged the comment with a shade too much arrogance.

"Darcel Kinlafia and I have much in common in this way. I do for Uromathia what I can to protect the people from those who would wish us ill. And sometimes, regrettably, always regrettably, there is a conflict of understanding in the need for these protective acts. And," Chava's accent was thinning as the interview went on, but Trebar suspected few viewers would notice, "Mister Darcel with his Voice report of the Arcanan brutality brings us warning of the danger. We must have this man in the Parliament. His warning must be repeated again and again until all of Sharona demands a leader who will defend our universes properly."

Trebar held back a blink and shifted focus to Drubeka who took the volley.

"Your Excellency, we all saw you agree to the Unification Treaty establishing the Empire of Sharona for the fight against Arcana. Are you saying Emperor Zindel *can't* defend our universes?"

"He tries." Chava shook his head as if in concern for a small child. "But we can see what it costs the Caliraths. His own firstborn dead already? And this after losing how many universes to the Arcanan horde? I say only that Sharona may not be able to afford the Calirath style of protection. Must we lose that many more universes for every one of the grand princesses? I would not see Sharona so splintered or let my friend and fellow emperor, Zindel, suffer so much."

Chava stood and perforce, Drubeka came to her feet as well even though this was far from the note on which she would have chosen to end the interview.

"My friends at the SUNN," his accent returned, "I must say goodbye and return to my work." He gestured at the audience chamber where the court page had brought in a young woman with three sobbing children. Trebar turned his head back to the emperor and correspondent quickly, not wanting to linger on the staged setup.

Drubeka made her bow, and the very smug court page saw them out.

*　　*　　*

An old friend at SUNN contacted a politician's wife with news of the Uromathian emperor's words, and Alazon Yanamar's eyes widened in shock, and then closed in disgust.

"A problem?" Crown Princess Andrin whispered in her ear. "We could cut back on the wedding flowers a bit, if you really hate them."

"Just a negative Voicecast piece, Your Highness" Alazon explained and tried to narrow her focus back to just this room of the Grand Palace. Ulantha Jastyr would be more than able to relay the newest set of aspersions being cast by Emperor Chava. Today Alazon was supposed to pretend to like wedding planning.

Lilies—enormous lilies, and piles of other flowers she couldn't begin to identify—bedecked a massive display the very proud florist had rolled into the center of the Tajvana main ballroom.

"Pretty! So pretty!" Nine-year-old Grand Princess Anbessa squealed in delight. The girl danced a circle around the thing pointing out this and that flower from places Darcel Kinlafia had worked survey missions.

Crown Princess Andrin patted Alazon on the shoulder. "They aren't actually from the border universes." She whispered. "Don't tell Anbessa."

"But we got all the right ones, yes? Picked from the geo-match locations here in Sharona." A young florist's assistant hovered, clearly concerned about a possible failure of diligence in meeting the latest elaborate wedding request.

Andrin reassured the young man, and he calmed immediately. The crown princess' falcon Finena nuzzled her beak into her feathers for a nap, expressing about the same level of interest as Alazon herself felt.

Still, there were roses in the mix, and Darcel had given her a massed bouquet of them the day after the election results came in. He didn't have to do that. They were psionicly-paired lifemates. She knew exactly what he felt and how much he cared for her... but he still sent flowers out of the blue, just to see if they might make her happy.

Anbessa completed another turn around the flowers and twirled around Alazon.

"Mistress Yanamar, you do like them right? Can we keep them in the wedding?" She looked uncertainly back and forth between Alazon and the florist. Empress Varena, Marithe Kinlafia, and Anbessa's other sister Razial stood a little way off, surrounded by a pile of silks, making some kind of plan for table linens—too preoccupied to make another wedding decision on Alazon's behalf this time.

Alazon laughed and pulled Anbessa in for a hug.

"I'm going to let your mom plan my wedding however she wants it," she whispered to the youngest grand princess, letting her in on the secret.

"Oh." Anbessa whispered back. "It is going to be really big. Lots and lots of flowers," the girl cautioned, wide-eyed.

Alazon nodded. The grand princess was more right than she knew. Empress Varena had been robbed of the opportunity to make a grand spectacle of Andrin and Howan Fai's wedding, so she'd redirected all that energy towards this one, throwing all the wedding planning zeal she hadn't been able to spend on her daughter's state wedding into the reception she and Zindel were throwing for Alazon Yanamar and Darcel Kinlafia.

She and Darcel got to keep the service itself simple and traditional, with full respect for the ceremony before the Holy Double Triad. And in exchange for this one hard line, the grand princesses and the empress (especially the empress) had an entirely free hand in the reception festivities.

Thank the Triad they were also *paying* for the reception, or

Alazon imagined she'd be indenturing her great-grandchildren to cover the price of the meticulously planned party. The newlywed Crown Princess Andrin gamely stayed at Alazon's side during these wedding planning sessions, offering few suggestions of her own. But, Alazon noted with some suspicion, the crown princess delighted in encouraging her younger sisters in their greater flights of fancy. She was beginning to suspect that Crown Princess Andrin had received exactly the kind of simple wedding she'd always wanted, and that she was delighting in redirecting all the hoopla onto another couple.

If Darcel's mother, Marithe, hadn't turned out to have a surprising appreciation for over-the-top festivities, Alazon would have put her foot down on a lot more than the ceremony. But since her future mother-in-law was also enjoying participating in the spectacle, Alazon left them to it.

Andrin winked and covered her exit, and at least being a Voice made it easy to arrange to sneak off with Darcel. She'd have to stop in again before dinner to agree with everything the four women had decided on, but in the meantime she got to spend a lovely afternoon walking with her fiancé: the Honorable Mister Kinlafia, Member of Parliament in the House of Talents.

She rather liked the ring of that. Perhaps she could attempt to introduce herself as MP Kinlafia's wife later and see if any of the other newly elected delegates were politically naive enough to accept that summation of her identity at face value.

She suggested as much to Darcel. He first laughed and then actually thought it through and agreed. Some politicians were elected because politics was simply what their families did and the voters were used to choosing that name, and most members of the new House of Talents were from long established political families. This test might be a way of finding out which of them had taken their seats with intent to actually *do* something. Anyone who intended to show up for debates and make their own choices about votes would know Alazon Yanamar had been the emperor's Privy Voice.

And she would be again, very soon. She'd actually tried to convince Emperor Zindel to retain Ulantha in the position, and he'd admitted she was doing very well. Unfortunately, she lacked both Alazon's experience and the strength of her Talent. Ulantha was a very good, very strong Voice, but she wasn't a *Projective*

Voice. Alazon was, and there were times when that could be a critically important ability for Privy Council meetings. On the other hand, Alazon had been thinking about her protégée's future, and it seemed more and more likely to her that Ulantha would make the perfect Personal Voice for Andrin, which would also guarantee the younger Voice's career.

In the meantime, it amused Alazon immensely that some people thought she'd become a quiet politician's wife.

The security concerns for the wedding nagged her a bit. Crown Princess Andrin and Prince Consort Howan Fai had discussed sitting in the balcony with most of the Calirath family to watch the ceremony, and she felt almost physically queasy at the thought of putting so many eggs into one basket. On the other hand, Telfor chan Garatz, the Chief of Imperial Security, had everything in his capable hands. Alazon had to trust him to outwit any threats.

Empress Varena was hosting the after party back at the palace. Surely the house guards would be in attendance in some form, but that particular chapel had been expressly nixed in favor of the Conclave floor for the Andrin-Howan Fai wedding because it lacked sufficient defenses. Alazon didn't think it had been reinforced in the meantime, and while Howan Fai's marriage to Andrin might have sealed the unification of Sharona, it hadn't brought peace to the tempestuous Ternathian relationship with the Uromathian Empire.

She hoped the Imperial Guard had a plan to see to the imperial family's safety.

*　　　*　　　*

The interview ran as the lead story in every SUNN market that evening with bits and pieces shared out for further discussion in the talk shows the next morning. And Privy Voice Ulantha Jastyr did indeed discuss it with the emperor. Meanwhile the SUNN correspondent team took the first train back to Tajvana.

Noriellena Drubeka's promotion had come through, but not for Features Correspondent. Instead she was offered Lead Uromathian Political Correspondent... along with a warning from corporate that an appearance of favoritism towards the emperor could result in firing.

Trebar sometimes wondered if corporate paid any attention to the news the company collected. If SUNN wanted a permanent political correspondent in Uromathia, they'd have to accept the appearance of bias in Chava's favor.

He also checked SUNN's staff directory. SUNN had no other permanent Uromathian political correspondents, but "lead" came with a significant pay bump, and as her assigned Voice, he'd get a raise too.

Drubeka suggested they think of it as a hazardous duty bonus and work as many features as possible from the seat of Parliament in Tajvana.

Trebar heartily agreed.

Now Drubeka grabbed her diner-train glass and toasted her reporting teammate.

"To surviving the election season!" She lifted the glass and gulped down half of it.

Trebar tilted his own and sipped while his partner gasped at the kick.

The harsh Uromathian liquor from the bartender hadn't been miraculously improved by the dining car's price markup. After a few gasping coughs, Drubeka tossed back the rest of the glass with a grimace.

"I don't understand how you can sip this stuff," she said.

Trebar chuckled and added his own toast. "And here's to getting out alive."

"Hey now, all that insinuation made for good copy, but—" She waved it away.

Miles away from Uromathia's capital city and on a fast train to their new office in Tajvana, she indicated with a wiggle of her fingers why SUNN supervisors always paired her with paranoid, or at least highly cautious, Voices. Noriellena Drubeka would never quite be brave—not with the cold-blooded courage which truly recognized danger and accepted it. Hers was the sort of personality which protected itself by *denying* threats, not grappling with them. In the moment, she'd know there was danger and do the work anyway, but in the in-between times, she never really acknowledged that that danger had existed. Trebar knew that perfectly well, and now he waited for the inevitable justification.

"You know what I think," she said. "This battle of the two emperors is all showmanship. Uromathia clearly accepted the Treaty of Unification, and the drama with the crown princess' wedding has all blown over. Yes, I agree with the VBS commentators that the wedding clothes left something to be desired. But really? Complaints about clothing hardly amount to a true attack on the Winged Crown, and we do have this multiversal war with Arcana going on."

She caught an attendant's eye and signaled for another round before continuing.

"I mean, surely all these people will put aside their local issues for the war. When all's said, we've got to make sure we still have a Sharona—we'll need something to fight over amongst ourselves after we smash the barbarians back into fairy dust! Speaking of which, did you see that new shooting gallery promo stunt?"

Trebar shook his head, giving her all the encouragement she needed to keep going. Running commentary was one of the things occasionally required when waiting for something truly newsworthy to occur. Thus some commentators needed to practice near monologues on random public interest topics just to fill the time. Drubeka didn't need any more practice, but Trebar let her talk anyway.

"What's the shooting gallery thing?"

"Well the reports are that Arcanans look pretty much like us, so they haven't been able to come up with any really interesting new targets to sell. But some of the Voice reports say the Arcanans' magic comes from some kind of crystals, so Tajvana's shooting galleries have taken to making sugar crystal targets. The first one called it Metal vs. Magic, but the competitor's branding of Crack the Crystal seems to sell a bit better. I gotta say, I like the idea. Triad forbid the Arcanans ever break as far back as Sharona, but at least if they do, all the shopkeepers will know what to shoot at!"

The chances that a crystal powering anything truly deadly would be marked off with concentric circles and held fixed at twenty paces struck Trebar as unlikely, but he grunted acknowledgement.

CHAPTER THIRTY-THREE

Cormas 26, 505s AE
(February 14, 1929 CE)

"...AND THE LAST OF THE STEAM DRAYS SHOULD BE SWAYED aboard by midday, along with their mud tracks, Sir." Battalion-Captain Rechair chan Ersam flipped his notepad closed with something between a grimace and a smile. "After that, gods only know what else will go wrong, but I don't *think* it's going to be my people's fault when it does. Of course, I've been wrong before."

"No! Really?" Brigade-Captain Desval chan Bykahlar looked back at his silver-haired Delkrathian quartermaster in mock disbelief.

"Really, Sir," chan Ersam replied solemnly. "Why, I remember the last time clearly. Three years ago, it was, I think, during those maneuvers at Fort Erthain."

"Actually," Regiment-Captain chan Therahk said dryly, "I believe there may have been at least a time or two since then."

"I'd hate to disagree with a senior officer," chan Ersam told 3rd Infantry Brigade's executive officer, "but I *distinctly* remember that it was three years ago."

"Are you sure you don't mean three *weeks* ago?" Battalion-Captain Fernis chan Klaisahn, 3rd Brigade's chief of staff sounded a bit more sour than the XO. Chan Klaisahn was a native Ternathian, six and a half feet tall and immensely strong, with huge hands, who'd won more than a few beers by straightening horseshoes without benefit of an anvil. Now he cocked his head at chan Ersam. "Something about Regiment-Captain chan Ferdain's tents, I believe it was."

"That was entirely TTE's fault," chan Ersam asserted. "*My*

people had all the right paperwork. It wasn't our fault TTE put them on the wrong train."

That won a chuckle from the officers seated around the utilitarian desk. That desk sat in the quayside office which had been made available to chan Bykahlar while the men of his brigade—and the mountain of food, equipment, and ammunition accompanying them—filed aboard the transports which would carry them across the Vandor to what ought to have been New Ternath. And while that chuckle was entirely genuine, it had a sour edge which had quite a lot to do with that logistical mountain, because the truth was that chan Ersam had a point.

The battalion-captain was a bit long in the tooth for his current rank (at fifty, he was only three years younger than chan Bykahlar and three years *older* than the XO), but that was entirely due to the six years he'd spent in forced medical retirement after losing his left leg below the knee in a training accident. It had taken him that long to browbeat the Personnel Board into letting him and his peg back into uniform. The sheer determination that accomplishment had required—coupled with his undoubted capability and the closeness of their ages—was one reason he got along so well with chan Bykahlar, and during his career, he'd probably seen just about every mistake a quartermaster could make. No doubt the Quartermaster's Corps was thoroughly capable of inventing new ones, but that hadn't happened in the case of the tentage for Hahlstyr chan Ferdain's 312th Infantry Regiment. It wasn't really the Trans-Temporal Express train masters' fault, either, chan Bykahlar supposed. They were shoving things into every nook and cranny aboard the torrent of trains pouring down the chain of universes from Sharona to Traisum, and it was inevitable that at least some of those things would end up misplaced. In its way, that was stupid—military logistics depended on things arriving where (and when) they were *expected*; simply getting them there early if no one knew they were coming was pretty useless—but he certainly understood why it was happening.

What bothered him, truth to tell, was less that the tents had arrived when they did—they *had* been early, not late—than the reason the space they'd been pushed into had been available. According to the official lading transmitted down the Voice chain, that train ought to have been full of Uromathian infantry, at least as far Frayika. In chan Bykahlar's opinion, the fact that it hadn't been didn't bode well.

"If pressed, I will concede—unwillingly, but concede—that I can't really blame you for that one, Rechair," he said after a moment. "Which doesn't mean I won't have your guts for gaiters if we have any major screwups on the move to the front."

"In all seriousness, Sir, I don't expect any." Chan Ersam's tone and expression were much more serious than they had been and he rested his palm on the closed notepad. "The truth is that all of the reports coming back from Shosara sound like this is actually going to work. Assuming TTE's people are their usual efficient selves, we ought to be detraining in about five weeks in Resym." He shook his head. "When I first heard about this brainstorm of the division-captain's, I thought he was crazy. I was much too respectful to say so, of course, but any experienced quartermaster could've told him the whole idea was insane. Push an entire corps down a seventeen-thousand-mile corridor through six different universes in only four months? With an ocean crossing thrown in for good measure, and with fifteen hundred miles of unimproved travel after we run out of railroad?" He shook his head again. "I suppose it's a good thing Division-Captain chan Geraith *isn't* a quartermaster. If he was, he'd never have tried it!"

"No one ever accused the division-captain of thinking small," chan Klaisahn pointed out. "And we have been playing with the Bisons and Steel Mules for a while now. Not that I don't think you have a perfectly valid point, Rechair."

"From the sound of things it's been going better than we had any right to expect it to," chan Bykahlar agreed. "But it's our job—read that as *your* job, Rechair—to make sure it *keeps* going that way."

"I know, Sir. And if I'm going to be honest, I'm more than a little nervous about how many steam drays we're going to end up using. I was joking when I said it was a good thing the division-captain wasn't a quartermaster, but he really is demanding an awful lot out of our logistics net. The Bisons and Mules seem to be having fewer maintenance issues than I'd expected, but the drays are making up for that. And given that long stretch through the Dalazan, I'm nowhere near as confident as I'd like to be that they'll hold up under the pounding."

"We'll just have to do the best we can," chan Bykahlar said. "And, speaking of doing the best we can, it's occurred to me that once we reach Shosara and start breaking bulk for the move to

Kelsayr, it might be a good idea to make sure the ammunition for the 37s and the pedestal guns is well to the front of the queue. So, what I want you to be thinking about Rechair, is—"

Cormas 27, 5053 AE
(February 15, 1929 CE)

IT WAS AS HOT AS IT HAD EVER BEEN AT FORT SALBY, ARLOS chan Geraith thought, and much, much, *much* more humid. He hadn't thought anything was likely to make him long for that remembered heat as a breath of cool air, but he'd been wrong.

He stood on the platform of his command car, sweating in the oppressive early afternoon sauna and smoking one of his cigars while he listened to the shouts of command, the snort of heavy equipment, and the clang of metal on metal as Olvyr Banchu's and Ganstamar Yanusa-Mahrdissa's work crews labored furiously. That labor continued rain or shine—and a lot of the weather was rain, not shine, here in the very center of New Farnal—driving even the enormously experienced TTE personnel past the brink of exhaustion.

The Trans-Temporal Express had laid track through the heart of the Dalazan Basin in at least half a dozen universes, and its engineers had all the maps, all the records, all the construction logs at their disposal. Without that, the current effort would have been a madman's dream. Even with it, it was a task to daunt the ancient tomb builders of Bolakin, but they were actually doing it.

The troop train upon which he'd arrived would be forced to back for over forty miles to the nearest triangle junction—the railroad men called it a "wye"—where it could be turned to head back the way it had come. Eventually, Yanusa-Mahrdissa had told him, there'd be balloon loops, or even proper wheelhouses and switching yards, spaced along the line at convenient intervals. But at the moment, he was also at what was—for now—the very end of the rail line from Traisum, and those improvements were a future luxury their frenetic present had to do without. And however primitive their facilities might be, they were working... so far, at least. At this moment, as he stood smoking his cigar and cradling a cup of tea in his left hand, looking out across the raw-edged railbed and muddy road hacked out of the rain forest, he was the next best thing to two thousand miles from the point at which he'd entered the universe of Resym.

Of course, I'm still seven hundred miles from the point at which I intend to leave Resym, he thought. *And when I do, I'll be going from all this nice heat into a godsdamned icebox.*

He snorted at the thought, but at least the reports coming back from Battalion-Captain chan Yahndar were hopeful.

Young chan Mahsdyr's Gold Company, the very tip of 3rd Dragoon's spear, was well into Nairsom. The weather had been just as bad as chan Geraith had been afraid it would, and if the Imperial Ternathian Army wasn't quite as accustomed to campaigning across the crazy-quilt geography of the multiverse as the Portal Authority's troops were, at least he and his staff had been able to pick the brains of people like Regiment-Captain chan Skrithik and Division-Captain chan Stahlyr's quartermasters back home in Sharona and had done their homework. They'd also consulted with Orem Limana's experts at the Portal Authority on equipment lists and requirements, and the decision to use Regiment-Captain Gerdain chan Malthyn's 12th Dragoons as his vanguard was paying a handsome dividend. The Army might not have seconded as many of its officers and men, proportionately speaking, to the PAAF as the Imperial Marines had, but the Army was *much* larger than the Marines. Even a relatively small percentage of its total strength was a surprisingly large number, and the nature of the PAAF's requirements meant the Army personnel temporarily assigned to the Portal Authority tended to be drawn from mobile units like the 3rd Dragoons. As a result, chan Geraith had discovered a surprising number of officers—including both chan Malthyn and chan Yahndar—who did have that sort of experience. The 12th had still suffered several cases of frostbite after crossing into Nairsom, but there'd actually been remarkably few of them.

And now it's time to see how the rest *of us make out,* the division-captain reflected more than a little grimly.

There was no doubt in his mind that weather-related casualties were going to climb once the 3rd Dragoons' main body hit the frigid reality of a Roanthan Plains winter. Not every regiment-captain or battalion-captain had served in the PAAF, and however good they might be at looking after their men back home, some of them would take time acquiring the...mental agility such an abrupt transition from rain forest summer to high plains winter required.

And while they were acquiring it, their men would pay the price, however conscientiously those officers tried to minimize their inevitable mistakes.

Well, you knew it was going to happen when you came up with your brainstorm, Arlos. It's not as if you've got a choice, and experienced or not, your boys're damned good. If anybody can pull it off, it's the Third Dragoons, and you know it.

Yes he did. He drained the last tea and stepped back inside the car to set the empty cup beside his lunch tray, then folded his hands behind him and stood gazing at the huge map pinned to the car's inner bulkhead.

The bold black line of Yanusa-Mahrdissa's steadily lengthening rail line stretched across it, and chan Geraith's mind went back over the wearisome train trip to his present location. There'd been plenty of signs of improvisation along the route, but it was good, *solid* improvisation. The speed with which the TTE's construction gangs could throw timber trestle bridges across rivers had to be seen to be believed. It was something they'd done countless times over the last eighty years, and even now the snarling scream of one of the mobile steam-powered sawmills drifted in through the compartment's open window. It was all going to have to be replaced with more permanent construction as soon as possible, and the trestle bridges couldn't handle trains as heavy as those booming down the mainline from Sharona to Traisum, but it was doing what needed to be done, and he'd settle for that joyfully.

He glanced out the window as another convoy of Bisons rumbled past, towing their enormous trailers. The trailers' outsized pneumatic tires had been designed to reduce ground pressure for better cross-country performance, but the designers hadn't visualized the abuse to which he intended to subject their brain children. The TTE, on the other hand, had a great deal of experience when it came to moving heavy equipment through difficult terrain, and Olvyr Banchu's workshops in Renaiyrton had improvised "mud tracks" for the trailers—continuous tracks similar to the Bisons' own tracks, with the tires functioning as bogies—to decrease ground pressure still further. They'd scavenged the material for the first few hundred sets from their own forward equipment depots, and the original design—sent up the chain to Sharona by Voice and slightly refined—had been put into crash production by Ram's Horn Heavy Equipment. Enough of them were coming forward to keep up (barely) with the Bisons and trailers being moved up from the Kelsayr railhead, but the heavy traffic was still pounding the jungle roadway into soupy mud. His own engineers and everyone the TTE crews could spare were dumping hopper cars of gravel into the task of keeping them moving—gods only knew how many thousands of tons of *that* TTE had shipped forward and stockpiled for railroad ballast!—but the farther they got from the railhead, the worse it was going to get.

The platoon of Bisons churned on up the path and out of his field of view. As the five behemoths disappeared, a longer column of Steel Mules followed. The half-tracked vehicles made heavier going of it than the fully tracked Bisons, but reports from farther down-chain confirmed that, on firmer terrain, the Mules were both faster and more maneuverable. They were also considerably quieter, which might prove a significant factor once 3rd Dragoons ran into the Arcanans. That didn't make it any easier to wrestle them through the rain forest, unfortunately, and the commercial steam drays had an even harder time of it than they did. On the other hand, TTE and the Portal Authority had turned up Chindarsu's own horde of the things. Even with mud tracks turning them into improvised (and much less capable) siblings of the Steel Mules, they were restricted to rear areas where there'd been at least some improvement of what passed for a roadbed, but they were helping enormously.

Of course, none of Regiment-Captain chan Kymo's original calculations had included hauling the kerosene to fuel that many boilers. For that matter, his estimates for fuel consumption for the Bisons and Steel Mules were proving at least thirty percent low, mostly because the vehicles were spending more time slogging through mud than he'd allowed for. The abundance of steam drays eased much of the strain in that respect, and there were enough more of them than expected to manage—barely, but to manage—to haul forward enough fuel to meet the higher than anticipated requirements.

And at least fuel expenditure at the spear point of the movement should be dropping again soon. The one thing a high plains winter would provide was good, solid going once they got into Nairsom. Of course, they still had dozens of rivers—including the upper reaches of the Dalazan itself—and another seven hundred miles of jungle to cross before they got there.

But many of those rivers had already been bridged, and although the Bison's tracks were taking a worse hammering than he'd hoped, they were also holding up extraordinarily well. Breakdowns were deadlining perhaps twenty percent of his total forward Bison strength at any given moment, but most of the problems were directly related to the pounding their tracks were taking. They'd been designed for the beginning for fast replacement of broken links, and the spares situation was actually better than chan Kymo had anticipated. The parts they needed for repairs were there; it was the time required to *make* those repairs which posed potential serious problems.

But we'll do it, he told himself, settling behind his desk to deal with the day's paperwork. That was one thing he wasn't going to miss when he abandoned the train for one of the Steel Mules and headed forward tomorrow morning.

We'll do it, he repeated, *and when we have, the frigging Arcanans will damned well wish they'd never been born.*

*　　　*　　　*

"*Chan Wahldyn!* Vothan's Chariot, man! We're supposed to be *building* the godsdamned road!"

Company-Captain Hyrus chan Derkail, CO of Silver Company, 1407th Mounted Combat Engineers, looked up. Senior Armsman Tyrail chan Turkahn, the senior noncom of his second platoon, stood atop one of the parked Bisons, hands on hips, glaring at another Bison which had just slithered across fifty feet of muddy roadway and demolished the approach to the crude felled-tree bridge across yet another of the Dalazan rain forest's innumerable waterways.

It really wasn't Armsman 1/c chan Wahldyn's fault, and chan Turkahn undoubtedly knew that as well as chan Derkail did. Expecting him to admit anything of the sort was futile, of course. Senior armsmen simply didn't do that. As the junior armsman of chan Derkail's own first platoon had explained to him, one might be able to accomplish more with a spoonful of honey than a cup of vinegar, but one could accomplish even more with the toe of a boot applied smartly to an errant trooper's arse.

At the moment, however, chan Derkail was more concerned with getting chan Waldyn's Bison back out of the stream—or off the wreckage of the bridge, at least—and getting that bridge repaired. The Bisons could ford this particular river without undue difficulty, and the Mules could probably do the same, but the commercial drays couldn't, and they were carrying a lot more of the logistical load than the operations plan had originally called for.

Fortunately, Senior Armsman chan Turkahn realized that as well as chan Derkail did. For all his red-faced outrage, he was already clambering down and wading into the confusion—and the waist deep stream—to sort things out. Platoon-Captain chan Gairwyn, 2nd Platoon's CO, wasn't afraid to get his own boots muddy, either. He arrived in a splatter of mud on an even more mud-splattered Shikowr gelding, and dismounted quickly beside chan Derkail.

"Sorry about that, Sir," he told his company commander. "Chan Wahldyn knows to be more careful than that. That's why chan Turkahn's playing traffic director."

"Not his fault," chan Derkail replied. "Or yours or Senior Armsman chan Turkahn's, either." He shrugged. "We're getting at least two thunderstorms a day, Ersayl, and that stretch is more like porridge than mud at the moment. No wonder the Bisons and Mules wallow like pigs in shit trying to get through it! We just need to make a note to move the tracked vehicles' fords farther from the bridges to give us a little more slack."

"Agreed, Sir. And chan Farcos is already on it."

The platoon-captain pointed, and chan Derkail grunted in satisfaction as a Mark 2 Bison came churning up the roadway. The massive vehicle was over twenty feet long and ten feet wide, and its kerosene-fueled monotube boiler produced almost twice the steam pressure of the Mark 1's pelletized coal-fired boiler. In fact, it had better than twice the horsepower of the TTE's famous "Devil Buff" bulldozers, and Battalion-Captain chan Hurmahl had decided to fit a quarter of the 1470th's Mark 2s with bulldozer blades of their own. Now Junior-Armsman Urmahl chan Farcos, the senior noncom of 2nd Platoon's third squad, lowered the blade on his vehicle and went grinding forward.

Jungle trees toppled and deep, soft rain forest loam rose in a bow wave as the Bison began broadening the cleared approach to the stream, and chan Derkail watched it with a sense of wonder experience had yet to dull. He'd grown up as a combat engineer of the Imperial Ternathian Army well before Division-Captain chan Stahlyr had first proposed his radical concept of "mechanization." In those long forgotten days—all of five years ago—scores of men and dozens of horses would have spent the better part of two full days laboring on the task chan Farcos and his Bison would accomplish in no more than a couple of hours. There were times—many of them, especially when he found himself cursing a breakdown or dragging yet another of the massive vehicles out of the muck when they hit a swamp deep enough to mire even them—when he missed those simpler days of muscle-powered shovels and transports with hooves. But without the Bisons, without the additional bulldozers, graders, steamrollers, and steam shovels the TTE was driving forward behind the spear point of the 1407th Engineers, this entire operation would have been flatly impossible.

As it was, it was simply very, very difficult.

So far, at least.

The company-captain removed his hat and mopped at the perspiration coating his shaven scalp. It didn't make any difference, of course. By the time he put the hat back on, the sweat would be just as deep and just as irritating. But at least it gave him the temporary illusion of having done something about it.

At the moment, Silver Company was five hundred miles from the current railhead and barely two hundred from the Nairsom portal at Lake Wernisk. According to the Voice messages from their rear, the TTE was doing wonders improving the roadway behind them, as well as extending the rails, but that was still five hundred miles of heat, snakes, monkeys, insects, crocodiles, and mud. Frankly, chan Derkail was astounded they weren't suffering even more delays.

More trees crashed down as chan Farcos bulldozed them into the river, and chan Derkail nodded in approval. Even with all the powered equipment, they were the better part of a week behind schedule. The good news was that the schedule had built in a certain amount of cushion for slippage. The bad news was that they were rapidly using up that cushion, and somewhere far out in front of them, on the far side of the Nairsom portal, Battalion-Captain chan Yahndar's patrol was already nearing Lake Wernisk. It would be weeks yet before 3rd Dragoons main body overtook its 12th Regiment, but when that happened, this muddy, mucky, hot, humid, rain soaked, bug-infested wound gouged through the rain forest would be the entire division's logistical lifeline.

The task of building and, even more importantly, *sustaining* that lifeline was in the hands of Hyrus chan Derkail and his men, and they weren't about to fail at it.

He shoved his sweat-sodden bandanna back into his pocket, settled his hat on his head, and nodded to chan Gairwyn.

"I'll be moving up towards the head of the line, Ersayl. If you need me, have chan Kostyr Flick a note to chan Dorth."

"Yes, Sir. I'll let you know as soon as we've finished widening the ford, as well."

"Good." Chan Derkail patted the platoon-captain on the shoulder. "And don't forget we'll need four or five hundred more feet of timbers tomorrow. It might be a good idea to start felling the trees while chan Farcos is working on the ford. Company-Captain chan Kilstar will be coming along behind you later this afternoon. He should have the transport to haul the logs forward."

"Yes, Sir." Chan Gairwyn saluted, and chan Derkail gave his shoulder another thump before he climbed back onto his own horse and started across the stream.

CHAPTER THIRTY-FOUR

Cormas 28, 5053 AE
Molidyr 25, 206 YU
(February 16, 1929 CE)

"WELL," NAMIR VELVELIG SIGHED, DISMOUNTING TO LEAN against the side of his unicorn, "there it is."

The trees around him rattled mournful, leafless branches that did absolutely nothing to cut the frigid wind. He'd been far colder than this upon occasion back in Arpathia, but that made the current weather no less unpleasant. Getting wagons through the broad belt of woodland hadn't been a happy experience either, even with the Arcanan levitation spells, and it had slowed them considerably. The trees had also provided welcome cover for the last several miles, however, and he'd been careful to halt well back within their concealment before he dismounted.

"You sound surprised, Regiment-Captain," Therman Ulthar said, looking down from his own saddle with a tired, crooked smile. "Someone might almost think you hadn't expected to get here."

"They might, might they?" Velvelig cocked his head to give the young Arcanan a moderate glare. "Can't imagine why they should've."

"Neither can I," Ulthar assured him, and swung down from his unicorn.

A growl rumbled deep in the beast's muscular throat, and the fifty swatted its nose with a casual assurance Velvelig still found disturbing. He wasn't accustomed to "horses" with five-inch fangs capable of effortlessly removing a man's hand... or his *head*, for that matter. That wicked ivory horn was equally daunting; he'd seen spears that were less sharply pointed, and the thing was over two feet long. It would never have done for an Arpathian septman to admit fear of anything that went on four feet, but he knew damned well he wasn't the only Sharonian in the column who hadn't entirely come to grips with the notion of riding a seven or eight hundred-pound carnivore. Nor had any of them developed the degree of comfort—or the confidence to smack them to remind them who was in charge—Ulthar and the other Arcanans demonstrated.

Yet whatever reservations he might retain, he'd become devoutly thankful for their presence. Without them, the mutineers and escaped prisoners would never have made it this far, and certainly not this quickly. The unicorns were just as fast and just as hardy as Ulthar and Jaralt Sarma had assured him they were. Keeping them fed was a greater challenge than simply grazing a horse or a mule normally presented, but given the season and the speed with which they'd been moving, the chore wasn't that much worse than hauling along fodder would have been. And little though the horse lover in him cared to admit it, he suspected that something with a predator's instincts probably made a better combat mount than a creature whose best natural defense to a threat was to run away from it. Of course, there *were* downsides, and one thing he'd observed was that unicorn dung had the reek of carnivore excrement, rather than the homier scent of horse manure. Fortunately, that hadn't been much of a factor on their open air jaunt, but he really didn't like to think about mucking out a stable full of unicorns.

He smiled wearily at the thought and uncased his binoculars as he gazed at the portal between Thermyn and New Uromath.

And however . . . unpleasant that might be, the critters really are tough as hill demons, he reflected. *They aren't as sensitive to sudden climate changes as horses are, either. More of that damned magic, I'll bet. They sure as hell didn't grow any sudden furry coats along the way!*

And that was one more thing to be profoundly grateful for, he acknowledged. For that matter, although their gait took some getting used to—a man who'd learned to post on a horse had required quite a bit of minor adjustment before his mount had stopped complaining and his own arse and thighs had acclimated—it was actually smoother than any he'd ever before experienced. And those clawed feet made them incredibly surefooted and nimble in rough terrain. The Arpathian in him resisted being seduced away from the horses he'd always loved, but he couldn't deny there were profound advantages to these unnatural beasts.

He raised the binoculars and suppressed a desire to wince as the skin around his eyes made contact with the rubber eye shields and his gloved fingers adjusted the focusing knob. At this time of year, the average temperatures here on what should have been the location of Wyrmach ought to have averaged well above freezing, but that was an *average* temperature. Daily highs and lows peaked twenty or thirty degrees outside that range, and the town was subject to occasional bouts of bitter cold...one of which they—of course—had arrived in the middle of. And just to make the situation even better, the Thermyn side of the portal was a thousand feet higher than the New Uromath side. Although this portal was old enough for the portal wind to have stabilized quite a lot, the current of air pouring through from New Uromath remained far too powerful to call a "breeze," and while that would normally have been a good thing, the weather on the far side of the portal had decided to drop well below *its* normal range, as well. It was marginally warmer than the Thermyn side, but not enough to evoke any handsprings of delight.

He gazed through the binoculars, sweeping his gaze steadily across as much of the fourteen-mile wide portal as he could see from his present location. The combination of the way the woods straggled off and the nice, flat terrain around Wyrmach meant he could see most of it, which didn't make him especially happy as he contemplated the small cluster of chinked-log structures parked on a low rise almost squarely in the center of the portal's arc.

Miserable as it might have been to cross, the rugged terrain between Bitter Lake and Fort Ghartoun had given a lot of cover. The fact that the best land route—indeed, the only truly practicable land route, especially this time of year—had wandered far afield from the straight-line route available to dragons had helped even more. Despite which, Valnar Rohsahk, Ulthar's "recon crystal specialist," had detected six separate overflights by dragons. Rohsahk was what the Arcanans called a "javelin," according to the literal translation their talking crystals provided. That was roughly the equivalent of a junior-armsman, and despite his youthfulness, the Arcanan—who was from what ought to have been the Republic of Syskhara in New Ternath—had the solid, unflappable competence Velvelig normally associated with strongly Talented noncoms. The regiment-captain had no idea how the Arcanans' "spellware" worked, but he was willing to take their word that it did. They had as much to lose as the Sharonians did if they were overtaken, after all, so they had no vested interest in pretending it could accomplish things it couldn't. And it didn't hurt his confidence in their abilities any that Under-Armsman Haryl chan Byral, his own junior headquarters clerk-specialist (who was even younger than Rohsahk), had been assigned as Fort Ghartoun's Distance Viewer. Despite his youth, chan Byral was powerfully Talented, and twice he'd Seen the passing dragon Rohsahk had detected.

Fortunately, none of them had flown directly overhead, and apparently none of them had been actively seeking the fugitives at the time they passed. All of those near escapes had occurred in the first few days of their flight, however. By Ulthar and Sarma's most optimistic estimates, Thalmayr must have gotten his story into someone senior's hands by now, which meant any additional overflights were unlikely to be benignly negligent. And the terrain had been depressingly open for the last four or five hundred miles. In fact, here in the approaches to Wyrmach, it reminded Velvelig of a pocket-ball table, and he felt remarkably like the strike-ball as he stood surveying the portal. He'd done his best to keep clear of that straight-line flight path between here and Fort Ghartoun, but trying to balance the extra time to circle wide of crossing dragon traffic against the threat that orders to find them might come racing down-chain from Two Thousand Harshu at any moment had been a nerve-racking business.

Now, unfortunately, they had no choice but to move squarely back onto the flight path. The portal was the critical bottleneck, the funnel through which they *had* to pass to reach New Uromath . . . and through which *any* Arcanan traffic, whether specifically searching for them or not, must also pass.

"What do you see?" Ulthar asked, and Velvelig's lips gave the slightest of twitches . . . which would have been a broad grin in anyone who wasn't Arpathian.

He and his Sharonians found the Arcanans' casual use of magic fascinating, yet the *Arcanans* seemed at least equally fascinated by routine, everyday bits and pieces of Sharonian technology. They'd never seen anything like a pair of binoculars, for example. Instead of learning to grind and polish lenses, they'd learned how to polish and enchant "*sarkolis*" crystals to let them see distant objects. And as nearly as Golvar Silkash and Tobis

Makree had been able to figure it out, their "magistrons" could Heal nearsightedness, farsightedness, and even cataracts, so no one needed spectacles. The thought of being able to duplicate a Distance Viewer's Talent with a shiny piece of rock was certainly impressive—and seductive—but Velvelig was well content with his binoculars, and Ulthar and his people appeared to be just as deeply impressed by the notion of a distance viewing apparatus that required no Gift to produce or use.

"Nothing in the air, right now," he replied, answering the fifty's question. "What about your Rohsahk?"

"Nothing," Ulthar said. "Unfortunately, there could be fifty dragons hovering on the other side of that portal and Valnar wouldn't be able to detect them from here."

Velvelig grunted in combined understanding, unhappiness, and worry. It was interesting that the Arcanans' Gifts and spells were no more capable of crossing a portal threshold than a Sharonian's Talent. Learning that minor fact had made it abruptly clear how Balkar chan Tesh had managed to ream what were clearly elite troops so easily when he'd attacked the Swamp Portal. Of course, it had helped that the idiot in command of those elite troops had been Hadrign Thalmayr. Velvelig remembered a conversation with Silkash in which he'd tried to explain his suspicion about the quality of the prisoners chan Tesh had sent up-chain from Hell's Gate. Now he knew he'd been right, although he supposed he ought to cut Thalmayr at least a *little* slack. The man *was* an idiot, and his defensive deployment and tactics (such as they were and what there'd been of them) had reflected that, but they'd been based on his understanding of his own weapons. None of the Arcanans at the Swamp Portal had ever imagined that anything more lethal than an arbalest bolt or a grenade could be thrown *through* a portal. Velvelig liked to think a Sharonian commander wouldn't have made any comfortable assumptions about that, but the fact that the Arcanans had taken five entire universes with such absurd ease suggested he might have been wrong about who had a monopoly on overconfidence.

What mattered at the moment, however, was that the handful of Arcanans who were now his allies couldn't tell him anything more about the far side of that portal than he could see with his own two eyes and the assistance of his binoculars, and that was limited enough to make anyone unhappy.

What he *could* see from here was that the Arcanans appeared to have placed their picket on the Thermyn side of the portal rather than the New Uromathian side. Given the normal weather in New Uromath, Velvelig completely agreed with their decision. The rainfall and seasonal temperature variation in Malbar, the Sharonian city nearest to the New Uromathian portal's site, was less pronounced than in Wyrmach, but Malbar also got around four times the annual precipitation, and he preferred surroundings which were a bit less damp. It did leave him with a bit of a problem, though.

"You were right about where they put their fort," he said, studying the offending structures through the binoculars. "It's right damned in the middle of this side of the portal." He lowered the glasses and showed the Arcanan his teeth. "I suppose there's only one way to be sure they haven't switched things around on you on the far aspect, though."

"Part of me hopes they have," Ulthar admitted. "Not the *smart* part of me, of course. It just offends me to think that the Union Army could be sloppy enough to've left things this way."

"Peacetime thinking dies hard," Velvelig replied. "Here on the frontiers, it's always been *our* policy to locate our forts on the down-chain side of each portal as we explored it, so it's probably not too surprising your people operate the same way in what they think are their rear areas."

Ulthar nodded, although his expression remained an odd mixture of hopefulness and disgust.

The New Uromath Portal was fourteen miles across—what Ulthar had described as a Class Six portal. Sharonians didn't bother about classification systems; they simply measured a portal's diameter and got on with exploring it. This one happened to be quite a bit wider than most and aligned roughly on a north-south axis...on this side. On the *far* side, it was aligned almost exactly on an east-to-west line, however, and that was where the "counterintuitive" nature of portals came into play. Standing west of the Thermyn aspect of the portal and gazing through it, one looked due south into New Uromath; if one circled around to the *eastern* aspect of the portal, however, one looked due *north* into New Uromath. It was impossible to look across or through a portal within a single universe—all you could see was the *other* universe, as if you were peering through a picture window, and in this instance, vision was as useless as spells or Talent. The only way for an observer in one universe to find out what was happening on the far side of a portal in the *same* universe was to move around the perimeter of the portal until he had a direct, unobstructed line-of-sight.

Which meant that unless the Arcanans had gone ahead and constructed a second position—a lookout post, at least—on the far side of this portal, they'd left a fourteen-mile wide blind spot. The blind spot in question happened to be fourteen miles *high* at its tallest point, as well...which didn't do Velvelig any good since he didn't have any handy dragons of his own.

Personally, he damned well *would* have put at least an outpost on the far side of that portal if he'd been going to war against another multi-universal civilization, no matter how far in his rear it might happen to be. But he'd known dozens of Portal Authority officers who probably wouldn't have, too.

"I suppose it all comes down to how crazy your Two Thousand Harshu—or whoever the hells is behind this frigging cover-up of yours—thinks we are," he said finally. "If anyone who's looking for us thinks we might be big enough lunatics to head even deeper behind your lines instead of hiding out in the mountains west of Fort Ghartoun and Snow Sapphire Lake, he'll damned well have put somebody on the other side of this portal to watch its eastern aspect. If he doesn't think we're crazy enough to try sneaking into New Uromath in the first place, he won't be worrying about watching for us here."

"Especially not if they're trying to keep what happened at Fort Ghartoun from leaking out," Ulthar agreed. "They wouldn't want to issue any orders that might make people wonder what the hells is going on, I suppose. I wish I had a better feel for whether or not they *will* try to keep the news from getting out, though. In a way, I'd feel a lot better if I knew they'd decided to go as public as possible about it. It'd make sneaking past them harder, but at least then I'd assume they weren't thinking in terms of making us quietly disappear before Duke Garth Showma starts asking awkward questions."

"Does make it a little harder to catch someone when you're trying to keep the truth about why you're hunting them from your own troops," Velvelig acknowledged. "You can probably come up with plausible orders to cover a lot of contingencies, but if the man on the spot doesn't know what you're *really* trying to do, he won't do a very good job of adapting or modifying those orders to cover a contingency you didn't think of when you gave them."

"Agreed. On the other hand, if Jaralt and I are right and mul Gurthak is the one who set all of this in motion, he at least managed to find someone like Alivar Neshok when he needed him. I don't like to think he could have found a *lot* of other officers who were . . . equally apt, let's say, to his purposes. But he might not need many of them if the ones he does have are in the right positions. Or, from our perspective, the *wrong* positions."

"Like on the other side of this portal?" Velvelig arched his eyebrows, and Ulthar nodded. "Well," the regiment-captain said more briskly, sliding his binoculars back into their case, "there's only one way to find out, isn't there?"

He swung back up into the unicorn's saddle and squinted up at the sky through the branches. Like many Arpathians, he wasn't especially fond of trees, but under the circumstances, he was willing to make an exception to his usual attitude.

"Gets dark early, this time of year," he observed. "Light'll be gone in another couple of hours, and there's no moon tonight—on either side of the portal. The troops in that fort of yours are going to be showing at least some lights, which should help us keep wide of them while we creep around to the other side, but it'll be slow going without lights of our own. Still, I figure we should get chan Byral far enough around the western end of the portal to get a good Look for any outposts covering the southern aspect in, say, three hours. And if he doesn't see anything, we may just be justified in thinking this mul Gurthak of yours doesn't realize how crazy we really are. And if he *doesn't*"—the Arpathian grinned suddenly and broadly as Fifty Ulthar climbed into his own saddle—"we may just have a straight dash from here to Hell's Gate after all!"

CHAPTER THIRTY-FIVE

Fairsayla 20, 5053 AE
(March 8, 1929 CE)

"WELL, SIR, CAN'T SAY I'M LOOKING FORWARD TO THIS next bit," Tersak chan Golar said.

"Whyever not?" Grithair chan Mahsdyr asked with a smile. Chan Golar, Gold Company's company senior-armsman, was from southern Jerekhas, accustomed to the Mbisi's mild summers, and the company-captain had a pretty shrewd notion of the reasons for his discontent.

"Might say nobody but a pure and simple lunatic would go anywhere near Lake Wernisk in th' winter if he had any choice about it, Sir," chan Golar replied glumly. "If I was inclined t' complain, that is, which gods know I'm not. And according t' my cousin Rhodair, not even bison're stupid enough t' spend the winter at Ulthamyr. Migrate south into Benteria, he says, like anything else with a brain. But us?" The lean, grizzled noncom shook his head in disgust. "We're not only goin' to Lake Wernisk, *we're* goin' the next best thing t' six hundred miles cross-country to Ulthamyr. Gods bless the poor sodding cavalry!"

"I swear, Tersak, you'd complain if they hanged you with a golden rope!" chan Mahsdyr said, and the senior-armsman's chuckle acknowledged the hit.

Chan Golar had been with chan Mahsdyr for almost two years now, and he and the senior-armsman understood one another well. At the moment, they sat in their saddles on the bank of the Rathynoka River in what ought to have been the Darylis Republic in New Farnalia, gazing west at the never-boring spectacle of yet another door between universes. The Resym side of the Resym-Nairsom Portal was several miles west of the location of the town of Shdandifar, but the *Nairsom* side—as chan Golar had just none-too-obliquely observed—lay just outside what would have been the small bison-ranching town of Ulthamyr in the Republic of Roantha, well over three thousand miles north of and twelve hundred feet higher than their present location. Here in Shdandifar, the afternoon temperature was in the high nineties; in Nairsom, the temperature was well below freezing, with lazy snowflakes drifting down a steel-gray sky. This particular portal had obviously been around a while, since the portal wind speed was no more than ten or twelve miles per hour, and what there was of it was out of Resym and into Nairsom. That produced a bubble of warmth on the far side in which there was no accumulation of snow...but it was a rather *small* bubble.

"Awful cold 'round a man's neck, those golden ropes, Sir. Or so they tell me. Never tried one, m'self."

"Yet, at least." Chan Mahsdyr observed cheerfully. "There's always time."

"True enough, Sir. On the other hand, it really is goin' t' be a shock for the horses, not t' mention the men, you know."

"Now there, Tersak, you've got a point," chan Mahsdyr acknowledged less than happily.

His dragoons had brought along the heavy winter uniforms and cold weather equipment they'd need for the six hundred-mile trek between Lake Wernisk and Ulthamyr, but their horses had not. And those same horses had just completed a grueling twenty-eight hundred mile journey between Shdandifar and Paditharyn, during which the temperature had seldom dropped much below seventy degrees and had occasionally risen into the high nineties. They were thoroughly acclimated to *that* climate, and not even the Imperial Ternathian Army's Shikowrs were going to take the sixty-degree drop in average temperature anything like well. They'd brought along plenty of heavy blankets to keep their animals well rugged when they weren't actually riding, but he wouldn't be at all surprised if they lost some of them over the next week or so.

"At least the Mules have held up well," he said now. He wasn't referring to flesh and blood mules, and chan Golar nodded in emphatic agreement. "The Bisons've done better than I really expected, but the Mules have been the real surprise," the company-captain continued. "I'm beginning to think Division-Captain chan Stahlyr might have a point about those 'mechanized troops' of his."

"Wouldn't go that far, Sir," chan Golar said, stubborn despite his agreement of a moment before, and leaned forward to pat his mount's shoulder. "Horses've been around a lot longer nor tea kettles. Mind, they've done well enough *so far*, and I'll not deny it, but they've got no *heart*, no guts. Had my skin saved more'n once by a good horse that was too damned stupid t' know it couldn't keep goin', begging your pardon. It'll be a while before I'm willing t' trade in *my* saddle for good."

"I don't doubt that for a second," chan Mahsdyr agreed with a grin. "And I'm not suggesting we shoot them all next Marniday, either. But just between you and me, I thought the division-captain was smoking things he shouldn't have been when he first came up with this brainstorm. Now—assuming we get across the Stone Carve at Coyote Canyon without the Arcanans spotting us while we're about it—I think he's about to go down in history as a military genius. I sure as hells don't know anyone else who's ever proposed a frigging *eight thousand*-mile approach march with a single division!"

"All due respect for the division-captain, and all, but I b'lieve I've heard as there's a thin line, sometimes, 'twixt genius and crazy," the noncom observed. "Never a doubt in *my* mind which the division-captain is, you understand, Sir!"

"I'm sure," chan Mahsdyr said dryly. "In the meantime, I think we'll go ahead and bivouac. Take time to break out the cold weather gear and inspect it properly before we poke our noses into that nice, cool climate on the other side."

"Good idea, Sir," chan Golar agreed in a considerably more serious tone. "Your permission, and I think it'd be another good idea t'put at least a picket on the far side, though."

"Agreed." Chan Mahsdyr nodded. "Send chan Parthan and chan Ynclair with it. I'll want to talk to both of them before they cross the portal, though."

"Yes, Sir."

"Good. And ask Platoon-Captain chan Sabyr to join me here, as well."

"Yes, Sir."

The senior-armsman nodded, reined his horse around, and trotted back along the column, and chan Mahsdyr dismounted to take the weight off his own horse's back while he waited. Folsar chan Sabyr's 1st Platoon was scheduled to take the lead when they set off into Nairsom, and chan Mahsdyr wanted to be certain chan Sabyr and his men had properly prepared themselves. The platoon-captain was experienced, but he was also young, and his senior-armsman was from coastal Teramandor—a long, long way from New Ternathia—and a bit new to his duties as the platoon's senior noncom. It wouldn't hurt to tactfully remind both of them of some of the unpleasant realities of winter in Roantha. For that matter, it might not be a bad idea to send chan Sabyr's entire platoon through as chan Golar's "picket." They'd spend a milder night in close proximity to the portal, given the portal wind blowing through from Resym, but it would still be chilly enough to find any holes in their preparations and . . . underscore the desirability of plugging said holes before they set out for Ulthamyr.

And it definitely *won't be a bad idea to get chan Parthan and chan Ynclair over to the other side for a looksee*, he reflected.

Chan Parthan was the youngest of the half-dozen Plotters assigned to Gold Company for this little foray, but he was also the most strongly Talented, with by far the greatest range. And chan Ynclair was one of the strongest Distance Viewers chan Mahsdyr had ever encountered. If chan Parthan detected any of the Arcanans' damned dragons hanging about, chan Ynclair would be able to spot them without difficulty.

One interesting discovery they'd made in the course of their journey was that a Plotter's range seemed greater against airborne creatures . . . and got greater still the higher the altitude at which he searched. Chan Parthan's current theory was that the "background noise" of other living organisms—including plants, chan Mahsdyr had been surprised to discover—became less and less a factor at higher and higher altitudes. Without that distraction, he could simply Plot farther and more clearly.

Of course, that might not have come as a surprise to *every* Plotter. The detection of flying creatures wasn't something with which anyone except bird watchers and a relatively small number of Plotters assigned to various park services or ornithological research organizations had much experience, however, because most of them were normally concerned with landborne or seaborne critters. Chan Mahsdyr had come to the grim conclusion that it might very well be that neglect of watching for *aerial* threats which had let the Arcanans take out Company-Captain chan Tesh's men in New Uromath without anyone's getting a warning out up-chain. *Something* had certainly let them get into range and eliminate chan Tesh's assigned Voice before any alert could be sent, and since chan Tesh's Plotters and Distance Viewers had almost equally certainly been anticipating *landborne* threats...

Whatever had happened in New Uromath, chan Mahsdyr had no intention of allowing that to happen to Gold Company. He did wish he had a better notion of just how far someone on dragonback at an altitude of a few thousand feet could actually see, though. He knew it was possible to see as much as fifty or sixty miles—sometimes even farther—from a high enough mountain, and even with the greater range chan Parthan had been able to achieve against aerial targets, that would exceed his reach. On the other hand, how much *detail* could anyone see from that sort of elevation?

No one knew the answer to that, and ever since they'd emerged from the rain forest on their way to Shdandifar, he'd been acutely aware of the lack of any sort of measuring stick by which to judge the threat's true parameters. That was the main reason he'd had binocular-equipped lookouts backing up his Plotters every weary mile of the way. He intended to go right on backing them up, and he devoutly hoped the present overcast visible through the portal would remain with them all the way to Ulthamyr. However he might worry about the horses' vulnerability to cold, he'd prefer anything much short of a howling blizzard to clear skies and good visibility for any aerial spies the other side might have left behind.

The handful of hardy souls in Resym who'd ignored the evacuation orders sent down-chain from Lashai had reported no Arcanan presence in that universe to any of 12th Dragoons' scouts, but chan Mahsdyr was none too certain any of the stay-behinds would have recognized a dragon or an eagle-lion even if they'd seen one. The idea of such creatures remained profoundly unnatural to chan Mahsdyr even after all these weeks, and he'd actually examined their carcasses at Fort Salby. Even if someone here in Resym had seen one of them, why should anyone who'd never heard of them have realized that what he was seeing was much larger than any bird and simply far farther away than he'd thought?

That thought had loomed large in his mind ever since they'd left jungle's tree cover, and he was more grateful than ever for the Steel Mules which had been sent after him following his discussion with Ganstamar Yanusa-Mahrdissa in Shosara. They'd overtaken his mounted men without any difficulty, and he'd redistributed his supplies as they'd arrived. The half-tracked Mules could keep up with his dragoons effortlessly, and without the betraying banner of coal smoke a Mark One Bison emitted. So he'd loaded the Mules with fifteen days of everything his mounted troops would require and left the remainder of his supplies aboard the Bison-towed trailers. That should be more than enough to get him all the way from Lake Wernisk to Ulthamyr before he had to call the Bisons forward, and he was all in favor of remaining as invisible as possible while he did just that.

He hoped none of his men were stupid enough to think he was truly as unconcerned and confident as he pretended, although the game required *them* to pretend that he'd fooled them. Yet the truth was that everything at least *appeared* to have gone extremely well so far. Now if only things *stayed* that way....

CHAPTER THIRTY-SIX

Chesthu 3, 206 YU
Fairsayla 8, 5053 AE
(February 24, 1929 CE)

"WELL, ANOTHER DAY, ANOTHER PORTAL."

Therman Ulthar looked up from his steaming mug of bitterblack as Jaralt Sarma sat on the large rock beside him. It was a gray, cold evening, moving steadily towards full dark, with a miserable drizzle dusting downward, and the vista through the portal before them was less than welcoming, to say the very least. Especially for Ulthar.

"The last time I was this way," he said, "there were trees on the other side of this one. Mind you, I wasn't paying them a lot of attention at the time. Getting shot with one of those damned rifles puts a damper on your sightseeing. But this..."

He shook his head, and Sarma grunted in agreement, although the last time *he'd* crossed that portal the land on the other side had been blackened and still smoking while hooves and dragon wings stirred up torrents of bitter, clinging ash. It had been like a foretaste of Shartahk's own hell, but he had to admit that even that had looked more welcoming than this.

It was winter on both sides of the portal, but the other side wasn't just much colder, with snow falling heavily on a steady wind from the northwest. It was also far bleaker, with snags of burned stumps sticking up through the snow. Some of the bigger forest giants seemed to have survived the torrent of fire which had burned out a thousand square miles of woodland, but if they had, they were clearly in the minority. Either way, it would be impossible to be certain until spring, when they'd either leaf once more...or not. For now, the universe both Arcana and

Sharona had agreed to call Hell's Gate looked very much like its name: a barren, blackened drift of dead trees, burned snags, and blowing snow where the current temperature hovered far, far below freezing.

"It's not too late to change our minds and head for Fort Rycharn," Sarma said after a moment. Ulthar looked at him sharply, and the short, stocky fifty shrugged. "I'm not saying I think it's a wonderful idea, but at least it'd be warmer. And once we cross over into that"—he twitched his head at the uninviting terrain beyond the portal—"we're going to be moving hell for leather and any air patrol that spots us is going to wonder what the hells we're doing. If we made for the Mahritha portal we'd at least be heading *towards* our people instead of obviously avoiding them! And I'm pretty sure Five Hundred Klian would at least listen to us before he slapped us into the brig."

"Something to be said for that, I guess," Ulthar replied after a moment. "Personally, though, I think the idea really sucks."

"That's one of the things I like about you, Therman. That tact and exquisite sensitivity to the sensibilities of others."

"Screw tact. Are you seriously suggesting we do that?"

"No." Sarma sipped his own bitterblack. "The notion does possess a certain comfort quotient, though. We've been completely off the grid ever since the mutiny, in more ways than one. Don't you find it at least a little tempting to consider getting back into a world we know about?"

"No, not at the moment." Ulthar leaned forward to lift the bitterblack pot from the heating crystal and refresh his mug. "And not just because I don't think for a minute that the five hundred could keep us alive long enough for anyone *else* to listen to us. We still owe Regiment-Captain Velvelig and his people for the way they were treated, Jaralt. We both gave the regiment-captain our word to accept his orders, too, and all the Sharonians have more than pulled their weight getting us this far. Besides, I've come to the conclusion the regiment-captain's probably smarter than both of us put together."

"And trying to change plans at this point would be a really good way to touch off a firefight we might not survive. You forgot that bit," Sarma said dryly.

"I'm damned *sure* it would touch off a firefight." Ulthar snorted. "For that matter, at least some of our boys would side with the Sharonians. They've done the math on what's likely to happen if whoever's behind all this gets his hands on us before we hear back from Duke Garth Showma."

"You're probably right. But I didn't broach the idea to suggest we should do it, Therman. I'm bringing it up because it's occurred to me that it's entirely possible one or two of our people might be thinking that making a run for Fort Rycharn and turning the rest of us in would be a way to get their own arses out of the dragon's reach."

"I don't think I like that thought very much," Ulthar said after a long pause.

"I don't either, but we need to be thinking about it. And as you just pointed out, Regiment-Captain Velvelig's smart enough to be thinking the same sort of thoughts. I think it would be a really good idea for the two of us—and Sahrimahn—to make sure we're on the same page he is."

"You're probably right." Ulthar scowled down into his mug and grimaced. "Damn, I don't like that thought. I really don't."

"The good news is that I'm probably worrying more than I ought to," Sarma said. "I mean, if anyone really wanted to desert, he could've done it when we crossed into New Uromath."

"Yeah, but at that point they'd've been in the middle of nowhere, with the rest of us wondering where they'd gone," Ulthar pointed out. "The entire garrison at that excuse for a portal fort couldn't've been more than fifty or sixty men. If we'd had to take it out instead of sneaking around it, we sure as hells had the firepower for it, and that was the only place they could've gone. I'm pretty sure most of them are smart enough to figure out what the rest of us—and especially the regiment-captain—would've done if we'd figured out they'd gone running to the fort to report us. No," he shook his head, "if anybody's really thinking about turning his coat on us, he'll wait until he has a clear run for Mahritha."

"Probably," Sarma acknowledged. "If it's any comfort, anybody who might be thinking that way's almost certainly one of my boys or Sahrimahn's cavalry. Your Second Andarans are about as all in on this as it's possible for someone to be!"

"Well, of course they are!" Ulthar's frown turned into a grin. "Unlike the rest of you, we know *exactly* what the duke's going to do. By now Arylis has to've delivered my report to him, and none of my boys have any doubt about what's been heading down-chain towards us ever since. So we're not in any hurry to be throwing ourselves into the dragon's mouth in the meantime."

"Faith," Sarma observed, sipping bitterblack, "is a wonderful thing. I just hope to Hali it's not misplaced."

* * *

"Ready to proceed, Regiment-Captain," Therman Ulthar said an hour later as he reined in his unicorn beside Namir Velvelig and Company-Captain Traisair Halath-Shodach, Velvelig's senior surviving subordinate. His tone was rather more formal than the one he normally used when addressing the Sharonian he'd come to know so well over the last several weeks. Sarma and Fifty Sahrimahn Cothar came cantering up behind him, their unicorns moving with the almost feline stride to which Velvelig had finally become accustomed.

"Any cold feet on your side?" he asked now, raising one eyebrow by perhaps a thirty-second of an inch. For a moment, Ulthar looked blank, then grimaced once the spellware came up with the Andaran equivalent of the cliché.

"Not that we know of, Sir," he replied, glancing at his fellow Arcanans. "Everyone's present and accounted for at the moment, at any rate." He looked back at Velvelig and shrugged. "Actually, Jaralt and I were rather hoping that particular concern wouldn't have occurred to you. Not that we figured there was much chance it wouldn't."

"People are people, Therman, whether they're Arcanan or Sharonian. Much as I didn't think I'd ever say this while I was locked up in my own brig, your lads are about as good and solid troops as I've ever seen. They'd be more than human if at least some of them weren't thinking about it, though."

"The thought had occurred to me, too, Sir," Halath-Shodach said, stroking his flowing mustache with a gloved finger. "But to be honest, I haven't seen any sign of its occurring to any of Fifty Ulthar's men." He smiled a bit crookedly. "Maybe they're just not as corruptible as Sharonians."

"Oh, we're just as corruptible," Ulthar replied a bit more grimly. "That's what we're all doing out here, after all—coping with *someone's* corruptibility."

"But not *your* boys' corruptibility," Halath-Shodach said. As a Shurkhali, he'd been filled with just as much hate for all things Arcanan over Shaylar's death as any *garthan* in the Arcanan

Army had been infuriated by Halathyn vos Dulainah's "murder" at Sharonian hands. And like his Arcanan trail companions, he'd had to do some profound rethinking once he learned the truth. In the process, he'd become something suspiciously close to an Arcanan sympathizer.

Where *some* Arcanans were concerned, at any rate.

"I don't know if I'd go as far as Traisahr, Regiment-Captain, but I think we're good," Cothar said, meeting the Sharonians' eyes levelly. Velvelig gazed back at the cavalry officer for a moment, then nodded.

"In that case, I think it's time we were going. I trust your little navigating rock is ready?"

"It is," Ulthar assured him, lifting his navigation unit and showing him the activated display. At the moment, it was still oriented to New Uromath; the instant they crossed back into Hell's Gate it would shift to the stored navigational data for that universe, although only a sixty-mile radius around the Mahritha portal had been mapped and loaded when Sarma and Cothar passed through on their way towards Thermyn. A broader upload was undoubtedly available by now, but what they had was enough for their present need.

Velvelig glanced at the glowing display and nodded. He wasn't fully enamored of trusting his navigation to someone who was technically the enemy, but the Arcanan device was clearly better than anything *he* had. And at least he knew the rough compass bearing to their destination, which should tip him off if they started steering him in the wrong direction for some reason. Of course, *seeing* his compass was going to be just a bit difficult under the circumstances, he reflected, unable to suppress a stab of envy as he looked at that lighted display.

Oh, come on, Namir! he told himself. *What kind of sorry excuse for a septman needs a compass to find his way around even on the darkest night? And in the snow? When he can't see a damned thing? Anyway, the damned glow's probably visible a thousand yards away in the dark! Not exactly the best thing in the world when you're sneaking around in the shrubbery. Assuming the damned forest fire'd left any shrubbery, anyway.*

His lip twitched in the fractional lift that served him for a smile and he raised one hand, waving at the darkness before them.

"After you, then," he said.

*   *   *

The snowfall thickened as full night fell. It didn't quite qualify for the term "blizzard," but it was clearly headed that way. In fact, it ought to reach it in the next few hours, which pleased the fugitives no end. Dragons didn't mind snow, but few of their riders were particularly fond of it. And even if the inclement weather didn't ground any potential overflights, not even a dragon would see much on a night like this. The snow which already blanketed the burned-out forest was more than a little treacherous underfoot, and it was deep enough to hide the kind of obstacles which could break a horse's—or even a unicorn's—leg entirely too easily, but it also made the night seem less dark.

They produced what seemed like an incredible racket slogging through the snow. In fact, Velvelig knew, there was actually very little noise, considering the number of men and vehicles moving through the dark. It was only tight nerves and adrenaline that made it seem so loud. And even if it had been just as loud as it seemed, the Hell's Gate portal was what the Arcanans called a Class Eight, just over thirty-six miles across. There was no way in all the Arpathian hells the Arcanans at what had been Fort Shaylar could hope to cover *that* kind of frontage on a night like this—and he didn't care if they *did* have magic to do it with!

He'd never heard of portals as close together as the Hell's Gate cluster, but he thanked his ancestors' ghosts for it. The swamp portal to the universe the Arcanans had dubbed Mahritha was thirty miles from the Hell's Gate itself, but one of the other portals was barely half that far away. In fact, it was close enough that they ought to reach it easily before what ought to have been sunrise, assuming the cloud cover broke enough for there to *be* a sunrise.

Namir Velvelig was Arpathian, born and bred to the steppes, and he hated close country. He *especially* hated jungle, if he was going to be honest, but under some circumstances, jungles had a great deal to recommend them. For one thing, they offered lots of hiding places. And, for another, as hard as rain forests could be on equipment and clothing, they never got cold enough for hypothermia to kill his men.

*   *   *

"Marshan's mercies, but that feels good," one of the Arcanans said, and Master-Armsman Hordal Karuk nodded in profound agreement.

He had no idea at all who "Marshan" was. As an Arpathian, he had too many demons of his own to keep track of to worry about all the other *Sharonian* deities be, much less about heathen Arcanan pantheons! But he was heartily in favor of staying on the good side of any divine being who specialized in mercies, and the blessed warmth blowing into their faces constituted the greatest mercy he'd encountered since leaving Fort Ghartoun.

"Does feel nice," he agreed. "But let's hold up for a minute till the rest catch up a bit."

"Right, Master-Armsman," the Arcanan replied. Or, rather, his crystal replied for him. What he'd actually said was probably something like "Sure, Master Sword," but by now Karuk was almost accustomed to the damned twinkly rocks.

He chuckled mentally at the thought and eased himself in the unicorn's saddle. Unlike his regiment-captain, he'd decided early on that the horned beasties were vastly superior to horses. As an Arpathian, he wasn't supposed to admit anything of the sort. As someone whose arse had spent entirely too many hours making the acquaintance of entirely too many saddles, however, he approved enthusiastically of unicorns. It might be a tad inconvenient to have a mount who might nip off your arm if it got hungry, but that was a small price to pay for all of the other good points.

He'd also decided, much to his own astonishment, that he rather liked most of the Arcanans in their ... diverse party. He hadn't expected that, even after they'd broken him and the other POWs out of their own brig, yet it was true. He'd spent too many years in uniform not to recognize the Arcanans' hard core of professionalism, and those same years told him how hard it must have been for them to turn against their own superiors, whatever the provocation, over what amounted to a matter of principle and conscience. He wasn't sure he bought into the notion that someone with motives of his own had deliberately fanned the flames for the current war, but he'd found he had no choice but to believe these men were simply doing their duty the best way they could in one hell of a messy situation. And the fact that they were said some things which were at least hopeful about the society and military which had produced men willing to run such risks in the name of their army's honor.

"Have we lost anybody, Master-Armsman?" a voice asked quietly from beside him, and he snorted.

"Now why should we be losing anybody, Evarl?"

"Are telling me Regiment-Captain Velvelig didn't discuss that possibility with you?" Thermyn Ulthar's senior surviving noncom replied. "Fifty Ulthar and Fifty Sarma sure as hells both discussed it with *me!*"

"Ah, well, that's the sort of thing officers're paid to worry about, isn't it?" Karuk turned to glance at the Arcanan, whose face was faintly visible in the backwash from his navigating crystal. "You and me, we're a bit closer to the lads than that."

"Have to admit that once they brought it up I was a little nervous," Evarl Harnak acknowledged. "Couldn't think of anyone who was likely to hightail it, though, once I put my mind to it."

"Me neither," Karuk told him. "Seems to me your boys are pretty solid."

"Yours, too. 'Course for mine there's the problem that if that bastard Thalmayr's story's gotten out, anybody we go running to might just shoot first and wonder whether we were innocent bystanders second. That's got to weigh on the mind of any bastard who'd turn on his squad mates in the first place."

"That kind does like to keep his skin in one piece, doesn't he?" Karuk chuckled harshly. "Nice to know some things don't change from universe to universe, isn't it?"

"Kind of wish some of them *did*, just between you and me," Harnak said.

"You think this duke of yours really has the reach to straighten this mess out?" It was the first time Karuk had actually asked any of the Arcanans that question, and Harnak cocked his head, green eyes glinting in the light from his crystal.

"I'm not saying I don't think he'll try, understand," Karuk continued. "I've got a pretty good idea about you Second Andarans by now, and I reckon your duke's probably about as stubborn as the regiment-captain. I know damned well what Regiment-Captain Velvelig'd do in a situation like this, and I expect your duke'll do the same. But seems to me that whoever's pushing this thing probably has a line or two in his plans for dealing with the duke, too. And even if he doesn't, won't having his own son right in the middle of this make it harder for him to get a hearing?"

"Trust me, the fifty's thought about that, too, whether he wants to admit it or not," Harnak said after a moment. "On the other hand, *I* sure as hells wouldn't want to be the poor sod who got in the duke's way when he thinks the Second Andarans' honor is on the line. Sure, having Sir Jasak 'in the middle of it' may... complicate things for him, but not Shartahk himself could *stop* him in a case like this. And if there's one Andaran duke in all the multiverse you *don't* want pissed off at you, it's Duke Garth Showma."

Karuk nodded with immense satisfaction. It wasn't as if Harnak had just said anything he hadn't already heard before from Thermyn Ulthar and Jaralt Sarma, but over the years Hordal Karuk had seen quite a few officers with touching faith in fables, magic charms, moonshine, and the honesty of their superiors. Some of them seemed to feel there was some kind of code that required them to believe the official truth even when they knew better. He hadn't thought Ulthar or Sarma fell into that category, but it was always a relief when a good levelheaded noncom who'd seen the bison confirmed their judgment.

"Well, in that case—" he began, only to stop in midsentence as Regiment-Captain Velvelig and Fifty Ulthar appeared out of the snowy darkness.

"Chelgayr, that feels good!" the regiment-captain said, and Karuk heard something suspiciously like a smothered laugh from Evarl Harnak's direction.

"Yes, Sir, it does," the master-armsman agreed, pointedly not looking at his Arcanan colleague. And it was true. The portal's vestibule was a bubble of blessed warmth. The steady portal wind wasn't especially strong—or, rather, most of it was going straight up instead of blowing outward at ground level—but there was at least a ninety-degree difference between its starting temperature and snowy northern New Ternathia. That heat bled off quickly, but not before it had produced a zone perhaps three hundred yards deep in which there wasn't a trace of snow, and the sky on the other side—actually visible, thanks to the clearing that abutted the portal—was a deep, moonlit sapphire sprinkled with the stars of another hemisphere.

"I suppose we should get our arses over where it's warmer, then," Velvelig continued and glanced at the two senior noncoms. "Should I assume in your customary efficient manner the two of you have confirmed our nose count?"

"Yes, Sir," Karuk replied. "Evarl and I've been the sort of keeping an eye on that all the way here."

"I thought you had." Velvelig produced another of his infinitesimal smiles. "Good noncoms are an officer's greatest treasure, Hordal. Now we just have to find me one."

"You go right on looking, Sir," the master-sword said easily. "Be a comfort to retire and put my feet up in front of the fire when you finally find one."

Velvelig snorted, conceding the exchange, and twitched his head at the portal.

"Take us through, Hordal."

"Yes, Sir! Chan Byral!"

"Here, Master-Armsman!"

The tall but slightly built—and very young—Distance Viewer appeared out of the darkness.

"I apologize for disturbing your beauty rest, young Hanyl," Karuk said in his most fatherly tone, "but if it would be possible for you to spare the Portal Authority a moment of your time, I'd appreciate your taking yourself to the other side of that portal and Looking around. I'm sure Sword Harnak would be happy to ride along and keep you out of mischief."

"Yes, Master-Armsman." The youthful Distance Viewer glanced at Evarl Harnak, and the Arcanan shook his head with a smile.

"No rest for the weary," he observed. "Oh well, Hanyl, I guess we'd best be about it before the Master-Armsman thinks of something else for us to do."

Chan Byral smiled and sent his unicorn pacing forward.

Behind him, the rest of the column was closing up with remarkable speed, given the weather conditions and terrain. The Portal Authority wagons, floating on the dwindling Arcanan levitation spells, had moved through the treacherous, burned-out, snow-covered forest with an ease the Sharonians still found profoundly unnatural. Welcome, yes, but *definitely* unnatural.

From Namir Velvelig's perspective, those levitation spells had offered another advantage. The passage of so many unicorns had churned the snow badly enough, but not to the same extent wagons would have under normal circumstances. Given the current heavy snowfall, the traces of their journey between portals should be completely obscured by dawn. He hoped so, anyway. He had a suspicion that tracks in the snow would be glaringly visible to an aerial observer once the clouds broke, and the last thing he wanted were any arrows pointing in the direction of their flight.

Platoon-Captain Sedryk Tobar and Platoon-Captain chan Brano, the most junior of his four surviving line officers, brought up the rear. None of the Arcanans had commented on the fact that their column's rearguard was solidly Sharonian, or on the fact that Company-Captain Halath-Shodach and Platoon-Captain Larkal just happened to be commanding the scout parties on either flank for tonight's march. To be honest, he wouldn't have expected them to complain about it, but he'd seen no sign of *silent* resentment on their part, either. He doubted very many of them could have failed to understand why Tobar and chan Brano were keeping an eye on things, but rather than resenting it, what he'd seen the most evidence of was satisfaction. They knew what would happen to them if they fell into the wrong hands, and they were strongly in favor of anything likely to prevent that from happening.

Now the regiment-captain watched through the portal as Harnak and chan Byral rode into the humid, blessedly warm rain forest and paused. Not for the first time he wished they had at least one Plotter, although a rain forest was probably so stuffed with living critters as to knock any Plotter's reach back to little more than range of sight. He also would have liked to send chan Byral through the portal's other aspect, as well, to let him get a good Look around the huge blind spot it created, but they didn't have enough time for that.

Several minutes passed. Then chan Byral's unicorn came trotting back across into Hell's Gate.

"I don't See anything I shouldn't, Sir," he told Velvelig with a salute. "I'm not saying there isn't anything out there—just that if there is, it's well enough hidden I'm not going to pick it up in the dark. There's no sign of any Arcanan pickets, anyway."

"I suppose that's the best we're going to get," the regiment-captain said simply. "Let's go."

He touched his unicorn with his heel and started across the interface between universes. The air grew steadily warmer as he approached the actual portal; by the time he crossed it, he was shedding his gloves, unbuttoning his heavy coat, and already sweating heavily. Not that he had any intention of complaining.

The damp, powerful, earthy smells of riotous vegetation enveloped him, and the sound of night birds and gods only knew what other night-roaming creatures filled the darkness with a welcome chorus of living things. After the cold winter weather of their journey, the sudden flood of noise was as welcome as the gentle breeze stirring the night and he drew rein to remove his coat completely and hang it on the pommel of his saddle while he turned and watched the rest of the column follow him into the nameless universe.

He couldn't see much, and all he really knew about this particular universe was that the portal *probably* opened somewhere in the Dalazan Rain Forest. There'd been no time for any further exploration before everything went to hell, which meant that probability had never been definitively confirmed. They'd probably get a chance to do something about that, assuming they could find another break in the overhead canopy and establish exactly when local noon occurred. The PAAF was as accustomed to taking noon sights to establish latitude and longitude as any mariner, for obvious reasons. The problem would be finding the aforesaid break. The area immediately around the portal was choked with thick, luxuriant herbaceous varieties: vines, leafy ferns, low-growing shrubbery. Clearly something—possibly the formation of the portal itself—had killed back the towering hundred-foot high trees beyond that tangle and let in the sunlight which had created such an explosion of growth. He had no intention of hanging about this close to the portal, however, and once they'd gotten a few hundred yards farther in-universe, they'd be back in typical triple-canopy jungle, where undergrowth was blessedly uncommon and the sun and stars were seldom seen.

The column flowed past him, not without difficulty given the thickness of the ground cover. Even the floating wagons found the going difficult. The vegetation was dense enough—and tall enough—to catch at their wheels as they floated over it, and even if it hadn't been, the draft animals had to work hard to force their own way forward, far less haul the wagons with them. Velvelig was trying very hard not to glower at the column's glacial progress when one of Platoon-Captain Zynach Larkal's men trotted up to him.

"There's some sort of game trail to the east, Sir," Armsman 1/c Shalsan Thykyl reported, and Velvelig wasn't even tempted to ask how he could be so sure of that in the dark. Thykyl was the best of the 127th Regiment's scouts and the finest hunter Namir Velvelig had ever seen anywhere. If he said there was a game trail, there was a game trail.

"Is it wide enough for these damned wagons?"

"'Pears to be, Sir." Thykyl turned in the saddle to point back the way he'd come. "Wouldn't be if they had to run on their wheels, but on the Arcanans' crystals the unicorns should be able to get 'em through. There's a nasty steep ridge up there ahead of us, too. Trail looks like our best way up it." He turned back with a smile. "Always trust animals to find the easy way, I say, Sir."

"Or the eas*iest* way, at least," Velvelig agreed. "All right. Go find Master-Armsman Karuk and tell him we're changing course. Then show him this trail of yours."

"Yes, Sir." Thykyl saluted and sent his unicorn in search of the master-armsman while Velvelig moved back to the very edge of the portal to halt the rest of the column until they got its head straightened out.

* * *

"Well thank Hali Thykyl found that trail," Therman Ulthar said with profound gratitude.

He rode once again at Regiment-Captain Velvelig's side, as the weary column reassembled itself back into a semblance of order behind them. There'd been times while they wrestled the wagons through the undergrowth—even with the game trail, that had been no picnic—when Ulthar had entertained serious doubts about the practicality of using this universe as their refuge. Dense jungle might be as ideal for evading pursuers as Velvelig said it was, but one had to get *to* it first and it had seemed unlikely the wagons would let them do that.

The game trail had made it possible, but no one in his right mind would have called the task easy. Once or twice, he'd been tempted to suggest simply abandoning their vehicles. The thought of leaving behind all of the Sharonian weapons and ammunition they'd hauled with them—especially the mortars and machine guns—had been unpalatable, but they probably could have packed the truly essential supplies on unicornback. Of course, leaving the wagons just inside the portal would also have been a dead giveaway to anyone looking for them who happened to glance this way, and there were plenty of things in those wagons which might not be truly essential but were certainly very good to have along. So it was fortunate they hadn't had to abandon anything after all.

"Agreed," Velvelig said now. "Of course, it's fairly obvious which way we went, for now, at least. The one good thing about jungle like that, though, is how quickly it grows back. Give us a few days—a couple of weeks at the outside—and somebody would have to look really, really closely to see that anyone had passed through."

He sounded, Ulthar thought, like a man trying to convince himself he was being clever rather than a man who didn't care to admit how much he hated this kind of terrain.

"You're right about that, Sir," he said helpfully, then shook his head. "I never would've thought of heading this way on my own, but Jaralt was right. If you're looking for a place to hide from dragons and recon gryphons, this kind of jungle takes some beating."

"I know." Velvelig's tone was undeniably sour. "I know, but the rain and the humidity are going to play hell with our equipment."

"They won't do ours any favors, either," Ulthar admitted. "We don't have as many moving parts to rust solid as you do, but *sarkolis* doesn't really like this kind of sustained heat and humidity, either. The crystals issued to the Army are as climate-proofed as anybody can make them, but we still have to take Graholis' own extra precautions. And you *don't* want to see what the gearing on an arbalest looks like after a couple of weeks of this kind of weather. As for sword blades—!"

He rolled his eyes, and Velvelig chuckled.

"Probably not any worse than what it does to our bayonets," he suggested. "Axe blades and machetes, too, for that matter. But at least it gives the noncoms something else to keep the men busy with!"

"I think that's what they call finding a bright side to look on, Sir," Ulthar said dryly, and Velvelig chuckled again, harder.

"Oh, I don't know. When you come to it—"

CRRAAAACK!

Namir Velvelig froze, his head jerking around in astonishment, as the single rifleshot set twice a hundred birds into raucous, terrified flight. The racket was deafening, but that wasn't what froze him in place. No, what stopped him dead in his tracks was the fact that the shot had come not from any of his men but from somewhere in the jungle *ahead* of them.

"Column, halt!"

Halath-Shodach headed their column at the moment. His bellowed command stopped their entire party as effectively as the gunshot had already stopped Velvelig, and the regiment-captain nodded in approval. Then he sent his own unicorn cantering—except, of course, that unicorns didn't "canter;" they *loped*—to the front, Ulthar at his side. By the time they reached the column's point, Halath-Shodach had dismounted and was peering through his binoculars.

"Can't see a damned thing, Sir," he confessed, looking up as Velvelig halted beside him. "Has to be out there somewhere, though. And whoever it is, it's sure as hell not an Arcanan, unless he's acquired a Model 10 somewhere."

"What it sounded like to me, too," Velvelig agreed. He was staring intently into the dim, shadowed depths of the jungle while his mind raced. Was it possible someone had survived the destruction of Balkar chan Tesh's Copper Company after all? But if they had, how in Kreegair's name had they gotten *here?* They were the better part of fifty miles from the swamp portal! Besides—

"Regiment-Captain Velvelig! I certainly didn't expect to see *you* here!"

The voice—raised to carry but almost conversational in tone—floated out of the jungle. It was a voice, Velvelig realized incredulously, that he recognized... and speaking Arpathian.

"It seems you're an even harder man to kill than I thought, Platoon-Captain Arthag!" he shouted back after a moment in the same language, and it was difficult to maintain a proper Arpathian imperturbability. "Would you care to come out and talk to me, or should I come in and talk to you... wherever the hells you are?"

"Oh, I imagine I can come out. And I hope you won't take this wrongly, Sir, but until we're sure you're in charge, the rest of us will just stay out here with our rifles and keep an eye on things."

"I wouldn't have it any other way, Platoon-Captain," Velvelig replied with a faint smile.

* * *

"So when we spotted you and saw the unicorns and the wagons floating a foot off the ground, then saw all those fellows in Arcanan uniform, we were pretty sure the bastards had finally gotten around to hunting us down. Fortunately, our lookouts spotted quite a few PAAF uniforms, too, and the people wearing them didn't seem to be prisoners. Then Hulmok got a good look at you through his binoculars, Sir. After that, it seemed like a good idea to at least give you a chance to explain what in Saramash's name was going on instead of just shooting you."

"I'm glad it did, Platoon-Captain chan Baskay," Velvelig said dryly. "I've discovered I have a constitutional objection to being shot. And you can't have been any more surprised to see us than we are to see you. We didn't think anyone had gotten away."

"Not many did, Sir," Dorzon chan Baskay, Viscount Simrath, said grimly, and his expression as he looked at the three Arcanan fifties seated behind the regiment-captain could have been carved out of flint. "If not for Hulmok's Talent, they'd have caught us as flat-footed as they must've caught Company-Captain chan Tesh. As it was, sixteen of his boys didn't make it."

"I can imagine." Unlike chan Baskay's face, Velvelig's was expressionless—he *was* an Arpathian septman, after all—but his voice was equally harsh. "Most of my men at Fort Ghartoun didn't have any more chance than yours did. And I'm fairly certain what you're thinking. But Fifty Ulthar was already a prisoner in my custody at the time of the attack. He didn't have anything to do with it, and Fifty Sarma and Fifty Cothar—and all their men, for that matter—put their necks right into the noose to get what was left of my people out alive. For that matter, my own Sifter's confirmed that everything they've told me is the truth. And none of my people would be here now if not for them and their assistance."

Chan Baskay glared at the three Arcanans for another few seconds. Then his nostrils flared as he inhaled sharply.

"Point taken, Sir," he said quietly. "And, to be honest, we've had confirmation of our own that something about this whole attack stinks to high heaven. Besides the fact that it was a treacherous, cold-blooded ploy from the very beginning, I mean."

Sarma and Ulthar winced slightly at his last sentence, but they met his hard eyes levelly, and something like a tinge of approval flickered in the depths of those eyes.

"We took three of the Arcanan 'honor guard' alive, and all three of them were regular troopers, without any idea what Fifty Narshu and his 'Special Operations' assassins had in mind. I didn't want to believe that, but Trekar"—he twitched his head at Under-Captain Trekar Rothag, sitting beside him—"Sifted them the same way your Sifter did for the fifties." He shrugged. "So

I'm at least open to the possibility that the Arcanan command systematically lied to its own men. In fact, I'm godsdamned certain it did."

"Excuse me?"

Velvelig cocked his head. The man in front of him looked very little like the immaculately groomed Ternathian cavalry officer who'd passed through Fort Ghartoun on his way to Fallen Timbers as Zindel Calirath's diplomatic representative. It wasn't just the inevitable weathered raggedness, either. Unlike his own people, chan Baskay and the survivors of Hulmok Arthag's guard detail hadn't been given the opportunity to pick through Fort Ghartoun's supply rooms before heading off cross-universe, and the jungle had been less than kind to their clothing and uniforms. Their weapons and equipment, however, were spotless, meticulously cleaned and cared for. But the endless weeks he'd spent keeping his tiny command of fugitives together in this jungle, never knowing if—or when—an Arcanan pursuit would come through the portal after them, had toughened more than just his exterior. There was good, solid metal inside Platoon-Captain chan Baskay, and that metal had been hammered into something hard and lethal.

"It happens that one of the Arcanan 'diplomats' also survived the ambush attempt," the platoon-captain said now. "He almost didn't, but Master Skirvon's been remarkably . . . forthcoming, and he's had ample proof Trekar knows when he's lying. And that he really, really doesn't want to lie to me ever again."

Namir Velvelig was an Arpathian, yet something in the younger man's tone sent a shiver through him. Somehow he didn't think *he'd* want to lie to Dorzon chan Baskay, either.

"Forthcoming, is he?" The regiment-captain's tone was no more than mildly interested, and Hulmok Arthag, standing behind the seated chan Baskay, grunted.

"Told you you wouldn't put him off stride, Dorzon," he said, and chan Baskay snorted a brief laugh.

"Yes. Yes, you did, Hulmok," he acknowledged, then looked back at Velvelig.

"Yes, 'forthcoming' is about the best word for it, Sir. As a matter of fact, he's tried very hard to come up with something new I'd like to know every day. He seems to be under the impression that his ability to do that has a direct bearing on his longevity."

"I see. And while he's been so 'forthcoming,' what exactly has he told you?"

"Well, besides the fact that Shaylar and her husband survived the massacre—" He broke off and arched an eyebrow. "You already knew about that, too, Sir?"

"I told you Fifty Ulthar and Fifty Sarma have been as honest with us as they could. For that matter, they didn't know *we* didn't already know they were alive. Would it happen that your 'forthcoming' diplomat's told you why they were so idiotic as to lie about it in the first place?"

"For several reasons, apparently, Sir. The most immediately pressing one was that they didn't want us to realize how much they'd already learned about the Voices. Not until they were ready to attack and start shooting them out of hand, anyway. But Skirvon's pretty sure there was more to it than that. In fact, what he's said dovetails very neatly with what Fifty Ulthar and Fifty Sarma have told you. According to what he's had to say, they're absolutely right that someone is deliberately manipulating the situation. Skirvon doesn't know for certain *why*, although he's fairly sure it has to do with politics back home, but he's pretty damned positive his own government would be really, really pissed off by the way things are being handled out here...assuming it knew the truth, that is. According to him, it's probably about a confrontation between what he calls the Mythalans and the Andarans—I'm guessing your friends here can give us a better idea of what the hells he's talking about in that regard—even if he doesn't have a clue what the end game is supposed to be. But if he's not sure exactly what the 'why' is, he's pretty damned sure about the 'who' who's behind it. According to him, it's someone named Nith mul Gurthak, the local governor."

CHAPTER THIRTY-SEVEN
Fairsayla 20, 5053 AE
(March 8, 1929 CE)

SOOLAN CHAN RAHOOL SETTLED INTO HIS FAMILIAR JUNGLE cabin after another easy day of tree climbing and eating his fill of nuts and fruit. His arms still twinged a bit from building back the muscle mass lost during travel, but no gorillas had been waiting for him on his return to the chimpanzee clan.

The work of arranging transportation for any of the gorillas who chose to travel out-universe was done. Now he hoped they'd leave him alone. Larakesh had been a blast, especially meeting with the stevedores, but hunting up and down Ricathia to find the right gorilla clan to report to had been excessively like Ternathian Army work.

His own Minarti chimpanzees seemed much as they'd always been: dedicated to moving about in the triple canopy to follow the food supply while negotiating among themselves for the best and having as many baby chimpanzees as they could manage to feed.

He sat up fast nearly slamming his head on the guest's bunk above him. *Babies!* A string of curses ran through his head until he fixed on the core problem. *They're nearly all pregnant.* And that wasn't normal at all. The Minarti clan grandmother was ironfisted about controlling the size of the clan to keep it within the resources available to it. As far as chan Rahool knew, the range territory hadn't increased—and he was pretty sure he'd have been made aware of that minor fact if it had—but the clan was obviously growing, anyway.

The manual from Combined Simian Embassies was in the drawer under his bed somewhere. He tossed the detritus of study notes onto the floor, shoving crinkled papers and reports out of the way until he found the old green book with CSE printed on the cover. He was sure there'd been something in there about increased pregnancies, and that it was *not* in the "everything normal, don't worry" section of the book!

He cut his finger flipping too fast through the front half of the book. The thing really ought to have been better organized. Calamity events should have been in the front. Or at the very least all together in one section instead of spread throughout the book as though some back-office CSE administrator imagined simian ambassadors were able to spend time reading this tome in the breaks between swinging between tree branches.

Ah! Here it is! He read the section carefully. Then he read it again, even more carefully.

It didn't get any better the second time through.

CSE had documented several cases of primates and higher order monkeys increasing their populations without a change in food supply. In the seasons that followed the clans invariably began organized conflict. As a consequence, CSE "strongly advised" ambassadors to carefully monitor the fertility of their assigned clans and to advise clan leaders to limit procreation.

Chan Rahool snorted. Teach the Minarti clan grandmother to suck eggs why didn't he? The bureaucrats had the worst ideas. Still someone needed to know about this.

He abandoned the mess in the sleeper half of the cabin to go write Dorrick a note. Dorrick needed to know about this immediately, but chan Rahool knew he'd have to find someone at CSE himself. He had to tell them about the pregnant chimps, and this wasn't something that could wait for normal channels.

Of course, whoever he told about it was going to want to know why it was happening, and he didn't have a clue. The Minarti had seemed peaceable towards Dorrick's clan, which were their closest simian neighbors, and no humans had done anything idiotic lately, so why in the gods' names was—?

Wait. *Humans.* Oh no! Arcana. Chan Rahool cradled his head in his hands. The Minarti clan grandmother was preparing to defend her holdings in case the Arcanans managed to get this far. But if the war didn't reach them, the chimps would have to start a fight of their own to secure the resources their enlarged populations would require!

Chan Rahool grabbed his travel satchel and started throwing things into it. This was bad. This was very, very bad.

*   *   *

Cetaceans also prepared, though no stevedores had bought their human representative any drinks, and their ambassador hadn't been nearly as warm to the TTE staff as chan Rahool had been. But then, she was also much, much harder to surprise.

The orca took that as a challenge.

Teeth Cleaver sprayed water in triumph to announce his arrival by the pier. Shalassar Kolmayr-Brintal, Cetacean ambassador, reluctantly went out to meet the large orca.

<I report. The large-minds hear. They will sing on it.>

Teeth Cleaver launched himself into the air to twist and look along the railway leading up to the Cetacean Institute. The rails were free of cars at the moment, but a large train happened to pass on the cross line visible in the distance while he was airborne, and he landed with a satisfied splash.

<Three of those to start. With feed cars. My sisters and brothers must not arrive too weak to hunt in the new oceans.>

Shalassar tossed the black-and-white a fish from the feeding barrel by the pier. Teeth Cleaver swallowed it whole and opened a wide toothy mouth for the next installment. She tossed in a half dozen more.

<I'd like to hear what the large-minds sing of this,> Shalassar said, finally.

The orca smiled. <They will sing and sing and sing. But in the end we orca will go.>

<Do you know where to go?> Shalassar asked.

Teeth Cleaver said nothing. That was a no then. Orca didn't care to admit ignorance.

<The portal is at Larakesh. I've made arrangements with a team at the port there to load aquarium cars. If>—she held up a flat hand and gave it a wiggle to indicate a cetacean's dorsal fin signing uncertainty—<the large-minds sing that you should go. You'll need to swim up through the Ylani Strait to get there, but it's a deep ocean path and we can make arrangements to temporarily stop shipping.>

Teeth Cleaver made a dismissive noise with his blowhole. <Porpoises swam it. Scared little porpoises went there and back. Orca need no 'stop shipping.'>

Shalassar considered him. The portals were hardly a secret, but she hadn't expected an orca to consider logistics enough to have another cetacean do a trial run. And why had the porpoises been "scared?" Orcas seldom thought much of porpoises, but still—

A squeal distracted her, sounding in the distance and followed by white crested splashing from a fleeing porpoise pod. Teeth Cleaver's tail twitched, and Shalassar saw a host of black fins rise in the incoming tide.

The orca whales were eating the distance at attack speed and crisscrossing their own wakes. Even from this far out she could sense something harsh about the group. These weren't the playful types who routinely visited the Cetacean Institute out of simple curiosity.

<Are these your sisters and brothers?> Shalassar asked.

Teeth Cleaver gave a tail and body wiggle of negation. <Cousins these. These hunt the white sharks. But sharks swim alone. These hope for shark pods in the new oceans. More fun better fight, say these.> The orca snorted water in derision. <Don't eat all their kill, these.>

Shalassar furrowed a brow. Cetaceans were not normally so wasteful. What kind of outcasts were these? <Why not eat the whole shark?>

<Taste bad,> he supplied. <Except liver. All liver tasty, even shark. Also these leave shark bits for smaller whites. Want small white shark eat, eat, eat so grow big and be strong for hunt again later.>

<But not I.> Teeth Cleaver turned a large smile at Shalassar. <I, I shall eat all. Taste and sing of Arcana flesh. I swallow all.>

She was not relieved.

*   *   *

Lady Merissa had stopped wearing the excessively pungent citrus perfume. Andrin Calirath, crown princess and heir to the Empires of Sharona and Ternathia, was deeply, deeply grateful.

Her lady-in-waiting's normally light scent had begun to stink. Or, rather, Andrin's nose had become exceptionally sensitive. And of course Lady Merissa's eyes had lit entirely too brightly when she'd first complained of the smell. Everyone but her was enjoying this.

It could just be a horrid stomach bug, but they were all utterly convinced a new prince or princess was on the way.

Though "everyone" in this case was limited to those who knew: Howan Fai, Lady Merissa, her mother, her father...and Lazima chan Zindico and Munn Lii. The two lead bodyguards couldn't be left out. One or two maids might also have figured it out, but if so, they hadn't breathed a word of it. Andrin had even managed—barely—to keep herself from telling her sisters and writing letters to Eniath about it. She and Howan Fai would at least wait for a doctor's confirmation. And they would once again pretend absolutely nothing was going on.

Andrin held the carved arm of her chair in a white-knuckled grip under the table, held her breath against the wave of nausea, and forcibly relaxed her upper body to nod politely at the courtier addressing her father. Parliamentary hearings lasted too long.

And more than any physical discomfort, Andrin was worried about what she knew was going to happen during the next recess.

Doctor Gynthyr Morlinhus had a minor appearance before the committee, but that wasn't the real reason she was here today. Andrin had never doubted her father would move mountains to protect her, but this time it was Empress Varena who'd arranged to get one of the top doctors anywhere in Sharona into Tajvana and make it possible for her to examine Andrin undetected.

Publicly just a shadow of her husband the emperor, few people truly took Varena seriously. In many ways, the empress found that convenient, but the truth was quite different, and she was the one who'd insisted a board of the best medical practitioners be formed to study the needs of the new Sharonan Army and set policy for medical care of the sick and wounded. Even some of Emperor Zindel's staff had questioned whether that might not be an overreaction of a grieving mother. Not even the miraculous healing abilities the Arcanans had used on Prince Janaki's comrades at Fort Salby could have saved the prince, and no amount of healthcare policy improvements was likely to reduce deaths during battle.

But collecting bandages and assembling medicine kits gave the families left behind something to do, and maybe, just maybe, they could make an impact on the number of deaths *after* the battles. The recommendations so far from the new Imperial Board of Healers had been hugely popular. So much so that some were beginning to suspect Empress Varena of political savvy after all.

But no one seemed to have guessed that while all of that was useful, the true reason it had been arranged in that manner was to get Doctor Morlinhus to Tajvana once every four to six weeks expressly to see Andrin . . . very, *very* quietly.

As long as Chava could continue to claim that an unfruitful marriage was essentially unconsummated and thus legally void, Uromathian opposition to the Calirath dynasty stayed a broad threat, dispersed over a thousand ways to widow her, discredit her husband, or attack her father. Once it was known a child was coming, all plotting would focus immediately solely on her.

Glimpses were strong, clear, and utterly unforgettable. What she was having now weren't Glimpses, unless they were some kind of spillover from an unformed Talent that might or might not be growing in her womb. That happened occasionally with the Calirath Talent . . . or so legend said.

Andrin had seen in fitful nightmares hundreds of ways Chava might attack her to try to kill her or destroy her unborn babe. Those panicky dreams lacked the eerie clarity of a Glimpse, thank the gods. But still Andrin had her nightmares and woke to Howan Fai holding her and whispering her sweetly back to sleep.

But before Uromathia could threaten the child, there had to be one. So far all she knew for sure was her monthly flow was late by several weeks. Lady Merissa had gone so far as to bring in a jar of pig's blood and soil the linens normally used during Andrin's monthlies so any spies working in the palace laundry would have misinformation to report.

She'd need to repeat the subterfuge again in a week . . . unless Andrin simply started bleeding again on her own. That did happen, her mother had warned. Sometimes a pregnancy simply didn't hold. Though Empress Varena always added with a prayer to the Mother, she hoped that never happened to any of her daughters.

The hearing break was called and Andrin left for the restroom several doors down the hall. Behind her, the closest women's facility immediately formed a line, and Doctor Morlinhus was snatched from the end to follow a servant to another facility being opened.

The doctor walked through the door, which was immediately— and firmly—shut behind her, and took one long look at the crown princess.

"I should've known that palace staff wouldn't go out of their way to help a random visitor find a lady's restroom." She looked plaintively around. "I do really need to go."

"Of course, Doctor." Andrin bit down a demand that the woman tell her first what her Talent showed and pointed at the carved screens that shielded a line of necessities.

The Grand Palace did do luxury remarkably well. The Order of Bergahl had maintained that aspect of it in their centuries-long stewardship. A small fountain in the waiting area filled and drained hand pools, offering easy wash-ups and a soft splashing that also covered any undignified noises those using the necessities might need to make. After what seemed like an eternity, Dr. Morlinhus reemerged and set to washing her hands thoroughly.

"I'm sorry to rush you, Doctor," Andrin said, "but we've only got a few moments before this meeting starts to look suspicious. I believe my mother explained that she needed you to give me an exam."

"She said a woman in need. She did *not* say the Crown Princess and Heir to the Throne of Sharona carrying the next Heir to the Throne of Sharona."

"Really? I'm pregnant?"

"Of course you're pregnant." Dr. Morlinhus shook her head. "Everything feels fine. Just one mind in there though. I hope you don't expect me to try to make it two or change the gender for you. No one can do that."

"Oh no. Of course not! But can you tell what I'm having?"

"Too early. In another month maybe, depending on the growth between now and then. And even then I might get it wrong." Dr. Morlinhus gave her a sharp look. "I expect the empress will be arranging a reason for me to come back regularly?"

"I expect," Andrin agreed softly.

"Yes, dear." Doctor Morlinhus softened. "You'll do fine, Your Highness. It's just hard work expecting. Don't wear yourself out too much pretending not to be."

Andrin crushed the woman in a hug.

"My Talent only covers so much. All I can do is listen to how the little ones are feeling and measure how developed their minds feel. Do try to maintain a healthy level of exercise and keep away from sick people. I can only See how things are going, not what will happen if you do foolish things. Make sure to eat a good quantity of fish. It's poor people's food here, but it's good for you. Lots of vegetables too. I'll give your mother a list if she doesn't have one already."

"Of course. Thank you, Doctor!"

Lady Merissa knocked once on the door, and Andrin left with her, in a hurry to get back to the council chambers before anyone realized she'd just had a prenatal consultation with one of the universe's most Talented doctors. Lady Merissa had to remind her to slow to a calm walk lest she return out of breath.

*   *   *

That night Andrin dreamed of waddling.

In the fuzziness, she couldn't see her feet. Then the dream took on crystalline, almost Glimpse-like clarity and she saw a great mound of belly hid her feet from view unless she stuck them straight out. She wiggled the tips of her toes at herself. They were clean, scrubbed and painted in delicate pastels to match the baby's sleeping room. The playroom, she was suddenly certain, had a much bolder more vibrant paint scheme, inspired by the lush plant life and bright ocean colors of Eniath, for all that the room was here in Tajvana.

A dark shadow blocked the sunlight streaming through the window. Glass shattered and knives struck her even as she turned to shield the precious bump with her back and spine. The movement was too slow with heavy weight wrapping her body in an aching layer of sustenance for her child, and hideous scarlet splashed the sundrenched playroom.

The dream reset. She'd moved the baby's chambers to an inner suite. No windows this time, for better security. Attacks still happened, as she'd expected, but the Guard stopped each of them before they could reach the nursery or her. She rested easily with the large tummy. No elaborate painting on the toes this time, but she still wiggled them back at herself.

Again the dream reset. She sat down to a breakfast tray delivered by Lady Merissa. Some berries Andrin didn't yet recognize filled half the tray. Somehow she knew they'd quickly become her favorite food, during her pregnancy—she'd want them day and night for their mix of tartness and sweet lusciousness—for all that they were seasonal and increasingly difficult to procure.

Fast work with the spoon emptied the entire bowl. She only barely noticed the off flavor at the end. Then the cramps came sharp and hard. Blood splatter coated the hands she tried to use to hold the bleeding back and stop the too early, far too early birth. She vomited bile mixed with breakfast, but too late. Vomit and blood clogged her senses as she lay weeping on the matted child's rug.

The dream reset a dozen more times. Until finally she gave it all up for utter secrecy. No suite prepared, no special food requests. She vomited, normal healthy vomit, multiple times a day and hid it. Lady Merissa increased her makeup to hide the sallow tinge to her face. Her middle sister, Razial, pretended a renewed love of sweet jams and included the favorite berries in the mix. But the jar was tested carefully and measured out a bit at a time in no more than the consumption rate a boisterous young princess could reasonably manage. Andrin bore the pregnancy in deepest stealth. She had to keep this child alive.

And still she failed. Again and again, she failed.

She rose from the depths of sleep, weeping, and her tears stirred Howan Fai awake beside her. She hadn't wanted to do that, but she clung to the strong, loving comfort of his embrace as she poured out the horrible dreams. And not simply because she needed his comfort. These weren't Glimpses; she knew what they looked like entirely too well, and only Death Glimpses revealed the fate of the person to whom they came. She *did* die in some of the nightmares, but in most, she survived to grieve bitterly over the yawning ache of her murdered babe. Yet they were more than simple nightmares induced by anxiety: she was equally sure of that. She dared not trust the details of the fast changing dreams to paper, yet she needed to be sure they were remembered properly in the morning, and so she poured out her nightmares to him in a bare whisper while he held her sobbing body.

"It will not happen, my love," he told her sternly, kissing her earlobe while he stroked sweat and tear-soaked hair from her forehead. "Upon my life, it will *not* happen! We will keep our child safe and your pregnancy secret. Chava and his accursed agents will learn of it only when our babe is born!"

Andrin nodded against his shoulder, limp with emotion, wrapping his love and his promise about her like another blanket. The Caliraths had already given up one heir to the throne, willingly and at great cost, she thought. But she and Howan Fai would see that *this* child reached Janaki's years.

"We can keep the secret for a while without too much trouble, I think," she said after a moment. "If we're careful, it'll be at least two months, maybe three, before anyone's going to notice anything just looking at me. But you know Chava's watching like a hawk for any sign of something like this, and I'll still have to attend state dinners. Won't he start to wonder if I suddenly stop drinking the wines at them?"

"No doubt you're right about that viper," Howan Fai agreed grimly. "But I think the solution to this problem is near at hand, Sister of White Fire. We will get you a Taster. Your father has Kallen, and as rare as Precogs are, Tasters are among the more common. They only need to Know food and drink with a Precog range of a few minutes, and you *are* the heir. We should already have assigned one specifically to you, too, and no one will be surprised if we correct that oversight. The Taster can switch any wine for juice of the right color, and with enough care we'll be able to keep the news from leaking that way."

"Yes. That should work." Andrin hugged him. "Thank you. I'm so worried, but you're right. We can make this work. But what about after that? I'd hoped that because I was tall the baby would just sort of stretch out lengthwise, but that doesn't seem to be this child's intention. In all my dreams, I get *huge*."

Frustration and dismay mingled with the worry in her tone, and Howan Fai chuckled and kissed her fingertips.

"Large you may get, My Lady, but you can never be anything save beautiful to me. And how could you be anything but lovely in my eyes when you carry the child of both our hearts beneath your own? But even if you are to become 'huge,' it need not present an insurmountable difficulty. We could take a honeymoon cruise. Go visit Eniath maybe? My mother's family's island is closer to Uromathia, but it's isolated and a virtual citadel. We can defend it, and keep the wrong people out much more easily than we can here at the Grand Palace. I think we could keep you safe. Were any of the nightmares in an island fortress?"

Andrin pondered that.

"No. I recognized all the rooms. Every time we tried another place it was within Tajvana. We could do that. We *should* do that. Take me home, Howan. I just need a safe place to have this baby. I don't know why this can't be made to work at Tajvana, but there doesn't seem to be a single way to have the child here safely. And in some of the dreams a lot of the Imperial Guard die, too.

"They serve to save us, but they shouldn't die for nothing."

CHAPTER THIRTY-EIGHT

Fairsayla 28, 5053 AE
(March 16, 1929 CE)

IT WAS EVEN COLDER THAN HE'D EXPECTED IT TO BE, AND the ice-edged wind didn't help a bit.

The snow-covered plains stretched away in every direction, as far as the eye could see. It was no longer actively snowing—there was that much to be grateful for, he supposed—and a brilliant sun burned down out of a cloudless blue sky. It offered at least the specious illusion that there was warmth somewhere in the world, and Arlos chan Geraith stood on the running board of his Steel Mule headquarters vehicle, his head haloed in sunstruck breath steam, and slapped his gloved palms together for warmth.

He stopped pounding his hands together, pushed back his parka's fur-lined hood, and raised the field glasses hanging around his neck to sweep the impossibly distant horizon, although that was purely a reflex action on his part. His scouts were ten miles out from the main column, with Plotters and Distance Viewers scattered among them; nothing was going to get past them unnoticed.

He lowered the glasses and glanced around their overnight laager. Tiny vortexes of white danced above the previous day's powdery snow, which had covered without concealing the deep tracks scores of vehicles had cut into the virgin prairie, and he grimaced. That pounded-down swath gave new meaning to the term "bison wallow," and he doubted even a blind Arcanan dragon pilot could miss that broad spoor if he happened to pass overhead. That hadn't happened yet—that they knew of, at any rate—and hopefully, it *wouldn't* happen, either.

He snorted at the thought, expelling another spurt of steamy breath, and looked at the vehicles parked around him. The Bisons and Mules were firing up for the day's travel, sending up the wind-shredded scent of burning kerosene, and heat shimmer danced over their exhausts. The Bisons were all the Mark Two, kerosene-fired variant; their flash boilers could produce enough pressure to be up and moving from a cold start in less than five minutes even in these weather conditions, although it took a bit longer to reach full pressure, and he imagined more than one crew had the heavily insulated hatch into the boiler compartment latched back this morning to take advantage of the welcome heat.

The Bisons' tracks were heavy with snow, and he heard sledgehammers pounding as the crews broke up the ice that had a tendency to form around drive sprockets and track bogies before firing them up. That ice had broken—or thrown—more than a few tracks, but the Bison's tracks seemed more tolerant of that particular form of abuse than the Steel Mules'. The halftracks' crews had to spend even more time and effort on keeping them moving, and the long route back to the railhead was dotted with over a hundred and fifty abandoned Mules. No doubt most of them would be recovered and put back into service eventually; in the meantime, they—like at least fifty or so Bisons—had been stripped for spares to keep their more fortunate brethren running.

At the moment, the broad, flat backs and the roofs of the Bisons around him and the enclosed box trailers were crusted with snow, and more snow had gathered in the folds of the canvas tarps covering the flatbed trailers. Many of the flatbeds had been fitted with an adapted version of the PAAF's and Trans-Temporal Express's cold-weather wagon covers: multiple layers of canvas separated by tightly woven blankets of Kyaira cotton from the Chuldair tree. The fiber was light, water resistant, and a good insulator, and the covers provided a shell that was both weathertight and windproof and did an excellent job of retaining heat. Fitting the Steel Mules with the covers had been relatively straightforward; since the always logical Portal Authority had sized their wagons to the same dimensions as a standard steam dray and the Mules were based on the same standard dray chassis, the covers could be easily fitted to them. The Bison trailers were harder, since no one had considered providing that sort of protection for something *that* size, but the Authority and TTE workshops had managed to provide at least enough of them to meet the Army's minimal needs.

The Steel Mules were just as snow burnished as the Bisons, and he saw several vehicle crews doing morning walk-around inspections. Two of the Bisons were parked to one side with their outer engine hatches hooked back on both sides while mechanics leaned in and did something to the boilers or the fire boxes. He wasn't sure which it was, but he knew they were lucky to have only two of the massive vehicles on the disabled list this morning. Breakdowns had been manageable, so far, at least...but they were suffering more than enough mechanical failures to make him nervous. Worse, the breakdown rate was increasing, and it had become evident several weeks earlier that the 3rd Dragoons still didn't have enough trained maintenance people of its own. He'd borrowed all the mechanics he dared from Ganstamar Yanusa-Mahrdissa, and he knew the TTE engineer would have given him more if he'd asked for them, but it was even more important to keep the logistics corridor behind his advance open and steadily growing. The TTE crews who'd taken over responsibility for that corridor and the chain of supply dumps dotting his back-trail needed enough mechanics to keep their own drays and the Bison Ones they'd acquired from 5th Corps up and running. If the price of supplying his men with all the supplies—especially fuel—they needed was to slow their rate of advance, he'd just have to smile and bear it.

And at least he hadn't had to do that yet, he reminded himself.

His command group was traveling with the 16th Dragoon Regiment—Regiment-Captain Teresco chan Urlman's command and the second regiment in Renyl chan Quay's 1st Brigade. The 12th Dragoons, 1st Brigade's other regiment, was six days and six hundred miles east of his present position, closing in on the Thermyn portal, while the 9th Dragoons, leading Brigade-Captain Shodan chan Khartan's 2nd Brigade, was about twenty-five miles behind him. The 23rd Dragoons (2nd Brigade's second regiment), followed just thirty miles behind the 23rd. But the lead elements of Brigade-Captain chan Sharys' 3rd Brigade, unfortunately, trailed almost a hundred miles behind the 23rd, while Brigade-Captain chan Bykahlar's infantry brigade had only reached Kelsayr the day before yesterday.

A foot crunched, breaking through last night's fresh snow

to the crusty layer of ice beneath it, and he turned his head to look over his shoulder.

"Why do I think you have another message from Corps-Captain chan Rowlan, Lisar?" he asked with a slightly skewed smile as Company-Captain chan Korthal came to attention and saluted.

"Perhaps because of my cheerful expression, Sir," his staff Voice replied.

"Oh, come now!" chan Geraith chided. "The corps-captain isn't *that* bad!"

"It's not so much the corps-captain. Or not as directly him as it is Platoon-Captain chan Valdyn, anyway," chan Korthal said. "He's a very good Voice, you know, Sir, but he does like to add his personal commentary on how the corps-captain's day is going. I think the phrase he used this time was 'snowbear with a sore tooth,'" he added with a grin which might have been just a bit devoid of sympathy for his fellow Voice.

Chan Geraith shook his head reprovingly, but his heart wasn't in it. Chan Korthal and Zendar chan Valdyn, Corps-Captain Fairlain chan Rowlan's Voice, were very close friends. Unlike the dark-haired, dark-complected chan Korthal, who'd been born within sight of the Fist of Bolakin in southern Narhath and thought a day below fifty degrees was a foretaste of the Farnalian demon Gynarshu's frozen hell, the red-haired, very fair-skinned chan Valdyn had been born and reared in the northern reaches of the Republic of Hanyl in New Ternath. *He* probably would have found their present surroundings downright balmy . . . which, of course, was why he was still stuck at Fort Salby, where Corps-Captain chan Rowlan had established his current forward headquarters.

It was difficult to imagine two people who looked less like one another, but the Voices were very much alike under the skin. In particular, both of them shared the same . . . respectfully irreverent outlook, and chan Geraith was very much afraid that chan Valdyn's chosen simile was probably well taken. Of course, chan Rowlan wasn't exactly a towering giant—not for a Ternathian, at any rate; he was only a few inches taller than chan Geraith himself—but his growing impatience at being stuck so far behind his corps' lead elements probably made him seem quite a bit larger. In fact, on a bad day, he probably *did* remind chan Valdyn of the enormous white bears of his homeland.

"I think it would be wise of you and the platoon-captain

to refrain from exchanging observations about the irascibility of your superior officers," he said now, as severely as he could.

"Yes, Sir. Of course, Sir!"

The earnest sincerity of chan Korthal's response was undermined by the twinkle in his eye, and chan Geraith sighed. He hadn't expected anything else, nor did he truly want it. The Imperial Ternathian Army was less invested in excruciating military courtesy and protocol than many militaries—the Imperial Uromathian Army and (for that matter) the Imperial Ternathian Navy came rather forcefully to mind. It understood discipline and the consequences of insubordination, but as a rule, it preferred its people got on with the job rather than salute one another at the drop of a hat, and both he and chan Rowlan were even less concerned with taut punctilio than was the Ternathian norm.

There were times when that bit both of them on the arse, but it also produced enthusiastic, engaged subordinates. All things considered, that was well worth any...minor quirks in those subordinates' gallop.

"So how, aside from his irascibility quotient, is the corps-captain this fine morning?" he asked. "I assume your good friend chan Valdyn didn't contact you *just* to describe the state of the corps-captain's dental work, you understand."

"Actually, Sir," chan Korthal said much more seriously, "Tymar's transcribing the latest dispatches right now. He should have the morning's traffic in the next half hour or so."

Chan Geraith nodded. Chan Korthal was fully capable of reproducing every Voice message he'd received verbatim, or even relaying them mentally to anyone who (unlike Arlos chan Geraith, who lacked even a trace of Talent) could Hear them directly. Normally, however, unless the message was truly urgent, he delivered it initially not to its addressee but to Javelin Tymar chan Forsam, chan Geraith's staff Scribe. Scribes were capable of producing flawless transcriptions of anything they'd seen or heard, which was essential for message distribution and record purposes. What made chan Forsam especially valuable was that, unlike all too many Scribes, he also had a minor Talent for Mind Speaking. That meant he could take "dictation" directly from a Voice, and he was a highly skilled typist, capable of over a hundred and fifty words a minute. In fact, that typing speed and his Mind Speaking Talent were the primary reason he'd been assigned to the unTalented chan Geraith. The division-captain *couldn't* Hear chan Korthal directly, but between them, the Voice and the Scribe could get him written copies of any critical dispatch very quickly indeed.

Of course, the current message traffic was enough to keep even the two of *them* busy for several hours a day, chan Geraith reflected.

"Just give me the highlights for now, then."

"Yes, Sir. I don't think there's anything really critical at the moment. Tymar will have the complete movement report for Regiment-Captain chan Isail and Regiment-Captain chan Kymo shortly, but Brigade-Captain chan Bykahlar's brigade should be detraining at the Resym railhead by sometime tomorrow afternoon, our time. Everything else is pretty much where it was with last night's situation report."

Chan Geraith nodded. No surprises there, thank the gods! In fact, chan Bykahlar was a bit ahead of where he'd expected him to be, based on the 3rd Infantry Brigade's last reports. He and his people were still a long slog behind 3rd Dragoons' spearhead, but they'd made up time. Whether or not they'd keep on making it up once they reached the end of the rails would be another matter, of course.

"That's good to know," he said after a moment. "And what have we heard this morning from Battalion-Captain chan Yahndar?"

"Company-Captain chan Mahsdyr's lead platoon's reached Tesmahn, Sir." The Voice looked around at the icy snowscape, his expression a bit sour. "According to Company-Captain chan Mahsdyr, it's unseasonably warm. He says it's a good thing they're having thunderstorms to cool things off a bit."

Chan Geraith hid a smile behind his mustache. A certain irreverence was required for a successful dragoon officer, and young chan Mahsdyr had it in ample quantities. The division-captain never doubted that he'd included that weather report—and commentary—with malice aforethought.

"Well, maybe the thunderstorms will help keep the dragon problem down, as well," he observed, the temptation to smile fading.

"The company-captain says they haven't seen any sign of Arcanans on the ground yet, Sir. And his Plotters and Distance Viewers haven't spotted any in the air, either."

Chan Geraith pursed his lips thoughtfully at that.

He was glad chan Mahsdyr hadn't seen any evidence of an Arcanan ground presence, but he hadn't really been too worried about that in the first place. Given the way Gold Company's Distance Viewers and Plotters had been reinforced, they were almost bound to detect any ground threat well before it came into visual range. According to the prisoner interrogation reports being passed down-chain in a steady stream, the Arcanans had spells which were considerably superior to binoculars, but they had no equivalent of Plotters or of the Distance Viewers' ability (depending on the strength of their Talent) to See far beyond normal visual range. Unfortunately, he didn't know what "visual range" might be for someone mounted on a dragon and several thousand feet in the air. He suspected it was probably greater than any but the most powerful of Distance Viewers could match, and on the broad, level plains between Tesmahn and the Nairsom-Thermyn portal, his advancing patrol would stand out like bugs crawling across a tabletop if one happened to fly over them. So the fact that chan Mahsdyr hadn't spotted any Arcanans yet didn't guarantee the Arcanans hadn't spotted *him*.

Well, we'll just have to go on hoping they haven't any operating on the worst-case assumption that they have...*or will sometime very soon now, at any rate*, he thought.

"I'll want to pass a formal message down-chain to Battalion-Captain chan Yahndar and the Company-Captain after breakfast," he said out loud, and chan Korthal nodded, making a mental note to remind his superior in the extremely unlikely event that chan Geraith forgot.

"In the meantime," the division-captain went on, "I assume Master Yanusa-Mahrdissa's been his usual efficient self and updated our vehicle availability numbers?"

"Yes, Sir."

"In that case, if you'll step into my office," chan Geraith twitched his head in the direction of t his headquarters Mule, "we'll just get out of the cold and enjoy a mug of hot tea while you bring me up to date on that."

CHAPTER THIRTY-NINE

Fairsayla 29, 5053 AE
Chesthu 24, 205 YU
(March 17, 1929 CE)

"SIR, I'M THINKING YOU'D BEST HEAR THIS."

Grithair chan Mahsdyr looked up at Senior-Armsman chan Golar from the sustaining (but not very appetizing) ration can of lima beans and yellow corn. Under normal circumstances, he would have been pleased by any excuse to divert his attention from its overcooked contents, but chan Golar's expression wasn't that of a man who'd come to exchange idle pleasantries.

"Hear what, Tersak?" the company-captain said, mess kit fork still in hand. He swallowed and pointed the fork at the young junior-armsman at the senior-armsman's heels. "Should I assume I won't like whatever chan Ynclair has to tell me?"

"Probably not, Sir," chan Golar replied.

"In that case, Ignathar, you might as well get started." He stuck the fork into the can and set it aside. "Whatever it is, at least it'll distract me from lunch!"

Chan Ynclair smiled at the company-captain's tone, but his eyes were serious. "Tairkyn got close enough to the portal for a good Plot, Sir," he said, and chan Mahsdyr's lips tightened.

"And when he did, he found something, right?"

"Right, I'm afraid, Sir."

"And did you get close enough to See what he'd Plotted?"

"Yes, Sir."

"Well, don't make me pull it out of you one 'Yes, Sir,' at a time," chan Mahsdyr said a bit tartly.

"Sorry, Sir. We didn't See anything on this side of the portal, so we crossed the threshold to take a look at Fort Rensar.

Once we were over the threshold, Tairkyn got a good Plot and told me he'd picked up forty or fifty men, a couple dozen of those unicorn things of theirs, and something he'd never Plotted before, so I took a look. I make it forty-five men, ten of their unicorns, and a coop full of what I guess are those 'hummers' you've had us looking for. Well, 'a coop full' is probably a bit of an overstatement. There're only six of them."

"Wonderful." Chan Mahsdyr sat back on the rock he was using as a chair and gazed sourly for several long, thoughtful moments into the small fire over which he'd heated his unappetizing meal. Chan Golar and chan Ynclair stood waiting patiently until he looked back up at them once more.

"Are they parked in Fort Rensar?" he asked.

"Not exactly, Sir. Looks like the fort burned to the ground when the Arcanans came through. These boys're camped out on the hill behind it."

"Camped out this time of year?" Chan Mahsdyr smiled nastily. "They're actually under canvas?"

"Yes, Sir, they are. And they don't seem too happy about it, either."

"Can't blame them for that, Sir," chan Golar put in. Chan Mahsdyr glanced at him, and the senior-armsman's expression was sour. "Not 's bad as it was crossing Nairsom, Sir, but I still wouldn't half like spending the winter under canvas in these parts. Unless these bastards have some kind of magic windproof tent!"

"That they don't, Senior-Armsman," chan Ynclair said. "They do have some of those glowing rocks they use instead of fires, but these are some *very* unhappy troopers, and I don't think blue's their natural color."

"Well, that's nice to know, anyway," chan Mahsdyr said thoughtfully. He scratched his chin, then looked up at chan Golar. "Go find Platoon-Captain chan Sabyr, Tersak. I think this might be right up First Platoon's alley. And tell him I think we'll need chan Gyulair."

"Yes, Sir!" Chan Golar's eyes gleamed with satisfaction as he touched his chest in salute and turned on his heel. As the senior-armsman headed off through the damp chill, chan Mahsdyr turned his attention back to chan Ynclair.

"And while the senior-armsman's doing that, Ignathar, you can start drawing me a sketch map."

*   *   *

"What a sorry-arsed collection of fuck ups," Armsman 1/c Fozak chan Gyulair observed. "Bastards're acting like they didn't have an enemy in the world!"

"Sort of the point to our having snuck up on them, Fozzy," Armsman Wendyr chan Jethos replied. He lay on his belly beside chan Gyulair on a hilltop just over a mile east of the Tyrahl River, peering down through powerful field glasses at the burned-out shell of what had been a Portal Authority fort. The fort had been built on moderately high ground between their present position and the eastern bank of the river, far enough above the normal water level to keep its garrison's feet dry during the spring floods. The enormous arc of the portal connecting this universe to the universe of Thermyn towered above them, effortlessly dominating the entire horizon. It was three hours earlier on the Thermyn side of the portal, and that vast arc was still purple with the light of early dawn. Its extreme northern end crossed the riverbed at an angle to their left, just south of the roughly two mile-long island below the ruined fort. It was unusual for a portal to actually intersect the course of a major river. For all the blue lines crawling across any topographical map, *major* streams were relatively few in number compared to the amount of space in which a portal might appear. When they did intersect, however, interesting things could happen. In this instance, the mile-wide Tyrahl simply poured itself into the portal and disappeared, leaving its bed downstream from the portal dry and empty. It also created a trans-universal river on the Thermyn side, where it met—and just about doubled the flow of—the Sand Rock River about eight miles south-southwest of Chindar.

The bed didn't stay empty forever on the Nairsom side, of course. The Tyrahl was the longest river in all of New Ternath, longer even than the mighty Vandor which flowed all the way from the Inland Seas to the Gulf of Cordara. A riverbed that long, draining that much watershed, could always find enough water to resurrect itself over the six or seven hundred miles from their current location to the Vandor. Still, it was impressive to watch that much water go pouring from one universe to another. And the fact that the riverbed was dry vastly simplified the problem of how to get the company—and the rest of 3rd Dragoons—across it when the time came.

Their attention wasn't on the river just now, though.

"Looks like Ignathar's sketch was just about perfect," chan Jethos went on, rising on his elbows as he swept his field glasses across the encampment. Unlike his partner, he was no Distance Viewer. He *was* a very powerful Plotter, however. "I See the coops for their 'hummers' about fifty yards due east of their bivouac. Got 'em?"

"Got 'em," chan Gyulair confirmed in a grimmer, harder tone and smuggled down behind his big, bipod-mounted Mark 12 rifle. The weapon had a barrel just over thirty-four inches long and a double-set trigger. In trained hands it was capable of delivering a killing shot at over a thousand yards...and in *some* people's hands, it could do the same thing at *two* thousand yards.

Fozak chan Gyulair had the hands—and the Talent—to take full advantage of his weapon's capabilities.

"Don't See anyone moving around near them at the moment," chan Jethos continued, his voice taking on a faintly singsong note as he closed his physical eyes to focus more fully on his own Talent. He was chan Gyulair's regular spotter, with a Talent which was relatively short ranged but capable of very fine degrees of discrimination over the range it had.

"Just let me know if that changes," chan Gyulair said flatly.

*   *   *

"Who's got lookout duty this afternoon?" Nyk Phiery asked.

He was the squad shield for 1st Squad, 2nd Platoon, C Company, 2nd Battalion, 451st Regiment of the Union of Arcana Army, and he didn't sound happy.

"That would be Dhugahl, I believe," Sword Kilvyn Forstmir replied. "Why?"

"Because it's an hour past chow time and no one's relieved Jelmart and Vermahka. They're getting a little *hungry*, Sword."

Forstmir frowned, and not at the bite in Phiery's voice. The 1st Squad leader did his best to keep his own people on their toes and sharp, just as Forstmir tried to do for the entire under-strength platoon, but both of them were fighting—and losing—an uphill battle. It wasn't surprising the platoon should feel thoroughly crapped on, stuck out here at the arse-end of nowhere and under canvas in the middle of a northern Yanko winter. It was the most miserable, godsforsaken assignment Forstmir had ever caught, and gods knew he'd caught more than a few in the course of his fifteen-year career. And it didn't help that every member of the platoon knew Commander of One Hundred Thimanus Gorzalt, C Company's CO, had chosen them for this blissful duty because he'd taken a profound dislike to Commander of Fifty Zakar Ustmyn.

Forstmir wasn't supposed to know that, but it would be a cold day in Shartahk's hell when a platoon sword didn't know everything that might affect *his* platoon. Forstmir knew all about the feud between Gorzalt and Ustmyn. He also knew Thousand Carthos had left Gorzalt—who might most kindly be described as a bit of a dud as an officer—to keep an eye on the "backdoor" portal between Nairsom and New Uromath because he'd figured not even Gorzalt could do much harm stuck way out here. It wasn't as if the dragon-less Sharonians were coming pouring through Nairsom anytime soon, after all, especially when they had their hands full with Two Thousand Harshu and the rest of the AEF in Traisum. Unfortunately, Gorzalt seemed to be aware of Carthos' reasoning, and he resented the hells out of it. And, also unfortunately, Commander of Fifty Ustmyn was not the most socially adroit youngster to ever don the Union of Arcana's uniform. In fact, he was pretty *mal*adroit, when you came down to it, and he'd managed to put his foot squarely on Gorzalt's injured pride in an overheard conversation with one of the company's other fifties.

Now, personally, Forstmir couldn't fault Ustmyn's opinion of their CO, but he wished to Seiknora that the fifty had been able to keep his mouth shut when Gorzalt was in hearing range. And, truth be told, the sword was more than a little pissed off with his own fifty at the moment, too. Zakar Ustmyn was only twenty-three, but he was generally serious about doing his job and did it one hell of a lot better than Gorzalt did his. At the moment, though, he was spending most of his time resenting Gorzalt's decision to stick him out in the wreckage of the old Sharonian fort—under canvas—while the rest of the company not only enjoyed a much nicer (and far better sheltered) campsite on the local equivalent of the Jerdyn River, six miles away, but also monopolized the limited number of chansyu huts Thousand Carthos had left behind. In fact, Ustmyn was spending far more time resenting the unfairness of it all than thinking about his own responsibilities.

Forstmir didn't mind kicking the platoon's arse when it needed kicking. After all, everyone knew the senior noncoms actually ran the Army while the officers simply commanded it! But he did like to think that his own fifty had at least some notion of which arses needed kicking and why. At the moment, it appeared Ustmyn neither had nor wanted a clue about that. And there was always someone like Shield Mahk Dhugahl, 2nd Squad's leader, who'd see just how far he could exploit a superior's lack of interest.

"I'll go kick Dhugahl's arse up between his ears," he told Phiery now. "Tell Jelmart and Vermahka that their reliefs'll be on the way shortly. *Very* shortly."

*   *   *

"Not a sound." Junior-Armsman Saith chan Kilvaryk's voice was barely audible, but none of 2nd Squad's men had any trouble understanding him. "The senior said he'd have your guts for boot laces if anybody gives this away, but I wouldn't worry about him. First you'd have to live through what *I'll* do to you."

The squad nodded as one. They didn't really think chan Kilvaryk would murder them out of hand...but they weren't prepared to place any bets on that.

"All right," the junior-armsman said after sweeping his dark eyes back and forth across them for several seconds. "Chan Nysik, a lot of this is on you. You need to get into position fast."

"Gotcha, Junior."

Chan Nysik was a couple of years older than chan Kilvaryk, and while he'd never had any ambition to rise above his present rank of Armsman 1/c, he was as solid and reliable as the rocky crags of his native Mulgethia's mountains. He was also very tall and powerfully built. The Faraika machine-gun weighed over a hundred and twenty pounds, but he carried it with little apparent effort while his assistant made heavy going of its tripod, which weighed barely fifty. Now he gave chan Kilvaryk a lazy, confident smile.

"Don't you worry, Junior," he said. "Once Larthy and me are in position with old Maragleth"—he hefted the machine gun in his arms with a smile which showed a missing tooth—"ain't none of them Arcanans getting past us."

"Glad to hear it," chan Kilvaryk said dryly. He gave his entire squad one more beady-eyed look, then jerked his head in a "follow me" gesture, turned on his heel, and started forward.

*   *   *

"I hope this works as well as I've convinced everyone else it will, Doc," Grithair chan Mahsdyr muttered to the man beside him as his company moved forward.

Platoon-Captain Fezar chan Birhahl, Gold Company's senior healer, snorted in amusement.

"Well, you certainly didn't sound to me as if *you* had any doubts about it, Sir," he said.

"Of course I didn't!" Chan Mahsdyr shook his head. "First thing they teach you is to always *sound* like you know what you're doing even if you don't have a clue. In this case, I'm pretty sure I do have a clue. I'm just not sure what else I have."

"Surprise, for one thing," chan Birhahl replied much more seriously, and chan Mahsdyr grunted.

"Looks like it, anyway," he acknowledged. "And that's the most dangerous weapon there is, really, when you come down to it."

Chan Birhahl was a Healer, but he'd been around soldiers who *weren't* Healers long enough to understand exactly what the company-captain meant, and he nodded in agreement.

All the Distance Viewers attached to Gold Company agreed that both the Arcanans in the ruins of Fort Rensar and those in the far more substantial—and comfortable—permanent bivouac in the valley of the Graystone River showed absolutely no awareness that there were any Sharonians in their vicinity. It was remotely possible they knew all about Gold Company and were setting some sort of subtle trap based on yet another unknown magical ability, but it seemed unlikely. This was one of the times when chan Mahsdyr passionately wished that he had at least a touch of the Distance Viewer Talent himself and could have avoided the need to rely on the reports of the observations of others.

Isn't any different from relying on any other report from a forward scout, Grithair, he told himself firmly. *Just keep remembering that.*

And, if the Distance Viewers were correct about that element of surprise, it meant Gold Company and the rest of 2nd Battalion had gotten all the way to the very doorstep of Thermyn without any Arcanan seeing a thing.

Of course, that just puts even more pressure on us to make sure the bastards behind them stay equally fat, dumb, and ignorant. It's still thirteen hundred miles to Fort Ghartoun, even after we're through the portal. Plenty of time for them to arrange something nasty if we fuck up at this point!

At least the terrain favored them. The only really tricky bit was getting past the miserable, cold squad or two of Arcanans who'd staked out the ruins of the fort. The dry riverbed below the portal provided quite a lot of cover for men as well trained at wringing every possible advantage out of any terrain feature as those of the 3rd Dragoons. Its depth gave excellent cover against anyone at the level of the riverbank, at least until they were most of the way across. Better yet, the angled portal itself created a huge blind spot. If he'd been in charge of picketing it, he'd have had positions for two or three section-sized outposts stretched across each aspect, but especially on the southern side, where the river had disappeared into Thermyn. That would have given him an excellent chance of spotting anyone trying to sneak across the river towards him.

But the Arcanans hadn't done that. Fort Rensar had been designed as an administrative node, not a serious defensive work, and while it had an excellent view of the portion of the Tyrahl River which still had water in it, its view of the empty bed beyond the portal was badly restricted by the portal itself. By moving a mile or so downstream, chan Mahsdyr's men had been able to cross the channel without anyone at the fort seeing a thing. Worse—or, actually, *better* from his perspective—it was obvious the idiot who'd picked the location for their main encampment hadn't thought about the fact his forward pickets had such an enormous blind spot. If there'd been one approach route chan Mahsdyr would have worried about, it was the *empty* riverbed, not the one that was still full of icy cold, rushing water, yet the southwesternmost edge of the portal completely concealed it from anyone in the Graystone's valley just as completely as from Fort Rensar. They literally couldn't see anything coming around the portal's eastern aspect. Why in Chindarsu's name they hadn't pulled their encampment all the way back to the Thermyn side of the portal if they weren't going to picket this side *adequately* was more than chan Mahsdyr was prepared to guess.

He wasn't about to complain, however. His maps were both detailed and highly accurate, updated by the TTE's surveyors to account for any discrepancies between the purely local geography of Nairsom and that of Sharona. With that advantage, it hadn't been difficult to pick his approach route to the spot he wanted. He imagined his men—especially those of the mortar platoon—were inventing imaginative curses for him at the moment as they struggled across the rugged terrain, but he was fine with that. And they'd be fine with it, too, if they managed to get into position without being spotted.

"Well, Doc, I guess it's time we were heading out, too."

*   *   *

Commander of Fifty Gilthar Vurth closed the door of 2nd Platoon's mess hall chansyu hut and stood on the front step, idly picking his teeth with a toothpick. It was getting on towards evening—days were short this early in the year and this far north—and the cooks were about ready to start serving dinner. As Thimanus Gorzalt's senior platoon commander and acting executive officer, it was one of Vurth's self-appointed duties to sample each meal and make certain it was worthy of the Union of Arcana's fighting men.

It wasn't like he had anything else to do out here in the middle of absolutely nowhere.

He grimaced at the thought and wondered once again what god or demon he'd offended to end up under Gorzalt's command. Of course, the 451st Regiment was a far cry from one of the Army's elite units, like the 2nd Andaran Scouts. No doubt there was some sort of seismic settling process which inexorably moved less than scintillating officers into its ranks and away from those more elite units. The only problem with that theory was that while it explained how Gorzalt had ended up in the 451st, it didn't explain what *Vurth* was doing here.

Or I hope to hells it doesn't, anyway, he reflected.

He shrugged and turned toward the barren, unkempt "parade ground" Gorzalt had insisted on laying out between the mess hall and his HQ hut. It hadn't gotten a lot of use since Thousand Carthos pulled back to rejoin the main expeditionary force in Traisum. Vurth tried to make sure all the men were inspected at least weekly and got at least some time on the firing range every week. It shouldn't have been difficult, but Gorzalt seemed to have withdrawn into a sulk when he realized who was being left behind to picket the portal, and the rest of C Company appeared to have caught the malaise from its CO. Well, aside from Zakar Ustmyn, at least, and look what Ustmyn's attitude had gotten him!

Vurth shook his head in disgust—disgust directed almost as much at himself as at Gorzalt—and started across the "parade ground" as the shadows cast by the high ground to the northwest began to creep over it.

*   *   *

"Platoon-Captain chan Urhal's in position, Sir."

Grithair chan Mahsdyr took the hastily scribbled note from Armsman 1/c chan Tylwyr, his company Flicker, and managed—somehow—not to say "At last!" It would have been unprofessional, unfair to Jersalma chan Urhal's 3rd Platoon, and a case of blaming the wrong person, anyway. He'd been right about the way the terrain would cover his approach, but he'd made insufficient allowance for how it would *slow* that approach. For the last hour or so, he'd been afraid he was going to lose the light before all of his men were in place. That would have left him with the choice of mounting a night attack or waiting in position—without cover and without bedrolls—until dawn. Neither was a palatable alternative, although he was pretty sure he'd have gone with the first if it came to it. Surprise and darkness should let them sweep up the entire Arcanan encampment, but that same darkness would make it much easier for someone to get away with word of Gold Company's presence.

Now, fortunately, he wouldn't have to. He still had at least forty-five minutes, more likely an hour and a half. That should be plenty of time.

"All right, Shodan," he told chan Tylwyr. "It's time. Pass the word."

"Yes, Sir!"

The Flicker gave him a quick, broad smile, and then concentrated on the neat row of metal message tubes laid out in front of him. They vanished in rapid, silent succession, as quickly as a Faraika spat out bullets, and chan Mahsdyr raised his field glasses and looked down from the ridgeline.

He stood barely eight hundred yards from the center of the Arcanan outpost, looking down from the top of a five hundred-foot hill. The Graystone's valley widened at this point, so its farther side was almost fourteen hundred yards from his present position. That was farther than he really liked, but the contour lines were also much steeper and he'd gotten chan Urhal's platoon down onto the valley floor itself. That was one reason this had taken so long; 3rd Platoon had been forced to swing substantially wider than the rest of his attack force. That was the bad news. The *good* news was that chan Urhal had managed to use the Graystone's bed to infiltrate to within little more than three hundred yards of the encampment without being spotted.

Now, as chan Tylwyr's Flicked message tubes reached their destinations, half a dozen mortars opened fire.

* * *

Gilthar Vurth was halfway across Thimanus Gorzalt's parade ground when the first mortar bomb landed.

The two support platoons assigned to Gold Company were equipped with light, three-inch mortars, not the much heavier four-and-a-half-inch weapons of a heavy mortar company, and chan Mahsdyr had brought only one platoon across the riverbed. The three-inch projectiles weighed less than a third as much as those of their bigger brethren and, at four thousand yards, they had only two thirds the range. But they had ample reach for the task in hand, and their seven-pound bombs came sliding down the frigid air with the sound of whispering silk.

Vurth just had time to register the mortars' muted coughs. It wasn't much to hear, really, because they were emplaced in the dead ground behind the hill upon which chan Mahsdyr had taken up his position. The fifty's head came up, turning as he tried to determine the peculiar sounds' direction. Unfortunately for him, he'd never heard mortar fire before. He had no idea what he'd heard, and the incoming fire arrived long before he could figure it out.

He'd never heard mortars firing before, and he'd never hear them again, either. One of the plunging bombs landed barely fifteen feet from him and the blast hurled his broken, bleeding body back into the front wall of the mess hall. He oozed down it in a broad, crimson streak of blood, his eyes already settling into the dull, fixed stare of death.

* * *

Commander of One Hundred Thimanus Gorzalt jerked upright in his chair as the explosions thundered. He sprang to his feet, eyes wide, expression incredulous, and wheeled toward the single window in the chansyu hut's southern wall.

He got there just as another mortar bomb impacted on the hut's roof almost directly above him.

* * *

Sword Trymayn Ilkathym heard a voice bellowing orders, fighting to bring some sort of order out of the sudden, terrifying chaos. It took him a moment to realize the voice belonged to *him* ... and that he didn't hear a single one of C Company's officers. He knew he wouldn't hear Gilthar Vurth's. He'd been waiting for the fifty on the far side of the parade ground when the first Sharonian fire exploded like Shartahk's own thunderbolts. He'd seen his fifty blown backwards, seen him smash into the mess hall's wall and ooze down it, and he'd seen more than enough dead men to recognize one more.

Then he heard something no Arcanan had ever heard before. He heard the high, fiercely snarling wolf's howl of ancient Ternathia and the wild music of the war pipes of the mountains of Delkrathia. The Imperial Ternathian Army had adopted those pipes more than two millennia ago, and their savage voice had played Ternathia's soldiers to victory on more battlefields than even the best military historian could have counted.

And then the Faraika machine guns which had been wrestled forward opened fire from the ridgeline on which Grithair chan Mahsdyr stood watching.

"Move, gods damn you! *Move!*" Ilkathym's sword was in his hand, somehow, and he jabbed it at the steep valley side from which that spreading thundered came. "Get your weapons and fucking follow me!"

Perhaps a half-dozen voices answered, and he snarled. He already knew how this was going to end, but he'd been a soldier for seventeen years. That was more than half his entire life, and here at the end, he discovered that he didn't know how to be anything else.

"*Follow me, boys!*" he screamed and charged across the valley.

He got fifty yards before a .40 caliber bullet hit him squarely at the base of his throat.

*   *   *

"Mother Jambakol!"

Kilvyn Forstmir whirled towards the sudden sound of explosions and gunfire, his face gaunt with shock in the afternoon light pouring through from the far side of the portal. The main encampment was over four miles from Fort Rensar's charred remains, but sound carried extraordinarily well in the cold, still air. He'd never heard anything like it, and he didn't really know what he was hearing now, but he knew who had to be behind it.

How? How in the names of all the gods could Sharonians have gotten this far down-chain from Traisum so *quickly?* And how could they have done it without *anyone* spotting them?

The questions hammered through him, and his jaw tightened as he realized the answer to the last one, at least. They'd gotten into position to attack Hundred Gorzalt's position because C Company had *let* them. He'd known—*known*—Gorzalt hadn't even tried to properly picket the portal. And instead of trying to do anything about it himself, instead of finding some way to prod his own fifty into doing something about it, he'd sat on his own mental arse and wasted his energy bitching at his officers. It was damned well an officer's job not to let something like this happen, but when they didn't step up and do it, someone else had to.

And he hadn't.

"What the hells is all that racket, Sword?"

He turned to see Fifty Ustmyn bursting out of his tent, buckling his sword belt as he came.

"Only one thing it can be, Sir," he said grimly.

"But how in Shartahk's name could Sharonians have gotten all the way down-chain to Nairsom?"

"Don't know, Sir." Forstmir's tone was flat. "Hells, maybe they *do* have their own version of dragons! Doesn't really *matter* right now though, does it?"

"You're right about that," Ustmyn said after half a breath and squared his shoulders. "If they're here, they're twenty-five hundred miles closer to Hell's Gate than Two Thousand Harshu. And if they got here this quickly—"

He and his platoon sword looked at one another sickly. To get to this point, the Sharonians had traveled almost eighteen thousand miles—six thousand of them across the Treybus Ocean in the middle of winter—in no more than four months...and that assumed they'd started instantly. And if they could reach Nairsom that quickly, they could almost certainly beat Two Thousand Harshu to Hell's Gate and cut his communications behind him.

"Must've missed us somehow, Sir," Forstmir said quietly. "Either that, or they figure they can tidy us up anytime after they deal with the rest of the Company. But they'll be coming."

"I know." Ustmyn rubbed his chin, then inhaled sharply. "Get the men turned to, Kilvyn. It probably won't matter, but we can at least try. And in the meantime, these bastards must not've realized we have a hummer cot of our own."

"Yes, Sir."

"Tell Galvara I need him."

"Yes, Sir!"

Forstmir slapped his breastplate in salute and headed off into the gathering twilight, shouting orders to the shaken men of 2nd Platoon. Ustmyn looked after him for a moment, then sat on one of the fort's burned timbers, pulled a recording crystal out of his belt pouch, and began dictating his report.

* * *

"You wanted me, Sir?"

Ustmyn looked up as Lance Gordymair Galvara, the leader of the three-man hummer section Hundred Gorzalt had attached to 2nd Platoon, slid to a halt beside him. Gorzalt hadn't sent his most capable hummer master out to share 2nd Platoon's misery, but at least Galvara didn't seem to be panicking.

Probably lack of imagination, the fifty thought mordantly.

"Yes, Galvara," he said out loud and extended the crystal. "Get this transferred and into the air as soon as possible. It's critical this message get through, so copy it to every hummer you've got."

"But if we send them all off, Sir, we won't have any left for additional messages," Galvara pointed out.

"No, we won't," Ustmyn said almost gently. "On the other hand, I don't really think we're going to need them. Do you?"

Galvara stared at him. Then his eyes widened and he swallowed.

"No, Sir. Don't reckon we will," he said, reaching for the crystal.

"Which makes it especially important to get this one right." Ustmyn gripped the lance's shoulder. "Make sure you do, Gordymair."

"Aye, Sir. I'll do that thing."

The lance's Limathian accent was more pronounced than Ustmyn had ever heard it, but his jaw firmed and he nodded sharply.

"Good man." The fifty squeezed his shoulder again. "Now, go get it sent," he said and turned to follow Forstmir as Galvara ran towards the hummers.

* * *

"Oh, laddie, that's a bad, bad idea," Wendyr chan Jethos said softly.

"Can't blame them for trying," Fozak chan Gyulair replied and drew a deep breath as he settled even more squarely behind his Mark 12. "And it's why we're here."

"I know." Chan Jethos shook his head. "Doesn't hardly seem fair, though."

"And what those bastards did to every Voice between Hell's Gate and Traisum *was* fair?"

"Didn't say that." Chan Jethos closed his eyes, concentrating on his Talent. "Good news is there's only one of 'em so far. Might be the others'll take the hint."

"Maybe."

Chan Gyulair had his own eyes closed as he squeezed the rear trigger, transforming the one in front of it into a hair trigger that could be touched off almost with a thought. He ignored the bulky, powerful telescopic sight mounted atop his rifle. In fact, he hadn't even opened the protective lens caps. There were times he needed that sight, because his was a very special Talent. He was a Predictive Distance Viewer. His range was too short to be useful for the artillery, where ranges of up to fifteen or even twenty miles might be required, but it was more than long enough for other purposes, and the Army aggressively recruited men like him for its snipers. He had to know where to Look, which was why he was normally paired with chan Jethos, whose Plotting Talent located his targets for him. Without that sort of spotter, he had to search for them the old-fashioned way, using his eyes first and his Talent second, which explained the sight.

But today, he *did* know where to Look, and as he Watched Gordymair Galvara racing towards the hummers, he recognized the exact moment when he'd be in exactly the right spot.

Of course, it wasn't enough to simply know where the target was. No Talent could provide the breath control, the steadiness, the ability to gauge the range and put a bullet precisely where it needed to be precisely when it needed to be there. That took years of training and constant practice, but Fozak chan Gyulair had invested those years in mastering his trade.

*   *   *

The 320-grain bullet was still traveling at almost nine hundred feet per second when it struck Lance Galvara directly above his right eye like a five hundred and seventy-pound hammer.

CHAPTER FORTY

Vandiyahr 4, 5054 AE
[March 23, 1929 CE]

"YOUR BOYS HAVE DONE ONE HELL OF A JOB, RENYL," ARLOS chan Geraith said, exchanging a forearm clasp like hammered steel with Brigade-Captain Renyl chan Quay. "I knew I was asking a lot of you, and you've done all of it and more. Especially chan Malthyn and young chan Mahsdyr."

"They have done the Brigade proud, haven't they, Sir?" Renyl chan Quay was almost a foot taller than chan Geraith, with hazel eyes and the dark hair of his Teramandorian birth, and white teeth flashed against his dark complexion as he smiled broadly, pleased with the division-captain's well-deserved praise.

"They've done the whole damned *Army* proud," the division-captain corrected. "I couldn't even begin to count how many things could've gone wrong with this march. I'd say probably at least a third of them *did* go wrong, for that matter. But the entire corps pulled my arse out of every hole we almost fell into, and your brigade's done more of that than anyone except—possibly—chan Hurmahl and the other engineers."

Chan Quay nodded, his smile fading into a more sober expression, because chan Geraith had a point.

Breakdowns had accelerated at an alarming rate over the last couple of weeks. Third Corps was down almost half of the Bisons which had been assigned to it at the beginning of its epic march. Some of those losses had been made up out of additional Bisons sent down-chain as replacements, but the corps remained thirty percent short of its theoretical establishment and the Steel Mules and steam drays couldn't compensate for the missing Bisons' massive hauling capacity. It was like using switching engines in place of one of the TTE's Paladins, and it was beginning to bite their logistics badly.

Despite that, there'd been enough redundancy—barely—in chan Geraith's original planning to compensate for their losses. So far, at least.

Unfortunately, that was subject to change.

"I've been following all your Voice reports," chan Geraith continued, "but it's not the same as a face-to-face briefing."

Chan Quay nodded again, his expression neutral. Unlike chan Geraith, the brigade-captain was a Voice, although his range was only a few hundred yards. Had chan Geraith been equally Talented, the two of them could have conferred directly through their staff Voices, despite the distance between them, a point he had no intention of making. The division-captain needed no Talent to read his non-expression, however, and snorted dryly.

"Wasn't the first time I've regretted being deaf as a post when it comes to Hearing reports, Renyl. Won't be the last, either . . . I hope. So why don't you just step over to my office and my maps."

"Yes, Sir," chan Quay said respectfully and followed chan Geraith back to the division-captain's HQ Steel Mule.

Unlike the icy winter in Nairsom, the weather here, about midway between what should have been the towns of Carotal and Simaryn, was clear, dry, and much, much warmer. The early afternoon temperature hovered in the mid-fifties, though chan Geraith's staff Weather Hound predicted it would drop well below freezing overnight. At the moment, however, and with the brilliant sunlight striking down to heat the shell covering the Mule's cargo bed, it seemed almost unpleasantly warm to the division-captain, and the windows were cracked to let in the brisk southeasterly breeze.

That breeze ruffled the corners of the map paperweighted down on chan Geraith's desk as he and chan Quay bent over it.

"We're here," the division-captain said, tapping a point roughly two hundred miles west of Chindar and a thousand miles southeast of the Failcham portal and Fort Ghartoun. The long line of the Sand Rock River, snaking from northwest to southeast, lay a hundred and thirty miles to the south, and the terrain offered firm, relatively easy going for their vehicles as they rolled along, throwing up a vast plume of dust—which he hoped to every Arpathian hell there were no Arcanan eyes to see—from the dry soil.

"Yes, Sir," chan Quay acknowledged. "As of twelve hours ago, Regiment-Captain chan Malthyn had the rest of Second Battalion here at High Rock City, a couple of hundred miles behind chan Mahsdyr's Gold Company," he touched a spot just over two hundred miles northwest of their current location. "Chan Grosyar's been holding First Battalion here, about ten miles west of us, at Broken Shoe Butte, for the last couple of days." He tapped another spot. "He'll be moving up to join Second Battalion tomorrow morning. He's been waiting for that load of engineering supplies Battalion-Captain chan Hurmahl needs. Assuming nothing untoward happens, he should reach chan Mahsdyr day after tomorrow."

Chan Geraith nodded slowly, leaning forward to take his weight on his arms, his palms spread on the map while he considered the positions of the rest of his division. The 9th Dragoon Regiment had closed up with Teresco chan Urlman's 16th Dragoons five days ago, and the 23rd would overtake the main body within another seventy-two hours. At that point, two of his three brigades would be concentrated in a single fighting force, ready to hand.

That was good, but the erosion of his Bison strength worried him—a lot—in the case of Brigade-Captain chan Sharys' 3rd Brigade. So far, chan Sharys was managing to maintain his planned rate of advance, and at least he had only about two-thirds as far to travel as chan Geraith's other brigades, but if *he* hit a cropper, the consequences could be . . . unfortunate.

I really should be with chan Sharys, he thought. *Not that I could do one damned thing he isn't already doing. And not that he isn't perfectly competent. And not that—Oh, shut* up, *Arlos!*

"Chan Malthyn's left Battalion-Captain chan Hyul at High Rock City to mind the store while he moved up to Battalion-Captain chan Yahndar's command group," chan Quay continued, oblivious to his CO's internal soliloquy, "and chan Yahndar still has chan Mahsdyr's Gold Company out in front. According to chan Malthyn's last Voice message, Gold Company's actually on the rim of Coyote Canyon now."

"Ah?" Chan Geraith looked up. "When did that come in?"

"About fifteen minutes ago, Sir." Chan Quay grinned. "I thought I'd just save that news to give it to you personally."

"It's a little late for a Midwinter gift, but I'll take it," chan Geraith replied with an answering grin. "Any sign the Arcanans've been poking around the bridging site?"

"None, Sir." Chan Quay shook his head.

"Good," chan Geraith said. "Good."

Of course, dragons flying overhead wouldn't leave any convenient tracks for chan Mahsdyr's men to spot, but if the Arcanans had noticed the preparation work TTE's advanced construction parties had done they would almost certainly have landed to inspect it in person. Or that was what *Sharonians* would have done, anyway. Gods only knew what sort of "magic" Arcanans might use to carry out detailed reconnaissance!

Stop that! he told himself firmly. *You've already had plenty of evidence that there are limits to what they can do. Don't start giving them godlike powers at this stage!*

"Is the site in good shape?" he asked out loud.

"Chan Hurmahl says it is, Sir." Chan Quay straightened and propped his hands on his hips as he and his superior gazed down at the crooked blue line of the Stone Carve River.

Coyote Canyon was scarcely as great a terrain obstacle as the enormous chasm of Vothan's Canyon, a hundred miles farther south, but it was daunting enough to be going on with. Fortunately, the Trans-Temporal Express had realized it would have to bridge the Stone Carve *somewhere* if it meant to run a line across Thermyn from Failcham to New Uromath, and, since it had already bridged Coyote Canyon in one other universe, its engineers had chosen to use the same location in Thermyn. It wasn't on the shortest route between Fort Ghartoun and Fort Brithik, to say the least, but TTE was intimately familiar with its terrain, and the best news from chan Geraith's perspective were the steep, rough ramps crews staged through Fort Ghartoun had already blasted down from the canyon lip on both sides of the river. They'd been intended to get construction equipment down to river level when the time came to build bridge pylons, and anywhere construction crews could go, his Bisons and Steel Mules could go... when they weren't broken down, at any rate.

"Has Battalion-Captain chan Hurmahl been able to evaluate the water level?" he asked after a moment.

"He says the river's a little higher than we'd hoped but not enough to make problems. He's confident he can throw the bridge across within forty-eight to seventy-two hours once chan Grosyar catches up with Second Battalion and hands over the bridging material."

Chan Geraith nodded again, stroking his mustache with a thoughtful index finger. The construction crews who'd blasted the gaps into Coyote Canyon's walls had also surveyed the riverbed itself. The Trans-Temporal Express and the Portal Authority had learned the hard way that terrain was never identical from universe to universe. It was usually very similar, enough so that routes could be picked from maps with a fair degree of certainty, but the gods clearly delighted in variations on a theme. Even without the often bizarre effects generated in proximity to portals, each universe enjoyed its own subtly different but always unique geological history. In this instance, the painstaking survey of the Stone Carve had allowed the fabrication of steel supports and a plate steel roadway that would let chan Hurmahl's men throw a bridge capable of supporting Bisons and Steel Mules across the rocky riverbed. Chan Geraith didn't like to contemplate the amount of labor involved, but in addition to his own battalion of highly trained engineers, chan Hurmahl could draft additional bone and brawn from chan Quay's entire brigade. In theory, that gave him three thousand more strong backs, and when 2nd Brigade came fully up, he'd have the next best thing to seven thousand additional sets of hands available.

Of course, if it takes that long, the chance of the Arcanans happening by overhead goes up a lot, doesn't it? the division-captain thought, then snorted harshly. *There you go, looking for problems again!*

Vandiyahr 7, 5054 AE
(March 26, 1929 CE)

THE RACKET, THE HEAT, AND THE HUMIDITY HIT WITH the force of a hammer as Brigade-Captain chan Bykahlar climbed down from the rail car. It had been hot enough inside the car—the "air-conditioning" available for luxury rail traffic back home was a relatively recent development, and the Trans-Temporal Express didn't send its most sophisticated rolling stock to the arse-end of nowhere—but at least the train's steady motion had driven a cooling breeze through the cars' open windows and wind scoops. Now that breeze had disappeared, and the steam bath of the Dalazan rain forest had to be experienced to be believed.

The racket, on the other hand, was purely man-made. No

self-respecting jungle bird or animal would have been caught dead within ten miles of the railbed being driven through the primeval jungle. The sheer volume of noise produced by steam locomotives, steam bulldozers and graders, steamrollers, track cars delivering endless lengths of rail, sledgehammers, wrenches, steam drills, rivet guns, and the occasional roar of explosives from the advanced parties had sent any local wildlife packing in short order.

At the moment, the railhead was two hundred-plus miles farther north than it had been when 3rd Brigade embarked for its trans-Vandor crossing and it was being driven steadily farther north even as he watched. The TTE's track-laying crews, with well over three-quarters of a million miles of railroad construction on their logbooks, were the most experienced in human history. When *they* decided to drive a railhead, it advanced at a rate which had to be seen to be believed, and the current railhead was the site of yet another burgeoning supply dump. The same trains whose troop cars had moved chan Bykahlar's regiments forward had hauled enormous loads of freight along with them. Now TTE's steam-powered mobile cranes were transferring that freight to the existing mountain of supplies, where a fresh line of steam drays and Bisons with their enormous trailers waited to haul it yet farther down-chain towards 5th Corps advancing spearhead.

"This way, Sir!"

Chan Bykahlar turned his head at the sound of Battalion-Captain chan Klaisahn's shout. The brigade's chief of staff had located—or possibly stolen—a Steel Mule with a boxy superstructure built over its cargo bed. The brigade-captain recognized one of the mobile command posts Division-Captain chan Geraith had ordered fitted up, and he eyed it a bit sourly. Certainly it would be nice to have those walls' protection once they hit the weather waiting for them in Nairsom, but chan Bykahlar was an officer of the old school. The proper means of transport for an Army officer was either his own two feet or the saddle of a Shikowr. He fully appreciated the theoretical advantages of moving companies, battalions—even entire divisions—at the speeds steam made possible, but he had his doubts about how restful the ride would be over the so-called "roads" which had been hacked out by the engineers.

He had no doubt at all about how restful the ride *wouldn't* be once they started heading cross-country.

He pushed that thought aside as the Mule came to a halt. It was already liberally streaked with mud, and after watching a conventional steam dray slither off the pounded-down track and bog almost instantly in the mud beyond it, he decided there was much to be said for its half-tracked suspension.

Chan Klaisahn hopped down from the running board and trotted over.

"I've got the maps and dispatch cases aboard, Sir," he said, saluting crisply. "We can move out as soon as Gershyr's transferred your personal gear. Regiment-Captain chan Ferdain's already loading the Three Hundred Twelfth aboard its Bisons and Mules, and TTE's mating the heavy equipment and artillery with the transport. Of course, we won't dare move until Gershyr tells us *he's* ready!"

He rolled his eyes, and chan Bykahlar chuckled. Senior-Armsman Gershyr chan Lorak had been his batman for five years, and he ruled the rest of the brigade with an iron will. It would have taken a hardier soul than any mere brigade-captain to deflect Gershyr from The Way Things Ought to Be where the care and feeding of one Desval chan Bykahlar was concerned.

"Actually, Sir, I doubt even Gershyr's going to delay our departure today," chan Klaisahn continued, and shrugged when chan Bykahlar raised a questioning eyebrow. "I don't mean to suggest he's suddenly decided to turn over a new leaf and become *reasonable*, Sir. It's just that we won't be ready to move out in less than at least ten hours, no matter what we do. Not only do we have all of our own baggage and heavy weapons to cross-load, but I understand Master Yanusa-Mahrdissa's sending a fuel convoy along with us. It's going to take a while to top off the kerosene drays from the tanker cars."

"Sounds like a good idea to me," chan Bykahlar agreed. "Gods know the last thing we need is to run short of fuel in the middle of the godsdamned Roanthan Plains in the middle of winter! But only kerosene? Not coal, too?"

"Not this trip, Sir. Rechair's in the midst of a deep discussion with the freight master, and I expect he'll emerge with more detail than I have now. From what I understand, though, they've decided to hold the coal-fired Bisons farther back, where the bulk of their fuel requirements—and their funnel smoke—won't be as big a problem."

Chan Bykahlar nodded. Aside from its tendency to leak, kerosene was actually far easier—not to mention one hells of a lot cleaner—to transport, and while he strongly suspected that several hundred Bisons and Steel Mules churning across the plain would produce enough dust to make their presence obvious, he was entirely in favor of not adding dense clouds of coal smoke to the mix.

Not that it's likely to be much of a factor where we're *concerned,* he reflected. *It's the poor bloody dragoons who have to worry about being spotted by the damned dragons. And if we* are *spotted,* they're *the ones who're going to draw the first dragon attacks, too, I imagine.*

"All right," he said, squelching across the mud to the step built into the Mule's rear bumper, "I suppose I should survey my new domain while it's still standing still."

CHAPTER FORTY-ONE

Vandiyahr 8, 5054 AE
[March 27, 1929 CE]

DIVISION-CAPTAIN CHAN GERAITH STOOD ATOP THE CANYON wall and peered down at the bustling anthill so far below through his field glasses.

At the moment, he was seven hundred and eighty miles northwest of Chindar, but that was in the sort of straight line possible to one of the Arcanan dragons. To get there, the 3rd Dragoons, had been forced to cover the better part of *thirteen* hundred miles in the eight days since crossing into Thermyn, and every bone in his body knew it. The five hundred and ninety miles from Chindar to High Rock City hadn't been all that terrible ... except for the extra hundred and ten miles (and endless climb up to High Rock) the terrain had imposed. Covering the remaining six hundred miles—which would have been only three hundred, for the godsdamned Acanans, of course—from there to Coyote Canyon had been far worse, however. But at least the Bisons and Steel Mules which had preceded the main column had pounded the worst of the ground flat, and the weather hadn't been all that bad. In fact, the temperature hadn't fallen below freezing for the last week and there'd been plenty of sun, but lack of water and the dense, choking pall of dust had more than made up for that. Civilians who'd never tried to move a few thousand men and horses across an arid waste had no concept of just how much water they'd need. The engineers had dammed the Sand Rock River where it flowed through High Rock City to create a reservoir, but even this early in the year the Sand Rock was scarcely the Dalazan River. It helped a lot, but he knew the quartermasters spent a lot of time worrying over breakdowns among the water tankers.

Fortunately, that problem was in a fair way to being alleviated here at Coyote Canyon itself, given the amount of water brawling its way along the Stone Carve. The engineers had set up a water collection and purification point five miles upstream from the bridging site, and through his glasses he could see several hundred men splashing around in the river itself. He suspected the water was a bit too cold for his own tastes, but he was glad to see them washing away the dust. No doubt at least some of them were also trying to soak up as much moisture as they could through the pores of their skin, he thought with a grin.

He moved his attention to the bridge itself. He couldn't hear much from his present position except for the constant, sighing voice of the wind, but the bridge's prefabricated steel spans swarmed with workmen. It was almost completed, and the bulldozer blade-fitted Bisons were improving the approach to it. More of them, as well as hundreds of men with shovels and picks, were working to improve the steep, rugged ramp up to the notch blasted out of the canyon's farther wall.

Tomorrow, he thought. *Yahnday at the latest. And that's when the race* really *starts.*

He lowered the glasses and turned to look back to the east. The sprawl of vehicles, orderly rows of tents, and industriously employed soldiers stretched as far as the eye could see, and the inevitable cluster of shirtless, sunburned mechanics swarmed over a half-dozen Bisons, shielded from the desert sun by overhead canvas flies. From the occasional curse riding the stiff breeze to his ears, at least one of the recalcitrant vehicles was likely to find itself cannibalized to get the others running again. He hated the thought of losing yet another of them, but his instructions to Therahk chan Kymo's quartermasters had been uncompromising.

The next six or seven days were critical. The indefatigable Company-Captain chan Mahsdyr and his Gold Company were once again far out ahead of 3rd Dragoons' main body. In fact, he and his men were ensconced in the rugged country along the White Snake River east of Fort Ghartoun, keeping a cautious and surreptitious eye on its Arcanan garrison. As long as they stayed at least a few miles back, the rough terrain—made considerably rougher by the violence of the portal wind which must have come screaming through the Failcham portal, probably for centuries, when it originally formed—offered an abundance of concealment for troops as experienced at keeping out of sight as Ternathian dragoons. Chan Geraith knew that. And despite knowing that, his nerves tightened every time he thought of all of the ways in which they might betray their presence to any semi-alert Arcanan.

Fortunately, there seemed to be few of those in Fort Ghartoun. Nor had chan Mahsdyr's Plotters or Distance Viewers seen any dragons attached to the fort. For that matter, they hadn't seen any of the eagle-lions the Arcanans appeared to use as unmanned reconnaissance vehicles, either. That undoubtedly explained how the thousands of Sharonians along the Stone Carve, barely four hundred miles from them, had so far eluded their attention. Unfortunately, Fort Brithik, at the New Uromath portal, lay almost directly east of Fort Ghartoun while he and his dragoons were approaching from the *south*east.

The good news was that dragon traffic seemed to be far lighter than he'd feared it would be. Every pound of supplies for the Arcanans in Karys had to transit the Thermyn-Failcham portal, and he'd expected dozens, if not hundreds, of dragons to be moving up and down the Karys Chain. Yet Chan Mahsdyr and his Plotters had seen only a handful of them pass through Fort Ghartoun, which argued that Harshu's logistic situation was worse than chan Geraith had ever allowed himself to hope.

Unless, of course, he reminded himself conscientiously, *the godsdamned Arcanans turn out to have their own magical equivalent of the Bison or the Mule and we just haven't seen the damned thing yet!*

Under the circumstances, that seemed less than likely, however. Surely if the Arcanans *did* have an alternate means of transporting supplies, chan Mahsdyr would have seen some sign of it, given the voracious appetite of a force the size of Harshu's. The logistics needs of an Arcanan Army couldn't be that different from a Sharonian one!

And if they *don't* have something like that and chan Mahsdyr's seen—what? Only four?—freight dragons while he's had the fort under observation, maybe Harshu's supply chain's really as fucked over as it looks. And wouldn't *that* be sweet?

Unfortunately, while the flight path across Thermyn still lay comfortably over two hundred miles north of his current position, it also formed the long sides of an isosceles triangle with his march from this point to Fort Ghartoun. That meant the distance between the two would drop sharply once the 3rd Dragoons resumed their advance...and vastly increase the chance of one of those dragons straying far enough south to see it coming. He'd cheerfully have sacrificed his left hand for the sort of aerial reconnaissance capability the Arcanans enjoyed, but in its absence, the best he could do was to take the threat into consideration and try to plan around it.

And that was why the next several days were going to be critical.

According to chan Mahsdyr's reports, the entire garrison of Fort Ghartoun couldn't amount to much more than half a battalion. There was perhaps a company of their unicorn-mounted light cavalry and what looked from the Voice reports like no more than a couple of infantry companies. It was obvious, reading between the lines of the company-captain's reports, that chan Mahsdyr was confident Gold Company could have successfully seized the fort out of its own resources, and given how expeditiously they'd secured the entry portal from Nairsom, chan Geraith was confident he was right. He had no intention of finding out, however. When the time came, Battalion-Captain chan Yahndar's entire battalion would storm the fort. Hopefully, 2nd Battalion's attack would come as as much of a surprise to Fort Ghartoun as chan Mahsdyr's assault had been for the Arcanan encampment on the Tyrahl River. Unfortunately, the Fort Ghartoun hummer cots were inside the fort's sturdy walls. Not even a Talented sniper like Fozak chan Guylair could hit a target on the other side of a solid, clay-reinforced timber palisade, and the engineers who'd chosen Fort Ghartoun's site had picked one which offered no handy vantage points simultaneously high enough and close enough to target the fort's interior over its walls.

Chan Yahndar had devised a plan to deal with that, and chan Geraith had approved it because it offered an excellent chance of success. Without the ability to specifically and directly target the hummer cots, however, no one could *guarantee* that the fort's garrison—chan Geraith hesitated to use the noun "defenders" to describe a body of troops which appeared to spend so much time sitting on its collective arse—couldn't get off a message. That was unfortunate, for several reasons.

It would be...awkward if the garrison got off a message to Harshu, but Harshu was in Karys, over twenty-five hundred miles from Ghartoun. Even with dragons, it would take him time—and lots of it—to do anything about the force which had suddenly severed his supply chain.

Unfortunately, it was also well over a thousand miles from Ghartoun to Fort Brithik on the New Uromath portal as a bird—or a dragon—might fly it, and more like fifteen hundred for the Bisons and Mules. Crossing that distance would have required the better part of three weeks of hard slogging even with the tracked vehicles and even assuming he'd been able to haul forward enough fuel for the trip...which he couldn't. But Brithik's recapture was essential to his plans. As the barest possible minimum, he needed to shut down that portal to protect the Thermyn/Failcham portal and his own supply line from Chindar to Fort Ghartoun. If the Arcanans managed to break loose a couple hundred of their dragons here in Thermyn, it would be child's play for them to find a place to sever that supply line, at which point the 3rd Dragoons would find themselves even more disastrously cut off than Harshu in Karys.

But settling for shutting down the Thermyn/New Uromath portal was definitely his second choice. That portal was fourteen miles across. Dominating that much space with fire would be a...problematical task even for the Third Dragoons, especially assuming the Arcanans had the rudimentary sanity to push their dragons through it in the dark. He had no doubt he could hugely constrict the Arcanans' use of the portal, given his Distance Viewers, organic artillery, and machine guns, yet that wasn't remotely the same thing as *shutting it down*.

But if he could hit Brithik before the Arcanans knew he was coming, the remaining distance to Hell's Gate was only another two hundred and fifty miles. Through heavy tree cover and con-stricted terrain, yes, but only two hundred and fifty miles. By his worst-case estimate, based on painstaking analysis of the detailed terrain maps Balkar chan Tesh had sent home before his death, the Bisons and Mules could cover that distance in no more than six days. And if they *did* cover those miles and got to the swamp portal chan Tesh had seized immediately after Fallen Timbers before the Arcanans could muster a force to stop them....

That would be an entirely different seine of fish. Given the miserable, marshy terrain on the far side of that portal and its smaller size, he was fully confident of his ability to hold it indefinitely. Certainly until he could be relieved by the infantry following in his division's wake. The truth was that the swamp portal was the real strategic prize of his entire advance, and the dearth of traffic moving up-chain towards Karys meant his chances of taking it might well be greater than he'd originally assumed.

The problem, of course, was that the same force couldn't hit two objectives, twelve hundred air-miles apart, simultaneously.

That was why Brigade-Captain Losahl chan Sharys' 3rd Brigade hadn't followed 1st and 2nd Brigade west to Coyote Canyon. No, *3rd Brigade* had headed north-north*east* from Chindar, directly toward Fort Brithik. Despite the fact that chan Sharys' brigade had been the last to move forward, it also had a far shorter distance to travel—Fort Brithik lay only eight hundred miles from Chindar—through much easier going.

At the moment, chan Sharys was less than two hundred miles from his objective. Given the terrain he faced, he should be able to cover that distance in little more than fourteen hours—call it thirty-six, given the hours of daylight he'd have to work with—and he'd be coming in at almost a right angle to the east-west flight path between New Uromath and Failcham, which meant a much lower threat of someone simply happening across him. And once he had Fort Brithink, assuming he *got* Brithik....

Of course, chan Geraith had no idea how big an Arcanan reaction force might be ready to hand at Hell's Gate. Logic said that if they had the troop strength to maintain a sizable force this far to the rear they would have powerfully reinforced Harshu. Everything they'd seen so far seemed to support his original analysis, that Harshu represented everything the Arcanans had had available. But it was also possible—unlikely, but clearly possible—that they had far greater troop strength available in Hell's Gate and simply lacked the transport to move it to Karys. In either case, chan Sharys needed to hit Hell's Gate with as little warning as possible.

At least less traffic means fewer godsdamned eyes to see him—or us—on the approach march, the division-captain told himself.

And at least he could count on the Arcanans' lack of Voices. Fast as their hummers were, they were far slower than a Voice message, so it would take any Arcanan reaction force—or Harshu—a lot longer than it would have taken a Sharonian commander to respond to any message from Fort Ghartoun. Unfortunately, once they *did* respond they had those never-to-be-sufficiently-damned dragons, so it would be a race between his powerful, concentrated ground force and a dragonborne Arcanan force which would *probably* be far more scattered initially than his own.

It would be an interesting challenge in a training exercise, he reflected, *but it's a pain in the arse when I have to do it for real. How close can I get to Fort Ghartoun before one of those transiting dragon riders glances down and happens to notice several hundred vehicles churning towards it? And how close to Brithik can chan Sharys get before they spot him? The closer we get to the portal, the more likely it is that somebody flying across Thermyn's going to spot us and our damned dust clouds. And chan Sharys' terrain south of Fort Birthik's a hell of a lot more open than our approach terrain is.*

He'd decided that fifty miles was absolutely as close as he could hope to approach without being detected. He'd already spotted Plotters and Distance Viewers along his route to Fort Ghartoun, tied together by Flickers and Voices to warn him of any dragon which might chance close enough to detect them, and chan Sharys had Distance Viewers out seventy-five miles in advance of his own column. But once either force got within fifty miles of its objective...

At least according to chan Malthyn the idiots garrisoning Ghartoun aren't doing a dawn stand-to. And if they aren't, it's likely the Fort Brithik garrison's being just as stupid, he told himself, then grimaced.

It probably really wasn't entirely fair to think of the Arcanan garrison troopers as "idiots" this far in their own army's rear. As far as they knew, the nearest possible threat was thousands upon thousands of miles away. Still, he liked to think Ternathian COs would have taken more precautions than the Arcanans appeared to be taking.

And whether they're really idiots or not, the fact that they're sleeping in instead of manning the firing steps is going to cost them when the time comes, he reflected more grimly.

His smile would not have looked out of place on a hungry lion, and he raised his glasses once more, gazing down at the bridge and willing the engineers to work even faster.

Solyrkain 14, 206 YU
Vandiyahr 18, 5054 AE
(April 6, 1929 CE)

COMMANDER OF ONE HUNDRED VERCHYK GORSATAN CON-
templated the day's paperwork with sour disgust. It wasn't
that he objected to paperwork *per se*; as an officer who'd come
up through logistics, he was really more of an administrator than
a warrior, anyway, and he knew it. In fact, he was very good at
paperwork, and as a general rule, he took a quiet pride in the
fact that it was men like him whose ability to manage supply
chains, troop movements, and transportation resources—and
generally massage the system—who made possible advances like
the one Two Thousand Harshu had driven so brilliantly forward
until that unfortunate business at Fort Salby.

Which, although he had no intention of pointing it out, had
clearly been the fault of the warriors, not the despised bureaucrats
who kept them fed.

No, the reason Gorsatan objected to the reports floating in
his crystal's depths this morning was that warrior or not, he
recognized the shit storm certain to descend upon him at some
point in the thankfully indeterminate future. What made it even
more revolting was the fact that none of it would be *his* fault,
despite the fact that he was the one who'd be holding the can
when that storm made its inevitable landfall.

The only good news, he reflected, was that even more of it
would descend upon Hadrign Thalmayr, who deeply deserved every
single thing that was going to happen to him. That had become
abundantly clear to Gorsatan since his arrival as Thalmayr's
replacement at Fort Ghartoun. Fifty Varkan and Fifty Yankaro,
the senior officers of the fort's rather tattered garrison, had done
their best to gloss over Thalmayr's excesses. Their very silence
on the subject of prisoner misconduct, torture, and violations of
the Kerellian Accords spoke volumes, however. Gorsatan was well
aware he wasn't regarded as one of the Union of Arcana Army's
sharpest blades, and he suspected he'd drawn Fort Ghartoun at
least in part on the theory that he wouldn't poke into matters
which predated his own assumption of command. For that matter,
he didn't *want* to stick his nose into things which were none of
his affair, and he especially didn't want to turn over any rocks

that might reveal scorpions ready to sting his hand...or Two Thousand Harshu.

Much as he respected Harshu, however, he knew those scorpions were waiting, and that their venom was going to be painful. And, despite that same respect, he'd come to the conclusion Harshu would merit whatever came his way. Gorsatan was well aware Harshu had never approved Thalmayr's personal, vicious cruelty. But he was equally well aware that Harshu had, at the very least, turned a blind eye to the activities of Alivar Neshok. How the two thousand could have thought for a moment that men like Thalmayr wouldn't take Neshok's brutality as a license to commit their own atrocities passed Gorsatan's understanding. Verchyk Gorsatan had never seen a better illustration of the old Chalaran proverb about a fish rotting from the head.

And when it all hit the fan and the inevitable investigators arrived at Fort Ghartoun, *he'd* be one who went down in the Army's memory either as the man who'd provided the information that started the catastrophic implosion of the career of an officer he deeply admired or else as the man who'd tried to conceal evidence of profoundly criminal activity in an effort to *protect* an officer he deeply admired.

Whichever way it worked out, it was exceedingly unlikely he'd ever advance beyond his current rank. Assuming, of course, that it wasn't suggested very strongly to him that he might, perhaps, seek a civilian career, instead. And civilian career opportunities for Andaran officers effectively drummed out of the Army were few and far between.

It was ironic, but the officers who'd actually mutinied and for all intents and purposes gone over to the enemy actually had far better long-term career prospects than Gorsatan, who hadn't had a single thing to do with Thalmayr's excesses. If, that was, they survived long enough for events to exonerate them, and the fact that they'd managed to get clean away suggested they might. Two Thousand Harshu had detached an entire air-mobile battalion to search for Fifty Ulthar, Fifty Sarma, and the escaped Sharonian prisoners. They hadn't been able to begin their search until Thalmayr reached Karys, however, and by the time they did, the mutineers had vanished. Precisely how they'd accomplished that remained a mystery, although Gorsatan inclined toward the theory—shared by Valchair Stanohs, the thousand who'd been detached to find them—that the Sharonians must have devised a way to mask or deactivate the casualty recovery spells. They'd certainly managed to elude the most assiduous searches, not just in Thermyn but in Failcham and New Uromath, as well, and they obviously hadn't passed through Hell's Gate into Mahritha. That meant they damned well ought to be in range for the overflights to trigger the recovery spells if they hadn't been turned off somehow, and those spells were specifically designed to be impossible for anyone except a highly trained magistron with the security keys to deactivate.

The chances of finding them without those recovery spells was nonexistent, and Two Thousand Harshu needed every dragon—and man—he had in Karys, so Stanohs and his battalion had returned to the front, leaving the fugitives to whatever concealment they'd found. There were times Gorsatan suspected Thousand Stanohs had ended that search as soon as he had because deep inside he didn't want the mutineers found.

That was one thing that *wasn't* his problem, however, and he allowed himself one more grimace before he drew a deep breath and called up the first report.

*   *   *

"You realize we're about to use a sledgehammer to crack a walnut, Sir, don't you?" Company-Captain Traivyr chan Fyrkam, 2nd Battalion, 12th Dragoon Regiment's executive officer, observed with a wry smile.

"Actually," Battalion-Captain Hymair chan Yahndar replied judiciously, "we're about to use a sledgehammer to *pulverize* a walnut, Traivyr. Or I damned well hope so, anyway."

Chan Fyrkam nodded. Chan Yahndar's verb was a better choice, and if it had been in the company-captain to feel sympathy for any Arcanan ever born, he probably would have felt at least a modicum for the aforementioned walnut. Unfortunately for Arcana, chan Fyrkam had actually met Crown Prince Janaki and fallen under the Calirath spell. Janaki's death was even more personal for him than it was for every other member of the Imperial Ternathian Army. The Union of Arcana's soldiers owed Sharona a debt, and Traivyr chan Fyrkam looked forward to collecting it in full.

"Is Company-Captain chan Esmahr ready, Tahnthair?" Chan Yahndar asked, turning to his battalion operations officer.

"Waiting for the order, Sir," Platoon-Captain Tahnthair chan Lyscarn said.

"And Company-Captain chan Mahsdyr and Company-Captain chan Lyrkad are in position?"

"Yes, Sir." Chan Lyscarn sounded just a tad overly patient, but chan Yahndar could live with that. The ops officer had done his usual excellent job of coordinating the attack plan's details, but while making sure those plans functioned properly might be chan Lyscarn's job, it was chan Yahndar's *responsibility*.

The battalion-captain looked down at the large-scale, detailed, and painstakingly accurate map of Fort Ghartoun on the flat rock before him, its corners weighted down by handy stones.

The fort lay in the White Snake Valley, the depression running roughly northeast to southwest along the serpentine course of the White Snake River. The portal to Failcham cut diagonally across the valley on a northwest to southeast line little more than a mile south of the fort. Like the much larger Tyrahl River, the White Snake flowed into the portal and disappeared, but Fort Ghartoun was three miles from the stream's nearest approach. Although the terrain east of the fort offered valleys, ridgelines, and seasonal watercourses for cover, it was nowhere near as heavily forested as the steeper, more rugged slopes between the fort and Snow Sapphire Lake, eight or nine miles to its north-northwest. That made approaching it from the east without being detected a ticklish propositional—though they were still at least not on the direct aerial route from New Uromath to Failcham—and chan Yahndar had been glad he was using horses, not Bisons, for the final approach. Hiding those vehicles would have been a much more ticklish proposition, and even on horseback he'd been unable to get his men as close as he would have preferred. Still, they'd gotten one hells of a lot closer than they ought to have against an alert opponent...even one who didn't have dragons and eagle-lions.

Now, as he gazed down at the map his Distance Viewers had last updated less than two hours earlier, a meditative index finger tapped the crayon mark which indicated Grithair chan Mahsdyr's Gold Company. Given how successfully—even brilliantly—chan Mahsdyr had led the advance all the way across four universes, there'd been no question who'd earned the opportunity to spearhead the assault on Ghartoun, and Gold Company lay roughly three and a half miles southeast of the fort, between the White Snake and a ridgeline hiding it from the flat terrain around the fort. Ulysar chan Lyrkad's Silver Company was deployed on Gold Company's right flank, a mile and a half farther back—the ground was more open and less forgiving northeast of the fort, and he hadn't been able to get as close—while Company-Captain Lerkhali chan Dasam's Bronze Company had circled around to deploy another three miles north-northeast of Silver Company, more to prevent anyone from scampering off in that direction than to participate in the attack itself. Company-Captain Vynchair chan Zelmahdyn's Copper Company formed 2nd Battalion's reserve, although a reserve was probably about as necessary as teats on a boar hog. The Distance Viewers had spent the last twenty-four hours further refining their detailed estimates of the fort garrison's strength, and the Arcanans had little more than *two* full strength companies. Even better, it was obvious they had no idea what was coming.

He snorted at the thought, and his finger moved back to the position of Company-Captain Temyk chan Esmahr's 103rd Battery, Imperial Ternathian Horse Artillery, located on a bend of the White Snake six miles east of the fort. The mortars of Company-Captain Namair chan Jersyk's weapons company had been moved up to support chan Mahsdyr and chan Lyrkad, but chan Esmahr's horse artillery had its part to play, as well, although it had proved impractical to get his six Ternathian 37s into position for direct fire on Fort Ghartoun. Fortunately, chan Esmahr had been reinforced. In addition to the pair of 4.3" howitzers of his own Steel Section, the Steel Section of the 116th Horse Artillery had been attached to his command. That gave him four of the weapons, and they had the range to reach Fort Ghartoun easily from their present position. Which meant eighteen mortars and four howitzers were poised to open fire on the fort the instant he gave the command. He was sure chan Jersyk and chan Esmahr would have preferred to register their weapons ahead of time, but one couldn't have everything, and chan Yahndar had complete faith in their gunners.

And the poor bastards've humped their guns and mortars over sixteen thousand miles to get here. It'd be a shame if they didn't get to fire a shot.

That was good for an actual chuckle, not just a snort, despite the tension singing in his nerves. This was the point at which the race really began, he thought. The instant his attack kicked off, Division-Captain chan Geraith's Voice would pass the word to Brigade-Captain chan Sharys to begin his own advance on Fort Brithik. And as soon as someone got word to the Arcanan forces in Karys or Hell's Gate....

He inhaled deeply and looked back up at chan Lyscarn.

"Well, if everybody's ready," he said calmly, "I suppose we should see about passing that order, Tahnthair."

*   *   *

Temyk chan Esmahr twitched as Battalion-Captain chan Yahndar's Flicker dropped the message canister neatly into the basket by his elbow. He snatched up the small steel tube, twisted it open, and glanced at its contents. Then he looked up at Platoon-Captain Horahstyr chan Wayshyr.

"Open fire!" he snapped.

*   *   *

"Open fire!" Company-Captain Namair chan Jersyk barked, looking up from the message slip in his hand.

*   *   *

Arlos chan Geraith looked up as the Flicked message landed in Merkan chan Isail's in-basket. The division's chief of staff opened it quickly, but even before he could scan it, the sudden bark of artillery told the division-captain what it said.

"All right, Lisar," he told Company-Captain chan Korthal. "Inform Brigade-Captain chan Sharys' Voice our attack's begun. He's to begin his own advance immediately."

"Yes, Sir!"

*   *   *

Verchyk Gorsatan had exactly zero warning.

One instant he was dashing his signature across the latest report from Fort Ghartoun's cooks; the next instant four howitzer shells and eighteen mortar bombs came slicing out of a cloudless morning sky. It was true chan Esmahr and chan Jersyk had been denied any ranging shots, but their Distance Viewers, Mappers, and Plotters had established ranges and bearings as accurately as if they'd actually paced off the distances, and there'd been plenty of time to position their weapons' range and bearing stakes with finicky precision.

Two of the 3" mortar bombs fell outside the fort's palisade.

They were the only shots that did.

None of Gorsatan's men had any more warning than their CO. Half were still in the mess hall, and aside from the dozen or so sentries on the walls and in the fort's watchtower—none of whom had seen a single thing—not one of them was even armed. The cascade of high explosive and steel thundering down upon them was as terrible—and just as totally unexpected—as any attack the AEF had launched on its way up-chain to Fort Salby, and the gunners and mortar crews had all the ammunition they could want.

Explosions and deadly splinters of steel turned the fort's interior into a holocaust. Commander of One Hundred Gorsatan's chair crashed over backward as he leapt to his feet, his eyes wide. It was impossible. It couldn't be happening! Not *here*—not so many thousands of miles behind the front line! But it *was* happening, and warrior or not, it was his job to do something about it.

His mouth tightened and he crossed his office in two strides, yanked the office door open, and started through it.

The thirty-two-pound 4.3" shell sliced through the cedar shingles above him at a velocity of approximately eight hundred and ninety feet per second.

*   *   *

"Now!"

The bugles sounded—high, fierce, and strong—and 1st Platoon, Gold Company, 2nd Battalion, 12th Dragoon Regiment, came over the ridgeline in a line of mounted men. The company's other platoons followed them, dust rising from the hooves of the horses which had carried them so far. The Imperial Ternathian Army's cavalry were dragoons. Oh, there were still officially "lancer" regiments in the ITA, but they were indistinguishable from dragoons these days, except for their uniforms. No Ternathian mounted formation had delivered an actual cavalry charge in seventy years, but there was a time and a place for everything.

Gold Company had five miles to cover, and it was in a hurry.

*   *   *

"Mother Jambakol!"

Sword Falstan Makraik clutched at the observation tower's railing as the interior of Fort Ghartoun erupted like twice a dozen volcanoes. Blast fronts and shrieking splinters ripped through the observation tower's floor, and he heard screams behind him. The fire seemed to be coming from the east, and he raced around to that side of the platform, ignoring the white-hot steel death hissing past him, trying desperately to locate its source.

Nothing. He could see *nothing*, and he swore again, even more foully than before. The godsdamned Sharonians and their godsdamned artillery! No Arcanan heavy weapon could fire *over* obstacles that way, but the *Sharonians* could! Only how could they *be* here?

The screams, the chaos, and the blood raging across the fort's parade ground in bubbles of Shartahk's own hellfire was total. The garrison was already disintegrating, at least a dozen men flinging themselves through the open gate, running madly away from the inferno towards the beckoning safety of the portal to New Uromath. Makraik twisted around in that direction, lips drawn back in a furious snarl. He understood exactly why they were running, and it wasn't simple cowardice, whatever his emotions might insist, but that couldn't change the way he felt. He opened his mouth to curse them . . . then closed it with a snap as a solid line of mounted men came sweeping in from the southeast behind the high, shivering howl of the Wolves of Ternathia, sabers gleaming in the morning light.

* * *

"Battalion-Captain chan Yahndar has the fort, Sir!" Company-Captain chan Korthal announced sharply.

Arlos chan Geraith looked up from his discussion with his staff and brigade commanders, brown eyes narrowed, and chan Korthal grinned hugely.

"Second Battalion didn't lose a *man*, Sir—not *one*—and the Distance Viewers and Plotters confirm that none of the Arcanans got away!"

"Arcanan losses?"

"The Battalion-Captain says initial indications are that they were very heavy, Sir." There was less delight in chan Korthal's reply, but he met chan Geraith's eyes unflinchingly. "His current estimate is that at least half the garrison was killed, and many of the survivors are wounded."

"Not too surprising, given chan Yahndar's artillery, especially if the bastards never guessed it was coming, Sir," Brigade-Captain chan Quay remarked. The 12th Dragoons was one of his regiments, and his expression was grimly satisfied.

"No, it isn't," chan Geraith agreed. "Your boys did well,

Renyl." He looked back at the chan Korthal. "What about their hummers?"

"The Distance Viewers say a shell or a mortar bomb must've landed directly on the hummer coop early in the attack, Sir." Chan Korthal shook his head. "None of the Arcanans got to them to send off a message."

"Good." Chan Geraith's voice was even more satisfied than chan Quay's expression, and he turned back to his senior officers.

"As of this moment, we've cut the Arcanans' line of communications, gentlemen," he said, resting the heel of his left hand on one of his bone-handled revolvers. "It'll take them a while to figure that out, though—or I hope to all the gods it will, anyway! And there's always the pesky little problem of their dragons, isn't there?"

His staff and brigade commanders chuckled harshly, and he thumped the palm of his right hand on the map before them.

"Renyl, your boys've had the lead all the way from Fort Salby. I don't see any reason they shouldn't keep it now. I want you on the way to Fort Mosanik within six hours. And I hope you won't mind the fact that I'll be tagging along with you."

"Oh, I think the boys and I can stand that, Sir!" chan Quay assured him.

"Good. Shodan," chan Geraith turned to Brigade-Captain chan Khartan, 2nd Brigade's CO, "I want the Twenty-Third on its way with Renyl. Three regiments should be enough to look after themselves, especially if the Arcanans are as lax in Failcham as they were here in Thermyn. I hate leaving you and the Ninth behind, but someone has to mind the store here at Ghartoun until Brigade-Captain chan Bykahlar's infantry can get here to relieve you. As soon as they do, I want you on the way to Karys, too. In the meantime, there may well be dragon traffic through this portal sometime in the next day or two even if chan Sharys nails Brithik as cleanly as we just did Ghartoun, and what I really need you to do is to stop it dead, if you can. Clear?"

He looked back and forth between the two brigade-captains, his eyes hard, and they nodded back.

"Clear, Sir," chan Quay said for both of them, and chan Geraith frowned at the map again.

It's fifteen hundred miles from Ghartoun to Mosanik, he thought, *but if the gods love us and every single thing breaks our way, we'll be halfway to the Karys portal before Harshu finds out he's lost this one. In the real world, unfortunately, some frigging dragon's going to fly right over us in the next few days and tell the bastards we're coming.*

That was not a happy thought, but it could have been one hells of a lot worse. Especially if chan Sharys did take Fort Brithik out cleanly.

If we have to fight our way to Fort Mosanik, that's why we've got the Bison-mounted pedestal guns and the 37s. And the Arcanans won't have the advantage of surprise this time, either. If they want to fuck around with my lads when we know they're coming, they're welcome to try it!

"All right," he said now, returning his attention to his brigade-captains, "chan Bykahlar's infantry ought to be on the ground here in Thermyn in the next week and a half, and Brigade-Captain chan Gorsad's only five days behind chan Sharys. "Gentlemen," he met their eyes levelly, "it looks to me as if we've got Thermyn and Hell's Gate in the bag. And one way or the other, Third Brigade's going to be rolling into Fort Mosanik in about eight days."

He showed his teeth in a sharp edged, hungry smile.

"I would *love* to see Harshu's face when he hears about *that!*"

CHAPTER FORTY-TWO

Solyrkain 18, 206 YU
Vandiyahr 22, 5054 AE
(April 910, 1929 CE)

NOT FOR THE FIRST TIME, COMMANDER OF FIFTY YORIL
Jerstan wished he were a battle dragon pilot. They got all
the prestige, all the shiny medals, and—for that matter—all the
girls. What transport pilots got was plenty of hard work, precious
little thanks, and windburn.

Transports lacked the cockpits formed into the backs of battle
dragons' enormous, tree-trunk necks, and transport pilots got to
ride in saddles, without the carefully sculpted scutes designed
to protect strike dragon pilots from the airstream when their
mounts reached maximum speed. Visored helmets and heavy
leather flight suits made the transport pilot's lot endurable, and
there were times when the wild rush of air around his body as
Grayscale's mighty wings swept onward was as intoxicating as
any whiskey. But over the long haul, day after day—especially
given the hectic schedule necessary to keep the AEF supplied—
windburn got old.

Quickly.

He snorted at the familiar thought and reached down to rest
one hand fondly on Grayscale's warm scales. The big transport
was slow and not very maneuverable, compared to the swift,
agile battle dragons, but he was steady as the sunrise, and just
as reliable. And he was in a good mood today, because he knew
they were headed down-chain towards the bison herds. He might
not be a battle dragon, but he was a canny and capable hunter.
Thousand Toralk's decision to send his dragons to hunt for themselves might not be the most efficient way to keep them supplied,

575

but it worked, and Grayscale thoroughly enjoyed the freedom to chase down his own meat.

The truth was it didn't take a lot to make Grayscale happy. He had an unusually placid temperament, even for a transport, and he was normally as cheerful and willing as the day was long. Even his disposition had developed a few rough spots over the last few months, though, especially since the Sharonians stopped Two Thousand Harshu's advance dead in front of Fort Salby. The sheer drudgery of one endless flight after another—without a sufficient stockpile of levitation spells, the transports' carrying capacity was so small they had to fly twice or three times as many missions to ferry the same quantity of supplies forward—would have taxed the patience of a saint, and transport dragons were anything but saintly.

Of course, Grayscale had no way to understand *all* the downsides of their present situation. He knew he was working harder than ever in his lengthy life; he *didn't* know the entire AEF was stuck at the end of an impossibly extended supply line, that no one seemed to be killing himself to provide the additional dragons and spell support Two Thousand Harshu needed, that the Sharonians had demonstrated just how dangerous their bizarre weapons and Talents actually were, and—according to scuttlebutt Jerstan absolutely believed—that they'd managed to kill the Sharonian Empire's crown prince at Fort Salby. He didn't even want to think about how *that* was going to further fan the Sharonians' fury at Arcana's "sneak attack"! The *last* thing they needed was—

Fifty Jerstan's thoughts broke off and he frowned, squinting into the late afternoon sun. What in Ekros' name was *that?*

He pressed the sarkolis crystal embedded in his flight helmet. A circular window appeared in the center of the helmet's face plate, and the earth far below snapped into sharp focus as the helmet linked with the sarkolis embedded in Grayscale's hide, allowing Jerstan to see what his dragon saw. The cross hair in his field of view was more of an aiming mark than the sighting system it would have been for a battle dragon—Grayscale had enough red dragon in his ancestry to generate a fireball of sorts on command, although it was a pallid, feeble thing—but the principle was still the same, and so was the helmet linkage.

Now Grayscale turned his head in tandem with Jerstan's, guided to follow the crosshair by the helmet spellware. Dragons' eyes were capable of picking up incredible detail even from four or five thousand feet, and Grayscale obediently refocused his vision on the strange, low-lying cloud which had attracted Jerstan's attention.

For a moment, it failed to register. His brain simply refused to process the preposterous input. But then Yoril Jerstan snapped fully upright in his saddle despite the buffeting slipstream as he realized what that low-lying cloud was.

*   *   *

Gerun Hostyra was bored.

He wasn't about to complain where any of his superiors might hear him, and he thoroughly understood the importance of keeping the dragon trains moving. But given how thin 1st Provisional Talon's combat strength had become after Fort Salby, it made no sense at all—in his opinion—to detail a pair of desperately needed battle dragons to play "escort" for the transports.

On the other hand, he was only a lowly commander of twenty-five. It was unlikely Thousand Toralk would appreciate his opinion if he wandered by headquarters to share it with him. Besides, whether or not the transports needed an "escort" this far from the front lines, Sky Sabre wasn't going to complain about the opportunity to eat fresh bison, and the gods knew a well-fed battle dragon was far less proddy than one with an empty belly. So, on balance, he supposed it was possible Thousand Toralk knew what he was doing, after all.

Which didn't make the three-day flight from Traisum all the way back to Hell's Gate any less boring. For that matter, why couldn't he and Sky Sabre stop here in Thermyn, spend three or four days hunting, and then pick up a fresh transport flight on its way back to the front? It wasn't as if—

The abrupt flash of a double crimson flare above Fifty Jerstan's transport jerked his attention out of its familiar rut, and he frowned as a second pair of flares burst. He glanced to his left, where Helok Bersil, his regular wingman, flew on the far side of the lumbering transports, and saw Bersil's head come up into the slipstream, craning around towards the flares. He seemed just as surprised as Hostyra.

What the hells did Jerstan think he was up to? He was the senior officer of the flight, as well as Hostyra's superior in rank, but he was a *transport* pilot. A trash-hauler. Maybe he had delusions of grandeur, and maybe he thought this was a good time for some weird practice drill, but even he ought to know the *double*-crimson was never used in training exercises. It was a live-action signal, reserved for actual combat, not a toy for a transport pilot to flash around just because he was bored!

Then a *third* double-crimson flashed.

Hostyra muttered a curse and hit his helmet crystal rather harder than was necessary. He turned his head, staring at Jerstan, and Sky Sabre's eyes focused on the fifty. Jerstan—and Grayscale— were staring back at him, and as soon as the fifty realized he had Hostyra's attention, he pointed urgently to the southwest.

All right—all right, idiot! Hostyra thought grumpily. *YSo you want me to see something. What the hells is so frigging impor—*

His eyes widened. Dozens—*scores*—of bizarre vehicles ground towards him in a huge, rolling cloud of dust. He'd never imagined anything like them! Not even Sky Sabre's vision could pick out actual numbers through the incredible, low-lying pall of dust, but there must be hundreds of them! Some were enormous, towing huge trailers behind them; others were no bigger than a large freight wagon. But all of them came surging across the barren, blasted desert without any sign of the draft animals upon which the Sharonians relied. They were moving on their own, as surely and steadily as any slider, and if their speed was far lower than a slider's, it was obvious each of them was picking its own course across the rolling prairie. They were being *individually* steered, advancing with no indication of whatever bizarre force might be propelling them, and he swallowed as he saw the artillery pieces—the "field guns"—some of those vehicles towed.

They couldn't possibly be here, yet they were here...and they were headed directly towards the ruins of Fort Mosanik and the Karys portal, barely seven hundred miles to the northeast.

Gerun Hostyra stared at the impossible sight for long, endless seconds, trying to digest it. He was only a commander of twenty-five, yet the danger of that enormous column—he and Sky Sabre could see yet another dust cloud rolling along behind the one closest to hand—was abundantly clear. The picket on what had been Fort Mosanik consisted of only a couple of platoons of infantry, and there had to be thousands of men in that oncoming horde. How in Shartahk's name they could be here, coming from the AEF's *rear*, was more than he could even begin to imagine, but he knew exactly what was going to happen when they reached the portal.

But they're not there yet, he thought harshly. *And they're not in one of their godsdamned forts with all their frigging artillery dug in to cover its approaches, either!*

He dropped down, pressing even closer to Sky Sabre's spine, and the big red banked hard left as his fingers stroked in the control grooves.

* * *

"No, you idiot!" Yoril Jerstan shouted, even though there was no way in the world Hostyra could have heard him. He groped for his flare projector, triggering off the yellow-yellow-green sequence that ordered Hostyra to break off, but the young twenty-five paid no attention. His dragon's dive angle only steepened, increasing his airspeed, and Jerstan swore again.

He fired the break off sequence a second time, and banked Grayscale hard to the right, *away* from the oncoming Sharonians. The other transports followed him promptly, but Hostyra's wingman hesitated. He held on in Sky Sabre's wake for a handful of seconds before he slowly, grudgingly brought his own dragon around to follow the transports back towards Fort Mosanik.

* * *

"Action left! *Action left!*" Platoon-Captain Seljar chan Werkan shouted through the dust-clogged bandana over his nose and mouth, and the drivers of the Steel Mules on which Copper Section's two field guns had been mounted halted almost instantly, turning away from the column and its blinding dust storm.

Quickly as they responded, the gun crews were even quicker, stripping off the muzzle covers and breaking open the ammunition locker. By the time the Mules stopped moving, looming up out of the fogbank of settling, wind-shredded dust like sunbaked steel islands, the slim muzzles of the 3.4" "Ternathian 37s" on their specially modified carriages were already swinging towards the black dots so far above them and rising sharply.

They'd practiced the evolution more times than chan Werkan could count during the long, weary march from Fort Salby and they moved with the smooth efficiency of all those endless drills. Unfortunately, this was the first time they'd had actual *targets*, and no one—least of all Seljar chan Werkan—knew how well all that training might be about to pay off.

The training and elevating wheels blurred, spinning under the gunners' hands, while the barrels angled up to a preposterous seventy-five degrees.

"Load!" he shouted, and breechblocks clicked with crisp, metallic smoothness.

Fifty yards to chan Werkan's right, Silver Section's gun muzzles tracked the same targets.

*　　*　　*

Better stay away from those, *Gerun*, Hostyra thought as Sky Sabre's eyes picked out the multi-barreled guns mounted atop some of the bigger vehicles. He hadn't been at Fort Salby himself—he'd been with Thousand Carthos' command—but he'd had the weapons—"pedestal guns," he thought the Sharonians called them—described to him in detail.

Now his steady fingers guided Sky Sabre into a deeper left bank, bearing away from the "pedestal guns" towards the smaller, wagonlike vehicles on the Sharonian column's flank. Some of them mounted some sort of "gun," too, but whatever they were, each of them had only a single barrel. They couldn't be as dangerous as the rapidly firing multiple-barrel weapons.

*　　*　　*

Most of the Arcanan dragons had broken off, and chan Werkan's jaw tightened as they headed back towards the Karys portal through which they must have come. So much for surprise, but it was too late to do the bastards any good. There were no horses in the lead echelons of 3rd Dragoon's column, it was only early afternoon, they were making even better speed across the desert than had been expected, and it was clear, open going all the way to Fort Mosanik. The Bisons and Mules could cover the remaining seven hundred miles in little more than thirty hours, and unless there was already a godsdamned Arcanan Army on the portal, they were damned well screwed.

And in the meantime—

*　　*　　*

Three of the 4.3" shells detonated well below Sky Sabre, spraying their potentially lethal clouds of shrapnel harmlessly across the heavens.

The fourth detonated barely twenty yards from its target.

CHAPTER FORTY-THREE

Solyrkain 23, 206 YU
(April 1415, 1929 CE)

IT WAS VERY QUIET INSIDE THE CHANSYU HUT. THE TICKING of one of the Sharonian "clocks" would have been deafening, and Klayrman Toralk wondered what thoughts were running through Mayrkos Harshu's brain. It was impossible to tell from the two thousand's expression, but they had to be grim.

Fifty Jerstan's frantic hummer message, sent from Fort Mosanik, had reached the AEF three days ago. Jerstan himself had arrived with his personal report a day later, his transport dragon obviously exhausted from how hard his pilot had pushed. That arrival had dashed any lingering hope that the original message might have been born of panic and overreaction, because Jerstan had engaged the recording function in his helmet crystal and spent the better part of three hours circling the oncoming Sharonian column...from beyond its apparent artillery range, thus avoiding the fate of yet another overly aggressive young pilot. Commander of One Hundred Tamdaran had analyzed that imagery carefully, and his conclusion was the same as Toralk's own analysts: there were at least five thousand Sharonians in that column, supplied with scores of artillery pieces.

Toralk had no more idea than anyone else how they could have gotten there. It was obvious they must have followed the Kelsayr chain, but nothing the AEF had seen on its advance to Fort Salby or learned in prisoner interrogations had suggested the Sharonians had the capacity to move an entire brigade over seventeen thousand miles in barely four months! Nor did he understand how *none* of the pickets along that enormous approach

581

route had managed to get off a single hummer message warning of the enemy's coming.

Not that it really mattered, he supposed. No. What *mattered* was that the Sharonians wouldn't have been stupid enough to send what looked like a single brigade of their dragoons so far into the Arcanans' rear. The force which had annihilated Fort Mosanik's garrison a day and a half after Jerstan had spotted it, was a powerful formation, but it was also operating twenty thousand miles from the nearest major Sharonian base at Fort Salby, and its own communications would be vulnerable to air attack... assuming, of course, Toralk could find the battle dragons to attack them and get past Forth Mosanik to *reach* them. And that meant there were damned well more Sharonians coming up-chain to support the troops who now owned the Karys-Failcham portal.

"Well," Harshu said finally into the silence, "at least we know why they've been content to sit at the top of the Traisum Cut all these weeks, don't we?"

His tone was almost whimsical, although his expression certainly wasn't, and Toralk's teeth ground together as he thought about the lost months while they'd waited here, confident they could savage any frontal attack. And it had seemed obvious such an attack *had* to be forthcoming, anyway. There was no other way the Sharonians could get at them, and their threadbare supply of recon gryphons had amply confirmed a steady, massive buildup around Fort Salby. The size of that buildup had made it abundantly clear that his staff's initial estimates of Sharonian "railroads'" cargo capacity had been hopelessly inadequate. The enemy had taken longer to get his initial units into position than an Arcanan commander would have, but once those initial units had arrived to stabilize the front, Sharonian strength in Traisum had grown explosively. Coupled with their obvious preparations to assault down the Traisum Cut, there'd been no doubt that they'd read the unpromising menu of their tactical options the same way Harshu and Toralk had.

Yet as the size and power of the impending assault grew steadily and the reinforcements promised by Nith mul Gurthak equally steadily failed to materialize, Toralk had come to doubt the strategic wisdom of holding their position here. The sheer weight of the attack, whenever the Sharonians decided to unleash it, promised to be enormous, and if they did manage to carry the Cut, the AEF was likely to find itself in serious trouble, even with its maneuver advantages. The steady, annoying trickle of operational losses among Toralk's transports had only increased his uneasiness, since each dragon in the Dragon Healers' hands or sent to the rear to recuperate was one less dragon for troop movements if the Sharonians ever once broke free in Karys.

But as uneasy as Toralk had become, that very lack of transports had only underscored the importance of keeping the cork in the Traisum Cut. There, at least, the Sharonians were restricted to a single narrow avenue of attack through an all but impossible terrain obstacle. It was the *only* place the AEF could hold an attacking army as powerful as the one building up on the Fort Salby side of the portal. The only other option would have been to fall back, let the Sharonians in, and then operate as aggressively as possible against the enemy's ground-bound supply columns. That would have been a purely delaying strategy, however, one which conceded the initiative entirely to the enemy, and the ugly truth was that there wasn't a single spot between Traisum and Hell's Gate itself that offered the defensive strength of the Traisum Cut.

"Do we have any better estimate of the enemy's strength in Failcham, Sir?" Thousand Gahnyr asked. The AEF's infantry commander was tight-faced and he couldn't quite to keep an anxious edge out of his tone.

"Not really, Sir," Five Hundred Mahrkrai answered for Harshu. The chief of staff met Gahnyr's eyes levelly. "Our best estimate is still that this is a single reinforced Sharonian cavalry brigade with additional artillery attached. And, of course, those vehicles of theirs. I think we can take it for granted that there's one hells of a lot more coming on behind them, though. The fact that they never let a single one of those big vehicles of theirs anywhere in range of our recon gryphons in Traisum suggests they've been planning this all along. This isn't some panicky, last-ditch ploy, so we can be damned sure they sent along a force they think is strong enough to look after itself in the face of anything we could throw at it."

"Herak's right," Harshu said. "It's obvious—now—" his smile was knife-thin and cold as a Lokan winter "that they've planned all along to mousetrap us here in Karys, and that means using a force strong enough to hold the portal against us."

"In that case, Sir," Gahnyr asked quietly, "what do we do?"

"A good question." Harshu nodded. "Unfortunately, we don't have a good answer, only a choice of *bad* answers. Not only are the Sharonians between us and home, but the speed of their communications is a hells of a lot faster than ours. Fort Mosanik sent a hummer to Governor mul Gurthak at the same time they sent one to us, but it won't reach him in Erthos until tomorrow. I'm sure as soon as it does he'll pull out all the stops to get our reinforcements forward."

His tone, Toralk reflected, indicated something less than rousing confidence in mul Gurthak's doing anything of the sort.

"That's not going to help us in the next couple of weeks, though," the two thousand continued. "I'm afraid we have to assume the Sharonians' arrival on the Karys portal indicates they're about ready to pull the trigger on their counteroffensive from Traisum, too. I'm still confident we can hurt them badly if they come down the Cut into the teeth of our defenses, though, and they may not realize just how bloody we can make it for them. So the question is whether or not the force *behind* us is powerful enough to press an offensive into our rear. If it's intended *only* as a blocking force—if it was meant to panic us into falling back without a battle or simply to hold the portal once their frontal attack drove us out of our positions—it's unlikely to get too frisky any time in the immediate future. If that's the case, we still have some time to work with, although getting supplies forward just got a lot more complicated."

Now that, Toralk thought, was a generous understatement. Getting heavily laden transports past Sharonian artillery would be about as "complicated" as operations came.

"In the meantime, though, we need to plan for a rapid withdrawal," Harshu went on unflinchingly. "I know it goes against the grain to give up all the ground between here and Thermyn, but I'm afraid we're unlikely to have much choice. We do still have the advantage in tactical mobility. It took them four months to reach the Karys portal; we could've made the same movement in two weeks, assuming we could've gotten across the damned ocean in the first place. Not only that, we have to assume they moved as quickly as they could from the moment Fifty Jerstan sighted them to the moment they hit Fort Brithik, and that tells us that moving cross-country those vehicles of theirs can't have a speed much greater than, say, twenty miles an hour. If we pull back from here, we'll have to fight our way through the portal into Failcham, and that's going to be ugly. The transports will have to make at least three trips to ferry all our people through the portal, and we'll take losses every time they do it, but at least we won't have to fight a rearguard all the way across Karys. Once we break contact here, we'll have the speed to stay in front of any pursuit they could drive down the Cut even if we hadn't seeded its walls with demolition spells to close it behind us.

"I've already sent hummers to Governor mul Gurthak telling him that if we're forced to retreat from Karys I hope to fight a mobile campaign against any Sharonian forces in Failcham and Thermyn until a fresh offensive from Hell's Gate can reach us. In the meantime—"

He paused, his eyes narrowing, as someone rapped very lightly on the office door and his eyes narrowed. Then the door opened and a message clerk stepped through it hesitantly.

"Yes?" The one-word question was sharper than usual, clearly irritated by the interruption, and the clerk came to attention and saluted.

"I'm sorry, Sir," he said quickly, "but I thought you'd want to see this message as soon as possible."

Harshu's face smoothed into non-expression as the clerk's tone registered and he held out his hand to accept the message crystal. He gazed down into it for two or three heartbeats, then his jaw tightened and he nodded to the clerk.

"You were right, Javelin," he said, handing the crystal back. "Dismissed."

The clerk disappeared, and the two thousand looked bleakly at his senior subordinates.

"It would appear our options are even more limited than I'd thought," he said. "That was a hummer message from Five Hundred Klian in Mahritha. Apparently the brigade sitting on the Failcham-Karys portal isn't the only bunch of Sharonians operating in our rear. Another brigade—or possibly an even stronger force—rolled over the Hell's Gate picket two days before the hummer from Fort Mosanik could reach them. Twelve hours later, they hit the Hell's Gate-Mahritha portal in overwhelming force. The thousand commanding the portal garrison had less than four hours' warning before the attack rolled in, and according to Five Hundred Klian, he was probably outnumbered by at least three to one."

Icy stillness hovered about him, and his nostrils flared.

"It would seem, Gentlemen," the words came slow and measured, "that the Sharonians now control every portal between us and Mahritha."

CHAPTER FORTY-FOUR

Kleindyr 7, 206 YU
(April 27, 1929 CE)

"SPECIALIST VOS HOVEN," COMMANDER OF TWENTY THOU-
sand Sogbourne said, peering intently at the prisoner in the
witness box, "you were present, were you not, at the confrontation
which has been dubbed 'The Battle of Toppled Timber' in the
popular journals?"

"Yes, Sir, I was there." The prisoner's manner was very humble, very un-*shakira*-like. Helfron Dithrake mistrusted it—and vos
Hoven—more every time the man spoke. He supposed it was possible for the close relative of two line-lords and a clan-lord to learn
humility after spending several months in the brig. But he was more
inclined to believe such a man would have spent his time brooding
on the wrongs done to him and his exalted pedigree...unless a
caste superior had shown him the error of his ways, so to speak.

Given the *other* Olderhan mess involving that yellow dragon
and the deaths surrounding it, Helfron Dithrake was inclined to
believe someone had either coached vos Hoven or had put the
fear of eternity into him so effectively to permanently break his
pride. Whether it had ensured his honesty remained to be seen.

"I understand you were transferred into Hundred Olderhan's
company at the same time as Fifty Garlath?"

"Yes, Sir, I was."

"I understand, as well, that you'd served under Fifty Garlath
for some time?"

"Yes, Sir. Several months, Sir."

"What is your evaluation of Fifty Garlath's ability as a commander?"

587

Bok vos Hoven pursed his lips and appeared to give the question serious consideration. "Well, Sir, I'd have to say Fifty Garlath wasn't nearly as able a commander as Hundred Olderhan."

"Really? What prompts that evaluation?"

"Well, Sir, under Hundred Olderhan's direction, the fifty was a lot more efficient than he'd ever been. And he followed book procedure a lot more closely. We certainly got things done a lot faster than we ever had, before."

"I see. In your estimation, then, Garlath was a better officer under Hundred Olderhan's direction than he was under his previous Commander of One Hundred?"

"Yes, Sir. Absolutely, Sir."

"Very good. Now, then, how would you evaluate Fifty Garlath's efficiency the morning your platoon trailed the Sharonians to their camp?"

"Well, Sir, I know this much. The hundred kept the fifty on a very short leash. He quoted book regulations repeatedly, in a very abrupt manner."

"Then the hundred's temper was fraying?"

"Yes, Sir, I'd say that, Sir."

"Due to?" Sogbourne invited speculation, curious to see how vos Hoven would respond.

"We were all under stress, Sir, wondering what had killed poor Osmuna, wondering what other terror weapons these people—or creatures—might possess, how far ahead of us they were, how many of them there might be. It was nerve-racking, Sir, for all of us, and the hundred seemed affected more than the rest of us."

"Are you saying," Sogbourne asked in a curious tone that masked his intense disgust, "that the hundred was overwhelmed by fear?"

"It certainly looked that way to me."

"Why?"

Bok vos Hoven blinked. "Well, Sir, he was jumpy as a frog in a pond full of crocodrakes, for one thing."

"Jumpy as a frog?" Ten Thousand Rinthrak echoed. "In what way?"

"He kept watching the trees, nervous-like. Kept barking at the fifty to stay on point, to stop dawdling. I was worried we were going to run up their backsides before he was satisfied."

"The general idea, when trailing an escaped killer," Rinthrak said in a severe voice, "is to catch him."

"Well, yes, Sir. That's true. But there's hasty prudence and there's hasty folly, Sir, and I can tell you I wasn't too happy about the way he was rushing us ahead, like that, with barely a moment's pause to consider any nasty surprises they might've laid in our path."

Sogbourne frowned. Given the charges this man faced and the source of those charges, he'd expected vos Hoven to characterize Jasak Olderhan's actions in the worst possible light, and so far those expectations hadn't been disappointed. Unfortunately, there was a serious dearth of eyewitnesses to question, let alone question closely about nuances like vos Hoven was trying to impart. Or, perhaps, insinuate.

He made a brief notation in his PC to question the few witnesses they did have on this subject, but even there, he anticipated trouble. While Bok vos Hoven could not, by any stretch of the imagination, be considered an impartial witness, neither could the other three witnesses available to him.

Trooper Sendahli could have been impartial immediately after Toppled Timber, but he was only in Portalis to be interviewed because of his status as a victim of Lance vos Hoven in a case against the *shakira* soldier that hinged heavily on Hundred Olderhan's testimony. It was a mess.

Battalion Chief Sword Threbuch was almost even more of a mess, from a legal perspective. Sogbourne had no personal qualms at all about Threbuch's honesty, but his ties to the Olderhan family went back decades. He'd served under Hundred Olderhan's father, earning high commendations and an income for life for saving the life of the current Duke of Garth Showma. Threbuch was ordinarily an honest and impartial witness, with an unimpeachable record for scrupulous honesty and meticulous accuracy.

However...

The situation wasn't much better with Magister Kelbryan. Just for starters, she wasn't a soldier. In fact she wasn't remotely *close* to a soldier! Not only was she a civilian, she was a Ransaran who didn't understand military protocols, regulations, and duties or even the standard operating procedures of a platoon—let alone the emergency procedures necessary to deal with a serious crisis. Had she been Andaran, trained to understand military realities, he would have been more inclined to trust her assessment of the hundred's performance.

But the gods had seen fit to give him a Ransaran, and Ransarans were notorious for their total lack of understanding of all matters military. Ransaran scholars, in particular, were noted for their appalling lack of military savvy and their inordinate pride in that lack, as though willful ignorance was a virtue. Amongst Ransaran academicians, it *was*.

So Sogbourne patiently took vos Hoven through the entire chase Olderhan had conducted through that distant forest, on the trail of unknown killers with weapons that struck horror into the very souls of the men doing that trailing, and tried to sift truth from skillful, vindictive manipulation of fact. Either vos Hoven was a great deal smarter than his personnel scores indicated or he'd received some highly skilled coaching from *someone*, because he managed to paint an ever blacker, damning picture of a rattled commander jumping at shadows, without quite crossing the line into outright fabrication and triggering the courtroom's verifying spellware.

When they reached the fateful moment of arrival at the wind-toppled pile of twisted timber, Sogbourne asked vos Hoven to describe exactly what had transpired.

"Well, Sir, as nearly as I can recall, Hundred Olderhan ordered Fifty Garlath's squad to search the clearing for concealed enemy personnel. Fifty Garlath had already lodged a strong protest over the advisability of pursuit, given the potential for a large number of the enemy to overwhelm our platoon. The hundred told him that falling back to wait for reinforcements was out of the question. Magister Gadrial actually accused Fifty Garlath of cowardice, which was a dirty lie. The fifty was only concerned for the safety of his men, and it turned out he was right to be. We *were* overwhelmed by enemy firepower and damn near lost the entire platoon as a result of the hundred's hasty actions."

The lie-detection light might have flickered just slightly, but Sogbourne couldn't be sure. Anger or hatred could be used to partially beat the truth spells if the speaker had enough boiling emotion to convince himself of a false reality, and vos Hoven had more than enough rage towards Jasak Olderhan to attempt it. For that matter, he probably had enough to achieve it completely spontaneously!

Sogbourne narrowed his eyes, but decided against pursuing the line of questioning *that* pile of dragon manure warranted.

Not yet. Instead, he said, "The hundred ordered the clearing searched. What was Fifty Garlath's response?"

"Why, he complied, of course. It was plain suicide, sending men into the open, like that, but the fifty did his duty, did it bravely, I'll tell you!"

This time lie-detection light behind the witness did flash. But before Sogbourne could react, vos Hoven continued his embroidered-for-effect tirade.

"The fifty obeyed the hundred's orders and he died for it, Sir! I know what you're thinking of me, standing here in chains, but I'm telling you plainly, the hundred sent the fifty out there to die. Hundred Olderhan conceived a hatred of the fifty almost from the moment he arrived in the hundred's company. I'm convinced the hundred deliberately sent Fifty Garlath out to be killed, to rid himself of the problem his own prejudice had created!"

The light behind vos Hoven flashed again.

"Really?" Sogbourne murmured. "That's an interesting theory, Specialist vos Hoven. Perhaps you'd care to explain to this Court why you've lied twice in the past ninety seconds?"

Vos Hoven's face went totally blank, then collapsed into a sick expression as he realized what he'd done in his zeal to convict his nemesis. He started to jerk around to look at the lie-detection light behind him, then controlled that instinctive reaction and got himself turned around again, facing the officers of the court. Before he could say anything further, Commander of Five Hundred Anshair Kolthar, vos Hoven's assigned defense counsel, was on his feet.

"Sir, counsel for the defense respectfully requests that all mention of the lie-detection alarm be stricken from the record."

"On what grounds?" Sogbourne asked coldly.

"On the grounds that a lie-detection spell cannot be used to penalize a witness expressing opinion, rather than fact. Specialist vos Hoven was expressing his personal opinion that Hundred Olderhan bore a grudge against Fifty Garlath, a grudge moreover that was strong enough to send an inferior officer into harm's way to rid him of a troublesome problem. While that opinion may be unpleasant to the majority of listeners, it's still merely an opinion and cannot be used to the detriment of the witness expressing it. Again, counsel for the defense requests that all mention of the lie-detection spell's alarm be stricken from the record."

"An interesting request, Five Hundred." Ten Thousand Rin-thrak's tone was cold enough to freeze fire. "An outright accusation of murder is not an expression of opinion, however. It constitutes libel, false witness, and a violation of the military code of conduct while under oath before a court-martial.

"Furthermore, the lie-detection spell didn't register because the witness stated an opinion. It registered because the witness uttered a *false* opinion. If the accusation Specialist vos Hoven leveled at Hundred Olderhan had been vos Hoven's true opinion, his statement wouldn't have triggered the alarm.

"This court is left with the inescapable conclusion that Specialist vos Hoven lied about his 'opinion' as part of a premeditated attempt to destroy his commander's career. His action is contemptible and your protest, Five Hundred, does not even merit a hearing, let alone being sustained.

"Be warned that you're treading on extremely thin ice even raising such an objection when you know the mechanics of lie-detection spells and the regulations regarding them as well as you know your own name. If you *don't* know them, you have absolutely no business being entrusted with the defense of anyone, not even someone who stands self-convicted of lying under oath about his superior officer. Do I make the Court's displeasure sufficiently clear, Sir?"

Sweat had popped out along Kolthar's brow. "You do, Sir," he said in a flat monotone.

"Very good. Sit down, Sir, and save your protests for legitimate points of statutory merit."

He sat.

Bok vos Hoven swallowed hard under the Court's stony stares, and Sogbourne pinned him with a glare that had reduced grown men to gibbering shakes more than once.

"Need I remind you, vos Hoven, that you already face serious—indeed, perhaps capital—charges? If I were in your shoes, I wouldn't utter so much as one syllable that might be misconstrued as additional deliberate falsehood. Be advised that your false accusation of attempted murder against Hundred Olderhan will be added to the charges you already face."

Sogbourne hadn't thought it possible for a man to look more thoroughly terrified than vos Hoven already did, but that admonition did the trick. For a moment, he feared the *shakira* would slide to the floor and grovel on his belly. He got himself under control, however, and nodded in a movement made jerky by muscles locked tight against bone.

"Very well, I suggest you reconsider your testimony about the events leading to Fifty Garlath's demise. Do you wish to re-phrase your account of them?"

Another jerky nod.

"Then proceed," Sogbourne said coldly.

Whatever the lying bastard said, it ought to be interesting.

* * *

Commander of One Thousand Arnith Janvers, Count Tisbane, was—like most Andarans, when viewed from a more normal Ransa-ran height—tall enough to scrape the sky with his hair. Gadrial had begun to feel so small and so intimidated by the towering male bodies surrounding her everywhere she went that her temper had begun to simmer. Not that her temper needed much excuse, given the unholy circus which had enveloped people about whom she'd come to care deeply. The information Duke Garth Showma had shared with all of them was enough to fill anyone with fury; adding the stress of Jasak's court-martial to it only made things worse, and the way in which so much hatred focused on Shaylar and Jathmar—the only two true innocents caught up in the entire rolling disaster—was sickening. It had taken her considerable self-control to refrain from incinerating some of the people behind that hatred—like that loathsome slime toad Minister vos Durgazon—on the spot. Just one well-placed levin bolt would've done it. There was, she thought darkly, a reason Magisters of the Hood took such binding oaths to use their Gifts for nothing but humankind's good.

Eliminating vos Durgazon would *serve humankind's good*, the back of her brain whispered to the front. Temptation was a ter-rible thing. At the moment, however, she faced a very different challenge. Count Tisbane was one of the finest attorneys money could buy. He was also a senior officer in the Judiciary General's office who carried a reputation as a scrupulously honest man who was ruthless to adversaries and fiendishly intelligent.

If Tisbane had been assigned to this case as prosecutor, rather than Jasak's defense attorney, Gadrial would have tasted despair. Instead, she took her seat in the witness' box with a fair appearance of equanimity, folded her hands in her lap, swore the required oath of truthfulness, and waited for him to speak.

"Magister Gadrial," he said in a soft, cultured voice that could have charmed bees into handing over honeycombs and dragons into rolling over to have their belly-plates scratched, "there are two main questions this court must resolve: was Hundred Older-han derelict in his duty and did he perform his duties with good judgment.

"As a civilian, you won't be able to assist the court in determining whether or not he was derelict in his duty, as that determination is made under a complex set of criteria embedded in Andaran military code and the Articles of War."

She nodded, having already been briefed on that point.

"What you can do, Magister Gadrial, is assist the court in determining precisely what happened that day and whether or not Hundred Olderhan used good judgment in the performance of his duties as an officer, before the crisis, during the crisis, and after the crisis.

"You were present, either within view or within earshot, of all the main events this court must consider. As Hundred Older-han's defense attorney, I'll ask a number of questions related to the issues the court must resolve. After I've questioned you, the prosecutor will cross-examine you on many of those same points and, potentially, on issues I haven't raised during my initial examination. If that's the case, I'll then be given a chance to discuss those new points with you, to clarify your testimony on behalf of my client's defense. Is that clear and is that acceptable, Magister Gadrial?"

She drew a deep, silent breath and nodded. "Yes, it is."

"Very well, let's begin. How well did you know Hundred Olderhan when he took out the platoon that escorted you in the search for Halathyn vos Dulainah's Class Seven Portal?"

She answered gravely. "We'd barely met, Defensor." From the corner of her eye, she caught several surprised expressions from the officers of the court. They hadn't expected a Ransaran to know the proper title of the defense counsel in a military courtroom. Well, that was fine with her. She intended to surprise them again, before this was done.

"What was the extent of your interaction with him?"

"Sir Jasak departed on the same transport ship I'd arrived on, when I joined Magister Halathyn in the field. We spoke briefly on deck, where he wished me a pleasant and productive research mission, and I left the ship after wishing him a safe and speedy journey. I wasn't even aware, at that time, where he was headed. I knew only that he wasn't expected to return for some time, which I learned when one of the ship's officers mentioned it while welcoming him aboard."

"So you spoke briefly when he departed, leaving Fifty Garlath in acting command of the company until Hundred Thalmayr's arrival?"

"That's what I was told, yes, Defensor. Hadrign Thalmayr was due to arrive at any time, aboard a special courier dragon, since his connecting transport had been delayed, causing him to miss the ship's scheduled departure. Fifty Ulthar's platoon was at the coast, on R and R, which left Shevan Garlath in charge of the camp at the Swamp Portal."

"And what was your assessment of Fifty Garlath's capabilities?"

"He was an arrogant, lazy, shiftless, ill-mannered, power-mad, incompetent twit."

Gadrial heard a stifled squeak from someone on the bench that sounded suspiciously like laughter stuffed down before it could burst loose.

"Ah, yes, that *is* a very clearly stated opinion," Count Tisbane said. Despite the serious mien of his long, square face, Tisbane's eyes twinkled with carefully restrained mirth. "Could you enlighten this court with specific details that would illustrate this somewhat remarkable opinion?"

"I'd be delighted to, Sir."

And she did. For the next eleven minutes. Without even reaching, yet, any description of the events surrounding their departure on the ill-fated search for Halathyn's portal.

"Please, Magister," Count Sogbourne finally pleaded. "You've made your point. Eloquently and convincingly. Shevan Garlath will be entered into the court records as a—what did you call him?"

She smiled sweetly. "An arrogant, lazy, shiftless, ill-mannered, power-mad, incompetent twit."

"Ah, yes, that was it. Let it be noted that the court designates Commander of Fifty Shevan Garlath as, ah, seriously deficient in the criteria which define a competent officer of the Union of Arcana."

Gadrial smiled, but her heart seethed with hatred of that arrogant, lazy, shiftless, ill-mannered, power-mad, incompetent bastard. If he hadn't shot an unarmed man through the throat...

They wouldn't all be sitting here in judgment of the man she loved.

"Magister Gadrial," Count Tisbane's voice jolted her attention back to the courtroom, "your powers of observation and recall are clearly substantial and—to judge from comparison with other witness' testimony—accurate.

"What was your overall impression of Hundred Olderhan's command judgment during the preparations for your journey into what proved to be the contact universe?"

"Hundred Olderhan told Fifty Garlath to have the platoon ready to march within the hour," she said flatly. "Fifty Garlath was incapable of complying with that order. In the two weeks Fifty Garlath spent in charge of the camp, he managed to reduce his command to a state of total chaos. His platoon was physically incapable of reorganizing and repacking its equipment, supplies, and even personal gear, which Fifty Garlath had insisted the troops lay out in constant 'surprise inspections' that he sprang without warning every other day or so."

Her lip curled in remembered disgust.

"Those inspections were apparently designed to show his favorite cronies which troopers had the gear most worth stealing. A number of troopers complained viciously within my earshot that someone had stolen various items after each surprise inspection."

"They complained of stolen gear?" Tisbane asked softly as every officer on the court-martial board went rigid with anger. "What kind of gear, Magister?"

"Yes, Defensor, they most certainly did. One soldier complained about losing a spell-powered canteen that purified water in one pass. Another had deluxe nav-gear stolen from his pack—gear he'd paid for with personal savings. I heard a number of similar mutters over the course of those two weeks, ranging from the theft of expensive equipment to the filching of specialty crossbow quarrels and popular snacks sent by family members. They'd just arrived in the mail sacks that were delivered from the ship I sailed on, traveling to meet Halathyn. That was bad enough.

"But one night I overheard one of Fifty Garlath's cronies whispering to another of his favorites that he had enough gear stashed away to earn several thousand in profits when he went on leave.

"When I brought that conversation to the fifty's attention, he told me civilians had no business butting into military affairs and warned me that civilians who did so invariably had their noses bloodied. He gave me breezy assurances the troopers would be questioned and their gear would be searched, but those assurances were as worthless as the rest of him. They were never questioned, never searched, and certainly never censured.

"*That* was the reason the platoon was in such wild disarray when Hundred Olderhan gave the order to march. Garlath had ordered a major inspection that morning, to include a full layout of field loads. Not just personal gear, but field dragons, the spell accumulators to power them, medical equipment, you name it. They'd only put away half of it when Hundred Olderhan returned to camp."

Gadrial shrugged. "I would have taken it up with the hundred at an opportune moment, but both men involved in the stolen gear incidents were killed in the fighting at Toppled Timber. So was Fifty Garlath. We were far too swamped after that battle, just trying to keep the wounded alive while Hundred Olderhan sent men ahead to verify the portal and pulled the rest of us back to the Swamp Portal, to bother reporting it. Truth to tell, I'd completely forgotten about it until I sat down to prepare for this testimony."

All eyes had darted to the truth detection light as she spoke. It never so much as flickered, and now the entire panel of officers stared at her in white-lipped rage. Sogbourne leaned forward with a furious demand.

"Were you aware of any other illegal dealings by Shevan Garlath or his 'favorites' among the platoon?"

"Not that I could prove, Sir. Fifty Garlath and Specialist vos Hoven were very tight, having apparently served together in another platoon. But I heard and saw nothing that could serve as evidence that would hold up in court, either military or civilian.

"By the time Hundred Olderhan arrived, I was so disgusted with Shevan Garlath and his nasty little games—including constant belittling of men he or his cronies disliked—I would have turned him in to Hundred Olderhan in a heartbeat if I'd *had* sufficient evidence. Shevan Garlath was the most repulsive man I ever met, including the *shakira* faculty and students at the Mythal Falls Academy."

Sogbourne actually winced.

Solvar Rinthrak and the other officers scowled like gorgons.

Count Tisbane took Gadrial carefully through the events of that terrible day, from the moment of their departure to the first, fateful rifle shot in the distance. She described Jasak's efforts to rehabilitate the officer, forcing Garlath to do his job to at least minimally acceptable standards. She described Garlath's insubordinate behavior and language and Jasak's attempts to protect the safety of his command as well as her interpretation of his decision to leave Garlath in command of the platoon despite his patent inadequacies.

"I'm not a soldier," Gadrial said carefully, "but I've worked with military men on a number of occasions during my tenure as assistant director of NAITHMA. The academy's housed on a military base, after all, and derives a high percentage of its funding from military sources. During the early years, almost *all* its funding came from the military, in fact, and I was responsible for meeting with a wide variety of officers to secure and administer those funds. I've seen any number of officers interacting with subordinates, whether they were visiting my lab or I was visiting their offices on one military base or another."

Tisbane nodded. "Understood. Please continue, Magister."

"When trooper Osmuna was found dead and no one could even make a guess as to *what* had killed him, let alone who, the troopers were visibly rattled. Some of them were terrified. For that matter, so was I. Everyone was jumping at shadows for those first few minutes.

"When one of the cartridge cases was found on a stream bank overlooking Osmuna's body, alongside footprints that looked very much like human feet had made them, a lot of the fear dissipated, but the men were still shaken. Hundred Olderhan ordered me to stay back during the preliminary investigation of Osmuna's body, with two troopers as bodyguards. When we finally joined the rest of the platoon, I overheard one of the soldiers say he was glad Hundred Olderhan was back, but he was just as glad the hundred had left Garlath in command."

"Why, Magister Gadrial?" Tisbane asked.

"I thought it was an awfully strange remark, until the soldier he was talking to said, 'Yeah, me, too. With Garlath giving the orders, at least we'll know what to expect. It'll probably be the coward's road, but we'll know what he's likely to do. Now the hundred's back, he'll straighten the fifty out if Garlath tells us to do something *really* stupid.' And that's exactly what Hundred Olderhan did, on several occasions. The men weren't happy, Your Worship, but they settled down to perform their duties very effectively."

She bit her lip, then. "The worst moment was when we reached that clearing and Hundred Olderhan ordered Garlath to search it."

"He ordered Fifty Garlath to search it?" Tisbane asked sharply. "Not the point squad?"

"That's correct, yes. He ordered Garlath *and* his point squad to search the clearing for enemy personnel. He believed our quarry might be hidden in all that timber blown down by the wind. I wasn't close enough at that point to *see* what was happening, since he kept me back the same way he had before. He stationed me in a gully, out of the line of possible fire, with a pair of guards to watch over me if the enemy *did* spring an ambush. I couldn't see, but I could hear what he and the other members of the platoon were saying, very clearly."

"And what did you hear Hundred Olderhan and Fifty Garlath say?"

"Fifty Garlath didn't say anything. I could hear men crunching through dead leaves and dried, brittle branches as they searched all that timber. I could hear someone curse under his breath for some reason, a miss-step, maybe. Then I heard Hundred Olderhan shout at Fifty Garlath."

"What did he say?"

"He said, 'Hold fire! Hold fire, Fifty Garlath! Damn it, I said hold—' Then I heard the thwack and twang of an arbalest."

"He ordered Fifty Garlath *not* to fire? You're certain of that?" Trisbane pressed, and she nodded, her face like stone. The lawyer waited a breath or two, as if to let that settle into the court's mind. Then he said, "Continue, please. What happened next?"

"Next?" She rubbed her arms, cold to the bone. "Next, I heard a hideous, meaty thump. And the most horrifying, choked scream I'd ever heard in my life."

She shuddered in memory.

"Then it sounded like the gates of hell opened. The whole clearing erupted in thunder and horrible screams and more arbalest fire. I heard Fifty Garlath screaming, again and again. Much as I despised him, hearing him die like that... It was ghastly," she whispered. "No one should die in that much terror and pain."

Her fingers had tightened into fists in her lap.

"But it got worse. As Rahil is my witness, I will never, ever forget those terrible minutes. All I could do was lie there and listen while men I'd come to know and respect died just a few yards away." She unclenched her fingers to wipe her face, which was wet. Her fingers shook. "They died because of one man. One screw-up of a man, an insubordinate, insolent *idiot* who disobeyed his commander's direct orders. Disobeyed and shot down an unarmed man.

"I couldn't believe he'd done it. Even having watched him for two weeks, I couldn't believe he'd done it. That he'd disobeyed orders like that, orders that important. That *critical*. It was almost like he'd done it on purpose, to be deliberately defiant. As though he wanted to make Hundred Olderhan look incompetent or maybe to hog some kind of glory for himself. To be the man who caught Osmuna's killers, so Hundred Olderhan wouldn't get the credit."

The officers ranged along the bench studied her with thoughtful frowns tugging at the corners of thinned lips, and Gadrial shook her head.

"I don't know why he did it. But I do know he *had* to've heard that order. I was fifty yards away, down in a gully, and *I* heard every single word of it. I've called Garlath an idiot, but he wasn't actually stupid. He had a brain, a decently agile one; he just didn't use it very often.

"You could tell he was smart, but he was sly, playing mind games to get out of doing his job, instead of just *doing* it. To defy his superiors and find ways to make them look bad, to cover up the fact that he'd never done an honest day's work in his life and had no intention of *ever* doing one."

She bit her lip and wiped fresh tears.

"Even Magister Halathyn detested him." She drew a ragged breath. "I will never, ever forgive Shevan Garlath for starting this war. For setting in motion the events that killed Halathyn vos Dulainah." Her voice shook as she said that, shook with pain and grief. "He started a chain of events that destroyed Hundred Olderhan's whole company. He caused the slaughter of innocent Sharonian civilians in that clearing. And thanks to what he did there, hundreds of more Sharonian civilians have died, needlessly, in an invasion *we* started."

Absolute silence gripped the courtroom.

After a moment, Count Tisbane spoke quietly again, in his beautiful, cultured voice.

"Magister Gadrial, there's not a man in this room who doesn't bitterly regret the pain and suffering you've endured because of this war, because of this man you've testified started it."

"He *did* start it," she snarled, eyes flashing.

Tisbane lifted both hands in a conciliatory gesture. "Peace, Magister," he murmured. "Believe me, Magister Gadrial, I understand your reasons for feeling the way you do. But at the moment, we're speaking in legal terms, for the sake of this court-martial. Bearing that in mind, what more can you tell us about the events that transpired and Hundred Olderhan's role in them, after Shevan Garlath shot down the Sharonian crew leader?"

Gadrial nodded and drew a long, steadying breath.

"All right, I'll do that. Everything was really crazy for a couple of minutes, with people shouting and screaming and the crack and thunder of the Sharonian weapons sounding like a thunderstorm without rain. A lot of the shouts were from the Sharonians. They sounded . . . astonished. Furious. Terrified.

"And right in the middle of all that confusion, I heard Hundred Olderhan shouting orders to his men. Very clear orders. He shouted at them to encircle the clearing, to contain the enemy. To prevent their escape and stop anyone who tried to run for the portal with a message. He also ordered his best arbalest shots to try creeping forward under cover, to take out as many enemy shooters as possible, but their rifle fire was relentless. There was never a lull in the shooting, not once, not until every last Sharonian had been shot down.

"I heard Hundred Olderhan shouting to bring the field dragons up, which was the only thing that saved the platoon. I heard him order three separate firing lines. The artillery crews kept screaming in agony and Hundred Olderhan kept shouting for replacements, ordering specific men forward by name to man the dragons. I was cowering in terror on the ground, listening as he directed that fight. I couldn't believe my ears, he was shouting orders with such clear-headed deliberation. I'd never heard anything like it.

"My bodyguards were swearing a blue streak. Not because they were angry. They were frustrated, mostly, because they were stuck babysitting me. But even that wasn't the whole reason. I was curled up on the ground, shaking in my robes, while they stood over me with cocked and locked arbalests, and the most amazing thing was *how* they were swearing. They sounded the way my brothers did when their *jarrca* team made some great play. The kind of play that netted the point that propelled them into a championship game. It sounds crazy, probably, but that's what it sounded like."

"Thank you, Magister, for your testimony," Tisbane said formally. "If there are no direct questions from the bench, I'll turn the witness over to the prosecution."

Gadrial steeled herself for the moment she had dreaded for weeks.

She watched Commander of Five Hundred Ghulshan Vreel, Jasak's Accusator, closely as he rose and left the table where he'd sat since entering the chamber. Five Hundred Vreel wasn't a typical Andaran. He was tall, certainly, but his uniform clothed a frame just shy of skeletal. His eyes were banked down coals, eyes that pierced to the quick, probing for the secrets one hid from the entire world, and Gadrial controlled a shiver by dint of sheer willpower as those eyes focused upon her.

"Magister Gadrial," he said slowly, his voice as cadaverous as the rest of him, "your testimony's been extremely complimentary to Sir Jasak Olderhan."

Gadrial didn't rise to the bait, whatever he was fishing for; she merely looked at him, waiting for him to make his next point.

"Your status as a theoretical magister is beyond reproach. And despite your relative youth, you've suffered great adversity, great emotional pain. Your professional and personal lives have been a source of both satisfaction and upheaval, none of it your fault."

Again, she merely looked at him, not liking what he was doing, but unsure where he was going with it.

"I would say—as would most people—that you've earned a little joy, a little personal happiness."

"What is your point, Sir?" she asked coolly.

"My point is merely this. Your name has been linked with Sir Jasak Olderhan's in more than a professional capacity. There are rumors, Magister Gadrial, that a romantic liaison is part of your relationship. A woman who aspires to becoming Duchess of Garth Showma is likely to say a great many things in defense of the man destined to be the Duke of Garth Showma."

Gadrial narrowed her eyes. His ploy was contemptible, but not entirely unanticipated. If he'd hoped to break her, he'd be waiting a long, long time.

"Whatever the status of my relationship with Hundred Olderhan may be, Accusator Vreel, these are the facts. I wasn't in love with Sir Jasak Olderhan the day Shevan Garlath shot an unarmed Sharonian engineering professor through the throat and started a war. I didn't 'aspire' to anything, that day, except survival. As to my testimony today, might I inquire whether or not the lie-detection alarm has gone off even once during my testimony?"

"That is beside the point, young woman—"

"I am a senior Magister of the Hood, Sir. I'll thank you to remember that when you address me."

"You're an aspiring gold-digger angling for the Olderhan billions, an aristocratic title, and a secure social position for life, which throws suspicion on every syllable you've uttered! And as a Magister of the Hood, you're more than skilled enough to short-circuit a simple lie-detection spell!"

Gadrial stared at him for several silent seconds while the officers of the court held their collective breaths, waiting for the explosion.

They weren't prepared for what they got instead.

"*A secure social position for life?*" She laughed out loud and shook her head, her expression incredulous. "Rahil's toenails, d'you think I *want* to be saddled, snared, and roped into a life-time of impossible duties and obligations to a social code I find suffocating, medieval, and positively *insane*? You think I *want* to be trapped in a marriage where every move I make, every word I say, every garment I wear is dictated by a thousand years of protocol? Where any children I might bear would be treated like little automatons to be programmed like—like *ants* in a hill? My God, if Jasak Olderhan wanted to marry me, he'd have to go down on his knees and swear to me that my life would remain mine. That I'd live by Ransaran precepts unless I *chose* to honor that crazy hodge-podge of rules you Andarans call a society.

"And he'd have to put down in writing that my career and my family would be under *my* control, not some cabal of aristo-crats with nothing better to do than sit around trying to figure out how to control one another's lives every waking moment!"

She leaned back in her chair. "Sorry, Accusator, but the only people who think being part of the Andaran aristocracy is the most fabulous lifestyle in the world are other Andarans. And *I* am not, thank Rahil, an Andaran."

The accusator stared down at her, eyes wide in his cadaverous face. Then *he* started to laugh.

"My dear," he said, "you're thoroughly and delightfully Ransaran. If Hundred Olderhan does ask you to marry him, do us all a favor and hold him to that set of demands. I believe you just might be a breath of fresh air."

He smiled at her a moment longer, then glanced at the officers of the court.

"No further questions, gentlemen."

"You may step down, Magister Gadrial."

She blinked in surprise. "That's it?"

"For now, Magister." Count Sogbourne smiled. "If we need to recall you, we'll be in touch. Please be assured that your testimony's been most helpful. And, ah, rather educational, as well. It's always enlightening to see one's self through the eyes of others."

Her cheeks scalded. "I didn't mean any disrespect, Sir."

"Of course not. You're Ransaran."

She blinked. Then she realized that, in his stodgy Andaran way, he was teasing her, and she grinned.

"I could almost come to like an Andaran or two, now that you mention it," she told him.

"That's very flattering, Magister Gadrial. But now, much as it pains me, we must return to our very serious duties and you, I fear, must return to yours."

She bit her lip; then drew a swift breath and nodded. "Yes, you do. And so do I. You know where and how to reach me. I'm not planning to go anywhere," she added grimly.

She retrieved her business case, nodded to the officers of the court, the attorneys, and even the long-suffering clerk in the corner, whose eyes widened when she included him in her silent farewell. She dropped a solemn wink on the flustered young soldier, then squared her shoulders, marched out of the courtroom...

...and promptly dissolved into tears. She was desperately afraid for Jasak, for his future, and the life she hoped to somehow build with him, if these mad Andaran officers didn't destroy him over their mad, medieval rules and if his mad Andaran pride didn't stand in the way of *asking* her, if things went against him.

She scrubbed her eyes with a savage gesture, furious with herself for falling apart like this. She respected the men on that court-martial board. Under other circumstances, she might even have liked one or two of them. As it was...

She sucked down a deep, shaky breath. As it was, she had a

job to do and a society to save from another group of people she respected, two members of whom she'd come to care for as very dear friends. For the first time in her life, the knee-jerk, automatic Ransaran dislike of war had a profoundly personal basis.

War was hell.

Particularly when it was your job to win it.

*   *   *

It had been hours.

More than a dozen hours.

Gadrial had paced the floor. Chewed her nails ragged. She'd destroyed her carefully arranged hair, redone the styling spell to rearrange it into a neat coif, then destroyed that, as well. At least twenty times, now. If word didn't come soon, she was going to start tearing the draperies down from the walls and hurling breakables across the room.

Would they find Jasak guilty?

Or innocent?

She couldn't bear the suspense much longer. The calm, very nearly serene poise of the duchess, seated beside her, drove Gadrial nearly mad. How could Sathmin just *sit* there, gazing down into the street?

Because, Gadrial's conscience whispered, *she's a great deal stronger than you are.* She bit her lip. Then made another frantic circuit around the room, nearly ready to climb the walls with a sticky-spell that would let her crawl out across the ceiling like a fly and scream from the center of the chandelier.

I can't bear this! Not another moment!

The door opened.

Gadrial jerked around, heart beating so hard, she couldn't breathe. For one long, stupefied moment, she simply stood there, staring at the figure in the doorway. It wasn't the duke, with word about his son. It was *Shaylar.*

Gadrial hadn't even seen the other woman since the terrible night Thankhar Olderhan had unflinchingly told all of them what he'd learned. The Voice had withdrawn to the apartment she shared with Jathmar to weep for her dead, to cope with the horrible knowledge she'd never wanted yet had needed to know. One or two of the Garth Showma staff had seemed irked by her refusal to leave her chambers, but they'd followed their employers' example and left her to the privacy she so desperately needed.

And so had Gadrial. She'd longed to try to comfort Shaylar, but when she'd quietly suggested that to Jathmar, he'd shaken his head sadly.

"Not now, Gadrial," he'd told her. "She...she just needs to be alone for now. It's hard, especially for a Voice, to cope with all of this—" he'd waved vaguely at the townhouse around them in a gesture which took in everything beyond it, as well "—without knowing what's happening in our own universes. And just now...just now she's too raw and wounded to want to see anyone. Even you."

His words had cut her like knives, but she'd understood. And now, as the door opened and she looked up, she froze. She wanted to run to her. Wanted to throw her arms around the other woman and beg her to forgive Gadrial for being on the wrong side in this awful war. She wanted—

She didn't have to do anything.

Shaylar, tears streaming, crossed the room and embraced *Gadrial*. "I couldn't bear it any longer," Shaylar said softly. "Knowing how much this wait was hurting you."

"But..."

Shaylar's arms tightened down; then she stepped back.

"But you're my friend, Gadrial. My *only* friend here. I need you, Gadrial," she whispered. "And I think you need me?"

Gadrial hugged her again. "Gods, yes," she said equally softly. "But I wouldn't blame you if you never wanted to speak to an Arcanan again!" She felt her own eyes prickle. "After what the duke's found out so far, knowing there could be even worse to come, I—"

Shaylar drew a deep, ragged breath. "No, Gadrial. I never felt that. I needed to be...alone for a while. It's been terribly hard for me. For Jathmar and me, both of us. But I never felt like I didn't want to see you, ever again."

Gadrial's eyes filled with tears. "Shaylar, there's nothing I can say that can tell you how horrified I was by that news. How horrified I still am. Nothing justifies that. Nothing."

"Thank you, Gadrial. That...helps."

Gadrial touched Shaylar's hair, tucked a lock of it behind her ear. "Thank *you*, Shaylar. For still being my friend."

Shaylar nodded.

"Jathmar?" Gadrial asked after a moment.

"He's...thinking it over," Shaylar said softly, and Gadrial nodded. Of course he was.

"I hope he decides to join us, too," the duchess said, rising to put her own arm around Shaylar and hug her tightly. "But in the meantime, my dears, why don't we all have some tea and send for something to eat?"

"I think that sounds like a very good idea, Your Grace," Shaylar replied, and if her smile was wan and just a bit watery, it was also real.

*　　*　　*

Three hours and seventeen minutes later, the drawing room door opened again. Everyone jerked around, and Gadrial's heart shuddered to a halt when she saw Jasak standing in the doorway. For long moments, she was frozen to the chair in which she'd been sitting for the past two hours, too exhausted to continue her pacing. Her eyes met his and the blaze of fire in them left her pulse shuddering, wondering if that fire was the look of a man filling his eyes with the sight of her for the last time or the fire of a man out from under the cloud that had dogged his heels all the way from that pile of wind-wrecked trees. Not to mention the man and woman sitting beside her, whose capture had wrenched Gadrial's life—and everyone else's in this room—inside out and upside down.

Then Jasak spoke. He whispered hoarsely, "The verdict was not guilty, on all charges."

Gadrial sobbed aloud once; tears filled her eyes. Someone else was weeping, as well, close by. But then Jasak spoke again, and she stared at him in shock.

"I . . . can't stay in the army," he said.

"I don't understand!" she cried. "You're innocent! They cleared you! Cleared your name, your reputation, completely! Why can't you stay in the army? We'll *need* good officers!" Even as she said it, a flutter of terror—and raw, selfish gratitude—tore through her. *He won't be going to war!* Even though he needed to . . . and *wanted* to, being a mad Andaran. "I don't understand," she finished, miserable for failing to understand even *this* about the man she loved, and a strange little smile touched his lips.

"Yes, I was cleared, completely. But the Army needs someone to take the blame, even so. Someone besides Garlath, who's been officially found responsible for starting the war, but who's inconveniently dead and therefore not an ideal candidate. Much of the verdict hinged on his failure to obey my order to hold his fire, as we suspected it would. But that was a two-way sword. They determined that I was in command and that Garlath's refusal to obey that order started the war. They also determined that my decision to leave him in place was reasonable and correct, given the circumstances surrounding his...attitudes and behavior. Your testimony tipped those particular scales very firmly in the direction of the final verdict, Gadrial.

"But because I was in command, ultimately the blame for the war rests in part on my shoulders. And however...fraught any decision of mine to summarily relieve him might have been, I didn't do it. The fact that I obeyed regulations by leaving him in command clears me of *legal* responsibility, but a lot of people who weren't there are going to be wise after the fact and second-guess my judgment. There'd probably be fewer Andarans like that than Ransarans or Mythalans, but there'd be more than enough of our own people. Any future military career for me would probably be a disaster, and if I tried to stay in uniform, every single one of Father's political enemies would have a custom-made club to beat him over the head with in Parliament and public opinion. So I'm resigning my commission to enter politics."

Another strange smile curled around his lips.

"I've already been approached, in fact, after the verdict was read, the probable consequences to my career—and the war effort in general, given whose son I am—were discussed. Consequences which I brought up, in fact, when I tendered my resignation on the spot. After the dismissal of the court, Sogbourne approached me, privately."

He shook his head. "He begged me to enter the political arena, suggesting I'd be an asset to the Commandery, not because of who my father is, but because of my voluntary resignation. If Father will have me," he glanced over to meet the duke's gaze, which hadn't left his son's face since he'd entered the drawing room, "I'll work as an assistant or a page until the next election cycle."

"Gladly," the duke rumbled. "And Sogbourne's right. We'll get you qualified in a proper Andaran district and you'll win that election, make no mistake about that."

"Why are you so certain?" Shaylar asked, puzzled, and the duke grinned.

"Because an officer who voluntarily shoulders the punishment and the responsibility for a serious act he didn't commit is seen—rightly so—as the most honorable of men. The sacrifice of an army career under those circumstances is the greatest one a man can make, other than to lay down his life. Oh, yes, Jasak *will* win that election. By a landslide."

Gadrial shook her head.

"That's nuts!" she protested, and Jasak chuckled.

"That's Andaran," he corrected. Then the mirth faded from his eyes and he crossed the room in three swift strides. Went down on his knees. Took both her hands in his.

"Gadrial, I'm pleading with you to consider becoming my wife. I swear by all that I hold sacred that you'll be free to live your life by whatever precepts, whatever mores and beliefs you choose. Your career is the second-most important thing in my life."

Her cold hands began to tremble in his.

"If you'll agree to tolerate these crazy Andaran rules I live by, I'll agree to let our children choose which world they want to live in. Yours or mine."

Tears were coursing down her cheeks.

"You crazy, mad, adorable Andaran," she whispered. "You were listening, weren't you? To my testimony?"

His face went red. "Guilty as charged, Madam. It's an accused man's right, to hear the testimony for or against him. He just doesn't sit in the room, because his presence might prejudice or intimidate the witness."

"*That* makes sense, at least," she said with some asperity. Then she slipped one hand free of his grip and ruffled his thick hair. "Our children, Jas Olderhan, will live in *our* world. Rahil alone knows what it'll look like, but it will be *ours*."

In the next moment, Gadrial was in his arms, and she discovered that the kiss he'd bestowed on her in the slider coming into Portalis had been little more than a peck on the lips. The kiss he'd delivered the day she'd gone tottering off to her lab on campus had been a simple buss on the way out the door. What Jasak Olderhan's lips wrought here and now was probably illegal in every single town and village in Andara. *Hah! Just let them try tossing us in jail,* she thought in a muddle somewhere in the middle of that life-altering kiss.

Then she couldn't think at all.

And that was just fine with her.

CHAPTER FORTY-FIVE

Noristahn 14, 5054 AE
(May 3, 1929 CE)

ANDRIN LEANED AGAINST THE SHIP'S RAIL, HAIR FLYING in the wind as she and Howan watched the glorious fireworks display overhead. The dark waters of the Ylani Straits were a mirror reflecting back the explosions of light and color. The sharp crack and rumbling boom, followed by the staccato crackle of secondary explosions, rolled across the black water like the voices of the very gods lifted in celebration. They'd stopped Arcana!

The Voice message announcing the recapture of Fort Ghartoun, Hell's Gate, and the portal to Mahritha had reached Tajvana two days ago. All of Sharona was still awaiting confirmation that Fort Brithik had been retaken, as well, but no one in the entire multiverse seemed to doubt it had been done by now.

She hugged the joy of it to herself, just as she hugged all her good fortune from these past few days. She'd needed that good fortune, every drop of it. She'd faced so very much, these last months: terror, horror, anguish, numb grief, cold rage...so many emotions foreign to her life, she ought to have been exhausted.

But the fireworks sparkled in the night sky as brightly as Andrin's happiness, which knew no bounds, tonight. She knew they still faced danger and pain, but for now, for these few moments, she let herself simply be happy. She felt almost giddy, like a child at Spring Coming. Sharona was safe, Chava Busar had failed to destroy her life in his quest for power, and she'd married a man whose love for her was so deep she knew already she would never taste the bottom of it.

Each day, each hour they spent together, Andrin realized

she'd joined lives with a man as worthy of her respect and love as her father was. For all that he was a reserved and quiet man, he deliberately drew her sense of humor into the open, made her smile and laugh more than she ever had in her life. He sought her opinions and found them sound, agreeing with her a surprising percentage of the time. When they *didn't* agree, he said so ... and made his case in calm, measured tones, although she could sense the temper that sometimes boiled beneath the surface.

She glimpsed it, now and again, when some officious twit said or did something that pushed the limits of his patience. He'd come close to losing control of that temper at the last crossing of the swords, so to speak, with Prince Weeva. His Highness would smart for months to come under the sting of Howan Fai's cold-voiced opinion, which had endeared him to her all the more. Andrin detested that particular son of Chava so deeply it was nearly pathological.

She put him deliberately out of her mind. She'd much rather think about her husband—his sense of humor, his respect for her opinions, the strength of his *own* convictions, his soul-shaking tenderness. ...

She didn't know if this was love or some other emotion, since she'd never felt this way before, but whatever it was, she wanted more of it. And she wanted an excuse to slip away to their cabin and share a little more of that delicious intimacy. She sighed. It had been dark for barely half an hour, and she was only too aware of the eyebrows that would rise if she suggested retiring to bed *this* early. She nearly giggled aloud, shocked by her own indecent thoughts.

There'd be time enough for *that*, later.

For now, she leaned against the rail, watched the fireworks, stroked Finena's glossy white feathers with absent fingertips, and stole occasional glances at her husband. Their child was growing well. Not a hint of a belly showed yet, though Dr. Morlinhus warned her that even at her height, a bump was to be expected in the next couple of weeks. The dreams had faded as the child grew, but Howan Fai was slipping her away to safety, she hoped.

Let it be so, she prayed silently. To that prayer, she added, *And please, let me hold onto this happiness, let me hold onto this wondrous man you've given me. Grant me this much, at least: a chance to spend my whole life with him, for him to spend his whole life with me. There's so much we can do, together, to protect the people of our worlds. Grant us the time to do that work together.*

Howan Fai turned to peer into her eyes, sensing a change in her mood. He gave her arm a reassuring squeeze and lifted his chin slightly in inquiry.

She was afraid to say it, for fear that once uttered, some malevolent demon would hear the words and smash them to pieces. So she merely smiled and said, "It's nothing."

She sensed that he understood her reluctance to speak, that he knew at least some of what she'd been feeling so strongly and concurred with her decision not to voice it aloud. Of course, that might simply have been a caution that was instilled into every man, woman, and child born of Eniath, particularly its aristocracy and royal family. With neighbors like Chava Busar, *not* voicing certain thoughts had become an ingrained and necessary habit.

But tonight, those fears and worries were far away and dim. Tonight, the stars were brilliant, the sea and sky were a glorious riot of bursting colors, and joy filled the air. Millions of people stood along the shoreline, on the housetops, in the windows of shops and tall buildings. Every single one of those millions of people shouted and rang bells and set off long chains of fire-poppers. The noise came rolling across the water like a solid wave of sound, filled with bursting happiness.

It wouldn't last, she knew; but for tonight, at least, the worlds that had sprung from Sharona—and all the people in them—were safe from the threat of Arcana. That simple, profound truth moved her nearly to tears. She gripped the railing as her yacht moved slowly and softly through the darkness, past the crowd of boats bobbing on the water where even more Sharonians celebrated the halting of the Arcanan menace.

She smiled as the *Peregrine* slipped through the dark, color-splashed water, with her security men nearby, her hawk on her arm, and her heart full nearly to bursting with happiness and hope for their future. She turned to tell Howan Fai how very happy she was—

And the Glimpse struck.

* * *

Zindel chan Calirath wandered across the long stone balcony overlooking the Ylani Straits, ostensibly to obtain another glass of wine after draining his first one in toasts to the newly married couple: MP Kinlafia and Voice Yanamar. His real motive was the view. This portion of the balcony gave a better view of the western end of the Straits, where they led into the Imbral Sea and eventually down past Imbral's Blade and out to the Mbisi Sea. The Straits and the harbors on either side were filled with boats of every size in a confusing jumble that was lit every few seconds by the strobing light of fireworks.

None of that mattered. The *Peregrine*'s profile was etched into his memory. He'd learned a deep appreciation of the sailing master's craft aboard that trim, lovely little ship. She was moving under sail, tonight, creeping softly, silently through the crowded harbor, toward the open channel at the center of the Straits. Her escort destroyers steamed fore and aft—under power at slow speed to follow the rules of the road that granted sailing vessels right of way—as if they'd merely happened to be transiting the Ylani Straits at the same time as *Peregrine* instead of following careful, Voice-coordinated transit orders. A convenient port call at Larakesh had held them at the ready, and now they were immediately at hand to defend the *Peregrine* if anyone dared threaten her.

Zindel had wandered along the length of the balcony several times already, this evening, careful to spend just as much time gazing out across other vantage points. He didn't want observers to notice his keen interest in the ship moving so slowly toward the deep channel. The fireworks offered the perfect cover under which the *Peregrine* could run, taking his daughter to a place where she and her husband could learn one another in greater privacy. It was difficult enough for ordinary newlyweds to learn how to live together. For an imperial heiress, the job was ten times harder.

Still, he couldn't help worrying. So he strolled the balcony, watching the *Peregrine* make her way towards the open sea. He wondered again if he'd made the correct decision, sending her on the yacht, rather than the *Windtreader*. The *Windtreader* was harder to attack, certainly, but part of his intention had been secrecy. It would have alerted most of Tajvana, had the *Windtreader* steamed out in the middle of the victory celebration.

So he'd arranged for Andrin and Howan Fai to take the sailing yacht, instead, relying on the brand new engines installed in her hull, the Imperial security team onboard, and her destroyer escort. She might be a romantic little ship, but she carried a genuinely nasty sting for anyone foolish enough to attack her, and the two destroyers could blow anything short of a major warship completely out of the water. And for the possibility of major warships, two armored cruisers were waiting to add themselves to the escort once they were safely out into the Mbisi.

The *Peregrine*, which had nearly cleared the tangle of small craft clogging the harbor, carried a marine detail, in addition to a full squad of Imperial Guardsmen, but he still couldn't help worrying. *I shouldn't have let her go,* he found himself thinking as he gripped the stone balustrade. *This is stupid!* he snarled at himself a moment later. *You're being an overprotective father. She's a woman grown, married, now. She has enough firepower around her to take out half a city. And there hasn't been so much as a whisper of trouble out of Chava, let alone anyone else.*

When he caught himself worrying his lower lip with his teeth, he took several deep, slow, calming breaths. He was being paranoid. Chava Busar had behaved with extreme prudence and every outward appearance of unhappy acceptance. Security had been watching him, his sons, his wives and daughters, his supporters, and his high-ranking security officials, every second of every day and night. They'd even been watching the officers of Chava Busar's so-called "imperial police," who constituted a private army under the Uromathian emperor's control.

A spate of cheering prompted him to glance down at the broad flagstone terrace just below his balcony. This portion of the palace had been built along the slope of a hill which had been terraced with a series of gardens, staircases, and open flagstone pavements where garden parties were held throughout Tajvana's long social season. The palace's gaslights had been dimmed for the firework display, but more than enough light spilled across the terrace from open doorways and windows to reveal the identities of the revelers below.

Various members of his Privy Council chatted with one another and their families, pausing now and again to cheer a particularly spectacular burst of fireworks, and musicians played. The bright sounds of military marches, the patriotic tunes of every nation on Sharona, and celebratory hymns of thanksgiving and joyous praise for the deities which watched over them splashed across the terrace and eddied out into the night, and temple bells tolled solemn jubilation in the distance. All of Tajvana was filled with joy, tonight.

Zindel spotted First Councilor Taje, head bent in conversation with Darcel Kinlafia. Kinlafia wasn't a member of his Privy Council, but his new bride was. Alazon Kinlafia had been reinstated as Privy Voice and was radiant tonight. Zindel approved of that match, very much, and a faint smile touched his mouth. From the reports he'd been receiving, Kinlafia had weathered the transition from survey crew Voice to Imperial Parliament MP with great success.

He'd been selected to several important committees in the House of Talents, including Foreign Relations and Budget, and he was vice-chair of both the War Caucus and the Talent Mobilization Board. That sort of authority was rare for a novice politician, but he owed it only partially to his fame as the sole surviving member of the Chalgyn Consortium crew and the Voice who'd relayed Shaylar Nargra-Kolmayr's last Voice transmission. It turned out—to Kinlafia's own surprise, Zindel suspected—that he had very good political instincts even without his wife's guidance, and his fellow MPs had quickly realized he was smart, thoughtful, and well-informed on the critical issues not only of the war but of conditions in the border universes, as well.

And he was using that stature to keep the House of Talents focused on creating the structures they'd need to recruit and train Sharona's Talented citizens to assist with the war. Whether at home or at the battlefront, Talents would be essential to Sharona's war effort, indeed, to Sharona's survival. Darcel Kinlafia understood that. It was a great relief to have him in the House of Talents, advocating and browbeating and persuading his fellow Talents to do the hard work necessary to prepare Sharona's Talented citizens for war.

Servants wended their way through the crowd, carrying trays of beverages and sweets. One of those servants caught his attention. The young woman was familiar to him, but he couldn't quite place her. A frown touched his mouth as he tried to recall who she was—

And the Glimpse struck.

He staggered, nearly collapsing under the shock. *Fire!* There was fire everywhere. A blazing inferno blowing the room behind him to hell. His whole body was engulfed in flame and there was no time, it was right on top of them . . .

"VARENA!"

His wife jerked around as he began to run.

"Zindel—?"

"The girls! *Get the girls!*"

His wife blanched and whirled. Armsmen were running toward her. Razial was beside her mother. But he couldn't see Anbessa.

"Telfor!"

Telfor chan Garatz, Chief of Imperial Security, had already scooped Razial out of her chair. He jerked around at Zindel's shout.

"Get my family off this balcony! *Not through the room!*"

"Yes, Sire!"

Chan Garatz was already moving...moving so quickly he didn't notice that the emperor was headed the opposite direction.

Headed directly *into* the room he'd ordered his armsmen to avoid.

"'Bessa!" Zindel chan Calirath thundered, his mind full of fire and blast, his body already screaming protest of the agony he knew was to come. He should have been paralyzed, should have been lost in the crushing power of his Death Glimpse, but his Talent had always been powerful. Now, like his son at Fort Salby, he was in fugue state. He Saw the world about him, Saw the future, Saw the agony, Saw his daughter's death, Saw his own, Saw the slim possibility that Anbessa might live, and he threaded the needle between those futures—all of them potential; each of them in that moment as real as any other—and raced towards her.

"Daddy?" she looked up at the sound of his voice, and even in fugue state, his heart spasmed with terror.

She was standing in front of a tray of chocolates. *In the room.* Oh, gods...

"'Bessa! *Run!*" he shouted. "Get to the balcony! *Now!*"

She dropped the candy and ran towards him, but his own armsmen had realized which way he was headed. Two of them hurled themselves at him, desperate to tackle him and drag him bodily to safety, but he was in fugue state. He Saw them coming, knew exactly where they'd be, where their hands would be, and he went through them like smoke, smelling the fire, racing to embrace it. He was at the door, *through* the door, and Anbessa was six feet from him and running hard when he saw the terrible flash of light. It started at the back of the room. The table of candies exploded. The whole back of the room exploded.

The blast cracked open the room's gas lines and the entire enormous salon ignited. The guards who'd tried to stop him vanished into a boiling inferno, flame belched through the room, and Anbessa was still three steps away. The blast front roared over him, and he reached into it, closed his hand around her outstretched fingers. Heat crisped all around them, and Zindel chan Calirath pulled with all his massive, bull-shouldered strength, all the desperate power of a father who would *not* lose another child. He spun, his baby girl somehow in his arms, and hurled his daughter through the air, threw her violently forward, a living javelin.

The second explosion blew out the doors.

And part of the wall. It picked him up, hurled him back toward the balcony like a toy, swept everything *off* the balcony. It blew out the stone railing and hurled *all* of them out and down in a blazing ruin of flame.

*   *   *

Andrin gripped the ship's railing. The Glimpse struck her like a club and she fought to see details. It was like seeing two different events through one set of eyes. She saw the Grand Palace, cracked open, fiercely ablaze. *Papa!* she screamed in silent horror, watching the flames engulf her father, watching the explosion sweep him off the broken balcony like a shattered doll. But there was fire all around her, as well, fire above her, fire and black water, deep and terrible and her lungs were bursting, but she couldn't breathe for the flames and terrible black water that was dragging her down while hell blew up around her—

"*Get off the ship!*" she croaked.

"What?" Howan Fai asked, staring at her.

"Off the ship! A Glimpse—just now—I was in the water. There was fire everywhere, all around, I couldn't breathe, oh, God—"

She saw two things simultaneously.

Men in black, form-fitting clothing. They charged across the deck, converging on *her*. And a massive explosion behind them. An explosion that sent fire belching into the night from the heart of Tajvana. The Grand Palace had blown open. Fire belched out of it.

"*PAPA!*" she screamed.

Gunfire erupted—

—and she plunged over the rail. Was *shoved* over the rail. Finena launched from her wrist. The falcon screamed. *Andrin* screamed as she fell. As she plunged down the long, long hull. Toward the cold, black water of the sea.

And then the vicious shock of impact smashed through her.

The water was hard as stone. She'd turned instinctively to protect her belly and her side struck brutally. The cold shocked her whole body, and then she was *under* the water, down in the terrible black depths. Her gown was pulling her even deeper and she fought its weight. Ripped at the buttons, the seams. She couldn't fight free of it. Her lungs were bursting. Panic throbbed through her. Gripped her throat. Stabbed through her, knife-sharp with every pulse of her wildly racing heart.

Someone had her wrist. She flailed wildly. Hands pulled her from behind. Then the heavy weight of her gown ripped away. She felt suddenly light as goose down and she kicked frantically. Swam madly up—*hoped* she was swimming up, not deeper into the endless black water. She was suddenly propelled upwards by the strong grip of whoever had torn off her heavy dress. Her lungs were on fire. She couldn't stand it. Had to gulp *now*—

Her head broke water.

She sucked down air—huge, shuddering lungfuls of it—and Howan Fai was beside her, face lit by the exploding fireworks overhead as they were jostled in the wake of the passing ships. Her yacht was already fifty yards ahead of them and pulling away steadily as the wind in her sails and the current in the straits carried her forward. The first destroyer was even farther away, out in the main channel; she couldn't even spot the other one in the dark waters, but she could breathe—*she could breathe!*—and Howan Fai was with her. They hadn't—

A sparkle of light erupted on *Peregrine*'s decks. Gunfire! Those men in black swarmed across the yacht. Fighting Andrin's armsmen. Fighting Imperial Security. Fighting the *Marines* her father had stationed aboard. Andrin drew breath to cry out for help—

Peregrine exploded.

The whole yacht blew apart. Flaming debris arced high through the air, hurled violently across the water, came flying down in a lethal rain.

"Breathe!" Howan Fai shouted.

She gulped air—and her husband dragged her under. He swam frantically down, as frantically as they'd just swum up. The water lit up, bright as daylight, and saltwater burned her barely slitted eyes even as she tried to make out the dark shapes sharing the cold waters.

A shockwave tumbled them through the water. Something massive slammed down past her, plunging its way toward the bottom, and the water blazed above them.

Great sheets of flame spread far and wide overhead, and Howan Fai swam hard sideways, towing her frantically toward the darkness. She started to kick that same direction, and for the first time in her life, Andrin was grateful she was large and strong, with more power in her body than grace. She swam with a single-minded determination toward the dark water beyond the flames, and when she reached it, she swam madly *up*, lungs nearly bursting yet again.

When her head broke water a second time, she sucked down air in gasping, painful shudders. *Oh, Triad, help us, please . . .* She searched wildly, trying to find Howan Fai again. Then he was beside her, gulping down air, as well, treading water at her side. She gripped his hand, gripped hard, trembling and crying as the emotional and physical shocks hit her.

Beyond them, the sea was an inferno. The fuel gushing from *Peregrine*'s ruptured hull spilled across the surface of the water, turning the waves into a raging sheet of flame. The yacht was nothing but wreckage. She'd broken in half and the two halves were sinking, still fiercely ablaze. Andrin heard people screaming in the flames, heard the engine-throb of the destroyer closest to them.

She was opening her mouth to scream for help when Howan Fai covered her lips with his hand and shook his head urgently. He nodded with his head and she saw another boat—one with a haze above it, visible only when it rose on the very crest of a wave and instantly gone again when it slid into a trough. A smaller craft than *Peregrine*, it sat rocking in the waves less than thirty feet from them.

It was a pleasure boat, one of the new power cruisers rich men liked to speed in, racing across harbors and bays, kicking up spray behind them in gleeful abandon.

This boat wasn't kicking up spray. It sat silent and dark, ominous in the black water. Then she heard the voices. Men's voices. Low, rapid, speaking in a language she recognized as the Othmaliz dialect of Shurkhali. What they said riveted her entire attention.

"—no one could've lived through that," an angry voice snarled. "Gods *damn* it! How could those fools have bungled the job so badly? It was a cinch! Board in the darkness, snatch that cut-cha, and dump her over the rail. Aruncas knows the fishes are hungry, and I Masked this job, neat as anything. We should've been halfway across the Straits before the bomb blew. But no, they *botched* it! That was a godsdamned *gun battle*, raging up there, before it blew apart!"

Another voice, no less appalled, said, "The Seneschal will be furious. His Eminence wanted that—what was your word, cutcha?—to *vanish*. Swallowed by the waves and never recovered!"

"Dead is dead," the Masker chuckled nastily, "and that frigging explosion won't leave much in the way of identifiable bodies! But if they can't trot out every tall fisher girl up and down the Ylani as the missing heiress for the next decade, that's the Seneschal's problem, not ours. We did our part. Let's finish this."

A large form blocked Andrin's view of the boat for a moment and then slid on by.

"Good enough," said one of the Bergahldians.

"Fine," replied the Masker. "Get us out of here before those fucking destroyers decide to strafe every boat within a thousand yards."

"I thought they couldn't see us," said a third voice showing a little more fear.

"They'll see us just fine if you let a stray bullet hit me. Finish Calling your hungry little friends, and we can get out of here," said the Masker.

"I'd really rather we got to shore first."

"Do it!" snarled the Bergahldian.

The boat didn't race away. That would have attracted too much attention. Instead, it chuffed slowly away under low power while the destroyers raked the flaming wreckage with searchlights, looking for survivors. Andrin realized quite abruptly that she was nearly naked in freezing cold water. She'd begun to shiver while listening to those murderous ghouls and those shivers were rapidly turning into shudders.

"Swim, Andrin," Howan Fai said grimly beside her. "It will help keep us warm until we're close enough for someone to hear us or see us."

She nodded. Then she reached across the dark water and touched his face. "You saved my life. Again and again, tonight." There was more salt in her eyes than the sea could account for. "Oh, Triad! Howan, Daddy and Mama and the girls..." She was crying, fighting desperately for control, but the pain was tearing her in half. "I'm not ready to be empress! Not like this!" she cried.

Howan Fai hooked one arm around her and churned the water with his legs to hold them both up. The strength of his arms and his ease in the water calmed her even before he started speaking, and Finena, circling in the air above, invisible in the darkness, cried out her fury. Andrin had almost forgotten her falcon.

"Sister of White Fire," her husband said in a stern voice, "you're strong enough to do anything. To endure anything. You're Talented enough to protect your life and my life and this whole world we love. If not for your Glimpse, we would both be dead. Your warning gave me time to act. To throw you over the rail before those murderers could reach you. If you can save us from a plot *this* well orchestrated, Andrin, you can do *anything* you must!"

His voice was fierce. His eyes, lit by the fires raging across the water, were as hot as the flames that had nearly killed them both, and that fierceness steadied her. She was still shaking, but the hysterics were draining away and what was left was merely the shudders of icy water and reaction.

"I'm c-cold, Howan," she chattered. "Let's s-swim."

This time, it was his grin that was fierce.

"That's the woman I love. Swim with me, Andrin. We have but a little way to go." He pointed to the closer of the two destroyers, which had left the deep channel in the center of the Straits to search for survivors. She heard shouts as sailors from both ships lowered lifeboats and she saw searchlights sweeping across the flaming ruin of her beautiful yacht. She wouldn't think, yet, about the people who'd died aboard that yacht. Her servants, her security men, her crew...

She started to swim.

It seemed such a short distance, but it was a long, brutal swim in the cold water, with her body shuddering and her teeth chattering. They swam five yards beyond the edge of the burning fuel, having to skirt debris floating in the dark water. Some of that debris had been human and she closed her eyes and kept swimming, trying to blot out the numb horror of what she was seeing.

She swam slowly, exhausted as the adrenaline rush wore off, and Howan Fai matched her pace stroke for stroke.

"Keep going," he encouraged her. "Almost there."

They watched another lifeboat hit the water and push off. Its crew had lit rescue torches, looking frantically for survivors. The flames were so fierce the lifeboats couldn't even get close to the sinking wreckage and she heard them, faintly, calling out across the wreckage and the crackling of the flames.

"Hello! Hello! Can anyone hear me?"

She and Howan Fai were too far away, yet, to be heard above the secondary explosions that ripped periodically through the yacht's broken hull. Mixed in with those hopeful shouts were curses, raging and frantic as men swore in savage tones. She could even hear what sounded like weeping. She'd never heard grown men cry, before. *They're crying for me*, she realized through her numb weariness. Her lungs hurt from the gasping breaths she pulled down, trying to force her flagging body forward.

One of the lifeboats began moving toward them. It was skirting the wreckage, trying to get at the debris from another direction. They didn't expect to find anyone out here, this far from the ship, but their maneuver brought them unknowingly closer to Andrin and Howan Fai. She gritted her teeth and kept swimming. If they could just get a little closer, so the men in the lifeboat could hear them shout above the noise of the burning yacht...

Something bumped Andrin's leg.

Something large. Something rough as sandpaper. Something *alive*. Then a fin broke water, a *big* fin. And a tail fin appeared, as well, nearly fifteen feet away from her. Andrin froze in place, water rising around her.

"S-shark!" she gasped. "Oh, Merciful Triads—Howan—*sharks! I wasn't supposed to *drown* here! They wanted me eaten alive!"

The fins sped up and knifed past her. A chunk of debris—*human* debris—floating ten feet away vanished into the black water. Howan Fai watched in wide-eyed horror. Then he shouted with all his strength.

"HELP!" The bellow raced across the black water.

Andrin shrieked as more fins appeared in the water. "*Help!* Sharks!"

Someone shouted. A man stood up in the lifeboat. A light caught them full in the eyes. The man standing in the boat was lifting something. Throwing something. Right at them. A life ring smacked down beside them. They lunged for it, grabbed hold as still more fins cut through the water. Some of those fins were far larger than others, and she sensed a mad swirl of violence all about her.

The instant they gripped the life ring, the men in the lifeboat hauled on the rope, and Andrin and Howan Fai shot forward through the water. Something big grazed her kicking legs again. Scraped it raw. Something else brushed against her and rolled pushing her hard. She screamed—

—and then something was *under* her, heaving, sending her hurtling up like an elevator. Whatever it was literally *threw* her over the lifeboat's side, into the startled arms of one of the sailors. The man's arms closed instinctively as her hurtling weight knocked him flat. She landed on top of him, and an instant later, Howan Fai was beside her, coughing and shaking.

Andrin sprawled across the bottom of the boat, across bits and pieces of several men, shuddering violently with cold and terror. Her leg bled where the shark had hit her the second time, but she shoved herself up on an elbow, staring back out at the water. The searchlights picked out more and more sharks teeming the strait, yet something else was out there too. Massive fins were ripped down under the waves not to emerge.

Andrin clung tight to the gunwale watching the sea battle. Something towed a corpse in Imperial Guard uniform and lifted it with surprising gentleness—once, twice, and three times until the searchers overcame their shock enough to pull it onboard.

A black and white orca's face with a rough scar over the left eyespot examined her for a long solemn moment before twisting back towards the maddened swarm of shark fins. Whatever the Order of Bergahl's Talent had done, the cetaceans were aware and fighting.

She heard a blur of voices as the boat rocked violently under her.

Then someone had a blanket wrapped around her. She allowed herself to be lifted again, turned and propped against a shoulder. Someone pressed a metal rim to her lips, exhorting her to sip, to swallow whatever was in the flask he held, and she gulped down fiery liquid. The whiskey tore down her throat and left her coughing and wheezing, but it warmed her up and steadied her down.

The blur of voices resolved into the sound of men weeping in wild relief. Someone was saying, over and over, "Oh, thank the Triads, Shalana's mercy, oh, thank the Triads…" and someone else was cursing in rough tones that she slowly realized were an expression of shock and a release of stress too deep to endure. Someone else was shouting through a megaphone. "We've got her! We've found the crown princess! She's alive, we've got her safe, she's all right and the crown prince consort is with her..."

Andrin found herself looking up into the face of the sailor she leaned against. He was just a common seaman, a rough-faced, ordinary sailor in his early forties, from the look of him, but there were tears in his eyes and on his weathered cheeks, and he held a whiskey flask.

"Need another swallow?" he asked gently.

She nodded.

He had to hold the flask to her lips, again, and she swallowed another deep gulp, shuddering as it ripped down her throat and tore into her belly. But it helped ease the painful shudders. The cold of the water, the cold of physical exhaustion, the cold of deep and desperate terror had left her shaking so violently, she couldn't even control her own arms and legs.

The sailor brushed wet hair off her face with a gesture so tender it brought tears to her own eyes. He pulled the blanket more closely around her shoulders and urged her to sip the whiskey again.

"Thank you," she croaked out, voice little more than a hoarse rasp. "Oh, Triads, thank you so much..." She was dissolving into tears again, sobbing and shaking as the terror caught her in its teeth. Howan Fai leaned against her, wrapped in his own blanket. He held her awkwardly, made gentle hushing sounds, rocked her slightly while she clung to him and cried helplessly.

When the hysteria had finally run its course, she knew a long moment of stinging shame for having broken down in front of all these people, still working to clear the wreckage and find whoever else might have survived. But a gentle touch and the tears streaking down Howan Fai's own face told her she was more than entitled to a little bawling. She sighed softly; then lifted her face.

The expression of the sailor still holding the bottle had twisted with anguish as he watched his crown princess and consort weep, and she gave him a tremulous smile.

"Thanks," she whispered. "Ever so much."

For some reason, those words and that shaky little smile caused a fresh rush of tears to well up in his eyes. "You're welcome, Your Grand Highness," he choked out.

She turned her head and looked around to find every man in the lifeboat watching her. She managed another smile, then turned again to Howan Fai. His blanket was slipping, his cold-numbed fingers having difficulty holding it one-handed. His jacket was gone. He must have wrenched it off on the way down, when he'd jumped overboard with her. He was still wearing the sheath he'd worn since the day of their wedding, but the knife was missing.

He must have used it to cut away her gown, she realized slowly. No wonder he'd managed to rip it off her back so quickly. Then he'd lost the knife, somewhere in the wild confusion when the ship had blown up. He cradled another whiskey flask in his hands, and his shoulders drooped in exhaustion, but his eyes shone fiercely, fixed on her. They might be huddled in the bottom of the lifeboat, shaken out of their wits, but they were still alive and still together.

The rush of love she felt for the quiet, courageous man she'd married filled her heart to bursting, and then, suddenly, there in that crowded lifeboat, a wall went down. That turbulent tide of love lifted her, reached out, opened what she realized must be the marriage bond Darcel and Alazon had described to her. But how? Howan Fai wasn't Talented! They *couldn't* forge a marriage bond, yet they had. They *had!* And as her emotion swept across him, through the bond they now shared, the look in his eyes shifted, gentled . . . and somehow blazed more fiercely than ever.

Until now, she realized, she'd only tried to love Howan Fai. She'd liked him immensely, enjoyed his company, been enthralled by his touch in the night. But not until this moment, crouched nearly naked in the bottom of a lifeboat, wrapped in a blanket and leaning against him . . . not until now had she truly realized how much she'd come to love the man she'd married.

"You are my heart," she whispered fiercely, gently, deeply. "I'll need you forever."

A moment later, she was in his arms, shuddering against *his* shoulder. He choked out her name again and again, his heart slamming against her ear, his lips buried in her wet, tangled hair. When the shudders had finally run their course, again, he touched her face with wondering fingertips; then he kissed her lips, very gently.

"I may be your heart," he whispered, "but you are my soul, Andrin."

She clung to him, needing the quiet strength of him more than she'd ever needed anything in her life, and he braced himself carefully against the gunwale beside her, then pulled her down to rest against his shoulder. She leaned into him, longing to simply sit in the safe haven of his arm forever, yet she couldn't. She knew she couldn't, for the cruel echoes of her Glimpse were still upon her. She didn't want to face what came next—more than she'd ever wanted anything in her life, she wanted *not* to face it—but she was a Calirath, heir to the Winged Crown of Ternathia and the throne of Sharona.

She bit her lip, then faced the sailors who'd pulled them from the water.

"Does anyone know if my parents are alive?" she asked in a shaky voice. "The Grand Palace exploded just before my prince jumped overboard with me."

She watched shock wash across their faces. They'd been so desperately focused on the search for her, they'd forgotten about the explosion at the Grand Palace. She could all but hear the next thought reflected on their faces: *We might be guarding the empress...*

Firelight from the burning fuel revealed the shift from shock to hard, grim determination.

"Get us back to the *Striker*," the petty officer in the prow barked. "*Move*, damn it!"

The oarsmen bent over the shafts of their oars, and they shot across the black water like a sculling boat in a regatta. Andrin had never imagined such a heavy boat could move so quickly without steam, but then the destroyer's hull rose above them like a steel cliff, blotting out the stars. Their helmsman brought them alongside with the polished efficiency that was the Imperial Navy's hallmark, and then the falls from the davits were being hooked on. A steam winch clanked, and the lifeboat rose smoothly, water running from its keel to the water below as it rose to deck level while Andrin clung to Howan Fai, exhausted and so deeply afraid she could hardly breathe.

When they reached the deck, the captain, himself, helped her out of the boat while Howan Fai steadied her. She clutched the blanket around her as the captain said, "Vothan be praised, Your Grand Highness! Let's get you both someplace safe and warm."

Someone else turned up—a grizzled Marine chief armsman, with four enlisted men at his back. There was a heavy Halanch and Welnahr revolver at the noncom's side, all four of his men carried both revolvers and slide-action shotguns, and their faces were grim, their expressions harsh in the light of *Peregrine*'s fires. They fell in about her and Howan Fai as the captain escorted them across the swarming deck. They passed sailors who stood rigidly at attention, faces wet, but eyes shining as she passed, and she tried hard to smile at them.

They were met part way across the deck by another officer, running to meet them. He carried a surgeon's bag, and several medical assistants were right behind him with stretchers. The moment the ship's surgeon touched her, Andrin knew she was safe, in the hands of a master healer. A wondrous rush of warmth and strength washed through her, and then she was lifted up, carefully, and placed on one of the stretchers.

"I can walk," she protested.

"So you can," the surgeon nodded, sounding her pulse, "but I won't be letting you, so just rest quietly, Your Grand Highness. We'll have you in sick bay and feeling better in no time."

She didn't want to let go of Howan Fai's hand, but the surgeon ordered him onto the other stretcher after the briefest touch on his shoulder. The stretcher bearers lifted them, and she suddenly realized they were taking her away and the captain wasn't coming with them.

"Wait!" she cried. "Captain, I need to tell you something! Urgently!"

He was at her side in an instant, even as the surgeon sent another flood of healing energy into her, inducing drowsiness.

"We heard two men on a cabin cruiser out there," Andrin said, gripping the captain's hand. "While we were in the water. They'd planned this whole monstrous thing. They might still be out there. They have a Masker and"—her mouth twisted—"someone who Calls sharks."

The captain's face flared with sudden blazing interest.

"You *know* who did this, Your Highness? Was it agents from Arcana?"

She shook her head, wishing it were so, but Arcanans didn't have Talents and they didn't speak Shurkhali.

"No," she said in a hoarse rasp. "It was the Seneschal." Her voice went harsh with hatred. "We heard his filthy hirelings talking about it, not thirty feet away. He sent men to board the *Peregrine* in the dark to throw me over the rail to the sharks.

They meant to make *certain* I was dead before the bomb went off—they probably didn't know the yacht had so much fuel aboard and they were afraid I might have survived the explosion somehow—but I had a Glimpse just seconds before they attacked. We saw men swarm up over the rail and come running at us across the deck, right before Howan Fai threw me over the rail. My armsmen and Marines were shooting back in a gun battle as we went overboard."

The captain turned from Andrin to Howan Fai then spoke roughly, "Your Grand Highness, you have my gratitude and deepest respect." He saluted Howan Fai, sharply.

"Thank you, Captain. But if not for Andrin's Glimpse, the Seneschal's plan would have worked and I'd be dead, along with all the rest."

Water started to stream down Andrin's face again—the inhaled ocean water stung her eyes and nose now that she had time to notice it—but her tears more than that. Raw fury clawed at her throat.

"That evil man has to be found, has to be punished! His people blew up the yacht, killed my staff, my armsmen. And Lazima!" She remembered her personal armsman turning to face the running dark figures, the revolver spitting flame in his hand, the way he'd stepped directly between her and the threat. "Did chan Zindico—? Has Lazima chan Zindico been found? I don't remember having time to tell him. He was right there not two steps away from us. No, no, he wasn't in the water. One of them threw something at us in the Glimpse and he moved into it. He couldn't have jumped, or if he had he would have already been bleeding, and the sharks—"

She froze, her throat closing in anguish for just a moment, but then something went through her—something hard, and deadly, and icy cold, and her voice went hard as flint.

"That bastard arranged *all* this. My yacht, my servants, my armsmen, and, and—The palace! I saw it burning too. Are my sisters...?" She turned to look towards the coastline where orange firelight flickered too brightly on the spot where the Tajvana Palace should have shone with festival lighting.

She was sobbing again, as grief and fear lashed through her. She was responsible for those deaths. She'd been the target. The target to destroy. It hurt so deeply, she couldn't breathe against it, but that freezing tide of lethal fury bore her up, turned her quivering sinews to iron and her will to steel.

"Find them!" she rasped. "Find them and *arrest* them!"

"Your Grand Highness," the captain gripped her shoulders, peering down into fiery gray eyes which streamed with tears and flashed with fury, "my Voice will flash that message to every law enforcement agency, every military base on Sharona. Those bastards will go down. I swear by Vothan, they *will* go down. *Tonight.* There's no hole deep enough to hide them, not anywhere on Sharona."

"Thank you, Captain," she whispered.

Then she turned her gaze helplessly to stare at the burning palace on the shore and that terrible, supporting rage flickered and she sagged as the agony whipped through her again. The surgeon's hands touched her, urging her to lie flat, and the moment his hands touched her, the terrible pain in her heart eased away, grew dim, disappeared. He was murmuring softly to her.

"Rest, now, Your Grand Highness, close your eyes, yes, that's right, we've got you safe, hush, now. Breathe softly ... softly ... light as down feathers from a gosling ..."

Her eyes closed over unutterable weariness.

Andrin's last thought was a plea to Shalana. *Have mercy, Lady, please. Let my parents and sisters be alive. Please, I can't bear this burden alone. ...*

Then even that disappeared.

*   *   *

Relatha Kindare had come a long way from Estafel and the servants' quarters at Hawkwing Palace. *Trainee Healer.* Those two words meant more to her than anything ever had in her life, and she had the crown princess to thank for it. Not only had she been accepted into the training program at the legendary Tajvana Healing Academy, one of the Imperial Healers had volunteered to give her extra tutelage in his spare time.

But for tonight, she was just Relatha the servant, again, by choice. She'd wanted to be part of the celebration at the Grand Palace, and gods knew the Grand Palace staff needed all the help they could get! Since she was already well known and thoroughly vetted by Security, it had been relatively easy to be added to the duty roster for the evening.

So here she was, in the midst of the glittering assemblage on the stone terrace, carrying a tray of drinks, enjoying the fireworks, and surreptitiously stealing glances at the Ylani Straits. She hadn't learned until just a few minutes ago that the crown princess and her husband were leaving Tajvana for a few weeks of long delayed honeymoon.

If she looked sharp, she could just pick out the dark silhouette of the royal yacht slipping out of the harbor, to be joined by the destroyers waiting in mid-channel, and her eyes went watery. Such a good man, she'd found. Relatha had gone nearly out of her mind thinking about Andrin in the hands of one of Chava Busar's unholy brood. During her work at the clinic attached to the school, she'd heard horror tales of girls who'd come in for medical help and emotional counseling after running afoul of the Uromathian emperor's sons. The thought of *any* of them with Crown Princess Andrin had made Relatha's blood run cold.

She was just passing Mister Kinlafia and his bride, the Privy Voice, who were talking to First Councilor Taje about some piece of legislation, when shouts erupted on the balcony above the terrace. Relatha jerked her gaze up to see the emperor running toward the Palace, shouting at the empress to get off the balcony.

She froze, unable to breathe, even, when Security started to run, as well, converging on the Imperial family. The emperor was shouting for Anbessa, but Relatha didn't see the youngest imperial grand princess anywhere on the long marble balcony. She raked her gaze along the whole, immense length of it—the marble balustrade ran for at least fifty or sixty feet along the open doors of the Grand Imperial Salon—but there was no sign of Anbessa anywhere.

Relatha gripped her tray of wineglasses hard enough to hurt when Security lifted the Empress Varena and Grand Princess Razial over the side of the balcony rail, lowering them to the armsmen below. What was wrong, up there? Why hadn't they just retreated into the safety of the Grand Imperial Salon? Was there a crazed gunman in the salon? Surely not—Security would've been on top of him long before this and there hadn't been a single gunshot. But if everyone else was running *away* from the salon, why was the emperor running *into* it—?

The empress touched the terrace first, followed an instant later by Razial. More Calirath armsmen were vaulting the rail, jumping down to close in around the empress and her daughter. They were shouting at everyone to get back, away from the building, and Relatha stumbled backward, her hands unsteady on the tray. She needed someplace to set it down as more people crowded back, away from the palace walls, but her eyes were locked on the emperor as he slid between two or his armsman like an eel and disappeared through one of the Grand Imperial Salon's dozens of doors.

The armsmen charged after him. She could hear them calling his name, but the emperor's voice rose over theirs like thunder, shouting at Anbessa. The girl must be inside the Salon, Relatha realized, and craned her head, trying to see as more people crowded around her, partially blocking her view—

The Salon exploded.

Relatha screamed. She dropped the tray as the whole, long room filled with fire. The Salon was a raging inferno—an inferno licking out to envelop the Emperor of Sharona and his armsmen. There was fire everywhere—*only* fire, roaring and hissing like one of the Arcanans' dragons—and then a small, familiar figure arrowed out of the furnace, thrown high into the air. She cartwheeled out above the crowd, her gown smoking and trailing cinders.

"It's Anbessa!" someone screamed, even as a heavier, far more massive body came charging out of that flaming hell.

And then there was a second explosion.

The blast front picked up that heavier body and flung it out across the night in a corona of fire.

Dozens of people were reaching up, trying to catch the grand princess as she fell, but Relatha's gaze tracked that second, heavier body. She knew exactly where he'd come down, and she started to run, shoving her way through the stunned crowd, even as the Salon blew apart in a third massive explosion.

Flame and death belched out into the night, an overpressure of sound and debris roared across the terrace at treetop height, and the entire balcony came down.

Chunks of marble slammed down into the crowd, and Zindel chan Calirath plunged down like a boulder as shocked spectators screamed and scattered. He crashed into the elegant little tables set with crystal and candles, punchbowls and wine and fancy pastries. He smashed down across them. Slid through them. Tumbled and rolled sickeningly off the end. Vanished into a large flowerbed filled with trees and shrubbery and flowers.

Panic-stricken people slammed into Relatha. Heavy bodies almost knocked her down, and she cursed and shoved people aside.

She ran frantically forward, toward the spot where the emperor had fallen. More of the balustrade crashed down around them, sending people running in wild terror, but Relatha Kindare didn't care. She fought her way to him. She hurled overturned tables out of the way, climbed across tumbled chairs, heaved burning debris aside with her bare hands as she searched frantically through the shrubbery.

There!

He lay at a grotesque angle, and he was frightfully still. Horribly still. *No!* she cried in denial, and dropped to her knees, nerved herself to search. Her fingers shook as she reached for his wrist....

A pulse! She sobbed aloud just once. Then she closed her eyes, concentrated...and whimpered.

There was pain everywhere. Pain from broken bones—*dozens* of broken bones. Some of those breaks lay near major arteries, too close for her to dare to move him, even though his pulse was thready, fast, and weak. Shock was dropping his blood pressure, far too quickly, and she concentrated hard. Energy flowed through her body, down through her heart, where she filled it with as much love and strength as she could muster.

She sent that healing flood through her arms, out through her hands, and her life force merged with his. She absorbed some of his shock, reeled under the wave of agony that crashed through her, and her hands shook as it threatened to suck her under. But she refused to yield. She fought the darkness aside, sent more of her life force into him. Her training told her to stop—screamed that she *must* stop! She was pouring too much of herself into him, spending her own life force like fire, emptying herself into a cold, dark void of death. She knew that...and she didn't care. He was the Emperor, *her* Emperor. She would die before she let him go, and she turned her back on her teachers' warnings. She emptied herself against his pain and the savage injuries of his broken body.

And it wasn't enough.

She could feel him slipping away, under her fingers.

"NO!" She screamed at him, but her voice emerged as little more than a hoarse, rasping whisper. Tears blinded her. "Don't you *dare* go!"

She moved by raw instinct now and lunged for his feet. She jerked off his shoes, jammed both hands hard against the balls of his feet, locked what her instructors had called the "wellsprings of life" in the soles of his feet. Energy centers there drew energy in and let energy flow out. When death came, her instructors had said, a person's energy bled away to nothing through those wellsprings.

"*You may not leave!*" she screamed at him, her voice stronger, and his soul hesitated, trapped by her hands and her will. "We *need* you," she cried. "We need you too desperately to let you go! Oh, goddess...Shalana, give me strength, we *need* him. *Please*, Your Majesty, stay with us..."

A terrible spasm went through him. Then he started to shudder, violently. The shuddering lasted for several terrifying seconds. Then he relaxed with such suddenness, such totality, she thought for a moment he'd died, after all. She drew breath to howl in anguish, when a low, deep groan tore from him. He tried to move under her hands, and pain flared, cruelly. He cried out in agony.

"Don't move!" she cried. "You have broken bones!" She didn't dare release her grip on the wellspring points, but he was trying to move, trying to thrash around.

"Anbessa..." The name tore from him, raw with anguish.

She searched the terrace with a frantic gaze, trying to find someone—anyone—in an Imperial Security uniform. There were so many people running in panic-stricken horror, she could see nothing but total confusion. But then a face she recognized resolved itself from the wild melee and she screamed out a name.

"*DARCEL!*"

*   *   *

Darcel Kinlafia jerked around, yanked out of his efforts to help the dozens of injured, sort out the panic, by the sound of his name. The scream cut through the chaos and the confusion with an impossible clarity. He knew he couldn't possibly have heard it through the chaos and the bedlam, but he didn't need to hear it with his ears, for he Heard it with every fiber of his Talent and he wheeled, eyes searching for its source.

"Down here, Master Kinlafia!" Relatha Kindare shrieked. "*Help me!*"

His gaze dropped to the flowerbed. It focused on her—then on the shape she crouched over, in that flowerbed—and his face turned paper-white in the ghastly light of the burning palace. He charged forward, tossing aside tables, chairs, and people with equal abandon, and Alazon was right behind him.

"Find a healer!" Relatha gasped, as he slid to his knees beside her. "Please! I can barely keep him stable, I'm just a student, oh, Goddess, I'm so scared..."

Both Voices went glassy-eyed. It took her gibbering mind a long, horrified moment to realize they were sending out a broadband distress call. She tried to feel grateful, tried to hope someone would Hear in time, but the battle to force the emperor to live consumed her and despair tore at her as she felt him slipping away once more.

The Privy Voice came out of "send mode" first and her eyes focused on Relatha once more, huge and dark in her ashen face, glittering reflections of savage firelight.

"What can I do?"

"Don't let him move, don't let him thrash around. He's got broken bones. If he moves, he'll tear things open, inside. And he's asking for Anbessa."

"Alazon," Kinlafia said.

"Got it," she replied immediately, and set a light hand on Relatha's shoulder. "I'll find out how the grand princess is. Darcel will stay with you."

She disappeared into the wild confusion, but her husband stayed close by Relatha's side, searching, for injuries. The emperor's arm had a ghastly break, a compound fracture pumping blood, and Kinlafia's face blanched even whiter. He ripped off the capelets of his formal court dress and used a strip torn from them to tie a tourniquet around the emperor's right arm. A jagged splinter of bone had torn through flesh and skin and sleeve. There was blood everywhere, so much blood...

"More cloth strips," Relatha said, her hands still clamped like death on the soles of the emperor's feet. "And something for splints."

Kinlafia tore more strips from his capelets. His explorer's good sense kept his nerves steady and the emergency medical training which went with it told his hands what to do, and Relatha held tight to Zindel's life force, trusting him to staunch the wounds while she refused to let her emperor slip away.

Kinlafia bound Zindel's right arm to his chest so he couldn't move it, then smashed a tumbled chair to bits for splints to secure the shattered arm more securely. Then another chair went to pieces as he splinted the emperor's right thigh and left calf.

He'd just finished that when several uniformed armsmen came running from another part of the terrace, and Relatha heard fire alarm bells clanging as fire wagons fought their way through the victory celebration crowds, trying to reach the burning Grand Palace. A ponderous crash marked the collapse of the Grand Imperial Salon, and she flinched as a fresh shockwave of heat, flame, and smoke belched across them. Cinders rained down like hailstones.

Every one of the armsmen had a gun in his hand.

"Get away from His Majesty!" one of them barked, and another reached down to snatch the emperor's shoulders, but—

"*NO!*" Relatha screamed.

"*Don't move him!*" Kinlafia snarled. "You'll *kill* him if you move him!"

"The fire—"

"He's got broken bones!" Relatha shouted over the roar of the fire. "They'll slice open arteries if you snatch him up like that. I'm training as a Healer; I can *sense* the damage in there. He's barely holding onto life, just from the physical shock. If I move my focus off the wellspring points, he'll die! He needs pain medication, emergency surgery. God's mercy, where's the Imperial Surgeon? *Any* surgeon, *any* Healer?"

Alazon Yanamar-Kinlafia shoved her way through the guards with kicks and curses.

"Let me through!" When she finally broke through the cordon they'd thrown around His Majesty, she dropped to her knees beside Relatha. "Dr. Sathron's on his way from the palace clinic. He's nearly here. I've called for a whole trauma team and an ambulance. Is he conscious?"

"Barely."

The Privy Voice leaned across to speak directly into her ear. "Will it help him or hurt him to let him know Anbessa is alive?"

Relatha bit her lip and blinked helpless tears. He might be holding onto life just long enough to know his child was safe and would let go of the struggle and die if they told him. Or he might be reassured enough to ease the strain of terror and guilt, easing the stress on his laboring body, now that he no longer needed to fear for her life. She didn't know, wasn't trained, didn't have enough experience.

"I don't know!"

When she tried to explain, someone—Security Minister chan Garatz himself, she realized suddenly—spoke decisively.

"Tell him!"

"Yes," Kinlafia agreed. "It's sheer hell, never to *know*."

He wasn't talking about the emperor and Anbessa. He was talking about Shaylar, Relatha realized with a sudden surge of pity and compassion, even through the chaos and the fight to save the emperor's life. When she saw the pain etched into his face, burning in his eyes, she nodded.

"Yes. Tell him."

She braced herself for the worst.

"Zindel!" Alazon crouched low over him, speaking directly into his ear. "Zindel, it's Alazon. Anbessa is safe. I've seen her, talked to her. She's alive. She'll be all right. Can you hear me? You saved her, Zindel, she's going to be fine. Please, Your Majesty, don't give up, 'Bessa needs her father, she needs you. We *all* need you. Dr. Sathron's on the way. He's nearly here. He'll give you something to take away the pain. Just hold on a little longer, *please*."

Tears ran down her lovely face, and a moan escaped the emperor. Then the heavy head moved, in the tiniest of nods, and Relatha felt the surge in his life force as he gathered reserves of strength from his massive, powerful body. He dug in, hung grimly onto life, defying the pain of torn tissue, shattered bone, and burns.

Relatha sobbed aloud in relief, and then someone else was shouting and shoving the guards aside. Dr. Sathron had arrived and other Healers rushed across the flagstones behind him. The ambulance had arrived. Stretcher-bearers came running behind the Emergency Medicine Talents rushing toward the emperor.

"Move back, please," Dr. Sathron said crisply, "give us room to work." He glanced at Relatha, saw where her hands were, and blanched. "Shalana's mercy, child," he whispered.

Then the others were there and a trained medic slipped her hands under Relatha's, taking over for her. Relatha gabbled out, "There's a break in his right femur, a bad one, right beside the big artery. I can Feel it. We didn't dare move him. Master Kinlafia splinted it and his arm..."

The medic met and held her gaze.

"It's all right, girl," the EMT said. "It's all right. Back out now, child, and let me take it. Your quick thinking saved his life—not many students remember the wellspring points—but move back now. Let us work, love. You can rest. We've got him."

Relatha sighed, relaxing her concentration, felt the other woman's fully trained Talent take up the load she'd supported for an eternity. She sagged back, sitting on her heels, head reeling, and then tried to stand and move out of the medical team's way.

She couldn't. She tried again and made it halfway, then staggered and went down, her head swimming and her muscles water. But Kinlafia caught her. He murmured something—something she couldn't hear through the tumult around her—and then he was helping her totter unsteadily out of the way. He supported her on one side and his wife took her arm on the other while they guided her faltering footsteps across the wide terrace.

The firefighters arrived, at last, bells clanging and horses snorting. Men were scrambling down, connecting hoses to the Palace's water supply, yanking open the valves and racing with long hoses toward the blaze. Water shot upward in massive jets as the hoses filled and sprayed it into the raging inferno.

Men with ladders scrambled up to reach windows on the rooms not yet burning, trying to contain the blaze before it spread to the rest of the immense structure, and streams of people were evacuating, carrying out art treasures, government records, anything they could salvage.

Watching the destruction of such a beautiful place made Relatha sick inside, and she wondered, numb with agony, how many people had been killed in the explosion. Servants she knew, maybe even her own mother and cousins, and all those Guardsmen who'd been on the balcony and in the Grand Imperial Salon. And there must have been many others in the corridors surrounding the Salon. How many of them had been injured? Perhaps crippled for life? Heavy chunks of the balcony had smashed down into the crowd out here, as well. People could have been badly injured by that falling debris.

By the time they reached the stairs leading down the hillside toward the street, she was shaking so badly she could barely stand. She didn't know where the two Voices were leading her and she didn't much care, so long as it was away from the horror behind them.

"Who could have done such a thing?" Kinlafia asked in a

voice harsh with horror. "Surely not even Chava Busar would have conceived of something this foul!"

"You think not?" Alazon snarled. "You don't know him the way I do, Darcel. He's *evil*! Chava Busar is interested in just one thing—Chava Busar! He'll stop at nothing, he'll—"

Her voice chopped off. She stopped dead in her tracks. Stared out across the dark waters of the Ylani Straits. Horror twisted across her face. Relatha followed her gaze....

A ship was ablaze, out there. Pieces of a ship. Fuel burned in a sheet of flame that danced insanely across the waves. Two hulking destroyers flanked the sinking wreckage.

"Oh, dear God..." Alazon whispered. "That's *Peregrine*."

A whimper broke from Relatha's throat.

It couldn't be real. She couldn't bear for it to be real. But how could anyone have lived through *that*? The yacht had been blown to *pieces*. Kinlafia was cursing. Endlessly. Brutally. With words so foul, Relatha blanched. Some of them, she'd never even *heard*, before. Relatha turned stunned eyes toward him, saw the wreckage of grief and agony in his face, and wanted to comfort him. But she couldn't. Her throat was locked tight. She couldn't breathe past it.

Then she was falling. Collapsing like a house of cards. Sobs ripped through her. The burning ship and the dark water and Darcel Kinlafia's voice gyred insanely around her, slid and whirled in crazed circles like a cork caught in a whirlpool. She couldn't bear it. She found herself sitting on the cold stone steps, huddled in Alazon's arms, and both of them were crying.

Kinlafia crouched beside them, one arm around each. Relatha heard another massive crash inside the burning palace. Firefighters were shouting. More fire bells were clanging as additional fire wagons and crews arrived. It was all dim and distant and strange. When a fire crew hauling hoses charged up the steps toward them, Kinlafia lifted Relatha in his arms and simply carried her out of the way while Alazon hurried after them.

They stepped out into the garden that sloped its way down the hillside, and Kinlafia set her down carefully. He actually went to one knee so that she was sitting down when he let go, rather than standing. She clutched his hand tightly.

"Thank you," she choked out.

"For carrying you?"

She shook her head. "I'm just a servant..."

"Just a *servant?*" he echoed sharply. His hands tightened on hers, painfully. "Don't you dare say that!"

She gaped up at him, stunned.

"By the Triads, you saved the emperor's life! You're a Talented Healer, girl, powerfully Talented. Even if you're only a student, you knew exactly what to do. And you *did* it. Most of us were running in blind panic. But you kept your wits. Shalana's mercy, girl, if you hadn't..."

He shuddered. Then he brushed wet hair back from her face, pulled loose long strands caught in her mouth.

"People call me a hero," he whispered hoarsely. "All I really did was sit in perfect safety at the portal and receive a message. But you..." He touched her cheek. "You ran forward, right toward the explosion, with debris falling all around you." He tipped up her chin, *made* her meet his eyes. "There's only one real hero on this hillside and I'm looking at her."

"But—"

Alazon hushed her. "He's right, Relatha. It is Relatha, isn't it? Your name?"

She nodded, astonished a member of the Privy Council knew *her* name.

"Relatha," Alazon laid one hand against her cheek, "all of Sharona owes you a tremendous debt. One we can't possibly repay—"

And then she broke off suddenly and whipped around to stare at the blazing debris in the dark waters of the Straits.

"Andrin!" The shriek tore loose, high and wild and...exultant?

"She's alive! *Andrin's alive!*" The Voice was laughing, weeping, gabbling in wild excitement. "That was the captain's Voice. The Captain of the HMS *Striker*. The ship's Voice just contacted me. The *Striker's* crew pulled her out of the water. It was the prince consort! He saved them both! Howan Fai threw her overboard. *Dragged* her overboard, just minutes before the *Peregrine* blew up. Vothan's mercy, *he jumped off the ship with her!*"

Kinlafia let out a crowing, triumphant whoop and grabbed Alazon and kissed her. Grabbed Relatha and hugged *her*. He was all but dancing in place, nearly jumping out of his skin in his own wild relief.

"My Gods," he gasped, "how in Vothan's holy name did he *know?*"

"Andrin had a Glimpse!" Alazon's eyes blazed with incandescent joy. "She knew the ship was going to blow up. She was choking it out to him when a boarding party rushed at them, trying to snatch her."

Relatha gasped.

"The prince jumped overboard with her in the middle of a gun battle. Oh, Darcel, they're *alive*, both of them!"

"But—" Relatha said in confusion, "but Her Grand Highness should have drowned! Her gown must have weighed close to sixty pounds! I know it did! I've helped her dress, before."

Alazon grinned hugely. "It's sixty pounds at the bottom of the Strait now! Howan Fai cut it off her back, in the water. With his sheath knife. He's carried it everywhere since the wedding. They were pulled from the water by a search party in a lifeboat. They're safely aboard the *Striker*. That one," she pointed to the destroyer on their left, bathed in the lurid red flames from the burning fuel and the wreckage of *Peregrine*. The destroyer on the right was mostly obscured by the thick black smoke boiling up from the fire.

Numb shock vanished. Relatha started to cry again. But *this* time, oh, gods, *this* time, her heart was wild with joy, not grief.

"We have to find Empress Varena," Alazon said, dragging Relatha to her feet. "We can't tell the emperor yet, not till his life's out of danger, but we have to tell the empress and Razial and Anbessa. We have to tell all of Sharona. The crown princess is alive!"

They were the sweetest words ever spoken.

EPILOGUE

Noristahn 14, 5054 AE
Kleindyr 13, 206 YU
[May 3, 1929 CE]

THE SENESCHAL OF OTHMALIZ LOWERED HIS FIELD GLASSES
with a wide, satisfied smile and the flames blazing out
in the harbor shrank once more to a patch no larger than the
palm of a man's hand. The blaze consuming the Imperial Grand
Salon was much nearer to hand, though not so near as to pose
a threat to him, and far brighter. The Grand Palace's gas mains
had contributed so nicely to the unfortunate disaster.

The flames were really quite lovely, he thought smugly. It
was a pity there'd been no opportunity to stretch out Zindel's
suffering, but one couldn't have everything, and what he had was
quite good enough, really.

The Uromathian emperor had been most helpful, even if he
was a crass, boorish man without a proper sense of retribution.
And Faroayn Raynarg fully intended to repay him. At the moment,
of course, the entire Order of Bergahl was as horrified, shocked,
and surprised as anyone else in Tajvana! They had *no* idea how
this could have happened, how an attack could have slipped past
the Calirath's highly trained armsmen and security staffs! But,
equally of course, they would be eager to aid in determining how
this heinous crime could have been committed. So would the
highly trained Imperial Uromathian Police. And in the course of
their investigation, they would produce a dead "Arcanan agent"
with secret orders written in the Arcanan language on his body,
orders instructing him to murder the Imperial family of Sharona.

The yammering pack of fools who were even now doubtless
sobbing in anguish would be so grateful to the Uromathian for

"saving" them, he'd end up ruling in his own right. Whereupon the Seneschal would have restored to him what was rightfully his. Chava Busar's sons wouldn't get to bed the imperial heiress or produce an imposter, but that didn't concern the Seneschal in the least.

He'd hated that nasty hulking cow. She and that damned bird. She'd thought it was funny, watching him sweat in fear of that vicious predator on her arm. Ternathian Imperial falcons were big, mean birds that could tear a man's face off. There'd been no way to feed it to the sharks alive like its owner, but he could always hope it had at least been crisped in the explosion.

He poured a celebratory glass of wine and sipped in genuine delight, visualizing the crown princess' brief horror—but not, one could always hope, *too* brief horror—when she discovered what Chava's shark Caller had summoned to meet her. He chuckled aloud at that thought and dipped up a spoonful of the prized Ylani caviar. He spread it on a crisp cracker, biting into the delicacy with gusto and sipping more wine. Ah, such simple joys were finally sweet, once more, without the bitterness of rancor and hatred on his tongue.

He was mentally planning the move back into his quarters in the Grand Palace when the door crashed open. He jerked around and snarled at Acolyte Raka, who was stumbling into the room, white-faced and shaking. Water dripped from his clothes onto the thick carpets.

"Your Eminence—"

"What the hell do you think you're doing?" he shouted. "I told you I wasn't to be disturbed!"

Before he could snatch up something to throw at the intruder, the Acolyte gasped out, "I tried to stop them. I swear by Bergahl I did! They just tossed me into the ocean. I barely survived!"

"What are you babbling about?"

Before the shaking fool could answer, the door flew open again. Soundlessly.

Other acolytes sauntered into the room. But, no, they *weren't* acolytes. They wore the garb of his own Order, and they were strong, obviously capable men...yet he didn't recognize a single face.

Wineglass and caviar crashed to the floor as he whirled towards one of the chamber's other doors, but he wasn't fast enough.

The men spread around the room blocking all exits—even the windows. He turned, tried to lunge for a weapon—

—and froze in place.

A blade protruded from his belly. A strange symbol was embossed on the pommel. Ever so slowly the Seneschal recognized it as a piece from the Arcanan replica weapon set he'd supplied. A rough twist tore it out of his gut and spilled more than wine on his fine rugs.

*　　*　　*

Drindel wanted more than anything in his life to run. The men with him were indubitably in Service to Uromathia, and they were worse than sharks. The Acolyte Raka, older in death than he'd seemed while alive, had at least stopped that awful neck bubbling.

Remarkably, few others had even noticed their entry. Drindel began to suspect the team he was with of boredom. Their Masker had covered their initial approach, but not even a Masker could pass a dozen men through the halls of the Seneschal's residence without being seen. Their acolyte robes had gotten them through unchallenged, though, and the Masker could easily cover them once again if they left through the chamber's windows and simply filtered through the ornate garden down to the shore of the strait. Drindel didn't quite understand why Raka hadn't raised the alarm or warned his fellow acolytes he might be pursued. Apparently it hadn't occurred to him that they might be right on his heels. Perhaps he could be excused for not thinking that bit through, though. He hadn't realized he was a dead man from the moment he'd stayed on the pleasure boat instead of joining the Talent-masked assault team who'd climbed the ropes up the side of the *Peregrine* and proceeded beyond the range of the Masker's focused Talent, but he'd probably caught on pretty quickly when one of the other Uromathians kicked him over the side for the sharks.

Who had somehow missed devouring him...among others.

Drindel had been distracted in the slow transit back to dock. Monsters he didn't know were devouring his sharks, and it had taken every bit of his ill-used Talent to conceal the failure from the Masker. Many, many sharks were fighting for their lives even now in that teeming deep-water channel of the Ylani Strait. He took up the field glasses from the dead Seneschal's table and examined the surface of the water more closely. The flickering bits of charred boat debris didn't interest him. Only the fins mattered. Drindel desperately wanted to know what was eating his sharks.

The glasses weren't good enough and the night was too dark. He couldn't make out enough in the waves—not beyond the reach of the fires which were finally dying, at least—to guess at the fight under the surface. But the search effort was all wrong. In fact, one of the two destroyers had obviously abandoned the search entirely. It was headed back into port—at a speed which was dangerously high in such crowded waters—and Drindel's heart skipped. He could only think of one reason an Imperial Ternathian destroyer wouldn't still be scouring the water for survivors.

We missed the princess. That was his first thought. *They're going to kill me,* was the second.

"Boy!"

A gruff voice called him away from the ocean disaster. It was the Masker, and Drindel made himself set the glasses down as steadily as he could. They didn't know the sharks hadn't finished off all the *Peregrine*'s survivors—not yet, at least. They *couldn't* know yet, and Drindel did his very best to calm his panic.

"Sir," he replied as respectfully as he knew how. He still didn't know any names, and they'd refused the offer of his own. He regretted very much now that offer of his own name.

The Masker set a fisherman's wet bag in his nearly limp hands. He took it without thinking and checked the seals and closure out of pure reflex. The bag was intended to hold wet bait or a fresh catch, and his stomach clenched as he looked down at the Seneschal and realized what was in it. Obviously the others had been busy while he'd been staring out at the channel, but the outside of the bag—thank goodness—was dry.

Drindel was the only member of the group not dressed as a Bergahldian. He was just in normal fisherfolk clothes—of good quality, of course; Maman wouldn't supply him with anything less, but it was much the same as anything worn by the men who harvested the two seas to feed Tajvana.

The others had covered up in acolyte robes after leaving the boat, which was why he was certain they'd planned to kill the Seneschal all along. The robes fitted them far too well to be a last minute improvisation. Of course, no one had mentioned any of that to *him*, which suggested some very unpleasant possibilities, but it seemed their plans didn't—yet—include anything that involved his own demise.

As long as he didn't piss them off, at least.

Drindel weighed the bag containing Faroayn Raynarg's heart in his hands, uncertain of his next move.

"Go." The Masker pushed him towards the back stair. "Feed it to your fish. It's the sort of thing an Arcanan would do to counter their Healers."

Drindel stumbled the first step and then ran. Laughter followed him for a few steps, until his range from the Masker deadened all sound from the Seneschal's office, but he didn't care. Let them think he was just new to this sort of work, and that he'd had no experience of getting his own hands dirty. Let them laugh—that was fine with him! All Drindel wanted was to get far, far away, and hope no one ever remembered his name as having any connection to this.

That Seneschal had been a powerful man, who'd been allied with Uromathia...and whose heart Drindel now carried in a fisherman's bag.

If *he* could become...inconvenient to the Emperor of Uromathia, then so could a Shark Caller who knew too much and whose sharks had failed in their task. Under the circumstances, all he wanted was to be somewhere else.

Quickly.

*   *   *

When the door at the end of the corridor opened and Bok vos Hoven realized who was coming toward his cell, he slid onto the floor so quickly he left skin on the side of his bunk. That didn't matter. His skin was no longer his own to worry over. He lay kissing the floor while a multitude of footsteps echoed their way down the long corridor that led to his cell.

He wanted to offer an apology for having inconvenienced His Exalted Line Lord, Skollo vos Diffletak, by having been placed in a cell so far from the door, but that inconvenience was so minor beside all his other offenses, he didn't even dare whisper it. That would only put His Exalted Line Lord to the additional effort of having to respond to it. So he lay with his belly on the floor and awaited his doom.

Footsteps came to a halt beside his cell door. His Exalted Line Lord hadn't arrived alone. Vos Hoven hadn't expected him to, since no Line Lord ever traveled anywhere without a retinue of the Loyal ready and waiting to serve in whatever manner His Exalted Line Lordship required. On visits of great import, His Exalted Line Lord would travel with a retinue of a hundred or more retainers; the higher the status of the one visited, the greater the number of retainers.

On a visit to view the unworthy, His Exalted Line Lord would travel with the minimum number required to ensure His Exalted Line Lordship's personal comfort and preserve his public status as a man of great worth and importance. Vos Hoven had counted ten retainers—the absolute minimum necessary to preserve His Exalted Line Lordship's dignity on an errand of little or no worth.

Bok vos Hoven grieved that he'd forced His Exalted Line Lordship to interrupt his sacred schedule. He wasn't worth even the ten retainers, let alone the man they served. A man who'd dandled the nephew who'd failed him so utterly on his knee, expecting great things of this new babe born to his line. Now that nephew had failed his mother, his father, his Line Lord, his line, and his entire caste so profoundly, he could not—ever again—so much as view their faces.

"Vermin," the voice of the man he'd once called uncle hissed down from His Exalted Line Lordship's height.

"L-Lord," he cringed, barely whimpering the word in just enough of a whisper to let the man standing in judgment know he'd been heard.

"Do not degrade my title by uttering it with fouled lips!"

Vos Hoven shook his head frantically, leaving bloody scrapes in his nose and cheeks. They wouldn't have time to heal.

"The officers sitting in judgment upon Jasak Olderhan have reached their verdict."

He held his breath. He hadn't heard that the son of a jackal's trial had gone to deliberations already. Now he waited, breathless, to hear the outcome. He'd entered that trial with only one purpose. Had he succeeded? Or failed, yet again?

"The son of a demon has been acquitted. Never again profane our line with your worthless blood."

His Exalted Line Lordship turned on his heel and strode away. His retainers filed past Bok's cell. One of them, he had no idea which, tossed something into the cell with him. It bounced with a metallic clang and skidded to a halt against his brow. The knife was so sharp it creased his scalp with a thin line of blood.

When His Exalted Line Lordship and all ten retainers had retreated through the doorway at the end of that long corridor, Bok vos Hoven sat up.

He picked up the knife. It was heartlessly plain: just a steel blade and a wooden handle. He wasn't allowed the honor of dying with a beautiful knife in his hand. He hadn't earned that honor, and he closed his eyes, so deeply shamed he could barely breathe.

He took solace in the knowledge that His Exalted Line Lord would never rest until the man who'd just been acquitted had paid for his part in his Line's disgrace. He took solace, as well, in knowing that the great plan he'd been a part of, that he'd failed so dismally, was still in place.

The Mythalan officers in the field now were only a small portion of that great plan, which would reshape the Union of Arcana in ways no one living outside Mythal could even imagine, on this ordinary day. But Bok vos Hoven could. And because he could, he wept, for he'd denied himself the chance to birth that world he could see so clearly in his mind's eye.

I offer apology for all the failures I have committed against thee, Bok vos Hoven told the ancestors who would stand in judgment over him in just a few moments, and kissed the knife in his hands.

Then slashed his throat.

The pain and the death that rose to meet him were a relief. This death would free His Lordship for the great task at hand, and so Bok vos Hoven lay bleeding out on the stone floor... and smiled.

PUBLISHER'S NOTE

Expanded versions of the Glossary and
Cast of Characters are available online at
www.baen.com/theroadtohellextras

GLOSSARY

Aeravas—a Sharonian city in Harkala; located in approximately the same place as Shiraz, Iran.

Alathia—one of the provinces of the Ternathian Empire, it is the trans-temporal analog of Italy.

Andara—the Arcanan equivalent of the continent of North America. Andara is the home of the warrior kingdoms of the Andarans and provides the backbone of the Union of Arcana's military.

Arau Mountains—the Sharonian analog of the Yoblonovy Khrebet mountain range east of Lake Baikal.

Arcana—the home universe and Earth of the Union of Arcana. Its physics are based on "magic."

Arcanan days of the week—Firsday, Seconday, Thirday, Fourday, Fiday, Sixday, Sevday.

Arcanan Expeditionary Force (AEF)—the Arcanan force sent to attack Sharona's frontier universes under Commander of Two Thousand Mayrkos Harshu.

Arpathia—the Sharonian analog of the area stretching from the Caspian Sea through the Siberian tundra north of Mongolia to the Pacific Ocean. While there is no united government for this region, it is often referred to as the Septentrion, which is a trade union developed by the septs (see Septs and Septentrion, below).

Aruncas of the Sword—the Uromathian god of war.

Automoticar—a new, personal form of transport recently introduced in the Union of Arcana; essentially, small, private sliders capable of delivering individuals to their destinations.

Baranal—literally, "protector" in old Andaran. A baranal is the individual responsible for protecting a shardon (see below).

Barican Valley—the Sharonian analog of Mason Valley, Nevada.

Barkesh—a city in Sharona located at the approximate trans-temporal site of Barcelona, Spain.

Bearcat Valley—the Sharonian analog of Reveille Valley, Nevada.

Benteria Union—a republic in New Ternath (North America) consisting of most of the states of Kansas, Oklahoma, Missouri, Arkansas, and Illinois.

Bergahl—the dominant deity of the Order of Bergahl. Bergahl is a god of both war and justice. His order is a militant one, which has traditionally provided the judges and law enforcement mechanism in the Kingdom of Othmaliz.

Bergahl's Comforters—an ironic nickname for Berghal's Dagger (see below).

Bergahl's Dagger—a highly militant cult within the Order of Bergahl. The Dagger was officially disbanded over a hundred years ago.

Bernith Channel—the Sharonian analog of the English Channel.

Bernith Island—the Sharonian analog of the island of Great Britain.

Bernithian Highlands—the Sharonian analog of Scotland.

Bile toad—a large, venomous ugly, ground-dwelling amphibian from Mythal on Arcana. Bile toads are a brilliant green in color with black "leopard" bars and represent an arcane genetic manipulation experiment which went awry and escaped the laboratory.

Bison—the steam-powered tractor portion of the Ternathian Army's recently adopted (and still in process of development) mechanized transport. The Bison comes in two models: Model A is the personnel transport while Model B is a pure tractor intended to tow heavy loads cross country. Both are in 20 to 25-ton range and very powerful units. The original Mark I Bison was coal fired; the newer Mark II variant uses kerosene as its fuel and has over three times the operational radius of the Mark I.

Bitter Lake City—the Sharonian analog of Salt Lake City, Utah.

Bitter Lake—the Sharonian analog of the Great Salt Lake, Utah.

Bitterblack—the Andaran name for coffee. See also Mythalan tea and cherryberry.

Black Rhino—the most powerful bulldozer manufactured by Ram's Horn Heavy Equipment (see below). See also "Ricathian Buffalo" and "Devil Buff."

Blade of Ibral—the Sharonian analog of the Gallipoli Peninsula.

blood debt—an ancient Ransaran concept of justice based on the principle of "an eye for an eye and a tooth for a tooth." It also has personal connotations of vengeance, but has been renounced by modern Ransarans as a barbaric and horrific basis for true justice. The term is sometimes still used as a slang phrase to describe a highly personal form of redress for wrongful actions.

blood vendetta—Shurkhali blood vendetta is triggered when a massive miscarriage of justice leads to someone's death. Shaylar Nargra-Kolmayr's apparent murder by Arcanans triggers a blood vendetta reaction in every Shurkhali alive.

Bolakin, Queens of—the queens who collectively rule the ten Bolakini city-states which control the southern shore of the Mbisi Sea.

Bolakini Strait—the Sharonian analog of the Strait of Gibraltar.

Book of Secrets—one of the two seminal holy books of the Mythalan *shakira* caste.

Book of the Double-Three—the holy book of the Church of the Double Triads, the imperial religion of Ternathia.

Book of the Shakira—one of the two seminal holy books of the Mythalan *shakira* caste.

Broken Shoe Butte—the Sharonian analog for Elephant Butte, Utah.

Busnara—the capital city of the Uromathian Empire, located approximately on the site of Changsha, China.

Calirath—the imperial dynasty of Ternathia. The Caliraths have ruled Ternathia for more than four millennia.

Carotal—the Sharonian analog of Ft. Stockton, Texas.

Cejyo—the Sharonian's port city in the Haysam Universe at the trans-temporal location of Wenzhou, China.

Celaryon II—King of Ancient Ternathia who negotiated the treaty which bound Ternathia and Farnalia as allies in the year 203 of the Ternathian calendar.

Central Bank of Mythal—the largest, wealthiest, and most powerful of the Mythalan banks. The CBM, unlike the private Mythalan banks, is directly subject to government supervision, and a full third of the seats on its Board of Directors are held by government appointees.

Cerakondian Mountains—the Sharonian analog of the Altai Mountains.

Cetacean Institute/Shurkhali Aquatic Realms Embassy—the Sharonian research institute and embassy founded and operated by Shaylar's mother, Shalassar Kolmayr-Brintal, who is a cetacean translator. Similar embassies serve the sentient great apes and higher primates of Ricathia (Africa), Uromathia (Asia), and New Farnal (South America, with its New World monkeys).

Chairifon—the Sharonian analog of the Eurasian supercontinent.

Chalar—an Arcanan maritime empire, based on the island of Chalar (Cuba) and dominating the Chalaran Sea (Caribbean Sea) and Gulf of Hilmar (Gulf of Mexico). Chalar is the dominant naval power of Arcana.

Chalgyn Consortium—survey company that employs Jathmar Nargra and Shaylar Nargra-Kolmayr. The Chalgyn Consortium is an independent survey company based in Shurkhal.

chan—"veteran" in Ternathian. This is an honorific indicating someone who is currently or has been a member of the Ternathian military.

Chansyu—a creature of Arcanan legend, originating in Ransar, the chansyu is a rough analog of the ancient Greece phoenix. Like the phoenix, the chansyu represents an eternal cycle of life-death-rebirth. Unlike the phoenix, the chansyu is a two-headed winged lion which is reborn in a flash of lightning rather than fire.

Chansyu hut—the Arcanan analog of a Quonset hut, erected quickly using pre-stored spellware.

Chemparas—a major city in the Arcanan universe of Basilisk at the portal connecting Basilisk to Manticore, located approximately on the site of Addis Ababa.

Chernoth—a small city in the Benterian Union located approximately on the site of Hays, Kansas. Location of the portal between Traisum and Kelsayr.

Cherryberry—the more common Arcanan name for coffee and the one customarily used by Ransarans. See also Mythalan tea and bitterblack.

Chindar—a small town in the Kingdom of West New Ternath approximately on the site of Comstock, Texas.

Chinthai—a Sharonian breed of horses very similar to Percherons.

Chuldair tree—Sharonian analog of the kapok tree.

Code of Housip—the formal statement of Andaran honor obligations attributed (probably apocryphally) to Housip Kerellia, the drafter of the Kerellian Accords.

Commandery—see High Commandery.

Conclave—The formal multi-nation crisis-management organization established when the first portal opened in Sharona. Its members are the heads of state of every sovereign nation in Sharona and, on paper, Sharona's new, independent colony universes.

Coyote Canyon—the Sharonian analog of Glen Canyon, Arizona.

Cratak Mountains—the Arcanan analog of the Sierra Nevada Mountains.

"Cross the Vandor"—the Sharonian analog of the phrase "crossing the Rubicon" as an expression of irrevocable commitment.

Crown of fire—the Sharonian term for our own volcanically active "ring of fire" in the Pacific.

Cutcha—a (very) derogatory Uromathian term for a woman.

Daggerstone—a sarkolis crystal used to store short-range combat spells. Maximum range is no more than twenty feet, and they are impossible to conceal from any Gifted person, but they can store antipersonnel spells of great power.

Dalazan Rain Forest—Sharonian analog of the Amazon rain forest.

Dalazan River—the Sharonian analog of the Amazon River.

Darnifa—a Ransaran republic in the Andaran analog of China consisting of Xinjiang Province and the extreme northwestern in and of Gansu Province.

Darylis Republic—a republic in New Farnalia consisting of southern Nicaragua, Costa Rica, Panama, Colombia, Ecuador, Peru north of (and including) Lima, Venezuela, Guyana, Suriname, and the extreme northern portion of Brazil north of the Amazon River.

Daykassian—the premier Arpathian breed of cavalry horse. Very similar to the Turkoman.

Dead Mule Valley—the Sharonian analog of Depression Valley, Nevada.

Delkrath Mountains—a mountain range in Delkrathia Province; the Sharonian analog of the Santa de Guararrma Mountains of Spain.

Delkrathia Province—a province of the Ternathian Empire north of Narhath and east of Teramandor; it consists of the equivalent of central Spain, from just south of Madrid to the Bay of Biscay.

Devil Buff—another name for the Ricathian Buffalo, or Cape Buffalo.

Djadja berry—a type of Uromathian persimmon, commonly used to treat fabric to produce heavy duty, water-resistant, and mold-resistant clothing for dailywear and traditional ceremonial garb favored by Eniathians.

Dosaru—the Uromathian god of justice. Also known as "Dosaru of the Watching Eyes" and "Dosaru of the Scales."

Duchy of Wahred—a duchy in New Farnalia consisting of a lobe of northern Peru and extreme northwestern Brazil, most of Bolivia, Chile north of Mount Aconcagua, a portion of northwestern Argentina, and the extreme northwestern corner of Paraguay.

Dynsari Sea—Arcanan analog of the South China Sea.

Dynsari—Arcanan analog of Borneo.

Ekros—an Arcanian demon; the equivalent of our own Demon Murphy.

Elath—an Andaran kingdom whose territory covers roughly the area of the United States as far west as Kansas and Nebraska and extends as far north as Newfoundland.

Elder Triad—the most ancient members of the Ternathian Double Triads, consisting of the original Ternathian ruling gods: Vothan, Shalana, and Marnilay.

Emergency Transportation System—a Sharona-wide teleportation system capable of transporting very small groups of passengers. The ETS is designed for the emergency use of heads of state and diplomats in time-critical crises.

Emergency Voice Network—a planet-wide network of Voices capable of linking all Sharonian heads of state in a real-time conference.

Emperor Edvar Mountains—the Sharonian analog of the Pyrenees Mountains.

Empress Wailyana II—Wailyana Calirath, Empress of Ternathia, 4172–4207. Generally referred to as Wailyana the Great.

Eniath—a technically Uromathian Kingdom in the eastern region of the analog of Mongolia. A land renowned for its falcons, its people are as much Arpathian as Uromathian and not particularly fond of the Empire of Uromathia.

Eraythas Mountains—the Sharonian analog of the Cantabrian Mountains along the Biscay Coast of Spain.

Erkahlan—a coastal Sharonian city in the Republic of Faltharia in New Ternath, on the site of Norfolk, Virginia. The location of Shosara, the seaport developed in Traisum to reach the Chernoth Portal between Traisum and Kelsayr.

Ermandia—a province of the Ternathian Empire, corresponding to Austria.

Erthain the Great—semi-legendary founder of the House of Calirath and the Ternathian Empire.

Esferia—the Sharonian analog of Cuba.

Estafel—the capital city of the Ternathian Empire.

Evanos Ocean—the Arcanan name for the Pacific Ocean.

Falcon (abbreviated TF)—Ternathian unit of currency. Coins are issued in triple falcons, double falcons, falcons, half-falcons, fifth-falcons, and twentieth-falcons (commonly called twenties).

Faltharia—a republic in New Ternath, located in the general vicinity of the Great Lakes. The homeland of Jathmar Nargra.

Farnalia—the Sharonian analog of the Scandinavian peninsula.

Farnalian Empire—a Sharonian empire stretching from its home Farnalia across the northern periphery of the Sharonian analog of Europe to the analog of the Sea of Japan.

Farnalian Sea—the Sharonian analog of the Baltic Sea.

Farsh Danuth—an Arcanan kingdom ruling the area between the Farshian Sea in the west, the Tankara Gulf in the east, the Shansir Mountains in the northwest, and the Urdanha Mountains in the northeast. Farsh Danuth is Mythalan in population, societal institutions, and attitudes.

Farshal—a Hilmaran Kingdom in Arcana whose territory includes the analog of Guyana, Surinam, and French Guiana.

Farshian Plain—Arcanan analog of the Red Sea coastal plains of Saudi Arabia.

Farshian Sea—Arcanan analog of the Red Sea.

Finger Sea—the Sharonian analog of the Red Sea.

Firsoma—Uromathian goddess of wisdom and fate. Also known as "Firsoma of the Shears" and "The Cutter."

Fist of Bolakin—the Sharonian analog of the Rock of Gibraltar.

Flicker—a Talented Sharonian capable of teleporting, or "Flicking," relatively small objects over long distances with considerable precision.

Flight—an Arcanan Air Force formation consisting of four combat dragons, organized into two pairs of wingmen.

Fort Brithik—Sharonian portal fort in the universe of Thermyn, covering the outbound portal to New Uromath. Located roughly on the trans-temporal site of Lincoln, Nebraska.

Fort Emperor Erthain—the Imperial Ternathian Army's premier military base on the continent of Chairifon (Europe) in the province of Karmalia (Austria).

Fort Ghartoun—Arcanan portal fort (formerly Fort Raylthar) in the universe of Thermyn, covering the inbound portal from Failcham. Located roughly on the trans-temporal site of Carson City, Nevada.

Fort Losaltha—the Sharonian portal fortress protecting the entry portal of the Salym Universe. Located approximately at the trans-temporal site of Barcelona, Spain.

Fort Mosanik—Sharnonian portal fort in the universe of Karys, covering the outbound portal to Failcham. Located roughly on the trans-temporal site of Astana, Kazakhstan.

Fort Rycharn—the Arcanan coastal enclave in the universe of Gharys, serving the swamp portal to Hell's Gate. Located roughly on the trans-temporal site of Belém. Brazil.

Fort Salby—Sharonian portal fort in the universe of Traisum, covering the outbound portal to Karys. Located roughly on the trans-temporal site of the Sharonian city of Narshalla, or our own Medina, Saudi Arabia.

Fort Saylar River—the Sharonian analog of the Pecos River.

Fort Shaylar—Sharonian portal fort in New Uromath commanded by Company-Captain Halifu.

Fort Talon—Arcanan fortress in Erthos located roughly on the trans-temporal site of Ust Ilimsk, Siberia.

Fort Tharkoma—Sharonian portal fort in the universe of Salym covering the outbound portal to Traisum. Located roughly on the trans-temporal site of Sofia, Bulgaria.

Fort Wyvern—the Arcanan fortress and base in the universe of Gharys at the entry portal from the universe of Erthos. Located roughly on the trans-temporal site of Manzanilla, Cuba.

Gariyan VI—the Ternathian emperor who began the phased withdrawal from the easternmost provinces of the Ternathian Empire.

Gariyan VII—the son of Gariyan VI; the last Ternathian emperor to rule from Tajvana.

Garmoy, Sunhold of—a Sharonian dukedom in southeastern Uromathia. Roughly analog to the country of Laos.

Garouoma—a Sharonian city located on the Narhathan Peninsula; roughly analog to Cordoba, Spain.

Garsulthan—a Manisthuan word which translates roughly as "real politics." Its practitioners believe that all international relations ultimately rest upon the balance of military power and that morality and ethics take second (or third) place to that reality when formulating foreign policy.

Gartasa Mountains—the Sharonian analog of the Iberian Mountains in Spain, separating Teramandor from Delkrathia.

Garth Showma—a large and powerful duchy and city in the universe of New Arcana. The city is located at the Arcanan analog of Niagara Falls and the headquarters site of the Arcanan Army.

Garth Showma House—the townhouse and official residence of the Duke of Garth Showma in the city of Portalis.

Garth Showma Institute—the Academy established by Magister Halathyn vos Dulainah at the site of Showma Falls in New Arcana. It is the second largest magical academy anywhere and its prestige is rapidly overtaking that of the Mythal Falls Academy.

Garthan—the non-magic users of the Mythalan culture. They make up at least eighty percent of the Mythalan population but possess only extremely circumscribed legal rights.

Gerynth—a city in the southern portion of the Andaran Kingdom of Yanko roughly analogous to Durango, Mexico.

Goose Mountains—Sharonian analog of the Coastal Ranges Mountains in the Pacific Northwest.

Gorhadyn Protocol—a Mythalan assassination technique.

Graholis—Andaran god of chaos.

Grand Ternathian Canal—the Sharonian analog of the Suez Canal.

Graystone River—the Sharonian analog of Bad River, South Dakota.

Great Hilmar River—the Arcanan analog of the Amazon River.

Grocyra—the Sharonian analog of Siberia.

Grocyran Plain—the Sharonian analog of the West Siberian Plain.

Gulf of Cordara—the Sharonian analog of the Gulf of Mexico.

Gulf of Shurkhal—the Sharonian analog of the Gulf of Aden.

Gyrfellan Plateau—the Arcanan analog of the Najd Plateau of Saudi Arabia.

Gystair Mountains—the Sharonian analog of the Gabbs Range Mountains, Nevada.

Gystair's Valley—the Sharonian analog of Gabbs Valley, Nevada.

Hahnahk Mountains—the Arcanan analog of the Hawaiian Islands.

Haimath Island—the home of Drindel Usar, it is the trans-temporal analog of Hainan Island, China.

Halnach and Welnahr revolver—the standard sidearm of the Imperial Ternathian Army, a 7-shot, .436 caliber weapon with very good stopping power.

Hammerfell Lake—the Arcanan analog of Lake Huron.

Hanahk Mountains—Arcanan analog of the Hejaz Mountains.

Hancytha—Hilmaran goddess of mercy and plenty.

Hanthyria—Sharonian analog of the Greek island of Andros.

Hanyl—a republic in New Ternath (North America) which consists of eastern Alberta, Saskatchewan, Manitoba, and the Northwest Territory.

Harkala—the Sharonian analog of India. The ancient Harkalian Empire extended from India through Afghanistan and into Iran.

Hell's Gate—the Sharonian name assigned to the universe where their survey personnel first encountered the Arcanans. Later adopted by Arcana, as well.

Hesmiryan Sea—the Arcanan analog of the Mediterranean.

High Commandery—the high command of the Union of Arcanan's Army. Essentially, the analog of the Pentagon and the Chiefs of Staff, rolled into one. Traditionally, the High Commandery is heavily dominated by senior Andaran officers.

High Rock City—the Sharonian analog of Albuquerque, New Mexico.

Hilmar—the Arcanan analog of South America.

Hinorean Empire—the smaller of the two empires which dominate Uromath. The Hinorean Empire includes the Sharonian analog of western India and Bangladesh, Burma, Thailand, the Philippines, and Malaysia.

Hook of Ricathia—the Sharonian analog of the southern side of the Strait of Gibraltar; the trans-temporal equivalent of Morocco and Ceuta, Spain.

Horn of Ricathia—the Sharonian analog of the Horn of Africa between the Gulf of Aden and the Indian Ocean.

Hummer—a magically enhanced bird developed from normal hummingbirds by Arcanan sorcerers as high-speed, highly aggressive "carrier pigeons."

Hurkaym—a small town/communications post located at the trans-temporal site of Palermo, Sicily, in the Salym Universe expressly as a Voice link between Fort Tharkoma and Fort Losaltha.

Hurlbane—a Ricathian deity associated with the Queens of Bolakin. She is a warrior goddess who protects the Bolakini (see Bolakin, Queens of), and her clergy have always been very influential in the Bolakini city-states. Hurlbane's High Priestess, for example, advised the Queens of Bolakin to ally with Ternathia thousands of years ago.

Hyrain Valley—the Sharonian analog of Tikaboo Valley, Nevada.

Hyrythian Sea—the Arcanan analog of the Mediterranean Sea.

Ibral—ancient Sharonian god of earthquakes worshiped in Nessia (Greece).

Ibral Strait—the Sharonian analog of the Dardanelles.

Ibral's Blade—the Sharonian analog of the Gallipoli Peninsula.

Imperial Board of Healers (IBH)—a board created to set medical policy for the Sharonan Empire at the behest of Empress Varena Calirath.

Imperial Ternathian Peregrine—a highly intelligent peregrine falcon bred specifically for the Ternathian imperial house. They approach but do not quite reach the intelligence level of humans or cetaceans. The breed (which was crossed with gyrfalcons) is by far the largest of the peregrine species.

Indelbu—Ternathian port city; the trans-temporal analog of Belfast.

Inkara—the Arcanan analog of the island of Great Britain.

Inland Seas—the Sharonian analog of the Great Lakes.

Iryshakhia Islands—the Arcanan analog of the Philippine Islands.

Iryshakhian Sea—Arcanan analog of the Philippine Sea.

Isseth—a kingdom situated between Harkala and Arpathia in the Sharonian equivalent of Kashmir, Tajikistan, and northeastern Pakistan.

Isseth-Liada—a portal exploration company owned/sponsored by the Kingdom of Isseth.

Ithal Mountains—the Sharonian analog of the Hejaz Mountains.

Janu River—the Sharonian analog of the Rhine River.

Jarrca—a Ransaran field sport combining elements of field hockey, soccer, and lacrosse.

Jerdyn River—the Arcanan analog of Bad River, South Dakota.

Jerekhas—the Sharonian analog of the island of Sicily.

Journeyman—a formal rank for Arcanan practitioners of sorcery who have completed their formal education but have not contributed a new application of sorcery. The majority of sorcerers do not progress beyond this rank. (See also "novice," "magister," and "magistron.")

Judaih—a city in Sharona located on the site of Ghat, Libya.

Judiciary General's Office—the Union of Arcana military's equivalent of the Judge Advocate General. The section of the military responsible for enforcing military regulations and law and prosecuting those accused of wrongdoing in uniform.

Jukali—a volcanic island on Sharona; the Sharonian analog of Krakatoa.

Kanaiya—a duchy in central Lokan, consisting of much of the central portion of the equivalent of Manitoba. Its capital, also called Kanaiya, is located on the eastern shore of Lake Kanaiya.

Karmalia—the Sharonian analog of Hungary.

Kerellian Accords—the Andaran military accords drafted centuries ago by the Andaran Commander of Armies Housip Kerellia and adopted by the Union of Arcana as the official standard for treatment of POWs and as the code of conduct to be followed by Arcanan personnel who become POWs.

Kershai—the ancient Mythalan word for "lightning"; the release code for a black dragon's breath weapon.

Kingdom of Limathia—a Sharonian kingdom in southern New Farnalia consisting of most of Argentina and Chile south of Mount Aconcagua.

Kingdom of Shartha—a Ricathian kingdom in Sharona; it occupies roughly the area of Somalia, eastern Ethiopia, and most of Kenya. (See also "Lubnasi.")

Kingdom of Valsha—a small kingdom in the Yamali Mountains. Its people are a mix of Uromathian and Harkalan genes, but are culturally Harkalians.

Kosal River—the Arcanan analog of Spain's Ebro River.

Kraythnar Federation—an Arcanan federation of almost a dozen small states occupying the analog of Tajikistan and Kyrgyzstan. Some are kingdoms, some are principalities, some are republics or direct democracies. The Federation is culturally Ransaran, but tends to be much more socially conservative than most of Ransara. It is violently anti-Mythalan in sentiment.

Kyaira cotton—Sharonian name for the fiber of the Chuldair tree.

Kyaria Island—the Sharonian analog of the Island of Java.

Kythia—a region of Arcana roughly analog to Gujarat, India.

Lake Arau—the Sharonian analog of Lake Baikal.

Lake Kanaiyar—the Arcanan analog of Lake Winnipeg.

Lake Shyngilar—Sharonian analog of Lake Washington in Washington State.

Lake Syrana—the Sharonian analog of Walker Lake, Nevada.

Lake Wernisk—Sharonian analog of Lake Winnipeg in the Republic of Hanyl.

Lake Wind Daughter—the Arcanan analog of Lake Michigan.

Larakesh—the site of the first Sharonian trans-temporal portal on the Ylani Sea. The Sharonian analog of Varna, Bulgaria.

Large-mind—the Sharonian cetaceans' name for blue whales.

Larkima—the ancient Mythalan word for "strangle"; the release code for a yellow dragon's breath weapon.

Levin bolt—a potent Arcanan combat magic; a lightning bolt.

Lifter—a Sharonian telekinetic Talent. Most Lifters can handle only very small objects; a very small percentage of exceptionally powerful Lifters can manipulate objects weighing as much as thirty or forty pounds.

Limathia—a kingdom in New Farnal, located between the Sharonian analog of Chile and Argentina. One of the Directors of the Portal Authority is from Limathia.

Lissia—the Sharonian analog of Australia; the main landmass of the Lissian Republic, which also includes New Zealand, the islands of Oceania, and a fair percentage of the South Pacific Islands of Polynesia. Shaylar Nargra-Kolmayr's mother is Lissian.

Lokan—an Andaran kingdom whose territory covers the equivalent of most of Canada and Alaska, but sweeps down to include Oregon and most of California, as well.

Losaltha—the Sharonian city located at the entry portal of the Salym universe. Located roughly at the trans-temporal location of Barcelona, Spain.

Lubnasi—an ancient independent city-state located within the boundaries of the Kingdom of Shartha (see above) in Sharona. Like the Bolakini city-states (see "Bolakin, Queens of"), Lubnasi was an ancient treaty partner of Ternathia, which is the historic guarantor of its independence.

Lugathia—a province of the Ternathian Empire, equivalent to France.

Lusaku Island—the Sharonian analog of Sumatra.

Lyndara Mountains—the Sharonian analog of the San Antonio Mountains, Nevada.

Magister—a formal title earned by Arcanan practitioners of sorcery. It requires the completion of an arduous formal education and the creation of at least one new, previously unknown application of sorcery. There are additional ranks within the broader title of magister. (See also "novice," "journeyman," and "magistron.")

Magistron—a formal title, equivalent to "magister," but reserved for those whose Gift and training are specialized for working with living things. There are additional ranks within the broader title of magistron. (See also "novice," "journeyman," and "magister.")

Mahritha—the Arcanan-explored universe connecting to Hell's Gate. Named by Magister Halathyn in his wife's honor.

Malbar—a Sharonian multiverse coastal city in the Madahn Association in western New Ternath on approximately the same site as Seattle, Washington.

Malbar Sound—the Sharonian analog of Puget Sound.

Manisthu Islands—the Arcanan analog of Japan.

Manisthu, Kingdom of—the dominant political unit of the Manisthu Islands.

Mark 10 rifle—the standard-issue bolt-action rifle of the Imperial Ternathian Army. It is a .40 caliber weapon with a 12-round detachable box magazine. Official designation is Rifle of 5047 from its year of introduction.

Mark 12 rifle—a specialist sniper's weapon built for the Imperial Ternathian Army. It is a .34 caliber weapon with a 34" barrel, firing a necked down version of the black powder Halnach and Welnahr .458 cartridge designed for Ricathan Buffalo and other dangerous big game. Official designation is Rifle of 5049 from its year of introduction.

Marnilay—a Sharonian goddess, "Sweet Marnilay the Maiden" is one of the Ternathian Double Triads, which are the foundation of the religion for at least half of Sharona, as Ternathia once controlled and/or colonized so much of that world.

Masked whales—the Arcanan term for orca.

Mbisi Sea—the Sharonian analog of the Mediterranean Sea.

Melwain the Great—the Andaran analog of King Arthur. Melwain lived well over a thousand years ago and is revered as the perfect example of Andaran honor.

Merikai—a Ransaran socialist republic roughly equivalent to southern Mongolia, China's central Gansu Province, and most of Neimongol Province.

Mind Healer—a Sharonian with a complex of Talents which permits him to treat mental disorders.

Mithanan—the Mythalan god of cosmic destruction.

Monarch Lake—the Arcanan analog of Lake Superior.

Monkey Tail Peninsula—Sharonian analog of the Malaysian Peninsula.

Mother Jambakol—an Arcanan evil goddess or demoness, both worshiped and feared in Hilmar. She is the personification of destruction, vengeance, and hatred.

Mother Marthea—a Sharonian deity. In the Shurkhali pantheon, she is revered as the water-bringer and life-bringer. She is called the Mother of Rivers, the Mother of Springs, and the Mother of the Sea. Revered as Mother of the Sea, she brings wealth in the form of pearls and coral, and watches over Shurkhali ships. She is viewed as a mother of abundance, whether from the sea, agricultural crops, or herds and flocks.

Motic—the shortened version of "automoticar" applied to a new class of personal vehicles recently introduced in the Union of Arcana.

Mount Chansyri—the Arcanan analog of Mount Dhaulagiri, Nepal. Birthplace of the legendary Ransaran chansyu two-headed, winged lion.

Mount Karek—a mountain peak west of Fort Salby in the Ithal Mountains.

mul—"warrior" in ancient Mythalan. As a part of a Mythalan's name, it indicates that he springs from one of the family lines of the *multhari* warrior caste. If the individual is also *shakira*, the higher caste indicator vos is used for most purposes instead of mul, but the proper formal usage is "vos and mul," so a *shakira* officer named Sythak of the Yuran line would properly be "Sythak vos and mul Yuran," but would normally be referred to as "Sythak vos Yuran."

Mulgethia—a Ternathian province, equivalent to Germany/Switzerland.

Multhari—the second most important caste group of Mythalan society. The *multhari* are the military caste. Some members of *multhari* are also *shakira*. These normally tend to dominate the upper ranks of the Mythalan military.

Myndakor Mountains—the Sharonian analog of the Rocky Mountains.

Mythal—the Arcanan analog of Africa. Mythal is dominated by a caste-based society which enshrines the total superiority of the shakira magic-using caste to the garthan caste of non-magic users.

Mythal Falls—the Arcanan analog of Victoria Falls.

Mythal Falls Academy—the oldest and most prestigious magical research and teaching Academy in Arcana.

Mythal River—the Arcanan analog of the Nile River and Zambezi River. By the will of the *shakira* and the work of many generations of *garthan* the two waterways are connected in the Arcana Prime Universe.

Mythalan Hegemony—the supranational Mythalan political body representing all Mythalan states. Effectively, the governing body of the Mythalan Empire, although there is no *official* Empire of Mythal.

Mythalan tea—the Arcanan analog of coffee, although it is most commonly known outside Mythal as cherryberry or bitterblack.

Mythal's Stool—Arcanan analog of the Sinai Peninsula.

Nansara Island—the Sharonian analog of Mercer Island, Lake Washington, Washington State.

Narash Islands—Sharonian analog of the Philippine Islands.

Narhath—an affluent province of the Ternathian Empire, consisting of the equivalent of southern Spain and Portugal.

Narhathan Peninsula—the Sharonian analog of the Iberian peninsula.

Narisma—an Arcanan republic roughly equivalent to Kazakhstan, minus the southwestern corner of Kazakhstan which belongs to the Kingdom of Shendisfal.

Narshalla—a Sharonian city located approximately on the site of Medina, Saudi Arabia.

Nessia—easternmost modern Ternathian province, equivalent to Greece.

New Farnal—the Sharonian analog of South America.

New Ramath—the port city built specifically to serve the rail line to Fort Tharkoma in Salym. Located on the trans-temporal equivalent of Durrës, Albania.

New Sharona—the first additional universe surveyed from Sharona.

New Ternath—the Sharonian analog of North America.

Norgamar Works—one of the great locomotive foundries of Sharona. A prime supplier to the Trans-temporal Express.

Nosikor—a Sharonian city located at the southwestern end of Lake Arau.

Novice—the title awarded to a Gifted student in Arcana. A student remains a novice, regardless of age, until his or her graduation from formal training. (See also "journeyman," "magister," and "magistron.")

Nymara—a city and important seaport on the Mbisi coast of Ricathia on the approximate site of Alexandria.

Order of Bergahl—the religious order of the war god Bergahl (see above). Because of its special position in the Kingdom of Othmaliz, the Kingdom's Seneschal must, by tradition, be selected from the Order's priesthood.

Osmaria—the Sharonian analog of Italy.

Othmaliz—the kingdom which dominates the eastern end of the Mbisi Sea and the outlet from the Ylani Sea. It is roughly equivalent to the western half of Turkey and the southern third of Bulgaria. Its capital is Tajvana, the ancient Imperial capital of the Ternathian Empire.

PAAF—the Portal Authority Armed Forces. The military units of various Sharonian nations placed under the Portal Authority's command for frontier security operations.

Padith River—the Sharonian analog of the lower Parana River (south of its junction with the Pantanal River) in Argentina.

Paditharyn—a city in the New Farnalia Kingdom of Limathia, located on the Padith River (Parana River) on approximately the same site as Rosario, Argentina.

Paerystia—a region of Arcana roughly equivalent to Oman.

Pairhys Island—the Sharonian analog of the Isle of Man. The premier training camp of the Imperial Ternathian Marines is located there.

Parnatha—Arcanan analog of the Italian peninsula.

Pigfish—Arcanan term for Bottlenosed dolphin.

Plotter—a Sharonian with the "Plotting" Talent. Plotting is a specialized sub-variant of the Mapping Talent which is particularly useful in military service. Plotters, unlike Mappers, detect the presence and location of living creatures, like human beings.

Pocket-ball—the Sharonian analog of billiards or pool.

Portal Hound—a Sharonian psionic sensitive to trans-temporal portals.

Portal wind—term for the wind which blows through portals whose aspects are at different altitudes in the universes they link. A portal wind blows at a constant velocity from the lower elevation to the higher and, depending on the elevation differential, can be extremely powerful.

Portals—portals are the naturally occurring access points between universes. In Sharonian practice, they are not formally classified by type; simply referred to by their measured size. Arcanan practice is somewhat more formalized (though essentially similar), using the following classifications broken down by portal diameter:

Class 1 = 0-1 mile.	Class 5 = 9-13 miles.
Class 2 = 1-2 miles.	Class 6 = 13-19 miles.
Class 3 = 2-5 miles.	Class 7 = 19-25 miles.
Class 4 = 5-9 miles.	Class 8 = 25-40 miles.

These classifications are based less on the diameter of the portal (although that is the most easily observable aspect of them) but rather by the strength with which they register on the spellware used to detect them.

Porter—a Sharonian Talent with the telekinetic ability to teleport (or "Port") passengers or limited freight via the Emergency Transportation System.

Princedom of Traylis—a monarchy in New Farnalia; analog of the area consisting of northern Brazil south of the Amazon River in the east and south of the Rio Negro River in the west, northeastern Bolivia (north of Trinidad) and central Brazil west of the Xingu River.

Projective—a Sharonian psionic with the ability to project detailed and accurate mental images for non-telepaths. All Projectives are also Voices, but less than .01% of all Voices are Projectives.

Puma Valley—the Sharonian analog of Stone Cabin Valley, Nevada.

Queen Kalthra's Lake—the Arcanan analog of Lake Ontario.

Queriz—a city in Arpathia, located at the equivalent position of Astana, Kazakhstan.

Queriz Depression—the Sharonian analog of the Caspian Depression.

Rahil—the Great Prophetess, the founder of and patron saint of mercy and healing in the Fellowship of Rahil, one of the dominant religions of Ransar.

Rahilian—an adherent of the Fellowship of Rahil.

Ram's Horn Heavy Equipment—the preeminent manufacturer of heavy construction equipment (bulldozers, steam shovels, etc.) of Sharona, headquartered in the Ternathian province of Mulgethia (Germany).

Rankadi—Mythalan ritual suicide.

Ransar—the Arcanan analog of Asia. Ransar is home to a highly humanistic, democratic, and innovative culture which places an extremely high value on the worth of the individual. This makes Ransar an uncomfortable fit with the Andaran warrior aristocracy at times, but an even more uncomfortable fit with Mythal's caste-based society. Ransarans enjoy the most comfortable life styles of any Arcanan social group.

Rathynoka River—the Sharonian analog of the Orinoco River in Venezuela.

Razinta Basin—the depression between the Gartasa Mountains, Teramandor Mountains, and Emperor Edvar Mountains of the Narhathan Peninsula; drained by the Razinta River.

Razinta River—the Sharonian analog of Spain's Ebro River.

Recon crystal—also called "RC"; a sarkolis-based reconnaissance device capable of recording and storing visual imagery and sounds within specified radii of the crystal. It is a *storage* device, and has no ability to transmit reconnaissance data across any distance.

Redberry—a vine fruit cultivated in Sharona similar to heirloom tomatoes.

Renaiyrton—the small city around the major shipyard in Traisum, located on the same site as the Sharonian seaport of Nymara (Alexandria).

Rendisphar—a republic in New Ternath (North America) which consists of Alaska, the Yukon Territory, British Columbia, and western Alberta.

Renisyl Mountains—the Arcanan analog of the Kopets Mountain on the frontier between Turkmenistan and Iran.

Republic of Faltharia—the oldest nation in New Ternath (North America), consisting of the eastern seaboard of North America from New York State to Florida and as far inland as the Mississippi River.

Republic of Varnath—a republic in southern New Ternath consisting of the southern tip of Texas, all of Mexico south of Chihuahua, and all of Guatemala, or El Salvador, Honduras, and northern Nicaragua.

Republic of West New Ternath—a republic in western New Ternath consisting of California, Nevada, most of Utah, Arizona, New Mexico, roughly the southern half of Colorado, most of Texas, the Mexican states of Baja California Norte, Baja California Sur, Sonora, Sinaloa, and Louisiana where it reaches the Gulf of Cordara.

Republic of Ysar—a republic in New Farnalia consisting of Uruguay, the eastern two thirds of Paraguay, and southern Brazil to the line of the Paranaiba River.

RHHE—the commonly used acronym for Ram's Horn Heavy Equipment (see above).

Ricathia—the Sharonian analog of Africa.

Ricathian Buffalo—the Sharonian name for the Cape Buffalo, which are also referred to as "Devil Buffs" because of their uncertain temper and ferocity. Also the name of a powerful steam-powered bulldozer manufactured by the Ram's Horn Heavy Equipment works for the Trans-temporal Express.

Ricathian Desert—the Sharonian analog of the Libyan Desert.

Rindor Ocean—the Sharonian analog of the Indian Ocean.

Roantha—a republic in New Ternath (North America) consisting of roughly the area of the states of North Dakota, South Dakota, northern Nebraska, northeastern Colorado, Wyoming, southern Montana, Idaho, Oregon, and the western third of Washington.

Roanthan Plains—the Sharonian analog of the Great Plains of North America.

Rokhana—a nation of New Ternath on Sharona which occupies the western coast from what would be our own Oregon to just about the line of the Mexican border.

Saint Taiyr—also called Taiyr of Estafel, the patron saint of the House of Calirath.

Sand Rock River—the Sharonian analog of the Rio Grande/Rio Bravo.

Sankhar—Arpathian demon twin of Vaylar, patron of war. See also Vaylar. In many ways, Vaylar and Sankhar are the Arpathian analogs of Scylla and Charybdis.

Saramash—the Shurkhali devil.

Sarkolis crystal—the extremely strong, quartzlike "stone" (actually an artificially manufactured crystal) used as the matrices and storage components for Arcanan spell-based technology.

Sarlayn River—the Sharonian analog of the Nile River.

Sarthan Desert—the Sharonian analog of the Sahara Desert.

Saylian—a Ransaran constitutional monarchy roughly analog to northern and central Mongolia.

Scurlis Sea—the Sharonian analog of the Sea of Japan.

Sea of Ibral—the Sharonian analog of the Sea of Marmara.

Seadrake—an aquatic equivalent of a dragon created by Mythalan breeders.

Seadrake Owners Association—a professional organization, based in the universe of New Mythal, supporting the efforts of breeders of seadrakes.

Selkhara—Arcanan analog of Medina, Saudi Arabia.

Selkhara Oasis—Arcanan analog of the Sadiqiyyah Oasis in Saudi Arabia.

Septentrion—Most septs of Arpathia do not have a formal government outside the ruler of each tribe/clan-based sept. Their territories are somewhat fluid, particularly in the region of the Siberian plains. The septs banded together in the matter of trade, however, creating the Septentrion as a trade union that protects the financial interests of all the septs. The representatives of the septs who serve in the Septentrion deal with outside merchants and bargain the best prices for Arpathian goods, including the legendary work of Arpathian goldsmiths. The Septentrion established regional trade centers along the borders with Arpathia's neighbors. The Septentrion also sends a delegate to serve as a director of the Portal Authority and assists septmen who want to join the PAAF as soldiers or to apply to the Portal Authority for training to explore the multiverse as members of a civilian survey crew.

Septs—Arpathian clan-based social units, most of which are nomadic herders. Arpathian septs breed some of the finest horses in Sharona. Septs are mistrustful of outsiders, due to unscrupulous traders who sought to take advantage of "nomadic barbarians" and due to the tendency of other cultures to view them as primitive and make them the butt of unpleasant humor.

Serikai—"City of Snow," a lakeside city in Sharona, which is the equivalent of Buffalo, New York. Serikai is the capital city of the Republic of Faltharia.

Serinach—the northernmost state of the Republic of Rendisphar, consisting of almost the entire state of Alaska.

Serinach Peninsula—the Sharonian analog of Alaska.

Serinach Strait—the Sharonian analog of the Bering Strait.

Sethdona—the capital of the Sharonian Kingdom of Shurkhal. Located at the trans-temporal equivalent of Jiddah on the Arabian peninsula's Red Sea shore.

Shaisal Air Base—a major Union of Arcana air base located outside the city of Chemparas in the universe of Basilisk.

Shakira—the magic-using caste which totally dominates and controls the culture of Mythal. These are the researchers, theoreticians, etc., and control virtually all of Mythal's "white collar" occupations.

Shalana—"Mother Shalana" is one of the Ternathian Double Triads and one of the most-revered and powerful deities of that Double Triad. Blue is her sacred color, which is why her Temple in Tajvana is covered with lapis lazuli and sapphires. She is also known as Shalana the Merciful. Her priestess-hood is one of the wealthiest in Sharona.

Shaloma—The Arcanan analog of Western Europe.

Shansir Mountains—the Arcanan analog of the Taurus Mountains.

Shardon—a technical term, from the Old Andaran. It translates literally as "shieldling," and indicates an individual under the protection of an Andaran warrior and his family. (See baranal, above.)

Sharona—the home universe and Earth of the Ternathian Empire. Its physics are similar, but not identical, to our own, and its society is largely based upon highly developed psionic Talents.

Sharonian days of the week—Vothday, Shaladay, Trygday, Marniday, Yahnday, Zymday, and Mariday. Vothday is the first day of the week.

Sharskha—the battle at the end of the world in Arcanan mythology.

Shartahk—the main Andaran religion's devil.

Shartha Highlands—high, rugged mountains in northwestern Shartha; the Sharonian analog of Ethiopia's Eastern Highlands.

Shartha—a kingdom in eastern Ricathia (see "Kingdom of Shartha," above).

Shdandifar—a small town in the Darylis Republic in New Farnalia located about 20 miles down the Rathynoka River (Orinoco River) from the location of Puerto Ayacucho, Venezuela. The portal connecting Lashai to Resym lies a few miles outside Shdandifar.

Shehsmair—Arcanan analog of India.

Shendisfal—an Arcanan kingdom consisting of Turkmenistan, the northeastern corner of Iran, Uzbekistan, and the southwest corner of Kazakhstan. It is predominantly Ransaran but with a substantial minority population of Mythalans, especially in the southwest. This area has been a flash point between the Ransaran and Mythalan cultures for better than a thousand years.

Sherayn's River—the Sharonian analog of the Santa Clara River, Utah.

Sherkaya—the ancient Mythalan word for "fire"; the release code which triggers a red dragon's breath weapon.

Shikowr—a breed of riding/cavalry horse developed in Ternathia over the space of several thousand years. The Shikowr resembles the Morgan horse in conformation and stance, but stands between sixteen and seventeen hands in height. The name is taken from a type of Shurkhali cavalry saber which was adopted by the Ternathian cavalry.

Shosara—a seaport developed on the continent of New Ternath in the Traisum Universe to support extension of the Trans-temporal Express across Traisum to Kelsayr. It is on the site of Erkahlan, a major coastal city in the Republic of Faltharia in Sharona's home universe.

Showma Falls—the Arcanan analog (in New Arcana) of Niagara Falls. Site of the Garth Showma Institute of Magic.

Shurkhal—a Sharonian kingdom, roughly equivalent to Saudi Arabia, Jordan, and the Sinai Peninsula. The Kingdom of Shurkhal is the largest of several "Shurkhalian" kingdoms, closely related culturally to Harkala, but clearly a distinct subculture, which dominates the area of Syria, Iraq, and most of Iran.

Sifter—a Sharonian psionic whose Talent allows him to determine whether or not any statement is the truth or a lie.

Simaryn—a moderate sized Sharonian city in the Kingdom of west New Ternath, approximately on the site of El Paso, Texas.

Sky Blood Lode—the Sharonian name for the Comstock Lode.

Sky Blood Mountains—the Sharonian name for the Sierra Nevada Mountains.

Slide rail—also "slider." The Arcanan equivalent of a railroad.

Sniffer—another term for a "Tracer." (See "Tracer," below.)

Snow Sapphire Lake—the Sharonian name for Lake Tahoe, Nevada.

Snowbear—Sharonian term for polar bear.

SOA—Seadrake Owners Organization (see above).

South Uromathian Sea—Sharonian analog of the China Sea.

Steam dray—Sharonian term for a wheeled, steam-powered truck or lorry.

Steel Mule—the Halftrack, Mark 1 (also the Halftrack of 5050, sometimes referred to as the Halftrack 51), is an 8-ton Halftracked modification of Ram Horn's Heavy Equipment's standard 7.5-ton steam dray. Maximum payload is 3,400 pounds; maximum speed is about 45 mph; maximum unrefueled range on roads is about 300 miles; maximum unrefueled range on unimproved surfaces is about 200 miles.

Stone Carve River—the Sharonian analog of the Colorado River.

Strait of Bolakin—the Sharonian analog of the Strait of Gibraltar.

Strait of Junkari—Sharonian analog of Straits of Malacca.

Strait of Tears—the Sharonian analog of the Bab el-Mandeb Strait connecting the Red Sea with the Gulf of Aden.

Strike—an Arcanan Air Force formation consisting of three "flights," for a total of twelve dragons.

Strike-ball—the ball struck by the "striker" (equivalent of a cue stick) in the Sharonian game of pocket-ball.

Striker—the equivalent of a cue stick used in the Sharonian game of pocket-ball.

Stun bolt—a special arbalest bolt used for crowd control which can be fired even by un-Gifted personnel and carries a spell which renders its target instantly unconscious. The exact duration of the unconsciousness can be adjusted up to a maximum of 24 hours.

Sunhold—the Uromathian feudal territory held by a "sunlord" (see below); roughly equivalent to a duchy or grand duchy.

Sunlord—a Uromathian aristocratic title roughly equivalent to that of duke.

SUNN—Sharona's Universal News Network, the largest news organization in Sharona's multiple-universe civilization, with both print and telepathic broadcast divisions.

Synthara River—the Sharonian analog of the Willamette River.

Syrana River—the Sharonian analog of the Walker River, Nevada.

Syskhara—a republic in New Ternath (North America) which consists of Ontario, Quebec, Maine, New Hampshire, Vermont, and Nova Scotia.

Tahlsar—a minor deity of Ternathia associated with nature and hunting.

tahlsara suit—a camouflage garment, the Sharonian analog of a ghillie suit, developed in the mountains of Mulgethia and named after Tahlsar, a nature god native to Ternathia.

Tairynak Mountains—the Sharonian analog of the Cascade Mountains.

Tajvana—the capital of the First Ternathian Empire at its height; the Sharonian equivalent of Constantinople or Istanbul.

Talon—an Arcanan Air Force formation consisting of three "strikes," for a total of thirty-six dragons.

Taniaport—a city in the Sharonian Republic of Rendisphar located approximately on the site of Anchorage, Alaska. Location of the portal between Kelsayr and Lashai.

Tankara Gulf—Arcanan analog of the Persian Gulf.

Taryka Valley—the Sharonian analog of Ralston Valley, Nevada.

Tayrmek—an Arcanan city in the Kingdom of Shendisfal near the site of the city of Ashgabat, Turkmenistan.

Temple of Saint Taiyr of Tajvana—a temple in Tajvana, commemorating Saint Taiyr of Estafel, built by Empress Wailyana I in 3016. Traditional site of Calirath coronations for almost two thousand years.

Teramandor—a province of the Empire of Ternathia located in northwest Narhath; roughly analogous to Catalonia and western Aragon, Spain.

Teramandor Mountains—the Sharonian analog of the Cataluna Mountains of Spain.

Ternath Island—the ancient homeland of the Emperors of Ternathia; the Arcanan equivalent of Ireland.

Ternathian Empire—the most ancient human polity known in any of the explored universes. The Ternathians established an effective world-state during the Copper and early Iron Age eras of Sharona, largely through the recognition, development and use of psionic talents. Originally located on Ternath Island (Ireland), it is the largest, oldest, most prestigious empire on Sharona. Its major component states include, besides Ternath Island: **Alathia:** Italy; **Jerekhas:** Sicily; **Bernith Island:** Britain (Scotland, England, Wales); **Delkrathia:** part of Spain; **Ermandia:** Austria; **Karmalia:** Hungary; **Lugathia:** France; **Mulgethia:** Germany/ Switzerland; **Narhath:** part of Spain; **Nessia:** Greece; **Pairhys Island:** Isle of Man; **Teramandor:** part of Spain.

Terohma—the Sharonian analog of New Zealand.

Tesmahn—a small Sharonian city/large town located near the site of Humestan, Iowa.

Tharkan—a grand duchy in Shaloma, an imperial territory of the Kingdom of Elath located in the Arcanan analog of Poland where the first Arcanan trans-temporal portal was discovered.

Theskair—a city in the Arcanan universe of New Ransar. Theskair is built at the portal between New Ransar and Basilisk, located approximately at Ulaambaatar in Basilisk and at Riyadh in New Ransar.

Thunder-fluke—the Sharonian name for blue whales.

Time of Conquest—the period of ancient Ternathia's most sustained, militant expansion. Generally dated by Sharonian historians as extending from approximately 2025 to 3650.

Tophyr—a Ransaran constitutional monarchy roughly equivalent to the coastal Chinese provinces of Liaoning, Hebei, Shandong, Jiangsu, Zhejiang, Fujian, and Guangdong. This is the most powerful single Ransaran state, with a strong maritime and naval tradition which has led to several conflicts with Zyntahra. For the last two hundred years or so, however, the two states have been firm allies.

Torakreg Mountains—the Sharonian analog of the Monitor Range Mountains, Nevada.

Torkash—the chief deity of the ancient Manisthu pantheon in Arcana.

Tosaria—an ancient Ransaran kingdom on Arcana. Its capital was located in the same approximate geographical spot as Shanghai. Tosaria had attained a high and sophisticated level of civilization while most of the rest of present day Ransara was still in a state of primitivism.

Tracer—a Sharonian with the Tracer Talent. One who is sensitive to the current location, or at least direction to, another individual or object. They are also called "Sniffers."

Trans-temporal Express—a privately-held corporation responsible for building and maintaining the primary rail and shipping connections linking the Sharonian home universe to the expanding frontier. Although it is the single largest, wealthiest privately-held corporation in Sharonian history, the TTE is subject to close regulation and oversight by the Portal Authority, which has granted—and retains the legal right to revoke—the TTE's multi-universal right-of-way.

Trembo Fire Heel—messenger of the gods and patron of geographers in the Andaran pantheon.

Treybus Ocean—Arcanan analog to the Atlantic Ocean.

Triad—common colloquial reference to the six deities formally known as the Elder Triad and Veiled Triad. *Elder Triad*—the most ancient members of the Ternathian Double Triads, consisting of the original Ternathian ruling gods: Vothan, Shalana, and Marnilay. *Veiled Triad*—the "junior" of the Ternathian Double Triads, consisting of deities which entered Ternathian cosmology as Ternathian culture and the Ternathian Empire spread across the ancient world. They are mother Marthea, Sekharan, and Tryganath.

Trombo Mountains—the Sharonian analog of the Monte Christo Mountains, Nevada.

Tsykantha Island—Sharonian analog of Borneo Island.

Tukoria—the largest and most powerful of the Hilmaran kingdoms, consisting of the equivalent of most of Argentina and Chile. Tukoria was the only Hilmaran state which maintained its independence against Andaran conquest and colonization.

Tumble Rock River—the Sharonian analog of the Virgin River in southwestern Utah and stream southeastern Nevada.

Tyrahl River—the Sharonian analog of the Missouri River.

Ulthamyr—a small bison-ranching town in the Republic of Roantha in New Ternath, located on the Tyrahl River (Missouri River) a few miles from Pierre, South Dakota.

Union Arbitration Commission (UAC)—a quasi-diplomatic commission which answers to the Union Senate's committee on inter-universal disputes.

Union City—a city at the entry portal into New Sharona, located about fifty miles east of Bloemfontein, South Africa.

Union Mark (abbreviated UM)—Arcanan unit of currency issued by the Union of Arcana. It is subdivided into half-marks, quarter-marks, tenth-marks, and hundredth-marks, usually referred to as halves, quarters, silvers, and coppers.

Union of Arcana—the world government of the home universe of Arcana.

Union Trans-temporal Transit Authority—the agency of the Union of Arcana's government charged with overseeing trans-temporal travel and commerce, including regulation of sliderails and maritime transport infrastructure.

Urdanha Mountains—Arcanan analog of the Zagros Mountains.

Uromathia—a general term applied to the Sharonian equivalent of Asia south of Mongolia and west of India. This area is divided into many smaller kingdoms and two empires, all of which share many common cultural traits.

Uromathian Empire—the larger of the two empires found in Uromathia. It occupies the Sharonian equivalent of China and includes the equivalent of Vietnam and Cambodia.

Usarlah—a Sharonian city located in the Delkrath Mountains (just north of Madrid) in the Ternathian province of Delkrathia.

UTTTA—see Union Trans-temporal Transit Authority, above.

Vahlstahg Mountains—the Sharonian analog of the Tonquin Mountains, Nevada.

Vandor Ocean—the Sharonian analog of the Atlantic Ocean.

Vandor River—the Sharonian analog of the Mississippi River.

Vankaiyar—a city in Ricathia located approximately on the site of Mogadishu. Location of the portal between Traisum and Salym.

Vaylar—Arpathian demon twin of Sankhar, patron of pestilence. See also Sankhar. In many ways, Vaylar and Sankhar are the Arpathian equivalents of Scylla and Charybdis.

Vaylar and Sankhar—Arpathian twin demons, patrons respectively of pestilence and war. In many ways, they are the Arpathian analogs of Scylla and Charybdis. (See also Sankhar.)

Veiled Triad—the "junior" of the Ternathian Double Triads, consisting of deities which entered Ternathian cosmology as Ternathian culture and the Ternathian Empire spread across the ancient world. They are Mother Marthea, Sekharan, and Tryganath.

Verdynal Valley—the Sharonian analog of Ione Valley, Nevada.

Volmyria—an Arcanan empire roughly equivalent to Pakistan and Afghanistan. Although it is considered a Ransaran state and is predominantly Ransaran racially, it possesses a military tradition almost as powerful as Andara's and is centered around a very powerful (and well organized) imperial bureaucracy. Although it is in many ways an uncomfortable fit with the predominant Ransaran fetish for individual rights and elective government, it has stood as a bulwark against Mythalan expansion for centuries.

vos—"of the line of" in ancient Mythalan. The use in a Mythalan's name indicates that the individual is of high *shakira* caste. (See also "mul," above.)

Vothan—the Ternathian deity called "Father Vothan," who serves as Ternathia's war god, is one of the Ternathian Double Triads. "Father Vothan" protects the Empire in military combat and is therefore also called Protector Vothan or "The Protector" by the people of Ternathia and those regions colonized by Ternathia.

Vothan's Canyon—the Sharonian analog of the Grand Canyon.

Vothan's chariot—the armored chariot of the Ternathian Double Triad deity who serves as Ternathia's Protector, or god of war.

Voyager-**class transport**—the *Voyager* is a modular design steamship developed by TTE engineers to be shipped through portals aboard enormous railcars and assembled in universes where ships are needed to cross the water gaps. Similar in concept and design to the *Liberty* and *Victory* ships of World War II.

Vyrlair—an Arpathian region of Sharona roughly equivalent to our own Turkmenistan.

Western Ocean—the Sharonian name for the Pacific Ocean.

Western Plains—the Arcanan name for the Great Plains of North America, lying along the boundary of Elath and Yanko.

Whiffer—a Sharonian with the Whiffer Talent. One who is sensitive to residual psychic impressions.

White Mist Lake—the Arcanan analog of Lake Erie.

White Rush River—the Sharonian analog of the Columbia River.

White Snake River—the Sharonian analog for Carson River, Nevada.

White Snake Valley—the Sharonian analog for Carson Valley, Nevada.

Willow Creek—the Sharonian analog of Willow Creek, Nevada.

Wind Peak Mountains—the Sharonian analog of the Wasatch Mountains.

Windhold—the feudal territory held by a Uromathian "windlord" (see below); roughly equivalent to an earldom.

Windlord—a Uromathian aristocratic title, roughly equivalent to that of earl.

Windscrub Valley—the Sharonian analog of Sand Spring Valley, Nevada.

Windstorm Lake—Sharonian analog of Lake Washoe, Nevada. Noted for its often extremely violent winds.

Winged Crown—the imperial crown of Ternathia. This ancient crown (still used in coronations) was made by Farnalian goldsmiths almost

Chan Byrnal, Under-Armsman Hanyl, Portal Authority Armed Forces—[TRTH] HQ Section, 127th Regiment, PAAF. Regiment-Captain Velvelig's most junior "clerk" and a Talented Distance Viewer.

Chan Calirath, His Imperial Majesty Zindel—[HG, HHNF, TRTH] Zindel XXIV, Duke of Ternathia, Grand Duke of Farnalia, Warlord of the West, Protector of the Peace, Wing-Crowned, and, by the gods' grace, Emperor of Ternathia.

Chan Calirath, Platoon-Captain Crown Prince Janaki, Imperial Ternathian Marines—[HG, HHNF] the eldest child and heir of Emperor Zindel chan Calirath of Ternathia. CO, Third Platoon, Copper Company, Second Battalion, 117th Imperial Ternathian Marines, assigned to duty with the PAAF.

Chan Carthad, Junior-Armsman Padrair, Imperial Ternathian Army—[TRTH] 1st Recon Section, 3rd Dragoon Division, ITA, a Talented Distance Viewer attached to Gold Company, 2nd Battalion, 12th Dragoon Regiment.

Chan Cyrmyn, Platoon-Captain Symahrn, Imperial Ternathian Army—[TRTH] 2nd Battalion, 12th Dragoon Regiment, 3rd Dragoon Division; Hymair chan Yahndar's staff Voice.

Chan Dasam, Company-Captain Lerkhali, Imperial Ternathian Army—[TRTH] CO, Bronze Company, 2nd Battalion, 12th Dragoon Regiment, 3rd Dragoon Division, ITA.

Chan Derkail, Company-Captain Hyrus, Imperial Ternathian Army—[TRTH] CO, Silver Company, 1407th Mounted Combat Engineer Battalion, ITA.

Chan Dernal, Junior-Armsman Jakys, Imperial Ternathian Army—[TRTH] 2nd Battalion, 12th Dragoon Regiment, 3rd Dragoon Division, ITA; a strongly talented Distance Viewer assigned to 2nd Battalion for its advance down the Kelsayr.

Chan Dersain, Armsman Thakoh, Portal Authority Armed Forces—[TRTH] HQ Section, 127th Regiment, PAAF; Regiment-Captain Velvelig's clerks at Fort Ghartoun.

Chan Dorth, Under-Armsman Lerthan, Imperial Ternathian Army—[TRTH] Silver Company, 1407th Mounted Combat Engineer Battalion, ITA; Company-Captain Hyrus chan Derkail's company Flicker.

Chan Ersam, Battalion-Captain Rechair, Imperial Ternathian Army—[TRTH] Quartermaster, 3rd Brigade, 21st Infantry Division, 5th Corps, ITA.

Chan Esmahr, Company-Captain Temyk, Imperial Ternathian Army—[TRTH] CO, 103rd Battery, Imperial Ternathian Horse Artillery.

Chan Evard, Under-Armsman Rodahr, Imperial Ternathian Army—[TRTH] bugler, 1st Platoon, Gold Company, 2nd Battalion, 12th Dragoon Regiment, 3rd Dragoon Division, ITA.

Chan Fairstal, Company-Captain Gerkar, Imperial Ternathian Army—[TRTH] CO, Bronze Company, 1407th Mounted Combat Engineer Battalion, ITA.

Chan Farcos, Junior Armsman Urmahl, Imperial Ternathian Army—[TRTH] senior NCO, 3rd Squad, 2nd Platoon, 1407th Mounted Combat Engineer Battalion, ITA.

Chan Ferdain, Regiment-Captain Hahlstyr, Imperial Ternathian Army—[TRTH] CO, 312th Infantry Regiment, 2nd Brigade, 21st Infantry Division, 5th Corps, ITA.

Chan Fyrkam, Company-Captain Traivyr, Imperial Ternathian Army—[TRTH] XO, 2nd Battalion, 12th Dragoon Regiment, 3rd Dragoon Division, ITA.

Chan Gairwyn, Platoon-Captain Ersayl, Imperial Ternathian Army—[TRTH] CO, 2nd Platoon, Silver Company, 1407th Mounted Combat Engineer Battalion, ITA.

Chan Garatz, Telfor—[TRTH] the Chief of Imperial Security.

Chan Gayrahn, Battalion-Captain Chimo, Imperial Ternathian Army—[TRTH] 3rd Dragoon Division, Imperial Ternathian Army; Division-Captain chan Geraith's staff planning and operations officer.

Chan Gelsayr, Senior-Chief-Armsman Hahkir, Imperial Ternathian Army—[TRTH] battalion chief-armsman, 2nd Battalion, 12th Dragoon Regiment, 3rd Dragoon Division, ITA.

Chan Geraith, Division-Captain Arlos, Imperial Ternathian Army—[HG, HHNF, TRTH] CO, Third Dragoon Division, Fifth Corps.

Chan Golar, Senior-Armsman Tersak, Imperial Ternathian Army—[TRTH] company senior-armsman, Gold Company, 2nd Battalion, 12th Dragoon Regiment, 3rd Dragoon Division, ITA.

Chan Gorsad, Brigade-Captain Resardan, Imperial Ternathian Army—[TRTH] CO, 2nd Brigade, 21st Infantry Division, 5th Corps, ITA; one of Division-Captain chan Jassian's brigade commanders.

Chan Grestayr, Senior-Armsman Junar, Imperial Ternathian Army—[TRTH] 3rd Brigade, 21st Infantry Division, 5th Corps, ITA.

Chan Gristhane, Captain-of-the-Army Thalyar, Imperial Ternathian Army—[HG, HHNF, TRTH] senior uniformed officer of the Ternathian Army, senior member of the Imperial Board of Strategy, and Ternathian Defense Councilor.

Chan Grosyar, Regiment-Captain Hyrneth, Imperial Ternathian Army—[TRTH] CO, First Battalion, Twelfth Dragoon Regiment, Third Dragoon Division, ITA.

Chan Halmar, Petty-Captain Frynak, Imperial Ternathian Army—[TRTH] CO, 1st Squad, 1st Platoon, Gold Company, 2nd Battalion, 12th Dragoon Regiment, 3rd Dragoon Division, ITA.

Chan Hopyr, Platoon-Captain Rynai, Imperial Ternathian Army— [TRTH] 3rd Dragoon Division, Imperial Ternathian Army; Distance Viewer attached to Battalion-Captain Chimo chan Gayrahn's intelligence staff.

Chan Hurmahl, Battalion-Captain Francho, Imperial Ternathian Army—[TRTH] CO, 1407th Mounted Combat Engineer Battalion, ITA.

Chan Huval, Platoon-Captain Hydyr, Imperial Ternathian Army— [TRTH] CO, 2nd Platoon, Gold Company, 2nd Battalion, 12th Dragoon Regiment, 3rd Dragoon Division, ITA.

Chan Hyul, Battalion-Captain Feryx, Imperial Ternathian Army— [TRTH] XO, 12th Dragoon Regiment, 1st Brigade, 3rd Dragoon Division, ITA.

Chan Ilkar, Master-Armsman Terays, Imperial Ternathian Army— [TRTH] regimental master-armsman (senior noncom), 12th Dragoon Regiment, 1st Brigade, 3rd Dragoon Division, ITA.

Chan Isail, Regiment-Captain Merkan, Imperial Ternathian Army— [HHNF, TRTH] 3rd Dragoon Division, Imperial Ternathian Army; Division-Captain chan Geraith's Chief of Staff.

Chan Jarkysa, Junior-Armsman Pryo, Imperial Ternathian Army— [TRTH] 2nd Battalion, 12th Dragoon Regiment, 3rd Dragoon Division; strongly Talented Plotter assigned to 2nd Battalion for its advance down the Kelsayr Chain.

Chan Jassian, Division Captain Ustace, Imperial Ternathian Army— [HHNF, TRTH] CO, 21st Infantry Division, Fifth Corps, ITA.

Chan Jersyk, Company-Captain Namair, Imperial Ternathian Army— [TRTH] CO, Weapons Company, 2nd Battalion, 12th Dragoon Regiment, 3rd Dragoon Division, ITA.

Chan Jesyl, Regiment-Captain Erykor, Imperial Ternathian Army— [TRTH] CO, 31st Dragoon Regiment, 3rd Brigade, 3rd Dragoon Division, Imperial Ternathian Army.

Chan Kersahn, Company-Captain Rafair, Imperial Ternathian Army— [TRTH] senior healer, 2nd Battalion, 12th Dragoon Regiment, 3rd Dragoon Division ITA.

Chan Kilstar, Company-Captain Chayrus, Imperial Ternathian Army— [TRTH] CO, Copper Company, 1407th Mounted Combat Engineer Battalion, ITA.

Chan Klaisahn, Battalion-Captain Fernis, Imperial Ternathian Army— [TRTH] chief of staff, 3rd Brigade, 21st Infantry Division, 5th Corps, ITA.

Chan Klanmyra, Petty-Captain Yancir, Imperial Ternathian Army— [TRTH] CO, 3rd Squad, 1st Platoon, Gold Company, 2nd Battalion, 12th Dragoon Regiment, 3rd Dragoon Division, ITA.

Chan Korthal, Company-Captain Lisar, Imperial Ternathian Army— [HHNF, TRTH] 3rd Dragoon Division, Imperial Ternathian Army; Division-Captain chan Geraith's staff Voice.

Chan Kostyr, Armsman 1/c Trendan, Imperial Ternathian Army— [TRTH] 2nd Platoon, Silver Company, Silver Company, 1407th Mounted Combat Engineer Battalion, ITA; Platoon-Captain Ersayl chan Gairwyn's assigned platoon Flicker.

Chan Kylsair, Senior Armsman Thestycar—[TRTH] Anbessa Calirath's personal guardsman.

Chan Kymo, Regiment-Captain Therahk, Imperial Ternathian Army— [TRTH] 3rd Dragoon Division, Imperial Ternathian Army; Division-Captain chan Geraith's staff Quartermaster.

Chan Lorak, Senior-Armsman Gershyr, Imperial Ternathian Army— [TRTH] HQ group, Third Brigade, 21st Infantry Division, Fifth Corps. Senior-Armsman chan Lorak is Brigade-Captain chan Bykahlar's personal batman.

Chan Loryn, Regiment-Captain Syth, Imperial Ternathian Army— [TRTH] CO, 16th Dragoon Regiment, 3rd Brigade, 3rd Dragoon Division, Imperial Ternathian Army.

Chan Lyrkad, Company-Captain Ulysar, Imperial Ternathian Army— [TRTH] CO, Silver Company, 1st Battalion, 5th Mounted Support Regiment, ITA; CO of the mounted weapons company attached to Gold Company, 2nd Battalion, 12th Dragoon Regiment, 3rd Dragoon Division.

Chan Lyscarn, Platoon-Captain Tahnthair, Imperial Ternathian Army—[TRTH] operations officer, 2nd Battalion, 12th Dragoon Regiment, 3rd Dragoon Division, ITA.

Chan Mahsdyr, Company-Captain Grithair, Imperial Ternathian Army—[TRTH] CO, Gold Company, 2nd Battalion, 12th Dragoon Regiment, 3rd Dragoon Division, ITA.

Chan Malthyn, Regiment-Captain Gerdain, Imperial Ternathian Army—[TRTH] CO, 12th Dragoon Regiment, 1st Brigade, 3rd Dragoon Division.

Chan Manthau, Division-Captain Yarkowan, Imperial Ternathian Army—[HHNF, TRTH] CO, 9th Infantry Division, 5th Corps, ITA.

Chan Manusahr, Junior-Armsman Sylan, Imperial Ternathian Army— [TRTH] platoon junior-armsman, 1st Platoon, Gold Company, 2nd Battalion, 12th Dragoon Regiment, 3rd Dragoon Division, ITA.

Chan Miera, Regiment-Captain Urko, Imperial Ternathian Army— [TRTH] 3rd Dragoon Division, Imperial Ternathian Army; Division-Captain chan Geraith's staff cartographer.

Chan Parthan, Junior-Armsman Tairkyn, Imperial Ternathian Army— [TRTH] 1st Recon Section, 3rd Dragoon Division, ITA; the senior of the six Talented Plotters assigned to Gold Company, 2nd Battalion, 12th Dragoon Regiment.

Chan Quay, Brigade-Captain Renyl, Imperial Ternathian Army—[HHNF, TRTH] CO, 1st Brigade, 3rd Dragoon Division, Imperial Ternathian Army, consisting of 12th Dragoon Regiment and 16th Dragoon Regiment; one of Division-Captain chan Geraith's brigade commanders.

Chan Rahool, Ambassador Soolan—[TRTH] a Voice with animal speaker Talent appointed as the simian ambassador to the Minarti chimpanzee clan in central Ricathia in Sharona.

Chan Raimak, Regiment-Captain Valsyr, Imperial Ternathian Army—[TRTH] CO, 23rd Dragoon Regiment, 2nd Brigade, 3rd Dragoon Division, Imperial Ternathian Army.

Chan Resnair, Petty-Armsman Torsun, Imperial Ternathian Army—[TRTH] 1st Squad, 2nd Platoon, Silver Company, 3rd Battalion, 9th Dragoon Regiment, 2nd Brigade, 3rd Dragoon Division, Imperial Ternathian Army.

Chan Sabyr, Platoon-Captain Fosal, Imperial Ternathian Army—[TRTH] CO, 1st Platoon, Gold Company, 2nd Battalion, 12th Dragoon Regiment, 3rd Dragoon Division, ITA.

Chan Sarsten, Company Captain Erikon—Empress Varena's personal guardsman.

Chan Sayro, Regiment-Captain Braykhan Imperial Ternathian Army—[TRTH] 3rd Dragoon Division, Imperial Ternathian Army; Division-Captain chan Geraith's staff artillerist.

Chan Selyr, Senior-Armsman Vrysin, Imperial Ternathian Army—[TRTH] 3rd Dragoon Division, ITA; the highly experienced and Talented Mapper assigned to Gold Company, 2nd Battalion, 12th Dragoon Regiment.

Chan Serahlyk, Regiment-Captain Lyskar, Imperial Ternathian Army—[TRTH] CO, 123rd Combat Engineer Battalion, Imperial Corps of Engineers, ITA; 3rd Dragoons' chief combat engineer.

Chan Sharys, Brigade-Captain Losahl, Imperial Ternathian Army—[TRTH] CO, 3rd Brigade, 3rd Dragoon Division, Imperial Ternathian Army; one of Division-Captain chan Geraith's brigade commanders.

Chan Sherstal, Company-Captain Sylahs, Imperial Ternathian Army—[TRTH] CO, Gold Company, 1407th Mounted, Combat Engineer Battalion, ITA.

Chan Skrithik, Regiment-Captain Rof, Portal Authority Armed Forces—[HHNF, TRTH] CO, 203rd Regiment, PAAF and CO, Fort Salby, in the universe of Traisum.

Chan Soldayr, Petty-Captain Wyryk, Imperial Ternathian Army—[TRTH] CO, 2nd Squad, 1st Platoon, Gold Company, 2nd Battalion, 12th Dragoon Regiment, 3rd Dragoon Division, ITA.

Chan Solmahr, Petty-Armsman Rydar, Imperial Ternathian Army— [TRTH] company clerk, Gold Company, 2nd Battalion, 12th Dragoon Regiment, 3rd Dragoon Division, ITA.

Chan Stahlyr, Division-Captain Lairkal, Imperial Ternathian Army— [TRTH] Quartermaster General, ITA; the officer in charge of supplies and all acquisitions for the Army; primary advocate of mechanization in the Ternathian military.

Chan Tahlyma, Regiment Captain Althero—[TRTH] Emperor Zindel's personal guardsman and the chief of his protective detail.

Chan Therahk, Regiment-Captain Ilas, Imperial Ternathian Army—[TRTH] XO, 3rd Brigade, 21st Infantry Division, 5th Corps, ITA.

Chan Turkahn, Senior Armsman Tyrail, Imperial Ternathian Army— [TRTH] senior NCO, 2nd Platoon, Silver Company, 1407th Mounted Combat Engineer Battalion, ITA.

Chan Tynaith, Platoon-Captain Jysahrn, Imperial Ternathian Army— [TRTH] logistics officer, 2nd Battalion, 12th Dragoon Regiment, 3rd Dragoon Division.

Chan Ukahli, Platoon-Captain Cymair, Imperial Ternathian Army— [TRTH] cartography officer, 2nd Battalion, 12th Dragoon Regiment, 3rd Dragoon Division, ITA.

Chan Urhal, Platoon-Captain Jersalma, Imperial Ternathian Army— [TRTH] CO, 3rd Platoon, Gold Company, 2nd Battalion, 12th Dragoon Regiment, 3rd Dragoon Division, ITA.

Chan Urlman, Regiment-Captain Teresco, Imperial Ternathian Army— [TRTH] CO, 16th Dragoon Regiment, 1st Brigade, 3rd Dragoon Division, ITA.

Chan Ursan, Brigade-Captain Estavan, Imperial Ternathian Army— [TRTH] CO, 1st Brigade, 21st Infantry Division, 5th Corps, ITA; one of Division-Captain chan Jassian's brigade commanders.

Chan Ustaff, Battalion-Captain Endar, Imperial Ternathian Army— [TRTH] a talented Plotter and well-trained engineer; cartographer, 3rd Brigade, 21st Infantry Division, 5th Corps, ITA.

Chan Verak, Regiment-Captain Syldar, Imperial Ternathian Army— [TRTH] CO, 9th Dragoon Regiment, 2nd Brigade, 3rd Dragoon Division, Imperial Ternathian Army.

Chan Visal, Senior-Chief-Armsman Lestym, Portal Authority Armed Forces—[TRTH] HQ Section, 127th Regiment, Portal Authority armed forces. Fort Ghartoun's armory sergeant.

Chan Vornos, Master-Armsman Caryl, Imperial Ternathian Army— [TRTH] 3rd Dragoon Division, Imperial Ternathian Army; Battalion-Captain Chimo chan Gayrahn's senior noncom.

Chan Wahldyn, Armsman 1/c Yerstan, Imperial Ternathian Army— [TRTH] 3rd Squad, 2nd Platoon, 1407th Mounted Combat Engineer Battalion, ITA.

Chan Waisyn, Chief-Armsman Sylbar Imperial Ternathian Army— [TRTH] 12th Dragoon Regiment, 1st Brigade, 3rd Dragoon Division ITA; Regiment-Captain chan Malthyn's regimental Voice.

Chan Wayshyr, Platoon-Captain Horahstyr, Imperial Ternathian Army—[TRTH] CO, Steel Section, 103rd Horse Artillery.

Chan Werkan, Platoon-Captain Seljar, Imperial Ternathian Army— [TRTH] CO, 202nd Battery, Imperial Ternathian Horse Artillery, attached to 19th Dragoon Regiment, 3rd Brigade, 3rd Dragoon Division.

Chan Westyr, Company-Captain Terahnc, Imperial Ternathian Army— [TRTH] Intelligence officer, 3rd Brigade, 21st Infantry Division, 5th Corps ITA.

Chan Yahndar, Battalion-Captain Hymair, Imperial Ternathian Army—[TRTH] CO, 2nd Battalion, 12th Dragoon Regiment, 3rd Dragoon Division, ITA.

Chan Ynclair, Junior-Armsman Ignathar, Imperial Ternathian Army— [TRTH] 1st Recon Section, 3rd Dragoon Division, ITA; a Talented Distance Viewer attached to Gold Company, 2nd Battalion, 12th Dragoon Regiment.

Chan Yordal, Regiment-Captain Sairek, Imperial Ternathian Army— [TRTH] CO, First Battalion, Sixteenth Dragoon Regiment, Third Dragoon Division.

Chan Zelmahdyn, Company-Captain Vynchair, Imperial Ternathian Army—[TRTH] CO, Copper Company, 2nd Battalion, 12th Dragoon Regiment, 3rd Dragoon Division, ITA.

Chan Zindico, Lazima—[HG, HHNF, TRTH] Princess Andrin's senior personal guardsman.

Crown Prince Janaki—see Janaki chan Calirath.

Darcel Kinlafia—[HG, HHNF, TRTH] a Talented Voice, a member of the expedition attacked at Fallen Timbers in HG, a newly elected member of the world House of Talents and life mate of Alazon Yanamar in TRTH.

Darshu, Lord of Horse Jukan, Sunlord Markan, Imperial Uromathian Army—[HHNF, TRTH] the senior of the Uromathian cavalry officers sent forward to reinforce Fort Salby; his title is roughly equivalent to that of a senior Ternathian duke.

Desval chan Bykahlar, Brigade-Captain, Imperial Ternathian Army— [TRTH] CO, 3rd Brigade, 21st Infantry Division, 5th Corps, ITA, one of Division-Captain chan Jassian's brigade commanders.

Dithrake, Helfron—[TRTH] Commander of Twenty Thousand and Andaran Count of Sogbourne.

Dolphar, Ratatello—[TRTH] a TTE stevedore working Larakesh Central Station and Port-of-Larakesh.

Dolphar, Ratatello—[TRTH] the day shift chief stevedore at Larakesh, Sharona.

Drubeka, Noriellena—[TRTH] a SUNN correspondent paired with Voice Trebar.

Dulan, Brithum—[HG, TRTH] Ternathian Internal Affairs Councilor.

Emperor Zindel XXIV—see Zindel chan Calirath.

Empress Varena—see Varena Calirath.

Fadar—[TRTH] stationmaster's logistics assistant at Larakesh, Sharona.

Fai Goutin, Prince Howan—[HG, HHNF, TRTH] Crown Prince of Eniath and husband of Grand Imperial Princess Andrin Calirath (see also Prince Howan).

Fai Yujin, His Majesty Junni—[HG, TRTH] the King of Eniath (see also King Junni).

Finena—[HG, HHNF, TRTH] Princess Andrin's peregrine falcon.

Fosdark, Horvon—[TRTH] the Earl of Brith Darma, Commander of Wings for the Arcanan Air Force.

Garsal, Second Lord of Horse Tarnal, Uromathian Imperial Cavalry—[HG, HHNF, TRTH] Windlord Garsal, Sunlord Markan's senior subordinate officer and XO.

Garsal, Second Lord of Horse Tarnal, Windlord Garsal Imperial Uromathian Army—[HHNF, TRTH] Sunlord Markan's second-in-command; a distant relative of Emperor Chava.

Garsal, Windlord of—see Tarnal Garsal.

Geraith, Misanya—[HHNF, TRTH] Division-Captain Arlos chan Geraith's wife.

Githrak, Shorbok—[TRTH] Commander of Legions in the Arcanan Army, head of Army Intelligence.

Gorda—[TRTH] a stevedore on the day shift at Larakesh, Sharona.

Gorsatan, Commander of One Hundred Verchyk, Union of Arcana Army—[TRTH] the officer sent in by Two Thousand Harshu to replace Hadrign Thalmayr at Fort Ghartoun.

Halath-Shodach, Company-Captain Traisahr, Portal Authority Armed Forces—CO, Gold Company, 2nd Battalion, 127th Regiment; Namir Velvelig's senior surviving subordinate after the Arcanan capture of Fort Ghartoun.

Halesak, Commander of Fifty Iftar, Union of Arcana Army—[HHNF, TRTH] CO, First Platoon, Able Company, Second Andaran Temporal Scouts. Commander of Fifty Ulthar's brother-in-law.

Harnak, Sword Evarl, Union of Arcana Army—[HG, HHNF, TRTH] senior noncom, First Platoon, Charlie Company, Second Andaran Temporal Scouts.

Harshu, Commander of Two Thousand Mayrkos, Union of Arcana Army—[HG, HHNF, TRTH] CO, Arcanan Expeditionary Force.

Helika, Commander of One Hundred Faryx, Union of Arcana Air Force—[HHNF, TRTH] CO, 5001st Strike; pilot of red battle dragon Firefang.

Her Imperial Highness Crown Princess Andrin Calirath—see Andrin Calirath.

Hostyra, Commander of Twenty-Five Gerun, Union of Arcana Air Force—[TRTH] 5001st Strike, First Provisional Talon. Pilot of red dragon Sky Sabre. One of the escort pilots for Commander of Fifty Yoril Jerstan's dragon train.

Imperial Grand Princess Anbessa—see Anbessa Calirath.

Imperial Grand Princess Andrin—see Andrin Calirath.

Imperial Grand Princess Razial—see Razial Calirath.

Isrian, Commander of Five Hundred Chalbos, Union of Arcana Army—[HHNF, TRTH] one of Two Thousand Harshu's senior infantry battalion commanders.

Janvers, Arnith—[TRTH] Count Tisbane and Hundred Olderhan's defense attorney.

Jastyr, Ulantha—[HHNF, TRTH] Alazon Yanamar's assistant Voice and protégée.

Jerstan, Commander of Fifty Yoril, Union of Arcana Air Force—[TRTH] 1076th AATC Talon, First Provisional AATC Aerie. Pilot of transport dragon Grayscale.

Kalcyr, Senior Sword Barcan, Union of Arcana Army—[HHNF, TRTH] senior noncom, Company Bravo, 901st Light Cavalry.

Karuk, Master-Armsman Hordal, Portal Authority Armed Forces—[TRTH] regimental master-armsman, 127th Regiment, PAAF; Regiment-Captain Velvelig's senior noncom at Fort Ghartoun.

Kelbryan, Magister Gadrial—[HG, HHNF, TRTH] former student of Magister Halathyn vos Dulainah; Department Chairwoman, Theoretical Magic, Garth Showma Institute of Magic.

Kindare, Relatha—[HG, TRTH] a serving girl from Hawkwing Palace and Ternathia who replaces Sathee Balithar as Princess Andrin's personal maid after Balithar's injury.

King Junni—[HG, HHNF, TRTH] Junni Fai Yujin, King of Eniath (see also Fai Yujin, His Majesty Junni)

Kinlafia, Darcel—[HG, HHNF, TRTH] the second Voice assigned to the Chalgyn Consortium crew which first contacts the Arcanans.

Kinlafia, Marithe—[TRTH]Darcel Kinlafia's mother. A college professor in New Farnal.

Kinshe, Halidar—[HG, TRTH] a director of the Sharonian Portal Authority and a Parliamentary Representative in the Kingdom of Shurkhal.

Klian, Commander of Five Hundred Sarr, Union of Arcana Army—[HG, TRTH] CO, Fort Rycharn, universe of Mahritha.

Kolmayr, Thaminar—[HG, HHNF, TRTH] the father of Shaylar Nargra-Kolmayr and husband of Shalassar Kolmayr-Brintal.

Kolmayr-Brintal, Shalassar—[HG, HHNF, TRTH] a Talented ambassador to the cetaceans for the Kingdom of Shurkhal. Shaylar Nargra-Kolmayr's mother.

Kordos, Fleet Third—[TRTH] the third highest ranked officer in the Union of Arcana Navy and a member of Jasak Olderhans's board of inquiry.

Kormas, Commander of One Hundred Surtel, Union of Arcana Air Force—[HHNF, TRTH] Thousand Toralk's senior gryphon-handler.

Krethva—[TRTH] a Uromathian VBS correspondent specializing in society news.

Lii, Munn—[TRTH] personal guardsman to Howan Fai Goutin.

Limana, Director Orem—[HG, HHNF, TRTH] First Director, Sharonian Portal Authority.

Mahrkrai, Commander of Five Hundred Herak, Union of Arcana Army—[HHNF, TRTH] Two Thousand Harshu's chief of staff.

Makree, Platoon-Captain Tobis, Portal Authority Armed Forces—[HHNF, TRTH] Company-Captain Silkash's strongly Talented Healer assistant at Fort Ghartoun.

Markan, Sunlord of—see Jukan Darshu.

Mesaion, Company-Captain Lorvam, Portal Authority Armed Forces—[HHNF, TRTH] CO, Copper Battery, 1st Battalion, 43rd Field Artillery Regiment, Regiment-Captain chan Skrithik's senior artillery officer at Fort Salby.

Morikan, Sword Naf, Union of Arcana Army—[HG, TRTH] Gifted healer, Charlie Company, First Battalion, First Regiment, Second Andaran Temporal Scouts.

Morlinhus, Dr. Gynthyr—a Talented Healer and one of Sharona's leading obstetricians; Crown Princess Andrin's personal obstetrician.

Myr, Commander of Five Hundred Cerlohs, Union of Arcana Air Force—[HHNF, TRTH] CO, First Provisional Talon, pilot of black battle dragon Razorwing.

Nargra, Jathmar—[HG, HHNF, TRTH] a Mapper assigned to the Chalgyn Consortium crew which first encounters the Arcanans. The husband of Shaylar Nargra-Kolmayr.

Nargra-Kolmayr, Shaylar—[HG, HHNF, TRTH] a powerfully Talented Voice, assigned to the Chalgyn Consortium crew which first encounters the Arcanans. The wife of Jathmar Nargra.

Neshok, Commander of Five Hundred (acting) Alivar, Union of Arcana Army—[HG, HHNF, TRTH] Two Thousand Harshu's senior Intelligence officer.

Nourm, Sword Keraik, Union of Arcana Army—[HHNF, TRTH] senior noncom, Second Platoon, Able Company, Fifth Battalion, 306th Regiment.

Olderhan, Commander of One Hundred Sir Jasak, Union of Arcana Army—[HG, HHNF, TRTH] CO, Charlie Company, First Battalion, First Regiment, Second Andaran Temporal Scouts.

Olderhan, Sathmin—[HG, TRTH] Duchess of Garth Showma, wife of Sir Thankhar Olderhan, mother of Sir Jasak Olderhan.

Olderhan, Sir Thankhar—[HG, TRTH] Duke of Garth Showma, planetary governor of New Arcana, father of Sir Jasak Olderhan.

Porath, Javelin Lisaro, Union Of Arcana Army—[HHNF, TRTH] a noncom assigned to Five Hundred Neshok's Intelligence section.

Prince Howan—[HG, HHNF, TRTH] Prince Howan Fai Goutin, Crown Prince of Eniath (see also Fai Goutin, Prince Howan.)

Raka, Acolyte—[TRTH] an acolyte in the Order of Bergahl.

Raynarg, Faroayn—[HG, HHNF, TRTH] the birth name of His Crowned Eminence, the Seneschal of Othmaliz.

Regiment-Captain Namir Velvelig, Portal Authority Armed Forces—[HG, HHNF, TRTH] CO, 127th Regiment, PAAF and CO, Fort Ghartoun. Crown Prince Janaki's regimental commander in HG. Senior POW Fort Ghartoun following its capture by Arcana (HHNF, TRTH).

Restmar, Gorda—[TRTH] a TTE shift manager, freight division, Larakesh Central Station.

Rihva—[TRTH] a court page for the Empire of Uromathia.

Rinthrak, Solvar—[TRTH] Arcanan Commander of Ten Thousand.

Sarma, Commander of Fifty Jaralt, Union of Arcana Army—[HHNF, TRTH] CO, Second Platoon, Alpha Company, Fifth Battalion, 306th Regiment; assigned to Two Thousand Harshu's Arcanan Expeditionary Force.

Seasprite—[TRTH] a drake owned by Emm vos Sidus.

Sendahli, Trooper Jugthar, Union of Arcana Army—[HG, HHNF, TRTH] Third Squad, First Platoon, Charlie Company, First Battalion, First Regiment, Second Andaran Temporal Scouts. Sendahli is a *garthan* who has fled Mythal and enlisted in the Union Army.

Shelthara, Fadar—[TRTH] a New Farnalian TTE employee. Shelthara is an Assistant Freight Manager at Larakesh Central Station.

Silkash, Company-Captain Golvar, Portal Authority Armed Forces—[HHNF, TRTH] Regiment-Captain Velvelig's surgeon at Fort Ghartoun. A.k.a. "Silky." A skilled surgeon, but not a Talented Healer.

Silverstreak Fleshrender—[TRTH] a vos Belftus House bred seadrake owned by Kon vos Vacus. Her assigned *garthan* rider is Ullery the Fool.

Skirvon, Rithmar—[HG, HHNF, TRTH] a representative of the Union Arbitration Commission, an internal, quasi-diplomatic organ of the Union of Arcana. He is the senior diplomat available for negotiations with the Sharonians.

Taje, First Councilor Shamir—[HG, HHNF, TRTH] head of the Ternathian Imperial Privy Council; effectively, Zindel chan Calirath's prime minister.

Taleena—[HG, HHNF, TRTH] Crown Prince Janaki's peregrine falcon.

Teeth Cleaver—[TRTH] an orca with an interest in travel.

Terasahn, Commander of One Hundred Bismair, Union of Arcana Air Force—[TRTH] CO, 23rd Composite Strike, First Provisional AATC Aerie.

Thalmayr, Commander of One Hundred Hadrign, Union of Arcana Army—[HG, HHNF, TRTH] CO, Charlie Company, Second Andaran Temporal Scouts, Fort Ghartoun's Commander after its capture by Arcana.

Threbuch, Chief Sword Otwal, Union of Arcana Army—[HG, HHNF, TRTH] Battalion Chief Sword, Charlie Company, First Battalion, First Regiment, Second Andaran Temporal Scouts.

Thykyl, Armsman 1/c Shalsan, Portal Authority Armed Forces—[TRTH] 1st Platoon, Silver Company, 2nd Battalion, 127th Regiment, PAAF; a member of the Fort Ghartoun garrison.

Tobar, Platoon-Captain Sedryk, Portal Authority Armed Forces—[TRTH] CO, 4th Platoon, Gold Company, 2nd Battalion, 127th Regiment; one of Namir Velvelig's junior officers.

Tobar, Platoon-Captain Zynach Larkal, Portal Authority Armed Forces—[TRTH] CO, 1st Platoon, Silver Company, 2nd Battalion, 127th Regiment, PAAF; one of Namir Velvelig's junior officers.

Toralk, Commander of One Thousand Klayrman, Union of Arcana Air Force—[HG, HHNF, TRTH] Two Thousand Harshu's senior Air Force officer; senior Air Force officer, Arcanan Expeditionary Force.

Torrash, Rinlin—[TRTH] Larakesh Central Stationmaster, TTE.

Torrash, Stationmaster Rinlin—[TRTH] the train stationmaster at Larakesh, Sharona.

Trebar, Kylmos—[TRTH] Noriellena Drubeka's assigned Voice for SUNN.

Tumanau, Minister—[TRTH] a *garthan* on the Arcanan Parliamentary War Operations and Intelligence Committee.

Ulantha Jastyr—[HG, HHNF, TRTH] Alazon Yanamar's assistant Voice, protégée, and official keeper. Acting Privy Voice in much of TRTH.

Ullery—[TRTH] a *garthan* drake rider of Silverstreak Fleshrender. Also called Ullery the Fool. Owned by Kon vos Vacus.

Ulthar, Arylis—[HHNF, TRTH] Commander of Fifty Therman Ulthar's wife.

Ulthar, Commander of Fifty Therman, Union of Arcana Army—[HG, HHNF, TRTH] CO, Third Platoon, Charlie Company, Second Andaran Temporal Scouts. Commander of Fifty Halesak's brother-in-law.

Urlan, Commander of Five Hundred Gyras, Union of Arcana Army—[HHNF, TRTH] CO, Seventh Zydor Heavy Dragoons.

Usar, Drindel—a young Uromathian Talent; a Shark Caller who is in Service to Emperor Chava Busar.

Vankhal, Lady Merissa—[HG, HHNF, TRTH] Princess Andrin's chief lady-in-waiting and protocol instructor.

Vaynair, Commander of Five Hundred Dayr, Union of Arcana Army—[HHNF, TRTH] the senior Gifted healer assigned to Two Thousand Harshu's Arcanan Expeditionary Force.

Velvelig, Regiment-Captain Namir, Portal Authority Armed Forces—[HG, HHNF, TRTH] CO of Fort Ghartoun.

Vos and mul Gurthak, Commander of Two Thousand Nith, Union of Arcana Army—[HG, HHNF, TRTH] CO, Fort Talon, universe of Erthos, senior officer for a nine-universe command area running from Esthiya through Mahritha. He is both *shakira* and *multhari*.

Vos Diffletak, Skollo—[TRTH] Line Lord to Bok vos Hoven.

Vos Durgazon, Minister—[TRTH] a *shakira* on the Arcanan Parliamentary War Operations and Intelligence Committee.

Vos Hoven, Lance Bok, Union of Arcana Army—[HG, TRTH] a Gifted *shakira* combat engineer assigned to Charlie Company, First Battalion, First Regiment, Second Andaran Temporal Scouts.

Vos Sidus, Dre—[TRTH] a *shakira* child of the Sidus line, younger sister to Emm vos Sidus.

Vos Sidus, Emm—[TRTH] a *shakira* gentleman of leisure with a drake breeding hobby.

Vos Sidus, Kellbok—[TRTH] a *shakira* lady, aunt to Dre vos Sidus and Emm vos Sidus, known for her advances in dragon breeding. Also called Aunt Kellbok by her close family.

Vos Vacus, Kon—[TRTH] a *shakira* drake breeder, purchaser of Silverstreak Fleshrender and her *garthan* rider, Ullery.

Vreel, Ghulshan—[TRTH] the prosecuting attorney for Hundred Olderhan's case.

Worka, Commander of One Hundred Sylair, Union of Arcana Army—[HHNF, TRTH] CO, Company Bravo, 901st Light Cavalry.

Yanamar, Alazon—[HG, HHNF, TRTH] Emperor Zindel's Privy Voice, chief of staff, and trusted political adviser. Marries Darcel Kinlafia in TRTH,

Yanusa-Mahrdissa, Ganstamar—[TRTH] TTE SEIC in the Kelsayr Chain.

SHARONIAN TALENTS

This is a partial list.

Animal Speaker—a Sharonian with a Talent which permits him to communicate with nonintelligent animals. No one is quite certain whether this is a form of telepathy, a form of telempathy, or a combination of the two. Animal Speakers have sufficient telepathic ability to receive Voice broadcasts and communications from Mind Speakers.

Coal Hound—a specialized sub type of Mineral Hound (see below) sensitive to the presence of coal and/or oil.

Detail Viewer—a Detail Viewer is a rare subtype of a Distance Viewer. Unlike a standard Distance Viewer whose viewpoint is *always* located in midair above whatever he or she is Viewing at any given moment, a Detail Viewer can locate his or her viewpoint wherever is desired in relationship to what is being Viewed. That is, a Detail Viewer could locate his viewpoint on the ground, looking up, or even project it into a solid mountain to View a tunnel or mine shaft. A Detail Viewer is still hampered by physical obstacles between his/her viewpoint and what is being observed, but he/she can move his viewpoint to the far side of the obstacle in order to defeat that difficulty. Ranges for Detail Viewers are approximately the same as those for standard Distance Viewers.

Distance Viewer—Distance Viewers are clairvoyants capable of Seeing specific distant objects and terrain. Unlike Plotters or Mappers, they See as if looking through their physical eyes. The vast majority of Distance Viewers See as if they were looking down from a point in midair above whatever they are observing. From a greater height, they can See a broader area, although with less detail, just as if they were using their eyes. And, as if they were using their eyes, cloud cover, bad weather, etc., can and does limit what they can See.

They can control the altitude of their viewpoint, "zooming in" from a lower altitude for greater detail at the expense of sacrificing the general area they can observe. Most Distance Viewers can project their viewpoint to a range of no more than 20 or 30 miles (altitude is not a factor), but the strongest of them can project their viewpoint to distances of up to 200 miles. There are at least two major (and much rarer) variants of this ability: the Predictive Distance Viewer and the Detail Viewer. The rarest variant of all is the Predictive Detail Viewer.

Drafter—Drafters are capable of producing freehand versions of plans, maps, or virtually anything else which can be diagrammed. They are not necessarily skilled at painting or producing representational art (see "Sketcher," below), but can produce detailed exploded diagrams and schematics of anything within the range of their Talent. They need not be able to see inside or dismantle an object to diagram its interior, but their range is generally limited to no more than 100-200 yards and they must be able to physically touch anything whose interior is to be diagrammed. Drafters with a secondary Mind Speaker Talent can produce detailed diagrams/plans transmitted to them by another Mind Speaker. The most powerfully Talented of Drafters can use their Talent to diagram anything which can be seen or touched by another Mind Speaker (or Voice) with whom they are in communication as if the other Mind Speaker had the Drafter talent.

Flamer—a pyrokinetic, someone who can generate and control heat and/or flame. Flamers, in differing degrees of strength, and the most powerful of all are the Sunhearts, who can literally burn their way through armored steel. The Flamer Talent is among the most dangerous of Talents, and those who possess it are required to be tested and bonded. Perhaps fortunately, there are limitations on the range at which this Talent can be used, and the range is inversely proportional to the power of the Talent. A Flamer whose greatest power amounts to the ability to slowly and gradually heat a cup of coffee, say, can normally employ his power on any object within his visual range. A Sunheart capable of burning through a plate of face-hardened armor must be close enough that he could actually touch the armor in question. Sunhearts are highly prized in foundries and as welders.

Flicker—someone who can teleport small objects, such as tubes containing written dispatches. Range is limited, seldom exceeding much over 30-40 miles, and the Flicker must know exactly where he is sending it. Some of the most powerfully Talented Flickers have attained ranges of up to 50 miles or more.

Glimpse—a Glimpse might be thought of as a Precog on steroids, though the two Talents do not appear to be directly related in any way. Glimpses are restricted to members of the Calirath family (and only the Ternathian priesthood knows how to "activate" this Talent among those who potentially possess it) and are restricted to the ability to See the consequences of *human actions*. That is, someone with the Glimpse Talent could not See a naturally occurring forest fire or earthquake in advance but *might* be able to Glimpse such a disaster by Glimpsing the actions (and consequences of those actions) of humans *confronted by* the disaster. For most Glimpsers this Talent is uncontrollable, fragmentary, and offers little opportunity to determine exactly when that which is Glimpsed is to occur. (So far as is known, all Glimpses have been of future events, not past ones.) In addition, an individual experiencing a Glimpse is normally oblivious to his or her actual physical surroundings during the Glimpse. That is, he or she is so caught up in—almost entranced by—the Glimpse as to be literally deaf and blind to actual events around them. A Glimpser is unable, for unknown reasons, to Glimpse his or her own future, with one exception, although a Glimpse of *someone else's* future may provide highly revealing clues about his or her own. No Glimpser can control Glimpses of events more than a very few hours into the future. Those more distant Glimpses come without warning, cannot be "focused" or controlled, and tend (there have been some notable exceptions) to be fragmentary and often chaotic. Some of the most strongly Talented Glimpsers have experienced Glimpses scores or even hundreds of years into the future, and a handful of the most strongly Talented of all have experienced clear, coherent, and detailed Glimpses. All Glimpsers are capable of a "Death Glimpse," if their deaths are the result of human action. (Note that the action in question need not be deliberate; a Glimpser might very well experience a Death Glimpse as the result of a traffic accident or a pharmacist's mistake in filling a prescription.) Not every individual capable of a Death Glimpse will necessarily experience one, although that is very uncommon and Death Glimpses tend to be very, very strong. It is possible for a Glimpser to effectively *summon* a Glimpse into the short-term future, i.e. up to 5-10 minutes from the present moment. To do so, however, requires the Glimpser to enter what is known as "fugue state," which consumes large amounts of energy (physically, the equivalent of a 200-yard dash, let's say) and leaves the Glimpser even more oblivious than usual to his/her actual surroundings. For the vast majority of Glimpsers, a fugue state Glimpse means that they are effectively paralyzed, unable to see through their own eyes and unable to move. For those with a weak Talent, it is very difficult or even impossible to enter fugue state *except* in association with a Death Glimpse. Those with an extraordinarily *powerful* Talent, on the other hand, remain aware of their surroundings and the most powerful of all have actually been able to move and even fight in fugue state, which makes them extraordinarily deadly in close combat.

Healer—one who has the Healing Talent is able to perceive injuries and disease and to augment the natural healing process to deal with them. This is not the same as an Arcanan magistron's healing Gift, which can actually *command* the body to heal and recover from serious or even mortal injuries or fatal poisoning. A Talented Healer is able to accomplish seemingly miraculous results, but those results must have been at least potentially obtainable by the patient without the Healer's assistance. That is, a Talented Healer could cause a cut to close and began healing with extraordinary rapidity but would be unable to regenerate damaged or destroyed nerves or to save someone who had taken a bullet through the heart, whereas a magistron with a sufficiently powerful Gift *could* save someone who'd been shot through the heart if he/she could reach the wounded individual before brain function ceases. Talented Healers can (and do) serve as assistants and "guides" for un-Gifted surgeons.

Lifter—someone who can move objects with his mind. This is a short-range Talent; a Lifter can move an object from one location to another location which he can physically see at the moment he Lifts.

Live Tracker—a Live Tracker has a subtype of the Tracker Talent and can follow the trail of any living creature. The strongest Live Trackers have been known to follow trails as much as a full year old, but most Live Trackers cannot follow a trail much more than two or three months old. To use this Talent, the Live Tracker must know exactly where the trail he is following begins (or where he can intersect it, at least) and must know what sort of creature (including human beings) he/she is Tracking.

Mapper—someone who can see the terrain which surrounds him rather as if he was using imaging radar or sonar. Range varies with the strength of the Talent. A Mapper cannot detect living creatures; only terrain features (which includes trees and similar fixed, and moving plant life).

Metal Hound—a sub-Talent in the Mapper family. A Metal Hound can detect bodies of ore and give a very fair estimate of their purity and probable value.

Micro Viewer—a Micro Viewer is able to View objects on a microscopic level. This is a highly unusual Talent, but a very useful one in the medical and scientific professions. The most useful of all are Micro Viewers who have at least some Mind Speaker Talent and are able to work in tandem with Voices who can then distribute their actual observations to anyone who possesses a telepathy-based

Talent, such as a Drafter who can then produce a detailed drawing/ chart of the observation.

Mind Healer—a Sharonian with a complex of Talents which permits him to treat mental disorders.

Mind Speaker—Mind Speakers are relatively common among the Talented. Mind Speakers are telepaths, normally limited to a range of no more than a couple of miles. They normally cannot match the vibrancy, texture, and "completeness" of a Voice transmission and they do not have a Voice's perfect recall. Some Mind Speakers, such as Shalassar Kolmayr-Brintal, Shaylar's mother, can communicate with intelligent nonhumans (in Shalassar's case with cetaceans).

Mineral Hound—The Mineral Hound talent is very similar to that of the Metal Hound, but he can detect and estimate the purity of nonmetallic minerals, rather than metals. They are especially valued for their ability to find gems and critical industrial materials. A particular subtype of Mineral Hound, sometimes referred to as a Coal Hound, is capable of detecting fossilized carbon and/or oil.

Object Tracker—an Object Tracker has a subtype of the Tracker Talent and can follow the paths of *inanimate* objects (i.e., vehicles). An Object Tracker can follow only the object which *left* the path he is Tracking. That is, he could follow a wagon but not a single bag of potatoes which was carried in the wagon. Object Trackers can track even boats or ships through (relatively) shallow water, in which case they are following the path's "shadow" on the bottom of the body of water in question. Most Object Trackers can track through 10-20 feet of water; exceptionally powerful Object Trackers can track a vessel's "path" through as much as 200-300 feet of water, but no Object Tracker has ever exceeded a depth of 400 feet. As with Live Trackers, very powerful Object Trackers can track a vehicle as much as a year after it has passed through, but most Object Trackers are limited to a time window of no more than two months.

Observer—an Observer has what might be called an extremely acute sense of situational awareness. An Observer generally knows exactly where persons and objects are in relation to him in his immediate vicinity, and Observers are renowned for their ability to catch balls thrown from behind them, to unerringly catch a falling glass as it leaves the table, etc. In some Observers, the basic talent is associated with a weak Precog Talent, allowing them to actually predict (in a window of a few seconds or, perhaps, a minute or so) what objects and persons around them are about to do. In a particularly strongly talented Observer, "situational awareness" translates into a sensitivity to detail and relationships which rivals or even exceeds that of the legendary Sherlock Holmes.

Plotter—a Sharonian with the Plotting Talent, a specialized sub variant of the Mapping Talent can detect the presence and locations of living creatures, like human beings. A Plotter's range varies with the strength of his Talent from a minimum of perhaps one mile to a maximum of 35 or even 40 miles for those with the strongest Talent.

Precog—a Precog, as the name suggests, is capable of pre-knowing or reaching into the future. Precogs are normally sensitive to specific *types* of pre-knowledge: weather, earthquakes, etc. About 15-20 percent of all Precogs, however, are General Precogs—that is, their precognitions can apply to almost anything. A Precog sensitive to a specific type of pre-knowledge, however, can focus his or her Talent in a way that a General Precog cannot. That is, the sensitive Precog can "focus" on his or her area of precognition (weather, earthquakes, forest fires, whatever). This ability to "focus" allows him or her to See farther into the future, up to as much as two weeks with a high degree of clarity and perhaps as much as a month with decreasing accuracy. A General Precog is unable to focus in a similar fashion and is much more likely to receive unexpected, unanticipated precognitions. A Precog should not be confused with a Glimpse, however, and the greatest recorded Precog extended no more than approximately 90 days into the future.

Predictive Detail Viewer—the rarest of all Distance Viewers, the Predictive Detail Viewer combines Precognition with the ability to locate his or her viewpoint wherever is desired in relationship to what is being Viewed.

Predictive Distance Viewer—this is a rare subtype of a Distance Viewer. This Talent combines limited Precognition with Distance Viewing, allowing the Viewer to See a specific location *as it will be* in the immediate future. The degree of Precognition varies from Talent to Talent, and is normally measured in no more than minutes (an interval of 30 seconds to around 6 minutes is most common) but can in some cases be as much as 25 minutes. The rarest of all Predictive Distance Viewers are limited to a *fixed* time window: that is, they always See the same exact distance into the future.

Predictive Observer—this is a rare subtype of an Observer. This Talent combines limited precognition with the basic Observer's sensitivity to "situational awareness," to such an extent that the Predictive Observer can actually predict and anticipate where persons and/ or objects in his/her vicinity will be in the next several seconds or (for extremely powerful Predictive Observers) as much as two or three minutes. Individuals with this Talent have *extremely* difficult childhoods as they must learn to "turn it off" in order to interact with their environment and other people in "real time."

Projective—in a sense, all Mind Speakers, Voices, High Sensitives, etc., are Projectives, but the term refers to a specific Talent which is capable of sharing sights, sounds, etc., even with those who are not Talented. Like Voices, Projectives have perfect recall.

Receiver—a Receiver is almost the opposite of a Voice. Or, to put it another way, a Receiver is a Voice with a very, very short transmission range (seldom much over 100 yards) but the ability to receive Voice transmissions from extraordinary ranges (up to 2,500-3,000 miles in some cases). Receivers are even more unusual than Voices and are usually reserved for the Voicenet where they are teamed with regular Voices to overcome significant water barriers or other major terrain obstacles. The Receiver is capable of receiving Voice transmissions from the far side of the barrier and sharing them with his or her normal Voice partner, who then relays the transmission to other Voices on their side of the barrier.

Rememberer—a very rare Talent, a Rememberer is able to "remember" scenes which he has never actually seen. He must be able to physically see the location where the scene to be Remembered occurred and must know approximately when the events he is attempting to Remember transpired. The most rare of all Rememberers (and the most prized for their forensic capabilities) have sufficient telepathic ability to share what they Remember with a Voice or a Mind Speaker so that it can actually be Seen by other investigators.

Scribe—Scribes are thought to be in some ways a sub variety of the Drafter (see above). They are able to produce a detailed, scrupulously accurate written version of anything they have read or heard. Most Scribes have a "window" of no more than 6 to 12 hours in which they retain the ability to transcribe the material without errors or corruption, although some very rare Scribes have been known to retain such information indefinitely. Scribes are often paired with Voices in the military or in business applications where written copies of messages are necessary for distribution or for filing.

Sensitive—Sensitives are empaths. They can detect (and share) the emotions of those around them. Projective Sensitives are much rarer and are capable of projecting emotions to those around them. A High Sensitive (and the rarest of all) can both detect *and* project the emotions of others.

Sifter—someone who can tell whether or not a specific spoken statement is true or false. A Sifter cannot read minds, but particularly sensitive Sifters can detect and accurately estimate degrees of tension in those being interrogated.

Sketcher—a Sketcher is a Talented individual who can produce photographic quality drawings and/or paintings of anything he or she observes. A Sketcher with a secondary Mind Speaker Talent is capable of Sketching anything another individual with the Mind Speaker Talent has seen or is currently seeing. Sketchers should not be confused with Drafters (see above), although a Sketcher could produce a faithful and accurately scaled rendition of a diagram produced by someone else. Sketchers are highly sought after for newspaper illustrations. They are also highly valuable working with Distance Viewers or Micro Viewers, and are often at least as valuable as Mappers for military purposes, since they are capable of rendering what terrain actually *looks* like.

Sniffer—see "Tracer."

Sunheart—a Sunheart is an especially powerful (but short ranged) type of Flamer (see above), capable of projecting and concentrating sufficient heat to burn through heavy armor plate or weld objects together. A Sunheart's effective range is normally limited to objects he or she can/could physically touch. That is, such concentrated foci of heat cannot be projected very much beyond arm's-length of the Sunheart.

Tinker—a Tinker is a Sharonian whose Talent provides him or her with a pronounced "knack" or intuitive feel for various areas of engineering, technical design, etc. Many of the best Sharonian inventors are Tinkers.

Tracer (see also Sniffer)—a Tracer or Sniffer is a specialized version of Finder who is sensitive to the current location, or at least direction to, another individual or object. They are range-limited and must have a strong "feel" for the individual they are Tracing. Tracers with a particularly powerful Talent can work from a description of the individual or object from someone else who is familiar with that person or object; the majority of Tracers can work from an accurate image (or photograph); the weakest of Tracers require previous physical contact/proximity to the individual or object. *All* Tracers who are also Mind Speakers can work from Voice images of the individual or object. Tracers' ranges vary from a low of 5-10 miles to a maximum of approximately 80 miles.

Tracker—a Tracker should not be confused with a Tracer or a Sniffer. A Tracker is psionically gifted in following literally someone or something's tracks or trail. Trackers come in two varieties: Live Trackers and Object Trackers. A Tracker of either type must know exactly where the trail he/she is following begins and exactly what it is he is Tracking.

Voice—a Sharonian with the ability to project mental images and messages over great distances at the speed of thought. Voice range varies widely, with the strongest Voices able to transmit perhaps 700-800 miles. The shortest "commercially useful" Voice range is considered to be about 5 miles. The average for Voices in the Voice chain's connecting universes is around 350 miles. Any Voice has a photographic memory.

Water Witch—also sometimes called a "Water Hound," a Water Witch is sensitive to the presence and behavior of water in his or her vicinity. This Talent is very useful in digging wells for water, but it can also the extremely useful in mapping and charting currents and volumes of flow in rivers, streams, lakes, and even oceanic tides.

Weather Hound—a Precog subtype who is sensitive to weather. A Weather Hound does not appear to depend solely upon his precognitive ability, however. Weather Hounds are sensitive to wind directions and conditions, both current and future, in ways which do not seem to be completely reliant upon precognition. Weather Hounds are highly valued, especially aboard ship.

Whiffer—a Talented person sensitive to residual psychic impressions. A Whiffer normally focuses on a specific object and is capable of Seeing (and feeling) what an individual associated with the object saw or felt.

A NOTE ON CALENDARS

Arcana:

The official Arcanan Calendar is derived from the ancient Ransaran Calendar, although the Mythalans continue to use their own ancient calendar internally. The months of the official year are:

Hayrn	31 days
Molidyr	30 day
Chesthu	30 days
Solyrkain	28 days (29 days once every 4 years)
Kleindyr	31 days
Morkasa	31 days
Slynderas	31 days
Jyrdahna	30 days
Verikas	31 days
Noryka	31 days
Ursikahn	31 days
Inkara	31 days

The year begins Hayrn 1st, which falls on the Northern Summer Solstice, which is also Midwinter Day. Arcanan years are now dated from the creation of the Union of Arcana, abbreviated YU for "Year of Union."

Sharona:

The Ternathian calendar is used by virtually all of Sharona, although the Uromathian Empire has its own "official" calendar which is used internally (primarily in official documents). The names and length of the months are:

Vandiyahr	31 days
Noristahn	30 days
Valkar	31 days
Jumora	30 days
Erthanos	31 days
Maligair	31 days
Sorchala	30 days
Temisthian	31 days
Ternathal	30 days
Darikhal	31 days
Cormas	28 days* (29 days once every four years)
Fairsayla	31 days

The year begins from the date of the Northern Vernal Equinox.

The Ternathian calendar is also divided into PE and AE (Pre-Erthain and After-Erthain). The dividing point is the year tradition assigns to the first manifestation of Talent in the reign of Erthain the Great.

*   *   *

In *The Road to Hell*, section dates are given using the calendar of the people in the section. When both Arcanans and Sharonians appear in the same section, the first date given is for the first "nationality" in the chapter. For the benefit of the non-Arcanans and non-Sharonians in our readership, an "index date" using the Gregorian Calendar is also appended.